ALLEN
P9-BIJ-112
3 1833 04398 0530

Praise for *Nineteen Widows Under Ash*

'Wilkins reminds me of some of the great American
writers—Faulkner, Lowry, Richard Ford—where the simple
story you are apparently reading deepens and broadens and
throws out layers and shadows, and you are conscious of
an underwater life and a sky overhead, but all the time you
are immersed in what seems a limpid, even transparent
medium' *Evening Post*

'A meditation on the big issues, life and death, written with
an austere elegance this is, simply, a wonderful book'
NZ Herald

Praise for *Little Masters*

'*Little Masters* is an engrossing, fiercely readable book. It
deals with classic themes of parents and children, love and
exile, and the sadness of separation and dislocation. Damien
Wilkins writes brilliantly about streetwise, smart children
and adults searching for love and stability far away from
home' Colm Tóibín

'This lovely, loving novel is a double concerto for the voices
of gorgeously written children and the minds of the adults
they capture. It contains brilliant dialogue and strong
feeling. Mr Wilkins tells the truth' Frederick Busch

Praise for *The Miserables*

'An exhilarating read . . . This remarkable novel provides a
geography of a city and a country—and of a strikingly
individual sensibility' *Sunday Times*

'Wilkins has constructed a powerful portrait of family life
. . . He handles the temporal shifts of the narrative with
delicacy, precision, remarkable grace and apparent lack of
effort . . . the prose is controlled, elegant, almost deadpan
. . . A moving and subtle piece of work'
Times Literary Supplement

AUG 1 9 2003

Also by Damien Wilkins

The Veteran Perils (stories, 1990)
The Miserables (1993)
The Idles (poems, 1993)
Little Masters (1996)
Nineteen Widows Under Ash (2000)

Chemistry

Damien Wilkins

Granta Books

London · New York

Granta Publications, 2/3 Hanover Yard, Noel Road, London NI 8BE

First published in Great Britain by Granta Books 2002

Copyright © Damien Wilkins 2002

Damien Wilkins has asserted his moral right under the
Copyright, Designs and Patents Act, 1988, to be identified
as the author of this work.

All rights reserved. No reproduction, copy or transmissions of
this publication may be made without written permission.
No paragraph of this publication may be reproduced, copied or
transmitted save with written permission or in accordance with
the provisions of the Copyright Act 1956 (as amended).
Any person who does any unauthorized act in relation to
this publication may be liable to criminal prosecution
and civil claims for damages.

A CIP catalogue record for this book is available
from the British Library.

1 3 5 7 9 10 8 6 4 2

Printed and bound in Great Britain
by Mackays of Chathain PLC

Acknowledgements

The author gratefully acknowledges receipt of the Victoria University Writing Fellowship in 2000, during which time this book was written. Thanks also to Ross Carrick for his advice and generosity.

one

H E SHARED THE lift with a woman in a bed and the guy
who was pushing her. The woman was knocked out,
which immediately he saw as unfair. From the bag above her a
tube ran inside the blanket. Why her? She was grisly, with a face
that depended on control of the jaw, a light in the eyes. Something
critical was lacking. Consciousness, obviously. Why her, Jamie
thought, and not me?

Her surgical gown had slipped down on one side. He knew
such gowns did not obey the laws of clothes; it was like being
dressed in an envelope. Her shoulder bone—though she was in
her sixties, his mother's age—had the abiding youthfulness of

this part. A taut sheen. Lovely. But it was the bag he craved. To snatch it—the measuring marks like the seam in a football—and run. Could he run? At one time it would have been possible.

The orderly rested, hunched forward over the bed, breathing. Big bloke, defiantly unconditioned by his job. It was almost three, which the hospital had converted to early evening.

'Long day?' said Jamie. The orderly moved his eyes. Jamie was holding his piece of paper. It was always good to have a piece of paper. When he used to rip off office blocks, a bit of paper was like, I'm the invisible man!

The orderly looked at Jamie's paper. 'I've just come on,' he said.

'Hard night, eh?'

The orderly thought about this, failing to recognise himself for a moment in the other man's eyes. The orderly was a family man, with three kids. The other man—Jamie—was skinny and his jean jacket, with its fur-lined collar, was old, the blue rubbed to a sea green. In clothes, it was a young body—a little body—in the corner of the lift with him, shrinking back without seeming to move, with an old and beaten head, the orderly considered. Grey hair and sneakers. And the eyes full of a certain familiar agitation. Once stripped, the body would be skin and bones, a sunken pelvis, revealed hips. He'd wheeled such guys around. Even when they were dying they had something to say. He saw the floor he was headed to—what was that, pissing? Urology.

Jamie grinned back but felt himself unpicked. He had no feel for the social, they said, but he knew everything about what other people were thinking about him—wasn't that the social? Maybe he should hit the next floor, get out. Third floor, ladies underwear.

'What happened to her?' he heard himself ask of the woman in the bed. A kind of bruising ran down her neck.

'Surgery,' said the orderly.

'I've never had that.' The lie was fruitless. The orderly hadn't stopped looking. 'Time off work though, isn't it.'

'Not for me,' said the orderly.

Jamie didn't get it at first. He was jumping from the bag to the shoulder and back again. He felt hot in the lift. He hated Wellington Hospital. The guys with jackhammers had the job of their lives, levelling this piece of shit, and once he was fixed and nice he'd go watch some of that. They had bulldozers and cranes with wrecking balls. Amazing they still had those balls— like a fantasy of carnage. Then he heard the orderly's words, on a kind of playback he'd perfected. The words weren't in real time; this playback allowed you to review options, assemble an answer that didn't spook anyone. It was like having a video ref in your head. Go upstairs. He was upstairs now, amid his mind, then he saw it: 'Not for you because this *is* your work, right?'

He could have jumped that bag right then, fed the tube up inside himself until it came out through his nostril and back in his mouth.

With great dedication, Jamie studied his piece of paper, though in this state he couldn't read a thing.

The doors were opening. He was about to run but the bed swung forward. It wasn't his floor; it was their floor. The bag and tube were getting off! He stopped himself from crying out. Shame didn't stop him but the promise of his appointment. It was all there on the paper. He had a kidney stone. A real one too.

One of the bed's wheels got stuck and the orderly gave it a kick.

'Want me to hold the button?' said Jamie. But the bed was free and moving and the orderly gave Jamie a backward glance of such condescension that Jamie spoke a word just before he was sealed. 'Arsehole.' He was talking to the door now. 'It's my birthday, you cunt!' And it was. Jamie was forty-one.

EARLY ON IN the business, when they were sorting out how to deal with a bunch of degenerates and housewives and pilots and

truck drivers and town planners and musicians and doctors—
Jamie had come across them all—the criteria for admission into
a methadone programme used to include an upper age limit.
The age limit was forty. Jamie had turned forty on the programme
and his counsellor, thinking it would amuse him, told him this.
On his birthday it happened to be, in the middle of their little
celebration. 'Go back twenty years or something, Jamie, and
you're too old for this carry-on.'

The theory was, the counsellor said, that addicts *mature* out
of addiction.

Jamie was silent and the counsellor—good bloke, humane
sort called Chris—realising that he'd said something that maybe
wasn't so amusing, which had, in fact, the potential to damage
his client's feelings of self-esteem and self-worth, began to suggest
all the ways in which this idea of 'maturing' was both scien-
tifically wrong and morally repugnant. Since there was a rule—
an irritating rule, Jamie felt—that you took your cue from your
client, Chris wasn't laughing any more. 'The statistics on relapse,'
he said, 'tell us a truth about addiction that removes from the
whole picture any idea of guilt or anything.' Jamie was
motionless. 'Even the best-motivated, best-supported patients
who leave the programme can and do end up back on it. We're
not on methadone to learn how to get off it. We're on it to learn
to function properly, satisfyingly, in our lives.'

'We're not on methadone,' said Jamie.

'Sorry?'

'*We. We* are not on it, Christopher. *I* am on methadone.'

'Point taken.'

'You, Christopher, are on insulin.' This was something that
had come up early. Part of Chris's counselling technique, no
doubt—to stick a needle in his own gut in front of a client. I'm
one of you. I know about dependency. Then the conversation
could be had about disease. You and I have a disease. What are
the ways in which your opiate dependency is the same as my

3 1833 04396 0530

10

insulin one? What are the differences? How does your social context, your way of life, impact on your dependency? How does society view your dependency as against mine? Shall we talk about the delivery of medical services being about need not fault, and the programme being about help not blame? Do your experiences bear this out?

Jamie was disappointed in himself for returning to these worthwhile themes.

Watching Chris do his thing, he'd been mesmerised. The counsellor shot into folds of skin at his belly. Jamie had never seen such a fat junkie.

While Chris talked on encouragingly about the advance of scientific knowledge in understanding the brain, receptor dysfunction and so on, Jamie looked at the paper cups on Chris's desk. There was still some of the orange juice Jamie had bought—the fresh stuff, that went off in four days—and a few corn chips on a saucer. They'd been having a little party. The party of a child, he reflected, at the age of forty. On his fingers was the sticky orange dust from the corn chips, as though he'd been sanding. He felt a pang for the taste of alcohol such as he hadn't felt in months. It was like a paper clip on his tongue. He waited for it to pass and it did.

He thought of the people he knew who'd reached forty and their accomplishments. A few blokes from work, at the printer's, were over forty. Jamie had operated the paper cutter but he'd been laid off the previous week because of a downturn in business. His Dad. By the time his Dad was forty, he had two teenage sons. He also had just fifteen years left to live (Jamie was already at an age he'd never expected to see—a fact, embarrassingly, he'd told Chris after they'd had three or so orange juices, causing Chris, in an excess of feeling, to stand up as if to embrace him before sitting back down). Don, Jamie's brother, was past forty—forty-four. No kids but a wife and a business. Don was loaded now. Don lived in a sweet shop. When he was using, Jamie's mates couldn't believe he had a brother who was a chemist. What are we doing here? they said. Let's go see big brother! But big brother was in the South Island and that involved the booking of passage, the purchasing of tickets, the arriving on time and other technicalities. He never told them that his sister, Penny (way past forty, fifty nearly), was a GP, in case they rallied and actually made it down there. In his more lucid moments, Jamie was sure that his success in keeping himself and everyone he knew away from his siblings was something almost admirable, if inhuman.

He had to get off methadone. He would prove this diabetic wrong. This diabetic would never get off insulin but Jamie would get off methadone.

'You're doing really well, Jamie.' Chris lifted his paper cup. 'Here's to you, my friend.'

'Cheers,' said Jamie. His teeth were acting as a sieve.

IT WAS NEVER a room you waited in. It was always an area, usually a thoroughfare. You waited in a corridor or a leftover space into which someone had jammed a few sad brown seats. At the level the seatbacks touched the wall there was a line of broken plaster. When people stood up, they had these white marks on their clothes. This mark meant, you have been waiting for the correct length of time.

He thought of the wrecking ball. Somewhere else a TV was on. In the bigger thoroughfares they chained TVs to the walls and put masking tape over the controls. In this, the hospital was no different from the takeaway bar where he bought his dinner, if he was having dinner. He was in a smaller place—urology was about small places—and had to look at a travel poster for Samoa. The air wasn't moving. Air seldom reached the urethra. Two seats along from him an elderly man waited, moistening his lips every few seconds. From the small kitchen across the corridor a smell came, which made you thirsty: a sort of stainless steel smell. The Zip's whistle curdled the blood.

Within his jacket pocket, Jamie's fingers moved under his ribs. The stone was precious to him, its reality a sort of vindication. Six or seven years before he'd been in Nelson Hospital, in the toilets of A&E, spiking his urine with his own blood to give the right result. That, he'd said in counselling, was a low. Never again.

Now he had a stone to call his own. He'd relapsed—just as the stats, just as Chris, had told him he would. It wasn't Chris's fault he was back using. For a little while, as he came off the methadone bit by bit, piece by piece, he'd truly believed he was going to win. He was past forty. He was too old for this carry-on. But he wasn't. So when he felt the jab in his back one morning and threw up, he ignored it. He'd had worse mornings. The jab was a persistent companion, though. It could last a couple of hours and keep him in bed, which was a crisis since he needed to be places. He had people to meet and this jab was getting in the way. When he pissed blood the sixth day, Jamie was moved by the mystery, and felt a contentment.

His kidneys, master chemists of the body—smarter than Don, his brother—had made this for him. On his birthday, a small and solid gift. He was hoping it was a monster, the size of a tennis ball. That would mean surgery. Inside a hospital.

'Kidney stone,' he said to the old man. 'They don't know what causes them, right? But there's studies show *dehydration* increases the chances of having them.' Jamie pulled at his jacket, miming heat. It did not occur to him to take his jacket off; the hideous collar was a necessity. He liked it near his pillow, if he had a pillow.

The man's tongue ran around his lips again. He stared at Jamie, as if he was a mirage.

'You want some water?'

The man shook his head. No one of that generation, Jamie thought, ever wanted a damn thing. It was something to do with the Depression or the War. His father had been the same, impossible to help, offended by need, as if by a smell. 'I'm getting some. I'll get you a glass.'

Jamie stood up and walked across to the kitchen. The bench carried a single dried tea bag. The cupboards were empty except for a teapot lid and a flower vase. He looked in the vase; it was stained brown and smelled rotten. Since this was a hospital, he refrained from filling it, drinking from it. The empty drawers were lined with curling newspaper. To catch the dripping from the Zip, there was a saucer. He could take the saucer and get the codger to lap it like a cat. Jamie turned on the tap and scooped some water to his face. In fact, he couldn't bear to drink any. The stone was making him nauseous. He returned to his seat and the old man was gone. Called. Someone had been called. He was next.

Later—thirty, forty, fifty minutes? he didn't wear a watch— Jamie thought he heard his name. He listened again on playback, then he stood up.

The doctor was of the variety that wore bow ties, though today his neck bloomed with nothing but its own goitre. 'Have you got your—?' He held out his hand and Jamie gave him the piece of paper, which he glanced at then put on his desk. Jamie felt a sharp pain in his back, which he associated with losing the paper. The doctor put Jamie's X-ray up on the light-box, then he flicked through a file. 'Sit down.' Jamie sat. The doctor was now writing at his computer. He did this for a long time, though, without his watch, Jamie found he wasn't irritated. This close to the source, you didn't let feelings enter into it. Still without turning from the screen, the doctor said, 'You're on methadone?'

'No,' said Jamie.

'Says here you are, or were.'

'Were. Was.'

'Off methadone.' The doctor was typing. 'Since?'

'A year. No, eight months.'

14

'Eight months. Don't happen to know the date, do you? Not exactly but the month. What month was it eight months ago?' He was leafing through a calendar pinned to the wall.

'June.'

That was typed in.

'And how are you now?' The question or something went into the computer, and then the doctor paused above the keyboard.

'In a lot of pain,' said Jamie.

For the first time the doctor looked directly at Jamie, then across at the X-ray. 'No kidding, it's the size of a tennis ball.'

There was a surge of inner joy he had to clamp down on. While the typing resumed, Jamie asked, 'Will it be an operation?'

'It will.'

'No chance of ESWL?'

The doctor paused in his typing. Some liked it when a patient was up to speed—saved time. As a rule, however, surgeons hated to see their world comprehended. Jamie sympathised. 'Far too big. Really big one.' The response was this: drop the intelligence level further than it needed to go. While he went on typing, the doctor said, 'Shock wave only works on things less than about two centimetres. We're not going to crack this nut.'

Jamie knew again perhaps he shouldn't be asking, but it came out: 'So, an operation. Do we know when?'

'I can't do it myself.'

Well, that was a relief. 'But someone else?' He hoped he sounded not keen but needy, afraid, resigned, whatever was normal.

The doctor had finished his entering. 'Listen, you'll be in the outpatients' ward. There's nothing in the outpatients' ward. There's nothing to eat or drink, do you understand? And I'm not talking about the meals on trays.'

'Excuse me?'

'There will be no games. Unless you've swallowed something

15

or had it surgically implanted, you're a bona fide patient this time. Hurts like hell, probably.'

'Look—'

'Everything that happened in Nelson is on your file. Everything.' The doctor stood up.

'I'm clean,' said Jamie.

'Any normal person, that stone would lay them out flat. I don't know how you're still moving around.' He was at the door, which had remained open.

The stone gripped Jamie as he stood. 'I have a high pain threshold.'

The doctor answered by calling the next name.

FINALLY SHE FOUND the room. Truly they'd banished him and, as she pulled up a chair beside the bed and took out the patient's file from her folder, she had the question in her head: if this man is dangerous, why am I here alone? Quickly she assessed the situation. She was heavier than he was, if not taller, and she'd not had surgery. He was on heroin but that didn't make him depraved, only desperate and, she added to herself, deceitful question mark. Why the question mark, though? She had his file.

'I'm Kerry,' she said. 'I'm a dietician. Are you aware of the work of a dietician, Mr Webb?'

'It's putting cucumbers and stuff on your skin, right?'

'No, it's eating.'

'What am I thinking of? *Beautician*.'

'Dietician.'

'But you're beautiful. A beautiful dietician.'

Despite herself, she flushed. It was past seven in the evening and car-lights were coming on in the carpark below the window. Everyone going home. There was a bruising wind hustling rubbish and leaves into corners, lowering grey clouds to the north. You couldn't see the lights of the Hutt. She could go home soon, it made her feel vulnerable to think of it.

'Thank you but we're here to talk about this little problem you've got.'

'Which one?'

She referred to the file in an effort to break his gaze, which was almost leery. He was older than she'd expected, though his birthdate was here. She felt examined, as with a few of the more senior consultants. 'Kidney stones. I have some literature here that I'll leave with you.'

'Literature? What is it, Dickens? Balzac? Tolstoy, did he write on kidney stones?'

'Tells you all about how kidney stones form, what we can do about it and so on.' She put the brochure on the bedside table. 'The doctor's probably told you already about the chances of recurrence. Higher in males than in females.'

'Is that unfair or what?'

'There are, however, a few things we can do to minimise the chances of getting them again.'

'Excuse me, Kerry? Do you have them too?'

'Me? No.'

'Because I thought you said "we".' It was a minor point, this claiming of a shared experience, but it always made him speak out. It was his experience, after all; he had no other belongings except for it.

'Sorry,' said Kerry.

'Unless there's somebody else here. There is nobody else here, is there, or really within a mile of this bed.'

She wasn't sure whether this had more of the quality of a threat than a simple observation. 'I'm sorry, Mr Webb. Of course.'

'Thank you, Kerry. Please go on.'

She looked again at her notes. Her cellphone was in her bag, which was in her office about two miles away. 'Can I ask you, Mr Webb, if you've had kidney stones before.'

'One time I thought I had them.'

'Yes?'

'But I was badly impaired at that stage of my life. Turned out I was lying, pretending to have them.'

'I understand. But this time . . . ?'

'You want to see?' He was pushing the sheet away, lifting his gown.

'No, that's fine, Mr Webb.' Like the hull of a boat, he was covered in ribs.

'Listen,' he said. He drew himself up. This was the longest conversation he'd had with a woman in the vicinity of a bed in months, yet he had a strong urge to get rid of her. Perhaps he needed the bathroom; he couldn't feel his bowels properly, or his bladder, and had already peed himself the previous night. Decidedly, he was yearning and burning and he could no longer aim it in her direction. Anyway, he found her in the end pretty rather than beautiful. Her looks, once studied, were sort of exhausted. He was exhausted. The blonde hair in a bun, the white blouse tucked into the pants, the hide-and-seek bra. He couldn't get an erection until she left. Some delicacy, he remembered, had stopped him mentioning to the surgeon his haemorrhoids. 'What I got to do is, depending on my type, whether the stone was uric acid or calcium oxalate, there are some adjustments I could make in my diet. Basically, they don't know why the stones form but there's studies that show some link with water intake, so I'll drink more of that, and indications of links with calcium-rich dairy foods, red meat, tea, coffee, depending on the type of stone.' He reached out and grabbed the brochure, passing it back to her. 'I've read the literature.'

Kerry took the brochure, grateful and ashamed. She told him he was obviously well informed and that once they got the lab results back she would be in touch with him again. 'For the menu fine-tuning if that's required.'

'To be honest, Kerry, I'm not so big on cooking, you know.'

'So normally what do you eat? Lots of fried food? Takeaways, that sort of thing?' She was writing on her clipboard but doodles only—even he could see that. Her anxiety—unprofessional, unhidden—depressed him. She was afraid of him but not that much. The dangers he represented were fantastical, shadows of dangers. She couldn't rid herself of them, yet they meant nothing.

At the far end of the corridor—he couldn't walk further than to the bathroom—was the nurses' station. At night he'd looked down there and seen the light and almost wept like a child in a dark house. It hurt to fart and this alone, with its comedy, saved his life, protecting him from everything. 'If I break wind, I can leave,' he said to no one. Then he looked at the dietician. 'What do I eat? Is that the question?'

'On a normal night, say.'

'On a normal night, or a good night?'

'Normal night.'

'See, if it was a good night, that's different, you know.'

She couldn't meet his eye and didn't care that she showed him this either. He was the one who was fucked, not her. She had a car in the carpark, a home to go to. And though such things didn't go very deep with him, he registered a feeling of loss.

'But just regularly,' she said, 'what would it be?'

He leaned himself forward, which hurt. 'I'm going to answer the good night thing first, all right? What I eat on a good night. I like the shaved stuff.'

'Ham?' She was closing the folder, storing the pen. If only she could get out of here without hearing something awful.

He felt the dressing on his wound pull, or the wound itself. 'Ham? No, no, no,' he said. 'Pussy.'

Jamie's dietician stood up and walked out. He heard her shoes accelerating, though at no point did she break into a run.

THE LETTER THE hospital sent to the address Jamie supplied was returned 'not known here'. Inside it informed him that his kidney stone was a uric acid stone and that he should therefore cut down on red meat.

By the time the letter was back with the hospital, Jamie was on his way to Timaru, where his brother Don, the chemist, and his sister Penny, the doctor, still lived. The Magic Kingdom.

On the ferry, then hitching down the island, he knew this was about to be the lowest thing he'd done. He'd not been home in however long it was—another decade—though Don had seen him in Wellington a few times and Penny had tried to contact him. He still had her letters somewhere: Dear Shithead, Because I know you won't answer this or probably even read it or even get it (where the fuck *are* you!), I can tell you everything.

When the milk tanker dropped him off at the cheese factory turn-off, he had the sense to pause his journey in a barn. The rusticity was novel. Every minute he was woken by the factory siren. In the morning they were spraying whey onto the paddocks around the factory. The smell stood in for, and in fact banished, breakfast. Walking along the road, he found himself giving a wave to the bloke in the sprayer, who responded with a salute. Like all salutes, it contained a faint irony.

Jamie hitched into town and went to the house not of his good brother or his good harmed sister but to the flat of someone whose name he'd been given in Wellington, who admitted him with a shrug. Douglas. Douglas was in a mink coat. He wasn't queer, only cold. In actual degrees it was twenty-nine in the room—there was a digital thermometer fixed to the wall, its wires running through a hole to the outside, where it was twenty-six. There wasn't a window open in the place. The litter of old takeaways, newspapers, tin foil and used tissues failed to disguise the violence of the carpet, which was lime. The rubbish seemed not so much dropped and lying there but suspended on the surface, as if on a jelly. A lot of this rubbish turned out to be mail—there were heaps of identical-looking envelopes every-where, and cast-off handi-bags and boxes.

Resting against the wall was a single ski pole. 'The fuck's that for?' said Jamie. It was, somehow, a deeply offensive object.

Douglas went over to the pole and picked it up as if for the first time. 'Skiing,' he said. He wasn't joking. There were mountains: Jamie had forgotten. Even when it was hot there was snow. The South Island had always been escapist in this way.

They stood in the living room. Jamie had got some speed off the tanker driver. In the grate of the open fire and around the tiled hearth, cigarette butts—hundreds of them—made their own finger sculptures. He felt beckoned. On the windows, a yellowish substance coated the light coming through—the congealed exhalations of many afternoons and evenings. This room lacked mornings. There were no curtains. Douglas, in the mink coat, retreated somewhere, returning a moment later to snatch up a box of tissues from the floor. In a sort of horror, he pointed to the kitchen before leaving again. Already Jamie knew the chance of finding any food in there was nil. He felt, as he took a seat on the cushionless sofa and moved a pile of ash with his toe, perfectly at home.

He sat for a minute, then went into the kitchen, where he filled the jug. The jug was slow and he watched it—a watched pot, there was a saying his mother would know—and after ages he ripped the thing from the wall and poured the warm water into a cup. He watched the cup for a while before he remembered it wasn't hot, then he drank it. He drank another cup of the warm water and felt sick. He bent over with care and put his head between his knees.

Under one leg of the Formica table there was a phonebook. He pulled it out. Holding the thin book—it flopped around like a pamphlet—he was almost overcome. The thinness of the document was affecting, and something else too, the contents. In here were the people he knew and who knew him, or had once. He came from a small place and this was its census. Turn it over the other way, flip it round, and it was the Yellow Pages too. He threw it into the corner and went looking for Douglas in the mink. He needed Douglas. If that person couldn't help him— and he had no great hopes there: Douglas was of the younger generation—he'd go visiting. His mother was a few blocks away. She had a swimming pool. Also there were several prescriptions running around inside her cupboards.

two

AN AXOLOTL ONLY eats things he thinks are alive, Olivia was explaining. She was the head teacher at Don's niece's kindergarten. She spoke to a small group of parents and kids over by the tank. She'd been waving dinner around on the end of tweezers, she told them, and let it slip. 'Now I'm too chicken,' she said. As Don walked in, he had the feeling they were all waiting for someone to deliver them, and he knew he was not that person.

'Here's someone,' said Lucille, pointing at him and smiling. Lucille was always smiling. She was the youngest of the three teachers, barely nineteen. The reason Lucille was in a perpetual state of happiness, Tina said, was because she alone, at the end of the day, went home childless and slept a childless night and ate a childless breakfast. But so, Don thought, did they normally, unless Anna was sleeping over. Across Lucille's chest, written in red glitter, was the word 'TRY'. This teeshirt had been sighted before. Out by the sandpit, Don had once overhead a conversation between Lucille and a father.

'What?' said the father, nodding at the teeshirt.

'Sorry?' said Lucille.

'Try what?'

'Oh, pretty much anything.'

'Is that right?'

'Why not.'

'Why not,' repeated the father. 'I like it. Good attitude.'

The parents were backing away, letting Don through. Soon he stood beside Olivia.

'I think you might like to roll up your sleeve,' she said.

'I think I might not,' he said.

Inside the tank it was murky, indescribable. Don rolled up his sleeve. The axolotl waited, drifting on the bottom, ready to strike at whatever moved, while the sliver of meat lay on a stone right under his jaws.

Anna, his niece, stood at the tank. 'Don't!' she laughed. The children began to shriek. 'Don't! Don't! Don't!'

Olivia put her finger to her mouth: shush. And they were quiet. Olivia had that trace of severity in her that children liked, or perhaps it was only reassurance they felt; anyway, something in her manner made them want to please her. Don had the same feeling.

He'd never liked fish, handling them, the jerking life in their sweating bodies like reproachful bolts of electricity. This wasn't a fish, it was worse. It was like the tongue of an ox standing in soup. Why was he there in front of the tank? Why had they parted for him? He didn't even have a child here. He felt put-

24

upon, tested, important, actually happy. He asked whether it had teeth. No, said Olivia, just really nippy gums. The adults all laughed and Don laughed. Anna, in her excitement, half-tripped, and banged her elbow against the glass tank, causing the water to shiver. The axolotl turned and Don hooked the meat.

No one cheered. There was disappointment all round in his success. It seemed unclear what had happened. They looked as though they wanted him to do it again.

'Look!' said Anna. 'The axolotl farted.'

Don watched the string of bubbles rise to greet the surface, effervescing towards the laughter the girl had won. Clearly she knew how to work a room, and in this he considered her more like her father than her mother. Still, he couldn't fight the feeling of pride he had in knowing he was taking her home.

Simon, Anna's father, was an architect. For Don, 'practising as an architect' meant behaving as a liar, committing a fraud, going unpunished. Of course it had not always been that way. Simon himself had been quite happy to reveal the trickery of his trade. He'd once shown Don a 3-D model of a shopping mall extension he was working on. Everything was scaled to the matchbox cars that sat in the parking lot on the mall's roof. Simon himself was not a fan of such models. 'In miniature,' he said, 'things tend to look cute, like toys.' This diverted the attention from the true considerations of scale and context. At this point their cat had come into the room and leapt up onto the table. The cat belonged, more or less, to Anna. 'Favourite trick of city councils,' Simon said, watching the cat, ready to slap it away; he'd lifted his hand as a warning. 'They sell the punters their hideous designs through these toys. Under the cover of openness, they get these models made and set them up on display in the information centre. And I'm afraid the architects conspire with them. The God's-eye view is of tremendous and useless appeal. Despite what we may wish, none of us lives hovering fifty metres above a tiny world.' It was a view, however, that

Don now seemed to possess. He saw Simon laid out below him. Exactly crushable.

Anna was a hot ball, inflamed especially around her forehead. She was much hotter than he was, despite the coolness of the kindergarten's low-ceilinged, shaded rooms. Along the wall of north-facing windows, the leaves of the basil plants turned brown in the sunshine, kids' pictures sagged with paint. The kindergarten's two parrots were unmoving, as if stuffed. There was a smell of hamster and straw and algae, of the field and of the deep. Don was partially addicted.

He attempted to kiss her on the top of the head but she'd already spun out of his hold and was running into the cloakroom. Lucille caught his eye. 'Bit t-i-r-e-d today,' she spelled out, gesturing towards Anna, who was now rushing back with her bag, spilling things from it. Anna wanted another hug, further collisions. He stood up and she swung from his neck.

'Where are your shoes, honey?' he said. The girl giggled. 'Where are they, Anna?' He looked at the trail of spilled items— lunchbox, drink bottle, pencils. Of special and depressing note was the full lunchbox—she wouldn't eat. She was almost four, Penny liked to joke—on the Richter scale. 'You'll have to let go now, honey. We have to pick up all this mess. You find your shoes while I pick this up.'

'No,' she said.

'Fine, then you sit there and I'll do everything.' Olivia had come up behind them with Anna's shoes. 'Thank you,' Don said. 'Look, Anna, Olivia found your shoes. What do you say?' The girl pulled at one sock but refused to look up. 'Anna?'

'Never mind,' said Olivia, dropping the shoes beside them and walking into the story-room.

Tina had told him they should both refuse to feel let down by their niece, though that was a full-time occupation. He got one shoe on before Anna was away again. She told him she'd forgotten something. He had a good idea what: the stuff Tina never let Anna bring home and that he always allowed. Their basement housed a collection of rusty carpentry: blocks of wood with nails sticking out of them. Tina wanted to know why he wasn't throwing them out.

'Because,' Don said, 'that prick Simon comes round, I'll have something to use on him.'

Don had sometimes thought of removing Simon's glasses and standing on them. Then he would stand on Simon, on his puffy small man's chest, on his suits, on his shins. He had thought of stamping on his ankles, the diamonds on his socks. In fact, he'd passed Simon in the street a few weeks before—Simon hadn't seen him—and felt instantly immobile. A watchfulness grabbed him and pinned him in place, as if he was observing the walk of a dangerous beast, or a celebrity, an actor perhaps—since that's what he was, an accomplished player of roles—with fame's, or infamy's, forcefield repelling contact at the same time as it sucked in attention.

Simon continued, rather amazingly, to work at his office down by the railway station where he'd been for years, though now he lived in an apartment block carved out of a warehouse by the wharf. His own firm had done the work on the apartments, so no doubt there was some sickeningly favourable arrangement in the rent. Despite Don and Tina at first urging her to act, Penny wouldn't bring Simon down. Perhaps she would never act. Perhaps she would never send the letter to his firm or to the police, though Simon was not in a position to know this, which may have been the point all along. They had, anyway, stopped talking to Penny about it. Yet despite living on whatever time Penny chose to extend to him, despite his career and reputation nerve-wrenchingly in the balance, Simon, on the street, appeared typically confident and surefooted and untouched. It was all either an astonishing bluff or, revoltingly, he had confidence in his wife's clemency, or in her continuing fear. Between themselves, Don and Tina talked about Penny and Simon constantly, and in the misery of the situation they were grateful there was a single unambiguous and practical need: to help with Anna. However, though the need may have been unambiguous, their servicing of it was not. Tina, by her own admission, was struggling to like the girl. She'd inherited from her own mother a horror of the spoilt child; it made her harsh and indulgent, watchful and erratic. She was as likely to buy Anna an ice cream as give her time-out.

A Samoan boy, Patrick, stood beside Don. Patrick was Don's friend. 'I'm your friend, aren't I?' the boy had said one day. He was running from two smaller boys, surprisingly afraid.

There was an area outside with a workbench where the kids lined up to use the hammers. Patrick had been given his own hammer by the kindergarten. His one had a rubber head on it, whereas all the other hammers were steel-headed. It was apparently the best way of dealing with Patrick. What happened, of course, was that Patrick tried to swap his rubber hammer for a steel one, and some of the children didn't want Patrick's hammer, so the workbench was hell. On the worst days the teachers made the workbench out of bounds, and everyone seethed against Patrick.

Usually Patrick ran straight into Don's middle, bumping his head into Don's groin, sometimes painfully. With Don bent down, scooping Anna's things into her bag, Patrick looked lost. He could never remember Don's name.

'What's your name?' he said.

'Remember me, Patricko?' said Don.

'Patrick,' said Patrick.

'Petruchio!'

Don felt that Patrick saw him as a touchstone for maleness against the three female teachers and the predominantly female picker-uppers. He'd talked to Tina about it. There seemed, Don thought, a kind of thirst for information in Patrick's eyes. Tell me what I need to know about being a man, he seemed to say.

'And what do you tell him?' Tina asked.

'Well,' said Don, 'when Patrick rests his hand on my crotch I tell him, excuse *me*.'

The rubber-headed hammer was wrong, Don thought. An emasculated hammer! 'The thing about a rubber hammer,' Don said to Tina, 'is that you apply the right kind of force and all you get back is a nasty jarring in your hand.'

'Better than the nasty sound of another child's skull being crushed,' said Tina.

Patrick was always collected from kindergarten by his ten-year-old sister, who grabbed him by the jersey and urged him on with a foot. The sister had no need whatsoever of Don. In a few years Patrick's sister would be as big as a man. 'You should see this girl,' Don told Tina, 'a really tight jersey over this swelling upper body. Christ, she looks like a prop forward! And poor old Patrick will probably get that same jersey as a hand-me-down.'

'Where else should he get his clothes from?' said Tina.

The tone she'd used to close down the conversation made him aware he'd strayed down an old path. Perhaps she wasn't wrong in this. Don didn't think of Patrick as adoption material— the boy presumably had parents, or guardians at least—yet something in their relationship was a teaser of fatherhood, the same sort of unearned intimacy, the same spectre of injury and sudden warmths. Adoption had been on their minds at one time. But then friends had had an Indian girl, a beautiful, needy child, snatched from before their eyes in a hotel room in Delhi. 'I don't want to ever be in that hotel room,' Tina had told him.

He asked Patrick where his sister was and the boy shrugged. Patrick was leaning his body against Don's shoulder. The weight was something; Don braced himself with one knee on the floor. The boy needed him physically. Anything Patrick threw at him, he caught: that was their rule. Don stood—or squatted—firm. 'Talofa,' he said sometimes. 'Gimme five.'

Anna was back from the locker room carrying a chunk of wood with three nails sticking out of it.

'Look,' she said.

'Very nice, honey,' said Don.

Patrick reached out and touched the head of one of the nails.

'Don't, Patrick,' said Anna.

Don was trying to get the other shoe on. He wasn't quite convinced these were Anna's shoes, though of course he knew a child could pretty much decide on the size of its own foot at any given time. He pulled at her foot. Anna swung the wood out of Patrick's reach. The nail dug into Don's forehead.

A drop of blood fell on the kindergarten floor. Anna promptly stepped in it—to cover it up? Pretend it wasn't her, pretend it hadn't happened? She'd denied remarkable things in her time: toilet paper wrapped round her pillow, scissors in the video recorder.

The force of the blow to Don's head had been sufficient to almost dislodge the nail. Patrick took the wood off Anna and gave the nail a few more whacks by driving it against the floor to set it right, then he handed it back. Don was sitting on the floor, holding a handkerchief to the wound.

'See what I done?' Patrick said to Don.

'Good work,' said Don.

'Didn't even need my hammer.'

'No.'

'Are you her Dad?'

'No he's not my Dad,' said Anna.

'You didn't hurt your Dad,' said Patrick.

'I know I didn't,' said Anna.

Olivia had come out of the story-room. 'Is someone hurt?'

'No,' said Don, 'just an accident.'

She looked at Don's black-spotted handkerchief. 'You've got to be careful, Patrick.'

'It wasn't him,' said Don.

'Yes it was,' said Anna.

Olivia led the boy away by the hand.

'It was my fault, Olivia,' Don called out.

Olivia let him know she'd heard by lifting her arm and waving, though she didn't turn around. The familiar end-of-day economies were in evidence. Sweat loops showed on her shirt. He'd once seen Olivia kick a plastic cup on the kitchen floor, sending it sailing into the sink.

'Poos!' shouted Anna, pointing to the cage.

The parrots stiffened as if they'd heard the girl and were ashamed.

Apart from Olivia's van, Don's was the only car left outside the kindergarten. The little Starlet was decked in the pharmacy's purple and yellow, and bore—Don was usually happy about this—the name of the previous owner, Don's old boss Perry. As he was buckling Anna into her booster seat, he saw there was a ute parked across the street. He thought he knew it; he recognised the coloured bonnet that was clearly from another vehicle and had been rammed inadequately into place. He'd seen the ute outside the pharmacy, remembering how it was blocking the drive slightly and he'd had to go over the kerb. There was no one in it.

The bleeding from his forehead had stopped. The stinging pain was a dull ache. He put the soiled handkerchief in his pocket and closed the passenger door. Maybe there was more than one ute like this in town and the owner was a parent of a child at kindergarten. A hoon could be a parent, anybody could. His brother was a parent, or at least he'd fathered a child. Last time he'd seen Jamie they'd gone hunting for a late Christmas present for Jamie's son—it was April. Jamie calculated the boy was about eight. He insisted on visiting every toy store in the city. Finally, they'd settled on a twelve-dollar sword and Jamie had asked Don for a loan. Then later they discovered they'd left the sword in a pub. When they went back the sword was gone, and the toy store was closed. Don, who was flying back home in the morning, found he was far more upset than Jamie appeared to be about the loss. 'It's all right,' Jamie told him, 'I would have been struggling to wrap a sword. Actually, I would have been struggling to get an address.'

Don opened the driver's door to get in. 'I'm so thirsty,' said Anna. He was looking in the rear-view mirror; a scab was already forming on his nail wound. Vaguely he thought of tetanus but the nails at the kindergarten were all new, and he'd had a whole bunch of shots before they went on holiday the previous year. That had been their only big blowout. From the pharmacy purchase they'd acquired both huge debt and plentiful cash.

Then he saw someone—a young guy, aged about eighteen. He'd been sitting down against the concrete wall behind the ute, smoking. Don opened his door again.

'I'm *dying*,' said Anna. 'Why's your door open? Can I open mine?'

The guy was moving slowly round towards the driver's door, drawing on the last of his cigarette. He was packed into a black teeshirt and jeans; shorter than Don but bulked up, barely contained. Don shut his door and tried the fan again. It wasn't working. Of course no one had told him. Sharon, the shop girl, never told him anything about the Starlet, which she drove every day to do the deliveries. She always thought it was her fault if things happened to the car—a prophecy that neatly fulfilled itself. She waited wordlessly for permission and instruction, with the result that she'd run out of petrol several times on her rounds, and had once driven on a flat tyre until the rim was damaged. The car smelled—not unpleasantly—of her, of hair products and of the pharmacy. The glovebox contained Sharon's make-up and the logbook she never touched.

'Can I have some perfume?' said Anna.

'No,' said Don.

The ute was doing a three-point turn, the front wheels riding on the footpath as Don reversed out of his park. When Don straightened the car, the guy seemed to be waiting for them to pass. Expertly, he was letting the ute rock back and forth on the lip of the footpath. He looked at Don and grinned.

On the passenger seat the mobile phone rang. Don put the car in neutral to answer it. Tina spoke: 'Don, remember about the cup, won't you?' Tina had made it her personal crusade to get Anna off the bottle. In general terms, he supposed, they were trying to save her. The girl had an unsightly rash on her neck from where the milk dribbled down as she sucked falling asleep or watching TV. Idly she scratched it, inflaming the red spots. Often she took off her top because, she said, it was hurting her. Surely, Don thought, if it was a health risk, Penny, the child's mother, would have acted. She was a GP. Tina considered GPs to be more or less the worst people in the world at giving their own families proper health care.

'How's the madhouse?' he said into the phone. Sweat had stiffened the collar of his dispensary jacket. He felt it as a prod.

Tina lowered her voice so as to make herself indistinct to her workmates. She worked in an open-plan space above the art gallery, where she was Education Officer. 'There's been lots of hongiing.'

'Spot of brown-nosing, eh?'

She spoke without lightness. 'I hate that phrase.'

The heat had made him irritable, and the nail in his head, now this person across the street. 'It's horrible, isn't it.'

'Remember the cup.'

Don put the phone down and started moving his car forward. The guy in the ute leaned his head out the window as if he was about to speak. His right temple, Don saw, was tattooed, but these weren't the crude marks Don was used to seeing on his methadones. This wasn't prison calligraphy but something expert—a moko, was it? This relaxed Don suddenly. With its signal of political conscience, the tats gave Don courage. Yet the guy didn't look especially Maori.

Don flashed his lights and waved a hand: you go first. The guy pulled his head back inside, but the ute wasn't moving. Don drove forward and the ute lurched in front of him, forcing Don to hit the brakes, stalling the car. 'Hey!' said Don.

'We're so late,' said Anna. 'I'm going to miss my shows. I know I am. It's too hot in here.'

The guy grinned again, and then the ute was moving away from them at speed.

Don discovered he was trembling. He turned on the radio as Anna continued to grizzle about the television programmes she loved. He couldn't concentrate on either her or the radio; their voices blended unpleasantly. The Starlet, perfumed and close and cruddy, was a humiliating vehicle suddenly. Don decided they would get a new car. That was more or less how it was with his decisions these days—he decided something and it happened. He was aware that this could make him seem wilful or foolish in the eyes of those who'd known him for years as a mere employee. It was a sensitivity he shared with Tina, who nevertheless had proved herself a better spender of money than him, buying things for the house or 'reinvigorating' their wardrobes, or purchasing the paintings of local artists from group shows, thereby giving her indulgences the necessary gloss of community spirit. Neither of them was quite used to the idea of their own wealth; each spend was still accompanied by an excuse and they admitted everything to each other, even when they'd bought afternoon tea from a café for no good reason other than a sudden weakness for a blueberry muffin (her) or a lamington (him).

He could, he thought, get a replacement for the Starlet from the car dealer in Christchurch who was keeping an eye out for a replacement for their ten-year-old sedan. Every week the dealer emailed Don photos of likely candidates. The subject line of his messages always read 'Beamer Me Up, Scotty'.

AT HOME ANNA took up her usual position in front of the TV. She lay on the sofa with her head hanging over the edge, while her bare feet played with the curtains.

'I want a drink,' she said.

'What do you say?' said Don.

'I *need* a drink.'

'Do I hear the magic word?'

'It's so magic you probably can't even hear it.'

He filled a cup with milk and brought it to her.

'Where's my bottle?'

'Try this.'

'I want my bottle.'

'This is milk. Try this.'

The dialogue had been spoken on many occasions. She moved a cushion over her face and screamed into it that she wouldn't she wouldn't she wouldn't. He was mean, she shouted. He was so mean like Tina. She would be deaded. They were trying to make her deaded.

'No, no,' said Don. 'Deadened maybe.' Without another adult in the room his witticism struck a note of loneliness. He thought of calling Tina—not about the milk but about the incident at the kindergarten with the guy in the ute. But why? Such a silly thing really. Maybe he'd tell her when she got home.

He walked quickly back into the kitchen, decanted the milk from the cup into Anna's bottle and brought it to her. He placed the bottle on the little wooden stool beside the sofa, rather than handing it directly to her, giving in, he saw at once, to the temptation for useless punishment.

She waited a few moments. Then she peered out from behind the cushion and snatched the bottle.

Had she snatched things from Simon, her father? Had he taught her this? And had he made her suffer for what she'd learned from him? Penny had been singularly fierce on this point (in all other regards she was strangely circumspect, muted, though Tina thought this could be explained in terms of shock): Simon, Penny said, never laid a finger on Anna. She was indignant that Don had even asked such a question, her voice rising for the first time since she'd told them about Simon's violence. 'If you ask me that, have I stood by and watched him hurt my daughter, my child, I wonder what you really think of me. I wonder what I am in your eyes.' Naturally Don had apologised. But could Penny be trusted? The traumatised made all sorts of bad decisions. He'd thought this even while listening to her powerful and credible voice of motherly love in which there was bitterness too. She seemed savage for a moment, protective not just of her child but of the life she'd led for the past seven years; protective, finally, of Simon, whom she loathed. She did not wish any of that life to be understood by others since she did not understand it herself. All she wanted was for Don and Tina to pick up Anna from kindergarten on the days she couldn't get off work.

The urge to do Simon physical harm was not serious, though it was real and strong enough to break into Don's thoughts at inopportune times. The image of himself standing over the architect came to him when he was filling complicated prescriptions or when he was watering the garden in the evening. That is, when his mind was full and also when it was empty. Such imagery required no conditions of fertility, growing in all mental weathers, but he hadn't been thinking of Simon as he'd squared off against the tattooed driver of the ute. Only now did he sense a connection between the two events—someone whom he wanted to threaten and someone who wanted to threaten him: they were linked by his own timidity. Don was bigger than the guy in the ute and no less powerful. What he was, he supposed, was less willing, less practised maybe, less free with his power. Don's power sat on him like a layer—it was a fold of flesh, an application. It had, occasionally, encouraged others to test its resolve—pissed smaller men had jostled him in bars. The guy in the ute had a strength that was intentional, directional. It pointed outwards. Less an application than a need. But what was the intention, the direction, what was the need?

Had Don been followed from the pharmacy? Did they believe he'd been doing the takings, that the Starlet was on the bank run? It had happened to Cook's Pharmacy a few months back, though that had been a grab-and-run job right on the street as the bag was being walked to the bank. An opportunist's heist—and the thief easily caught, tackled to the ground outside Brownies Shoestore. Cars were something else. They required planning and careful execution. In this light the ute guy's actions didn't make sense.

Don had been bullied, that was all. He knew bullies. When he was young—twelve or thirteen—he had been approached at an intersection by another older boy who ordered Don to get off his bike. The older boy was on a bigger bike and had no need of Don's. He had need only of Don's fear. Once he had that, he rode off, leaving Don to pick up his own bike. The bike, transformed by the humiliation, reconstituted by Don's shame, was almost unrecognisable, and Don failed to find the handle-bars, pulling blindly at the frame, then at the wheel, which spun and caught his fingers against the spokes. It was like picking up the insides of a washing machine.

There was only one person he'd told this to—his little brother. He'd meant it to impress Jamie, to signal that he'd been tangling with ugly forces, true threats. They shared a bedroom and often spoke to each other in the dark while playing records on the little mono record player. 'Why'd you get off?' said Jamie. 'I can't believe you got off like he told you to.'

'Because, fuckwit,' Don said, 'I was in line for a pummelling, all right?'

The next day, Jamie told him he'd settled it with the older boy.

'What are you talking about?' said Don.

Jamie took out his pocketknife. He'd cut the boy's tyres. Not only that. Along the paintwork of the boy's bike, he'd scored the name of another kid who was always hassling Donny.

Don sat opposite Anna, watching the milk slosh around as she sucked. Later he was able to spread some cream on her neck, feeling under his finger the corrugations of the rash. Anna watched him as he did this. Usually he never felt her eyes on him, but now she looked. Was she judging this touch? Even when he looked back, she held her stare for a few moments. It was discomfittingly, inexplicably, adult—but not sexual. He never told Tina he was putting the cream on because they'd had that argument. Tina felt any treatment simply obscured the cause of the problem—the bottle drinking. Better that the rash got really nasty, completely unmissable, then Penny would be forced to act. For Don, any more force in his sister's life was unthinkable, even the force of good.

three

S HE WAS WASHING dishes, cups and saucers mainly, and
teaspoons and cake forks that were tiny but stabbed her
nonetheless. The normal kitchen hand was sick. You could
bounce a saucer and leave a dent in the linoleum. Sally scooped
a fistful of cutlery from the water and let it drain through her
yellow-gloved fingers.

'Change your water,' said Terry, the cook, without looking.
It was just the two of them since the waitress had knocked off.

Sally spoke in an automatic lie: 'I just changed it.' The lie
was recognised as such by the cook's refusal to say anything
more.

Terry was dicing onions. She held her left hand in a claw. It wasn't an action but a demonstration and more than that, a lesson. There were no tears since the juice remained with the onion. The skill was inspiring. For a short time Sally thought she would like to be a cook too, though not around here. Mostly the place was used by old women treating themselves to something sweet, or families after shade, kids gripping the sides of tall paper milkshake holders, treading food into the brown carpet. The cooking consisted mainly of toasted sandwiches.

'When did you check your baby?' said Terry. She wore the hat of a chef, though underneath it there was hardly any hair.

'He's all right,' said Sally. This was a topic, unlike the water in Sally's sink, in which the cook had an interest. They had the baby in the storeroom. When Sally had first arrived she'd gone round the alleyway, tapped on the kitchen window and passed the baby in his backpack through to Terry. Terry was a friend of a friend who was paying Sally two bucks less an hour than she was actually getting from Ange, the boss, for casuals. It was Terry herself who'd given Sally this information, proud of the margin. As a form of compensation Terry was showing a dyke's attention to motherhood—fussy, indulgent, kind. Already on a break she'd tried to feed him his bottle.

'I'll go in after I've done these,' said Terry. She spoke with a sigh.

Sally was too tired to consider this a criticism of her own methods.

They shut up the kitchen at 2.30. Ange had already gone home. She'd told Sally there wouldn't be any more work the next day because the sick kitchen hand had called in and she'd made 'a miraculous recovery'. The alcohol presumably having passed through her system, Ange said. Terry figured too that the boss must have cottoned on to the baby since it had not been the quietest mite in the world. At that statement, though it was delivered without vindictiveness or blame, Sally found herself in tears. The baby's faults were her own, and though she had never considered herself fragile she could, in an instant and against her own will, share his defencelessness. Terry took a step in her direction but Sally held out her hand as if to say, 'Whoa.'

There was half an hour before afternoon tea, when Sally would be the waitress as well, and Terry told Sally she had to come with her. At the door Sally asked if she could flip over the Closed sign and Terry said, 'Whatever turns you on.'

EVERYONE KNEW THE Bay Carnival needed night. In the daytime you understood what you were wading through: tickets and those milkshake containers, the paper napkins from hotdogs which looked bloodied. You saw the rust on the arms of the Master Whirl, oil in furry spills. Small blocks of wood had been jammed under everything. There were numbers stencilled at the joins of all construction. Four hooked up with 5, 5 with 6 and so on, but in one case—it was the merry-go-round—Sally saw that 11 was connected to 14. Was there a danger here that no one else had noticed? It didn't seem fair to put that on her and she refused to think about it. Anyway, the thing revolved so slowly, surely no one would be hurt if there was a collapse.

The bumper boats moved against their chains, waiting for a floodlit dark. Everything slept. Sensitive to this requirement, the operators lay inside caravans in the midday heat, broiling in tiny bunks, heating up their headaches. It had been Sally's first duty that morning to knock on such a caravan door and to be answered finally by abuse, a few things hurled, then silence. She'd gone back into the tearooms and told the boss that breakfast wasn't required. The boss had someone she was seeing in the caravan. At ten the door of the caravan was hot to the touch.

By day you saw the origin of everything—the big belly of the man whose breath appeared at your ear. Businessmen often strayed through the area, adjusting their belts, watching at the

41

fence while someone hit a shot at the mini golf. You saw exactly where the cigarette came from as it was tossed, and not just its flashing arc in the darkness. (It had been Sally herself, smoking, dawdling back to the tearooms.) Yet harboured as she was from the violence of all that was in plain view, she had not felt glad to be working inside. She had felt trapped—if you could feel trapped and, at the same time, strangely set loose. Someone at A&D, the rehab clinic, had told her it was like they had both been recently born—Sally and the baby. This was rubbish of the sort that still clung to your brain. She remembered crawling to the toilet she shared with the woman in the next room via connecting doors that couldn't be locked while the baby lay in its plastic bassinet and hospital sheets, behaving all the time—treacherously—beautifully. Not a sound, not a squeak.

At the paddling pool Terry took off Sally's sandals and rolled up her pants. When Terry had done the same they walked into the water. Sally was carrying her baby in the backpack. The kids in the pool looked at them as if they were strange, some sort of additive put in the pool. There was the faint feeling of a coating on the bottom. The tepid water had the effect, or close to it, of satin on Sally's shins. It gave no relief to her sore feet but she was grateful to be standing there with someone beside her, even this person. She would never have done such a thing by herself. As a recent former addict she felt strongly the desire to have all her decisions scrutinised by the group. Where was the group? She'd walked out of the group. At the last session she'd let slip that she was living with a person who still used from time to time. The information made everyone feel immediately good about themselves. She'd never seen them so fired up and alive. Did she know what she was doing? Was she clear in her head what the hell she was doing? They spoke in a rush, for once without prompting from the facilitator. Was she serious about recovery? Was she serious or just jerking everyone around, including her baby? At that she'd got up and walked out. Lots of people walked out but she had not imagined herself to be one of them. It was a humiliation to walk out, the walkout being itself a stage along the way, as was the humiliation. The difference here was that she was not going to walk back in. When you walked back in, your fiercest critics had turned into your closest allies. They hugged you and felt for your hand and gripped it and smiled into your face. Her hand, however, would not be held. She was without precedent.

The sun sat on her head. Against her neck she felt the prod of her baby's peaked cap. The backs of her arms were burning. Terry was holding her finger against the baby's mouth and asking him if he was hungry.

When she'd come home from group that evening, Shane was having breakfast. 'Thank God you're home,' he said.

'Why?'

'Because he's going to wake up soon.' He lived in fear of the woken baby.

'Do you want some vodka and Coke?' she said. She'd brought a can of it from the Super Liquor.

'I'm having my breakfast,' he said.

'Is that a yes or a no?'

He put the last spoonful of Ricies into his mouth and swallowed. 'A small one then.'

She poured herself a small one too—all her capacities were down—and waited for him to say something. He hated her drinking. Yet she'd snatched an advantage: he couldn't be overly sure of his ground since the drink had been so readily shared.

She sipped. 'I've got this plan,' she said.

One plan—which she did proceed with once Shane had left for work that night—was to pour the rest of the vodka into the sink. It wasn't his disapproval that made her do it but her own. She was hopeless with sugars now. Yet that wasn't the plan she told him about. That plan had to do with the chemist who was giving her methadone. (She'd only started keeping the methadone down once they stopped putting orange juice with it—sugars again.) When she finished telling Shane this other plan, and she'd been making it up, changing it as she went along, winging it in places because none of it had occurred to her before the group had attacked her for only wanting a father for her baby, he said, 'I don't like it.'

'Which bit?' she said.

'What do you think?' he said, lowering his head, rubbing his tattoo. There was something in the plan, involving the chemist and herself, which required the proximity of vodka. She knew she needed a drink handy to put it into words, and she knew Shane would require a similar sedative. He poured himself a second small one, bigger this time, finishing the can. It satisfied her and touched her that he'd had this reaction. He was an oaf but he was a human oaf. The extent of his feeling at this moment may have been only the briefest twinge from the spot where her proposal had wounded his male pride, yet she was glad to have the power to strike him even this weakly. The feeling—and her recognition of it—replaced the obliterating haze of earlier months. Neither of them was numb, this proved.

She brought his toast to the table.

'You know, Sal,' he said, 'I got the strangest feeling it'll work.' He kissed her. The kiss was a sign—of ownership of course but also of a limited sort of trust. He was, up to a point, handing things over to her. His resignation showed in the softness of his mouth against hers; its limits were understood by him keeping his eyes open throughout. She too was looking; it was how she discovered him watching her receive his agreement. They stared into each other's eyes, indecently close, and as a relief she made herself trace with her finger the lines he'd had applied to himself, a pattern which normally she could only see as the outcome of some workplace accident.

At once she believed the whole thing was a mistake. She'd planned it and spoken it aloud from some chemical depression, a 'stage' almost certainly, whose edge she could feel now, as if she was stepping back into real time—the time before this vodka, before the humiliation. In it was the outline of a kind of sanity which seemed as certain as a room. It was a matter of picking one's feet up and walking through. Perhaps he could meet her there in that room.

But she was tired. Her feet were sore. To have something between her jaws, she bit into his toast. She was still angry with the group. Shane was her support, as she was his. They had each other.

Then the baby started crying and he waited for her to go to it. He sat with his drink and waited, suggesting that no matter on what grounds she claimed superiority—he'd often said she was the smart one, the one who could talk—she was also and always and from now on tied to the whim of their speechless son. Shane believed he asserted himself in this realm, having no such ties. This time, however, she too waited at the table, forcing him finally to say something, making him ask her if she was going to get the little tike. In fact, she knew Shane was scared of the baby. He was always asking her to help the baby and look at the baby and feed the baby and check on the baby. He couldn't bear the baby's loneliness.

Shane would be out of bed by now; he was getting the video camera today, hitting on Mike, her brother, who couldn't say no. They took his car like it was theirs. But Sally had made a pact with herself: if she scored a job at the tearooms, they would call off the plan. She would go home and tell Shane to take the camera back to Mike and forget the chemist, since they could manage all right now they were both working, now she was well, now the baby was a few days older, a few days wiser. Everyone was wiser sooner or later, even Shane. But there was nothing for her at the tearooms.

Probably in the eyes of the other mothers watching from the side of the paddling pool she appeared as one half of a lesbian couple parading the offspring of a gay donor. If Shane could see her now, he would die. She experienced the urge to tell Terry the cook all these plans, all these permutations, how with Shane she had been on the point of turning herself into a criminal—though this was the wrong word, since it suggested she was already caught. What then was she on the point of becoming? In thoughtless experiment Sally put her arm around Terry's waist before claiming her as a support. 'Bit slippery,' she said.

'I don't want to think what's in this water,' said Terry. Of course she'd noticed the grope and had quickly worked it out. She was not being desired but only teased, and this teasing came from a deep misery. Terry stepped out of the pool and Sally followed her.

At the soundshell the stage was crowded with mothers and kids and babies. A sweating man with a microphone was offering a commentary while two assistants—women in matching yellow teeshirts and blue trackpants—arranged them in lines. The mothers with babies were being put in the front, just forward of the line of shadow extending from the soundshell's scalloped roof—something made Sally think of a guillotine.

'Go on then,' said Terry. She was already reaching behind to free Sally of the backpack.

'What?' said Sally.

'There's a hundred dollars there.'

'Piss off.'

'Come on, you stupid cow.' She spoke gently, getting the baby out of the backpack and holding him out to Sally.

'I'm not going up there.'

'Are you taking him or not?'

'I'm not going up there.'

The man with the microphone was calling for any last minute contestants to step forward. They had a busy programme and any baby not on stage when the judging started couldn't be considered. 'You know your baby's the best,' said the sweating man, 'and if he's not the best maybe the little blighter can fool our judge for a few moments.'

Sally's baby was colicky, a poor sleeper, a bad latcher and his normal expression suggested a struggle with wind.

'I'll take him up then,' said Terry.

'You?'

'Why not let me? We win, you can keep the money but it'll be my photo in the paper.'

A dyke holding her baby—the baby she'd almost died giving birth to: it had felt like that and not connected at all to the way everyone else in the room had become immediately amused once the thing was finally out, as if the baby was nothing more than a punchline. Here was the joke delivered again. If she was playing dyke, Sally thought, Terry was playing het.

Sally was feeling sick in the sun. She shrugged and Terry jogged up on stage, cradling the baby's head with a hand. A deep pelvic pain went through her watching Terry take her, Sally's, place in the line. She'd given up so much, she thought. Her habit and now this. Her freedom and now this. She'd given up even her newest burden. Her life consisted purely of renunciation. She was not even allowed to hold onto the thing that she had not chosen and which ruled her life. Yet she understood that was not true. Everyone said that, and she had said it too— that her life was over with this baby. It was an enjoyable, encouraging thing to say since it suggested the baby was in good hands, and the mother, in speaking, felt a rush of righteousness and self-pity which was also a form of energy. You needed that energy no matter how it was come by. But a baby did not rule her life as heroin had. For one thing, the baby lacked constancy. She could not attend to it as she attended to a regular and predictable need. It was an avalanche, or a placid white shape in the whiteness. It was everything at once, or almost nothing. For an hour one afternoon Sally had forgotten entirely that she had a baby.

The baby judge was welcomed onto the stage. This was the owner of a garden centre, a grandmother, a person in green gumboots, with silver white hair, as if from a drawing in a kids' picture book about sweetness, goodness. The sweating man was talking about the babies being saplings and buds as the judge made her way—she was embarrassed—along the line, scarcely able to look into the faces of either mother or baby. Some of the babies were crying, truly ugly. The judge could not pause here. The distressed and the serene should be viewed without preference, and she continued, her walk stooped, her motion full of apology. It was a stupid event, everyone felt, a hangover from years past. There was the aura of insult in this collection of women and children. Had this old woman in her day been part of it—as a young mother, as a baby?

Sally felt it then that they could win, they were going to win. They would have a hundred dollars from the green fingers of such a grandmother. Her baby had no one like this in his life, but he had found her and they had found each other and the fact that it was not his real mother holding him would make no difference.

She watched how Terry did it, how she would win. Terry did not hold the baby up as some of the mothers did, to offer the judge a view of the moving parts, the little legs waving in mid-air as though they belonged to a kitten or an insect. She had him modestly in the crook of her arm and glanced up only from politeness as the judge passed them, giving the bent and kindly woman the barest of nods. Some of the taller mothers were crouching down to bring their babies to the judge's eye level. Terry was stocky and did not move except to return her gaze to the baby once the judge was gone.

The baby appeared still and luminous. I love my child, Sally thought. They had been born together.

A photographer, presumably from the newspaper, went past Sally on his way to the stage. It was in the nature of motherhood that she, the real mother, would not figure in this photo. She watched the photographer moving among the women who were now out of the line. The man with the microphone was talking with the grandmother; the sound of their whispers was relayed around the soundshell. Terry was coming down the steps towards her.

'What happened?' said Sally.

'They went for a girl,' said Terry.

It was incomprehensible.

There was an announcement and applause. A new line of mothers was stepping forward, this time holding toddlers.

Terry was putting the baby in the backpack and hoisting it onto her own shoulders.

'I'll have him,' said Sally.

'No, you take a break.'

Sally took hold of one of the shoulder straps. 'Give me my baby.'

'Jesus, all right, all right.'

'He's my baby, you know.'

'You don't say.' Terry stepped back and looked at Sally. 'You all right?'

Sally nodded. She had him now. She was clinging to him, squeezing the backpack against her chest. Now she had him she didn't know what to do with him or what it meant to want to hold him like this. If he'd been older she might have thought she was comforting him. He had not been chosen. He was not the one. Someone else had been preferred ahead of him. He had not brought her the hundred bucks. He was hers and no one else wanted him—not even Terry, who'd walked off in the direction of the tearooms. Still she sensed it was also the other way round, as often it must be: he was comforting *her*, he was reassuring *her*. But of course he'd been perfectly calm and relaxed in the arms of another woman, a stranger. By gripping him Sally had actually spoiled that. He was beginning to whimper and wriggle.

Her smothering was a discomfort to them both; her arms had begun to ache.

She was aware of a man standing beside her. He was in his forties, balding, wearing a white short-sleeved business shirt. He carried his tie over his shoulder and faced the stage, pretending to study the mothers and toddlers. He was sweating through his head. He could not look at Sally yet. Once he spoke, she felt strong again, not giddy and ill but resolved and fierce, also wanted.

'You could win that, you know,' he said. It sounded, as intended, a somehow filthy proposal.

four

PENNY COULD BARELY speak when she arrived to collect Anna. She gave the girl a quick and awkward embrace, leaning over and putting an arm round her shoulders while Anna remained slumped on the sofa, the kiss ending in her ear. She told Don hello and went out to the deck for a cigarette.

At the back door he asked whether she'd been busy. Thirty-six patients, she said without turning to face him. He wondered how many he'd seen, how many scripts he'd filled—twice as many almost, though it was hardly worthwhile looking to a doctor for credit on that account. In name he and Penny were both health professionals. In fact she ranked him somewhere down the supply chain, with other retailers; he took his orders from her.

There was five years between them, which in their case amounted to a generation. As a 'battered wife', it seemed Penny had moved further away from him, from his generation and her own, and closer to that of their mother, who had never, to anyone's knowledge, been battered but who seemed to accept readily—perhaps too readily—the facts of her daughter's horror, as if Simon's brutality was a kind of talent that would one day surface, like the sudden appetite some have in middle age for running marathons.

Penny hadn't spoken to her mother in months. But who could speak to Ruth these days? She claimed to be sleeping no more than two hours a night, and certainly she had the credulousness of the insomniac, and the paranoia. Everything was a possible cure, everything a possible cause.

Penny was onto her second smoke by the time he brought out tea for them both, placing the tray down on the table underneath the sun umbrella.

'It's hot,' he said.

'I'm not drinking mine for a bit,' she said.

'The day I meant. The weather.'

'Oh.' His sister looked blankly out into the backyard. In the near distance the smokestacks of the hospital shone like rockets. Don had set up a swing for Anna from the branch of their kowhai. It had a red plastic seat that glinted in the afternoon sun. He had to wipe the seat down every few days from the birds that sat in the branches overhead. If Anna found out about the bird shit she would probably never use the swing again.

'Do they have air conditioning at the surgery?' he said. Penny didn't seem to take in what he meant. He found himself answering his own question. 'I think they must have or else you'd know about it. It's been bloody hot today, Pen.'

'Yes,' she said, suddenly revived, annoyed. 'Of course there's air conditioning, we're on the second floor.'

'Okay, I didn't know where you were working.' He cut a piece of cheese for his cracker—good, expensive, award-winning cheese, he made sure, since the pharmacy profits were now theirs. It was a weakness. The fat ran rather quickly to his gut. At his size, there was always the heart to think about, the family history. For a short time he'd taken up jogging, as a balance to the cheese, and he learned again that he thoroughly hated it. He settled on running harder at touch rugby, which he played most weeks down at the Bay. Right then an impatience stabbed at him; though he was clumsy at the game, he felt he was waiting out the week until he could play again. There was an urge in his legs.

Penny walked to the railing. 'Is that a swing? Christ, is that cheese?'

'You want me to make you one?'

'What sort of cheese? Yes, but I don't want a cracker.'

He cut off some and handed it to her. 'Anna goes on the swing.'

She put the cheese in her mouth as he read out the awards it had won from the wrapping. Penny was thinner than she'd ever been—this was probably lunch. If she carried a lunchbox to work, he could check.

'No wonder she wants to live here,' she said. 'With her own swing.'

She clearly disapproved. The swing seemed suddenly in the nature of a bribe. She was holding the end of her second cigarette—*this* was lunch—looking around for somewhere to put it. She gestured towards the deck. 'May I?'

'You already did one.' From the window he'd seen her toss it out into the garden.

She dropped the cigarette and rubbed at it with her shoe, then kicked it off the deck. 'Remind me, Donny, to go down there after and I'll clean up. Don't want Tina upset.' She turned back towards the doorway and looked in at Anna watching TV.

'Why isn't she on the swing now?' She called into the room. Anna didn't move her head. 'I haven't seen you on the swing yet. Have a quick swing, come on.' Penny picked up her cup of tea using both hands. There were cheese crumbs on her shirt. Her wiry thick hair was escaping at various points. The clips strained. Her eyes were bagged. Her skin was sallow. The perfect specimen of a health professional. She looked like she needed to see a doctor. Like most of them, however, she was a great self-prescriber. 'You go on back to work, Don, if you have to. We'll lock up.'

'I don't have to.'

'Go on. Let me have this and we're gone.'

'I don't have to, I'm the boss.'

'You're the boss.' In the echo there was a cold amusement.

'I say jump.'

'You still having those dreams, Donny?'

'What dreams? Did Tina tell you about them?'

'Wasn't she meant to?'

'I don't care.' He wasn't so vain he believed he was never talked about, yet it surprised him still and he didn't like it. Tina was discreet, unless asked directly; then she was helplessly forthcoming.

'I can see that.' Penny lifted the cheese knife. 'We'll leave now.'

'Stay as long as you like, Pen.' It was an effort to bring it out, though not because he didn't want her to stay—he did. 'Stay for dinner.'

'Dinner?' Somehow, Penny could always make him feel foolish for attempting a kindness. This wasn't a new skill and it wasn't cruelty, more like a hypersensitivity to anything insincere. His sister, like all cynical people, had set very high standards for the heartfelt.

Anna spun off the sofa and came running out to the deck. 'Yes!' she said. 'Goodie. Stay for dinner.' She walked back to the sofa and lay down on it, staring again at the TV.

54

'Tina's going to love this,' said Penny. She leaned across to finger the material of his white tunic. 'You look like a psych nurse, Donny. Like you're looking after me. I feel like I'm in the grounds of a nice institution. There are even swings available. Am I mad? What did you do to your head?' She forgot to stub this cigarette out but flicked it far into the bushes. Not quite immediately—with that delay typical of her—she realised what she'd done and volunteered to rush down and get it. She'd always made a point of underlining his conventionality. The middle child, naturally, had to be something of a bridge—in his case, between two kinds of victimhood. Don needed to be *their* victim, since they had no victims of their own. It was Tina who'd explained this to him. Did she think he was a victim? he asked. No, she said, he only had to *figure* as one for the purposes of, if he liked, the sibling story. He said he wondered if the story could be changed. Tina said she didn't know. All she knew was that she'd married the nice one in the middle whose life was not in crisis. The characterisation both pleased and disappointed him. He told her he thought that sounded boring. Yes, she said flatly, you're the boring one.

'Leave it, Penny. We'll watch the spot while we drink our tea and if anything bursts into flame we'll throw the teapot at it.'

Slowly Penny sat down and, without smiling, began to watch the bush. After a while she said, 'No you won't, that's a beautiful teapot. I know who gave you that teapot, don't I? It was me.'

'It is a beautiful teapot,' he said. He had never given the teapot a thought but now looking at it—they were both doing this—he believed it was probably either very valuable or worthless. It was done as a dragon, with the spout a fiery mouth and the handle a green tail. In this appropriation the pot might have represented a mild insult to Chinese culture, yet it was not quite kitsch. Something in its proportions gave it an unlikely elegance; and he knew it to be a brilliant pourer—the sole test he had of a teapot's worthiness.

Don thought his sister was probably mad and should be on something. Perhaps she was on something. He had never filled a script for her, as a matter of ethics, and privacy. At times he'd gifted their family bits and pieces from the overstock—perfume, teething rings and toys when Anna was small, sunscreen. Once, he gave Simon something for the eczema-type rash on his back and upper arms. He had inspected that creature's minor ailments.

'First I've got to take the car back to work,' he said. The pain from the nail had returned with Penny's question about it.

'What can I do, peel a carrot?'

The offer was plainly a courtesy. Don imagined Penny lying on the sofa, drinking his gin—an image that truthfully pleased him. He wanted his sofa inhabited, his gin swallowed, his mad sister made sane. 'Yes,' he said. 'All right. But nothing more.' Now she would have to do something more—make a salad perhaps. She tore a lettuce, however, as if she was boning a chicken; the leaves, as Tina once pointed out, bore those liquid bruises. Don, remembering this, made a point of taking the gin from the cupboard and the ice from the freezer and placing them with a smacking sound on the bench. If anything could drag his sister upwards it was ice returning uselessly to its original state.

T HE PHARMACY WAS still cooking. Inside a thousand bottles the temperature had risen further, it seemed, the air syrupy and sharp, a soup of vitamins, cosmetics, molasses. By midday it was usually druggy and unpleasant, headachy. Don thought again of having the air conditioning overhauled, a favourite staff complaint. He used to make it himself. But where was the economics in such a scheme? (Depressing to hear poor old Perry's arguments sounding so reasonable in his head.) Summer's uncomfortable peak lasted only a short time—two or three weeks perhaps—before the alpine winds, mild at first, came skidding across the farmland from the west, and from the south,

Antarctica sent miniatures of itself, burnishing the port with white-caps, swelling the streets with teams of Korean sailors. Early on Sunday mornings—Don sometimes went running then—you could find a sailor's hat in the gutter.

He hoped only to drop the keys in and take off again, but Graham was sitting in one of the chairs by the dispensary, looking mournful and keen, and there were a couple of phone messages to deal with. As he dialled the numbers Don motioned with his hand that Graham shouldn't get up.

They met for coffee every second Thursday. It wasn't their day. Graham was on the methadone programme so he came every morning but never lingered. He had two years of a PhD in maths from Cambridge, and his derangement was confined to certain quirks that Don found more or less tolerable. On Thursdays they always had to have the same table in the same café—the table closest to the toilets, from where Graham would sometimes issue false statements about the availability of the toilets to other customers. Generally, he'd tell attractive women that the toilets weren't free at that moment. Most other people he let through, though occasionally he told the same lies to children. Men and plain women got the okay.

Offsetting some of this craziness was the fact that Graham continued to hold down the part-time job Don had helped get him, doing data entry for Student Records at the polytech, which in turn allowed Graham to remain in the bedsit that Don had also managed to secure for him. Graham was, as Tina had put it, Don's 'project'. No, in fact they were closer than that.

Janet, Don's number two, was at the sink humming, though not with a tune. She had a small electric motor inside her, the motor of something deeper than happiness—the hum of orderliness, which of course was more important than emotion, in a chemist.

'Any emergencies? Anyone die?' he asked her, his hand over the receiver.

'Not that I saw,' said Janet. She looked up and noticed his head. 'What happened to you?'

'Spot of bother down at the kindy.'

In the style of an ice-tray—he thought of the one he'd left out for Penny—only cubes of solace were created in the pharmacy, distinct areas of cooled air, known by all: in the recesses of the dispensary, in the bathroom attached to the storeroom, in the far corner of the shop where Sharon, the shop girl and Starlet driver, had placed herself. (Don used to sit in the toilet, with his cup of tea, looking at the old car magazines Perry dumped there. Perry had once bought a sports car and with it the inevitable subscription to car literature.)

Rameesh, the intern, fiddled with the computer, rounding his shoulders protectively over the screen. Whenever Don approached the computer, Rameesh did something fast with the keys—a program was always just closing, a new task beginning. It was Rameesh who'd set it up so Don could look at the pictures from the Christchurch car dealer, so he wasn't completely useless; though it was also Rameesh who told him on an almost daily basis that the thousands they'd just thrown at upgrading their computer system was money down the drain. The intern, Don thought, took a quiet satisfaction in the 'teething problems' they'd had and continued to have.

'Who's winning?' Don asked.

Rameesh tapped away and didn't turn around. 'I'm running Norton.'

'I'm running a pharmacy, I'll swap you.'

Don thought if he sat down with the manual he could soon find what Norton was, and other incriminating evidence. Rameesh's father was buying him a pharmacy once he'd completed his training. It was hard to see the intern as a sympathetic figure.

Don felt a flush spread through him, up his back, his neck— where the collar of his white dispensing jacket still stuck into him—and through his hair, ending with a concentrated ping in his nail wound that was now covered by a plaster and a few puffs of antiseptic powder. The flushes had had him worried. The previous month his prostate had been checked and given the all clear. The sweat was sweat—he was hot, everyone was hot. Icebergs the size of cities were breaking off and floating free. Still they kept playing that prostate ad on TV with the guy watering his garden and the water suddenly stopping because of a kink in the hose. In Don's mind this was connected with the current water restrictions. 'Wear less clothes,' the doctor told him, 'keep up your fluids.' He'd had a water dispenser installed in the staffroom. The way the air rose in great pockets, it looked like the thing was drinking itself.

Finishing the calls, he couldn't put off Graham any longer, though he addressed him, strategically, from behind the counter, saying that he was in a hurry.

Graham stood up quickly, wiping his hands on his trousers. 'Did you notice a change in me?'

'When?'

'Now. Over the last few months.'

'What sort of change?'

'You didn't either.'

Don asked him if there was a point to all this because he truly had to be somewhere else.

'That I've been dropping pounds rather fast. I don't have bathroom scales, do I?' Graham was speaking to the plaster on Don's forehead. He had the hair of a former maths whiz—fairish and fine and too long. It was hooked at the ears behind the frame of his glasses.

'I didn't notice it,' said Don. Thin people lived on gradations of change too fine for his eye. Still, Graham, on closer inspection, did appear ill or more ill than usual. He was a periodic shaver, with the tanned face of the homeless. He spent many hours walking around the city. 'You're all right though?'

'Pancreas. They want to have a look inside as well.' He put his finger into his mouth, then mimed a tube going down his throat to his stomach.

'An endoscopy,' said Don.

'Which is a big problem for me.'

'No, it's routine. Everyone has them.'

'I don't.' Graham took a card from his pocket. 'You got to talk to this man. He's the man.'

Don took the card. 'This is who's going to do the procedure?'

'Not if I'm around to fight that bastard off me.'

'They give you a sedative.'

'I want you to talk to the man, Don, and tell him about me.'

'He knows you're on the programme, right?'

'I can't have surgery, can I?'

'Course you can. Who's having surgery anyway? You're getting ahead of yourself, Graham.'

'You ought to see my bowel movements, Don. They've got pancreatitis written all over them.'

From this method Graham, as a token almost of normality, had on several occasions convinced himself he had cancer. Don asked whether he wanted to sit in the back room for a little while, have a cup of tea.

'Would you have one too?' said Graham.

Don shook his head.

'No,' said Graham, 'I want to go home now. Digest this wonderful news. You'll talk to him for me, won't you, Don?' Graham reached out and gripped Don's arm. His hand was the only cool thing in the room, though still not attractive. The nails were dirty. Maybe there was less of the hand there now. 'The pancreas. Six inches of fucking nothing, can you believe it?'

THINGS WERE HOT at the gallery. Walls had been punched, threats and counter-threats circulated. Business as usual.

Tina was talking about it over dinner. In the basement, among the ancestors, there'd been weeping. Tina had been down there with a group of elders, looking at the paintings for the show, and the women had begun to cry and sing. Not everyone was so moved. The chair of the trust that administered the gallery's finances said he might pull the plug if he had to sit through another two-hour welcome in a language he didn't know and which the vast majority of the people in the place wouldn't know either.

'You know what he told us,' said Tina. '"Let them do their little dance or whatever, then get the bloody show on the road. I don't want to hear about their great-great-grandfathers buggering the rival chief in 1802 and how good he tasted. We've all got skeletons. We could all bore the pants off Job with genealogy." God, that man is amazing. What an idiot. And so successful! Every year on the rich list.'

Penny, thankfully, had not got to the salad. Don himself had done the dinner: puttanesca, with extra olives—something he could make in his sleep. Tina had insisted on a pudding, which she'd started the moment she entered the kitchen and without changing out of her work clothes. The apron was on top, the food processor was swung out from the cupboard. They'd just finished eating the result, her old stand-by, lemon meringue pie— 'the cheat's version' according to Tina, the base made from biscuit crumbs not pastry. Penny had told Tina it was delicious; in her book, she said, the cheat's version would be the one she bought from the supermarket.

They'd started talking about Maori artists as Don cleared away the plates. He was quickly out of his depth, his mind, anyway, filled with the events of the afternoon, the decorated guy in the ute. He thought about bringing it up but he didn't want to be mocked by his sister. No matter how he cast it, she'd be sure to draw out from the scene his immobility and lack of nerve.

Tina was laughing at something Penny had said. It was a

strange sound, since she was laughing encouragingly, with greater force than was warranted, trying to get her sister-in-law to express whatever feelings were in her. Penny was Tina's 'project'—they each had one. Penny knew this, but that didn't seem to matter much. Tina was the only person Penny allowed herself to be pampered by.

He heard a name. 'That's the guy who used to go over and watch the US Golf Open,' he said. It was information from Tina. Wealthy patrons, evidently, got the artist the tickets. Don enjoyed being this much in the know, though he seldom went to exhibitions except with Tina for openings.

Tina picked up her fork and used it to point in the air. 'Someone saw him once on TV, at the golf, watching Tiger Woods. Apparently you could see his face in the crowd.'

'Gallery,' said Don.

'What?' said Tina.

'People watching golf, they call them galleries.'

Tina turned back to Penny, who had taken up her pack of cigarettes in one hand and brought them to her chest. 'With Tiger Woods!' She'd had several glasses of wine. There was colour high on her cheeks, and her eyelids were threateningly prominent. Tina was someone whom alcohol, without trouble, found out.

'Two black geniuses,' said Don. He believed, on the evidence, they were, though having said it he was aware he'd sounded malicious or sly.

'See I don't think of either of them as "black",' said Penny.

'Well, they are,' said Don.

'I know they are. I just don't *see* them as black.'

'I know what you mean,' said Tina.

There was a noise from Anna, who slept on the sofa, lulled by the low din of her video, the cartoon *Pinocchio*. They'd already tried once to turn it off, and she woke immediately complaining.

What had they been talking about? No one, it seemed, knew

since the conversation failed utterly to revive. The whole thing belonged anyway to another time. It was that realisation perhaps which made them mute. They'd had these Maori discussions with Simon. Don looked at his sister's gaunt profile. Her almost permanently raised hands—they half-covered her face now—were the hands a boxer puts up in defence, with the difference that Penny had had no intention or no way of fighting back. If it had been boxing, what she'd gone through, she'd been the bag, with the bag's dull burden of abuse to carry and absorb.

The two women went through into the kitchen to do the dishes and they didn't want him in there. Penny snatched the tea towel from his hands and told him to go and sit down, read the paper or something. While Tina filled the sink, Penny guided him back into the living room, pushing playfully at his back. 'Go on, get.' Without the gin, without company, she wouldn't have touched him like this. It gave him pleasure to think they'd achieved that. 'Don't fall asleep, though,' she said. 'You'll have one of those dreams.' And that was Penny, too—for every silver lining, she created the cloud.

The dreams he was having were straightforward. Anyone burdened by new and demanding responsibilities surely had them. They were of disaster and error, and he recalled them most substantially not in their exact content but in their colour, their texture, their taste. They were blue tinged, powdery, acidic. They were routinely pharmaceutical. Frustratingly, typically, he woke in mid-accusation often. Other people's stupidity—Janet's, Rameesh's, Sharon's—was threatening to ruin him, to destroy the goodwill that was the most valuable component and that had been the most expensive item when he'd come to buy the pharmacy from Perry. He would be calling the names of customers who stepped forward showing two heads, open wounds. Weeping needles had been discovered in the face cream. The Mistake—in weighing, in counting, in speaking—was often dropped in the steel pan of his sleep. In one version, a little girl was at the pharmacy counter—at least her fingertips were—green liquid coming from her pants, and Don couldn't find her prescription though Janet was shouting at him that it had been done, it had been done. Then where was it?

He'd even phoned Perry one night. Perry's wife Camille had answered. Perry was sleeping. It was 8 p.m. He had his new heart of course. Perry told everyone he felt strong as an ox, though his thoughts seemed bovine too. At night he banged his head repeatedly against the headboard; he said he felt nothing nor did he remember it in the morning. Camille tied pillows into place. All around, Perry seemed a bad omen.

Don had tried the guest room to spare Tina his bolt-upright pronouncements, the strangely worded instructions that ran from his mouth. The duvet in his fists. It hadn't worked and she'd insisted he come back to their bed so she could at least keep an eye on him.

Don went through to the living room where Anna was sleeping.

Penny, he knew, had once confessed to Tina that when Anna was a baby, only eight weeks old, she had pressed her into the cot. It was the middle of the night. Anna had been crying for an hour and Simon refused to get up. Finally Penny had gone to the baby, picked her up and instead of laying her down she'd pressed her hard into the mattress of the cot, her hand coming down across the baby's chest—'Sleep, damn you, please sleep!'—until she could feel Anna's heart in her hand, which gave her a shock and made her stop.

Penny often used to joke about her difficulties with Anna. 'The threat of child abuse was palpable last night,' she'd say, and laugh. Had Penny, in fact, been trying to tell them about what was happening to *her*?

IT WAS NINE o'clock, still light and warm when Don carried the sleeping child to Penny's car. Her bare legs had a coolness like metal. Her shins shone. She smelled of her dinner—pieces were still stuck in her hair—and dried milk. She would always be one of those children people 'let go' despite their intentions. She would always, even as an adult, be slightly dirty, he thought, with the stain of this resistance and inattention. He longed to love her, and to be fair so did Tina. It was just that she did not think it was necessary to establish a rapport first. He felt Anna's weight through his bare feet, pressing his heels into the footpath.

'Where's the seat for her?' said Tina. 'Where's the car seat?'

Penny looked in the car, groggy from tiredness though certainly exaggerating her confusion. She mumbled something.

'I'll get ours.' Tina went to their car, which was parked beside Penny's. 'Where's ours, Don?'

'I had it in the pharmacy car.'

'Didn't you grab it out?'

'It must still be there.'

'Oh well,' said Penny.

Don was lowering Anna into the back of the car. 'She's not light.'

In the kitchen, the two women had talked together for another hour about artists: who was in and who was out. He'd heard laughter—lighter this time, a natural merriness. Penny and Simon had a small collection of contemporary photographs—chilly pictures of interiors abstracted into nothing; obscure blurry close-ups. It was perhaps the thing Simon would fight hardest for, besides the child, whom he didn't want. Now the mood was about to be wrecked.

'What are you doing?' said Tina.

'She'll be all right, Tina,' said Penny.

'There's no seat, Don.' Tina's cheeriness was gone.

Don propped Anna up and pulled the belt across her.

'It's just around the corner, Tina,' said Penny. 'I'll drive slow.'

'That's a pretty tight fit,' said Don. 'That's pretty stable.'

When he straightened and closed the car door, Tina was

already inside the house. She was punishing her sister-in-law by not kissing her goodnight; she was a fanatical kisser.

'Where is the seat, Pen?' he said. 'Why doesn't it stay in the bloody car?'

'It's not in the car!' She was lighting another cigarette.

'I know but why? Why can't it stay in the car?'

'I must have taken it out, okay!' She was moving around to the driver's door.

'Are you going to have that while you drive?'

'What?'

'You've got no seat for her, and now you want to be waving that around while you drive illegally. Do you want me to drive?'

'No.'

'Should I?'

'I do not want you to drive me home. I do not!'

Anna stirred inside the car. 'You're waking her,' said Don.

Penny took a final drag, then flung the cigarette away. 'There!' She got in the car and wound down the window. 'Please say goodnight to Tina for me.'

He waited until the engine started. 'So we're getting her on Monday, right? I'm picking Anna up?'

'If we're still alive.'

Don watched as the car crawled to the end of the street for its right-hand turn, and then he waited for the indicator to come on, but of course it didn't.

WHEN TINA UNDRESSED for bed, tipping herself out of her bra and lifting her breasts in inspection, she would often run her fingers over the clammy skin between them, always with an unhappy or judgmental look on her face. Unhappy about that clamminess? About the bra? Or dissatisfied with her breasts? Except it wasn't dissatisfaction. She was pleased she had them, when so many others did not. When they'd first got together, he'd been surprised by how often she mentioned this or that friend who 'had nothing'. When a flat-chested friend had her baby, of course, there was much astonishment at the new look, at the temporary rise. Tina, in all other matters modest to the point of reticence—especially about her knees, which she disliked showing no matter how encouraging Don was—had a deep pride in this permanence.

The 'unhappiness', he guessed, was Tina's modesty scrutinising such a public display—if a bedroom was public. Of course he was the public in this case and the look was certainly for him also. It was a kind of encouragement—'Look at me.' At the same time the invitation seemed to be withdrawn: 'But I'm really just looking at myself.' He never tired of it, the pull and the push, the advancement and the retraction of this display. He was not tired of it now, and yet he didn't watch her. She was angry with him over the car seat and, though she appeared not to be acting differently in any way, her anger effectively removed his viewing rights. He read his trade journal.

In bed her shoulder was so near to the page it was almost overpowering. He put his hand on it and she made a noise and turned to him, still holding her book. The two books touched. They had, he thought, the amorousness of a pair of librarians. Her bookmark was lost somewhere in the sheets. She made a half-hearted attempt to find it. These days he had little time for the novels she liked to push in his direction. To the usual pile of pharmaceutical journals were now added drug company brochures, management manuals and inspirational texts from business gurus—a pile of which Camille, Perry's wife, had brought round and which he was powerless to refuse. 'You have them,' she'd said rather fiercely, as though about to add 'and we'll see how *you* like it'.

They'd kicked the duvet off the bed and the window was open, yet still the night didn't deliver much relief. She handed him her book and he put it with his own on the side-table and turned off the light.

'Graham came in today,' he said. 'They're worried about his pancreas.'

'Who?'

He understood the tone; she'd meant 'Who cares'. Yet he went on. 'Graham. At the pharmacy.' Tina moved in the bed, banged at her pillow. 'Poor bloke,' he said.

'What is it?' Her question was almost swallowed in a yawn.

He waited a few moments then he said, 'Never mind.'

She turned over so her back was facing him. 'I'm so tired.'

Ten minutes later he heard her walking to the toilet. Neither of them had slept. When she got back into bed she cuddled up to him, gripping him round the stomach. She put her finger in his navel, a favourite haunt. 'Sorry,' she whispered. 'I'm so grumpy. I shouldn't drink.'

He turned to face her, kissing her on the nose and the forehead. 'No, it's me too. This weather.' In a little while he heard her breath begin to push through her nostrils—soon, astonishingly, she'd be asleep. 'I had this weird thing happen today at the kindergarten.' Tina grunted. 'This guy tried to freak me out. He was just a kid. With tattoos on his face. Moko.'

'Moko.'

Given her state, she'd pronounced it firmly. She needed to correct his pronunciation. She had claims here that were justified. He'd never been on a marae like she had. He'd never attended the te reo classes like she had. What did he know about the tangata whenua that wasn't from TV? He was as bad as his mother.

'What happened?' she said, waking a little more.

'Nothing. He just wanted to give me a scare, I suppose. In the car. Probably just some misunderstanding. He thought I was giving him the right of way, so he lurched out in front of us.'

'Is that where you got that cut?'

'No, I told you how that happened.'

'Oh, yes. Sorry. Brain getting slower. There's some horrible drivers out there.'

He sat up in bed. 'I forgot to ring Graham's doctor.'

'He'll be all right, won't he? Good old Graham.'

'Don't know.'

'I think he will,' she said.

'That's half the battle then, isn't it?'

She gave a sleepy laugh, a finishing sound which gently removed any intention he'd had to provoke her further—and indeed there had been a desire, mild and friendly but still faintly aggressive, to get at Tina. He lay down again. He'd felt faintly aggressive for a while now; it seemed to have arrived with the flushes—probably the result of not sleeping well. He turned over in bed to hold her around the thighs. He was thinking that whatever had been contested in this exchange, Tina had won. How could she be other than the victor when she was nearly asleep while he remained so uselessly alert? He shifted in bed, trying to get into a position that meant his head wasn't pressing down on his bandage.

When he got out of bed a few minutes later, she didn't stir. He went into the bathroom and, without turning on the light, found the bottle of Halcion tablets. It was some prophetic skill of his that even as a child he'd never needed water to wash down a pill.

five

BLACK WAS AN uncanny colour for a dog—even a Labrador—and when her husband died she'd given the dog away, rapidly and secretly. Ruth had the dog on her mind again because of the intruder. Donny was always on to her about getting a dog for security purposes, by which he meant an animal—walking it, feeding it, combing it—could keep her from her own thoughts. He believed his mother was going nuts. She spent sixty-five dollars a week on supplements and something called guidance.

Someone was in the pool. He yelled and splashed. He was expected.

For no particular reason, the kennel was there now—she could see it from the window. Henry had built it. Corrugated iron and four-by-twos. It was too heavy to move. Most recently it'd functioned as a playhouse for Anna, Ruth's granddaughter. And for two weeks thirty years before that, she recalled, Jamie had slept in it.

The day she got rid of the dog she'd had to watch as Jamie, who would have been eleven, put out the dog's dinner, and when he called the dog she had to remain silent. Later, he went looking for it. He pinned up notices around the neighbourhood. Lost: one beautiful black lab. He even drew, heartbreakingly, a picture of the dog, with a speech bubble coming from his mouth containing their phone number. She had to drive Jamie around town every evening for a week. And when he cried she held him, trying to forgive herself at the same time and actually succeeding. She knew she'd done the right thing in getting rid of the dog; her stealth had protected her youngest boy from worse pain, and besides, the grief he was showing was really for his father and not the dog. Hadn't she given him a more acceptable premise from which to launch his tears?

Then Donny had come home from school one day to find Jamie had done something that annoyed him—she couldn't remember what—and Donny, with whom she'd entered an unspoken pact on this, had told Jamie that wasn't it weird how the dog had run away with its lead and with its blanket and with its toy bone and everything. Jamie didn't get what he meant. Ordinarily, Donny was not malicious. He, too, was affected. The anger he felt at his father dying was turned on his little brother. She should have seen that coming. 'That's pretty amazingly prepared of a dog that's just taking off from its home, isn't it?' said Donny—which was when Jamie decided on the kennel for a bedroom. He crawled in and seemed at once more animal than anything. He received his meals through the opening.

Though Ruth had told her children no matter what you do

you can always come home, they never had. They did not, in their darkest hours, turn to her.

Without quite knowing why, she read their horoscopes—not the ones provided on syndication by the newspapers. Her naturopath, Lou, issued a weekly personalised report. Crazy— it was easy to see that; she saw it herself, thus establishing the opposite. The mad had no real insight. They were shut always within systems, occasionally of genius. Lou was mad; listening to her was nothing of the sort. Ruth believed contact with certain extremes gave her a sort of resistance, as inoculations carried a small amount of the disease.

Perhaps her children didn't come home because they sensed something else in her, some fearful need she was keeping from them which would be sprung once they moved back in. But they were wrong. She wasn't scared of being alone, of being left with all the other inmates. Inmates of gardens, she meant, of hobbies, of the blankets that covered knees just like hers gathered to watch a fifteen-year-old from Southland dressed simultaneously as a woman and a set of embroidered curtains sing 'Heart Don't Break' on a cooling night down at the Bay. It wasn't fear, it wasn't horror. It was intolerance, an old failing, indistinguishable from her pride. In the things she wouldn't put up with, Ruth was sometimes pleased to remind herself of a great aunt she was taken to visit as a child from time to time who said things like, Oh I don't like the radio because it's always on. That aunt had sat on a chair that was raised on a sort of platform to allow her legs to dangle a little—an aid to circulation. From this throne, she was haughty and funny and outrageous, sparing no one, though she was softer on people once they'd died.

The house Ruth stared out of was the largest in the street, two storeys, and desired by many—the fliers came through regularly, which she said she hated. They had buyers waiting. Phone calls woke her at nine at night. People, obviously without self-control, had come to the door, begging, apologising. They embarrassed her into giving the odd tour. Yes, the tiles on the hearth were the original tiles. In the hallway, the oak panelling. On the landing, yes, the leadlights. From the master bedroom, French doors—an addition of course—onto the balcony, original. The cult of originality saw her place as something of a temple. These were the worshippers—bank managers, accountants, lawyers. No, no, I can't see myself giving it all up just yet. Where would I go? This is where my children grew up.

Still there were little things she could have shown them. There were always little things in such a big place, even when her husband had been around. And she didn't want to be full-time maintenance. She vacuumed sometimes with a bag that needed emptying, dusted carelessly without using her finger to test. The old toys she'd brought out for Anna to play with—untouched for months—were still piled in the corner of the sitting room. It was a house after all, a building. There was nothing of her soul in it. She wouldn't be reduced like that. The proud widow rattling around in her tomb. She'd stopped using the downstairs toilet, for instance. The price of a plumber, when she'd rung, had convinced her to close the door and seal it with a draught-stopper. Fixed. Obviously there could be no tours now, since people always wanted to nosy into every corner and it was always the closed-off places that drew them most powerfully. You could walk them around a room so generous in its proportions they'd helplessly swing their arms in appreciation. But immediately after they wanted to investigate a cupboard no bigger than the width of a towel, and look and test the hinges on the cupboard door. In the kitchen, which was huge, with a skylight throwing illumination down onto a butcher's block of kauri, they opened the cutlery drawer and looked underneath to examine the drawer's two-dollar rollers. It wasn't, in the end, their delight she needed so much as their suspiciousness, which confirmed for her something basic and necessary: no one was happy. She was not and would never be alone.

Outside there were other things. The back fence, which kids had been pulling on for years. Again, she'd got a quote. Instead of repairs, she'd placed a large padlock on the gate to the pool. Behind the gate the pool may as well have been a wound, open to the world.

She told herself then she wasn't surprised that someone was in it. She'd been drawn to the kitchen window by the splashing and the voice. Someone divining water in the heat. What was that voice? It'd stopped her dialling for the police, though she still held the phone.

Behind the rose-covered trellis, the voice was calling, 'Muharm! Myah um. My arm!' Had he hurt himself? He would have climbed fences to get in, or the neighbour's tree with its branch that broke the boundary line, which she'd given up hacking off— it was a brute. There were always tennis balls floating, or balloons. Balloons seemed much more popular than they had been when her children were young. Everyone gave away balloons now, as vehicles of inane promotional messages, and her pool was where they all came to die. Had he cut himself somehow? If there was blood in her pool, she didn't know what she'd do. Would it flush out? What would happen to the chlorine? Donny would know.

Donny cleaned out the pool every month, and checked the equipment. Donny was good; she meant he was a good man. It did not seem to her at this moment, however, a clinching quality. Even without children of his own, her son appeared distracted, absorbed, dull. She had prepared for the years when she would help her oldest son with his family, when he would deliver them and a few hours later collect them again. Throughout this period she would be energetic and accepting and generous, and her son would be tired and grateful. Occasionally he would remonstrate with her over some small aspect of child-rearing. Don had married someone attractive and kind and intelligent, but also someone who was at war with nature. She knew that particular battle herself. Tina had had seven miscarriages—the number was grotesque—the last one on Christmas Eve, when she'd stood up suddenly from the dining table (Ruth had been around for a meal and early presents) and excused herself. Ruth didn't go to the hospital with them; she cleaned their kitchen, and after she'd done that—all the dishes and so on, not even using the dishwasher since that seemed slack and offensive—she'd sat by herself in her son's house in the dark. They were not home at midnight, which was the time Ruth started vacuuming. She had never made such a noise at midnight, the vacuum nozzle clattering over the wooden floorboards; surely someone would ring up to complain.

When he visited, Don ached to get down to the pool, to rest on the long handle of the net, to scoop at the water as though with a wand, stirring up a wish. But what wish? She didn't know what he wanted. Goodness had not delivered him much. That he owned the pharmacy now—and could travel and spend—struck her as insufficient to his being, changing the pattern on the surface without affecting what happened beneath. In summer he lowered himself into the water like a girl. Her son had breasts. They were brown pouches, pinkening at the aureole. He did not have his father's body at all. Jamie had had that—the athleticism; broad-shouldered, narrow-hipped, with thick strong legs; Penny also. Poor Penelope. Don was rather hulky.

'Marm!' called the voice.

Setting the phone down, she put on her sunhat and walked into the garden. It was blazing, awful; the concrete of the courtyard struck her in the face. She went back inside for her sunglasses, and was tempted again by the phone. She put on the sunglasses, and the phone, which was black, disappeared. This wasn't an omen—she was not usually prone to them, as Lou had said—though she felt it carried an unavoidable message: go out and face it. 'Our task,' Lou told her, 'is to interpret, not invent.'

From the shed she took her large gardening fork, but once

she was at the vegetable patch she stuck the fork into the soil. It fell, lifting dry clods of earth onto the path. She stepped over the fork and its mess. An implement could be used against her. The padlock was still in place. She could look safely enough at this menace through the trellis. The beast was caged, and in distress.

'Murmmm!'

She could see him now, or parts of him. The trellis and his jerky movements in the pool cut his head and arms into a strobe that hurt her eyes. She looked away, then looked back. Even cut up, she felt there was something familiar about the head, its shoulders. There were young men living next door. They attended polytech, the chef classes. She'd found paper hats in her garden. One time a group of them—drunk—had knocked on her door. 'Excuse me,' the ringleader spoke, 'we're chefs. Would you like toad-in-the-hole?' There was an explosion of laughter, then they staggered off back to their place. Chefs, in their kitchens for hours, had little access to normality; they suffered as women did.

She went forward. He'd stopped moving and gone silent, aware of her now. He lifted himself out of the pool and lay flat out beside it, as if sunbathing or dead. He was pale and stretched. Then he started to creep towards the fence, his head still down.

'Who's that?' she said. She was afraid. The fear tasted of the tines of the fork. 'Who's in there?' The thing was almost at the fence. 'This is private property. That pool is mine.' With this last statement she felt she'd committed an indiscretion approaching his—the pool, no matter that it sat at the bottom of her garden and was a 'feature' of those by-gone real estate tours, had never been hers. She couldn't swim. She hated the splashing. Such a collection of water to her was a hazard. She would have had it removed if it was practicable. A drained pool was no better, however—that added only eeriness to it. The pool was her husband's and the children's. Penny had been the best swimmer. She was not supposed to blame Penny, of course, for the tangle she was in. She was not to think of the meals she'd cooked the man who wasn't worthy to crawl into the kennel they had outside, where once Henry had kept his black lab and Jamie had slept. Still, she missed the little girl. Anna's unpleasantness somehow bound the girl to the house. She wasn't supposed to blame Penny but Penny somehow was blaming her. One of those offences had occurred which become so longstanding no one remembers what it is. A word, a gesture, or the absence of these, and a cold crust is formed, like the closing over of some creature's breathing hole in the ice. Ice! The idea partially revived her.

Ruth came a few steps forward and peered through the gaps in the trellis at the head.

'Mum,' it said. 'Ma.'

Yes, naturally, all along, it had been her name cried out. She felt a strange sort of embarrassed pride at the address, and a flush of self-pity, as though some private endearment had been uttered in public. She was at the gate but it was locked and the key was back in the house. He put his fingers through a gap in the trellis. Without thought, she gripped them.

'Bit hot,' he said.

He was wearing underpants, thank God, yet he looked naked in the way his brother never did quite. Donny's dark complexion clothed him, as did his fat—you could cast off fat. There was nothing to be lost from this person, surely. He was reduced to the elements—skin and bone. With a little twist he pushed his hand and his wrist and then his arm up to the elbow through the gap that had looked big enough for only the fingers. She felt sick, in the way any contortionist made you sick.

'I'll get the key,' she said. She didn't want any more of his body to come through the trellis at her.

He waved his arm. 'Hello,' he said goofily, as though it was his arm that was speaking.

'Hello.' She looked again at the arm, its inside. The skin

glowed white in the sunshine and its surface was ridged and untidy, as though it'd been through fire. The arm, of course, *was* speaking. I am yours, it said. I can pass through any barrier. I am home. I am Jamie.

HE DIDN'T WANT to sit anywhere except on the piano stool and he kept turning to strike a few keys. The first thing Lou, her naturopath, had done when she entered the house—a house call was necessary to the assessment—was walk over and open the lid of the piano. The ivory, with its discolourations, had always reminded Ruth of the fingernails of a smoker.

Extraordinarily, whatever progression Jamie hit sounded terrible. The piano seemed to give back only its ugliest capabilities, the notes unrelated, unmusical. She wished he would stop, and that he was wearing shoes. His long toes bunched at the carpet like a cat sharpening its claws. The nails, she noticed, were long—not just negligently so but extravagantly grown. Perhaps he was some sort of performer, a sexual thing. His readings were regularly about romance, while Donny's stuttered about business. Plainly the information she'd given out on her sons was dictating their paths through the stars, though that didn't make Lou a fraud. Ruth was satisfied to have a little intuitive flair added to the stories she provided. If someone insisted on calling this astrology, she didn't feel compelled to object. That it upset Donny so much gave it an extra interest, yet that was all it had for Ruth—interest. She was not about to change her life because a woman dressed in floral flowing garments and sneakers told her to swallow copper and magnesium, watch for a stranger and leave the lid of a piano always in the upright position. All these things she did, she did from boredom and curiosity. Still, here was her stranger. *Someone is on a journey in this direction.* As a commentary on Lou's offering, Ruth remembered, the milkman's truck had sounded its musical horn, the phrase incomplete of course. The world always answered in jokes, she thought, defending itself against revelation.

Her own feet were in sandals. She liked to see the veins above her ankle and press down on them with her finger. Go blood. Stop blood. Go blood. Juvenile, she knew. She'd been a girl when she'd first done it. She understood she was comforting herself with this little show of strength over her own body.

She'd made tea but Jamie wouldn't let her bring it to him. 'Leave it there,' he said. 'I don't like hot drinks.' Suddenly he had preferences, inabilities. He'd taken piano lessons for years. Well, she herself at one time had been an adequate flautist. She now knew more or less which end to blow in. There were wrong turns everywhere, the wreckage of abandoned obsessions.

'Are you down for long, Jamie?'

'Am I down for long?' He grinned at her. His teeth matched the piano's off-white keys. 'Not, "Would you like to stay?"' A fortune had disappeared on these teeth. It was not the money she missed but something else: the years in which decay had set about its work. When he'd left, there'd been none of this.

It seemed she'd been ready forever, though she'd long forgotten the rehearsed things. 'Would you like to stay? You're welcome to.'

'But you don't know for how long.'

'I don't care. There's plenty of room. As you know.' She regretted this last statement. She did not mean to punish or whine. He was a middle-aged man and mortal, not a child, and though he might behave like a child, she understood she tempted him in this direction not simply because she was his mother but because she so desperately wanted this all to work, and he knew that. It was what gave him his licence to be rude, ungrateful, appalling.

Beneath a disgusting denim jacket with a sheepskin collar, he picked at the material of his teeshirt, rearranging it on his chest. The neck of the teeshirt was stretched as though he'd used it for sleeping. Certainly there was no sign of luggage, of other options.

79

How had he arrived? There was a name and an image on the teeshirt but it was faded beyond legibility. His black jeans were holed at the knees. He got up from the piano stool and walked over to the mantelpiece. The family photos. She felt immediately vulnerable to his judging. Here, as with all such arrangements, were not only her photos but also her choices.

He paused over one at the back: Penny and Simon on their wedding day. Jamie, she guessed, would be in no position to reckon this a flaw. As far as she knew, no one had seen or spoken to him in years. It struck her then, however, that this might not be true. Her children operated, quite clearly, in secretive ways.

He moved quickly to the one of him she'd had out for only a short time—perhaps a month or so. It showed him as a boy of ten or eleven, riding his bike. He had the blondest hair and he was happy—smiling and reckless, his shoelace undone; it hung near the bike chain. Ruth knew immediately why she'd put this one out, having gone years without any picture of Jamie on display. It was because she thought she'd never see him again. Yet it had acted as a talisman to draw him back.

When Lou had looked over this area she'd repositioned several of the frames so they weren't 'talking to one another'.

'The fuck is that goon?' Jamie pointed at himself. 'Excuse me, I meant who is that fine-looking boy?'

'Remember that? Remember that bike, Jamie?'

He was nodding, though not in agreement, holding the photo in his hands, looking into it. He brought it very close. 'There's old Donny.'

'Where?' She stood up and walked across. It was the closest she'd got to him since she'd grabbed his fingers through the trellis. She was nervous, trembling. He smelled of the pool, other things. He pointed in the photo—there was the beginning of another bike wheel in the background. 'I never saw that before. Is that Donny's bike? I hadn't seen that before.' She couldn't tell if he believed her. She sounded too bright. Yet she was speaking the truth and her blindness was a shock, as was his vision. He'd never had an eye for detail. He grasped things at once or not at all; work and effort had never entered into it. It made him her favourite, once—and his father's enemy.

'There's old Donny. Coming up the rear.' Jamie laughed.

It was an unpleasant laugh and she disliked him for it. Her husband had always said they weren't a real family because of the spaces between the children. Every kid was a new beginning, an only child, a wandering soul. He understood he'd spoken thoughtlessly, forgetting what those spaces meant, only when she began to weep.

She didn't feel like sitting down again. Moving behind Jamie, she saw that his hair had wet his teeshirt. She picked up the towel from where he'd thrown it down on the carpet and patted at the back of his head. He swung round.

'Get off,' he said.

He was right and she was surprised at herself, recognising the shortcut she'd wanted. It was sloppy of her. The moment could not be manufactured.

'It's still wet,' she said, putting the towel down beside him on the stool. 'Have you seen Donny already?'

'Why?' He was walking through into the kitchen. She heard the fridge door opening. 'Got any beer or something?'

In the kitchen she opened a cupboard. 'It's not cold.' She did not tell him it was Sunday morning.

He was moving her out of the way, pulling a near-empty cardboard box of red wine from the cupboard. 'This is not beer,' he said. His head disappeared. He brought up an old bottle of sherry next. 'And nor is this. Right piss-head, aren't we?' Finally, he had the beer—it was in pint bottles. Leftovers from a Christmas or a birthday. Tina, her daughter-in-law, was always keen on importing such festivities into the house where her husband had grown up. She believed, wrongly as it turned out, she was restoring a merriness the house had lost.

81

Jamie stood up with three bottles in each hand, the necks of them expertly caught between his fingers. The skill was not auspicious.

'Do you want to put them in the fridge, James?' She didn't drink. Even the tea she'd poured was rare. Caffeine was a considerable enemy. 'Or in the freezer, would be faster.'

Now he had them on the bench, he seemed not to know what to do next. The bottles were a half-dozen dissatisfactions but it was not only their warm state that got him. He looked from the beer to her and back again. She thought she saw what they meant. If he conceded to their storage in her fridge or freezer, he was as good as stored himself. He was agreeing to stay—at least for the afternoon or the evening.

'I should, you know, get going,' he said. He'd spoken invitingly.

She snatched two of the bottles and put them in the freezer. 'Give them twenty minutes,' she said.

He looked at the freezer with a sort of fright. 'No, I really got to hit the road, Ma.'

'Shall I ring Donny and tell him you're here?'

The question, she saw, cast him adrift. He looked lost. Though she'd known for the twenty years that she hadn't seen her son he was sick, and though she'd read all she could about what his sickness meant, she now understood for the first time what previously she'd only ever processed as the kind of thing typically written about sick people—she saw he was incapable of making a decision which involved genuine choice. Truly he was an adept of compulsion. Nothing he did had the quality of judgement. All evaluation was tied to need. Did he want her to ring Donny? He didn't know. He lacked an opinion or even an opinion-making mechanism.

'What's that on your stomach?' she said.

This released him. He stepped away from her and the bottles. 'Where?'

He'd been showing her the area since they sat down, playing with his shirt. There was a dirty bandage around his navel. 'Were you hurt?'

He pulled up his shirt. 'Oh, that.'

'Let me see.' She didn't want to look.

He dropped his teeshirt, covering up. 'No, it's nothing. You should see the other guy.' The laugh again.

'Were you in a fight, Jamie? Is that properly taken care of? Let me look, won't you?'

He moved to the back door. 'I've seen someone, it's all right, Ma.'

'Really? A doctor?'

He clapped his hands together three times, then rubbed them. 'Only thing I need is some sleep.'

The clapping gesture, so at odds with the request, announced his deep fatigue—worse things perhaps.

'Come upstairs then and lie down.' She took his arm firmly and, to her surprise, he allowed himself to be led out of the room. Comically, he dragged his feet. 'Jamie, you want to cut those nails.' She regretted the statement, though she had a vision of them slicing through her sheets. She'd put him in the single room.

At the top of the stairs he turned her, with a sudden movement, into her own room, the master bedroom. She attempted to guide him back but he collapsed onto the bed and wouldn't move, his face buried in the duvet.

She'd not had the duvet on at night for months. Every morning she dragged it over the sweaty sheets. Lou had told her she wasn't to wash her sheets more than once a week. By sleeping always in clean sheets, Ruth was establishing an expectation that plainly couldn't be met—namely, that the sheets would assist her in achieving more than her usual two or three hours a night. Ruth, Lou said, was not to talk of herself as an insomniac. There was, in fact, no such category. What am I then? asked Ruth. You're

Ruth, said Lou. What was it in Lou's voice that made this idiocy sound significant and new?

'Would you like the curtains pulled?' Jamie was still, his eyes shut. Ruth closed the curtains and looked around the room. No one had been in this room with her for years, except Lou, of course, who'd found it to be highly conducive—for what, she didn't say. The French doors were the only problem. If they could come out, the room would be ideal. No, thought Ruth, they could not come out. French doors were what one put in—that was their essence. They did not get taken out.

She bent down and pulled the telephone jack from the wall. From the bedside table she soundlessly removed her primrose oil, her valerian and her melatonin—something she never did when Donny was in the house. Though the pharmacy sold the stuff, Donny disapproved of his mother taking them. In fact, he supplied her sometimes, though she never asked. He left her packages, discreetly. All the things he brought wrapped in gift paper he handed directly to her; the things she needed he slipped somewhere, as though ashamed. The wackier, pricier things she had on mail order from Christchurch.

In the ensuite, she tidied away a few items and lowered the toilet lid. Then she crept from the room, leaving the door open to aid the circulation of air, though there seemed none.

E LDERLY PEOPLE RANG, mothers of babies rang, out-of-towners who'd forgotten to stock up on their medication. There were even genuine emergencies. The phone was set to vibrate—Rameesh had located this function for him—and Don walked out of church to answer it.

It was his mother, who never rang. She was speaking in a hushed voice. 'Have you seen Jamie?'

'Jamie? No. Why?'

'You're not protecting me?'

He told her he didn't understand what she was saying.

'He's here.'

'Where?'

'He's right here, Donny.'

'In Timaru?'

'He's upstairs asleep.'

Don hadn't seen Jamie in more than two years. He'd told his mother nothing about that meeting, nothing about the son Jamie never saw. What was the point? Jamie was never coming home. Now Don felt annoyed with his brother—what a waste of time and emotion that had been, keeping it from their mother. Don didn't like to lie; his success at it seemed to whet an appetite. Yet still he didn't believe her.

'He's at the house?'

'I've just put him to bed.'

'Is he all right?'

'He's terrible.'

'I'll come,' he said.

'No.'

'I'll come. I can come now.'

'Come later.'

There was a twinge from his nail wound. That morning, on his pillow and sheets, there'd been smears of blood.

'Don't come now, Donny, he's sleeping. Let him. I'll ring and tell you when to come.'

When he put his phone back in his pocket it rang again. He expected it was his mother, about to recant the whole story. It was someone called Sally, one of their newer methadones, a girl of eighteen. She'd missed two days. Janet would have reported her to the clinic. She spoke rapidly, on the edge of a familiar panic. He was still thinking about his brother. Was it true? His mother now looked into the stars. She was full of herbal remedies. But she'd sounded excited, alive in a way he hadn't detected before.

Sally was at the end of everything, she said. She didn't know what she'd do with herself. Don cut in. He told her that if she came the following morning at the usual time her stuff would be ready and she'd be okay. Why didn't she take a long walk, or go outside, go to the beach, he said. Take her mind off it.

She was wailing at him now. No, no, no, he didn't understand. She was absolutely at the end. The next morning may just as well be the next year. Walk? She couldn't fucking stand! The beach? She was frying in her fucking house!

He explained that there were rules. The clinic had been through it all with her. Rules were the only thing that made the programme work. 'If I start giving out stuff on demand,' he said, 'I may as well be handing out heroin.' The strict logic of this escaped him but at the mention of heroin being handed out, Sally was at least silenced. Then she was apologetic. She said she knew he was right. She'd made fuck-ups. She was a fuck-up herself. She was sorry for ringing him. She'd probably got him at a bad time, right? A horrendous time, and it was such a beautiful Sunday morning. Sunday mornings, she remembered, were pretty special in her family. Immediately, her speech flowed out. There wasn't a break in it where he could interrupt.

Her dad, she said, used to come for them, pick them up and take them somewhere. He wouldn't say where. Christ, they weren't so dumb they didn't know the whole trip was based on fucked-up parent motives. They knew there was solid hatred in the tank, and that if there hadn't been a nasty divorce with all the stops pulled and scratch marks down her father's face on one occasion and worse on mum, if it hadn't been for two people at *war*, this suddenly attentive dad would have been ignoring them or worse as per usual, but who cared. They didn't care when they were in his car, driving somewhere on a Sunday. A lot of people hated Sundays. She didn't, which was funny.

'Dad's a redhead,' she said. 'Did you say beach? I'm too fair for the beach.'

'I could sell you some sunblock,' said Don. Unaccountably, he felt frivolous almost. With her rambling, his mood had become silly. The news of Jamie asleep in his mother's bed had set him off. Jamie had sworn he'd never come back, not even for his own funeral, he said—an event, at that time, of some imminence.

'You're not open,' said Sally.

'Come tomorrow.'

'What are you doing now?'

'What am I doing?' The question surprised him. He couldn't think of a reply that wasn't truthful.

'Yes,' she said. 'I bet you're doing something.'

A large dog in a car near the church entrance put his nose to the gap in the window and sniffed at him. There were smears on the glass. Don always came to church with Tina. They'd started going again a year ago. They'd been married in a church and, for the first few months of their marriage, they'd felt obliged to return there. The minister always sought them out with firm, lingering handshakes—as if feeling for a pulse, a commitment he knew already to be softening. Then they'd stopped going. Don didn't mind it now. There was a new minister who didn't know them, couldn't judge. It was for Tina they attended, and afterwards they went to one of the cafés on the waterfront and, like other couples, divided the paper up and read it, swapping sections with the fewest possible words exchanged between them, as though they were in bed together.

The café was his idea, as was the newspaper. He felt it offered a mild and necessary corrective to what happened—or, in his case, failed to happen—at church. Lurking somewhere within Tina, like her occasional wearing of items of clothing he'd thought she'd thrown out years before, was the possibility of religious fervour. She'd described the paintings of one touring show—it was the American abstract expressionists—as 'holy'. Jackson Pollock, to her, was something of a saint. Well, he could handle that. The first guy to hurl paint at a canvas. Still, it remained a deep consolation to him that she was not the sort of person who would talk of prayer even though she appeared to practise it. If ever she did start to talk about it, he'd know they were in trouble.

SALLY WAS WAITING for him in front of the pharmacy. She was not attractive, not any longer. He'd barely taken her in before, though he'd served her numerous times. She was tiny, dishevelled, pierced, with a grubby teeshirt hung on a sunken chest. There were cold sores around her mouth. Don was still scolding her as he unlocked the pharmacy back door.

'I'm in a bad way,' she said. She was very happy. He could see her happiness. It forced open her mouth on a surprisingly white set of teeth. The redness of the cold sores disappeared. She was smiling; she was lit up. It was a fine optical illusion. When she scored she would look like this. He'd seen it before in the faces of the methadones as they approached the counter—the anxiety that gripped their features and made them seem ugly, escaping like air from a balloon with each step they took so they appeared to rise on a draught of happiness. 'Hello, hello,' they'd say, giddy, loving. They could be a friendly bunch.

'You're so so kind,' she said as he held the door open for her. She touched the sleeve of his suit. Tina made him wear the suit—since she'd bought herself some new clothes and wanted not to cancel exactly, or conceal, her own purchase but to make symmetrical its effect—and finally he'd begun to enjoy it. 'Nice,' said Sally.

'Sit there,' he told her.

She sat on the sofa in the staff tearoom. The door leading to the storeroom was open and Don thought about closing it. There were boxes of supplies clearly visible from where Sally was sitting. How far could he trust her? She'd picked up a magazine from the coffee table and was flicking through it.

'It'll take me a couple of minutes,' he said. 'Don't you go anywhere.'

She didn't look up from the magazine.

When he came back from the dispensary, she was standing at the little window that looked out into the alleyway. She'd pulled back the curtains. 'What are you looking at?' he said.

'Nothing.'

'Why'd you open those?'

She held up the magazine. 'Going blind, aren't I?'

'Here it is then.'

'You're a god.'

'Before I give it to you, I want you to promise me something.'

'I promise, I promise.'

'I haven't said yet what it is.'

'Say it, darling.'

'Promise me that you'll never miss again.'

'I promise, lover.'

'Never call me again outside shop hours.'

'Promise.'

'Because I won't do this again, understand?'

She was close to him now, with her chin lowered. He was looking down on her hair, the pale parting, the vulnerable scalp like some private inner seam. He could smell her—something recognisable that didn't make sense. Without looking up, she raised her hand so it was level with his face. He placed the little plastic cup on her flat palm and her fingers closed around it. She was wearing several childish rings. Quickly she turned from him. The speed of the movement threw her hair against his chin. He watched her head tip back. Not even the sound of a swallow. As she turned to face him again, she was putting her fingers into his trouser pocket, pressing the plastic cup in there but then flicking it out. She left her hand in his pocket.

'What happened to your head?' she said.

'Nothing,' he said.

'Just looking for sympathy, were you?'

'That's right.'

She was bending down, opening his fly. He felt the air inside his pants adjust itself. The moment shocked him in its surrender. The opening up by other hands was as complete as surgery. He reached down and put his hands under her arms, lifting her up again.

'No,' he said.

She looked at him, confused. A rejected blowjob? Was he queer or something?

The redness was back—he made a mental note to give her something for the cold sores afterwards. He sat down on the sofa. Her arms lay across his stomach. He watched his belt being undone. The material of his suit, Tina had told him, reading from the brochure, actually breathed.

As a hand-job, it was terrifically painful, a real test of his character. Rapidly, he had tears in his eyes. She laughed as he whimpered, giving an aimless, thoughtless tug. It was all aimless. Thoughtless, however, was exactly the wrong word. He was consumed by thought.

He was forced to take over from her for a moment.

Tina was sitting in church. He was horrified at himself. Jamie was mixed up in this too. Stupidly Don felt as though something unfair had happened to him. This was unfair. He had had his opportunities—with shop girls especially. Weekend stocktakes. Drives home at night after working late. There'd been any number of unspoken offers, tacit propositions, indications through the eyes, the body—the entire semaphore of desire. He wasn't queer. They'd watched him being kind to old women. They'd seen his firm ways with difficult customers. When he changed into his running gear for the occasional lunchtime jog they'd seen his big thighs, his surprisingly slender calves. Penny had always wanted these calves. She'd got their father's instead.

Added up like this, he began to think of himself, with tender, pathetic self-pity, as unusually moral and self-denying.

With Sally, he didn't understand now why he'd turned down the earlier part. Her mouth would have been gentler, her pretty teeth. Cold sores—who was he to attempt such fastidiousness? His trousers were around his ankles; his underpants were at his knees. He had never had more than three or four pairs of underpants and a couple of pairs of old boxer shorts he rotated for bedwear. On buying the pharmacy, Tina had cleaned out his top drawer, replacing everything. He now owned underwear that was still in its plastic wrapping. When he stacked jerseys in his bottom drawer, there was the crinkling sound, the ingratiating whisper of unopened gifts.

So he was the boss, so he fucked whom he liked? Was that the new deal, the old new deal? Had Perry too, poor bovine Perry, used the room for this purpose? Was this part of the goodwill Don had purchased along with the building and the stock?

Sally was watching him with a humiliating curiosity. Maybe she too was now wondering what had happened, how she came to be here, how unfair it was. In the scheme of things, certainly she'd had the worse end of the bargain. Her hand glistened. He thought she was about to go to sleep.

He told her to reach over to the shelf above the sink for some handitowels. Immediately he regretted asking—she leaned, still gripping him. 'Get up, please,' he said. 'Go on, get up now.' She used him again—like the arm of a chair—to steady herself. He complained but she just stared at him blankly. She was gone. Through effort and will, or just through some helpless internal chemistry, the girl was absent.

He cleaned up, then threw the handitowels into the sanitary bin in the toilet. He washed his face and hands. In the mirror his face looked flushed. He was tracking his flushes—this one, at least, was easy. He led her to the sink and ran the water. 'Hold out your hands,' he said. She held out her hands and he squirted some liquid soap into them. 'Rub them together. Go on, rub them.' She looked at her hands. Was she kidding him? He felt suddenly he was being done, had. The zombie act was certainly elaborate—the girl hardly remembered how to walk.

He unlocked the back door and led her by the arm into the alleyway. There was a doctors' surgery behind the pharmacy. Sometimes the doctors had to come in after hours and would use the alleyway to park their cars. He noticed the surgery rubbish bins had been stacked against the wall of the pharmacy underneath the staffroom window. He'd mention it to the surgery receptionist, with whom he was on good terms. Most of their business came from this surgery.

Sally chose this moment to revive. She walked briskly round the corner. He wasn't sure whether to follow her. His cowardly hope was that she'd remember none of what had happened. She was zonked. She was suffering from an addiction. Weird shit you couldn't properly recall was always happening to you. People tampered with you—it was part of the game. Degradation was rife. He was part of the game. He was part of the degradation. Addiction was bad. He was a bad man. But could she really say what had happened this Sunday? She liked Sundays.

He walked around behind the building. He'd betrayed Tina in an instant. But it was just an instant. And now it was over, and he wasn't betraying her any more and she wasn't betrayed— not in this instant, not in this one, not in the next either. There was a lifetime of instants that had been and that were to come in which Tina, whom he cared for and loved and needed, was not betrayed. It was Sunday—day of the café and the big newspaper down on the waterfront. Car windows fogging up with the breath of dogs left for an hour. It was Sunday, with its soulful clash of the religious and the secular, belief and its opposite, faith and faithlessness. It was Sunday, when families of all persuasions, in love and in hate, went driving. It was Sunday in Timaru, when a foreign sailor's hat in the gutter was all that remained of the previous night's activities, its carelessnesses. It was Sunday and his brother was at his mother's house for the first time in twenty years. It was Sunday, and Monday would follow. He felt immediately full—he had plenty to be ashamed of. He would jog back to the church. In his mind also was the next game of touch rugby.

In a shadowy corner near the air-conditioning vents, Sally was bending over something—a baby's car seat. What was this? She tucked the blankets in, then she lifted the car seat up and started to walk back past Don.

'Yours?' he said.

'You think I found a baby here and I'm taking it home?'

'It was here all the time?'

'I was only gone a couple of minutes. Don't start on me for child abuse.'

The phrase carried a special charge—did she mean him? She was scarcely adult. He thought, confusedly, of Simon and Penny and Anna. The baby rocked him. Did he know she had a baby? Did he remember a pram when she'd come into the pharmacy before? The baby had been sleeping in the car seat in the alleyway while they'd been inside. It was a horrible scenario. If one of the doctors or a patient had come across the baby when they'd been inside . . . Don felt unsteady. His mess—some tiny portion of it anyway—was probably on the sofa where Janet and Rameesh and Sharon had their morning coffee, his DNA sitting beneath them. Had he cleaned up adequately? Swiftly, he had a politician's fear of the past, of the past's stains.

He couldn't think of what to say to her. The smell—the smell that was on her hair and on her clothes—was the baby. 'What's the name?'

'Richie.'

It was a cartoon, wasn't it? About a rich boy. This boy wasn't rich. The name was a joke. She was playing with him. Was the baby even hers? Was there a baby at all? He peered at it—yes, there was the top of its head. The satin fuzz.

'Richie? A boy then.'

'You're fast.'

'Listen,' he said. 'Sally.'

'He uses my name. First fucking time. Soon you'll be taking me to the movies. Soon we'll be having a fucking date.'

For a moment the ground seemed more solid beneath him. This switch to the abusive was something familiar. He'd been yelled at enough in the shop. As well as the methadones' happiness, their relief, there could be tempers. She was like them, was one of them. He knew them, their patterns. They flared up every so often but the real fire was pretty much out—or rather, the fuel having been removed, they were free to get on with that other conflagration, the one they'd been avoiding, namely life. Life could make you mad, unreasonable, vengeful, stupid. It could burn you, life, for sure. In giving up the dope you didn't gain any advantage. You got, in the hole the dope left, *time*. He'd lectured Jamie, his brother, on this stuff every chance he got—and still Jamie wouldn't do it.

'I've got guys trying to sell me methadone,' Jamie had told him. 'It's one more drug.'

That wasn't so, Don said. He tried to tell his brother about Graham. The dope, Don said, swallowed hours and days and months. 'What are you thinking of right now?'

'The beauty of the universe,' Jamie said. The late Christmas sword they'd bought for the son he hadn't seen in years was resting against Jamie's leg.

Graham had bought a calendar, Don said. He put it in the toilet. Nothing was more momentous than that purchase. He got another one—for the kitchen, so he could watch it over breakfast. Eventually he ended up with five of the fuckers. They were everywhere.

His brother nodded. 'I had a friend,' Jamie said, 'who gave up the booze. I met him and he said, "I've kicked it in the head." I said, "Good on you, mate." "Really," he said, "I'm going to make it. I'm down to forty-three cups of tea a day."'

In his mind, instead of his brother's case, Don was assembling his 'victories'. Once at the pharmacy Don had wrestled a knife away from a kid—it was a dinner knife, blunt and not even washed; it still had *butter* on it. He'd talked for two hours to a mother whose son had died from an overdose the previous night and she'd invited him to speak at the boy's funeral—which he'd done and done well. He'd been terribly moved and had wept in front of everybody.

'Sorry,' he told Sally. He meant it, though to his own ears he didn't sound as if he did. He sounded like those colleagues who wanted the problem swept off the city streets, the methadone patients corralled somewhere remote. Once or twice he'd been behind a counter-proposal to set up a dedicated central clinic, with patient rights the foremost consideration. The joke he was in cahoots with his clients—a secret user—was often the way his fellow chemists sought to move, without giving offence (they were an agreeable lot, kindly, dedicated, blinkered), through to the next item on the agenda.

'You know,' he told Sally, 'I'm so sorry about this. Okay?'

'Okay?' She spat it back at him. She was right about that too.

A car was coming up the alleyway. He heard its badly tuned engine. Not a doctor, he thought—recognising immediately the leap there, the easy assumption. He was in trouble for exactly this failing, for treating this person, if only for a moment, as someone less than she was—less deserving, less bright, less human. He didn't feel contrite—or not only contrite—he felt exasperated. He'd made himself so quickly, so completely, into his own enemy. He'd never registered the problem in such glaring close-up. He was looking at it. *He* was the problem. Big deal, he thought.

'Okay, Sally?'

The car was the beat-up ute from the kindergarten. The guy

with the moko—if it was that, if he was even Maori—didn't look at Don as he drove up alongside them. He put the ute in neutral but kept the engine running. Then he took something from the seat beside him and lifted it up, training it on Don. Don took a step backwards, alarmed for a moment that something was coming his way, that the guy was about to fire at him. It was a video camera.

'What's that?' said Don.

'Smile,' said Sally, 'you're on candid camera.'

Don was on the far side of the ute. He took a couple of steps round the front. 'What's all this, Sally?'

She was opening the passenger door, putting the baby in the middle. Did she buckle the seat in place? Moko raced the engine. Was Don going to be party to this as well—a car accident with a baby flying through the windshield? The guy with Sally was smacked up to the gills, he was sure of it. Most likely he'd stolen the camera and was going to sell it for drugs. Fuck the stereotypes: he was being got at. This pair had something going. He was a target. These were fiends he was dealing with, figures from some shitty dream he hadn't dreamt yet.

'Wait a moment,' he said.

Sally got in the car, and the ute was reversing fast down the alley. Don followed it, jogging stupidly alongside in his breathing Sunday summer suit. The ute moved away from him. It thumped over the kerb, rattling the baby's brain some more, then a gear was located and they were gone.

CONTRARY TO INTENTIONS, Jamie had slept. His wound hurt from lying on it. The sun was somewhere else in the curtains, which soaked the heat in a rose flavour. He supposed his mother doused the furniture in fragrances. A small panic of asphyxiation, like a noseful of grass, made him lift his head. The little bottles were gone from the table—he remembered them swept up in his mother's hand. She'd been depressed for years. She could chase a fly around the house all morning. Penny had told him in letters. This could mean neurontin, zytram, valium, prozac. Carefully Jamie pulled himself off the bed and went into the bathroom, his feet tingling.

In the mirrored cabinet he found the stash, not hidden but tidied. It was chamomile, something called skullcap, valerian and melatonin. He couldn't believe it. He fingered the bottles a second time and read their labels, opening the lids and rolling the useless amber capsules onto his palm. The oils within these tiny balls seemed to press against the insides, making a good case for their release. In bewilderment and slight hope, he ate three of the skullcaps, a couple each of the valerian and melatonin. He left the chamomile, which had always made him sick— the tea, he was thinking of. When he lived with someone—Ally perhaps or Renee—she'd tried to get him to drink the stuff. His antipathy—within a constitution that had no others—was, he guessed, the result of an ill-fated attempt, as a young person, to smoke herbal teas.

Downstairs he found a note his mother had left for him. She was at the shops, getting something for dinner. There was bread in the bin, and in the fridge cheese and ham, or fruit. This mention of food was sufficient to drive out his hunger. He took a couple of bottles of beer from the fridge and went into the sitting room. He dropped the bottles on the sofa, went back into the kitchen, got the red wine box, the sherry and two glasses, and returned to the sofa.

The TV, when he looked up from his pouring, was gone. They always had the set in the same place—the corner by the bookcase, where you got the best reception. The bunny ears would rest against the bookcase. Now the place was taken by a wing chair he'd never seen before, and beside that a pile of toys— his? Don's? Penny's? It was ghoulish. He carried his glass around the room, searching for the television. On a side-table he found the remote, as full as a calculator—a scientific calculator, they were once called. But where the fuck was the TV? He ran upstairs and into his parents' bedroom. Did she watch in bed? On the stairs, coming down, he spilled his drink.

He dragged the plastic bag from the wine box and massaged himself a half-glass of very stiff Chablis. He swallowed some of it, then mixed in the sherry as a sweetener. To clear his palate he drank the other beer. As a consequence of this, his head cleared and he picked up the remote once more and started firing it round the room. He walked into the kitchen, still pointing the remote and pressing the on button. Collecting the remaining beers from the fridge, he walked through into the laundry, then along the hallway, into the study, out again and into the spare bedroom, then back into the sitting room. He fired at walls, at the ceiling, at every object in his path, skipping the downstairs toilet, which had its door blocked by a dining chair. This he didn't question.

He knocked the top off a beer and continued to fire randomly. He may have been yelling now—it was unclear to him—though when he sat down on the sofa and put the beer to his lips he was aware of an astonishing quiet—of such purity and distance, he thought at once of the South Island, of the mountains especially and the lakes, snow and light. Could he truly be here? The liquid in his throat seemed suspended, eternal, all flowing—like a river originating in ice. His drinking was effortless.

Then within the quiet he heard—faintly—female voices, and laughter. He expected his mother was home and she'd brought someone with her. He was frozen—still stuck on that river of ice; or, like a glacier, he could move only a few inches a year. The wine box lay at his feet. There were empty beer bottles around him. He'd lost track of the sherry bottle, though its cap was in his lap. He waited for them to enter the room. Yet no one came.

The voices, however, kept on at the same volume, and the

laughter had a massed quality that made him think of something chilling and familiar. He walked across to a wooden cabinet on top of which was an arrangement of crystal ornaments. The sound was louder here. He bent down and turned the key in the lock of the cabinet doors, which swung open to reveal the television. How ugly everyone looked inside this antique cabinet, like finding a piece of raw steak inside a jewellery box. He was almost sick. Jamie stepped back to observe the pink, jabbering faces, then he kicked the doors shut again. The splintering gave a fine report. The wood split with such reality, he laughed and wished other people were in the room with him—his friends, all his old buddies, his mates, though he failed to name them in his head.

'What are you doing?' His mother stood at the doorway, holding packages. 'What are you doing to my things?' She did not drop the packages—which he expected, but only from TV— and she did not rush towards the damaged pieces to feel the evidence. She was economical, even in a crisis. And as she stared at him his prodigality seemed to recede. He was no longer the bad son returned and therefore released from blame and consequence. His shame was ordinary and juvenile, his mind choked with self-pitying excuses. Drearily, he was at fault. He thought of crying. In the hospital, after his surgery, banished to that distant, empty wing with its cruel view out over the carpark, he'd felt not cheated—not outdone by the doctors and everyone who'd sussed his plan—but alone. Not lonely either but fully separate. All ties had been cut. In such a state, he'd made a decision. Every twelve months or so he made a decision. And with the energy he could suck up from sentimentality, he'd made it to the ferry terminal.

'Where did you get these from?' She was near the sofa, indicating something that wasn't the alcohol. He saw her bottles of potions, her herbal extracts, which he believed he'd left upstairs in the bathroom cupboard. When he'd wandered with the remote, had he been back in there and brought them down? The whole scene was coalescing around the TV, which she'd hidden from him. That, in a nutshell, was the whole problem.

Now she released the bags and in a sort of panic was gathering up her gear. It was her first inefficiency, inviting him either to turn away or look more intently at this grovelling figure. One bottle spilled from her grasp and the capsules bounced out over the carpet. A cry of despair came from her. He'd seen women drop their handbags before in crowded streets and let out this same awful, senseless, terrifying sound as the contents scattered under feet. For a second they were paralysed. His mother was on her knees, collecting each capsule, the loose, puckered skin of her bare arms shivering with the movement. There was nothing for Jamie that wasn't commonplace in this moment: someone urging up her supply. But this was his mother. Her position on the floor gave him the oddest feeling—the feeling of usefulness. He'd come back, it struck him, to help. But he wasn't ready yet. He'd heard his name and he wasn't answering. Besides, he felt he would fall over if he tried to help her. She didn't need him was the shortest answer.

He stepped around her and walked to the front door, which she'd left open. Moving outside, as in some trick, the heat's wall closed completely around him until he was invisible.

six

THE BABY LIKED golf, which was pretty much the first thing it'd liked. At dusk they went looking for balls, she and the baby. Sally carried a bucket, while the baby slept in the backpack, lolling about. She liked moving over the gentle rolling grass and not just because the baby slept. It was peaceful—a car-ride feeling, with her freakily as the passenger.

On her picking hand she wore a glove she'd found on the course the previous week. It was decorated with breathing holes along the thumb and had a strap for tightening at the wrist. Its palm was marked with a black stain, from the rubber grip of a club. The glove was made of kidskin. She felt queasy pulling it on, but then it felt good. She didn't believe it bestowed an imaginary right on her—as if the presence of a single glove could turn her into a golfing lady. 'You don't have a big enough arse for it either,' Shane told her. It was Shane's bucket she carried, his baby also—yet the glove was something. Shane travelled with a club when he was ball gathering. Sally had the glove. They could have been married.

She went in under some low trees and pulled a ball from the grass, then another. Like picking apples—which she'd never done—she guessed the trick was not to think of the piddling money each ball represented but to keep her mind on filling the bucket, by which time she'd have enough cash to make it all seem a little less like the biggest waste of time she'd ever been involved in.

Occasionally—just as now—she came across a ball sitting completely in the open. Forgotten rather than lost. She picked up these ones furtively. You had to be sure there was no one around who might come running up saying what the hell was she doing with his ball. These people could arrive from a neighbouring fairway, and she never was sure which way to look to see them coming, since she failed to recognise the orientation of such a pointless and expensive thing as a golf course. Even Shane, with his familiarity, had been caught like this, which was the other reason he carried the club.

At the water, she didn't bother to take off her sandals. She waded in and bent down, scooping with her hand through the underwater weeds. There were always fewer balls here than she expected, apparently because the good players cleared easily and the bad ones took the long way, hitting out and around rather than over. Shane told her this, and it was something helpless in her always to disbelieve him and try to prove him wrong. She found nothing for some minutes. Her feet were getting cold in the water and she waded to the far end. As she stepped up onto the bank her trailing foot kicked against a ball, which happened to be tucked up beside another. It wasn't unusual, Shane told her, for a player to hit two balls in exactly the same wrong place. He knew golf—but he never found as many balls as she did. He disliked the activity. It was demeaning; he'd rather collect cans. On her own personal scale, she didn't find this demeaning. Golf was a sort of outrage, to do with money, but it was entirely separate from the demeaning universe as she experienced it minute by minute.

She walked the long dead stretch where the course crossed the road and then, unhooking the backpack, she sat down on a bench, with the baby wedged up against the seat. She adjusted his hat and felt his cheeks, which compared to hers were cold. He was a contrary baby, cold when it was hot and vice versa. From the side-pocket in the pack, she took his bottle of formula, unscrewed the top and drank some, almost gagging at the taste.

She took her bucket across to the ball-cleaner, fitted a ball into the slot and rammed the handle up and down. She liked this because it really worked. She repeated the action until all the balls were shining. Then she sorted out the duds from the near-news, putting the latter inside the pocket of the backpack. The baby groaned in his sleep as she hoisted him onto her back. Poor little bird, she thought. Poor 'little Shane'. The baby had his father's eyes when they narrowed in thought or displeasure, or when he claimed within his mouth all the phlegm his asthma produced and searched for a place to spit. There was an ashtray he favoured. The summer pollens made Shane sour. She liked the golf because it took them away from that—she believed in contagion, though Shane told her she was an idiot. Already the baby had a wheeze he practised at night.

She picked a ball from the branch of a tree, but the ball was split and she tossed it away. In the distance she heard voices and the swish of shots. The days had been so fierce and the evenings so warm, players were often out on the course until dark. It was best to keep away from them. The women would frown at the baby, and the guys—she wasn't sure about the guys. Some disapproved—maybe they didn't like to be reminded they'd lost balls or that this person was making a profit off their being so crap at golf. The young and talented were pricks of a special order, with lots of comments about her skill with balls. Yo ho ho. Gimme a three wood. I've got a wood already. Yet others—the older ones mostly—wanted to buy balls from her, and talk to the baby—or talk to her through the baby, making cooing sounds. She always felt she was being addressed with these babyish noises, and if they touched the baby she felt she was being touched.

On a distant green a sprinkler wafted water into the air, and far off by the clubhouse the greenkeeper—a man called Keith—rode his mower over the practice green in tightening circles. He was a cunt—and not only to Shane. If Keith saw them out on the course, he'd turn on sprinklers to get them, and he'd sometimes run his mower at them. 'Get off my fucking golf course! Get that baby home to bed, you little thieving witch!' Strange how every arsehole had some tip on child-rearing. At the age of sixty, Keith was cutting grass—which was the fact you had to remember. The one thing in their favour was that a deep and abiding hatred stood between this person and the person they sold the balls to—Marc the pro, who ran the shop in the clubhouse. He had a Swiss mother, he said, which accounted for the spelling. Marc was also barman and he gave lessons and he fixed the toilet when it clogged and he wiped every bum that came through the place in check trousers. He was a sad angry jerk but wrapped entirely in his own misery, and, alert to any opportunity to increase Keith's, he paid little attention to adding to theirs. He gave less per ball than the guy downtown at the sports shop but he was on site and you were saved a trip carrying the stupid bucket.

One problem with Marc, as far as Sally was concerned, was she thought at some stage he would rape her. He brought nips of vodka through to her from the bar while she waited for him to tally up the balls, and when he handed her the cash he always came out from behind the till and stood beside her, watching her counting it, allowing his hip to touch her side. Though she longed to and her back was aching, Sally would never take off the backpack when she was in the vicinity of Marc. The baby was invisible to him but it still represented a form of protection. He had the remnants of manners, and his Swissness stood vaguely to his credit—she did not believe it to be a country with a strong tradition in molestation. It was a mile home and the vodka lightened the load. Before home, she'd chew some gum so Shane didn't know. According to his calculations, if she had a double, baby was having a single. If she got ripped, they'd end up with a drooling moron as the inheritor of all their earthly possessions. Because he wasn't lactating, he could get ripped himself and it wouldn't have any effect on the baby. To see its father stumbling round pissed would have no effect on the baby.

She set off away from the players' voices and the clubhouse, towards the clay bank at the edge of the course where a collection of old railway sleepers often harboured booty. The baby had begun to cry, not full throttle, but this close to her ear and across the quiet grass, the noise seemed loud. She jogged a little, jerking the sound of the crying that didn't stop but picked up. 'Stop, baby,' she said. 'Stop that, Richie Rich. Quiet now, you hear?' She was in the middle of the fairway, exposed, and she couldn't reach round to grab the bottle from the pocket. 'Please, little man. Go back to sleep. Believe me, you don't want to know.' She continued across to the bank, running now, causing the sounds to be split up like a CD skipping. 'Ugh. Ugh. Ugh,' cried the baby, while Sally sang to it softly. 'Don't give up on us baby. Don't give up on us baby.'

When she was in behind the bank, she swung the backpack off her shoulders and plonked it down on the grass. The baby stopped immediately and looked at her, stunned. The pack stayed upright for a moment, then it toppled slowly backwards. Sally looked at it. There was silence and she put her hands in her face. Then the baby was screaming. She pulled him out and put the bottle in his mouth. His sucking was fierce, regular, like a farm machine. His eyes were puffy and red, and his chin was wet. In the folds of skin at his neck there was a rash. When she spoke to him, he continued sucking but lifted his eyes. 'You like golf, don't you?' She was weaning him and her breasts hurt. A crimson sky came out. She watched her baby fall promptly asleep. It was a miracle that made her cry.

Keith had gone and Marc was locking up when she arrived at the clubhouse. There was no one else about. Marc's car was the only one left in the carpark.

'Good evening,' he said ominously.

She stepped over a stream of water coming from the men's toilets. Marc hosed it out every day. 'Can you just do this for us?' She held up the bucket, which was nearly full. The pockets of her jacket also bulged.

He looked at his watch. 'Sorry,' he said. Though he wasn't rich any more, he had retained a few of the things from that era—the watch, the rings, a gold chain with a cross around his neck. He was thirty-two, washed up. Shane had told her that he'd had surgery on his back.

'Come on. Come on, Marc.'

'I'm logged out, Sally. I could open the door again but the till's closed.'

She was glad of the weeping she'd already done; it meant she had nothing left, though a low moan escaped her. She gathered the jacket around her. Her toes were dirty; pieces of grass stuck to the tops of her sandals.

Marc was padlocking the gate where the hire buggies were kept. 'What am I to do, Sally? I'd like to help.'

She was aware he'd converted this offer into a threat. 'Have you got any money on you?' she said.

'Of *my* money?' He smiled. In an ordinary setting, he would have been handsome. His occupation, his background—he would have been something to ponder. 'You think I want your stupid balls?'

'Fuck you, then.' She turned away and began walking up the path to the carpark. She heard him coming up behind her and tensed her body. He put his hand on her arm, stopping her. 'Get off,' she told him, twisting easily from his grasp.

He held his hands up in surrender. 'I said the shop's closed. I didn't say I closed the bar up yet. Bar's still open.'

She was ill with foreboding. Where was his pity? She had a sleeping baby on board. Slowly, he brought his hands down to sit on his hips and his head was nodding in appraisal of all the evil shit he would bring down on her skinny body. She felt beyond tired, up on another plain of need. Occasionally Marc had mentioned drugs to her, hinting at a personal predilection. She had always been careful to look stupid. Shane might have sold him stuff once, she believed. The bucket was leaden and the golf balls in her pockets poked at her organs. Her back had never stopped being sore from the day of the birth—or, the three days of the birth. A mile away the father of her child was sitting at home watching one more time a video of her with the chemist's dick in her hand. There was Pamela and Tommy Lee, and then this. Shane had wanted to make a copy, for insurance purposes— at which point she'd managed to get off a kick in the direction of the TV that had demasted the aerial, before he grabbed her and put her down on the sofa.

Inside her mouth the taste of formula sat dried on her tongue.

The bar was upstairs from the locker room. It was filled with the accoutrements of terror. A coin-operated pool table secured to the floor by a metal plate; a low rectangular jukebox with a tableau of palm trees and bikini-clad girls; a trophy cabinet, an honours board and, above the bar, a line of engraved tankards the colour of medieval concrete. Above each tankard a name was written in the style of a burn into the wood. Doug. Ash. Dippie. Les. Stu. Dave B. Dave L. Colin. The tankards provided the only relief in the room, since they announced that these particular arseholes were not presently in residence.

'What are you having?' Marc was moving round behind the bar, turning on the lights above the spirit bottles.

'A Coke or something,' she said.

'Rum and Coke?'

'No, just a Coke.'

'Vodka and Coke. Shit, I hate Coke.'

'Sprite then.'

'You're kidding me. Why'd I open the bar then?' He flicked off the lights and banged his fist on the bar, which didn't make much of a noise. The room was deadened with carpet and chunky wood panelling. They might have been on their way to getting buried and this was their transporter. 'Go to the fucking dairy, Sally.'

'Then a vodka, I don't care.' She recalled her aversion. 'But nothing in it.'

'More the party spirit.'

He brought the drinks to a table in the centre of the room. He still hadn't turned on the main lights. She didn't feel they were anywhere close to a golf course any more, or to nature in general.

'Can we see what we're drinking, please?' she said.

'Nope,' he said.

In the windows, the day was disappearing on her. It was light for ages, then it was dark suddenly and you found yourself sitting on a broken chair in the middle of the garden with nothing visible. She sat down with Marc at the table, perched on the edge of her seat because of the backpack. She put down the bucket and tasted her drink.

'Is there some kind of tube running back there? Does that baby ever come *off*?' He spilled his drink across the back of his hand.

'Please don't be unpleasant to me,' she said.

'I'm saying you'd be more comfortable sitting down if you had that thing removed. Can I help?' He stood up and moved behind her. She felt his hands on her shoulders, the straps easing back. She closed her eyes and drank again. When she opened them, he'd propped the baby against a nearby chair and was sitting facing her.

With some effort she connected the bucket of balls beside the table with this man. 'I've got like forty in there.' The numbers came to her; she was touching her pockets. 'The good ones, I've got nine or something.' She began removing the balls and placing them on the table. A couple rolled off across the carpet. Plop. Plop.

'Why do you do this, Sally?' It was not quite a criticism.

Her glass was empty and she was terrified to place it back on the table in this state. As a sort of reprimand, he was drinking terribly slowly. What was his question? With luck, he talked on, something about something else. He'd brought the bottle to the table. In the shadows she caught the gleam from the gold lettering of the honours board. All the trophies in the cabinet had sunk into a single puddle of dull mercury light.

'What is that around your mouth?' Gently he put his finger to her face. 'Can I catch that?'

At a point she asked, 'May we please sit near the window?'

He had her hand once. 'That glove is creepy,' he said. 'Take it off.'

Then her jacket was opened. 'Oh, mama,' he said. 'Look at you. You are *wet*.'

She touched the front of her teeshirt and began to cry. In the pocket of the backpack, she actually carried breast pads, though to get them would have woken the baby. She recalled making this explanation but not his reply.

SHE CRAWLED INTO bed in her clothes and lay as though in a harness until Shane turned on the light. 'Jesus, the curtains aren't closed,' he said.

She opened her eyes. He was wearing a towel around his waist and his hair was wet. 'You want to give everyone a show?'

She heard the curtains snapping shut, then his weight bringing down the bed on his side. 'You got to get up for the feed.' He was leaning over her with his lips on her ear. The smell of soap was powerful, like a dairy product. 'Hey, you. Mrs Milk Station, you got to give the little man his stuff.' He shook his head, showering her with drops, then he yanked the sheet off her. 'So when I wear my jeans in bed, it's ya ya ya, but when you don't want to get undressed.' He slapped her lightly on the backside.

'Leave me alone,' she said.

'What's the matter?'

'I'm sick.' She tried to get the sheet back up with her feet.

'You can't be.' He twisted her over so she was lying on her back, looking up at him. He wasn't without sympathy. A little concern now would save him in the long run.

'I feel bad, Shane.'

'You're a bad person all right. Where does it hurt?'

She looked past him, at the ceiling. She hated people walking on her head, and despised Shane for choosing the downstairs flat over the top. It was illogical. He said he couldn't be bothered with stairs, and with the shiftwork he didn't want to be creeping round trying not to wake anyone. Creak, creak, creak. But that, she said, was the noise *they* were going to have to put up with from now on! Like everyone on nightshift, he was selfish and disconnected from the world. Still she had to remember: he's working, at least that.

In the background she was aware of a sound. 'What's that?' she said.

'That's your baby.' He was drying his hair with the towel.

'How long's he been crying? Did you go in?'

'Don't think I'm set up for it, Sal.' He put his fingers to his own nipples and squeezed. 'You going to move or what?'

Her feet felt numb against the floor and there was a pain in her hip.

When she came back into the bedroom he was dressed in his puffy white boilersuit and his white gumboots. It was a prophetic uniform—already she was seeing him as an accused person, led from the paddy wagon into court, greeting everyone with a finger and a tongue, the tattoo given prominence.

'Baby, you look awful,' he said. 'Feed him and then go to sleep. I'm earning now. Daddy's the man now.' In his work clothes he had composure, self-belief. It was a scary thing.

Beside the bed there was a bottle of pills. He pushed his palm against his mouth, and then drank from the water bottle he carried in his workbag. He walked over and kissed her on the cheek. 'Plus,' he said, 'don't take offence, Sally, but you stink.'

She couldn't undress until she heard the door closing, the motor starting, the ute pulling out and fully evaporating. There was no water left in the shower, so she went into the kitchen, boiled the jug, poured it into the bucket and added some cold to it. She crouched in the bath and, using the soup spoon, began to wash herself. In this pose, she began to consider where she was. There was fifty bucks Marc had given her that she'd managed to hide from Shane. And there was the chemist. What was he doing? He was shitting himself. She hadn't seen him in a week. He was never there in the mornings. An optimism gripped her—not entirely of course. Her soreness went everywhere. When she went back into the bedroom the bottle of pills was gone and next door her baby was sleeping. Amen, she said. She was not anti-religion. Amen.

A GROUP OF them stood in the cooler, surrounded by racks of leghorns, the tubes of cheese that hadn't yet been cut. Shane, as the new boy, didn't know these people really, but they seemed like geeks, a few of them in glasses, pens sprouting from their pockets, citizens of the lab mainly, down here for rest and recreation. The one called Paul was handing out the pills.

Shane didn't know if he was entitled to see what was going on, let alone partake in it. They were pretending to ignore him, though with the tattoo he knew this to be more or less a ridiculous proposition. The cooler was where he worked, hauling the trolleys to and from the cutters, the leghorns like big cigarettes of an order similar to the pretend cheques they presented to lottery winners on TV or to children's hospitals.

Like him, the geeks all wore headphones over their plastic hats. Speech wasn't really possible anyway with the noise of the generators. It was all done with hand signals and looks.

He walked over to the group and held out his hand. Please, sir. Paul looked at him, then around the group. Anyone vouch for this prat? Over his white boilersuit, Shane wore the orange padded jacket that gave him his designation: cooler boy, trolley jockey, shit shoveller. He stood firmly on the ladder's lowest rung. No one among the geeks was giving Shane any support. They chewed and swallowed and looked away. Some, he knew, studied briefly the side of his face and wondered at the pain undergone to produce that sort of beauty. Paul put up his hands. Sorry, buddy. Shane fished out his bottle and held that up. An offering. Paul waited for several seconds, then he took the bottle from Shane and put it in his own pocket. The group were drifting off, leaving the cooler, rubbing their hands and blowing on them.

Shane followed Paul out of the cooler, along the corridor to the finishing tables. He watched Paul take off his headphones, then he did the same. It was quieter here. 'What are you?' said Shane. 'Like the big cheese, I suppose?' He was more strongly built than Paul, who nodded slowly as if to say, Yes I heard your joke, a million fucking times. Paul had a sunburned nose with skin that was peeling so you just wanted to reach over and pull.

In front of them the curd and whey slurry was being stirred by giant metal arms. Waves of oatmeal-coloured sludge rose and fell. Any factory, up close, cured you of its product. In the three weeks he'd been working here, Shane had sensed then adopted the prevailing shopfloor attitude—cheese was contemptible. He wouldn't touch it when Sally put it on meals.

'I don't think we've met,' said Paul.

'I'm Shane.'

'Like in the movie.'

'What movie?'

'*Shane*,' said Paul. 'The movie is called *Shane*. You've never heard of it?'

'Our video broke,' said Shane. This was not information he meant to give out. They had Mike's now anyway, and Mike's camera.

Paul indicated Shane's face. 'That have a meaning? Don't you have to be a chief or someone?'

Shane touched the grooves and decided something: enough banter. 'You've got something of mine.'

Paul held out his hand and, as Shane shook it, he discovered he was being given his bottle. 'I'd prefer, Shane, it's no offence, if you never talk to me again or come near me, okay?' Paul turned and began to walk out of the room.

'I might be useful to you,' Shane called out. 'But what the fuck use are you to me, you pasty cunt.'

Leaving the room, his shoes in plastic bags, Shane felt chosen, elevated above the many, like an astronaut.

He took his trolley up to the loading bay and watched the milk tankers roll in and the guy with the high-pressure hose washing their flanks till they shone like public monuments in sunlight. A driver came over and Shane sold him something for the ride to Dunedin. Then the driver took a cassette out of his shirt pocket and laid it on the ground under the front wheel of his rig. He walked over to the hose guy and said, 'This is a mercy killing. If I hear these songs one more time, I'm driving into a school bus.' He got back in his cab, started her up, and drove forward and away into the night on a diesel rush.

The cassette's obliteration did not register as a sound. In shape and texture it now resembled a pressed flower, possibly.

'What was that?' Shane asked the hoser, who was approaching the stain with his nozzle.

'That was a lady by the name of, wait for it, Rita Coolidge.'

'Never heard of her.'

The hoser was an old guy, in his fifties. 'She will drive you crazy if you let her.'

Shane thought of Sally and was about to offer an observation to the effect that he too was in such a danger, but the old guy had his hose blasting away recklessly, the spray punishing everything in its path.

In the bathroom, he couldn't piss because the guy who came in didn't think to take a cubicle but joined Shane right there at the wall.

'All right?' said the man.

'I'm fine, it's you I'm worried about.'

'Easy on, buddy.'

Shane looked at the man. They were dressed identically, both in their hats. Shane had taken off his orange jacket, though it was against regulations. 'Do we *need* to be talking at this moment?'

The guy was zipping up and stepping away. 'Fucking hell,' he said quietly at the door.

When finally he was able to piss it was as though soap had penetrated the end of his dick—unless he'd been given something, a disease. There was a factory doctor available at a discount, but if he went there news of his clap would be around the next day. In self-diagnosis, he looked into his eyes in the toilet mirror and from his bottle rolled two blue pills onto his palm and swallowed them, humming something he used to hum with Sally—before she went straight. I live with someone who's straight, he said to himself in a kind of wonder, and still she's a

114

sport. But Sally wasn't straight; she was just more dangerous, newly so. He sensed in her deep reserves of cunning and knowledge, once she'd got off it and had done this thing of giving birth. He'd lost her pattern now and didn't know where to find her. It was clear to him that he had to have his own trajectory—that was why he'd driven to the kindergarten and shown the chemist his face.

Mike was shutting off the vats. Mike's job was to see they were filled, then to watch the temperature as the milk coagulated. Shane observed Sally's brother from the doorway, thinking: where was the trick? Where did the hard bit come in? It didn't. Shane wanted to be working where Mike was. To be in with Mike, though, he needed qualifications—at least a diploma of some sort—and that was proving difficult. First he had to go back and make his peace with the polytech, probably pay for the phone he'd busted. It seemed a far-off proposition.

'How you doing, Mike?' Shane hit him on the back and there was no give. His almost brother-in-law was a solid person, slow and dim, but firm—like a calf-size lump of hard cheese. Mike lifted his eyebrows in greeting. Mike didn't have a diploma but he had about a thousand years' loyal service to the factory. As a token of this effort, he wore a hearing aid, which seemed to add to his weight. The vats hummed along.

'Keeping warm?' said Mike. He always said this. He'd got Shane the job in the cooler.

'Don't let the milk boil, Mike,' said Shane.

It was no pleasure to be aligned with Mike. In his locker Mike kept the painted figurines his wife gave him for no reason anyone could see except humiliation. They were her 'little people'—midget figures with goofy smiles carrying flowers, sipping from spoons, doffing their hats. At their feet always there were mushrooms. They sat on the top shelf of the locker, looking directly into the pornographic collage Mike had built up over the years. The suggestion had been made to Mike that his wife

115

should get him a little man carrying his dick in his hand and his eyeballs rolling back in his head. Mike said solemnly he doubted if they'd ever made such a one. There was more going on in the little people than in Mike. It was Mike who wondered whether the tattoo rubbed off.

'I can have my coffee now,' said Mike. He sounded like a child claiming a reward. He moved away from the vats to a space in the corner of the room where a single chair sat below a poster promoting work safety in a humorous manner. A guy had just guillotined his own hand off, and the slogan said Help Us Lend *You* a Hand. The severed hand was travelling along a conveyor belt. From a duffel bag, Mike pulled out a small thermos and unscrewed the cup. Then he sat on the chair and poured the coffee. All his movements—not just the things to do with hearing—were those of the deaf. He was inaccurate in everything he did. He was a liability. But it was his ute.

'Where's mine, you dozy prick?' said Shane.

Mike looked up. 'Eh?'

Shane squatted down beside the chair.

Mike was licking at his hand where he'd spilled the coffee. 'You want to get back, Shane, to the cooler. I don't want to have McKinley on my neck again. Where's your jacket?'

'Listen, Mike, the ute.'

'I seen it in the carpark. Good. I hope it's still A-okay, Shane. Gimme the keys.'

'We need it another day.'

'No.'

'One more day, Mike.'

'I given you the extension.'

Shane showed his son's uncle a finger. 'One day.'

'A day is not a day for you people.'

'What people? Your sister? All I'm saying is twenty-four hours, Mike. And it was never A-okay. It's a shitheap.'

'Gimme the keys, Shane. I turn a blind eye for Sally. But I

116

need my car back. You keep the keys, I got my own. What do you want it for anyway? If it's crime, I won't have it, and don't tell me a thing. I don't want to hear.'

'You *can't* hear, you stupid shit.'

'Just don't fucking tell me.'

Shane stood up and started walking away. Behind him he heard Mike calling out. 'You don't give me it tomorrow, Shane, I'm taking it and fuck Sally.'

'Done it already, my friend,' said Shane, 'I'd rather fuck the ute.' Mike didn't hear, which in the end was a good thing. The reason for talking like that had gone. Sally was a mother. Shane felt the presence of the baby, pictured in his woollen hat on the way home from the hospital, like a judge in a wig.

At the pay phone outside the poolroom he punched in his home number. No one answered. He let it ring and ring a second time: still nothing. Then he rang a third time and let the phone dangle while he walked over and looked in through the glass door at the empty poolroom. The rack of cues beckoned. He tried the door but it was locked. He returned to the phone and then finally she came on.

'Where'd you hide the money?' he said.

Sally pretended she didn't know who it was.

He repeated the question.

'Oh, shit, I was *sleeping*, Shane.'

'Thing is, baby, if we don't trust each other, I don't know why I'm bothering.'

She took a long time to speak again. 'I got it here, honey. I've got the money from the balls here. It's right beside the bed.'

'How much is there, Sally?'

'There's thirty bucks.'

'Thirty?'

'Yeah, about. Actually, let me see.' He listened to her hand moving across the receiver. 'There's thirty-four dollars, Shane. Please, I got to go to sleep before I get up again.'

'Tell you what, Sal, let's put *you* in a fucking cheese factory on the nightshift and I'll go golfing, how about that?'

'Shane, please.'

'Was it Marc who was there? I'm going to give him the bash, you know.' He'd begun to cough and draw in nothing. He bent over and hacked away, his eyes watering. When he drew himself up, he realised he still held the phone. He noticed the time getting eaten up on his card. He felt it was the video of Sally and the chemist that was interfering with his breathing. In truth he couldn't watch the video. He'd watched just enough to see them in the room, and a little more to know there wasn't a technical difficulty with the picture, then he'd killed it. He'd taken the video from the machine—his hands were trembling, look at that—and now it was in his locker. He felt the video was giving off a poisonous gas. It could penetrate metal. It was contaminating the products of the factory.

'Sal?' he said quietly.

'You okay, hon?' she said. 'You got your inhaler?'

He'd lost his inhaler. 'If we don't move on this thing, I'm going to do something stupid. I was going to ring him, you know.'

'What? No, no, no.'

'I was fucking on the brink.'

'No, you can't. You know you can't, honey. That's not in the plan.'

'Truly, I can't stand it. They piss on your shoes here, you got to thank them for it.'

'I know, honey, but you got to be good. We both got to be good.'

He waited, not speaking, while two guys passed him in the corridor. She was right; everything had gone so perfectly up to now. And they were a team. They had the tape; they had him. Did they even need the tape now? What they needed and had planted permanently in his head was the *idea* of the tape. The chemist had seen the video camera—he believed there was a tape. The belief was enough. Shane was suddenly happier, cleaner and fuller in his breathing.

Why didn't nightshift have use of the poolroom? Shane went over and gave the door a kick.

'Thirty-four bucks,' he said into the phone, which was now dead and beeping. 'Is that with or without the blowjob?'

He took the videotape from his locker and went to the loading bay. 'Here,' he told the old guy with the hose.

'What's this?'

Shane held up the tape. 'One of those Rita Coolidge things.'

'I'm not a fucking recycling station, you know.'

Shane walked around the side of the rig that was next in line and put the tape under a wheel. The driver spotted him and leaned out of the cab. 'The fuck are you doing, pal?'

'Drive on, man,' said Shane.

'Get away from my truck,' said the driver.

'It's nothing. I just want to see something crushed.'

'Get that out from under there and fuck off away from my truck else I'm reporting you.'

It was an unusual threat and it took Shane by surprise; the surprise was that he had something to lose by this 'reporting'— not the job foremost but perhaps the other thing. He didn't want the tape to become a matter of inquiry. Already he understood he'd made a mistake in bringing it to the loading bay to get rid of it. He picked the tape up and walked off. On his way through to the cooler he snapped the plastic casing open and pulled out a length of tape, mashing it in his fingers. Then he tossed the thing in a wheelie bin.

seven

SHADE WAS ONLY a place the heat had cooked and left. In front of them was a duck pond crossed by a humped bridge that led to a sculpture garden. The turmoil Don felt made him ravenous. He would have eaten Tina's sandwich too if she didn't have it in her hands. She never lifted a sandwich to her lips; she preferred to tear it with her fingers into mouth-size bits and feed herself that way, reversing almost the refinement she was looking for. Usually Don enjoyed watching it. In eating, the appetite stepped seriously forward. There was nothing but this. She pushed a piece of lettuce into the corner of her mouth. He thought, kindly though, of some sort of primate. He was one too—an ape with an appetite. His hand was in the bag with the tart.

'Thought that was mine,' she said.

He'd believed her eyes were shut. He broke the tart in two and easily forced himself to hand over the larger piece.

'No,' she said, 'I only want a little bit.'

'Take it.'

'No, no. I've got an apple in my drawer.'

There were office workers with their feet in the pond. The ducks no longer cruised but sheltered under trees, bobbing like wood.

Don's arrival had surprised Tina, which was the intention. As usual she'd packed her own lunch. There was a small argument as to which sandwich she should eat. At first she'd wanted to give the bought one away. The homemade, she was finally persuaded, could last a day in the gallery's fridge. If she finished all her sandwich, Don told her, there was a treat in the bag. Raspberry and lemon tart. In naming it, he was already desiring its sugars.

He watched her store the rest of her sandwich in the paper bag.

'You want that?' he said.

'I was going to have it for afternoon tea,' she said.

'With your apple?'

'Listen, Don, if you're still hungry you should get something else.'

'No,' he said.

He watched as she took off her shoes and socks. Automatically, he was doing the same. There was a surprising amount of relief in this action. He'd always, in the things that mattered most, followed her lead. It was Tina who'd urged him on in the wavering idea he'd had about buying out Perry. Where he'd seen risk, she'd seen opportunity. The status quo always had too much authority for him. His spirit, at root, was slothful. All his correct tendencies she highlighted for him, as with one of those fluorescent pens students used, so he would see what to do, where to go. Her slender feet, muddily brown, the pinkish toenails that hugged each toe—so different from his own ill-fitting square plates—stretched before him.

He almost spoke. That his act with Sally at the pharmacy, on consideration, stood in dumb isolation was causing him to feel courage. That it was a mistake and not a technique. He was not that person.

But they were seen, they were being greeted. It was Martin from the gallery; he was the registrar, checking the paintings in and out. 'I won't join you,' he said. Keys hung off his belt.

'You can if you want,' said Tina.

Martin looked at Don, who didn't speak. 'No, I won't,' said Martin. He was carrying his own brown paper bag and a bottle of juice. 'I want to be antisocial.' He wore prescription sunglasses in a red frame, which he adjusted on his nose. The shirt was determinedly Hawaiian. 'What did you do?' he said, pointing at Don's head.

'Banged into something,' said Don.

Martin spoke to Tina: 'Ouch.'

'Just a surface wound,' said Tina.

'I wouldn't mind inflicting a few surface wounds of my own on, you know.'

'Who?' said Tina. 'Oh. Yes.'

'Yes,' said Martin. He was smiling down at them, then casting his eyes meaningfully in the direction of the gallery buildings. Explanation was distasteful to him, a chore—that was a Martin word. It stood for almost anything. 'After you know what.'

'Yes,' said Tina.

Don was finishing the last of his tart. He had to get something in his mouth. There was nothing to be done with this coded conversation. He'd suffered enough of them to know not to ask. Asking was asking for it. 'See you, Martin,' said Don. Martin looked at him, a tiny seizure in the narrow nostrils. It came hatefully, easily to Don's mind that Martin was a very average-looking gay man—slightly buggy eyes, the slack shoulders, the basement tan—and yet he had sex at will, it seemed. Tina was Martin's sounding board for this. He'd taught her to say 'fucked' within sentences of some refinement and earnestness. Occasionally she repeated them to Don: 'When they came home from the play and they'd fucked, he began to look around Martin's flat and *critique* the furniture!' As for Don, Martin didn't know why anyone would want to be a chemist and be *privy* to all those grisly personal details about everyone, though this was exactly, Don had countered, why he thought Martin might have been drawn to it. Was this a stereotype raising its ugly head? Martin asked. Probably, said Don. 'You think I'm some gossipy queer?' Probably, thought Don.

Since that conversation a year or so back—they'd been thrown together at an opening—and because, Don supposed, they had Tina 'in common', he and Martin had quietly avoided each other.

Martin took his cue and walked away—the keys swinging—though not in the direction Don had suggested.

'Poor Martin,' said Tina.

Don wasn't rising to this either. He put the lid on his coffee cup, which he'd just drained. 'I spoke to Graham,' he said.

'How is he?'

Really he couldn't be bothered with Graham at this moment. He said something about Graham's fear of the endoscopy. The sun was hitting Don in the ear. He moved his head back to escape the blasting rays and closed his eyes.

'Tired?' said Tina.

He wasn't especially, though the idea of it appealed. But a shadow was on him. He looked. A mother pushing a pram moved slowly past them. Don knew her from the pharmacy but not her name. They nodded at each other. The baby, he believed, was colicky, or the mother anxious—or was she the one with high blood pressure?

'Who was that?' said Tina.

'Don't know.' He sat up. There was icing sugar on his pants. 'I had a call from Mum. Jamie's come back.'

'Jamie, your brother?'

Don felt the disappointment in his chest—precisely in the heart region. He was telling the wrong secret. 'He just turned up apparently but now he's taken off again.'

Tina had never met Jamie, which was a kind of absurdity. 'He saw your Mum though.'

'Briefly, she says. Then he took off.'

'What's he up to?'

'Who knows.'

'Did he leave a number or anything?'

'Jamie?' Don laughed.

'So he's gone back to Wellington?'

'I don't know, Tina.' The questions were irritating in their reasonableness. At each mention of his brother's name, he substituted in his head the name of the girl, Sally. Tina took the hint—the wrong one, of course. His anguish was a grim comedy.

She put her hand on his arm. 'Okay, honey.'

Don stood up, brushed himself down. He told her it was time to get back, then he bent and kissed her on the forehead, securing for himself the aura of a pain he now began to feel.

T HERE'D BEEN NO sign of the ute at the pharmacy. Don had taken himself off methadones for the rest of the week, explaining that it was time for Rameesh to step up to the plate. Janet could coach the intern while Don took care of the overdue paperwork. There was a stack of supplier invoices waiting, and a weight of Health Ministry forms. They were also behind on their re-ordering.

Sally and her friend needed time to think it through—whatever they had in mind. Now she was back on track with her dose, surely she would see there was nothing to be gained by putting the squeeze on. He'd learned she'd left her support group. The clinic was already watching her closely. One more slip-up and they'd revoke her take-home rights—she'd have to turn up on weekends. A word from Don to her case manager and she'd be in big trouble.

By removing himself in the mornings, he was sending a signal to Sally and her offsider not of defeat but of seriousness, and also truce. He knew what they were up to. He was admitting what he'd been up to. In the end, though, mistakes had been made, the consequences of which need never be faced. It was time for both parties, having peered into the precipice, to pull safely back.

Naturally, he had no confidence they'd read these signals correctly. They'd think he was running scared.

After lunch, Don checked the register and saw Sally's name ticked off. Then he questioned Rameesh on the morning—were there any problems, did anything need following up? Had everyone behaved? He didn't mention Sally's name, inquiring after others instead. Andy, for instance, who rode a Harley and liked to arrive early, before opening, and press his face against the glass. Andy's bike—and addiction maybe—had come from his years in TV computer animations. That was Andy's theory anyway—working in dark rooms in front of bright screens on odd shifts. He felt his retinas had been damaged and through his eyes—'the brain's outer skin', he said—his mind subtly influenced towards wrong choices. Perceptually he was about a frame off, he said. One-thirtieth of a second. At 9 a.m. he was often on his way home with a headache, a box of fried chicken.

But Andy was to be resisted. The doors didn't open till nine—like it said on the notice. Andy, in his leathers, could squeak around for a few more minutes. When the doors finally opened, there was something Andy always did—he pulled his riding gloves off with his teeth. He never did this while he waited, only as he was walking into the pharmacy. If Andy didn't do this, it meant something possibly was wrong. Rameesh wouldn't know this. He wouldn't look up and he wouldn't be able to tell even if he did. Occasionally Andy drank his methadone at the counter while wearing the gloves. That was when you had to ask Andy a question or two. Rameesh wouldn't ask a thing, nor would Janet.

'Andy?' said Don.

'Yes,' said Rameesh.

'What time?'

'Late.'

'Late?'

'Just been.'

'Rather late then.'

'Yes.'

'Any reasons?'

Rameesh looked across at Janet, who said, 'Who? Andy? I didn't see him.'

'Andy's never late, Andy's early,' said Don. He spoke to Rameesh. 'Tomorrow, I want you to note the time Andy comes in. If he's late again, say past 9.30 even, I'd like you to ask him something, a few questions.'

'Yes,' said Rameesh.

'What would you ask him?' said Don.

'Why's he late.'

'Don't ask him that. Not straight away. Ask him how's it going, how's work, how's life, you know? Don't ask him why he's late.'

'Okay.'

'Be an ear to him, Rameesh. These people don't need you treating them like children, do they?'

'Okay.'

'We're not the police, you know.'

'Okay.'

'Okay okay okay.' Don found himself holding Rameesh by the lapels of his white jacket. 'Okay.'

'Okay, okay,' said Rameesh, with impatience now.

'Got it?' said Don. 'Got it got it got it?'

Janet looked up from her work. 'All right, Don?' She was moving round the counter towards them.

He knew perfectly what he was doing. He still had the lapels in his hands, shaking. He'd become aware of the look of fright on the face of his intern, turning possibly to something else. And he continued to shake the boy, even with exaggerated force, as a way—clearly—of mitigating this outrage, turning it once more in the direction of the playacting that had begun the routine. Except the boy wasn't taking it in this spirit and so it was necessary to hold onto his lapels a little longer, squeeze tighter, until he got the joke.

'Don,' said Janet. 'Don, I think actually you're—'

'Yes yes yes,' said Don. 'Thank you, Janet.' He released Rameesh, who stumbled back against the wall and felt at his neck. In the corners of his eyes there was moisture. Don stepped towards him to smooth his jacket, but the intern backed away, holding his hands in front of him. 'Hey,' said Don. 'Listen, Rameesh, sorry. God. Sorry, mate. Sorry if I, sorry. Hey.'

'Yes, all right,' said Janet.

Rameesh allowed himself to be touched by her on the shoulder.

Sharon was standing by the sunglasses carousel, listening.

'Okay, mate?' said Don. 'Not hurt are you?"

'Nah,' said Rameesh.

'Won't report me to the Pharmaceutical Society or anything?'

'Nah.' He looked bashful now.

'Never shake an intern.' Don laughed and Janet joined him after a moment. Rameesh grinned at them both.

Don reached up to his own forehead and the scab from the nail wound came away in his fingers.

At coffee break, Don heard himself using Jamie once more. Janet didn't know about Jamie's drug habit. She knew him only as someone who was 'difficult', a drama-inducing figure whom Don, from time to time, had to take care of. She responded with sympathy. Maybe Don should take the rest of the day off, she suggested. He told her that wasn't necessary. He had to pick up Anna soon; he'd be back afterwards. She told him again to go home and stay home, sort things out—and this time he agreed with her that there were things he could look into, and he'd take some work home also. In the staffroom, he swallowed three Panadol for his head.

As he left, Don went over to Rameesh. 'See you tomorrow, Rameesh.' The intern, in farewell, raised his dark eyebrows. In near throttling him, Don had noticed the complexion changing to a reddish hue. A Red Indian, he almost said, aware then that he was beating down a kind of silliness, a delirium.

Sharon stood by the door. 'I'm going to buy you a new car,' he told her.

'Oh good,' she said unhappily.

'But you'll have to look after it.'

'Oh.' She moved her hands to her cheeks. 'Then maybe you shouldn't.'

'No, because I'll teach you.'

'Really, I don't want it.'

'Of course you do,' he said.

Outside, the sunshine descended on his head like a blade, causing his hair to lift slightly from his scalp, as baking rises. In the back of the car he found a straw hat with a drug company's name on the cloth band. The hat was too small, it cut like a crown, yet he pulled the brim down and peered forward through the windscreen. The roads were too wide, encouraging inattention that he fought with his fists and by leaning further into the light with unprotected eyes. His sunglasses were back at the pharmacy.

He thought of the axolotl. He was a figure at the kindergarten, a brave man.

For once he was early—only to find there was no one at the kindergarten. It was shut up. He put his face to the windows and saw that the chairs were stacked on the tables and the mats rolled in the corners. Then he remembered that it was the picnic day. Penny had moved her work around and she was with Anna at the kindergarten picnic. Without sense, he tried the door handle again, though he suspected he was courting the locked building as a punishment, a defeat he fully deserved.

He was reading the handwritten notice pinned to the window. The kindergarten had been broken into three times in as many months. The break-ins were violations of such cruelty and mind-lessness a few of the parents had pulled their kids out and sent them somewhere else. The notice addressed the perpetrators, who'd smashed in the door to grab the raffle money and to shit on the floor and to fill the fish tank with Lego and paint. They'd put the turtle on its back and hung the birds upside down with their feet bound. The notice read: 'We are part of your community. Whatever happens here affects everyone. Please honour yourself and leave our space as you found it. Thank you.' The reinforced glass had a crack running through it, as if someone had punched where the notice sat.

Walking up the path to the street, Don slowed down and listened for cars. At the gate he stopped and peered through the wire mesh. No ute, no one.

From his mobile he rang his mother. 'Has he called?' Don asked.

'No, he hasn't,' she said.

'I might come round.'

'He's not here if you think I'm hiding him.'

She'd told him that Jamie had run off—maybe he had. 'No but I'll drop in, okay.'

'When?'

'Soon. Ten minutes.'

'Where's Anna?'

'Anna's with Penny. I'll just drop in, Ma.'

'What's the time now? I was going to go out.'

He was sitting in the car outside his mother's house, making the call. But for the high fence, he could have looked in through the windows and seen her figure in silhouette, talking to him. He didn't know why she was still in the big house except to accuse him somehow of abandonment. To further interest him in her plight, he supposed, she was doing things like closing off the downstairs toilet. It made him think of Graham's mania. Don had told his mother he'd pay for the plumber but that offer had been turned down.

'Where d'you want to go?' he asked her now on the mobile. 'I can take you.'

'No.'

'Then I'm coming round.' He sank down in his seat and watched the house.

No one made a move. Jamie wasn't there. He waited for a few more minutes, then he rang his mother again to tell her something had come up at work and he couldn't make it round but he'd call her later that night to see if there'd been any news. Then he drove over to Graham's flat.

APART FROM WHEN he found the flat for him and helped move him in, Don had never been inside. His knock had not been answered. It was only when he called out that Graham came to the door.

'I didn't miss, did I?' said Graham.

'You didn't miss,' said Don. 'I was just passing.'

'A social visit.' Graham clutched a kimono-style dressing gown around himself. 'I should put on some underpants.'

'I'd appreciate that,' said Don.

Graham returned a few minutes later in a white shirt and black trousers. He was pulling on socks.

'Why aren't you at work?' said Don.

'I'm sick. Why aren't you?'

The cork tiles on the floor were worn black in places, and above the oven there were scorch marks on the wall. On top of the fridge in a saucer stood a small cactus in a plastic pot. The single item on the bench behind them was a water purifier. Graham took down two Arcoroc cups from their hooks and dispensed water. The cups, Don noticed, were cloudy with immovable stains.

On the kitchen table beside Graham's elbow was a beaten-up copy of the *Merck Manual*, the blue of its spine faded to white almost. Many of the pages were turned at the corners and there were yellow stickies throughout. Graham was one of the most famous hypochondriacs in town, a real baby, although as a sign of respect to Don he took all his prescriptions to other chemists. This kitchen, which was oddly at the front of the house and accepted the brunt of the afternoon sun, was the cauldron of his complaints. Today it burned liked a furnace. 'What can we do?' said Don. 'Can we open that?' He pointed at a louvre window, the only ventilation available. Its slats shelved the dust and grime of years—or was it merely months? They were sitting, in effect, on the shoulder of a road that passed across their vision just beyond a knee-high concrete fence. Every so often a car went by, like an experiment in sound.

Graham had told Don he spent most of his time in the bedroom where he had a small TV and a fifty-dollar computer that four years ago had been the most powerful personal computer in the world. He didn't have a printer, but that didn't bother him because he could use the one at polytech.

'Let's see,' said Graham. With a couple of tugs he had the first piece of glass out of the louvres. He laid it on the floor and turned to Don. 'How open do you want it?'

'Don't wreck it now,' said Don. Graham was laying the second slat beside the first. 'That's it, that's enough.' Above them the paper lantern swayed a little. 'Sit down.'

Graham caught Don looking at the *Merck*. 'My mother's copy. She has a newer edition. Many years ago I had a condition for which they said "avoid digital manipulation". I thought that was some sort of tricky doctor's machinery—a digital manipulator. So I kept touching and prodding. Jesus, I felt such a fool when one day I was looking at my own digit.' He held up a finger.

'How do you feel?' said Don.

'I'm sick. I don't feel too bad.'

'You don't look so bad.'

'You think?'

He'd spoken automatically and now he came to look at Graham, Don saw how wrong he'd been. There wasn't a true colour in his face. Don took a piece of paper from his pocket and put it on the table—but more in front of himself than Graham. 'Here's your appointment and everything.'

Graham didn't look at the paper. 'If you think I'm better, maybe I'll hang off that for now.'

'No, you won't.' Don placed a finger on the *Merck*. 'If you're going to keep consulting the book, you'd better get some proof that you've got what you think you've got.'

'My mother's new edition is far more comprehensive.'

'What does she think she's got?'

'Are you kidding? We more or less divide the book up between us.'

A cat walked into the room. 'Whose is that?' said Don. Vaguely, he recalled the no-pets lease.

They watched the animal move in a circuit around the table, rub against Graham's leg, then back out the door. 'I have no idea.' He put his finger in the cup and started working at the sides. 'Will you come with me, Don? You'll be with me, won't you?'

'I'll come if I can.'

'Can you?' Graham flicked the form around and read aloud

the date. 'Is that going to be possible for you?'

'We'll see.'

Graham was smiling at him helplessly.

'But first,' said Don, 'I want you to do something for me.'

'All right.'

'Are you still connected?'

'Connected?'

'I'm not trying to trap you, Graham. I just need to know if you're in a position to hear some news.'

'What news? Dope news? Drug news? You know I don't see anyone any more, Don.'

'I know you don't. But would it be impossible for you to learn a piece of information? Nothing that ties you into anything. Just are you able to hear, that's all.'

'I don't hear a thing because I'm not listening, Don.'

'I understand that, Graham. Good. *But*.' He was trying hard not to strike the table with his fist. Or grab anyone else by the lapels and shake them. The Panadol had no purchase.

'But if I put myself back in a position to hear?'

'Yes.'

'But I can't.'

'I see.'

'I can't. You know I can't. What sort of thing?'

'Someone called Jamie, we think he's a new arrival.'

'On the programme?'

'No, no. On the street. Someone new. Jamie. Is he still around? Who's he with etcetera. General inquiries.'

Graham looked unhappy, pained. He ran his finger along the metal edge of the Formica table, whose surface bore the cigarette burn marks that looked within the style of the period. 'No. Sorry, no. You're not asking that, are you, Don? You of all people.'

'Okay. Fair enough. I just thought if you happened to hear something.'

Graham stood up, cradling his cup. 'I don't hear anything. What's he done anyway, this Jamie person?'

'Nothing,' said Don. 'But we need to get in touch urgently. His family.'

'Try the cops.'

Don stood up and started to move out of the room, towards the back door. All around the smell of cat pee rose as if he was agitating it in the air with his steps.

'Give the bloody cops something to do, Don,' Graham called from behind him. 'All they do is help people who've locked their keys in their car outside the Warehouse.' Don was out the door, and Graham followed him. 'But you'll come when I have the thing, right?'

As he disappeared round the side of the house, Don was nodding his head very slightly. He was about to step over the concrete fence to the road when he turned back. 'What about a guy with tats, tattoos, on his face?'

'Who? I don't know people like that, Don.'

'Like a white guy, nearly.'

'No, no, no. This is someone else now? Where do you think I hang out? I work. I'm a nerd.'

'Not a gang guy. Listen, Graham. With a moko, you know. Professional work. Drives a ute.'

'No, no. A ute? No.' He was shaking his head. 'No way. I catch the bus, you know. I've got a Community Services Card for everything I do except taking a shit.'

HIS SISTER'S HOUSE had not been built so much as landed on its section, long and flat roofed, with wings that folded towards a central courtyard, sheltered by a pergola hung with wisteria and what were these—grapes? Lying back on the wooden recliner under the vines, his arms resting in his groin, cuddling his dressing, Jamie felt he might be stuck here forever in these wings. In the garden there were lemon trees and tomatoes. He thought of the Mediterranean, California. He hated it. Already he longed to be back in Wellington, though of course without having to spend time getting there.

At five he could meet Douglas, who it turned out was a postie. The mail in the flat had been stuff Douglas had failed to deliver, or had chosen not to for a variety of reasons. He was a far more promising person than Jamie had first thought, and there was now a small pressure for Jamie to prove his worth, add to the kitty of the flat. When he'd first got together with Renee, he remembered—it was Renee definitely—there was a real jar, with real money in it. For several weeks the reality of the jar prevented him from approaching it where it stood in the kitchen cupboard. With the whole house gone for the day, he felt even more strongly the jar's mission and its force—the glass was like something molten that gripped the dollar notes as in a paperweight.

The person who'd made this winged house, of course, had failed to disguise his own essence, which figured in the mirrored windows that collected the sky's vicious glare. It was brutal to look up there. Jamie had never met Simon, except in the photos that dropped from Penny's letters like advertising supplements.

The girl—also a photographed face—was suddenly above him. They looked at each other for a few moments, bound by curiosity, indeed by chemistry. She was seeing her uncle for the first time and he his niece in the flesh, and each was held by that little part they had in common—perhaps something in the width of the nostrils and the small ears, though here he was probably recalling Penny's descriptions. On the whole, he was no good at faces, only the broadest types of personality. Friendly. Hostile. Sarcastic. Naïve. With children, the mix was impossible.

'Jamie!'

The girl was gone, but he didn't need a face for this one. 'Gidday, Pen,' he said, sitting up faster than he intended. 'How're things? I'm Jamie.' He stuck out a hand towards Anna, who was holding onto one of her mother's legs. 'I'm your Uncle Jamie from long long ago. Once upon a time. Maybe you've heard of me.'

'I know you're in Canada,' said Anna.

'In Canada!' He checked with Penny, who nodded. 'Correct. It's Anna, right? Pleased to meet me and pleased to meet you.' This time she took his hand. 'And what class are you in?'

'I'm at kindy.'

'But you're so big. How old are you, Anna spanner?' He had never been an uncle before but clearly there was something in-built which produced the act.

'Three but I'm nearly four.'

'When's your birthday?'

Anna didn't know when her birthday was, and he didn't have any further questions.

'It's April,' said Penny.

'That's the same as me!' he said.

'No, it's not,' said Penny.

'Oh, am I thinking of Canada? They do things differently in Canada. When it's summer here, it's winter there. Believe that?'

The girl, bored finally, wandered off in the direction of the house. Penny was holding a picnic hamper and a rug. Jamie couldn't see her face properly because she wore a large-brimmed sunhat.

'I don't remember telling her that,' she said. 'Would you like to come in?'

'I don't know.'

'Come in for a drink.'

He looked at the house. He feared something.

'My arms are dropping off.'

He took the hamper from her and she saw him flinch.

'What's up?' she said.

'Nothing.'

She took the hamper back off him and put it on the ground, which was pebbles. You couldn't place a firm foot in front of you. Penny had a hand on his shoulder, straightening him carefully and lifting slowly at his teeshirt. 'What's all this? Is this from a knife? What happened? I don't care, Jamie, just tell me what happened.'

'It's not from a knife. At least not one, you know, raised in anger.'

Gently but with purpose, she touched the skin around the bandage, which was inflamed and red. He let out a gasp. 'This here is all infected, you understand? Let me look underneath.'

'No.'

'No?' She stepped back from him. 'All these years I've been thinking, is he dead, is he alive? Then Donny sees you, so you're alive. Then we don't hear, so maybe that's it. Now you walk in. You're alive. Big deal. With an abdomen full of pus. Really, I'm touched, Jamie. How considerate. Just for me. You shouldn't have, you know.' She picked up the hamper and the rug and turned away from him.

'Penny,' he said, 'I had a kidney stone taken out. This is from the surgery. All it is. You can look if you want.' He was lifting up his shirt, peeling at the bandage.

'Bring it inside,' she said, speaking over her shoulder.

They were in a bedroom now because there was a bed in it; otherwise it felt like an office where they were about to shift premises. Pictures were lined up against the walls. Packing boxes were stacked in one corner. The Venetian blinds were closed, filtering a corporate light onto the cream walls.

Jamie explained that he preferred to remain standing. Once he lay down, it was tempting not to change that position for some time.

Penny eased his shirt up and cut at the bandage with some scissors. He looked at the wound with interest. It was leaking a greenish substance that Penny mopped at with the edge of a towel. She peered closer.

'Will I live?' he asked, without flippancy.

'Not without a hospital,' she said. She was opening a sterilised bandage wrapper, fixing it to the area with some tape.

'Penny.' He held his sister's hand, stopping it in its work. Without her hat, he saw into her middle-aged face and neck. She looked more like him than he remembered. 'Is there something you could give me right now for it?'

'Like what?'

'I don't know, for the pain.'

'I know what you are, Jamie.'

'I can't take this pain, Penny.'

'I know you,' she said. She finished the dressing and pulled his shirt down.

It flared in his gut. 'Christ almighty, it hurts, Pen. It hurts like fuck!'

'If you've hit on me for drugs, Jamie, I'll let you die, I swear it. I'll walk out now.'

He was laughing in a sort of shock.

'We don't have anything here, all right?'

'Jesus, shit!' It grabbed him again and he felt nauseous. Somehow he stopped himself throwing up—that would have killed him. There were tears in his eyes.

'I'm going to give you something, Jamie. Then we're going to the hospital.'

As he stood, slightly bent, waiting for his sister to bring the stuff, he was aware of the girl at the doorway. She was some sort of spirit you had to charm or appease or kill. He tried to smile at her, while his stomach pulsed. 'Uncle Jamie's got a sore tummy.' The girl continued to stare. He felt in her the father, his low brow. 'Poor Uncle Jamie,' he said. He was weeping and weeping. He looked at the pictures on the carpet. They were photos but he failed to identify a single object. Their desolation rested in this.

eight

H E KEPT KNOCKING people over, women especially.
Don was not an athlete. He stood where he was told.
Usually Gary, who was a policeman and the tactical brain, told
him. Then Don ran after the ball carrier with great purpose and
no intelligence, often with his head down in desperate effort,
causing him to arrive a little late and with nowhere to go except
slap into the opposing player, who'd already offloaded.

'I'm not playing with Don any more,' said Helen.

Don had already bowled Helen over twice. She had a sore
shoulder, a limp, and she refused his offer of help as she lay on
the ground, clutching her knee with its grass-burn.

Karen came up and kicked him hard in the backside. 'Piss off, Don!' she said, bending to her friend.

Helen was Don's friend as well. Once before he'd nailed Karen so hard she couldn't play for a month.

'Gary, can you arrest him or something?' said Karen. Helen was crying, also laughing, with the pain.

'You're an ape, Don,' said Gary.

'Don gets a red card.'

'Off! Off! Off!'

Bruce, who was playing on Don's side, took him by the shoulders. 'We use the term "touch" advisedly, big fella.'

'I'm so sorry, Helen,' said Don. 'Are you all right?'

Karen told him to go away.

Troy was enjoying it. 'It's an early shower for Don. He's had his warning and that, quite frankly folks, was just plain awful.'

'Fuck up, Troy,' said Alan, who kept the results in a notebook.

'Oh, problem with discipline also. This must go back to the whole team culture, I'd say.'

'Take a breather, big fella,' Bruce told Don.

Don wandered to the edge of the grass and sat on the metal rail by the carpark. After a few minutes, the game resumed. Karen had taken Helen over to the far side of the field near the beach where, with their backs to him, they punished him by looking out to sea.

He undid the laces of his trainers and lifted his shirt at the arms where the sweat stuck the material to him. His face burned with exhaustion. He wasn't the only person to have hurt others on these Tuesday nights. There'd been injuries he had no part in, and shoving in the chest from time to time, and Troy had once taken a swing at Alan. But Don was certainly the most consistent offender and among his victims there happened to be more women than men. It was an embarrassment. Up to now they'd let him play because, in Bruce's words, he was totally

140

unco but by no means a vicious bastard.

He drank from his water bottle and tried to watch the game. From this vantage, his own participation seemed even more ludicrous than when he was playing. They were too good for him—even Bruce, who was fat and who now skipped into a gap and ran through to score. The high-fives cracked in the warm still night air. They called to him: 'See that? See fucking *that*?' He offered Bruce a thumbs-up sign. They had something: the ability to change a plan of attack.

Out at the port a container ship was lit up against a mauve sky. He took his sports bag and walked over to the car. Children were in the playground. Their shrieks came to him from behind the wall that separated the play area and paddling pool from the fields. He dumped his stuff in the car and made his way over to the noise. There was another sound too—a metallic scraping, unpleasant and distinctive.

The kids were racing a shopping trolley around the paths and over the bridge that crossed the paddling pool. The trolley contained three smaller kids, while the bigger ones—they were about ten or eleven years old—pushed. As the trolley took the corners, often two wheels came off the ground and the little kids were yelling with terror and excitement. The youngest kid in the trolley was no more than two years old—a little Maori boy—and the oldest and biggest was Patrick, Don's friend from the kindergarten. There were no adults around.

'Whoa, whoa, whoa,' said Don, standing in the path with his hand held up. 'Stop a minute.'

The trolley continued racing towards him. It came to a sudden halt a few metres away, and the passengers rocked forward, one smashing his nose into Patrick's knee.

'Okay,' said Don. The kid who'd hurt his nose gripped it but didn't cry. 'Big big fun. Who's in charge? Who's the oldest?'

'He is.' One of the pushers had stepped away from the trolley and was pointing at another boy, who still held on.

Patrick stood up in the trolley with his arms outstretched and said, 'I know you!'

'Hello, Patrick,' said Don. He moved to the side of the trolley and Patrick threw himself at Don's neck. The force of it caused Don to stagger slightly, and the kids laughed. Don let Patrick slide to the ground. He spoke to the oldest boy. 'Is someone here with you? Mum or Dad?' The question had no obvious merit. 'You're down here alone?' Don turned to Patrick. 'Where's your sister, Patrick?'

Patrick shrugged. He pointed to the trolley. 'Back. I want to get back.'

'Where'd the trolley come from?' said Don.

Finally the oldest boy spoke. 'Found it.'

'Found it?' said Don. 'Where?'

Patrick was climbing up the sides of the trolley, hooking a leg over the side. The oldest boy pointed vaguely in the direction of the carnival area.

'See this belongs to the supermarket. It's not a toy. May look like a toy but it's not. They shoot people for stealing these. They send up helicopters. Bruce Willis, you know. Machine guns, the lot.'

They were staring at him, waiting for him to finish so they could get on with it. Don lifted the two-year-old out and put him on the ground. Then he got the other kid out and finally Patrick. 'Okay, who owns this one?' He placed his hand on the youngest boy's head.

'That's his brother,' said the oldest boy, pointing at the kid who'd stepped away from the trolley first. They were all now drifting away from the trolley, as if it was tainted.

'You, too,' said the younger boy.

'You're all brothers?' said Don. 'Wonderful! And Patrick?'

'He's not,' the oldest boy said. 'We don't know that coconut.'

'Coconut, terrific,' said Don.

'We don't know that coconut,' the younger boy repeated and

all the kids, including Patrick, laughed.

'Then I'll take him,' said Don. 'I like coconut. You can take junior one and junior two and we'll all go home, all right?'

The kids looked at Don, disappointed there'd be no further opportunities for wit—theirs not his.

'Okay? Go!' He clapped his hands. 'Scram! Beat it! Go home!'

There was one more obvious question to be voiced. 'What you going to do with the trolley?' said the oldest boy.

Don clutched at the handle. 'I gotta do my shopping! Now move!'

Slowly the boys turned and started to dawdle off in the direction of the road.

'Hold hands!' he called out.

When they were twenty metres off, the oldest boy turned and called out, 'You a cocksucker, man!'

Don said to Patrick, 'Nice friends you've got.' Patrick put his hand against Don's bare leg. 'I've been playing touch rugby,' he told the boy.

'Touch,' said Patrick, pressing his finger into Don's thigh.

'That's right.'

'I want to ride.' Patrick gripped the trolley.

'No more rides, buddy.' The trolley, of course, was a hideous thing of unbelonging. It wasn't going to fit in the boot of Don's car and he couldn't haul it up the steps from the beach to the shops. The nearest supermarket was a couple of miles away and now he had Patrick also. 'Where d'you live, Patrick?'

'With my auntie.'

'And where's that? Do you know the name of the street?'

'I don't know.'

'Can you remember it for me?'

'I don't know.'

'How'd you get here?' Patrick pointed up towards the steps. 'Can you show me?' The boy nodded and began to walk in that direction. 'Hold on a moment, Patrick.' Don looked back to where they were playing touch. His phone was in his bag back in the car, but Patrick continued to walk away from him. Giving the trolley a shove that rolled it pointlessly a few metres across the grass, he began to follow the boy.

At the top of the steps, where they'd put in the piazza, Patrick had to stop for breath. Don sat him on one of the benches. 'Take it easy,' he told the boy, whose chest was rising and falling. Patrick leaned forward and spat on the paving between his legs. They were being watched by some outdoor diners at café tables under umbrellas. Don's grey teeshirt was swamped in sweat and his laces were still undone. He bent to tie them, then he stood up and took Patrick's hand, leading him off down the street.

They walked to the railway station end of town, then Patrick cut back and went up a side street, before rejoining the main road at almost the same point they'd been at before the manoeuvre. It was getting dark and Don was aware of the sweat cooling against his skin.

'Do you know the way, Patrick? It's okay if you don't. If you don't, we can find it.'

The boy nodded his head confidently and went off again.

They were in a residential area that led off a light industrial zone of furniture restorers, plumbing suppliers and garages.

'This look right to you, Patrick?' Patrick pointed down a street. 'This one?'

'Yes.'

Halfway down the street, Patrick stopped and looked back the way they'd come.

'You don't know? This is not your auntie's street, is it?' said Don. He hadn't spoken harshly, but the boy started to cry. 'It's okay, Patrick. It's okay. We'll find her.' The boy sobbed against Don's middle. 'There, there.' Of course he would have to take the boy home with him. They would have him overnight and take him to kindergarten.

Patrick pulled his head away and looked up at Don. 'No,' he

said. 'There.' He pointed at the house directly opposite them. 'Auntie lives there.'

They crossed the street. The door of the house was open and from inside came the sound of a TV. 'Hello,' Don called out. 'Hello-o.' Patrick held back behind him, as if it wasn't his house at all. There were no lights on. The passageway smelled of cooking. 'Excuse me,' said Don, advancing a few feet inside the house. Patrick remained on the doorstep. It was the wrong house.

Don looked inside the first room, a bedroom. There was no bed but several mattresses on the floor and clothes strewn about. In the corner was a pile of basketball boots. He continued on, towards the TV noise, which was coming from the back of the house. 'Hello there,' he called out.

He stepped into the kitchen, a long, narrow space illuminated only by the dull light coming through curtainless windows and the television's wild projections. Steam came from a pot on the stove. For a moment he failed to place a human form in the shape that occupied a bench-seat close to the TV. The shape was unmoving and angled towards the screen. The TV was on the table and its rabbit ears passed out through an open window. Suddenly a face was turned to him—a Samoan woman, who looked not at all surprised to see Don in her kitchen at nine o'clock at night. She was getting to her feet—a heavy-set woman in her seventies, wearing a tennis visor—moving as if he was her husband or son, requiring some service, some food. She paused, took off the visor, pulled two clips from her full hair, put them between her lips, gathered her hair roughly in her hands, then slipped the clips back in place and fitted the visor on again. The gesture stopped Don from speaking.

Patrick appeared at Don's side. The woman looked from Patrick to Don, then continued to the bench where she took a glass from the cupboard. She reached into the fridge, pulled out a bottle of milk and filled the glass. Patrick came forward and took the glass from the bench. He brought it to Don and held it up to him.

'So, this *is* your auntie,' he said to the boy. He turned to the woman. 'You're his auntie, yes?'

'Drink,' said Patrick.

'I think it's for you, Patrick.'

The woman shook her head. Patrick pressed the glass against Don's teeshirt.

'For me? Okay.' He took the glass and drank the milk. If he'd paused in his drinking, he thought, maybe it would have risked giving offence. In fact, he was still dehydrated from the touch rugby and the walk to the house. He hadn't had milk in this quantity for years. The creaminess and density was a shock. 'Thank you,' he said. Patrick was at his elbow to take the glass. The noise from the television was so loud, when he spoke he sounded formal and as if he was in charge.

The woman was checking on the pot, stirring its contents with a spoon. Then she was taking slices of bread and buttering them. This was not her home but her place of work, and he was simply one of the house's itinerant population. She put the buttered bread on a plate and moved the plate to the bench from where Patrick had collected the milk. The boy stepped forward and took the plate, bringing it to Don. 'No, no,' said Don. 'Thank you but I'm fine. I'm not hungry.' Patrick still held up the plate; it was tipping now and Don took it to prevent the bread from falling to the floor. 'Well,' he said. Don picked up the top slice and ate it. Of course he was hungry, he was starving. There was nothing to the bread. It was white and thin and the butter was slightly rancid. He put the plate down on the bench and again thanked the woman, who was now setting out soup plates and fishing in the pot with a ladle.

'Okay, Patrick, I'll go now and we'll see you at kindergarten, eh?'

The woman looked at Don. 'You don't want?' She was holding up the ladle.

'No, thank you. It's very kind.'

The woman shrugged.

'Have dinner,' said Patrick. The boy was holding Don's hand.

'I've got my own dinner at home,' said Don. He backed out of the kitchen and slipped his hand out of the boy's grasp. In the bedroom by the front door a man—Patrick's cousin?—was sitting on a mattress, with a boom box on his lap. He looked up as Don passed.

'I brought the boy home,' said Don. 'Patrick.'

The man spoke in Samoan to Patrick. He was telling him off. Patrick replied with a few mumbled words.

'It's not his fault,' said Don. 'He was with some other kids. I'm Don. I know Patrick from the kindergarten.'

Again the man spoke angrily to Patrick, who now walked off down the hallway into another room.

'No harm done,' said Don.

The man went back to the radio.

'Maybe you want to keep the door shut, eh? When there are little kids running round.'

'Too hot,' said the man. He lifted his singlet and stretched out his legs. Don saw the markings that went round his bare thigh in a pattern that looked like a painted Easter egg. The man sang, though not with the radio. He smiled to himself, then crooned more softly. 'Hot stuff, baby this *eve*ning. Hot stuff, baby to*night*.'

Further in, the room smelled stale, alcoholic. A cup containing some liquid was at the man's feet. 'I like that,' said Don, pointing at the leg. 'You know a guy with this on his face? A Maori guy, but white, like me?'

'They all white!' the man laughed.

'You seen someone like that around? I was thinking because of your tattoo there.' His own stupidity tumbled out of him. The milk rose again in his throat and subsided.

The man ran his hands down the sides of his body and

grinned. He spoke in Samoan and flicked the boom box up in the air with a thrust of his pelvis.

'I'm sorry,' said Don, 'I don't understand. What did you say?'

'Said I'm so darn hot, I wanna fuck my*self*.'

N ATURALLY THERE WAS a buzzer—rows of them—outside the apartment building. What did he expect—another open door? Did he hope to wander in and catch Simon in his underwear watching TV? Yes, in fact. He hoped for whatever was most demeaning and vulnerable.

Don didn't know the number of the apartment but he was rewarded by this prick's vanity: there was only one buzzer that was nameless. He held his finger over it, then pulled away as a young couple came down the stairs inside the building, laughing and tickling each other. Don was at the glass door, holding it open for them when they pressed the release. They thanked him and laughed again and he stepped inside the building. In his tracksuit and trainers, he looked like he'd just been out for a run. His car was parked a block away.

He recalled the apartments from a newspaper feature. Lengths of rope, nautically thick, had been hung along the exposed brick walls, and old signs from the wharves—or things that looked like old signs, perhaps they were copies—were suspended from chains that came off the ceiling girders. Onward Goods. Cool Store. Harbour Master. Massive wooden beams, joined by steel plates, ran everywhere. The shipboard atmosphere was capped by the deployment of portholes sourced, he remembered as he took the stairs, from a vessel due for scuttling. At each floor, one could look out and see—not much, as it turned out. The portholes were cloudy and bulged with streetlight.

The top floor was entered by means of a painted red door which appeared impossibly heavy, like the door of a safe, and whose surface was pocked with rivets, but which actually swung open on the lightest touch. Don looked up and saw the discreet black box. He hadn't needed to push at all. In the stairwell, security cameras had caught him climbing up.

Whether it was the old sweat he was activating—from the touch rugby—or new stuff, he couldn't tell. A line of it anyway ran down his spine and he rubbed at it before it reached the small of his back. His skin itched. He could smell himself now as he walked along a corridor lit by shippy lamps and carpeted in sea-grass matting. On the walls were photographs of early times—the port when it was only a beach, masted ships and horses pulling loads along decks. Each apartment door was red and had, in place of a viewing eye, a tiny porthole. Could he be seen? There was no sound except the building's loud whirring, carried above his head by pipes covered in insulating sleeves of silver foil.

The apartment was at the end of the corridor, the prime spot, looking out over the water. Its door was blue and it was without a porthole. That was Simon's superiority—to rid himself of the finicky details he'd given everyone else. There was no button to push, so Don knocked. In the sweaty tracksuit he imagined himself the perfect enemy of everything that lay behind the door.

Simon, of course, dressed in fine blacks—thin poloneck jerseys, cotton jackets with chrome zips. He didn't have a casual wardrobe and all his clothes, Tina said, carried designer labels. A few items from New York, where he'd been, without his family, to see, among other things, the big Modigliani show. A couple of years before that he'd been to Madrid, again alone, for a conference. (These solo flights—what did they think?) He was neat and small in large-looking, snub-nosed shoes (Spanish imports), and he had expensive glasses he changed frequently as models went out of fashion. Don also wore glasses, for reading, and kept his until they broke or he lost them.

'You probably just look through yours,' Simon had told him.

'Yes,' said Don. 'When I want to see something, Simon, I look through them and there it is.'

Simon had laughed—a surprisingly deep laugh for a small man, though his slight barrel chest probably helped. Simon knew the fashion of glasses because he was, he said, by temperament and by profession 'into style'. He had to be—so many of his clients had screwy ideas about door handles and kitchen sink mixers. A change in the optometry was always announced. 'The new Simon,' he'd say of himself, laughing and wiggling the new frame. He liked to encourage the idea that everything was ironic. There weren't many like him in Timaru. He was, by his own admission—the admission softening the crime, he hoped—a terrible poseur.

And in fact Don and Tina had always mostly liked him— that was the horror. It seemed a good match—Penny, if left too much to herself, tended to become sloppy, unkempt, a touch morbid even. Tina once said she was 'kind of gung-ho about cleaning'. Simon's energy lifted the household. He cleaned, even the toilets, relieving Penny, they thought, of the things that most depressed her. What a guy! He deposited stylish objects around the house. The most ordinary kitchen things—eggbeaters, mixing bowls, saltshakers—'spoke' a language. The apartment behind the blue door would be the same or worse, everything arranged and lovely, with an articulate surface.

When they went for meals at the old house and sat at the long lovely table (the tables also changed from year to year), Don would suddenly become restless. He knew the entire room would be packing its bags within eight or so months. When he got home, Don would look around him at the chairs they'd kept forever, at the sofa that was faded, at the clutter of lamps, cords, footstools. Of course it was all irreparably dated. It was also reassuringly mute and satisfyingly fixed. He remembered opening the pantry door and picking up the saltshaker, which looked capable of nothing more than the job it had been given. The holes, heroically, were a little gummed up and sweaty. There was a way, wasn't there, of stopping this moisture. A salt pig probably. Immediately he understood he was more or less free from an aesthetic sensibility. He liked to understand how things worked, though he was not a fiddler. His knowledge was therefore lazy and incomplete. He shook some salt onto his palm as a sort of useless proof. Salt, he thought. Here it was, all you needed, these humble crystals, and their humble container as old if not older than his own marriage. Where had the shaker come from? On closer inspection there were many objects in the pantry of mysterious provenance. Provenance was a word he'd learned from Tina. The provenance of this painting. He'd once heard someone on National Radio say 'providence'. The house, in its rambles, was probably a match for his mind.

Jovial, ambitious, successful, it turned out that Simon had been knocking Penny around for years. He'd broken a standard lamp over her head, pushed her elbow through a window. The gaps in Don and Tina seeing her, the unreturned phone calls—hazily explained, not chased up by them—now added terrifyingly up. What had they been looking at not to see this?

The humming old port building with its borrowed, corrupted atmosphere—its appeal was a sort of theft—carried the vibrations of all these terrors.

He knocked again. There was no sound of movement within the apartment. Then a woman opened the door. She was Don's age and she held a book and a tasselled bookmark. Her feet were bare. 'Yes?' she said.

Wrong apartment.

'I'm sorry,' said Don. 'I must have the wrong number.'

'I think so,' said the woman. Already she was backing inside the apartment, bringing her book up to her chest.

'I was after Simon.'

'Oh, then you didn't have the wrong place. But he's not in.'

'I see. So this is Simon's apartment?'

The woman repeated the information that he wasn't in. She was slim and handsome, and as she dipped her head her dark

151

full hair fell knowledgeably across her eyes. It seemed to him that in a practised way she'd bought herself a moment.

'When's he back, do you know?' said Don.

'Don't know. Are you a friend?'

'No,' said Don. 'I doubt that very much.'

She was looking at his clothes, the state of him. 'How did you get in, by the way?' Her suspicion had been voiced, though she'd spoken in such a way as to cover it, suggesting instead some cleverness on his part for being where he shouldn't be.

'Do you live here?' said Don.

'Did someone let you in?'

'Are you living with him?'

She put down her book on a small table by the door, inserting the bookmark first. He had the idea this sparring came naturally to her. It was how Simon often talked.

'You're the brother, aren't you?' she said.

He could see past her to where one of Simon's coats was hanging. It was a luscious, flecked grey—he remembered Simon's own description of it—and shockingly, the coat was more familiar to Don than his own clothes. That was it—he'd always listened to Simon somehow, even when rejecting what he heard, especially then. Simon was memorable, magnetic even. The attractive, strong woman in the doorway was further proof.

'Are you Don the chemist?' she said.

'I am.'

'And Penny sent you.'

'No.'

'Listen,' she said, 'it sounded all very messy with your sister, Simon told me. What I hope is that eventually things will settle down. It's a cliché, but with the passing of time I think we'll reach a state of more like equilibrium. Do you think, Don?'

This was plainly dismissive and it rankled. 'No, I don't,' he said.

The woman, in her turn, was now irritated. 'She can't keep sending those things.'

'Can't she? What things?'

'Simon could actually use them against her, if he had a mind to, you know.'

'Do you mind me asking, what's your name?'

'Caroline.'

He reached out and shook her hand. 'Hello, Caroline.'

'I'm glad you came, Don.'

'Really?'

'It shows the first thawing. A normality, I'm pleased.'

She was an intelligent person, a reader, but she knew nothing. Her ignorance was encouraging. 'I see,' he said.

She looked him in the eye, as if she was lying. 'My marriage fell apart too.'

'You can't marry Simon, you know that, don't you?'

'Christ! Well, thanks very much for your advice.' She retreated once more inside the doorway.

Don spoke very clearly, each word separate and strong. 'He beat her.'

She stared at him, then she laughed—it was the sign she was hurt.

'Simon beat Penny for years,' he said. 'He punched her in the face, he kicked her in the stomach and in the head. He threw her against walls. He beat the shit out of her. But maybe I'm telling you something you already know, if he's given you a little thump from time to time, I don't know.' He felt the unkindness of this immediately.

She was closing the door. 'I think you should leave.'

He stopped the door with his foot. 'Caroline, you shouldn't be with this person. But if you are with him, you should know what he is, what he does. He's an abuser.'

'What I think is abusive, Don, is you coming here on the orders of this Penny person, who's clearly deranged, and spreading slander to enact a revenge for Simon having ended a relationship that had no future.' It was something she'd worked out, though now, in finally saying it, she didn't look satisfied. She seemed by the end of it short of breath.

He spoke to the closed door. He knew she was still standing on the other side. 'Don't tell him I called. Don't, Caroline.'

TINA WAS COMING along the hallway towards him as he opened the front door. He was disappointed she hadn't allowed him to enter the house unseen. He required time by himself to prepare, though he didn't know for what or for whom.

'Did you get my message?' she said.

'What message?'

She kissed him. 'Jamie's in hospital.'

'Where?'

'Right in Timaru.'

'Oh, all right.' It registered purely as an address—hospital—as if he had something to deliver there. He turned back to the door.

'Wait, Don,' said Tina. She took the sports bag from him. 'Penny called, she's with him.'

She was speaking in a soft voice he found somewhat infuriating. 'Penny's at the hospital? Did they call her in or something?'

'Jamie turned up at her place.'

'So she's with him. Why?'

'Quieter, please. Why what?'

'In hospital. Why is Jamie in hospital? Why quieter?'

Tina nodded in the direction of the living room. 'Anna's here, sleeping.'

His mind went briefly back to Patrick, Anna's kindergarten mate. 'Penny dropped her, so you saw Jamie.'

'No, I went and got her from the hospital. Jamie was in surgery. He's all right, though. He had an infection. Come and sit down. Have you eaten? You look knackered. Why were you so late tonight? You weren't playing for this long, were you?'

He looked at the sports bag she was putting on the floor. He was aware finally of how badly his feet hurt. His toenails would be black. He understood he existed in a circle of fear. 'Christ, I flattened Helen.'

'Oh, no, not again.'

'Just crunched her.' He was speaking in an attempt to make this seem more real to himself; it had the distance of years to it. He slapped his palms together. 'Crunch!'

'They won't let you play and I don't think you should.'

'You're right.' Quickly he was sullen, as if she'd told him off.

'She's okay, isn't she? Helen?'

He nodded. 'Right,' he said, 'hospital.'

'Have something to eat first,' she said.

'I'll get something.'

'You don't have to rush off, Penny's there.'

'No, I should go.'

At the door he allowed himself to be kissed quickly, and she held onto his hand before he stepped towards the car. Her intention, he knew, had been for something of greater substance, some exchange between them, a few tender words to carry him into the night and towards his brother and his sister at the hospital. The hospital was such a bad place. He sensed he had become an irritating puzzle to his wife, one that could be easily solved were he to submit to the most straightforward questioning. He fled from these questions.

SITTING WITH JAMIE, Penny felt not simply the ordinary uselessness of the bedside relative. Her disengagement was more acute since she had things to offer yet no opportunity to contribute. The doctors on the ward talked to her as though she was a colleague, yet she felt only envy as they left Jamie's room to go somewhere interesting or at least different. She'd walked a few miles of corridor, returning to find not one thing changed about her brother or his room, except maybe his chart was at a slightly different angle. Noticing the angle of the chart was, of course, the first sign of craziness. The boredom was insane-making.

The nurses, some of whom she knew, offered her magazines from their own lounge so she might at least be in the right century. They had a little TV she could watch too and plunger coffee that was okay. She thanked them and turned them down. Behind their kindness—or within it—Penny sensed a curiosity about the GP with the junkie brother. She didn't begrudge them this pleasure. They were paid shit and they worked like dogs. She'd once been in the room when a senior surgeon had turned to a theatre nurse and said 'Heel!'

The surgeon who'd performed Jamie's operation was decent enough and had the degree of social awkwardness she liked; it guaranteed his technical proficiency. While Jamie was being prepped, he drew Penny aside and said, 'I don't know how much you want to know here.' Everything, she told him. 'Very well,' he said. 'In addition to fixing up the abdominal tearing and so forth, I'd like to do a hemorrhoidectomy.' Penny nodded. 'I think a ligation at this stage would be fairly much a waste of time.' Yes, said Penny. 'The prolapse is quite pronounced and it seems a perfect opportunity while we've got him there.' Penny told him, absolutely, he should go for it. 'I don't have his consent though.'

'Have mine then,' she said.

'I'd like to take it, but there are issues here.' She asked him to explain. 'Scenario one: your brother wakes up, he finds he's sore in places he never dreamed of.'

'Can I tell you something? My brother's been an arsehole all his life. If you can remove just a little of that offending part, the entire world will thank you.'

On her next walk she met Don, who seemed to want to hug

her in the corridor. 'Family reunion, Don,' she said as they held, briefly, the wrong parts of each other.

'How's it looking, Pen?'

Don himself was looking awful. 'You didn't run here, did you?' she said.

'Touch,' he said. 'Playing down at the Bay. Tina left me a message but I didn't get it. Where is he?'

He followed her to Jamie's room. They'd put him right outside the nurses' station, which was covered in balloons and flowers. One heart-shaped balloon—it was more like an inflated cushion—bore the legend World's Greatest Mum. Don also read the balloon. 'Does she know?' he said.

'I haven't spoken to her.'

They stood at the foot of Jamie's bed.

'He had piles,' she said.

'Piles of what?'

'Don't be dense, *piles*. Constipation's the junkie's bedmate, isn't it? This really is your area, Donny. What do a haemorrhoid and a cowboy hat have in common? Pretty soon every arsehole gets one.'

'Are you all right, Pen?'

'Look at the jerk.'

Don was looking. He moved round the side of the bed and peered closer. 'He looks so old, Pen. Like a dug-up person. His skin. He's so . . . *wasted*.'

'Good word for it,' said Penny. Both her brothers, it struck her, looked kind of exhumed. Don was red faced, red necked, sweating, as though he'd got out just in time from wherever he'd been trapped. She knew she was in bad shape too, closer to Jamie obviously than Donny. Food was tiresome to her. It had been Simon's realm. She'd caught the look in the eyes of a few of her longer-standing patients, wondering at her gauntness.

When Simon hit her, it was her insignificance that drove on the fury, her lightness and lack of presence, the bones he could

157

feel and which repelled him. 'Get up!' he yelled at her. 'Get up get up get up! I hardly touched you.'

Don had come to stand beside her again. 'Tina said something about an infection,' he said.

She then explained what had happened that afternoon, and Don asked again whether they should tell their mother. Penny shrugged. 'What would Madame Lou say?'

'That charlatan!' Don made balls of his fists.

'Take it easy, guy,' she told him.

'Shit, Pen.'

'Who are you going to punch?'

The nurse walked in and they both fell silent. She took a reading off the monitor and spoke to Jamie. 'How's it going, Mr Webb?'

Jamie opened his eyes.

'All right?' she said.

'One question,' said Jamie. His speech was slowed, slurred. 'To get out of here, do I have to fart?'

Immediately, he was asleep again and nothing Don or Penny said to him got any response. Finally, they drove in separate cars back to Don and Tina's place where it was decided—upon Tina's insistence—that Anna could stay where she was for the night.

nine

RUTH WATCHED LOU, who was looking in the bathroom
cupboard where the towels and sheets were kept. Her
feeling of invasion was gradually being replaced by the pleasure
she got from Lou's reprimands. It was what made her lonely
sometimes for her husband.

'This,' Lou told her, touching a purple towel.

'You don't like it?'

Lou removed the towel and handed it to Ruth, then she
continued. Lou never said 'I don't like this' or 'This is wrong' or
anything plainly derogatory. The offensive had a self-evidence
about it that required no commentary. She combed the house

like someone brought in for pest control—her inquiring eyes and hands had a single purpose. She wasn't nosy. There were nests, Lou said. Nets? Ruth had misheard. No, dear, nests, as in birds. Indeed, Lou looked into corners and underneath things as if fearful of disturbing the peace of something asleep. Just once, however, Ruth hoped Lou would flip and tell her unequivocally what was tragic about her life; that Ruth was under the sway, in fact, of the god of incorrect settings. Once, the gas had 'incorrect settings' and a man came and charged her four hundred dollars to put a new computer into the gas box so she could have hot water again. She supposed she needed hot water.

Holding the purple towel, she remembered it as part of a set given to her one Christmas by Penny and Simon. Lou had powers. Whether these were connected with an ability to sense deeper troubles, or simply to see that among the range of cream-coloured bathroom things the purple stood out, Ruth didn't know. Lou herself was always dressed rather garishly in colourful, flowing cottons of a vaguely Indian persuasion. Her sneakers contained bubbles of luminous orange—the 'air' on which she walked.

They were moving now to the medicine cabinet. The bottles Jamie had touched and raided had been wiped off and set back in the arrangement Lou had first advised would be most favourable. Ruth observed her checking all of this. She hadn't told Lou that Jamie had visited. On the phone she'd said only that she was sleeping badly again and a house call would be greatly appreciated, she'd be prepared to pay.

Lou took down a bottle and unscrewed the lid. She looked inside, then put the lid back on, replaced the bottle and closed the cabinet. The mirror caught them both—two women standing in an ensuite bathroom, looking for nests. Lou bent closer to the mirror and touched the skin beneath her eyes. 'I was up half the night with my daughter. She's got mumps.'

'Oh,' said Ruth. It wasn't information she'd expected to hear.

Ruth hadn't considered Lou to be part of all that—a family, nests of her own. The existence of a daughter was a shock. An ill daughter seemed a marker of even greater irresponsibility.

'I'm so tired,' said Lou.

Ruth's shoulders gave an involuntary twist. She herself was always tired; it just wasn't a subject. 'Mumps isn't so common now, is it?'

'She'll bounce back.' Lou moved past her and into the bedroom.

Ruth followed. 'I thought you got immunised for it.'

'Oh, Ruth, I'm too tired to talk about *immunisation*.'

The way she spoke annoyed Ruth. 'How will you treat her? She's home from school today, of course.'

'Poor thing's tucked up in bed. Rest is best. You know, if I had an opportunity ever to do some skywriting, that's what I'd write. Rest is best. Giant letters.'

'How old is she?'

'She's twelve. Vanessa.'

'And someone's there with her.' She'd neglected to turn it into a question.

Lou was heading for the stairs. 'Ruth, I noticed you're low.'

'Sorry?'

'Your supplies. I can't remember the dosage I prescribed but we didn't calculate anything heavy, I seem to remember. I've got my book and my things down here.'

Ruth stood at the top of the stairs. 'It's fourteen, isn't it?'

'What's that?' Lou turned at the bottom of the stairs and looked back up. 'Fourteen sounds high to me. A day? No.'

'No, I meant the age at which you can leave a child alone in a house. They have to be fourteen years old, Lou.' The moment she said this, Ruth thought she'd got it wrong. Fourteen was the age at which you could leave a child in charge of other children. Yet she didn't feel like correcting herself.

'Fourteen? Really? Well, Vanessa's a very sensible girl. I'm sure she'll be all right. She has my mobile number anyway.'

Ruth put the purple towel on the top banister and began walking down. 'I'm sure she will be all right, Lou.'

'Yes,' said Lou. She was irritated herself—Ruth heard it and didn't mind.

They both occupied the bottom step. Ruth could smell the other woman's scent—almondy. Nutty.

'Why don't you go home to your daughter now?' It was all Ruth had intended to say, but the way Lou ignored the question made her speak a thought. 'She wasn't immunised, was she?'

Lou attempted a laugh. 'I can see you've been brainwashed.'

This was surprisingly hurtful. 'How can you see? In my eyes?'

Lou took hold of Ruth's shoulders gently. 'What's the matter, Ruth?'

'Nothing.'

'What's the matter?'

'It's nothing,' said Ruth. 'It's Jamie.' She'd spoken without intention, though now the name was out Ruth felt a surge of relief—really it was more than relief. Something was jolted within her, as though she'd been conveyed in a lift that had arrived with a great exhausted thump a few inches short of its floor. 'My son came home.' The words were strange, wonderful, ancient. She sounded to her own ears as if the statement she'd made belonged to everyone—even to Lou—and that it included everyone. They were bound with the universal. Had she ever been so happy?

'You don't cry easily, Ruth,' said Lou, who wiped with her thumb at Ruth's tears.

'I try to be so strong,' said Ruth.

'You are strong.'

'I try to be.'

'Ruth means strength.'

'No, it doesn't,' said Ruth, laughing with her tears. 'It means compassionate, beautiful. And Ruth said, entreat me not to leave thee or to return from following after thee: for whither thou goest, I will go.'

'The Bible,' said Lou, happy to have got something right. 'Do you read the Bible, Ruth?'

She wasn't sure how the Bible fitted into Lou's world, or into her own. She had the quotation from the baby names book she'd bought for Don and Tina years ago and, for obvious reasons, had never presented. Don meant 'world-ruler' and Tina, from Christine, was 'Christian'. She'd never looked up Lou, or Louise. 'No. Sometimes. I don't know, I've always had a good memory, it's been my curse. I'd love to be able to forget, then I could sleep.'

Lou's face tightened briefly in response to this piece of self-diagnosis. Then she smiled at her client: if only things were that simple. 'And how is Jamie?'

Ruth slipped her handkerchief from her sleeve and dried her eyes, blew her nose. 'He's . . . *Jamie*, is how he is. He's still the same, you know.' But of course Lou didn't know Jamie.

'Ruth, was it Jamie who ate the capsules from your bottles?'

'That's right.'

'It was Jamie who upset you.'

'Yes.' Ruth was aware her hand had been taken.

'Our children are in trouble,' said Lou.

The inanity had the required effect on Ruth—she felt her brain pulverised, her watchful intelligence finally, fully released. She was ready to be stupid, and to be told what to do, how often, for how long, when, where, everything. Do it to me, she thought. Do it now.

Lou was leading Ruth along the hallway towards the living room. 'What's in there?' She stopped outside the barricaded toilet door.

'Nothing,' said Ruth.

'We've talked about obstructions, Ruth.'

'The plumbing is obstructed.'

'Can we get it fixed?'

'I'm waiting for the man.' Even in the dumb state, she still had the capacity for deceit.

'Don't let it build,' said Lou.

They sat side by side on the sofa as Lou opened her briefcase. Inside, it was customised to fit rows of bottles. A plastic moulding held each bottle in its hole. There were no names on the lids but Lou knew her stock by heart and ran her fingers over the identical black tops as if warming the keys of a piano. She hummed to herself. The mumbo-jumbo was an excitement, and Ruth listened to the advice and received the selected bottles with total concentration. She waited in grateful silence while Lou entered the details in her account book. When they were finished and Lou closed the lid of the briefcase, Ruth felt a ferocious pain, as though her finger had been caught in a door.

'Would you like a reading?' Lou also travelled with an artist's folder—a large, flat rectangular leather case that contained her astrological sheets. Ruth was less interested in this paraphernalia. At one time her daughter Penny had written the stars column for her high school newspaper, giggling at the kitchen table. Ruth could never completely rid her mind of this. Why should the stars, anyway, pity us? They burned and died, just as we did.

'I can't today,' said Ruth.

Lou put her folder under her arm. 'Then I better see if she's still alive,' she said.

'Who?'

'Vanessa, my daughter.'

The concept of Lou with a daughter had grown no more likely or likeable. 'Yes! I do hope she's better soon.'

Lou stood at the kitchen window. 'It really is a lovely house.'

Ruth sighed. 'It's far too big for me, I don't know why I hang on. I should sell.'

'Would you think of it?'

'My son—my other son—wants me to sell.'

'And would you?'

'It seems an awful effort. The agents, the open homes, the signs everywhere.'

Lou was close to her again. 'My husband, he's actually in real estate.'

'No, I could never sell. No, no.' How was real estate connected with all of this, Lou's work? A *husband*? People's choices were dismaying. To give Lou the message she should leave, Ruth began to walk towards the front door. 'We all feel from time to time we're in the wrong place, don't we?'

At the door, Lou turned to Ruth. 'If you move, Ruth, I'm sure Jamie will still be able to find you.'

'Jamie?' She regretted her outburst in the bathroom. Women like Lou fed on indiscretion as if it were truth. They were never listening to what you meant to say, only what you happened to blurt out. Through these accidents they advanced a diagnosis.

Lou had a speech. Behind her head, the sun caused the ends of her hair to grow translucent, pinkish, electrical. 'Many people, parents, hold onto the original home on the assumption that there is a line of breadcrumbs leading through a dark forest back to the first, the true and safe house. By leaving this house, they fear the trail will lead their children to a house of strangers.'

Ruth thought for a moment, during which time she believed Lou considered she'd made a crushing point. There was nothing, however, in the analogy that withstood scrutiny, though she was too tired—there! she was tired—too wrung out to think it through. Ruth's chief regret was that the euphoria of the brief-case opening and the medicine selecting had gone. She was her critical self once more. She saw helplessly how things failed. She was, as Lou had once said, Ruth.

Lou bent forward and kissed her on the cheek. Then she waited, smiling at Ruth. There was still the cheque to be handed over. 'I almost forgot,' said Ruth, retrieving the cheque from the side-table in the hallway and passing it to Lou, who took it with a little nod, as though she'd received a tip.

When she closed the door finally, Ruth discovered in her hand the card of Lou's husband with all his contact details. He was an Indian man, a real one, with obviously false teeth.

SALLY PULLED THE note from the windscreen. It said, Walk, you lazy cow. Beneath the message Shane had drawn a smiley face—the emblem on his acid tab. Already she had the baby buckled in. There was a slight dip in the drive down to the street. She took the handbrake off, straightened the wheels as best she could, then went round the front of the ute. Behind the window a few metres from her elbow, Shane was sleeping. Quietly, before leaving, she'd shut the top window in the bedroom. He'd swelter now and suffer, tossing in the sheets, unaware of the problem for some hours. Good job.

The ute wouldn't budge, however. She leaned against it and shoved, but it rocked backwards each time.

'Won't start?' a voice called to her.

Sally looked up to see the neighbour's boyfriend looking over the fence at her arse. He was wearing a suit and a white shirt but no tie.

'Need a hand?' he said.

Sally nodded, then held her finger to her lips, indicating the sleeping baby in the back of the car. He understood and held up his own finger, grinning.

He walked up the drive, taking his jacket off and rolling up his sleeves.

'Can you just push?' she said in a low voice.

'Hop in,' he said.

Sally got into the ute and, without closing the door, steered it down the drive and swung it onto the street. The boyfriend came to her window. 'Do you want to try it?' he said.

'I got it now,' she said. She was searching in the glovebox for the cigarettes she'd left there.

'You going to turn her over?'

'Thank you, we're fine.' There was the trash from Shane's fast-food meals but no cigarettes. 'Fuck you,' she said.

'Excuse me?'

'Not you. I meant someone else.'

'I don't know, I wouldn't complain.'

She looked at his head for a moment. For the hair he was losing on top he was substituting a moustache. From the top of his shirt, hair was also abundantly on view. The neighbour, whose boyfriend he was, sunbathed in slippers. Once, just after the baby was born, she'd brought across what she called a Greek salad. Shane had thrown the whole thing out since it contained cubes of rough cheese that he said were called fetid.

'Hey,' said the boyfriend, 'you wanna invite us to those parties some time.'

'What parties?'

'What parties! I swear to God I'm going to come over and smash that heavy metal shit record you've got.' He was laughing and shaking his head. 'Seriously, don't you have some good stuff?'

'Like what?'

'I could bring some over some time.'

'Like what?' She watched him take his tie out of his pocket and start putting it on. She understood he'd seen her struggling with the ute and rushed out to be of assistance and to talk to her. His shoelaces weren't even tied. Without a mirror, he was struggling.

'I like sultry music,' he said. 'I like summer evening music. The gentle sounds of Mr Brook Benton and Miss Anita O'Day. Classics, with a steady supply of alcohol.'

'Use the car mirror,' she told him.

'Why thank you,' he said, bending to the wing mirror near her door.

His bald spot was still pale, new. She touched it lightly with a finger. 'We don't have parties,' she said. 'That's just me.'

'Just you?' He stood up and touched the top of his head as if she'd left something there or taken something.

'Listening to whatever's on, you know. The baby just sleeps right through. He doesn't care.' It seemed to be true—the baby didn't like the quiet. 'My boyfriend works nightshifts.'

'Does he?'

'At the cheese factory.'

'Way out there.' His teeth, she saw, crossed slightly in front.

In the kitchen sink, she'd found two empty cans of baby dessert and the teaspoon Shane had used. He'd eaten the baby's food before the baby had even grown enough to try it.

'I don't get a chance to be loud all day,' she said. 'So I got to take my chances, don't I?'

'I think that's a good motto.' He reached his hand inside the ute. 'I'm Tony.'

She shook his hairy hand and said her name. 'I seen you round.'

'Yeah.' He was scratching his wrist. 'I mainly come for the cooking.'

They both exploded into laughter that caused the baby to stir, and then they watched him settle again. She felt they were waiting for a parent, her father, to go to sleep.

'You got a smoke?' she said.

'Yeah, in my pocket over there.'

While Tony went to collect his jacket from the driveway, Sally started the motor and drove off.

SHE WALKED TOWARDS the chemist's carrying the baby, who seemed lighter today. Maybe after trying to push the ute everything would seem lighter, though the baby was also sleepier. He'd fallen asleep at the bottle. He was awake now but dopey-looking. She resented this performance of his. At the chemist's they liked to look you over, and if they saw this drowsy baby there'd be added interest. She had the sunhat on him and she gave it a tug so it covered more of his face.

At the counter there he was, the chemist, in his white jacket. He said hello to her but he stared right through the baby. He didn't want to see a thing of such innocence associated with all this.

'You're back,' she said.

'How are you this morning?' he said.

Behind him the young black guy was bent over, mixing something in a beaker, and the woman was over by the sunglasses rack, talking to another customer. There was a customer she'd seen before sitting on one of the seats by the counter. She knew him from here but also elsewhere.

'Is this as private as it gets?' she said.

He put her plastic cup on the counter. 'You can swallow it through the back here, if you'd like.'

'I've done it before, haven't I?' she said.

He leaned forward so his elbows rested on the counter. 'I hope we're going to be sensible, Sally.'

'Perfectly,' she said. She felt his nervousness and vulnerability. Yet in the vicinity of all these chemicals her head was not as clear as it had been in the ute with the windows down. At a certain point a breeze had even come through, but that meant driving pretty fast.

He picked up her cup. 'I'll carry this for you.'

In the room where they'd been filmed he quickly took up a position by the door, as if for a rapid exit. She hadn't been prepared to be back in the room. The window she could only glance at, as if there was still a camera there. She was sheltering behind Richie. She was sure Shane would make copies of the video for sale—perhaps he'd already done it. Every arsehole at the cheese factory would be queuing up. Shane had put the video in a 'safe' place—she guessed his locker at the factory. It was certainly nowhere in the house. She'd ripped up everything trying to find it.

'Please,' said the chemist, showing her the cup on the bench.

She moved towards it while he began talking, in a low voice, about how well she'd been doing when things weren't easy, with the baby and everything, how hard it was but she was hanging in there, in fact more than that, she'd been making progress, which was fantastic. What did he know, he said, about how hard it must be for her, clearly he didn't know much, but he'd been doing this for ten years or more now and he had at least that experience with kids like her, not exactly of course, everyone was unique, but in similar situations, and what he'd seen told him how bloody hard it really was, so he had an inkling at least, the smallest understanding of the scale of her achievement. She brought the cup to her lips and swallowed the methadone while he talked on. He was full of shit, she knew. He was desperate to save his own neck. He was a weakling and a coward and a pretender and a cheater. His white jacket may as well have been a white handkerchief to show he was surrendering. He was afraid of her. He knew nothing about her. Yet in his mouth something of her life's path took shape. From his meaningless drivel a figure stepped forward.

The figure was not heroic but ordinary, not troubled but happy, not alone but loved, not despised but loved, not raped but loved, not forced but loved, not rejected but loved, not bad but good, not a mother but a child. It was herself, not as a ghost but as something less than solid. But she was there. She put the back of her hand to her mouth as a comfort.

SHE'D BEEN IN a taxi at night the previous week with her baby, and she'd started to cry—taxis could make her emotional easily. It was having someone drive you home through the dark. And that person, though a man usually, was more or less faceless and obedient. She'd buried her head in her baby's blanket and bawled, without much of a sound, for a few moments.

'What's the matter, love?' said the taxi driver. He was ancient, probably some old bus driver who'd yelled at her in another life. He had a silver and yellow frizz on the back of his neck. The skin there was sharply lined in a criss-cross pattern as though scored by a knife.

'Nothing,' she said. She looked at the baby, who was sleeping.

The driver's crooked eyes were in the mirror, studying her. 'Big job with a kid, isn't it? Lots of changes you got to do to your lifestyle.'

She nodded. Clearly he felt she hadn't begun to make these changes yet.

'You taking him home now, eh. It's pretty late for a little one.'

'Yeah yeah.'

'Big changes.'

'Know the biggest change?' she said.

'What's that?'

'I can't do runners so easy from taxis.'

He glanced at her in the mirror again, frowning. Then he was slowing down. 'I'm hoping you have some money on you, little lady, else we turn round and I drive you somewhere you don't want to go this time of night. I can dump you anywhere, you know, and I'd be in the right.'

'What about my baby?'

He laughed. 'That's your doing, isn't it.'

She found she was crying again, though not from anything he'd said. Her hormones were crazy; they washed inside her.

'Oh, Christ,' he said. 'Give it a rest.' He put his foot down and they were moving at speed. They were passing the golf course. In the green night, the fairways looked like a cloth thrown over the earth to hide something. She shuddered. He punched a few buttons on his taxi monitor and it made some electronic noises. She knew they had codes for safety. 'Anyway, what's the sprog's name?'

'Richie.'

'Richie.' The driver was shaking his head, smiling—she saw his ears go up.

'It's a positive name,' she said, which was what Justine at the A&D clinic had said to her. Richard, shortened when he's small to Richie—yes, Justine liked it. But they hadn't thought of Richard at all. On the birth certificate, it was plain Richie. And Shane had danced round the room with the baby, singing, 'We're in the money, we're in the money. My little Richie.'

'Well,' said the driver, 'you've got to say, don't you, hope springs fucking eternal.'

THE CHEMIST WAS still talking. He was on a roll. Maybe she should go back to the support group now, he was saying.

She missed the group suddenly. This made her think of Shane. If she had never said the thing about still living with a user, she wouldn't have walked out. She was, in the end and to her own surprise, an honest person and it was her honesty in front of the people she thought she could trust which had placed her in this particular universe. If she hadn't been living with Shane there would be no conversation with the chemist, no tape, no nothing.

'Listen a minute,' she told him. 'It was him that did it.'

But he wasn't listening. He wanted her to come and look at something. The chemist was motioning her to the door. 'Just stand here,' he said.

'I didn't want to,' she said.

'Ten years tells you a few things,' he said. 'Can I just point out one of them? Look there.'

She stood beside the chemist, looking at the guy on the chair. Her mind was filled with Shane, his stupid and meaningless tattoo that he'd got done when he was out of it and freaking over the baby and being a dad. Halfway through he'd wanted to have a word inserted into the design. The guy doing the tattoo was working from a book and he said there were never any words, it was impossible. The word, Shane said, was Nana. No, said the tattooist, there was no room for Nana. 'This is for my Nana,' Shane said. 'Tell you what,' the tattooist said, 'I'll do you a small

Nana somewhere else, for half-price.' But when one side was finished Shane didn't want to hang round for any more. He'd come home and gone to bed for fourteen hours. When finally he got up again, he told her, 'I don't want you to look at me.'

'It's beautiful,' she said, regarding the puffy mess.

'Don't fucking look at me.'

'I gotta look at you some time, Shaney.'

'It's not supposed to be beautiful,' he said.

'I didn't mean it like that.'

'It's designed to make you respectful and scared.'

Sally stared at him. He looked exactly like Shane, though after he'd come through a windscreen. Soon the swelling would go down and perhaps the effect wouldn't be so noticeable.

'I'm shitting myself,' she said. He poked out his tongue and waggled it. 'My big scary warrior.'

'There's someone who was once in a position like yours,' said the chemist. 'Not the same but like it. Let's not stare, but you see him.'

The guy on the chair noticed them looking. He crossed his legs and uncrossed them. He appeared to Sally, who'd worked as one herself for a few months before she spun out, like an office temp, slightly wrong and angry, and his face wouldn't be still. Yes, she knew him. He was like her.

'Now,' said the chemist, 'not too long ago he was in a very bad way. But he picked himself up. On the programme, through his own efforts, he turned it around, Sally. Just like you're doing. Stabilised. Got a job.'

'He looks like a loser,' she said.

'He *was* a loser.'

'He looks like a prat.'

'He's not a prat any more though. From the programme, he remade himself up again.'

'That geek?'

'You think someone's a geek because they have a suit on?

173

Grow up, Sally. If you're honest, you'd say you want that too, that stability.'

'That guy? No, he's gone, that guy. Up here.' She tapped her head. 'I know him. You got to avoid him, you know. Loo, we call him. Hangs around public toilets, doesn't he? Won't let you have a fucking pee! One day he's going to get beaten up real bad.'

The chemist sank back a little into the room, unsure. 'He's harmless enough.'

'That's who I'm aiming to be like?' she said. 'Jesus, maybe I shouldn't have had my swallow right now.'

'Listen, Sally,' he said, 'you and your mate, it's time to stop, okay?' The chemist sounded different now she'd shot down his methadone poster boy. 'I don't care about him, but if you get bumped off the programme that's a big loss. Do you want that old life back again?' He took the plastic cup she'd drunk from and dropped it in the rubbish bin. 'End of conversation.'

'End of conversation? My dad used to say that. "End of conversation."'

'I'm not your dad, Sally. I'm just a very stupid man. And I'm sorry, I really am. What I did was unforgiveable—stupid, stupid, and harmful—and I can't make it up to you, I know. But why should you suffer for my mistake?' He was close to her with his reddened face, and she moved the baby between them. 'Let me have the tape.'

She avoided his eye. She wasn't leaving the programme any time soon; it'd saved her life. 'I don't have it.'

'Where is it?'

'I don't know.'

'Will you get it for me?'

'It was never my idea.'

'I believe you. Will you get it for me, Sally?'

'I can't get it. He's got it. Shane's got it.'

'Where is Shane?'

She told him about the cheese factory, Shane's locker. The chemist asked her, apparently in all seriousness since his face carried that wounded look, to tell Shane he had to bring the tape in, or post it. Like in an envelope? she asked. Don nodded. Yes, she had to make him understand the game was up. She laughed outright at this, which finally seemed to connect with him. He continued nodding sadly. Yes, she said, she was sure Shane would see his point of view and it would all be over just like that.

There was a knock at the open door. The woman chemist stood there. 'Graham's getting anxious about the time,' she said.

'Thank you, Janet,' Don said. When she'd gone, Don turned to Sally and said, 'I don't want to put you in danger.'

'He'll kill me,' she said, and walked out of the room with its ugly eye and out of the pharmacy with its crackle of goods, into the glare of the footpath that rose like a platform bearing her up. Her feet felt quite unlike her own, and the baby was weightless, more or less reduced in her cradling arm to the burden of the blanket in which he slept. She understood she liked the baby because it was always on the verge of teaching her something about sleep, even though—especially though—it couldn't talk.

THE NURSE HAD invited Graham to take off his suit jacket but he'd declined.

'Take if off, mate,' said Don.

Graham shook his head and said he was fine.

They sat in a waiting area—a semicircle of chairs grouped around a toy castle. There were no children. The other patients were elderly. Some had magazines, some dozed, a few stared at the castle and the Viking-type toy soldiers that lay around on the square of carpet.

'I'm thinking,' said Graham, 'of something I can do after this. I'm trying to run my mind forward to *after* this.'

'Good thinking,' said Don. He'd picked up a magazine.

Graham's plan was to have a cup of coffee, and he invited Don to join him. Don said he had to get back to work. 'But you should have one,' he said.

'How?' said Graham.

'Have coffee by yourself, Graham.'

'With people watching?'

'Who?' said Don. 'No one watches anyone drink coffee.' Everyone watched Graham, though—Sally, everyone. *Loo*. It was depressing to think he was known. Somewhere Don had it in his brain that Graham was invisible or that he simply merged as other people merged and only Don could see into his troubles.

'You're so naïve, Don,' said Graham. 'That's all they do. We live in a café society.'

'Not in Timaru, we don't.' Don flicked through some more pages.

'I need to go to the toilet. Do you think they'll let me?'

'Go on,' said Don.

'What if I'm called?'

'I'll get you.'

Graham picked up his duffel bag.

'What do you need that for?' said Don.

'I need it,' said Graham.

'Fair enough,' said Don. 'Graham, don't cause any trouble in there.'

'What trouble?'

'Don't be stupid about who goes in the toilet or anything.'

Graham walked off down the corridor and Don put the magazine back on the table. He longed for there to be a child playing with the castle. He needed a distraction. He thought of Anna. On the way back from the hospital, after they'd seen Jamie, Penny had told him she was changing her work hours so she could do the pick-ups from kindergarten. She had to start seeing more of her daughter, she said. Too much of Anna's life was going by that she had no idea about. One day she'd wake up and find her borrowing the car or lying with her head on the toilet bowl—all those great parenting milestones. 'So,' Penny said, 'you guys are relieved.' Don knew this was an important step in his sister's life and he told her he thought it was a great plan but the first feeling he had was one of deprivation. He felt it again now. He missed the kindergarten: it was simple. He missed the axolotl. He missed the parrots. He missed Patrick.

In his mind then the figure of Shane loomed, and the cheese factory, where Don had never been. What were the ways, he wondered, of somehow getting into Shane's locker? As a health professional, were there reasons for gaining access without Shane's knowledge? He couldn't think of anything specific, yet an over-riding sense of the justice of such a search settled on him. He saw the factory manager nodding his head in acquiescence, leading him along some wide corridor to a stand of lockers, much like school lockers, and from a large collection of keys pulling out the master. He could drive out there today, while Shane was sleeping.

He stood up and followed Graham.

Don entered the toilets quietly, holding the door so it closed without a sound. The rope handle of the duffel bag trailed under the cubicle door. Don bent down and saw the soles of Graham's shoes pointing out. Graham was on his knees. Don stood at the basin for a moment, listening to the other man breathing. The pattern consisted of short intakes followed by deep exhalations. At the bottom of the near-empty bin for used paper towels he saw a single latex glove with blood on it, and the plastic wrapping of a hypodermic syringe.

Don reached down and quickly slid the duffel bag out from the cubicle.

'Hey!' There was fumbling at the lock on the cubicle door.

Don tipped the bag upside down and shook it. A magazine fell out on the floor. Graham flung the door open. 'You! What's all this, Don? Fucking hell!'

'What's all *this*, Graham?' said Don.

Graham's jacket hung on the back of the open door. He gripped his trousers in one hand. 'Can't a man have some privacy? Fuck.'

Don peered into the cubicle. A porn magazine rested on the toilet seat. 'What are you doing?'

'You know,' said Graham. 'What are *you* doing?'

Graham was tying his belt. Don said, 'You're about to have a procedure.'

'Exactly,' said Graham. He bent down and picked up the magazine, put it back in the bag. 'I was so tense. I'm over the abyss here. Jesus, what's with you?'

'What abyss?'

Graham struck his hand against his temple in the way of an idea occurring. 'You thought I was shooting up!'

'Look,' said Don. 'Sorry.'

'You thought that.'

'Not really.'

'How come you don't know a thing about life, Don?' Graham collected the other magazine off the toilet seat. 'You've gone weird, man.'

'Sorry.'

'This shit is all spooky anyway. The turn of events.'

'What events?'

'I was going to tell you afterwards.'

'What?'

'I found your brother, Don. This guy Jamie. He's your brother, right?'

'How'd you find him?'

'You could have said he was your brother.'

'Yeah.'

'I found where he was but he seems to have gone. I knew this guy Douglas.' He was feeling in his pockets. 'I got an address written down somewhere.'

'That's all right. He's here actually. He's in hospital.'

'Bummer,' said Graham. 'Or good, I don't know. I don't care.'

'Yeah,' said Don. 'Listen, Graham, I got you wrong.'

'You were so wide of the mark. I'm very upset with you.'

'What can I say?'

'To be on the programme this long and then you think I'm shooting up in a hospital toilet?'

'My mind made a whole lot of wrong inferences.' Don pointed in the direction of the rubbish bin. 'There was stuff in there.'

Graham was washing his hands. 'This undermines everything I thought about you.'

In the waiting area the nurse was ready with Graham's sedative. 'You know I'm on methadone,' said Graham.

The nurse nodded and told him the sedative wouldn't be a problem with his other medication. 'This is my medical adviser,' Graham said, indicating Don, who now sat across from him. He put the pills in his mouth and swallowed some water from the cup she gave him. 'What will I feel?' he said.

'Not much,' said the nurse. 'Pleasant. Relaxed. Nice.'

'Then can he have one too?' said Graham.

The nurse left them, saying she'd be back in ten minutes to collect Graham. They looked at the toy castle. Then Graham said, 'What are you still doing here? Go and see your brother.'

'You'll be all right?' said Don.

'Go and see your brother.'

'I can stay.'

'Frankly, Don, I find you oppressive.'

S HE DROVE THE ute aimlessly around, taking side roads and no-exit streets, and everywhere there seemed to be people or the possibility of someone watching from behind net curtains or from upper windows, forcing her to drive on. People had nothing to do in this town except suck the hem of their net curtains.

The baby woke and wouldn't take the bottle. Finally Sally

had to climb in the back with him and give him the breast. Then he was dirty and she tried to lie him down on the tray of the ute to change him, but he howled. Even through the thickness of the change mat and the cloth nappy she'd rested him on, the heat of the metal came through, scaring him rather than scalding him, but he wouldn't lie down there again. She ended up changing him on a grass verge in front of a church. There were prickles in the grass that stabbed her palm.

'Good morning!' The minister—she supposed he was that—stood above them. He wore a jersey with his shirt collar pinned underneath the V-neck, a style she associated with two classes, teachers and religious. In his hand he carried the gun-type nozzle of a hose.

'Sorry,' she said.

'No, no, be my guest. Can I help at all?'

'No, thanks.'

'If I'd been here sooner we could have used this on him.' He held up the hose and laughed nervously, removing his gaze, when she looked up at him, from the baby's still exposed privates.

She put a fresh nappy on him and pulled on the pants. Then she stuffed the dirty one in a plastic bag that she threw in the car. 'I need to wash my hands.'

'Okay.'

'You want to aim here.' She stood up and put her hands out to him.

'Right,' he said. He squeezed down on the lever and water shot out against Sally's hands, splashing up over her clothes and over him. 'Oh, dear,' he said.

She rubbed her hands together, then wiped them on her teeshirt. 'No worries.' She bent down and picked up the baby. The minister was offering to get her a towel. No, she told him, she was fine. The water was nice and wasn't he hot in that jersey? He looked at his jersey as if realising for the first time that he had such a garment in his wardrobe. And why was he watering in the morning? she asked. It'd all burn off by midday. While she put the baby back in the car, he was explaining that he and his wife were going away for a few weeks and this watering was just a vain attempt to give the place some chance of survival. He knew it was doomed. She was getting into the ute and she asked him where they were going. Surfers, he said, a little sheepishly. She said good on him and didn't he have a neighbour or anyone to come and do the watering. Alas, he said—she flinched when he used the word—alas, the neighbour was gone too, though someone from the church would clear the box every second day.

Maybe she was looking too intently at him now, or he'd thought of something else he had to do before leaving, or he understood in the bargain they'd struck after he'd wet her clothes they were more or less even—whatever the cause, the minister stepped rather rapidly away from Sally and the ute and waved them on their way. She was certain, as she pulled out, he knew he'd said too much about their going-away plans to this stranger and her dirty baby in the rusting heap. But with equal certainty she knew he didn't know why exactly this might be a problem. A mother and child—the omens, after all, seemed good.

She stopped at the next phone box and called home. She'd put their phone on automatic messaging—Shane wouldn't be up for hours—yet when it came on, she was so surprised to hear her own voice she rang off. It seemed freakily like her *inner* voice, or a voice from another time. 'Yo, you know the routine, dude.' She'd got written off one night and spent hours recording stupid messages. O happy days. She rang again and moved the mouthpiece away when she heard the message start. When it was over, she began speaking. She told Shane where the church was, how the minister was leaving on holiday and the neighbour was also away and how the house was tucked in behind the church, hidden from view. She was about to tell him good luck or something but at that moment a lump of bile entered her mouth and she was forced to put the phone down. The feeling

181

choked her that she had made a horrible mistake, and that it was one in a series. She staggered from the phone box, leaned against the ute and spat onto the footpath. She gagged once more and spat again. Then she wiped her chin with the back of her hand and got into the ute. She could drive home and erase the message. She could park the ute in the drive and get back into bed with Shane and begin the day again a couple of hours later—it was within her power. In the rear-view mirror she saw how her eyes were watering from the gagging and she was white. In combination with the sunshine she seemed, like paper under a magnifying glass, in danger of igniting.

Finally she found an empty street. There was nothing around except for the burnt-out body of a car sitting in a patch of stony grass. A hundred metres or so away, a wrecker's yard stood idle, a boarded-up house beside it. She turned off the engine and sat for a moment, listening to the baby breathing. She switched on the radio and tried to get a song she knew. It was too easy, so she tried to get a song she didn't know. Was there nothing new in this world? Was everything a fucking retread? Her youth wasn't over and it'd become a classic. Still, she sang along for a little while, mysteriously flattered to be in this company. It became a little test she passed again and again, which fact alone made her feel like she was cheating. Then she found herself in Nostalgia, which turned out to be the songs her father said he liked from a period after he'd finished listening to music. The radio would be on and he'd walk into the room and ask who it was. Paul Young or Bryan Ferry. And she was weeping. She saw them again, these suave singers in their immaculate suits. No one, it seemed, understood them, except their tailors.

She turned the radio off and stopped crying. She looked again, pointlessly, for the cigarettes. Out by the old car in the field there'd be butts—and with that thought she found she'd disgusted herself sufficiently. She crouched forward in the seat, then brought her head down hard against the steering wheel. The pain was intense, though not immediately in the area she'd hit. It felt like she'd been whacked behind her ear. She was crying again and the pain travelled slowly to the front of her head. She put her hand there and yelled sounds of self-consolation that, astonishingly, failed to pierce the baby's sleep.

JUSTINE AT THE clinic had her lying down in a room Sally had never been in before. The baby had been taken somewhere else. She had to make herself remember to ask about him.

'Don't you worry, he's fine,' said Justine. 'We'll get you both safe first. That's number one priority.'

The room was an internal one and painted white, and Sally was lying on a hospital-type bed with a plastic cover over the feet region and a paper cover over the rest. The point of this, she knew, was to save on the laundry bill. It also had the effect of making her feel temporary, like an object whose traces would soon disappear, consumed in the clinic's incinerator. She felt important and neglected at the same time, which was how she always felt in contact with the health profession. What had changed, of course, was the nature of this importance and this neglect. There was a pastel painting—not a real one—in a gold frame on the wall above her bed. Flowers. Sally was significant and meaningless in a different way, and she could tell from Justine's face that it was, however routine, a kind of excitement. There was gratitude in her concern. Her counsellor's morning had a fresh cast to it. Across Sally's forehead, a bulb of bruising had come out large enough to be on the periphery of her own vision, like the rim of a hat.

Justine took up a clipboard from a small desk in the corner of the room. She was writing as she spoke. 'There are some details we need, Sally. I know you probably don't want to talk about it now, and that's fine. I'm not going to ask you to go over everything when you're in this state.'

'I'm okay,' said Sally.

Justine looked up from the clipboard and smiled at her. 'Can I just ask, when did this happen?'

'When he came home from work.'

'Yes. And that was what time, roughly?'

'Fourish, this morning.'

'Four a.m. And how long did—how long was the abuse?'

'How long?'

'Over what time period, would you say? A few minutes, ten minutes, longer?'

'I can't remember.'

'No.'

'Not long.'

'Say, five minutes?'

'No. It was quicker.'

'All right.' Justine seemed a bit disappointed. She wrote on her sheet with a new emphasis, as if there was space there Sally wasn't letting her fill. 'What's Shane's last name?'

Sally sat up. 'Where's my baby?'

'Like I said, your baby's fine. He's in with Meredith.'

'Who's Meredith?'

'Meredith is the nurse. She's got your bottle. Would you like to see him?'

'I want my baby!'

Slowly Justine got to her feet and put the clipboard down on the desk. She approached the bed. 'All right, Sally.'

'That's my fucking baby you've got!' Sally was off the bed, heading for the door.

'And we can see him,' Justine told her, reaching for Sally's arm. 'Because he's your baby and we're doing everything to make you both safe. Would you like to sit back down, Sally?'

'No, I fucking would not like to sit back down, Justine!' In moving so quickly, however, she'd done something to the pain in her head. Now her eyes buzzed and jittered with movement of their own. Dizzily, she gripped the door handle. 'You fucking lock me up in here, I'll fucking kill you and anyone who touches my baby!' It registered with her somewhere that Shane had never hit her, had never pushed her seriously—had, in fact, always been strangely tender, with his hands at least. She vouched nothing for his mouth or his mind. He was an animal of a sort, as she was. Having a baby showed you that. She could have been attended to by a vet.

'Sally, it's not locked. The door isn't locked. Let's go and see little Richard then.'

'Richie!' she yelled. 'His name is Richie!' She was laughing. 'Little Richard is a rock and roll singer, you moron. My baby is called Richie!' The door then opened in her hand and she fell forwards into the corridor through an air that was different, less dense, more treacherous, since it failed utterly to hold her upright.

ten

A PNEUMATIC PULSE was operating in Shane's head. He was unaware as yet it had another location. He sat up in bed and grabbed the pill bottle from the table. The sheets gripped him damply at the shins, and at the band of his boxer shorts he was soaked—a terrible feeling. There was no air in the room. He put the pills in his mouth before he saw there was no water in the glass. In the bathroom he pushed his face inside a wet facecloth and gathered some water in his hands to wash down the pills. The mirror still presented him with a surprise. His face was two months old. Christ, he was a scary mother. As if in response to this conclusion, he felt a drip emerge from his penis.

He walked along the hallway and opened the front door onto the noise. The council weed-spraying truck was on its slow round, feeding poison to whatever wandered from the garden. A guy in goggles and breathing mask waved a sprayer that was fed to him from the small truck inching alongside. A light flashed on its roof without point in the bright sun. All of it seemed alien— as if organised by aliens, he thought. It was arrogance to think they were alone in the universe. There was humankind and then these wankers with their weed-spraying vehicle.

The air, with the poison, had little change in it—maybe it was sweeter. They seemed intent on killing stuff repeatedly at the edge of the front fence. The sprayer returned to a spot he'd already done. Of course behind his goggles he'd seen Shane standing at the door in his boxers. They were making his house out to be the noxious house, the house of things that needed to be eradicated.

The din of the truck was way out of proportion with the job—a job that Shane had, in fact, eyed up before he got in at the cheese factory. Now he saw the driver, who rested his chin on his hand, he was glad he wasn't part of that team. In the sinews of his arm, Shane could tell he was possessed of a wiry strength that would not yield in an arm-wrestling contest. Such contests weren't strictly about strength; they tested technique, a dying art. Everything about the old guy was dying. At this moment, he turned his head in Shane's direction and showed him a face without a flicker of interest in it. His soul had been blown through the hose.

'Don't kill my fucking lawn!' Shane yelled. The driver moved a hand to cup his ear, or scratch there. 'Kill it, then I don't have to mow it, who cares.' In fact, they didn't have a mower. The sun burned off the growth. Shane watched them move slowly off. It was like observing landscape from an airplane. He went back inside the house, without closing the door. Then he felt strange—robbed—and walked back out again, this time round the side of the house, where he stood on the burning white drive-way, looking at the space where the ute had been. The oil leak was there. The stain was damp. At what temperature would such a spill dry up? In what way would he punish Sally for this disobedience? He regretted leaving the note on the windscreen; she responded predictably to all the insults of authority.

He walked to the front fence and looked at the wet lines crossing the footpath. Sally had planted things—they looked no better than flowering weeds—in the dirt behind the fence. Shane put his bare feet into the dry soil and moved his toes under the first of these plants. When he kicked up, the roots came out easily. Yet this wasn't it. This wasn't a tender spot. Sally was no gardener. She'd stolen the plants from a roadside stall operating an honesty box. He himself had taken the box.

Inside, he swallowed some more pills with a can of beer before looking around for something to spoil or wreck or put his mark on. Where were these things by which a woman is known and made? Sally had nothing that wasn't already a disaster or heading that way. If she had a favourite shirt, he didn't know it. Shoes? They looked broken, still inhabited. The stuff in the wardrobe hung as if guilty. Her rings, her jewellery was all rubbish. The lava lamp on the chest of drawers no longer worked. He didn't feel he could touch her deodorant or the other bottles and cans in the bathroom. Some were leaking a froth, or had a rim of rust where they sat in little puddles. He held her toothbrush for a time and saw the flattened bristles splayed either side of the centre, as if her teeth had lain down there to sleep. She valued nothing, it struck him. She maintained nothing. Nothing was worth preserving and keeping nice. She was not nice. Often he'd been glad of this.

In the baby's room he fingered the mobile he'd got from an op shop. It was hung with sweets made of glass—the dumbest thing he'd bought ever, according to her. One look and you wanted to put the sweets in your mouth. Soon as the baby was able, he'd reach up, yank one off and choke to death. Yet with the light on it at night, there was a brilliance that she couldn't argue against, and Richie followed it like it was his life turning above him, his career in the stars. There was an ambition in the mobile that was transferred to whoever looked at it. It was the luckiest thing in the house.

Shane had a shower while still wearing his boxers. He put a towel around himself and took the boxers out to the clothesline where he hung them to dry. He heard music coming from a radio next door. Through the gaps in the fence he was looking at skin, some of it still not bad. She lay on her stomach, facing away from him, with the straps of her bikini undone and her head resting on her arms. Her bikini pants rode just above the cheeks of her buttocks. She must have been forty at least and coated even in her creases and cracks in a dark tan that looked ethnic. She was Greek or something. Lebanese, Sally said. No, he told her, because hadn't she seen the boyfriend. Ha, ha. There was always a drink in her hand. The glass now stood beside her on the arm of a beach chair. He watched her arse which, lying down, looked half its size. The satiny pants revealed the clear division of each cheek. In the towel he was hard. He coughed loudly. She turned her head suddenly and sat up. Her tits in profile were large and friendly looking. He fancied he saw veins running their length. He was off Sally's tits. Everyone was— Richie, the chemist. In the video—or in the few minutes he'd seen of it—the chemist had not attempted to get hold of them at all. Shane waited until his neighbour put her head down again, then he walked back inside the house.

In the kitchen he saw that the answering machine was flashing. He had to play it three times before he could gather in all the details. Sally's voice had never sounded stranger. Then he spoke aloud, talking back to the machine. 'I love you,' he said. For several moments he didn't feel in the least ashamed of this declaration.

189

WITHOUT A VEHICLE to sit in, it was impossible to assess the situation. He was sweating from the half-hour walk, but he couldn't stop—where could he wait? He turned directly into the church grounds, walking with purpose down the drive and round behind the church. He went up to the first door he came to and tried its handle. While he was doing this, he was looking at the windows and up onto the roof. It was a low building and through the net curtains he could see the walls were covered in kids' pictures. In one corner sat an electric organ and beside it a guitar case. He couldn't look at a collection of musical instruments without wanting to fool with them. His band days were over, and yet the desire was back in an instant. Already he saw his fingers on the keyboard, though he didn't play. Already he was stuffing an old blanket in the kick drum. There were little tables and little chairs. Sunday school. He'd been to Sunday school; his nana had taken him.

With less haste now, he followed the path round behind this building and went through a gate attached to a trellis fence covered in roses. The house was at the bottom of a sloping garden. He skipped down some steps and found himself tumbling towards a porch area. He did not quite have control of his body. There were large stones painted with flowers grouped at the front door. His bladder was suddenly full and the stones, with their suggestion of a river, commanded this next action. He was, however, erect—and, it hit him then, what if he'd arrived too swiftly or if the church people's plans had changed? Or what if Sally had set him up? With this last thought, he felt himself softening, and the urge to piss on the stones evaporated. He knocked on the door, just above the sign that said, 'We are All Tenants in the House of God'. The tenants, praise be, were not home.

For people of God, however, they lacked all trust. The house was shut tight and he was no burglar, though he'd tried to learn from a few. He'd brought nothing with him—how could he without the ute? The windows were deadlocked and the ladder he tried to pick up from beside the house turned out to be padlocked to a tree. There was a garden shed but that too was secured. The French doors at the back of the house were also deadlocked. A wave of tiredness passed through him, ending with a brief cramp in one calf muscle. He considered going home. He'd already done his work the previous night, real, honest work. What did Sally mean by leaving the message? She'd said she didn't want him involved any more in stupid crimes that could drag her and the baby down. He was a father now and he had to think of that whenever something cropped up. He had to bring every offer he got back to her. The thing with the chemist was all right because it was both of them and it involved hurting no one. There were no victims since the chemist had accepted through his own weakness Sally's offer, and he would simply end up paying them a fair and just amount, compensation for the wrongs he'd committed. It wasn't blackmail; it was a market opportunity.

Then this, too, he thought, must be a market opportunity, though he resented being the one who had to take advantage of it. The cheese factory had somehow softened him. He answered to an odd feeling—it was ambition. He coveted Mike's job or a better job and he knew he was capable of that. He could see himself climbing the ladder. In the face of this task at the window, he felt nervous, out of condition.

He stood again in the front porch and listened to the neighbourhood. It was still, the silence broken up only by the occasional car passing on the street in front of the church. He picked up one of the stones and held it in both hands. Already in his mind the stone was in flight, cast off from him. Once something is picked up and held in the hand, an opposing force is also felt and the object will soon return to rest. His mind sounded to him as though it now moved in the rhythms of that far-off Sunday school. He was listening to lessons.

He walked to the back of the house, and stood in front of a small kitchen window. Already the window was in pieces—he saw through the hole into the room, and he saw his hand moving through the hole. The stone gave him the gift of prophecy. Then somewhere close by a lawnmower started up. There was grass left after all in this burnt-out city. There was stuff living and green that needed to die. Shane raised the stone to shoulder height and lobbed it half-heartedly into the window. He viewed the result with a strange regret. He'd stood in front of such scenes before, of course. As a kid he'd never hesitated. Now he took a step away from the window and looked back up the path, saw back up to where he'd come from, looked along the tunnel of time which had brought him here, thought of the neighbour sunbathing topless, thought of each step he'd taken. It was possible to go back, he felt. The sheets on which he'd woken, with their smell of breast milk, still lay in their tangle, like an arm twisted.

Then he turned again to the task, taking off his sneaker and using it to knock away the glass that still remained. He went to pick off a shard with his fingers until he remembered he had brought something—he had the glove, Sally's golf glove. He took it from his back pocket and pulled it on. It was the left glove. Neither of them was left handed. It seemed immediately to rob him of the use of that hand, as if the glove indicated a deformity, the deformity that was his girlfriend and her baby.

'Hello, Shane.'

He knew the voice: it was Sergeant Burrell's voice, and it did not surprise him; his prophecy had contained this too, though he'd tried to block it. In every act was a shadow. Sergeant Burrell was the shadow that indicated something real had happened, something that presented an obstacle to the sun's rays and did not let them pass through.

They stood in a kind of red darkness created by the brick house. Burrell reached out for Shane's cheek. 'Gone a bit native, have we?' They hadn't seen each other since the tattoo. Burrell moved his stance a little wider, his shoes crunching down on the glass. 'If you'd wanted to borrow a Bible, Shane, I'm sure the minister would have loaned you one.'

Whenever he was arrested, Shane had a sudden desire for chewing gum. He was likely to bite his tongue otherwise. His jaws already seemed to be working at some rubbery compound, though his mouth remained dry as Burrell said what he needed to say about Shane's rights.

Shane was thinking of Sally and the responsibilities of fatherhood, and he was thinking of their plan in which there were no victims and it was not blackmail and it was about the future of their child. She'd spoken of creating an education fund for their child. Burrell knew none of this. Burrell didn't know that Shane had got rid of the videotape either. It was impossible to impress Burrell; he'd been in Vietnam. What mayhem they got up to as kids round Timaru—Burrell had known Shane since high school—meant nothing more than a nuisance to Big Bad Burrell. It was as a child now Shane appeared to the cop, in some dress-up version of a crime; he'd only broken a window after all. The markings on his face—these Burrell would see as pen and ink, like something scribbled on the bottom of a skateboard or on the back of a bus seat. Burrell would not grant Shane the five hours of torture, the days of pain. He would not give him a break. Even heroin, dirty needles under cushions, ambulance runs to the hospital, produced little in Burrell besides sarcasm. Peacetime nonsense. He'd picked Shane off floors in rubber gloves and carried him slung over one shoulder like a carcass to get his stomach pumped. Burrell was like a father to him, and Shane hated him like a father.

'I'm working at the factory now,' said Shane.

'Then this is even stupider than it looks,' said Burrell.

'Then let me go and I'll fix this up. I'll pay for the window.'

'Are you still using, Shane? If you're using I know I can't

trust you. The reason you've done this is because you're using, so that means I can't have faith in your word, can I? We're in the vicious cycle again, my friend.'

'My girlfriend is on the methadone programme and I want to get on too.'

'That's a start.'

'I've got a job.'

'Then it doesn't make sense, does it, Shane?' Burrell tended to be right—he'd never been wrong.

'No. But I can fix the window and the people won't be back and no one will know.'

'But *I* know, Shane, and I don't trust you yet.'

'We've got a kid too.'

'The poor shit.'

'No, fuck you, the kid's good.'

'I'm not talking about the kid, Shane. I'm talking about what he's been born into. His dad robbing churches and shooting dope.'

'Give us a chance.'

'What did you do that to your face for, Shane?'

'I don't know. I woke up, I had it.'

'Jesus, I'm going to take you in now. I feel like smacking you on the head, you make me so mad.'

'You don't have to take me in, do you?'

'Come on, let's go. I've got real things to do with my time.'

Shane still held one sneaker in his hand. He bent as if to put it on, then he picked up the stone with the flower painted on it, and smashed it down on the cop's foot. Shane did not believe the force of the stone could penetrate the leather of the police shoe, but Burrell cried out and began hopping around. 'You fuck,' he said. It didn't seem serious.

Shane again picked up the rock and hurled it down on Burrell's knee. The cop fell to the ground and began to make an alien noise. Shane had never stood above Burrell before. He looked down on him as if from the height of a building.

He endeavoured to bring an end to the noise.

He cast the rock, without looking, at Burrell's mouth. This was not in the prophecy nor in the lesson. He retrieved it—he did not examine the stone—and brought it down again, and still the rock was in his hand with its longing to return to the earth. It was getting heavier and heavier each time he picked it up. Much of what was emitted now from Burrell had the sound of internal, involuntary protest. On the surface, Burrell must have wanted to die—who wouldn't? Shane had thought about dying a few times and been surprised to wake up alive, still holding his life. Yet Burrell's organs refused finally to let go. Life, even at this point, was a matter of selfishness. With so much else available, it was Burrell's knee that had won out—the big hands still gripped there as if what had been sustained was some sports injury, possibly career-ending.

At high school one time Burrell had made them all play basketball, though Shane was never going to be tall. He even picked them up from their homes in a van and drove them to the gym. He said to Shane, 'You're a point guard.' He stood on the sidelines and he showed him how to be one, and for five months he was one.

This old point guard wept over his coach and mentor. He was down on one knee beside the great man. Burrell had been an outstanding leader, an outstanding coach.

Finally, as far as Shane could tell over the rush in his ears, Burrell was fully quiet. The neighbourhood lawnmower died and left a vast hole. Something was pounding in Shane's ankles—it was his pulse.

Burrell's blood was all over the golf glove. Shane removed the glove and put it in his back pocket. Then he walked quickly past the house, back up the path and through the church grounds. Burrell's police car was parked in the church carpark. From inside, he could just hear the sharp voices coming through on the car radio. When he was on the other side of it, he saw there was an old lady peering into the car. They gave each other a fright from which she was the first to recover.

'I seen him go in,' she told Shane, who nodded. 'They're away, you know.'

The woman began to stumble away from the car, noticing what? His tattoo? His manner? Something distinctive about him. He felt something leave him and go up into the old woman's shopping bag.

Shane kept walking. He was on the street now and feeling had returned to his arms and legs. His arms were sore as though he'd used muscles he hadn't used in years. He seemed to have come through a marathon, a coast-to-coast, some massive endurance achievement. The old lady, he knew, would appear again in his life. She had something of his. Leaving the neighbourhood, he almost looked forward to it. Since he'd never see Burrell again, the old lady would have to do. And she'd do fine; though she'd place his tattoo on the wrong side of his face and make up something about his demon eyes. He did not have demon eyes. He had kind eyes, as Sally had once said, though it was Sally's fault he was here now. Yet the old lady was the noticer that every crime draws out, as a snake is charmed from a basket, and you couldn't argue with it finally. He remembered, as if dredging something up from years before—as if *he* was the witness—that her shopping bag was tartan. She was not unlike his nana. Yes, he could identify her again. He could point her out in the courtroom if asked. There, that's her there. She was leaning into the cop car and acting suspiciously. You could hear the voices from the car radio. It was a real quiet day and the only sound was those voices, trying to make contact.

Some schoolkids passed him and giggled. He looked down at his jeans and saw that he'd wet himself. He began to run in the direction of the Bay. It wasn't far, and there was all that water waiting to receive him.

PENNY LOOKED AT the woman for the first time only after she said, 'I live with Simon.' The woman had been in the consulting room for at least two minutes, giving her details as Penny asked for them. Penny checked the name she'd typed on-screen: Caroline. The woman sat forward on her chair. Penny couldn't quite relinquish the keyboard though there was nothing further to type. She had to pick up Anna from kindergarten.

'I'm at work,' said Penny.

'I'll pay for the consultation,' said the woman.

'I've got real patients.'

'I took the last appointment. There's no one else. You can check if you want.'

'You took the appointment of a real patient.'

'If you want to look in my throat or something. I have actually had a sore throat for a while. If that makes you feel better, I'm willing to be a real patient.'

Penny moved her chair away from the screen and stared at her desk. Her own handwriting on various notes looked odd to her. Her day seemed on view only through a very tiny aperture. 'Why are you here?'

'I'm sorry for coming. It was wrong of me.'

'But you're here now.'

'I am.' The woman turned slightly away from Penny, adjusting the strap of her handbag across the back of the chair. 'Do you know why I'm here?'

'No,' said Penny. She thought of the envelopes she'd filled and sent to the address where this woman lived, the woman's hands on the envelopes though they were marked for him. Envelopes containing nothing much at all. Sometimes they might have appeared to be empty. A nail clipping, a hair, a piece of dried skin from her toe. What was she, a witch? It was probably the reason she could not go public with it—he was still forcing her to draw from a ghastly fund of superstition. She couldn't *think* about it, think it through. His violence had been a sorcery.

'Can you guess?' said Caroline.

'No.'

'Then maybe that's good.'

'What is?'

'If I'm here for the wrong reason or a nonexistent reason. If I'm here under . . . if I'm here because of something that was said to me which turns out to be false.'

'I don't follow.'

'I live with Simon, Penny.'

'You said.' The woman was older than she'd expected—older than Penny, though more stylish, infinitely so. What was her occupation—a judge? She looked legalistic but also wise, not at all pushy. Her nose was a perfect straight length. Despite the evidence that Caroline was a grown-up woman, Penny was pretty sure she could guess which school she'd gone to.

'I need to know if he abused you, Penny.'

She felt a familiar terror, not in remembering the beatings she'd suffered but in thinking she'd allowed it to happen to someone else—this woman. She lived with this terror. 'What do you do?'

'I work for the Local Government Association.'

'Where?'

'Christchurch is where the office is but I travel round quite a bit. Why do you want to know?'

She couldn't answer. There were no other questions to ask. 'Has he abused you?'

'No. No, he certainly has not. No.'

Penny felt like weeping and only the presence of the desk, its papers, the coffee cup—so clearly not the possessions of a stricken person—gave her the ability to swallow instead of howl. 'You find the idea . . . ridiculous.'

'No, not ridiculous.'

'But out of your range of . . .'

'Out of my experience. I haven't ever been abused, Penny,

it's true. However, I know it happens and I know it happens in the most unlikely—'

'Yes. The answer, Caroline, is yes.'

The woman put her hand across her mouth. Behind her hand, Penny could see that her mouth was moving, chewing at the palm.

'I'm sorry,' said Penny.

Slowly the woman tipped forward in her chair until she was bent in two and staring down at the carpet. She began to make small rocking movements.

'I'm sorry but we have to get out of this room now. I have to pick up my daughter.'

The woman raised her head. The solution had been received with gratitude. She'd been crying soundlessly and her eyes were red. 'Absolutely,' she said, smiling briefly. 'I'm so sorry to arrive like this.' She stood up and was trying to unhook her handbag from the chair; the strap had tangled.

'Let me,' said Penny.

'No, no,' said the woman. She jerked at the strap and the chair fell over with the bag still attached. 'Oh, oh.' The woman felt she was trapped; a panic came over her.

'Here,' said Penny. She bent down and unravelled the strap.

'All those things you sent,' said the woman.

'I've stopped.' Penny handed over her bag.

'He said you were demented and furious.'

'I was.'

The woman gripped the door handle. 'Thank you.'

'One thing,' said Penny, 'who told you?'

'It was a kindness, he meant it as, I think. He's decent. It was your brother, the chemist.'

J AMIE HAD BEEN sleeping when Don visited. He'd looked into the room briefly, and then he'd driven back to the pharmacy not exactly disappointed. He didn't know what he had to say to his brother. He was sort of sick of him already. He hadn't yet called his mother to tell her Jamie was in hospital. It was not his brother he was sick of, he thought again, but Jamie in this context—in the context of the town, of the family, everything he, Don, was involved with. To press even with the lightest touch at the top of his spine was to provoke a bitter pain.

Rameesh had gone home from the pharmacy, feeling unwell. 'Headache,' said Janet.

'I hope he didn't take offence,' said Don.

'When you shook his teeth out, you mean?'

'Was I too rough? I was rough, wasn't I?'

Janet rested the spatula on the counting tray. 'Is something wrong, Don? How's your brother?'

Immediately he felt more confident in his white jacket. 'Oh, there's always some crisis with him.' He swept a bunch of empty pill bottles from the counter into the open bottle drawer. Apropos of nothing, he turned on the tap over the sink and swept water around inside it. Janet was watching him. 'Some performance. Of course, you don't have siblings.' He realised it would have been quite possible for Janet, in other circumstances, to take this last statement as criticism of a particularly stupid kind.

'No, but Peter does,' she said. Peter was Janet's husband.

'Yes, so of course you get it through him. It's tougher probably on Tina too, when you come to think of it. If it's your sibling, you have all this practice at dealing with their nonsense.'

'How is Tina?' said Janet.

'She's good.' He was running his finger along the label-dispenser shelf, pulling out each little label box to check if they were running low. Rameesh had almost certainly done it in the last few days.

'I think it's my turn for lunch,' said Janet. 'I should ring her or else she'll think I'm a real cheapskate.'

'She's been busy with work and everything.'

'She's always busy. My job is to drag her away from that.'

Janet and Tina had lunch together every few weeks. Janet, it turned out, had had a miscarriage between her two children. That wasn't the bond—they'd been perfectly friendly before this came out—and it hadn't brought them closer. It had, however, created regularity in their contact. Previously, they'd been happy to chat whenever Tina called into the pharmacy. Once they began the lunches, it seemed neither of them had the power to go back to that other time. Lunch was now a powerful matter of loyalty between the women. They sat across from each other, waiting pleasantly for something—intimacy perhaps, Tina wasn't sure. After a few longish restaurant meals at the start, when they had to wait for the food to arrive, they moved the location to cafés. Janet would often come back to the pharmacy carrying a paper bag with her sweet inside. They'd established the discipline of a one-hour time limit and it was frequently shorter than that— Tina always had things on.

The impasse was clear to Tina. 'She works with you,' she'd told Don. 'And I live with you. There are too many things we can't talk about. We hold back.' Janet would chat about her own kids—teenage boys—until she figured she'd been going on about them enough, then she'd grow quiet. They couldn't talk about men, since Don was one. Tina could talk about the gallery, though Janet's niece worked on the front desk so that was another constraint. They were trapped but it wasn't horrible, just failed— and, Tina said, doomed to fail repeatedly. She told Don that they were no more likely to understand each other for both having had miscarriages than two people who'd lost their grand-fathers. 'I guess we also remind each other,' said Tina, 'that what we think is unique to us is actually everyone's and so widespread that our suffering is common and rather everyday, which is a good lesson but it's also bloody annoying.'

'Why don't you say that, then?' Don had asked. 'Talk about that.'

'She knows already without me saying it. There's nothing to say.'

'Then why do you keep on having lunch together?'

'Because I like her.'

'But why do you have to sit down and eat with her? You could like each other without food, surely?'

'I like to eat with people. I don't like to eat alone. You like to eat alone, Don, but I don't.'

This, he thought, was true. 'I don't mind drinking with people,' he said.

'You're not one of those chatty, jokey chemists,' she said suddenly. 'You're naturally inward, almost morose.'

'Thanks very much!' He laughed but Tina didn't smile. He had the impression these were things she'd worked at in her mind for a long time, and the fact that she was finally saying them made her not anxious so much as tender, as if she was providing a service that was difficult but utterly necessary. She, he thought, should have been the chemist. Or the doctor.

'You're not quite at ease. That's why certain people like you a lot for their chemist. I think they like you for some of the same reasons I like you for my husband. Though, of course, I also love you.'

'Yes,' he said. 'That last bit is a rather big difference, I'd say.'

'I'd say!' Now Tina laughed and put her arms round his neck. He saw she was flushed with the happiness of a revealed feeling and the pride in seeing it accepted.

'I love you too,' he told her. 'In my inward, morose way of course.'

Don had moved into the office while Janet served a customer. He rang Graham's number and left a message, asking that Graham should give him a call at home that night and tell him how it'd all gone at the hospital.

There was a knock at the open door. 'Sorry,' said Sharon. 'Can I ask you something about something?' She held up a bottle of contact lens cleaner. 'This says it's expired.'

'Yes,' said Don.

'Um, is it all right?'

'No, Sharon, it's expired.'

'We can't sell it, can't we?'

It wasn't worth trying to untangle the negatives. 'It would be a good idea not to sell it.'

'Someone wants it.'

'Is it the last bottle?'

Sharon nodded.

Don took the bottle from her and walked out to the counter. Rameesh's father stood there. He put out his hand and Don shook it. 'Is this for you, Mr Prasad?'

'It's for my wife.'

'Could we give you a different one this time?'

'This is the one she has. She has written it down.' He held up a piece of paper. 'All the others hurt her eyes.'

'I see. Well, it's only just expired. It'll still do the job, so I have no qualms about giving you this one, but we can order your wife one for tomorrow.'

'No, she needs it today. She says she's dying from the grit, I don't know.'

'All right.' Don handed Mr Prasad the bottle.

'How much?' said Mr Prasad.

'No, no, let's not worry about that. It's expired. Usually we'd throw it out.'

'No, I must pay you.' He had his wallet out and was twisting the bottle to read the price. He gave the bottle to Sharon, who was standing alongside him. 'Read that and tell me how much.'

Don took the bottle from Sharon and passed it back to Mr Prasad. 'Really, Mr Prasad, it's okay.'

Mr Prasad looked unhappy. He stood with the bottle in his hand. 'I said to her, get glasses, what are you doing, you're not winning any beauty prize.'

The topic had suddenly touched an area of Sharon's expertise. 'I think Mrs Prasad's a very attractive woman,' she said.

Mr Prasad studied Sharon for a few moments. '*You* are attractive,' he said sternly.

'And so is Mrs Prasad!' said Sharon.

Mr Prasad shook his head. 'Mrs Prasad has borne children. She's as ugly as me.'

'Can we help you with anything else?' said Don.

Mr Prasad led Don away from Sharon, holding his elbow. 'Rameesh is in the car. I brought him back.'

'Is he feeling better?'

'I said to him, you work in a pharmacy, how can you have a headache? If you have a headache, you take a Panadol. Do you work in a pharmacy it doesn't have a Panadol? So I brought him back.'

'Listen, Mr Prasad, if Rameesh is feeling under the weather, I think it'd be best for the pharmacy if he wasn't here.'

'Swallow a couple of Panadol. I eat it bloody every day! What does he think—the world doesn't work when you've got a sore head? My head is sore all the bloody time! Half my headache, it's him.'

'Still, I don't really want him here if he's not up to it. I'm fine with him going home. Tell him to come back tomorrow. He'll be fresh and ready.'

'And you can slap him, okay?'

'Sorry?'

'I don't have a problem with this discipline. You want to give him a little whack, I think that's good. I don't want him to be running home to his mother. Oh, that's a terrible sight to a father. You have kids?'

'No,' said Don.

'What a blessing,' said Mr Prasad.

'Would you like me to come out and speak to him?'

'I think now he's scared of you it will go better. I think

we're making progress.'

'He's doing fine,' said Don.

Mr Prasad laughed as though Don had said something funny. Then he shook Don's hand and walked out of the shop.

T HE CHEESE FACTORY, on its twenty-four-hour clock, rising through five storeys in parts and topped by silver chimney stacks, was visible for miles around. Don's car was soon in the line of milk tankers burning down towards it across disintegrating roads. He felt he existed inside a kind of pipe—all vehicles in the vicinity ran down the pipe at 100 kilometres per hour into the factory like a white-hot liquid.

The needs of the factory could be seen in the abandoned farmhouses and derelict barns that lined the route. The manufacture of cheese had an appetite that took up all other forms of life.

Don parked in the visitors' carpark alongside a tour bus. Inside, the woman at the reception desk was handing him a pair of goggles and a safety vest marked with luminous red strips. 'Up those stairs, and you'll meet them,' she told him. As he went to speak, she was answering the phone.

He found himself on the end of a guided tour. He still carried his vest and goggles, but the woman leading the tour, without looking at him, asked that all safety equipment be deployed in accordance with the Occupational Health and Safety Regulations. Don discovered he was obeying her, just as the land within an expanding radius obeyed whatever instruction issued from these walls.

They walked along a low-roofed corridor that shook slightly with their weight. It felt like the structures that exist in airports to convey passengers from terminal to terminal. There wasn't a distinct sound, but the noise of hidden machinery was continuous. At various points they were stopped by the guide in front of viewing windows too small to let the whole party of twenty look at once. This meant conversations began at the back of the group—where Don was—and the guide's voice became even harder to hear. The tour party was from Australia. They'd started in Auckland ten days before. From the snatches that Don heard of the guide's commentary, he understood she was repeating the production figures set out on a card beside the window. Once this was widely known at the back of the group, there was even less interest in listening to her.

One woman said, 'Wouldn't like to fall in there, Bob, would you?'

They were standing above the Brine Salt Hall, where large squares of cheese floated in pools.

Bob said he wouldn't mind.

'She said you'd float if you went in there.'

'Oh, yeah, like the Dead Sea, isn't it.'

'Now that's a bloody wonder, that Dead Sea.'

Someone asked Don whether he'd ever been in the Dead Sea.

'Greg loves salt. He says he can't taste anything unless it's got salt. He'd go in there quick as a flash.'

The voice of the tour guide was briefly audible. 'Moving right along, folks.'

An elderly woman had somehow attached herself to Don's side. 'I actually don't like cheese much,' she whispered to him.

They passed a glass door through which Don saw a line of grey metal lockers. He'd not forgotten why he was there. He'd taken a batch of home deliveries and left the pharmacy early. 'You're the boss,' Janet had told him. Was she taking the piss? He was a paranoid wreck. But now he was in, what was he to do? Peel off quietly, slip through the door and start trying every locker before he came to an open one? Of course the open one would be Shane's.

At the new window, they were looking into a huge room filled with racks of what the card on the wall identified as

Parmesan moulded into wheels. The Parmesan matured here for four months and had to be turned by hand several times a week. The racks were ten metres high and there were more than forty thousand wheels of cheese.

'Christ,' said one of Don's party. 'Job like that'd rot the brain, wouldn't it.'

The guide, who'd paused in her commentary, heard this and smiled. 'It's a big job all right,' she said.

There were five hundred people employed at the factory, but in all their looking they'd seen just three figures moving round the giant rooms. Finally it got to someone. 'Where's everyone hiding, love?'

The guide smiled more warmly this time; she'd heard the question before. She repeated a few things about the cutting-edge automation, state-of-the-art machinery and how many of the tasks that had been done by humans now could be done by machines. This answer naturally had the effect of only deepening the strength of the question. 'Yeah, but then what are these five hundred actually *doing*?' The guide paused and her eyes flicked briefly upwards as if she was waiting for her mind to forward to the next place in the tape. She was then explaining about shiftwork. She said that the workforce was rotated so as to maximise skills and interest.

'So their brains don't rot,' added a voice, and the party laughed while the guide looked out through the next window.

Here was a view of the outside world. It broke in on Don with a sudden liberating force. He felt himself take deep breaths, as if the sight of natural air was enough to fill the lungs. The group as a whole seemed to relax at this window, to bend towards it gratefully, greedily. Cloud, sky, even grass.

'It's a good day, isn't it?' someone said.

It seemed as if they'd been deprived of these things for a long time.

'We thought New Zealand would all be cold, especially down

south.'

The guide nodded. 'It's been so hot,' she said. It was her first statement that wasn't from the taped commentary. 'But we shouldn't complain.'

A man in a cap spoke to the guide: 'I'm originally from Townsville, we wouldn't call this a heatwave.'

In the foreground stood a line of three tankers. They were too far away to see the drivers. Again the scene contained no human activity, though apparently what was going on involved the draining of each tanker's milk supply. The guide recited the volume of milk required by the factory. 'Because of the hot conditions,' she said, 'we're under strict water regulations. The high-pressure jets that usually clean the tankers can't be used. The water ban is district-wide and carries with it serious penalties.'

One of the tankers was suddenly engulfed in a spray of water.

'Look,' said a woman at the window.

'Okay,' said the guide. 'That's me shot to pieces.'

As the party was led away to the next window, Don stayed and watched. A lone figure, dressed in white overalls and white gumboots and the same sort of vest Don was wearing, walked across the expanse of concrete towards the tankers. The walk was so deliberate and unhurried and the distance he had to cover so plain and huge, Don had the urge to speed up the whole scene. As he was about to arrive, Don heard the guide's voice calling to him. 'Thank you, sir. Sir? Thank you.'

They continued almost to the end of the corridor, with the guide giving out a stream of statistics about other products the factory produced apart from cheese. They passed a small, waist-high, domestic fridge plugged into the wall.

'That where you keep it all then?' a man asked the guide.

Many of the party, Don noticed, touched the fridge on their way past, as if patting the head of an animal to make friends.

Through the smallest window yet, they looked down into

the Whey Protein Concentrate Room. A figure—it was impossible to tell whether it was a man or a woman—stood beside a conveyor belt watching large paper sacks being filled with a white powder. The job was to look at the weight scales as each bag came past and with a metal scoop add or take out a little of the powder. Occasionally the person gave the metal rod above the bag a couple of hits with a rubber mallet. The noise from this small, enclosed area seemed to make the window throb. The figure was wearing headphones.

'The weight,' said the guide, 'has to be exactly right.'

As if hearing the guide's words, the figure looked up at the window. It was a Maori woman. She dropped her hammer on the ground and started flapping her arms and walking around the enclosure, shooting her head back and forth with her chin stuck out.

'Oh, jeez, she's doing the chicken,' said a man at the front.

'Look at this, a chicken!'

'Bwock, bwock, bwock.' A couple at the window waved down at the woman, laughing and making their own chicken noises.

'You'd probably be a bit mental, wouldn't you.'

'What a dag.'

The elderly woman was at Don's elbow. 'The Maoris are quite rare in the South Island,' she said.

Back at the reception area, everyone was handing in vests and goggles and a few were buying postcards from the woman at the desk. One of the party—the man wearing the cap—had been elected to give a vote of thanks to the tour guide. 'We've learned a heap. We've seen fantastic facilities. The automation is truly outstanding. Clearly the world knows all about your factory here, with the exports etcetera. And we're delighted to share in that knowledge. So thanks again for taking the time to show us around, and we promise we won't tell anyone about that water infringement.' He then kissed the guide on the cheek and everyone applauded, including Don.

When the tour party had filed out through the doors, Don stood at the desk. 'Excuse me,' he said. 'There's someone I know who works here. I've got to leave something for him.'

The woman turned around and slid shut the drawer of a filing cabinet with her knee. 'You want to leave it here?'

'Actually, I'm his chemist. I've got something from the pharmacy for him.' Don tapped his pocket.

'You leave it here, he'd get it. Who is it?'

'Shane.'

'Last name?'

'I don't know, unfortunately.'

'There's five hundred people here. Probably heaps of Shanes. I know two, three myself. What's he look like?'

A middle-aged man in a short-sleeved white shirt and tie had come out of an office behind the reception desk. He was listening to them.

Don put his fingers to his face. 'He's got a tattoo here. Just on one side, quite noticeable.'

'Is he a Maori?'

'Could be. Darkish complexion.'

'No.' The woman shook her head and adjusted her skirt at the waist. 'Don't you have some records of his last name?'

The man raised his finger in the air. 'Not Mike Waller's brother or something? Brother-in-law? Works nights, just started?'

'Oh, see, I don't work nights,' said the woman.

'Give Mike Waller a call, Maureen,' said the man.

'Where's he on?'

'Look him up.'

Maureen rolled her head, annoyed at being given the job. She stabbed at the computer keyboard. Then she picked up the phone and spoke to Don. 'Of course he's not on, is he, but let's see if we can find your Shane.' She wandered into the office behind the reception area, trailing the phone cord. When she came back she told Don the name was Castle. If Don left the package with them, they'd see he got it.

'Actually I can't leave it,' said Don.

'Thought you were leaving it.'

'Not in the open, like this.'

The man in the tie said, 'We could put it in the safe.'

'What is it?' said Maureen. 'Explosive or something? Put it in the safe then.'

'Does Shane have a locker or something?' said Don.

'Safe's right here,' said the man.

'There's this Ministry of Health thing, I can't hand it to anyone except the recipient. I'd love to throw it in your safe but my hands are tied.'

'Are you from Timaru?' asked the man.

'I'm Don Webb from Perry's Pharmacy.' Don shook hands with both of them. 'Thanks for your help, I appreciate it.' Now his real name was out the whole business seemed less deceitful.

The man looked at Maureen, who said that she couldn't take Don to the lockers. The man said he couldn't either.

'Could you point me in the right direction maybe?' said Don. They both ignored this.

'Security could take him,' said Maureen.

'Ring Ron,' said the man. 'Or I could stretch my legs.'

'No, it's not your job. I'll ring Ron.'

Ron, the Samoan security guard, led Don through a maze of corridors. Don thought: I may not ever get out of here again. He thought of the sky, the clouds, the trees.

They came to a door with a handwritten note stuck to it, 'Ladies Welcome at All Times!' The walls of both sides of the small room were taken up with lockers. 'Take your pick,' said Ron.

Don followed the nametags across one wall then, shifting to the other wall, he found S Castle. 'This is the one,' he said.

Ron came forward with his key and opened the locker. Don

waited for Ron to step back before looking inside. It was bare except for an empty plastic drink bottle and a sweatshirt, which Don carefully lifted out. There was no tape. He put the sweatshirt back in and picked up the drink bottle.

'They used to have this whole place in like playmates and stuff,' said Ron. 'Used to come in here and gorrrre! Then they had to take 'em all down. Which I agree with. I think a woman is something you don't see like that. I always say if the ladies have all these men up on their walls, you know, what would we think? Or if it was their daughters.'

Don put the bottle back inside the locker and shut the door.

'All done?' said Ron. He locked the door. 'That must be a good man.' He knocked a knuckle against the metal.

'Why's that?' said Don.

'Because there's no pictures, you know, inside the door. I think that's a good person with some respect in his life. A church person. Are you a church person, sir?'

'No,' said Don.

The guard nodded. 'That doesn't bother me. There's good outside and inside, I know that. There's the power everywhere.'

eleven

TINA DROPPED ICE into the three gins and cut up a lemon. She put the glasses on a tray. Janet, from the pharmacy, had arrived just before Penny. In ten years, Janet had been at their house no more than five or six times. Was a gin and tonic stirred? Tina got a teaspoon from the drawer and jiggled it inside each glass. A pip floated free and sank to the bottom of one glass. Having failed to retrieve it with the spoon, she moved this glass to one side of the tray, put on her sunhat and walked out into the sunshine. Already the ice in one of the glasses had fused.

'Here's our waitress now,' said Penny. She was running her hand roughly through her daughter's hair. Anna sat on the grass in front of Penny's chair. In Penny's other hand, which she kept down beside the chair at ground level almost, was her cigarette.

'Stinky old smoke,' said Anna.

'Anna's so big now,' said Janet, who'd got up from her chair the moment she saw Tina coming down the stairs. 'Can I help, Tina?'

'You can help by sitting down and taking your drink and drinking it,' said Tina.

'I like those sort of orders!' said Janet.

Tina supposed Janet had agreed to the gin only because they were having one. She seemed to regard her glass with regret.

Penny was already sipping from her drink. 'Did you put gin in this?' she said.

'Is it too weak?' said Tina. 'I stirred them.' She hadn't intended to confess this.

'Mine's fine for me,' said Janet.

'But you're not an alcoholic, Janet,' said Penny.

'Actually I was just saying the other night to Peter about how much we drink these days.'

'How much?' said Penny.

'A glass of wine every night.'

'I take it back,' said Penny. 'You guys are utter soaks.'

Tina watched her sister-in-law pick lemon from her teeth. She checked that the pip was still on the bottom of her own glass. Janet was in the shade of the umbrella that was attached to the picnic table.

'Where's Don?' said Penny.

Tina saw that Janet was about to answer but that now, as a courtesy, she waited. Don was Tina's husband after all. 'Deliveries, I think,' said Tina. 'Is that right?' Janet nodded, sipping— the gin seemed almost like a pain against her lips.

They drank or held their glasses in a silence that was soon too much for Janet. 'Look at your garden, Tina,' she said. In fact there was not much to be said for it—a point that now seemed to have struck Janet, who was turning in her chair from one undistinguished area to another as if soon she was bound to find something noteworthy. Janet's own garden was a real garden. Tina had been too busy at the gallery and the heat had been too fierce to work in it. The vegetable patch was all right. 'How do you keep everything so green?'

'They cheat on the water restrictions,' said Penny.

'We do not,' said Tina. 'It so happens that Don has a stockpile of distilled water from the pharmacy. He's had it for years in the basement. Every evening he goes out with his watering can of distilled water.'

'Clever Don,' said Janet.

Penny sat up in her chair, accidentally pulling Anna's hair, causing her to cry out. 'Don't you have a girl for the deliveries?' she said.

'Sharon does them mostly,' said Janet.

Penny drew on the last of her cigarette and looked questioningly at Tina, who nodded. Penny stubbed out the cigarette on the edge of the little brick wall that circled the vegetables. Tina looked more closely at the soil and saw a mound of cat's faeces.

'Then why's Don doing them?' said Penny. 'He owns the bloody thing now, doesn't he. He could tell you to do them, Janet.'

Janet crossed her legs. 'He could.'

'Would people like food?' said Tina.

'No, it dilutes the alcohol,' said Penny.

'How's your brother, Penny?' said Janet.

Penny looked at Janet through her glass. It was empty except for some ice; she'd swallowed the lemon; she could eat all of them: Janet, Anna, Tina herself.

Tina stood up. 'Janet? Cracker and cheese or something?'

'I'm hungry,' said Anna.

'We'll have dinner soon,' said Penny.

'But I want something now.'

Penny reached into her glass, fished out the ice and fed it into her daughter's mouth. 'My brother, Janet, is pretty much the same as he's always been.'

'Don said there'd been a bit of bother.'

'A bit of bother? Tina, does that sound like Jamie to you?'

Janet of course knew nothing about Jamie except that he was difficult. 'I'll get some crackers,' said Tina.

'I'll come and help,' said Janet. She was already moving. At the bottom step she drained her glass and set it down on the grass before thinking better of it and carrying it with her up the steps.

'I could go another,' said Penny, holding out her glass to Tina.

In the kitchen, Tina got Janet to unwrap some cheese while she found the crackers.

'I'm sorry for barging in like this,' said Janet.

'Don't be silly,' said Tina. 'It's good to see you.'

'She really hates me, doesn't she?'

'Who? Penny? That's just Penny after a hard day. She hates everybody, there's nothing personal in it.'

Janet tipped the cheese onto a plate. 'The reason I came, apart from to see you of course, is that—and this is going to sound silly—but I'm worried, or not worried exactly, but I want to give my support to Don, you know. Full support, so he can rely on me since things are getting . . . they seem to be getting more and more stressful, don't they? That's true of life in general. Certainly for Don, it's doubly true. He's "it" now, at the pharmacy, I mean. It's his baby, isn't it? And that's a great stress as well as, I think, a great opportunity for all sorts of excitement and growth.'

The woman was babbling. Tina arranged the crackers around the cheese. 'I don't think I quite understand, Janet.'

'I'm worried about Don, Tina.'

'You think it's too much for him?'

'No, I don't.'

216

'But he's taking on too much.'

'It's probably overwork. Have you thought of a break, a holiday?'

'We had a holiday last year.'

Janet touched the cheese with the tip of a knife. 'It hit me today, about poor old Perry.'

'You think Don could have a heart attack?'

Tina turned round and Anna was standing at the back door. 'Penny says can I have my bottle.'

'No,' said Tina. The first name thing had always irritated her. She turned back to Janet. 'What's he been doing, though? How's the stress manifested itself?' She thought of Don's nightmares—he hadn't had them in the last week. She considered his moodiness.

'I want my bottle,' said Anna.

'No, you can't!' Tina wheeled on the girl. 'You can have a glass of milk but I'm not giving you that dirty old bottle. No bottle!'

Tina understood that she'd yelled. Anna was staring wide-eyed at her. Janet was also taken aback. The idea had been planted—Tina saw it clearly enough—that whatever signs of stress Don was showing at work might have their origin not in the work itself, not in running a business, but here at home. Then the girl burst into tears and ran down the stairs.

When Tina and Janet went into the garden, Anna had her head buried in her mother's lap.

'What's up with the bottle?' said Penny.

'I'm sorry, Penny, but if she wants a drink of milk here she can have a glass.'

'I see, the milk police are out, are they?'

Janet put the plate of food down on the table. Tina was offering Penny her new drink.

'This is gin in a glass,' said Penny. 'So if I wanted to drink gin from the bottle, I wouldn't be allowed.'

'Gin from a bottle? I think you've got it, Pen,' said Tina. 'I just think on this issue it's worth trying a different tack.'

Penny stood up and took Anna by the hand. 'Listen, it's late. I think we'll go.'

'No, no,' said Janet. '*I'll* go. I was just going.'

'No one has to go,' said Tina.

'I want to go,' said Anna.

'She wants to go,' said Penny. 'She has spoken. Goodbye.'

'Penny,' said Tina.

Penny was already at the top of the steps, dragging Anna with her. She still had her glass in her hand, and before she went inside the house she drank it all in one go.

'I've ruined everything,' said Janet.

For a moment it was tempting to agree, if only to make her leave as well. 'I'm afraid, Janet,' said Tina, 'your power's just not that great.' She was halfway up the steps. 'Please wait a moment while I say goodbye to them. I'd like to talk with you.'

Penny had Anna in the car. 'I'm sorry,' Tina told her. 'I'm out of line. I'm a busybody. I'm sorry, Penny.'

Penny sat down suddenly on the bonnet of her car, as if she'd had a turn.

'Are you all right?' said Tina.

'She came and saw me,' said Penny. 'Simon's new woman.'

'I didn't know he had a—'

'She wanted to know if it was true. In fact she wanted to see me.'

'Yes.'

'You don't get it. She wanted to *see* me, to set eyes on the person who could allow another person to wander into that situation.'

'But she's an adult, presumably.' It was impossible to imagine anyone other than some young thing.

'You're right,' said Penny, standing up. 'I can't be responsible

218

for what other people do with their lives. I refuse to be tied to him like this.'

'Tied to him?'

'Through the constant worry of wondering who he's with and what they should know about him and so on.'

Tina tried to think about this and found she could not. There were rather large holes in her sister-in-law's viewpoint, but did Penny herself even believe it? Tina had sworn off advice anyway. 'How old is she?'

'She's older than me,' said Penny, satisfied.

They stood in a silence, which was really the only possible answer to the prurience which had made Tina pose the question and the ugly pride it had called up in response.

Finally Penny said, dejectedly, 'He hasn't hit her.'

Tina nodded, not trusting herself to say anything, even something routine such as 'Thank God'. The mood was so ambiguous and delicate. The delicacy had killed off the spontaneity. They waited and hoped. The sun as it left made them shiver, though it was still warm. And Tina had the vaguest sense of what it might have been like for Penny to have lived with Simon, to look out every window and see the view and also, on the glass as part of the view, to see the fingermarks.

TINA FOUND SHE was standing with Janet in the worst corner of the garden, where nothing seemed to work, and listening happily to Janet's good and knowledgeable observations on soil types. It was Janet who finally broke it off, saying that she had to leave before Don got home. Tina told her that wasn't necessary but Janet insisted. 'He can't know, of course,' she said. 'Can you please not tell him I came, Tina?'

'Rest assured,' said Tina. 'My husband will never know his life's in danger.'

'That's not what I meant,' said Janet. She touched her forehead. 'Actually I've got an awful headache from that drink.'

She'd forgotten for a moment that Tina had given her the drink.

'Listen,' said Tina. 'We should have lunch.'

'Yes!'

'If I haven't seen you or called, it's because of last Christmas and everything.'

'No, I understand. It was my turn to call anyway. Are you all right, Tina?'

'No.'

'No,' repeated Janet, nodding carefully.

'Yes, I'm all right.' Janet was waiting. Tina did not feel like speaking, though it was not a feeling she could commit to. She would never be that person who would not speak, no matter that she admired her sometimes and longed to be her. She was thinking mostly of Penny. 'Did I tell you,' she said, 'when I went to theatre, all the nurses were wearing something strange on their caps?'

'No, what was it?'

'Holly.'

'*Holly.*'

'It was Christmas.'

'And they had holly on their caps,' said Janet. She didn't know in which direction this was heading. She looked to Tina as though she was frightening herself out of the implied comedy of this hospital scenario. But maybe Tina meant it to be funny. Janet's confusion was to be cherished, then extinguished.

'I thought I was hallucinating at first. Here we go, I thought, I've brought the consultant out of some happy family occasion. He's going to be really pleased with me.'

'No, it's their *job*, Tina.'

'I thought he might have been tiddly.'

'No.'

'It was Christmas Eve, why not?'

'Because he was on call,' said Janet.

'Does that matter to you on Christmas Eve?'

'Of course. To a doctor, yes. They've sworn an oath.'

Tina looked at her friend and spoke with feeling. 'Thank God you came, Janet.'

Home from hospital the next day—Christmas Day—she'd told Don she'd been considering giving the babies names. They'd been lying on the bed; she was under the covers and he was in his clothes, actually still wearing his shoes. Why hadn't he taken off his shoes? The curtains were closed on the heat of the day. She'd been drifting off and waking up. She was disgusted with herself, and with the afternoon sunlight behind the curtains, and with Don. How could he be lying there and not have taken his shoes off! Her mind was in a million pieces. When she closed her eyes she saw disconnected things brought into tempting but elusive connection: the Ethiopian girl at the kindergarten whose hand Anna refused to hold; the Indian anaesthetist who'd seen her on a previous visit to the hospital. She spoke to Anna in her head just as she'd spoken to her at the kindergarten weeks before. The Ethiopian girl's father always wore a black knee-length raincoat—a very British raincoat, as if he was a London commuter. 'Hold her hand,' Tina told Anna. 'Be nice, Anna, and hold that girl's hand.'

The girl had tried to take Anna's hand, smiling.

Anna looked at her. 'I won't.'

The girl walked off.

'Why won't you hold her hand and be her friend?'

'Because she's always trying to hold my hand.'

Later Tina woke to the sounds of children's voices, and she thought of getting up to shut the bedroom door. She was convinced Don, who was no longer beside her, had organised something, or somehow let kids into the house. Perhaps they'd been selling raffle tickets door to door and Don had invited them in to wait while he found his wallet; one of them would secretly peel off, come upstairs for a nosy, or to steal something. She thought of Patrick, again from the kindergarten, in his big sister's stretched jersey, coming up the stairs. All the time she was having these thoughts, she was aware of their woeful cast. She knew but she was powerless. They aren't me but they are me, she kept saying. The anaesthetic is still in my system, the shit is still inside me. She wept and wept, and longed for Don to find her. Where the fuck are you? she said into the ceiling. No more HCGs at least, she thought. You get an intern and they can't hit a barn door. The inside of her left arm winced from the memory.

Then Don was back beside her and she'd said she wanted to remember them. Yes, he said. I want to remember them individually, she said. He made some sort of agreeing noise. I've been thinking, she said, of giving them names. He had sat up and looked at her, and for a moment he'd been unable to disguise his reaction. His reaction was this: *Don't you lose your mind too*.

S ALLY WAS LYING on her back and she couldn't lift her arms. It didn't cause her to panic. She would go back to sleep, or at least that state she'd been in just before she thought of her body. She was aware that she snored when she slept on her back. Shane used to kick her. But he didn't seem to be around; no one did. No one was going to kick her. It was peaceful, though she hoped someone would come soon and turn out the light. Such a light, it penetrated her eyelids—was she outdoors? Yet a hum associated with large buildings came through whatever she was lying on, stopping her on the point of absolute surrender. Vaguely, she was aware she was expected somewhere—an appointment of some terror, the dentist perhaps—and that she could never completely let go for fear of missing her name. Under her body she sensed a vinyl presence. Vinyl was the surface of terror, of transport but worse, of transit—the places of waiting. She recalled the chairs in the bar of the golf club and again she

222

struggled briefly to sit up. She knew who she was. She knew all about her baby. She understood she was on methadone and that her life was saved. Her entire life was not lost to her but it was distant. It seemed she'd embarked, or was about to. Then someone was dragging her back.

'How are you, Sally?'

Sally opened her eyes, which physically hurt. A nurse stood above her. Sally tried to bring her hands to her face but something was stopping her. Lifting her head, she saw now her arms were tied down. There were straps at her wrists. She tried to thrash loose—the same restraints were on her ankles.

'Easy,' said the nurse. She put a hand on Sally's arm. 'Just stay calm and I'll get someone so you can move, all right?' The nurse reached above Sally's head and pressed a red button on the wall. 'Just relax and we'll get those things off you.'

It felt to Sally as though her tongue had also been strapped down; she experienced it as a swollen obstacle and started to gag. The nurse lifted her head up and was murmuring consoling sounds as she moved Sally's hair off her face and stroked her cheek. Gradually Sally stopped heaving and sank back. She was still unable to talk.

'Good girl,' said the nurse.

Tears ran down Sally's face and the nurse watched them. Sally was grateful to the nurse for not wiping them away. This made her cry more. Then she thought how nurses and doctors weren't big on these bodily excretions—they didn't mop up blood from a cut or a wound if it was on the surface, but were happy for patients who'd been in accidents to lie in bed with dried blood on their faces. Sally stopped crying—in this context crying was unimportant. The tears dripped unpleasantly over her ears and ran down inside her neck; she rubbed at them by moving her shoulders.

A door behind her had opened and a woman she'd not seen before stood beside the nurse. 'Hello, Sally, I'm Kirsty Gordon.

I'm your doctor here. How are you feeling?'

Sally knew it was a trick question. The question really meant, how can I, with the minimum effort and time, remove you from my list of patients? Yet she responded as though this woman really did want to know and for no other reason than she was kind; she started to cry again, this time without bothering to hold anything back. She howled at the two women, holding her head still and staring through the tears at their faces. It was an audience—possibly Sally's last. The doctor was nodding, smiling gently, while the nurse—she'd had one performance already—looked a bit bored. After she'd finished, Sally found she could move her arms and her legs.

'Come on,' said the doctor. She was helping Sally sit up. There was a roll of handitowels on the bed, which the doctor gave her. Sally rubbed at her eyes and her cheeks, and the doctor took the paper from her, screwed it into a ball and, from several metres away, threw it in a bin in the corner of the room.

Sally thought, she's made a little game for herself from this.

It made her feel a kind of renewed strength and composure.

Hers was the only bed in the room. The curtains were closed across the windows. Opposite the bed was a brown door marked Toilet.

'Who'd I try to kill?' said Sally.

'No one,' said the doctor. 'You were upset, that's all. You've been through a terrible thing.'

'Who'd I try and hurt? Was it me?'

'We want to protect you and help you, and before we start anything I want to say your baby is safe and he's right next door. We can go and see him if you like. Would you like to see him now, Sally? He's sleeping.'

'I don't want to wake him,' said Sally.

'He's a beautiful baby.'

'I wanted a girl. A mate, you know.' That had been an old dream and she felt stupid to have brought it up.

'There are quite a few people here, Sally, who want to take him home, I can tell you.'

For a moment it seemed a solution. 'Really? Who?'

'Oh, just about everyone. So cute.'

Sally got the doctor's drift. There was no one. 'I need to have my 'done.'

'You've had it. Don't worry about that. We gave it to you.'

'I want to go to the toilet.'

'Of course.' The doctor helped her swing her legs over the side of the bed. 'I can get the nurse to go in with you, if you'd like.'

'Why don't you?'

The doctor looked flustered for a moment. 'I could, yes.'

'Don't bother,' said Sally. She walked with surprising ease towards the brown door.

In the mirror, the bandage on her head made her look like a paid-up loony. The view to the other side of her brain seemed at hand. Already in her career as a mental person she'd been strapped to a bed. There was a comfort in the idea. The mad were cooked for, looked after, tucked in. Finally, though, she couldn't be mad; there were too many people ahead of her in the queue—the really mad. Her mother, for instance, and her father. And being mad would be like jail. The windows wouldn't open; someone else would have their hands on your dirty washing. There would be something called exercise. Dykes would hold her down. The jail idea made her think of Shane and his final destination. He was probably insane. Many are called but few are diagnosed.

After jobs, she remembered, Shane would go to a bar and get faceless. She guessed he wouldn't have scored much from the minister's house but there was always the chance in those deadbeat places of hitting it lucky. There was still, in every neighbourhood, money under the mattress. Jewellery which old women were scared to take to the bank. In every location there was fear and dread. Fear and dread, fear and dread: it was a chant Shane had—the name, apparently, of some band he'd been in at school. They'd never played a gig, though they'd practised for two years. Shane was the drummer. The love he had for banging moronically on the side of the sofa during ads was based on this experience. Fear and dread was written in red ink on the bag he still carried to work. It made him seem fourteen. She wanted to save him.

She stepped back into the room. Her sandals were neatly set on the floor at the foot of the bed. She slipped these on. 'I want to see my boyfriend,' she told the doctor.

'Probably not the best idea, Sally,' said the doctor.

Sally walked to the door. 'Can I leave here? Am I being kept here or can I go?'

'Of course. We're not forcing you to do anything.'

'Fine-o,' said Sally, and she walked out of the room.

AFTER DINNER—WHICH he didn't have—Jamie found himself sitting up in bed, unvisited. The room was full, but not of his people. Who did he expect? His mother of course, brought in by Don. Penny wouldn't show up—she had her kid. The two guys across from him had their families there— grandparents, children, the works, all trying not to be raucous. They were telling stories and laughing, glancing across every now and then at Jamie to see if it was all right. It was all right, he didn't care. But he'd taken up a magazine so he didn't have to keep wearing a pleasant expression. They had the nurses running every way, looking for vases and extra chairs. Finally, he asked one of the kids at the doorway to pull across his curtain.

He'd expected his family but he missed Douglas in the mink coat. Where Douglas should have been there was a very white apparition. Jamie had called him earlier from the phone by the lifts, stressing his immobility. It would be difficult, he said, to get out on the street and be with the people he loved in the mighty and friendly city of Timaru. Douglas sneezed and said he didn't like hospitals, and Jamie had told him if he didn't make it during visiting hours or any hour soon, the ski pole he'd handled in the living room would find its way into a part of Douglas's body that was not especially designed for ski poles. He had to listen to Douglas blow his nose. How could Douglas be scared of him? His only advantage was that he wasn't so well known. Jamie might have been a nutter from up north, who knew? Douglas sighed and said he'd try to make it.

Jamie stepped gingerly out of the high bed. From the cupboard beside him he pulled out a plastic bag that contained the clothes Penny had packed for him when he'd been admitted. His own clothes—the teeshirt and jeans—were nowhere, probably destroyed. The loss of the teeshirt caused him a brief pang—a part of his history taken from him. These clothes in the bag were almost new. The short-sleeved shirt hung slightly large; it was of some shimmery blue material. At one stage of his life he thought he might have got right into clothes. The dark cotton trousers were short in the leg. The phrase for this outfit was 'casual but dressy'. It was the sort of get-up designed to cause you no trouble whatsoever at the doorways to nightclubs. Penny had even put in a pair of shoes close enough to his size. He looked bouncer-approved. He looked nothing like himself.

Jamie stepped out from behind the curtain, and felt the eyes of the room—all the relatives—fixed on him and his ridiculous costume. The stories and voices paused for a moment. But then, he thought, these people don't know me. They've never seen me dressed. To them I'm always to be found in shoes. They have nothing to compare me with. They don't miss the junkie teeshirt. They don't miss the old me. It gave him a shot of confidence. Already they were talking again. He smiled at them, and in this blaze of conspicuousness he sneaked out of the hospital.

Douglas was not at home and the door to his bedroom was

padlocked shut. A metal catch had been crudely nailed to the door and the padlock threaded through this. In the process, the wooden panelling on the door had been cracked. Jamie got a knife from the kitchen and tried stabbing at the cracks. The tip of the knife broke off. He continued to stab and the knife got stuck in the door so he couldn't move it. He looked at the door. He'd killed the door, though it wouldn't die. It was still standing. Carefully avoiding the knife, he tried ramming the door with his shoulder. This almost killed him. Back in the kitchen, he found a screwdriver. He worked this underneath the metal plate and levered it until the plate began to come away from the wood. When the door finally swung open, he was afraid of stepping inside. Suddenly he had the thought that Douglas might have rigged something up. Maybe *Douglas* was the nutter.

Jamie bent down and examined the ground. No tripwires. He then felt with his hand around the doorjamb and peered inside the room, still not stepping forward. He held the screwdriver and now he threw it into the room, checking for sensors. The screwdriver hit Douglas's futon and bounced onto the floor, scattering a pile of letters.

More of Douglas's undelivered mail cluttered the place. He was truly a bad bad postie. Videos and CDs, still in their plastic wrapping, spilled from international shipping boxes. These, Douglas had argued, were fair game, since punters got their money back on anything that failed to arrive. Jamie had never met anyone who didn't defend his work against the point of view of a hostile morality.

It was hard to step anywhere and not feel your foot sliding out on some paper. Birthday cards lay open, a few with ten- and twenty-dollar notes clipped to them and craggy, grandparent-type handwriting inside. Half-opened gifts—toys, shoes, dolls, knitted garments—were all about. Poster-rolls were stacked in one corner. He opened the wardrobe and there was more—a kid's tennis racquet in bubble wrap, books in cardboard, journals and magazines still sealed in plastic, and letters and papers in heaps. He did not feel safe standing among all these things. He felt the massive stupidity and cruelty of these thefts committed by someone other than himself. Jamie felt the crude forms, he believed, of guilt and remorse for his own thievings. Even while he continued his search, he felt these things—also a strong dislike of Douglas for having sufficient sense, amid all this mess, to hide his stash so well. The mind could suffer every disorder and still be a mind.

He returned to the wardrobe once more and picked up the kid's tennis racquet. He was thinking of his son of course. There had been presents he'd wrapped but never posted. He recalled a sword. Don, his brother, had bought that one. Something, he thought, was wrong with his brother. Don hadn't found him. He'd always sought him out and found him and he'd always made an effort—the effort was in vain but Jamie remembered it from time to time; in dark times especially it was of assistance. Jamie was dimly aware of someone like his brother at the hospital, but where was he now? Don was not himself if he wasn't helping someone. Maybe he was helping someone other than Jamie? This hurt.

In the end, it came down to a locked metal filing cabinet. Jamie shook it and kicked it a few times. The shoes were not kickers; he hurt his toes and also, through the operation of exquisite referral, his stomach. He squatted down in front of the cabinet and gripped the place he'd been cut into by the surgeon. An astonishing pain, like a punishment, straightened his back; he gasped. This came from his old friend, his anus. He was free, they'd told him, of the haemorrhoids, though the area would be active for a little while. Another part of his history gone.

A filing cabinet, in fact, was easy meat, as he now recalled. He swept his hand over the nearest pile of letters and turned up a membership card for a liquor chain. He knew the chain well and believed he'd joined this same club at some point—or perhaps he'd tried to join, then the thing had petered out when it came to the application form. All those questions. The club didn't offer discounts, it turned out, only the endless accumulation of points. Jamie inserted the card into the cabinet.

Douglas had misfiled his drugs; they were under 'P'.

THERE WERE TAXIS, she knew, but she was not of that generation who could act on the knowledge. Ruth set out for the hospital on foot. It was a forty-minute walk. In the material Lou had provided, there was a reference to the bathing of a red-and-white light. The phrase meant nothing to her; it meant a further fee so that Lou could interpret it. From somewhere then an ambulance had sounded and she'd phoned the hospital. She readied herself for the obstacles in such a call, but they told her straight away. She said she was the patient's mother and they said Jamie was resting comfortably. It wasn't their fault they didn't know her son.

The hospital lift was deep, rectangular—the dimensions of a bed or a box. Scrapemarks marred the paint at a regular height. Ruth was alone in the lift and immediately conscious of her hands, which were empty. Where were the grapes, the snack bar, the chocolate, the magazine? She became one of those people whose eyes fix on the roof of the lift as they travel up.

At her floor she had to push through a group who wanted to get in the lift before she'd left it. She was aware she had something of the state of invisibility about her, being old and small and a woman, a mother looking for her sick son. 'Let me,' she said. There were adults and children but no one in charge. 'Please, let me first.'

She waited at the information desk for several minutes before walking down the corridor. It seemed right that there should be no one to help her, that there should be people in fact to bruise and jostle her, ignore and fail to see her. She deserved it.

At the first room she tried not to look in but to read the name scrawled on the card attached to the wall. It was a long name so she moved on. The second room had two names written and these were easier to read. The third room had no names and she looked in it, as a sort of practice. She didn't want to be surprised by his room. She noted its contents.

The corridor turned a corner and Ruth went with it. She found his name on the second room in this wing. She peered in at the door, not shyly but out of respect. Visiting hours were over but the room was full of people. A few of them saw her and smiled. Neither of the men in the beds that were surrounded looked like her son, but she didn't pass on them immediately. She considered her own knowledge of Jamie's face to be sketchy, and she was familiar with the ways in which a hospital altered features, giving up an image of the person you loved that was less individual, less credible than the one you clung to. Her husband had been in these rooms. She waited until she was sure, then she turned away. In the far corner of the room a curtain had been pulled around the third bed. This was her son.

She walked towards it and stood, listening. Was he being washed? Was his dressing being changed? There wasn't a sound. Was he sleeping? What was the process? She could have ripped the curtain apart. She was his mother.

A young boy, who'd been with the other party, stood beside her. 'He's gone,' he said.

'What?' said Ruth.

'That man. He got his clothes on and he left.'

She thanked the boy and stepped inside the curtain. The smell of Jamie, trapped by the curtains, the bedding, made her lift her head until she was looking at a thing of perfect sense, the red button on the white wall. The bathing of a red-and-white light. Without thinking, she straightened the bed, striking the pillow a few times to bring it to life.

WITH THE MONEY he'd gathered up from the birthday and christening cards on Douglas's floor, Jamie went to one of the new bars overlooking the Bay—a place where he was unlikely to run into Douglas. Against the normal pattern of his inebriation, he agreed to take a table outside. Usually he needed walls around him but all the tables inside were filled up with diners. For a moment he was tempted by a barstool until a waitress went by carrying meals; he wanted to be as far away from food as possible. It was a warm evening, still and light. If he thought about it, he began to miss the proximity of the waitress—not because she was put on this earth to listen to what he wanted and to bring it to him but because she too was alone— and probably he missed another thing: the swivel of the stool. He enjoyed a seat that brought his knees into contact with a bar. In fact he couldn't sit; the pain was too great. He supported himself on his elbows.

The sea looked miserable, discoloured—a lesser sea than elsewhere, as if they received someone else's water once they were done with it. It struggled to make it very far in. Up the line someone, probably Lyttelton, was using too much. The sky was hazy, filled, it seemed, with smoke from a fire hundreds of kilometres off. He recalled something on a newspaper hoarding about a blaze, thousands of trees up in smoke. At the corner of the picture the cranes and general tangle of the port created the same feeling of restlessness he took from the nature here. His mother had always hated the Bay. She believed it to be crass, the carnival an eyesore. She wouldn't have minded a fire to rip through it. Below him, the ferris wheel turned and the lights were just beginning to show out on the stalls and rides. He drank to his mother, who'd always been afraid of pleasure. Down there, in another life, on the sandy grass with its scent of petrol and salt he'd had his first drink, fight, fuck, snort. He rolled his foot over the strange package he'd put beneath the table—a long, thin tube of bubble wrap.

When the waitress came past, he asked her for a phonebook and another whisky and soda. He didn't particularly want the drink—it was his third—but he wouldn't get the phonebook without it.

When she returned with them ten minutes later, she said, 'I could just tell you my number.'

He looked down at the blue shirt he was wearing; perhaps it was emitting its own kind of drug. The waitress was not young. She was not doing this while doing something else. 'You're like a real waitress, aren't you?' he said. He'd already placed a large tip on her tray.

She held out her arm. 'Pinch me, I'm real.'

In fact he did touch her skin, which surprised her. 'Then what is your number?' he said.

'Who are you anyway, buster?'

He thought of his next appointment. 'I'm Simon. I'm an architect.'

'Yeah? What'd you build?'

'Heard of the Sydney Opera House?'

'Yeah right. You aren't even wearing socks.'

'Neither are you.' Her feet were in sandals; she wore an ankle bracelet with little bells on it.

'You smell a bit too, I'm sorry to say. But I think I'll pass.' She started to move away from his table.

'I've been working all day,' said Jamie. 'Haven't you ever heard of honest sweat.'

The waitress stepped back. 'Tell me something about architecture then. Go on, anything. I keep this little notebook back in there. I like to write down things people tell me.'

'So wait on, you're a writer?'

'I'm not a writer. It's a stupid notebook with stuff I heard in it.'

'That means you *are* doing something else. You're not a real waitress.' He flipped open the phonebook, genuinely disappointed.

'The shit money I get for this, buster, you bet I'm real.'

'Yeah, yeah,' said Jamie. Moisture from his finger where it'd been in contact with his glass passed into the thin paper. Those numbers disappeared. He turned over a few pages and found it. Surprisingly, the waitress was still there. He asked to borrow her pen and wrote the address on a serviette. 'Thank you,' he said.

'I don't care, you can have it if you want,' she said.

'The pen?'

'My number.'

'Christ,' he said, 'we've hit it off so well, haven't we?'

She laughed. She was being called from inside. 'You like kids?'

He finished his drink and stood up. 'How many are we talking about?'

She leaned close to him. 'Fuck you,' she said.

'Seriously,' he said, 'I'd be a starter, only I'm recovering from surgery right now.' From his pocket he took the plastic bracelet that had been on his wrist, and held it out to her. He spoke with frankness to a person whom he believed could tell the difference. 'I'm not shitting you. From now on, I'm not shitting anyone.'

'Simon says he's not shitting anyone,' she said. 'How come that tag says James Webb?'

He touched the cloth of his shirt, Simon's shirt. 'I got swapped at birth.'

A WOMAN, CARRYING a load of shopping bags, was coming towards the door of the building. Jamie started his walk when she was nearly there.

'Need any help?' he said.

'Can't quite reach,' she said. She'd glanced at Jamie's own package. Her entry card was on the key ring which was half-trapped by her hold on one of the shopping bags.

'Let me,' he said. He took the other bag from her, and when

she'd passed her card over the electronic pad, Jamie pushed against the door, holding it open for her.

'Okay,' she said.

They were both standing inside the building. He pushed the button for the lift and gave her back the bag.

'Think I'll take these,' said Jamie, indicating the stairs. 'Healthier, they say.'

Having climbed the first flight and heard the lift leaving from the ground floor, he considered turning back and getting the next lift. To move up stairs required a new set of muscles and nerves, all seemingly connected to the site of the surgery. He tried using the package as a walking stick of sorts, but it bent and he was afraid of damaging it. He was forced to take several rests, leaning against the handrail, and, when finally he made it to the top floor, he put his back against the wall and slowly sat down in the corridor. He remained there until the pain eased off slightly and his breathing steadied. Then he got to his feet again, using the package carefully to prop himself up. When he was set, he began to pull the bubble wrap off.

He pressed the buzzer on the door. The walls were so thick there was no sound of footsteps, but he was sure someone was approaching. He felt they were locked in a kind of vault, Jamie and the person behind the door. Suddenly the vault contained nothing except these next few moments. His own pain was not stored here; it belonged somewhere else, where a figure such as he cut still existed—on hospital records mostly, in the files of government agencies, at the bottom of a variety of twenty-two-litre containers at needle exchanges. He did not exist at the door, only the moment in action, only his arm through the air. His thoughts were pure. They were arranged along these lines: *kapow kapow kapow*.

The door opened.

In his head Jamie had a scene playing. The scene involved Jamie ramming the ski pole at the man's face, using both arms and rushing at him to drive it home. The man would fall backwards and Jamie would be inside the apartment, kicking the door shut with his heel. They were no longer in the vault but in an expensive apartment with a great deal of wickedness all around and within, and some of it belonged to the other person. The man was not wearing shoes. On the sole of his foot was a red birthmark—sign of darkness. A strong small figure would be lying on the carpet, holding his face and screaming. An amazing amount of pain.

'Yes?' said the man, Simon. His feet were in slip-ons of the softest-looking leather, like fine shoes beaten and beaten until they became slippers.

A green sea chest with gold-painted locks stood on its end in the hallway. On its top was a large lamp with a heavy-looking ceramic base. Jamie wondered at the role these objects might have in his scene.

'Are you from Caroline?' said Simon. He took one step back and continued to hold the door.

The name was the wrong name. Jamie waited.

'Penny?' said Simon.

Jamie felt nauseous with this roll call; it seemed the names could go on—his sister was just one item in the catalogue. Now might have been a good time to act, he considered, bolstered by repulsion.

'You're wearing my stuff,' Simon said. He bent down and reached for the hem of the trousers Jamie had on, pulling. 'Those are my old clothes—are they? You're the brother, aren't you? You're Jamie.'

Jamie bent down so that their faces were level. 'I'll come again,' he said. 'When you think it's all over, I'll come. Understand, Simon? I'm addicted to drugs. It's a state that's gone on for twenty years or something. I can't shake habits easily, Simon, and now I'm addicted to you.'

Simon had retreated slightly inside the apartment.

'You're mine now,' said Jamie.

Jamie turned and left the place, abandoning the offensive ski pole. When he reached the stairs he knew the man was still standing in his doorway. The man had perhaps not been afraid but he'd been impressed. He had not recoiled in fright but he certainly had something to think about now. And there was the step he'd taken backwards. Recall the step.

In the port air with its fumes of journeying and far-off destinations, Jamie had a strong desire to see a movie—he hadn't seen a movie in years. Who could sit still for that long? That had been the telling symptom for the GP who'd diagnosed Jamie's kidney stone—a stone made the sitter move around a lot, seeking that elusive spot of comfort. Jamie didn't say, Doc, I've been like this my whole life.

Of course he'd have to get one of those inflatable ring cushions first.

Back at the bar, Jamie said to the waitress with all the kids, 'What's a good movie?' He was inside now, perched on a stool with his knees against the bar, speaking over the low music while trying not to be heard by the guy at the nearest table who sat alone, smoking and trying to listen.

She said, not unfondly, 'For you or for someone with taste?' She appeared to hover.

'What would you go and see?'

'I can't. I'm working till eleven.'

'I like something with a moral.'

She laughed at this—quite naturally, her teeth were showing and the roof of her mouth—making the other patrons turn and look. Apart from the smoker, there were two couples in the corners of the room. The laugh seemed to cause resentment. Then the waitress grew very serious. 'Don't let me find out something horrible about you, that's all.'

She was resigned to him, but he believed it could be better than that.

'I'll tell you everything now,' said Jamie. He felt he could and it would be the truth. He felt he could talk to this woman. He had a son, didn't he? It didn't matter if all they talked about was kids.

'Don't tell it to me now,' she said, moving off with her tray and cloth. 'Save it for later.'

S HE LET HIM have a shower and then eat dinner and then take the big glass bottles of distilled water around the garden, and then she let him open another bottle of wine—there'd been one at dinner—before she attempted to tell him about the afternoon. They were sitting in the living room, Don on the sofa with his drink and the newspaper, Tina with a pile of gallery papers at the little writing desk in the corner. She told him about the argument over Anna's bottle. He shook his head and returned to the newspaper. He was glancing at things, then turning several pages at once before going back to another section. He wrestled and slapped at it. She'd never seen him so aimless—or anxious, was it? She could no longer see very far into him.

'I wonder whether I should just give up about Anna and the bottle,' she said.

'Maybe,' said Don.

'You think so?'

'Like a brick wall, isn't it.'

'Then maybe I should give up. She's not my child after all.'

Don whacked the paper to fold it. 'It's aggravation.'

'Who?'

'Well I thought you wanted to give up on it? You don't need the aggravation.'

She stood away from the desk. 'How much wine do you intend drinking tonight, Don?'

'Whoa, I think I just missed that segue.'

'You've had a bottle.'

'Are we counting now?'

'What are you doing, Don?'

'Doing? I'm relaxing, I think.' He looked red and miserable.

'Janet came round,' she said.

Don sat forward and put down the paper. 'Janet? What did she want?'

'We had a drink. She's worried about you.'

'Why, what was she saying?' A spark came back into him.

'Nothing, that she was worried about the stress on you, overworking.'

'Really? Sweet of her.'

She regretted having waited to tell him. He was not drunk, just impervious, in a mood to deflect everything. 'Said we should think about a holiday.'

'We had a holiday,' he said.

'I told her that.' Tina walked over to the sofa and sat down beside him. 'She made me promise not to tell you she'd come. She came as a friend.'

'What did she say? Tales out of school?' He was pretending the spark had gone, that he was bored, that Janet was a humorous visitor. But she could feel the heat in him.

'No, nothing. Janet's, you know, she's very discreet. It drives me mad. What's to tell?'

'Nothing.' He put his hand on her knee and smiled.

She picked up his wineglass from the coffee table and drank some. She put the glass back down. 'Where were you tonight?' she said.

'Deliveries, like I said.'

'Then where?'

'Then I went to the hospital.'

'To see Jamie?'

'Exactly.'

'Don, I called the hospital. Jamie walked out of there tonight. What's going on?'

'When'd he walk out?'

'Why do you want to know? So you can say you were there at an earlier time than the time I say he walked out?'

'Jesus, I'm so sick of that guy. The mayhem.'

'Don! Are you going to answer me? Where were you just now? Why's Janet coming round? She never comes round, she never drops in, why's she warning me?'

'The truth is, Tina, I went for a drive.'

'Where?'

'Actually out to the cheese factory.'

'The cheese factory?'

'In the car you'll find some free samples I got. Go and look, if you want.'

'The cheese factory? But I don't understand. Why?'

'For the tour. Again, they had leaflets and stuff. It's all in the car.'

'Stop telling me about the car!'

'It corroborates what I've been telling you, Tina.'

'Corroborates? Don, listen to yourself! I'm not the police, am I?'

'Well, quite. "Where did you go on this certain night at this certain time?" "How much alcohol have you consumed?"'

They sat without talking. Somewhere along the way she'd collected Janet's headache. She loved Don. She loved him but she'd always known he had a sly centre. He lived more than she did in the public gaze, dealing with customers every day at the pharmacy, yet he retreated further and with more cunning. She could feel, from time to time, that even at home he was operating as the white-jacketed figure behind the dispensary counter—courteous, solid, and with just that touch of flippancy all chemists required. In short, he was good at hiding. He belonged certainly within that family. She hated them all, in a moment. She'd never met Jamie but she hated him anyway. That one had been hiding from her forever.

'I'm sorry,' he said. 'I'm just sorry, Tina, for being so horrible. I don't know why I went for a drive but I did. I was at the hospital in fact. But I didn't see Jamie. I was with Graham for his endoscopy.'

She regarded this somehow as changing the subject, yet she also felt weary and sympathetic. 'Maybe you do too much, Don.'

'Maybe.'

She said, 'You don't sleep at night.'

'I'm sleeping better.'

'No you're not.'

Tina knew there was a degree of self-description here—she'd been having bad nights as well. She regretted what she'd said to Penny that afternoon—about the bottle, about the woman Simon was with—but finally she did not regret attempting these conversations. It was only in their execution that she felt she was astray. It was not 'interfering' if one sought to improve a situation. The alternative was to sit and watch things get worse. Penny's business, in all its strangeness, was Tina's business too. They were connected, weren't they? And not just through marriage. They were connected in a way which was similar to the duty Don owed his customers at the pharmacy. There was a social contract she believed in. Typically it might bring, as Don suggested, 'aggravation'; it might produce misunderstanding, hostility, fear, withdrawal, silence. But it also had another side. She was not prepared to name this as hopefulness, that would have been insulting—she thought not only of Penny but of the old Maori women weeping and singing in the basement—yet the terms of this contract—stated simply, they meant that you were involved with others no matter what, no matter who—the terms retained some of hope's animating force, some of its efficacy.

'Maybe it is the pharmacy,' said Don. 'I don't know. We've had all these problems, with Rameesh and computer systems and all that stuff. Nothing we can't get on top of, but maybe Janet's right.'

'Can you hire someone?' The pharmacy was boring for Tina at this moment; she longed not to be talking about his work, or not in this way. Briefly she felt nostalgic for the time when Don was an employee and not the owner, before they'd been swallowed. It was easy to imagine that period as simple and straightforward. 'Now you can afford to hire someone,' she said, 'you may as well.'

'I could get someone in, I suppose.'

'The cheese factory,' she said, cutting this off. It was an odd detail.

'Yes.'

She saw he was uncertain how to proceed. She might have waited but she spoke. 'I haven't been in years,' she said.

He was used to being rescued; it hardly seemed to register with him that she'd taken over.

She said, 'When we were kids out there, you could wander through on your way to school and scoop your hand through the salt ponds.'

'None of that now,' he said. 'All very high tech and sealed off. Hygiene.'

'Someone had their schoolbag chucked in.'

He said, 'Have a drink with me.'

'I can't,' she said. 'My head hurts.'

'Can I get you something for that?' He stood up. 'Let me get you something for that.'

'Sit down,' she said. 'I don't want anything. Sit down now.'

He obeyed her.

'So,' she said. She watched him put his hands into his pockets. 'It's a huge place now, isn't it?'

'The factory? Biggest . . . something in the Southern hemisphere,' he said.

'Biggest what?'

'*Some*thing, I don't know. I wasn't paying enough attention.'

She laughed at this, and she saw how much of a relief her

laughter was to him. She understood he was terrified. It moved her straight into another story of her own. She began telling him about something that had happened at the gallery. Overnight some things had been moved mysteriously around in the basement—some of the Maori stuff for the new show. Big crates shifted from one side of the room to the other. And no one had been down there—not any of the staff—and there'd been no visitors. You couldn't get access without a swipe card. These were heavy items too—it would have taken more than one person to do the lifting. As she spoke she understood the transaction: she was offering him a kind of fuel for his scepticism; her own credulity had always been a delight for him. They both enjoyed the bait and he never mocked her outright, and she seldom grew offended. She went on telling him how everyone had been carefully questioned and there was no explanation for the weird shifting around that had happened.

Don listened to all of this, nodding and smiling, then he said, 'It was Martin, wasn't it? Playing around.'

'No,' said Tina. 'Martin was off sick yesterday.'

'Perfect. He came in after hours and did it. With a friend. This is not uncommon, is it?' They both knew Don was relying here on evidence Tina herself had introduced more than a year ago, when Martin had confided that he sometimes used the gallery for sexual encounters.

'We've got the security cameras,' said Tina. 'There's nothing on them.'

'Martin knows everything about that place. Easy enough to disconnect a camera or wipe a tape.'

It was true—Martin's favourite time was when he'd had a fuck underneath a big touring Warhol. The tape had been souvenired, replaced by another from the storeroom. Tina knew all this and so did Don. She also knew that Martin was bedridden with the flu—they'd spoken briefly on the phone and he sounded like death. Hard to fake that.

'But even if that was possible,' she said, 'why would Martin want to do it?'

Clearly the question of motive had no great pull for Don. 'Who knows?' he said. Then, thinking perhaps something more was needed to clarify this disengagement, he said, 'I don't know what goes on in Martin's head.'

She could hardly feel upset at the rationalist cast to his mind—she'd married him; he was a scientist after all—but she might certainly have found this last attitude offensive: that, in Don's eyes, Martin was capable of anything. Yet she pushed no further. Don bore the prejudice, in part, because he was jealous of Martin. He believed this gay man had managed an intimacy of relationship with her that he couldn't emulate. In the end Tina didn't mind the situation—Don's discomfort was worth keeping alive. It made him say things that were not in his best interests. It helped locate in the bedrock of his tolerance the small fissure of his bigotry. It stopped him, on occasion, being the sort of person he thought he was.

'Everyone's convinced there's a ghost,' she said.

'No wonder your funding's in trouble.'

This was spoken without the expected relish. She looked at her logical husband and saw that his high colour had drained off and he was sitting pale, exhausted and still.

twelve

SHANE WAS GLAD of the crowd, and some of them were even glad of him. He'd waded into the sea up to his waist and dried off in the sun and now he was enjoying the sounds of Miss Jessica Durant all the way from Clinton, while in the row in front of him a group of four girls, who may have been legal, appeared to be describing to each other the variety of ways in which they could please him or he could please them. In fact, he wanted their fish and chips mostly. The warm air was fat-soaked and salty. They were eating off their bare knees.

The music pumped along with way too much middle, drowning everything. Only Miss Jessica was 'live', though over the top he heard the occasional flare of laughter and denial, and he saw their heads toss back. Ponies, they looked like, with their pretty manes. They glanced behind from time to time. He'd given them the thumbs-up early, which made them rock forward.

Usually the grass around the Bay made his eyes and nose run. As a kid he avoided the place; this evening he felt fine in his sinuses and strong in his chest. Burrell was a big old nasty soldier and it made no sense for Shane to be bothered now by pollen or dust.

When the song finished—a fraction behind Jessica—Shane stepped over the seats and joined the girls. The one nearest to him was biting into a piece of fish.

'Catch that yourself?' he said.

The girl brightened with a blush and pushed the white flesh into her mouth. Bits fell off and landed stingingly on her arm; he saw her wince.

From the other end, an older girl spoke: 'Yeah and she put the batter on it too!' All the girls laughed, and Shane grinned back at them.

'Don't I get a chip?' he said.

The blushing girl looked at the older girl for permission. Then she offered the bag to Shane. He flourished his fingers in the air and put them carefully into the opening in the yellow paper. He didn't go far in. They were all watching. He removed a single long chip, which he held up.

'Who's got sauce?'

'Greedy greedy,' said the older girl. Again everyone was laughing and rocking forward.

He guessed they were fourteen or fifteen. The older girl moved her fringe away from her eyes. One of the straps of her cut-off top had slipped from her shoulder.

'I hate a dry chip,' he said, putting it to his mouth.

Someone giggled automatically, then stopped. The girls were

checking with their leader and eating their chips, looking at the ground. The older girl continued to stare at him, however. On stage Miss Jessica had started up again and he felt the urge to go and have a word with the guy on the mixing desk. They were all deaf, he knew; it was a requirement for mixers.

Despite present shortcomings, he'd always liked to be around amplification of this scale, to feel pulverised.

He shoved his hand deep into the girl's packet and pulled out a bunch of chips. He'd felt her skinny leg through the paper. She put the packet on the seat between them and stood up, moving along the row.

'Don't you want them?' Shane shouted, but the girl didn't turn around.

The next girl gave Shane a quick look and also stood up. She half-tripped over the third girl, who wanted to leave even faster. There were chips spilled on the grass.

'Ah, come back now,' he said. 'Do I smell that bad?'

The older girl remained in her seat, her hand inside the packet, looking straight ahead. There were three empty seats between them. Miss Jessica was belting it out—she was the same age as these girls, he thought. She had the thighs of a farmer, and the frilly dress she wore revealed suddenly white shoulders. Someone had told her she had to move around. Without rhyme or reason, Jessica stomped from one side of the stage to the other, turning sharply each time on the heel of her fringed suede boot. The back of her neck was burnt. She looked manic, like a country music robot. Shane felt quite hypnotised as she criss-crossed in front of him. Some of the crowd had begun to clap along.

He did not stop thinking of Burrell and the old lady with the tartan shopping bag. He did not stop thinking. He thought of his actions back at the church as set to this criminal music. Where was Sally? She deserved to be here with him, suffering.

He leaned over and spoke quietly and without sense to the girl with the fringe. She shook her head and pointed at her ear:

she couldn't hear. He gestured towards the seats between them and she shrugged. He moved along so he was sitting beside her. He put his mouth close to her ear and let his lips touch her hair. 'I hate this music,' he said. She laughed and nodded. She smelled of shampoo, soap. If only he could get her to talk into his ear. In his pocket he still had a bunch of pills. He'd had to hide them with his wallet under a rock when he went into the sea. He spoke to her ear again: 'Do you want to leave?' She pretended she hadn't heard him. He repeated the question and she shrugged. 'Are you thirsty?' he said. The question made his mouth dry. Still she wouldn't talk; she pursed her lips—maybe she was, maybe she wasn't. He ate some more chips and was at her ear. 'You're so pretty, you're beautiful. What's your name?'

She seemed to be thinking about this for several moments. Finally she turned to him and spoke into his ear, 'Miro.'

It was a beautiful sensation and she was beautiful. Even this music had the power to enter him. He wanted to play drums while she watched. He wanted to be on stage and look down into the audience and pick her. Of course the drummer never got to choose.

He offered her his hand to shake and she shook it. Hers was a limp and beautiful hand, the fingers warm from the chips and a bit damp. 'Shane,' he said. 'So, what say we get out of here.' Now she was shaking her head. 'Come on, Miro,' he said. 'Come fucking *on*, man.' He was prepared to insist; she looked like she wanted him to.

She pointed over her shoulder. 'Parents,' she said. 'Dad. Kill you. Kill me. He hates Maoris.' She put her hand to her throat, miming strangulation, and smiled at him. She was standing up, brushing at her backside.

Shane put his hand to his face. 'I'm not a Maori,' he said, but she'd moved off. He turned around and saw a woman and a man sitting on a rug on the slope of grass behind the seats; she was thin like her daughter and he was a slab of fried meat in a

248

towelling hat. The rug, he saw—he saw everything now—was tartan.

He believed his own blood—this was way back in time—was part Scottish. His dad used to drink Scotch. His nana had shortbread biscuits in a tin with a tartan design on its lid. Shane was of a clan, but not of this clan that rested on the tartan rug. He was at war with them and all their bastards.

The sideshows were packing up but he found himself drifting their way. He hadn't been down here since he was a kid. In the toilets beside the ferris wheel he scoffed a few methamphetamine tablets. Walking into the twilight, he felt not quite remarkable enough.

He had a go rolling rubber balls into holes—he figured it was the least bent of the stalls. On his second buck, he lit up all the coloured light bulbs and the old guy asked him what he wanted: a candy pack or a fluffy rabbit. 'The ladies love the bunnies,' he told Shane.

'Gimme the candy,' said Shane, 'I'm too hungry to care about fucking tonight.'

The guy slapped the candy down. 'Listen, sonny, this is for families, this carnival. Why don't you watch your language.'

Shane took the candy. 'Fuck off, Granddad.'

He walked across the concrete to the dart throwing. There were a hundred or so cards pinned to a board. 'Three darts one dollar,' the guy called out.

The guy's son or helper took it up: 'Can you hit a barn door? It's that easy.'

'I tell you there's prizes hanging on this wall that are *bored* with being there. You'd be putting them out of their misery to win them. That right, Davey?'

'That's right, Frank.'

Shane watched a loser throw some darts while his girlfriend still held him round the waist. The first two missed the board completely. He turned to her: 'I can't throw with you on me.'

She let go huffily, and he threw the last dart, which stuck in a card.

Davey pulled the card from the board and put it on the counter without looking at it. 'Tell me the worst,' he said.

'The best you mean,' said the old guy, Frank. 'I don't care now. I *want* someone to win big.'

The guy who'd thrown the dart picked up the card and read it. 'Unlucky this time.'

'Hard luck guys,' said Frank.

'He didn't win anything,' said the girlfriend. She spoke as though the truth had made her senseless.

'Hard lines,' said Davey.

The couple wandered off—a few metres apart—and Davey stuck the card back on the board.

'How's your eye, sir?' The old guy was talking to Shane, who put a dollar down on the counter. 'All rightee,' said Frank, leaving Shane's money there as though he wasn't interested in it.

Davey turned around and studied Shane. 'Look at this. This scares me.'

'You're right about that, mate,' said Shane. He took the darts from Davey and weighed them in his hand.

'Big chief pow wow,' said Davey.

'What?' said Shane.

Davey tapped his own face with a finger. 'That's some handiwork.' In doing so, the sleeve of his teeshirt rode up his bicep, revealing a small tattoo of an anchor with a chain curled around it.

Shane, in his beating Scottish blood, knew this was a pivotal moment. When he'd played guard and Burrell had coached him and yelled at him—yelled at everyone because his coaching style knew no quietness—that was what he used to say: This is pivotal, people. It meant, go hard or go home. 'Okay, you,' he said, pointing the darts at Davey. 'When I hit a card I want you to pull out each pin so slowly and carry the card really slowly so I can see it all the time down here, okay?'

The dart guys exchanged looks. Davey smiled at Shane. 'Really slowly all the way down. Got you, chief.' He turned to Frank. 'The chief here wants us to do everything really slowly.'

'We aim to please,' said Frank.

'No pun intended,' said Davey.

Shane flexed his throwing arm, then threw three times in quick succession. He hit two cards and the third dart bounced off. Davey picked it up and put it down in front of Shane. 'Go again, chief.' Shane threw again but missed. Davey went to the board: 'Yell out when you think I'm speeding up, chief.' He took out the two darts, then loosened the pins in each card and pulled them off slowly. Then he lowered the cards in front of Shane. 'All right, chief?'

'Don't call me that.' Shane still wasn't sure whether something had happened to the cards on the journey from the board. He looked down at the cards without picking them up. On one of them he'd won a toy from the second shelf.

'How'd you go?' said Frank.

'Read us the news, chief.'

'Why's he calling me that?'

'Don't call him that, Davey,' said Frank.

'What's the biggest prize?' said Shane.

'Uh-oh,' said Frank.

'Biggest prize on the board?' said Davey. 'Be the washing machine. Don't tell me you've won the washing machine.'

'What's second?'

'Second's like the Walkman, is it, Frank?'

'I think it'd be the Walkman *after* the car stereo.'

'The car stereo!' said Davey. 'I think chief here's won the car stereo.'

Shane looked up from the cards. 'You guys are the biggest fucking liars in this whole fucking lying carnival.'

'Hey there, chief,' said Davey. 'Easy on.'

'Easy on,' said Frank.

'You're a joke,' said Shane. 'You fucking cunts.'

'What's the problem here, chief?' said Davey.

Frank was leaning down under the counter—where was he going? 'Just a case of a sore loser, I think, Davey.'

Davey turned the cards round. 'Sore winner, you mean. Chief here's won a bear.'

'Un-fucking-believable,' said Shane.

'Give him the bear then,' said Frank, still crouched down.

Shane said to himself: I got to keep an eye on two wankers now.

Frank was still talking from below. 'I think we got a little kid here anyway, probably needs a good cuddle.'

'Oh, yes,' said Davey. 'You want to cuddle something tonight, chief?'

Shane snatched up a dart that was lying on the counter, and then it wasn't clear how far he got with his intention to pin it in Davey's face. A shadow was coming. Frank was swinging a softball bat into the side of his head. Shane thought: The other guy, the *other* guy, Shane. It struck him across the ear and he went down.

When he came round he was lying in the back of an ambulance, strapped to a bed. A cop sat beside him. 'Hey, Shane, you awake?' the cop said. 'How're you feeling?' The cop prodded him sharply and Shane grimaced. 'That hurt?' Shane nodded. 'Soon we'll be at the hospital and they'll fix you up, but right now? Right now and for the next few minutes, you're fucking mine, buddy.' The cop held his fist above Shane's face, and while Shane was figuring out why he couldn't get his arms free to defend himself, the cop brought the fist down hard into Shane's mouth. 'Heap of *shit*,' said the cop. 'Pile of fucking murdering shit.'

They'd found Burrell. Burrell was dead.

Shane hadn't tried to get away from Timaru. He wasn't a

252

mile from the place. There was a train running just above the soundshell, rattling the paving stones of the piazza, and he had not got on it. There was probably a bus too—he was not its passenger. And there was the open road and Mike's ute, wherever that was—he had not sought it either. He'd stayed more or less in the same spot, waiting to be found. And he was found. All of this would play in his favour. Yet he was scared too.

Okay, okay, thought Shane in the ambulance. Calm now. It's begun. We're rolling now. These, he said to himself, are the wheels of justice.

He noted, however, that the motion of the ambulance created nothing but a light rocking in the bed, a swing from side to side. They weren't travelling at any speed; they didn't have the siren on. They were going, more or less, nowhere.

The next blow struck him in the stomach and he coughed something up that remained on his face. He was close to an asthma attack. He experienced a terror thinking of that—the cop seeing him debilitated by nothing more than his own breathing. He rallied on that account, speaking some final words of insult and fearlessness.

'Fucking animal,' said the cop, and he beat with the side of his fist against Shane's injured ear.

Shane tried to speak again but his mouth wouldn't work.

'What? What's that, you tattooed piece of dirt?'

The cop's mouth was full of spit; it caught in his moustache.

In his head, Shane was perfectly clear. He was saying, 'I can't hear you.' Because truthfully he couldn't now. He was watching the cop's lips. He thought he'd been made deaf. 'Now,' he said to himself, 'I can mix sound at concerts.' He must have smiled at that or done something wrong because the cop staggered to his feet and seemed to be looking round for something else to use on Shane, then he heard the doors opening.

Someone said, 'What the hell happened here?'

The cop said, 'We went over a bump.'

SALLY DIDN'T FIND him at home and she called the factory but Shane hadn't shown up there either. She thought of driving to the church, but then the baby woke up and she had to feed him his bottle. Shane had left all the windows open anyway and that made her mad at him. It got hotter with the air circulating. She sat on the sofa in a singlet and a pair of his shorts watching TV, holding the bottle for the baby, feeling dozy with the fear and the dread and with the rhythmical sucking noises of the baby.

The news came on and she couldn't reach the remote. She closed her eyes and was jerked awake by the spluttering of the baby. She plonked him on her shoulder for his wind, which wouldn't come. He was more settled on her knee. They watched TV together. 'Balloons,' she said. Someone was up in one, trying to go round the world again. Someone had invented a new cure for asthma, but it wasn't that simple—it was years away. Then another item, another name, another face.

When he came on, she had a moment when she thought it was still the asthma cure story, as if he was a notorious asthmatic or a test case. They had him roped in to be a guinea pig for this wonder drug.

He was not identified and he was wearing one of those white boilersuits that looked like they were made of paper—different in fact from the factory clothes—and he held a cloth or towel over his head. But it was clearly him. He looked like he could be torn in half, ripped apart. There was a chain-link fence in the background, meaning that whatever he'd done it was major. The fence made her think of rubbish and dogs.

They pushed his head down as he got into the car. She winced as she watched this small moment: his head guided into the dark space by the hand of a stranger.

'Lookit,' she told the baby. 'Lookee. That's Daddy. That's your daddy.'

A cop, she thought. A cop in a religious setting. Oh Lordy

Lord. Shane had screwed up. She put the baby's forehead against her lips. She'd been very prepared for this moment. The shakes she had were pleasant for the baby. Okay okay okay, she said. Slow down, girl. Was she herself—had she *caught* it from him?— was she getting asthma too? The baby made a sudden noise and was sick a little down the back of her hand. Good boy, she told him. Good boy.

GRAHAM WAS SITTING at their usual table when Don walked in. 'I can't sit there any more,' said Don. 'You move or we can shout at each other.' He chose a table halfway along the wall.

'I've got all my stuff here,' said Graham. He looked at the orange on the plate in front of him and then picked it up, moving over to Don's table. Two police cars went past the window at speed. 'I don't know if I can handle all this law enforcement.'

'Terrible thing,' said Don. 'What a terrible, terrible thing.' He'd been saying these words all morning—to Tina, to Janet, to every customer who walked in the shop—and though they'd started out weak-sounding and inadequate, he felt that the language somehow through repetition deepened in colour, like a stone that's rubbed, until it shone with a sadness he began to feel. He knew Burrell by sight, everyone did; with his stature he was more like a landmark than a person. People were responding to a kind of unthinkable vandalism; his death was a public ugliness, like a building torn down for no good reason and behind people's backs. Don felt ill. The illness, though, had a source different from that of poor Burrell's fate. They hadn't identified the accused, but in getting into the car the face was partially uncovered. It was all over town now: his name, the cheese factory connection, his addiction.

Graham started to peel the orange. 'Have they talked to you yet?'

'Why would they talk to me?'

'You just have to walk out the front door, they want to know if you've seen anything, heard anything.' He put a piece of orange in his mouth.

'I take it you're no longer dying of some terrible disease,' said Don. On the phone, Graham had refused to tell him how it'd gone at the hospital.

At the counter, Don asked for six custard squares and a box to put them in—he'd take them back to the pharmacy for the others. Occasionally there were such treats. Janet had suggested it today, as a boost for morale. He opened the flap of the display case to get at the sandwiches but shut it again. The sandwiches lay under damp cloths as though with a fever. He looked down at the newspaper in the rack where the killing was the entire front page. The smell of the fryer came through from the kitchen, mingling with the sugar vapours of the cakes and sweets; he felt nauseous and put his head down on his chest, breathing deeply.

'What sort of person could do that?' May, the owner, stood behind the counter. 'To bash and bash like that. Awful. I'll bring your coffee over, love.'

At the table, Graham was wiping his mouth on a serviette. 'I'm okay inside,' he said. 'You were right, they didn't find a thing. You were right, it's all in my head.'

'That's really good news, Graham.'

'Oh, everything's fine, except I'm crazy.'

Don's coffee had arrived, and his box of custard squares. Of course he wasn't hungry. They waited while May cleared away Graham's plate of orange skin. She was not happy about this. 'Maybe one time you're going to buy something from here,' she said to Graham.

'One of these is his,' said Don, pointing at the custard squares.

'One day,' she said, still looking at Graham, 'I'm going to see that mythical beast, your wallet.'

May put up with them because Don had made a special trip to her house one holiday weekend to give her son something for a bee sting. He'd stitched the town together with these small favours. Sickeningly he thought, was there anyone who didn't owe him?

Graham said, 'In Europe, they don't have this pressure. A café is a place to sit and contemplate, or work, or just be with the world. No one wants to be with the world any more, do they?'

The argument was scarcely that; it was a routine.

'You don't want to be in the world,' she said. 'You want to sit near the toilet and scare off my customers.'

When she was gone, Graham gestured towards the custard squares. 'I can't have one of those.'

Don put them on the floor beside his chair. 'Anyway,' he said, 'great news that they didn't find anything.' He was trying to revive the sense of pleasure between them, even if it was only the other man's sense. His insides turned and turned along with his mind. Graham was watching him closely.

'I didn't tell them, Don,' he said.

'Tell who, what?' His visit to the cheese factory would be established. The witnesses came forward in his thoughts to point a finger. The last of them would be Ron, the Samoan security guard, speaking of the power that was everywhere. What power? Great weights were being thrown around in the basement of the art gallery. But this had an explanation and so did his role in the coming investigation.

'The police. That you were asking for that same guy.'

'What guy?'

'The one who killed the cop, with the tattoo down one side. Because you were asking me did I know this guy, and bang, there he is. I don't know what the connection is between you and this guy.'

On the far side of the café there was a fan on the floor next to a rubber plant. The leaves of the rubber plant barely moved.

'There's none,' said Don.

'But they were asking had I heard anything, and I had to stop myself. What possible connection, I thought to myself, could there be between Don and a person who'd do such a thing.'

'No connection at all.'

'That's what I was thinking, and so I stopped myself.' Graham was waiting, clearly, for an explanation, for a rope to be thrown to the spot where they were both sinking.

'It was a pharmacy matter,' said Don.

'I thought, he knows him as a client, as a customer from the shop. Tell me that scumbag isn't on methadone.'

'He isn't on methadone—not from us anyway.'

'Alleluia,' said Graham. 'Like you, I believe the programme should have standards. How's your brother?'

The question was so swiftly delivered, Don was answering without thought. 'I tried for years to get him on the programme.'

'I didn't know about that,' said Graham.

'I didn't tell you.'

Graham pushed back in his chair. 'How long's he been an addict?'

'Twenty years.'

Graham sat without moving his head or any part of him. 'That's why you do this, with me.'

'No, it's not.'

'That's what this is all about. Coffee, meeting me.'

'No.'

'It's all right, Don. It's about your brother. I'm a stand-in.'

'Rubbish. Don't be a psychologist. You're a mathematician.'

Graham stood up. 'Until you can learn to confide, Don, I don't want to see you any more.'

'What, are we breaking up?' He tried to make it a joke, but he felt something tearing inside him. He *was* breaking up.

'I want to arrange to have my methadone from somewhere else.'

'Come on, Graham, sit down.'

'I'm serious. I don't trust you any more. Tell me now that I can switch where I get my methadone from.'

'Of course you can, but you don't have to. Shit, Graham, I'm sorry. I'm sorry I didn't tell you about Jamie, but quite frankly I think that's my personal business, isn't it?'

'Personal business? What do you think we've been doing here all these years? We're friends, aren't we? Aren't we?'

'Of course.'

'That's what friends *do*. They do personal business.'

'I understand.'

'I take you to the hospital with me and you sit with me because of personal business.'

'You're right.'

'You bust into the toilet because it's all personal, Don.'

'Yes, I suppose you're right.'

'I am right. You've got to let people in, Don.'

Now Don wanted him gone, but Graham was moving the chair back into place and slowly sitting down.

'Anyway,' said Graham, 'let's talk about something else.'

They sat in silence until Graham said, 'I'm thinking of getting a haircut.'

'Great,' said Don.

'But I can't be in hairdressers'. When they sweep up the hair, oh man.'

'Do you want me to make you an appointment?'

'Don't find me anywhere weird, though.'

'I'll find you a place.'

FROM THE DISTANCE of the pharmacy door, he thought she was looking the best he'd ever seen her, or he was really seeing her for the first time perhaps. She was wearing a white V-neck teeshirt, blue shorts, sneakers and a cap. Her hair was done in a ponytail that poked from the back of the cap; it bounced as she walked. There was energy. In her sunglasses, she looked like a tennis mother, off for a few sets before the baby's mid-morning sleep. The baby was in the backpack, wearing—as all good babies out in the sun should—a hat.

Don told Rameesh he'd handle this one, and the intern backed off straight away. They'd made it a game between them now. Don was always threatening to throttle Rameesh, who was always ducking away or putting his hands up in fright.

'Come through,' Don told Sally. In the staffroom, he poured the methadone and handed her the plastic cup. When she'd finished, he asked her whether she'd like to sit down for a moment. She said she couldn't, she had to be somewhere. 'Just for a minute,' he said. 'It's important.' She perched on the edge of the bench-seat, sitting forward so as not to put pressure on the backpack. Don offered to help her off with it but she said no, she was all right. She hadn't taken off the sunglasses.

'I want to help,' said Don. 'I want to help Shane.' Sally shook her head. 'I want to do something for both of you.'

'You can't,' she said.

'A lawyer, I want to get him a proper lawyer.'

'That'll really help him,' she said sarcastically.

'It'll be better than what he'll get, Sally.'

'Why? Why do you want to?'

'Did he do it? Do you think he did it?'

'What difference does that make?'

'I want to know. Did he, Sally? What do you think happened?'

'I don't know what happened. Was I there or something?'

'No, but you know him best. Tell me what you think might have happened. Please?'

'I'll tell you what happened,' she said. 'I think he was put in a bad position.'

'Yes,' he said.

'I don't recognise the person that did it as the person who is the father of my baby. I think something snapped inside of him and he lost it. I don't think he knew what he was doing. I think he was in the wrong place at the wrong time and so was the cop. I think he was off his face was what happened.'

'He was using at the time?'

'I told him a million times, Come on the programme, and one time he actually looked into it. Really he tried and he wanted to—he went to the interview and they told him, You are a prime candidate, you should definitely be on the programme.'

For some reason Don had picked up a pen. 'Where'd he go?'

'He went here, A&D right in town. That'll be on the records. You don't believe me.'

He wrote something down—it was nothing, a scribble. 'I believe you, Sally. What happened?'

'He came home and he was so happy and excited, like a little kid. It was going to be this thing we did together, you know. Together forever together we're one. He went out and he celebrated. One last blowout, he said. I don't mind telling you I did the same thing when I went on it. You gotta say goodbye, don't you, otherwise it doesn't feel as though you've left.'

'But he didn't go on the programme?'

'Next day or something, I said, When's it happening, when are you getting on it? This was going to be so cool because we could come down here together, a little regular ritual like a married couple going off to work together. And he said, There's a waiting list. How long? I said. How long's the list? He said, Two years. I said, No, you've got that wrong. He said, Two years, I'm not kidding you. Two years? I couldn't believe it. I rang A&D and said something's gone wrong because my boyfriend is a prime candidate and they said there's nothing gone wrong. Two years, I told them, he could be dead or anywhere. They said maybe it would be eighteen months or something, but one thing they were not short of was prime candidates. I said, But I got on, and they said, Because of the baby.'

'That's right,' said Don. 'It's an inadequate service.'

She looked at him with contempt. 'Anyway, he couldn't get on and he wanted to get on and I was pregnant. Then after I had the baby, Shane just goes out on a bender and comes home, he's got this face. This half-face. I knew then he was in deep trouble and I began to expect the worst. He's got no Maori in him or any interest or feeling for all that and he's just as racist as anyone but now he's got half his face covered. And I knew straight off that he should have been on the programme because there was no one more prime than him.'

'I want to get him a lawyer,' said Don. He'd grown to love saying this. It was self-love probably but he didn't care because it was also another kind: the love one has for the people one has decided to help and who have decided to allow this to happen.

Slowly Sally took off her sunglasses, easing them past her ears with great care, and then she removed her cap which, he saw, had hidden a bandage. Bruising covered her forehead, spreading out from below the bandage. She pointed to her head. 'First thing,' she said. 'If you're planning on changing your mind about that lawyer, Shane didn't do this.'

Don stared at her. He said, 'Is that the truth?'

'Fuck you,' she said.

'Is that the truth, Sally?'

'I won't be demeaned and degraded by you for one more second.'

'I believe you,' he said.

'Big deal,' she said.

'WHO'S CAROLINE?' SAID Jamie.

Penny looked at her little brother. He was lying full-length on their sofa, a cushion under his head, and he had Anna, her daughter, on his feet. She was being jiggled and tossed each time she activated a button on her uncle's bare toe. 'Up,' she commanded, 'and *up*!' In return for each mission, she had to rub the soles of his feet and occasionally pass him the large glass of soda and ice that was on the carpet. They both had straws.

'Go easy there,' Penny told Anna. She didn't know how he'd broken through with his niece. Penny had left the room for only a few minutes. When she came back she saw at once what she'd forgotten from their childhood and after—that he could change a situation, its tone and temperature, in a flash. He could be loyal and faithful to nothing, not even a mood. To their father this made him some sort of reprobate, a person with the movements of a dragonfly, a succession of impossible turns. He left nothing the same.

'Caroline who?' she asked Jamie.

'Caroline,' he said. 'I paid Simon a call.'

'You did not.'

'I did. Who's Caroline?'

'His girlfriend, I think.'

'His ex-girlfriend.'

'Why, what did he say? Actually, I'm not interested.' She took out a cigarette.

'Outside!' said Anna violently.

'Hounded from my own home,' said Penny, standing up.

Jamie went to move but Anna lay down on his legs. 'No, you don't,' she said.

'Don't be too hard on your mum,' he said.

'*She's* killing *me*!' said Anna.

Jamie put his arms around her. 'Let me tell you a story,' he said.

'Let me walk outside,' said Penny.

Ten minutes later, he joined her in the garden. 'Where is she?' said Penny.

'In bed,' said Jamie. 'It's late.'

He was a marvel and she told him he was.

He looked into the roses. 'I had a terrible feeling of impatience when Tom was born. That's my son.'

'I've heard of this person.' She'd aimed, it seemed, to wound him but of course it hadn't worked. He went on talking.

'From pretty much day one, week one, I couldn't wait for him to get older.'

'The nappy stage.'

'No, not just that. I wanted him . . . bigger. I wanted him born like a horse or something, a foal. They take a couple of wobbly first steps and then in five minutes they can bloody gallop.'

'It would be easier.'

'I had no capacity to watch something, someone mature.'

'It does happen eventually, Jamie.'

'Christ, Pen, I'll take your word for it.'

'Do you see him? Do you get to see Tom?'

'Nah. One day though he'll knock on my door, I'm sure of it.'

'They seem to want that.'

'Yeah. I'll hear the knock and it'll be him, looking for his dad. I used to have this dream about it, Pen. Wonderful dream, I tell you.'

'I bet.'

'I'm lying in a state of utter degenerate bloody desperation in a complete cesspool of my own making. Do you mind? I'm about sixty years old but I look fucking a hundred, you know. Most of my vital organs are just going, "Let me outta here!" And someone comes to the door. It's him. Tom. And he just looks at me, you know. Pow! Just stands there, looking at me, seeing my whole life run across the screen—there's a sort of big video screen behind my head or something—and Tom is just taking it all in. This is Dad, so this is the man. In that moment, I am a complete goner. I am completely gone, no hope. Then he reaches out and somehow stops the tape. Tom stops the horrible bloody film and from behind his back he brings out something, like offering it to me, giving it to his old man. Like a gift? Something. He's travelled with something and it's all very important. Very hushed in the dream. I'm sweating and sweating. You know what it is?'

'What is it?'

'A bag of dope.'

'Oh, Jamie!'

'Big bag of smack.'

'Jesus.'

'True dream. Can I get a smoke off you?'

She shook the packet; it was empty. Then she passed over her cigarette to him and he took a powerful drag before handing it back. She was willing to be consoled, even by a dream. 'And that's when you decide to quit your addiction,' she said. 'Once your son turns up in your dream.'

Jamie looked puzzled. 'No,' he said. 'As far as I can remember what happens is we get stoned together.'

'Of course,' she said. 'Silly me.'

'All your letters, Pen?' he said. 'I read them.'

'You never replied.'

'I read them.'

'Why didn't you answer, even one of them?'

'I'm no good is why. I'm a self-centred person with a disease. I'm just too busy all the time, you know. The day just *goes*.'

'Did you really read them, Jamie?'

'I fucking read them and read them. They killed me, Pen.'

'I don't know why I wrote them.' She was aware that he didn't believe this. 'I hated you, Jamie, that's one reason I wrote them.' Did he flinch slightly at this? His eyebrows seemed to register a hurt in the way they popped up briefly. 'You had such a glamorous disaster on your hands, drug addiction. And mine was so . . . small and shameful and humiliating. You know what I thought sometimes? At least he has the highs. At least that. At least amid his muck there is transcendence. At least for some of each day, I thought in my fucked head, Jamie experiences pleasure.'

'That, I'm afraid, is not entirely untrue,' he said. 'For about two minutes, Pen, I can feel rather great.'

He looked unhappy and he'd started to jig his knee up and down. These pictures they were swapping didn't disturb him. She realised it was simpler than that—all this talk had set his brain off in the direction of its craving. He wanted drugs. The game with Anna—her pinning his feet down—had done double duty then. Jamie had used her to relieve this nervous motion. She found his resourcefulness almost poignant, almost unbearable. He was like her, she thought—allowing herself what she now recognised as the first compliment she'd paid herself in years. They were both alive. It made her feel strange but not sad at all. 'Are you all right, Jamie?'

'Jesus, Pen.'

'What is it?'

'I'm so scared.'

'Yes.'

'I haven't had a shit yet. I feel like if I go, the whole works are going to come flooding out, you know. All that's not supposed to.'

She was smiling. 'It's like after I had Anna. Give it time.'

'Okay, Pen. Nice one.' He beat on his knees with his fists.

'Why did you go and see Simon?' she said. 'You don't even know Simon.'

'To give him his clothes back.'

'What happened there, Jamie?'

'He thought it was about Caroline, that I'd come on her behalf. It made me see something.'

'What?'

'That when he beat you, it had nothing to do with you.'

'Except in the physical sense, I think you meant to add to that statement.'

'It was your body, Pen, but it had nothing to do with anything you'd done to him.'

'I didn't do any fucking thing to him.'

'That's right. You should know that and always believe that. He thought I was from Caroline come to beat the shit out of him for what he'd done to her. The prick is a serialist, doomed to repeat his nastiness, so rapidly we understood each other.'

'Jamie,' she said, 'tell me one thing. There was no violence, was there?'

'I don't think there's a thing to worry about.'

'You go round there, acting tough, of course there's something to worry about. He needs crap like that to show I'm not a decent mother to Anna. He wants her, you know. He'd take Anna from me just to prove a point.'

'Penny, who's going to give a kid to a wife-beating prick like that?'

'No one knows he's like that.'

'You know. Caroline knows. I know. Don knows. I fucking defy that secret to ever stay anywhere near locked up. It's out, Pen. Face it, it's out. The thing I don't know is why you never dobbed him in after you left him. I'm not judging you—I couldn't judge anything. But why is he walking round still in a nice apartment with a nice job, shacking up with new and unsuspecting women? The picture is wrong wrong wrong.'

'I always said it was for Anna, to protect Anna.'

Jamie nodded. She wasn't sure whether he'd even heard her answer. He was drumming his fists on his knees now as they went up and down. Round his mouth there was dried saliva. The blood had gone from his face. His head had begun to rock backwards and forwards.

She touched him on his cold, hard arm. 'I can give you something,' she said.

The offer seemed to be familiar to him. Jamie stood as if his name had been called and looked past her in the direction of the door. His eyes spoke: *Through here?*

'COME AND SEE Ma with me,' said Jamie. He looked quickly alive again, perched on the edge of the bath like a kid.

'That would be too much fun for this girl,' said Penny. She was washing her hands.

'Come on, Pen. Come and see Ma.'

'I could take my syringes here and give her a hit too.'

He'd taken her hand. 'Don't be mean like me. I want to see the old bird again, I do.'

'Anna's asleep.'

'She can sleep in the car.'

'She'd wake up and then it'd be hell.'

He leaped up and put his hands on her shoulders. 'You look wonderful, Penny. I love you like a sister.'

'You're very kind, James, and so is the stuff running round in your blood.'

'She's dying for you, Pen. That mad old woman is just this mess of wants and needs, and it's all to do with us.'

'No it's not,' she said. 'That's just what a child would say. You're not a child any more, Jamie.' As soon as she'd spoken she knew she was wrong. They were all children; it was permanent more or less. 'Anyway,' she added, 'she's got Don.'

Jamie showed no sign of having received the first part. It was as if on discerning a moralising tone he could turn completely off, not waiting even for the content. Any edifying sound closed him down.

'I'm ringing Don too,' he said with enthusiasm. 'I want us all there. I want us all.'

'I wash my hands of the whole thing.'

268

'Good girl,' said Jamie. 'There's germs everywhere. Good doctor.'

D ON WAS THE first one there, which annoyed him. He had no desire to sit with his mother and pretend it was a social call. She would know immediately something was up, and she'd grow more and more anxious, then hostile, as he sat there, dumb and getting dumber. He could easily find himself tossed out of the house within minutes. It was too late and dark to clean the pool. Yet what could he say? That Jamie, her junkie son, was coming round with Penny, her estranged daughter, for a 'catch-up'? It was exactly the word Jamie had used on the phone. Jamie, he knew, was high. He wouldn't answer any of Don's questions. Brother, Jamie kept saying. O Brother.

For small talk his mother, of course, would want to discuss the murder.

He waited in the car for them, starting to believe they weren't coming. Perhaps they too had figured out all this, the vision of Ruth in front of them, searching their faces for signs they were indeed hers—her children and not someone else's.

On his lap was the gift pack of aromatherapy oils he'd grabbed from the pharmacy on his way to the house. He found it impossible to enter this place without a meaningless token, some object to press into her hands so they—the hands— were engaged, taken up with the ribbon and the wrapping paper. She had a habit of hanging her arms at her sides and drooping her shoulders in a pose of abject and accusing loss. Always her body seemed to say to him: And where on earth have *you* been?

It had occurred to Don that he might intercept Jamie and Penny before they made it inside, and then they could reconvene at some other location—his place perhaps (Tina should meet Jamie to see him and believe that he was real). They could phone

Ruth and say they'd been delayed and she should go to bed, they'd ring in the morning.

He was thinking then, unhelpfully, of the lawyer he'd arranged for Shane. Another thing he would have to keep from Tina. He believed it was possible for the lawyer's fee to be put through the pharmacy's books, which Tina never saw. No one need know. That phrase, however, had an excruciating hollowness. Everyone knew everything sooner or later. It was extraordinary that after years of what he thought of as none of this, he now had what appeared to be a total commitment to dishonesty. And still he could think: I am doing a good. Truly, the human conscience was made of an astonishing elastic. Though he understood by providing the lawyer he was engaged in a form of barter for the incriminating videotape, Don also knew he was in fact going too far. He didn't need to do this. The most likely outcome was that, no matter what, Shane would go to jail for a long time. The lawyer might mitigate the damage but there was no question of Shane being 'saved'—and what would Shane want to do once he eventually came out of jail? Kiss and make up? Forget the whole thing? The game, surely, would begin again. No, it was sometimes possible for Don to see his own action not as some grasping and despairing bid to 'get off'—to buy the tape with a disreputable favour—but as something a little less calculating perhaps, as his response to someone in need. He could think of himself in these terms without too much self-conceit because for twenty years he'd acted more or less in this way. That wasn't a boast, was it?

Penny's car turned into the street and went clean past him, swinging fast into Ruth's drive. By the time he'd hurried across they were at the front door and Ruth was looking at them all, looking in a completely straightforward way at her children as if she'd been expecting them.

'Come on in, come in,' she said, waving them inside. 'You think it'll rain? Really? I can't believe how cool it is all of a sudden.'

She was right about the weather, though Don hadn't noticed it up to this point. No one had. He saw they were all dressed in the light summer clothes they'd been wearing for months. Penny gripped her bare arms.

Jamie hugged his mother with terrific force, grinning at Don as he did so. Ruth pushed him off finally and said hadn't he just had surgery, he should be careful.

'One more,' said Jamie, and he gripped Don around both shoulders and pulled him in briefly. They stood apart, looking at each other.

'How are you?' said Don. He put the aromatherapy gift pack on the sideboard.

'How are you?' said Jamie. 'Is that for me?'

'No,' said Don.

They'd reached an impasse, and they turned to Penny and Ruth who, as a way of avoiding each other, stood side by side.

'Ruth, this is Penny, Penny, Ruth,' said Jamie.

Ruth turned to her daughter. 'How are you, dear? How's Anna?'

'She's in the car.'

'Where? Out there?' said Ruth.

Penny turned to the door. 'I should go out and be with her, in case she wakes up.'

'Leave her,' said Jamie.

'It's not a warm night,' said Ruth. 'For once.' She'd also moved to the door.

'We put that many blankets on her,' said Jamie.

'We didn't leave her to freeze, Ma,' said Penny.

'I never said that,' said Ruth.

'I could go,' said Don.

Jamie brought his hands together with a sharp crack. 'Chris-sakes, won't you all give it up!' He moved past them, still smiling, and flung open the front door. 'Look. Look if you must. What do we see? Is there a crisis with the child in the car?'

Ruth said, 'Close the door, James, there's a draught.'

In the living room no one was prepared to sit down. They might have been at an open home, or waiting for someone to come in and give them the piece of sad news they were expecting, relatives at a deathbed. Penny was looking at the photographs that sat on top of the piano. Jamie gazed into a bookshelf. Don waited with his mother by the door to the kitchen. His mother, too, after the initial burst of sociability, was paralysed, expectant. It was Don who suggested they might have tea.

'Tea!' said Jamie, laughing.

Ruth scowled at him and left the room.

Don went across to his brother. 'What are you doing, Jamie? What's all this?'

'I'm visiting family,' said Jamie.

'What are you doing?' said Don.

'You've put on weight, Donny.'

Don looked at his wasted brother. Jamie must have believed he was making a comparison.

'That's what I've come for, the home cooking,' said Jamie. Then as if Don had offered a comment, he added, 'You look terrible yourself actually.'

The statement briefly shattered Don. He hadn't credited Jamie with even the weakest powers of observation. He was moving his brother into the hallway. 'I'm in trouble, Jamie.' He'd spoken nakedly and he knew at once that he'd made an error. Jamie looked worried—but not for Don.

'I don't know if I'm the right person, Don.'

'I know you're not the right person, Jamie.' Yet who else was there? Wasn't he in Jamie's world now? Couldn't he appeal to all that experience? His brother was mumbling something about listening if Don really wanted to tell him. Jamie held his hand to his throat, appearing to cringe. If he'd curled up on the carpet it wouldn't have been a surprise. Empathy had a sort of gagging effect on him.

272

'It's nothing,' said Don.

'Okay then,' said Jamie. He was backing off. 'Listen, I've got to see someone. I've got to go.'

'No you don't.' Don stepped towards him and took his arm, the bone of it. 'You stay and have your tea.'

Penny was carrying a photo across to them as they moved into the room again. 'Can you believe this?' She handed Don the photo, which showed Penny and Simon on their wedding day.

Jamie looked at it. 'It's good of you, Pen.'

'I don't believe it,' she said, taking the photo back.

Ruth was walking into the room with a tray of cups. She saw the photo in Penny's hand. 'I curse him every day, Penelope,' she said.

'Okay,' said Penny, 'so this is like your temple of bad people.'

Ruth breathed—some sort of technique she'd learned—and said to Don, 'That was a terrible thing that happened to the policeman, wasn't it?' Without looking in Jamie's direction, she said, 'He was a druggie, you know.' It appeared she'd added this automatically. It occurred to her now what this might mean. She seemed on the point of softening the blow but nothing came from her.

Jamie, accustomed to being accused, came fluidly back at her. He hadn't seen the TV or the paper—he said he never saw these things and didn't know what she was talking about. Ruth explained what had happened. 'See, Ma,' said Jamie, 'that's why you shouldn't read the paper or anything. There's too much that's awful in the world.' The irony and amusement was briefly missing.

'But I live in the world,' said Ruth. The statement was open to doubt and Don half expected a challenge to come from Penny, who still carried the wedding photo.

His sister lifted the photo once more and said, 'So why is this thing out exactly?'

'You might hate me,' said Ruth. The exasperating weight of this fell on everyone.

'Oh, Jesus Christ,' said Penny.

'You might have good reasons, but I curse that person with all my might and pray that he will be judged and punished as befitting his deeds.'

'You sound so biblical, Ma!' Jamie couldn't stop grinning.

'I keep that to remind myself of the pain you suffered.' Ruth was motionless with the tray, looking at her daughter, who sank down into a chair.

'Yeah, yeah, great, Ma,' said Penny. 'Whatever you say. But it was my fault too, right?'

'No,' said Ruth. 'I don't understand it, Penny. I don't understand it. How can anyone?' Her voice had become shaky. She'd liked Simon as well, or at least she'd recognised his value to Penny, who was easier to get along with as a married person than when she'd been single. Simon had earned a credit for this. The implication was inadmissible of course: that a battered Penny was the preferred option. It had been some fatally well-intentioned comment from Ruth on this confusing subject that had caused the rift with her daughter. Don took the tray and put it on the table. His mother's hands remained in mid-air, bereft, as it were, of their burden.

'That's right,' said Penny. She had her hand covering her face.

'I don't start a day without thinking of what he did to you and what you went through. Not a day, Penny. I miss your daughter so much. I miss her.'

Penny without warning began to sob. She cried quietly, with small shakes of her chin. It was a shocking scene. Had anyone ever seen the adult Penny cry? Don felt a muscle above one knee begin to twitch. Jamie was looking at his sister with his mouth open. His lips, Don saw, were dry to cracking. In his mind he was handing his brother the lip salve, his sister the box of tissues.

'Anyway,' Ruth said, as though interrupting, 'this will be the last time we'll all be sitting in this room.'

It took several moments for the statement to make any sense.

'Why, Ma?' said Don.

'Because I'm selling.'

Jamie stepped towards her. 'What are you selling?'

'This,' said Ruth. 'This house. I'm selling the house.'

'But why?' said Jamie, suddenly sober.

'When do you think you will, Ma?' said Don.

'Soon as I can. I've got someone coming to give me an appraisal.'

'Who?' said Jamie.

'I know him—or his wife, I know her. He's coming tomorrow.'

'Why the hurry?' said Don. He sounded to his own ears idiotically aggrieved. She should have sold years ago. He couldn't believe it was finally happening and it gave him a new feeling: things might begin now, though he didn't know what. The sense was there of a gift, if someone could take it. This was the piece of sad news they'd been expecting; it had arrived and soon they could leave.

'What hurry? I've been here forty-plus years.'

Penny stood up and wiped her face. 'Big move, Ma.'

'I thought you all wanted me to sell.'

'I don't remember expressing an opinion,' said Jamie.

'I don't remember you being around to give one,' said Don. He felt a wave of dislike for his brother but it was only the ordinary dislike of familiar things, of family things—a dislike of himself, in effect—and it closed a kind of gap between them. He understood he was punishing James for failing him in the hallway when he'd been about to spill his secret, but also that Don himself wanted to be punished for having the secret. It wasn't a secret; it was a symptom. Didn't he desire the symptom to be read and understood?

'Anyway, it's done. I'm selling. What am I doing in this castle?'

Castle. The word sounded nastily in Don's ear, as though his mother had spoken in a way that wasn't her own, or had tried an obscenity for effect. One time—it was over something that had happened at the supermarket—she'd said 'fuck' just to shock him, and it had, though not in the way intended. He was disturbed by his mother's need to shock him. It suggested she thought he had a complacent idea about the type of person she was—yet that was true of every son and every daughter. She was mean to single him out for a failure universally shared. Castle. It was obviously Shane Castle, the murderer, he was thinking about.

Penny stood beside her mother. 'You can come and stay with us, if you need to, during the sale and whatever.' All her effort was in the speech. She'd spoken haltingly, as though swallowing a sentiment exactly opposite to the one she finally forced from herself.

'That's very kind,' Ruth told her smoothly. 'But Lou says I don't need you any more.'

'Who's Lou?' said Jamie.

Penny stepped away. The disgust improved her fluency. 'She fleeces Ma every fortnight. Tarot.'

'Lou does *not* do Tarot,' said Ruth.

'Stars, astrology, healing,' said Don. He knew now why his mother had had that look of calm on her face at the front door. They *were* expected. Lou had read them already. Who knew but that Ruth didn't have a script upstairs, with all her lines written out. It was a stab of envy he experienced then, thinking of such certainty.

'You're kidding,' said Jamie. 'I think that's great, Ma.'

'Shut up, Jamie,' said Ruth. 'We all know why you came back. You came back for the money.'

'Money?' said Jamie. 'What money?'

'From when I sell the house.'

Jamie grinned—he was back again in that mode, untouchable now. 'Shit, if I'd known there was money here, Ma, I would have killed you with my bare hands years ago.'

Ruth took a step towards her youngest son and said the words evenly into his face. 'You can't kill me, James. You've been trying a long time and I'm still not dead.'

Jamie looked ready to cry but instead he raised his eyebrows to their fullest extension, preventing himself from blinking. 'Okay,' he said, 'I was on the programme but I fell off it.'

Ruth turned to Don. 'What's he saying?'

'Is that true?' said Don. The confession was tactical surely.

'I was doing great until I decided I could take early retirement.'

'What's he telling us?' said Ruth. 'Early retirement.'

'Methadone programme,' said Don. 'Like I do at the pharmacy for the addicts.' He turned to Jamie. 'Not smart, statistically, to leave.'

'You know the odds,' said Jamie. 'Now beat them.'

'But you have to get right back on it, Jamie,' said Penny.

'Course he does,' said Don.

'If it's good for him, why isn't he on it, Donny?' said Ruth.

'He fell off,' said Penny.

'Why isn't he back on it?' said Ruth.

'Good question,' said Don.

'Because I'm stupid, Ma,' said Jamie. 'Because I'm no good. Because I'm lazy. Because I'm rotten. Because I need help. Because a situation of dependency distorts one's judgement. Because I can't see a thing in front of my eyes.' The speech had the quality of a mantra—he'd spoken it before and in the presence of professionals. The words were genuine but also slightly routine—though this did not make them less meaningful, Don considered. At least his brother was telling the truth about having been on the programme. If the lines were learned, it showed he'd been near the script. In this Jamie was like his mother—a fact that seemed to settle in the room, drawing all of them more tightly into the same sphere.

'There's not a single objection to that,' said Penny.

Ruth took a step towards her youngest son. 'Why did you come back here?' she said. 'All this time. Why, Jamie?'

'I don't know,' said Jamie.

'Why? You know we love you, don't you? We all love you, Jamie.'

No one had touched the tea.

'He came back for me,' said Penny.

Jamie had his hand again to his throat. 'No,' he said, 'I can't claim that, Penelope.' His eyes weren't full of tears, though he looked as though he'd been crying for a long time and had just come down from his room. Of course his room was still upstairs. Everyone's room was upstairs.

'I don't care why you came back,' said Ruth. 'I'm just glad.'

'So am I,' said Jamie. 'In fact, I've met someone.'

'What are you talking about?' said Don.

'A lady. Don't be angry, Donny,' said Jamie.

'I'm not.' But he was—this was Jamie at his worst, at his most inappropriate and offensive. He felt a further insult had been administered—but to what or to whom? To the family? That was stupid. To feel this was to credit the family with a self-sufficiency it plainly lacked. This 'lady' would be another disaster, he was sure; but what could it mean, not to want Jamie to find someone? Probably it meant Don believed his brother incapable of making a good choice. This fault in Don—he finally saw—went much wider than Jamie. It was the shadow cast by his skill at helping people. From behind that particular murk had stepped Sally and Shane—and now the new Jamie.

'Who is this lady?' said Ruth.

'She's a lovely person called Hilary.'

'Here in Timaru, you mean?'

'That's right, Ma, a local girl.' Even this, though it came from him with a smile, had a startling sincerity to it. Jamie was speaking in self-surprise.

Penny said, 'And she's going to look after you, is she?' The bitterness wasn't fresh or even felt particularly—Don thought his sister's words were more of a nostalgic blast. Anyone could see Penny was pleased; Ruth too. Faintly, their mother beamed.

Jamie replied helplessly, 'Oh, I hope so.'

Don watched his brother being happy.

But Jamie wasn't finished. 'One other thing, Ma. I have a son.'

The place was silent, and in the distance, very softly, they heard another sound, like a cat or an opossum in the night.

They listened again to it, and heard a short fragment of the sound before it was obliterated by another noise: rain against the windows. Rain, like some piece of natural theatre. Did Lou also forecast weather?

The downpour stopped for a moment and they heard the cries.

'It's little Anna,' said Ruth, worried and tremulous. 'The poor child. She's out in the storm. Won't someone go to her.'

They all moved at once.

thirteen

I T SOUNDED ON the roof of the van like the drumming of
fingers. Shane and the guard both looked up. If he'd been
some other person, a rapist of old ladies or worse, a real scumbag,
Shane might have begun to feel fear. Of course he was afraid,
but the noise would have been the claws of a crowd scratching
at the vehicle to get at him and tear him up. As it grew louder,
he imagined they were being pelted—by fruit, something soft.
For a moment he had the sense of a large rage focused on him, a
storm arranged for his head. He knew he was special, wanted.
He would step into the hail of hands. The guard, he knew, would
slip quietly away. In none of his court appearances had he yet

experienced this. They were over so fast and seemed barely to be about him, like some Olympic sport where it was difficult to see the competitor for the arseholes in blazers and white hats.

It had felt for a while that he was being measured for something.

They listened, still watching the roof as if expecting it to burst in on them. The guard was turning his wedding ring; he'd been scared before the sounds on the roof, chatting about some rugby game. He was new on the run.

'Rain,' said the guard.

Was it that simple? Shane had forgotten about the stuff. Then the van was flooded with a rain smell—chrome and the concrete of footpaths—and it was coming down like fists and knees on the metal above their heads, and the guard opened his mouth but the sounds couldn't be heard. The van seemed to go into a small slide, a skid, before correcting itself. Shane was smiling, nodding. He loved it. With his handcuffs, he clapped along as best he could, and rattled the chains on his legs. The rain beat and beat, cooling the inside of the van until Shane was shivering. The guard had his hands over his ears, cowering.

Then just as quickly, it stopped.

'Jesus Christ, it never rains but it pours,' said Shane.

The guard was disgusted with himself and he told Shane, 'Shut up, you.'

'I'm talking about the weather,' said Shane.

'You won't see much weather where you're going.'

A similar point had been made to him many times over the previous weeks. He was not immune to it. The guard took Shane's silence for a victory and repeated the blow word for word.

Shane leaned towards the guard. 'I heard lots of good things about your wife inside.'

'Shut up.'

'Lots of good things.'

'From now on, that's all you'll be doing. Hearing about

women you can't have, you can't get to, you can't even fucking see.'

Shane sat back against the wall of the van; there was a strut against his spine. He had persistent earache, and vision that blurred from time to time in his left eye. He watched a trickle of water roll along the indentations in the floor and underneath his prison shoe. Then the van was taking an incline and the water rolled backwards and out under a crack in the door.

He didn't think often of Sally. He thought more of things like the next-door neighbour in her bikini pants or the pony girl at the Bay Carnival, even the pubescent country singer with her sunburned neck: namely the things he hadn't had.

'I WANT TO talk to you about the tattoo again, Shane.' The doctor crossed his legs and aimed his pen that he never wrote with against the closed cover of a black notebook. They sat in a windowless room on chairs you might get at a school—nothing but brown metal frames and a curve of varnished wood marked and gouged in places. They'd had a table once but Shane had thrown that against the wall. The guard from the van stood in the corner.

'I don't remember it.'

'You don't remember getting it?'

'Maybe I was insane.' He knew not to use that word but he wanted to cut to the chase today.

'Why do you say that?'

'I look hideous.'

'You regret getting the tattoo?'

'Sure.'

'What do you see when you look at yourself in the mirror, Shane?'

'A handsome devil.'

The doctor frowned.

'I'm lopsided.'

The doctor liked this more; he waved his pen encouragingly.

'I'm out of whack, aren't I?'

'Because one side is filled in and one isn't?'

'This uncle of mine. He had a stroke and the whole side was just, *whoomp*.'

The doctor looked very pleased. A comparison—one thing looking like another—always scored highly. A thing was not a thing until you'd made a connection. Occasionally Shane worried that these connections proved what he didn't want proved— that he was functioning in top order. But then he always got confused on this point anyway. Does a mad person know he's mad? He tried mostly to speak in surprising mixtures of bullshit and calm sense and always to keep the prick guessing.

'Do you identify with the Maori culture, Shane?'

At one session he had; at another they'd talked about the movie *Once Were Warriors*, which seemed to excite the doctor.

'They've had a good run,' said Shane.

'In what way?'

'Every way. I tell you, these Maori boys control the prison like you don't even need fucking guards.' This was clearly the wrong thing again but he'd felt genuinely impelled to say it. He'd had his head knocked against a toilet over some acid. They'd broken his cheekbone. The doctor checked his watch.

'Listen, mate,' said Shane. 'You know if I'm mad, if they say I was out of my tree when I did it, what happens to me?' He'd put the question to his lawyer, who'd first suggested the angle, and got an answer he didn't quite follow. It seemed the likelihood of them turning him into a vegetable was low. The lawyer didn't know whether Shane could be on methadone in a loony bin but he was sure there'd be a range of appropriate medication—and that had a nice ring to it.

'You mean legally?' said the doctor.

'Where do I go?'

'That's a legal question. I'm not qualified to say.'

'What do you mean, not qualified? Don't you do this for a living?'

'The court will decide, Shane. They decide different things depending on each case and its circumstances.'

They seemed to be through. The doctor stood up.

'When you look at me,' said Shane, 'what do you see?'

'I don't know,' said the doctor.

'Come on, not a diagnosis just what do you see? Come on.' Shane was also on his feet. The guard took a step towards him and he sat down again. 'Come *on*.'

SHANE WAS PLEASED she didn't have the baby with her this time; it gave them something to talk about. Richie was at a neighbour's. When Sally brought the baby in, they couldn't talk about him or anything much. Richie was evidence enough, though he couldn't speak obviously. He slept in the backpack against the leg of the chair—he was some dopey baby, probably stupid, Shane thought, but he didn't say this to Sally. She'd been using through most of the pregnancy and drinking. Without Richie there, Sally could say all the things he'd been doing. She made it sound like he lived a life of pure riot and adventure, and Shane had to stop sometimes and say to himself, Hey, hey, this is hardly a life form we're talking about. Tell me when he doesn't shit himself and I'll get excited. Still he truly enjoyed watching her mouth make the sounds. Christ, he could climb inside that mouth and lie down on her wet tongue. He sat very close to the reinforced glass screen, so he could smell the toothpaste coming through the little speaking holes. Smelling it made him see the tube, where it sat in the blue cup in their bathroom—the cup was flecked with white. His brush still next to hers. He always asked her, Please clean your teeth just before you come.

'Does my breath smell?' she said.

'Carry it in your bag if you have to and spread some on with your finger. All I want to smell is that toothpaste.'

She always started now by blowing in his face through the screen, though he had to ask her every time and every time she said, Oh I forgot.

'I don't believe how he's changed,' she said. The ends of her hair were slightly wet from the rain. He could have sucked that rain off. He could have bitten her head off.

She never used the baby's name, he noticed. He hadn't noticed that before but she was getting strange about it. He believed he was becoming a true inmate, since he was seeing as if for the first time the useless orbit in which he'd moved for years and years. The clarity was blinding.

'Always just cracking up, you know,' she said.

'Yeah, about what? What sort of things?'

'Oh, I don't know. Anything.'

'Tell me one thing.'

'Let's see. I can't remember. Just when I'm changing him, that mobile, you know.'

'I bought that mobile, you know.'

'I know, honey.'

'You said it was the worst fucking thing ever.'

'It's made of little bits of glass, Shane! Soon, I'm going to have to take it down.'

'Don't take it down.'

'When he's a little older.'

'Don't take it down, Sal, and test him, see if he grabs for it. I want to hear if he grabs for it.'

She smiled at him in a way he didn't like, in a way that said soon you won't know a thing about the place I'm living in with my son and you won't be able to change a thing. The mobile was in the rubbish, alongside his toothbrush. They were moving to somewhere cheaper and smaller. 'Okay,' she said.

He was brooding; she always made him brood by the things she said—or not the things but the way she said them. He couldn't help noticing that she was happy.

'How's your chemist boyfriend?'

'Yeah right,' she said.

'Cheating bastard.'

'Who happens to be paying for your lawyer.'

'Cheating bastard with a guilty conscience he wants bought off.'

She looked at her watch—this was another thing Shane figured was new, his sensitivity to other people always checking their watches. Sally saw him looking. 'I can't leave the baby too long,' she said.

'He's got a name, you know,' he said.

'What?'

'Richie. It's Richie is the name, in case you've forgotten.'

'What did I say?'

'The baby. You say "he" all the time or "the baby". Don't you like the name? We chose that name.'

'I didn't choose it.'

'Liar, you chose it with me.'

'I didn't choose it, you did. You said that was it, I didn't have a say.'

'You didn't have a say? What do you mean? Fuck.'

'All right, all right.'

'Fucking hell, Sally, I don't believe you.'

'All right, okay? Richie. Richie. It's a name, there. I don't know what the fuss is about.'

'Richie is my son's name.'

'Okay, fucking Father of the Year.'

'You cow, you bitch.'

She stood up. 'Bye, Shane.'

'Sit down,' he said. God, that was her power. 'Please. Sally, sit down. Don't go. Sit down. I'm sorry. Don't go, I'll fucking rip out the walls. Please.'

She sat down. 'Okay, sorry too.'

He looked at her pouty mouth. He waited until the beating

had stopped in his ear, or lessened a bit. 'At this point in the conversation, Sally would normally be reaching for a huge glass of vodka and Coke. Wouldn't that be great, Sal?'

She smiled weakly. 'Not any more.'

'Really?'

'Yeah.'

She looked bashful. She made him think suddenly that when he got out, he would go straight. There was a laser that would take off the lines of his tattoo and he would look like new almost, with some scarring. But he would be straight.

'I'm back at the group,' she said.

'Good for you,' he said. This made him immensely sad—he felt the sudden force of everything he was missing. He put his head down on the table that was bolted to the floor and wept into his arms. The crying made all the fear in him—fear of prison which was as boundless as the prison was not; fear of death which was bigger still but came to him in the shape of a blade, a thrust, something definite and small even—it all surged up and shook his shoulders as though he was being held and vibrated in a machine. If he was a lunatic—and why else did you kill another human being?—they'd surely strap him to a machine. He missed Burrell. Burrell had done things for him and he missed him, though this wasn't something he could say to anyone. No one came to see him except her.

When he sat up, she was looking at him dry eyed. He had no power, not even in his tears. She saw no deeper into him than when they'd lived together and fought over cleaning the house or going to the baby at night.

'Listen, Sally, that tape from the pharmacy.'

'Where is it? You won't tell me, where is it?'

'Promise me you won't do anything stupid.' He felt a strong desire to hold her neck as some sort of lie detector mechanism.

'Like what?'

'Promise me.'

287

'I promise. Now stop jerking me around. Where the fuck have you hidden it?'

'You know I didn't tell them about you, how you called me about the church.'

'This again.'

'I didn't pull you in, Sal.'

'I know, I know. Thanks.'

'Don't fucking mention it.'

'That was for your plea, Shane, to make it go better, if you were a lone wolf.'

'But I'm not a lone wolf,' he said. 'We're together, aren't we.'

She pressed her palm against the partition. 'That's right, we are,' she said. 'Now where'd you put the tape?'

He couldn't understand how any of this had happened, why he lived currently by the light of a funnel, why he was inside and she was not, why he was telling her something she would misuse. Yes, he was a crazy fucker, but even that seemed open, unfortunately, to doubt. 'There's no tape,' he said.

I T HAD RAINED all day, just as it had been doing the whole week, and then at about five the skies cleared, the sun was out again and Don got a call from Gary saying the game was on. He didn't have to think what game he meant. He left the pharmacy at six, as though he was going to enlist.

Water covered the grass. They stood in it. None of the women had come.

'A woman knows,' said Troy.

'A woman is not stupid,' said Alan. 'Why'd you call us, Gary?'

Troy answered: 'There were men going crazy all over town if they couldn't get out for a *run-round*.'

'That's true,' said Bruce. He was already stripped off and tossing a ball from hand to hand.

Though it pained him, Don walked back to his car and got

in, and the others did the same. Bruce threw the ball into the water, looked at it, picked it up and walked to his car, wiping at his splattered shins.

At the pub, which was empty except for some old guys with their bellies against the bar, they loaded up the table with jugs. They were sitting near a wall-size TV screen and they began to watch basketball, though none of them had ever played it. The crowd noise from the basketball was ferocious; a sound like static washed harshly over them where they sat. None of them showed any signs of discomfort. They drank and observed some things that caused them to speak briefly.

'Dunkin!'

'Free throw line.'

'Kidding me!'

'The shot clock.'

'From outside. *Whoosh*!'

They were men; there was not a sport whose rules they didn't know just enough to get into an argument with a giant screen. And they hadn't played their own sport, which made them even more cantankerously expert. Sitting with his friends, Don had a strong sense of how fights started.

Gary, the cop, was next to him. He knew the most about the game, so he said the least. But that wasn't the only thing. He looked exhausted, his eyes puffy and red, and he slumped in his chair with his glass resting on his stomach. Even when someone refilled it for him Gary didn't shift the glass over the table but kept it pinned against him. There was beer on his shirt. Everyone knew that Gary had worked closely with Danny Burrell, who'd been killed. Don guessed they'd also come out to the Bay to stand in a pool of water for Gary because the trial had started that day. He supposed they'd grabbed the table nearest the screen for a similar reason. It was all about being there and not saying anything. Don was struck by the wisdom of their plan, and its kindness.

Don stayed for an hour, then he said he had to get away.

'Hear that crack?' said Troy. 'That's the sound of a pussy-whip.'

Gary was also leaving and Troy held up his hand for a high-five. 'See ya, captain,' he said.

It was raining again, mightily, and Don stood with Gary under the awning at the rear of the pub, waiting for a break in the deluge. He felt he couldn't leave Gary. Though they'd played in the same game for four years, he didn't know him that well—or at all in fact. They regarded the rain as if it was a show featuring nothing but black asphalt, hard-to-see cars and lots of water effects. The doors of the pub opened and one of the old guys who'd been at the bar came through, walking at the angle his hours on the stool had hung him on. He stood beside them, leaning slightly against Gary, who said, 'Tell me you haven't got a car in this carpark, sir.'

'If I haven't, I'm calling the cops.'

'I am the cops,' said Gary.

The man looked quickly at Gary, then said, 'I think I forgot my umbrella.' He turned and went back inside the pub.

'One time,' said Gary, 'I saw Danny Burrell pick up a guy and put him on this roof here.'

'Yeah?' said Don. 'Why'd he do that?'

Gary appeared not to have heard the question. 'Speaking as a chemist, Don, I've got a medical mystery for you. How does a lawyer sleep at night? What sort of prescribed drugs could you give a creature like that?' Then Gary looked up at the sky and ran to his car through the rain.

R UTH DIDN'T GET a newspaper any more and didn't listen to the radio or watch TV; she'd been following her son Jamie's advice. And still she could understand what Lou's husband, the real estate agent she'd called, was saying. To glance in the windows of the dairy and see the covers of magazines satisfied her that a life without subscriptions was a rich one, yet even these glances informed. It was through such means that she'd been made aware of the trial of the policeman's murderer. Lou's husband—his name was Andrew and he wasn't Indian at all but from Sierra Leone—was very agitated about the case. He walked from room to room, writing on his clipboard, talking to her about the need for tougher penalties, the toughest, he said. Didn't she agree? 'A person like this, who kills a policeman?' he said. 'I have no worries about killing him in return. No worries. Absolutely. What can we say about the downstairs bathroom?'

Ruth told him she didn't use it any more.

He looked at her as if she was insane. 'For the people who buy your house, I mean.'

'Shall I get it fixed?'

He wrote on his clipboard. 'Excellent! Two bathrooms.'

'Where is Sierra Leone exactly?' she said.

'You don't want to go there.'

'No, but it's in Africa, isn't it?'

'Sierra Leone is in its own special hell. On maps you'll find it on the west side.' He went to the windows of the spare room. He was writing again. 'Sunny spacious fourth bedroom.'

'Or study,' said Ruth.

Lou's husband stopped writing. 'Oh, no, Ruth, a study is like a little corner somewhere. Not even a door is required. You put a desk there in the open home and some books, one of those cups full of pens. *I'll* find you the study in your house.'

They had tea at the kitchen table. 'These gangs,' he said. 'I'd wipe them off the face of the earth.'

'I didn't think he was in a gang,' said Ruth. She surprised herself with how much she knew.

'Or on drugs. It's the same thing.' The African shrugged. His skin colour didn't seem attached to that continent. 'You don't show mercy to us, we don't show mercy to you. Beautiful house,

Ruth. You know there'll be a lot of interest. A lot of interest. So many houses here are boxes. You could put an animal in them. But this house is a real property, you know. I'm proud to agent you.'

'Thank you,' she said, feeling decided. She liked him, Lou's husband, his dishonesty, and he had helped her decide. It had nothing to do with her children. She would never sell, never.

SALLY WAITED ON the street with her bag in the cool of a morning she'd wanted to come all night. Actually she'd gone to bed early, before nine, not to store up energy but to waste it in sleep, so she wouldn't be conscious of the hours. Of course it hadn't worked. She woke regularly through the night, looking at the clock. She even went and stood over the baby's cot in the hope he'd stir and give her something to do.

Mike's ute came round the corner and pulled up in front of her. Mike was sulking because she'd made him do this. 'He's your de facto brother-in-law,' she'd told him.

'That's no relation at all,' he said.

'I'll never speak to you again.'

'Except when you want to borrow something or use me for something like this shit.'

'Mikey,' she said. 'Mikey Mike.'

In the car she kissed him on the cheek; he smelled of milk powder. On the seat there were some old takeaway wrappings that she balled up and threw out the window. Mike refused to start driving. 'What?' she said. 'What?' He stared straight ahead. She got out of the car, walked to the rubbish and collected it. 'Okay, mein Führer,' she said.

They filled up on gas at Ashburton and Sally gave him twenty dollars.

'What's this?' he said.

'Shut up,' she said.

He was happier after that, telling her about a guy at the cheese factory who could identify the different clouds, the types of them—a real clever prick—and one day a few of the guys rigged his locker so when he opened it this smoke bomb went off. Mike struck his hand on the steering wheel and laughed. 'You know, they said, go on tell us what fucking formation that is, cumulus stratus fuckus something, and the guy is choking in these fumes. Shit.'

'Ignorant jerks,' said Sally.

He didn't hear her; he was adjusting his hearing aid. The factory had made her brother into an old man.

'What's with your little people now, Mike?' she said. 'How's the collection of hobbits?'

'They're not hobbits.'

Sally couldn't bear to be in the same room as Mike's wife. 'Shit, that's great. So she's still getting them?'

'It's a craft.'

'Oh, man.'

'Piss off.'

'Okay, okay.'

They were sitting behind a couple of milk tankers, wandering out to see if they could pass. 'Least I haven't got a live hobbit of my own,' he said.

'What's that?'

'Richie.'

She laughed and hit her brother on the shoulder as he put his foot down and swung into the other lane. Richie was at a neighbour's place. She liked the new flat; people said hello. They didn't know her. They made offers but they didn't invade you like you were a country. With neighbours like that she could have a life. In fact, someone had phoned her a few days before and said, How would you feel about a job? It was the employment woman from the A&D. She said there was a part-time position in a flower shop. 'Well, I don't know,' said Sally, 'everyone *hates* flowers.' The employment woman didn't get that, or it was the wrong attitude. 'No, no, like just tell me where and when,' Sally said.

The whole car was shaking as Mike tried to overtake the tankers. She could feel her chin shaking. The tankers went on forever and they seemed to be travelling in the wrong lane forever, as though they had to obey a different set of rules from everyone else. They had to. They were on a long straight, the road ahead deceptively clear. From the smallest rises and bumps she imagined the low roof of another car appearing. She leaned forward and patted the dashboard. 'Go!' she called out. 'Go, you old piece of junk!' She was thinking of her job in a flower shop. Mike had his window wound down and the air rushed in, pulling the hair off his head. They still had half a tanker to go. 'Wooo!' he shouted through the window. 'Owww!' Sally looked out her side; a giant wheel was turning close to her head.

Near Christchurch, Mike said, 'Can you believe it, Sal? Can you get a handle on this?'

'Nope,' she said.

'You act so cool.'

'Well, I'm not.'

'I don't know if I want to see him, you know.'

'You fucking are seeing him.'

'Shit,' said Mike.

They parked near the courts and Mike said he'd stay with the ute while Sally checked everything out. They probably had a lot of waiting to do, he said. She got out and he lay down across the seat and closed his eyes.

It had been Mike's first reason for not coming: no one knew when the jury would make up its mind. They'd had the previous afternoon for their deliberations, and then a night in a hotel, and she figured they couldn't take longer than another morning to come through. What's to decide? she'd said to Mike. Shane had killed the cop, so it was only the temporary insanity aspect.

Mike told her he thought that could take days if you got the right people sitting in a room. The right people sitting in a room could take a week to decide what colour grass was, he said. No, she said. They had to go up today, they didn't have a choice. She loved Shane, she said, starting to cry on the phone. Hey, Mike told her, he's an all right guy but with, as we all know, a heap of problems. Between sobs she told Mike she'd never forget how he got Shane the job at the factory when no one would give him the time of day.

'Well,' said Mike, 'to be honest, Sal, I didn't ever see him being like a cheesemaker.'

She laughed at that and said, 'I don't know what I'd do without you, Mikey.'

Mike was right, she thought. The court building looked like any other building on a Tuesday morning before lunchtime. One big zero. No crowd, no media. She watched the entrance for a while and saw a few people coming and going; none of them looked attached to an event of any magnitude. Probably they were paying parking fines or they worked inside at desks.

When she'd gone in for her methadone, she told the chemist they were driving up for the verdict, and he couldn't think of a thing to say or do except nod his head and look seriously concerned. Finally he told her, 'Good luck.' He still didn't have the tape—she'd said Shane wouldn't budge. The tape, of course, no longer existed but she wouldn't ever let him know that. It was offensive material and she was insulted whenever he mentioned it. She would say that to him next time: that if he didn't give up on it, she'd tell all, tell everyone, starting with his wife. She'd discovered that if she kept this misery between them he was a kind of friend to her. He had started to treat her as a normal person.

One time recently he said to her did she want to hear a dream he had. 'Nope,' she said.

'Fair enough,' he said.

'What dream?'

'I won't bore you. But I was wondering this. How would you feel if some things, clothes, got passed on to your baby?'

'Clothes?'

'From time to time.'

'From where?'

'I could buy them.'

'You'd buy him clothes how? Go into a baby shop?'

'How would you feel?'

'I don't know, I don't like it.'

'Okay.'

'I don't like the idea of being in your debt.'

'But you wouldn't be.'

'I know and I don't like that either.'

'Well, I had to ask you.'

Suddenly she was disappointed he'd stopped talking about the offer. 'What's this?' she said, in a reviving way. 'You buy my baby clothes and I have to hear about your dreams?'

'No, it's not like that.'

'I don't like the idea one bit,' she told him, less sceptical now. 'Except my baby gets clothes.'

'That's right. From time to time you could say, Well he needs a jacket or whatever, and that's all it'd be.'

'That's all it's going to be and this doesn't buy you a thing with me. It's all between Richie and you.'

'Exactly,' he said. 'You know my wife and I thought at one stage we'd adopt a baby.'

'Spare me,' she said. Sally's mind went quickly back to Terry the cook at the carnival tearooms. Everyone at some time or other wanted her baby but only for a little while to make themselves feel better, to fill a hole. 'My ambition one day,' she said to him, terminating his reverie, 'is to move somewhere, like Wellington.'

She'd been encouraged to have ambitions and to announce

them regularly, but her statement to the chemist had nothing to do with pleasing the teacher. She felt dragged—dragged screaming sometimes—in the direction of the future.

'I've got a brother in Wellington,' he said.

'Is that an offer of accommodation?' she said.

'It certainly is not. Actually I don't have an address yet. He's only just got back there following a break. He was down here for a while but it didn't work out.'

The chemist looked bleak. He seemed to have forgotten her.

'My ambition—' she began firmly, then she decided to spare him, the poor man, spare him the boring details. He had his own troubles.

SHE SAT DOWN on a bench opposite the court. A guy in his thirties, in a blue shirt and tie, was walking slowly to and fro in front of the doors of the building. Some sort of reporter, she guessed. He'd set his shoulder bag on one of the steps beside the little fountain; she watched him take a packet of smokes out of the bag and light one, then he was writing in some sort of notebook. He'd seen her too and raised his eyebrows in greeting. He shoved the notebook in his pocket and began strolling again. Gradually his circling took him closer to the bench where she was sitting.

He spoke to her from ten metres off. 'How's it going?' he said.

'What are you doing, waiting for this jury?' she said.

He moved closer, smiling. 'I am. You too?'

'I hate waiting,' she said.

'You got to think of something else.'

'Like what?'

'I don't know, anything.'

'What are you thinking of?'

'Me? I'm thinking of you.'

'Yeah, right.'

'I wasn't before but now I am.' He indicated the seat. 'May I?' He sat down. 'I like to make up a story or something. Who's this? Why's she here? Where's she from? You know. Passing the time.'

'And what have you made up so far?'

'Oh. Oh, boy. What have I made up?'

'Well who am I?'

'No, these are private, you know, stories in my head, where believe me they belong and deserve to stay.'

'Dirty stories.'

He laughed. 'What? Oh, no, no, no. No. Anyway, would I tell you a dirty story?'

'Then what would you tell me?'

'Well, you haven't been at the trial before. I think I'm right about that. You've come for the verdict only, which is interesting.'

'Why?'

'It means you're not family, not close family. But you want to see this bit. You want to see something done. Something final. You're here.'

'For who? What side am I on?'

'Don't take offence but I decided that one very quickly. Defendant.'

'Fuck you,' she said.

'Oh shit, I'm sorry.' He stood up with his hand on his mouth. 'I'm so sorry. What an idiot I am. I shouldn't have started. Look.' He was backing away. 'Look, I'm sorry. They should just lock him up and throw away the key, you know. That guy is the lowest. You have my complete sympathy, really.'

'Fuck you too.'

At midday people started emerging from the building and filling the seats around her, lying on the grass with their lunches. Mike arrived and she sent him off to buy them something to eat. He returned with nothing she could sink her teeth into—rolls hard as wood and inside them the bleeding flesh of the only vegetable she couldn't stomach: beetroot. With her fingers she scooped at the mayonnaise-coated strands of chicken that were tainted pink, and tossed the rest away. Then she had an Oddmint from a packet Mike had pulled from the ute's glovebox. He bit into his roll and chips flew off as though his mouth was an axe.

The lunch crowd disappeared, sucked back inside the building, and she waited again, looking out for the reporter guy who was now trying to avoid being in her line of sight. From time to time he appeared briefly from the side of the building, talking into his cellphone.

'Come on then,' she said to Mike. She was moving quickly across the concrete.

'What?' said Mike. 'How'd you know?'

The reporter had already entered the building. As if answering a force they were powerless against, people began to come from everywhere, heading in the same direction as Sally and Mike. At the revolving doors, there was shoving, a kind of panic and excitement as if space and time were limited. Sally felt it herself, an acceleration of her hopes, resentment towards these others. She trod on someone's foot—an older woman who yelled out but kept moving forward. Who was *she*, thought Sally. There was no one—no one—with more right than she had to be inside this place. Everyone else was ugly and spiteful. She almost said his name then, as if to prove her worthiness and make them see how foolish they were, how unnecessary and unwanted. The notion somehow produced him. It made him present in the building—she'd got inside, though Mike, who'd stood back, hadn't. Even Mike was surplus to the requirements of this place and this moment. She waited for him against her own will.

Shane, she knew, was here, in some buried part of the building, though he was being led right now through corridors and up narrow underground stairs towards the light. He was here.

'Jesus,' said Mike beside her, 'what a scrum.'

'I can't,' she said.

'What?'

299

'I don't think I can go in there, Mikey.'

'Course you can.'

'I can't, I can't.' Her head rolled on her shoulders and she looked into the panels of fluorescent lights above her. Someone shoved her in the back, just as she was about to fall, and she went forward with the surge of people, into the courtroom and along the row of seats and into her seat—she felt it was hers.

'There,' said Mike.

She couldn't breathe. 'I'm gonna die,' she said. She felt the furniture, its many wooden surfaces and its gleam, begin to shift around, as if being raised and lowered by hidden ropes. 'Oh,' she gasped. Mike pushed his hand against her head, forcing it down between her knees. She smelled the seat: vinyl. She put her tongue against it. Shane was moving towards this place. He was guilty as sin, and he was not mad just very very afraid.

When she opened her eyes, the jury was there. The judge. Everyone. His lawyer. She thought she saw his auntie, the nice one. She didn't see his mother of course. She saw people from Timaru and they looked scared and small. The family of the cop—she did not want to learn those faces. But she wouldn't look over there at that space she knew was also filled. She wouldn't look there. She felt her mind would collapse. She easily came up with an image of that—of walls falling in on her. With great effort she made herself think of her baby. She made herself think of the cot sheets she hadn't washed. She was a bad mother. With her fingernails she pressed into the skin of her arm. She wouldn't look where she saw in the corner of her eye, the shape of him, standing when everyone else was sitting. His shadow fell across her, across them all. He was here.

Despite everything, she felt a pride in knowing him.

The judge, a woman, asked some questions and then the foreman stood up. He held a piece of paper in his hands and the judge asked him how the jury found the accused on the charge of murder. The foreman made a movement of his neck—it was not clear whether he'd spoken.

'Mr Foreman,' said the judge, 'can I ask you to say again your verdict. On the charge of murder how does the jury find the accused?'

The foreman wore a suit but no tie—he looked to Sally like someone who ran a shop. He was in his early fifties and bald. This is not me, he seemed to say. This is not me and I am not here. A few of the other members of the jury were shifting in their seats, looking nervously at the foreman, who raised the paper closer to his face; his hands were shaking. There was a groan from the courtroom followed by other noises of pain, and the judge said, 'Quiet, please.'

Quiet please, as if it were a tennis match.

The foreman opened his mouth and made the same movement with his neck but still there wasn't a word.

'Would you like a glass of water, Mr Foreman?' said the judge. Someone sitting below the judge had stood up and was pouring water from a jug into a glass. The court was filled with the sound of the water.

She wouldn't look in that space where there was a shadow at the corner of her vision. She would not say she had known him because it was not true. He is a mystery as we all are, she said to herself.

The foreman shook his head, then spoke resoundingly into the ceiling of the room: 'Guilty.' Above the noise and the cries, as if it was a new word he'd learned and was showing off, he said it again: 'Guilty.'

'He *can't* say it twice,' said Sally. 'He can't say it twice.'

Near her, someone said, 'Holy God.'

She looked then and he was not looking anywhere, it seemed. Shane was swaying and his eyes drifted around the room. She held up her hand in the air, stretching it towards him, her fingers splayed, and she kept it there while he was turned around in the dock by the guard—he could not make it by himself—and led down the steps and through a side-door out of the court. She had her hand in the air still. She'd abandoned him for only a moment but that had been enough. There were others gesturing to him. She was one of many but she was one. The door closed on him and she saw that it was covered in wood panelling that matched the wall so that soon the door was hard to detect, and then it existed only in an outline which required great concentration to hold in her head. Door, she thought. Door. Door. Pretty soon the language for it seemed odd, like she was repeating a foreign word. Others were shouting at the door, where the door had been, but she was quiet, retaining everything in her mind. It appeared in her mind as though there was a chute down which he had been sucked. Her hand hurt but she kept it there, raised in the air of that place, displaying for anyone who cared to look the bones and veins that were hers to pledge and hers to take back.

n–Fri; beer and wine; reservations recommended; www.chezsovan.com; between
ryessa Rd and E Hedding St.

ht Forty North First / ★★

N 1ST ST, SAN JOSE; 408/282-0840 This restaurant with the no-nonsense name
rs to the San Jose power elite—say, isn't that the mayor exchanging pleasantries
h a justice from the municipal court? The food is eclectic, with Italian and Asian
ches influencing the contemporary American menu. Starters include a spicy sauté
oney prawns nesting on a bed of Chinese cabbage; a grilled portobello mush-
m atop Asiago cheese, roasted garlic, and sweet peppers; and a curried spinach
d with apples, peanuts, and golden raisins. Entrees include pastas (such as lin-
e with chicken and broccoli topped with a creamy sun-dried tomato sauce and
rinkle of feta and walnuts), fettuccine with smoked salmon, clams, artichoke
rts, and basil, and other temptations from the deep. A panoply of meat and
ltry dishes range from ostrich medallions to a grilled coconut and macadamia
ted mahimahi served with a tropical fruit salsa. By now, you've probably gotten
idea that chef/co-owner John Petricca takes chances here; sometimes he hits the
k and sometimes he misses. Still, his concoctions are always interesting, and you
wash them down with a selection from the extensive (and pricey) wine list. $$$;
DC, DIS, MC, V; no checks; lunch Mon–Fri, dinner Mon–Sat; full bar; reser-
ons recommended; www.840.com; between Mission and Hedding Sts.

ile's / ★★★

S 2ND ST, SAN JOSE; 408/289-1960 Catering to an older, well-heeled crowd
expense-account execs, Emile's has been one of San Jose's finest restaurants for
rly three decades. Chef-owner Emile Mooser offers a California version of the
ine he learned in his Swiss homeland, and his menu features classic French,
s, and Italian preparations as well as cuisine minceur (a somewhat leaner style
rench cooking). Using fine stocks and the best seasonal ingredients available, the
hen does a particularly good job with fish and game. Entrees on the seasonal
u may include a giant, open-faced ravioli with prawns, scallops, and fish in a
ter-brandy sauce; a fillet of beef with a roasted garlic and cabernet sauvignon
e; or even such exotica as wild boar with fresh fruit compote. The roesti—a
chy Swiss version of hash browns—is wonderful. Almost everything is made on
premises, from the house-cured gravlax to flawless desserts like the justly cele-
ed Grand Marnier soufflé. Emile's wine cellar contains more than 300 selections,
ging from the very reasonable to the very, very expensive. $$$; AE, DC, DIS, MC,
o checks; dinner Tues–Sat; full bar; reservations recommended; www.emiles.com;
een Williams and Reed Sts.

ombei Restaurant / ★★

E JACKSON ST, SAN JOSE; 408/279-4311 Among the many worthy restaurants
an Jose's Japantown, tiny, lively Gombei stands out with its unparalleled noodle
es and the near-volcanic energy of its devoted patrons and youthful staff. The
u offers everything from teriyaki and domburi to Gombei's renowned udon—
Japanese equivalent of Jewish chicken soup, which arrives in a huge ceramic

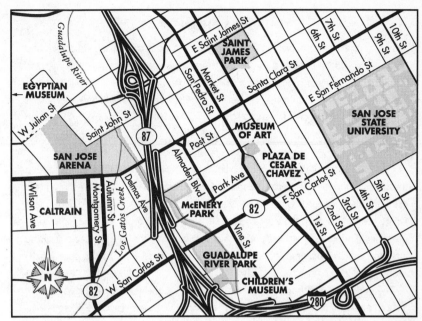

DOWNTOWN SAN JOSE

hip Blowfish Sushi offers tempuras, fresh sushi, and premium sakes until late in the
evening.

PERFORMING ARTS

San Jose has a thriving community of theater, ballet, and opera groups, most of
which may be found at the **SAN JOSE CENTER FOR THE PERFORMING ARTS** (255
Almaden Blvd at Park Ave; 408/277-3900). The **SAN JOSE CIVIC LIGHT OPERA**
(408/453-7108) puts on musicals and other frothy diversions, while **OPERA SAN
JOSE** (408/437-4450), the **SAN JOSE CLEVELAND BALLET** (408/288-2800), and
the **SAN JOSE SYMPHONY ORCHESTRA** (408/288-2828) offer more classical cultural enrichments. **LOS LUPEÑOS DE SAN JOSE** dance company (42 Race St;
408/292-0443) reflects the Spanish heritage of the city. For drama, the **SAN JOSE
REPERTORY THEATRE** (101 Paseo de Antonio St; 408/367-7266) offers innovative
productions of new works and classics. The **SAN JOSE STAGE COMPANY** (490 S
1st St; 408/283-7142) primarily showcases American contemporary drama and
comedy, while the **CITY LIGHTS THEATRE** (529 S 2nd St; 408/295-4200) follows
the more experimental route.

PARKS AND GARDENS

KELLEY PARK is a pleasant place for a picnic and a stroll around the **JAPANESE
FRIENDSHIP GARDEN** (corner of Senter Rd and Keyes St; 408/277-3664), complete
with a koi pond and a teahouse. If you have little ones in tow, they're sure to be
beguiled by the old-fashioned, low-tech charms of **HAPPY HOLLOW** next door, a

YOUR PC'S BIRTHPLACE

Two of the biggest babies on record were born in Silicon Valley—Microsoft and Apple—and despite the dot-com collapse three years ago, this area is still considered the unofficial high-tech capital of the world. Of course, where there are babies, there are albums to document their first steps, first words, what they might become. Such is the **TECH MUSEUM OF INNOVATION** (201 S Market St, San Jose; 408/294-8324; www.thetech.org) or, more simply, "The Tech"—a cache of technology's past, present, and future.

One look at the orange and cobalt blue museum building will make you chuckle at the now outmoded notion that "techie" was synonymous with "geek"—this is not a gathering place for nerds with taped glasses and pocket protectors. Instead, its modern facade seems to beckon the tragically hip to enter and get in touch with their inner programmer. The interior architecture follows suit, drawing one in, then catapulting the attention upward via a dramatic curved staircase and a massive supporting column lathered in gold leaf.

The Tech is divided into three levels. The ground level features an **IMAX DOME THEATER**—no museum is complete without one these days—and the Techstore, as interesting as the museum itself. The upper level contains the **INNOVATION AREA,** where you can, among other things, design and ride a virtual roller coaster or tour a computer chip lab, and the **LIFE TECH AREA**—an utterly fascinating look at technology's role in studying, diagnosing, and treating the human body. The squeamish and the recently lunched should avoid the video display that shows how a computer-generated image of the human body and all its internal organs is created by using a cadaver. The upper level also includes an interactive area called **IMAGINATION PLAY-GROUND** that dispels the notion that high-tech endeavors are always sedentary. A **Sneaks and Spies** exhibit boasts hideouts equipped with the latest and greatest surveillance equipment, so that visitors can be James Bond for a day. A **SHADOWS AND SANDS** display projects your movements on screen for an interactive media experience. The lower level is where you can catch a glimpse of technology's future. From robotic dogs with amazingly realistic movement—you can special-order one if you're willing to pay $3,500—and a robotic submarine you can pilot to a model Mars rover you can ride, it's a techie playground. Be sure to take a ride on the **SEGWAY HUMAN TRANSPORTER**—the stand-up scooter that is propelled by the way you shift your weight. Finally, the **CENTER OF THE EDGE** area showcases rotating exhibits of the newest state-of-the-art technology.

—*Brian Tacang*

zoo and amusement park aimed at the toddler-through-early-gra
GUADALUPE RIVER PARK is undergoing extensive renovations that
3-mile stretch of picnic areas and paved walkways that will extend
dren's Discovery Museum to near Highway 880 and the San Jose Ai
SAN JOSE DEPARTMENT OF PARKS AND RECREATION (408/
408/277-5998) for more information.

NIGHTLIFE

Once the red-light district, the area around Market and First Streets I
developed into a clean, hip home for many nightclubs and a slightly r
tive scene. If you gotta dance, you'll find live rock and recorded dance
CACTUS CLUB (417 S 1st St, two blocks south of the Fairmont hot
9300) and in the **B HIVE** (372 S 1st St; 408/298-2529). For live jazz and a
native rock, head to **AGENDA** (at the NW corner of S 1st St and E San
408/287-4087). Live rock, dance classics, and cheap draft beer are
TOONS (52 E Santa Clara St at 2nd St; 408/292-7464). For a mix of musi
rock, swing bands, DJ-spun rock, and '70s disco—check out **THE SPY** (4
408/535-0330). Coffee and attitude are dished out at **CAFE MATISSE** (3
408/298-7788).

RESTAURANTS

Agenda / ★★★

399 S 1ST ST, SAN JOSE; 408/287-3991 At this chic and beautifully design
rant in the city's SoMa district (yes, San Jose's got one, too), stylish type
mopolitans at the sculptured wood bar, Silicon Valley execs talk shop
flanked by arty souls, and jazz buffs check out the live (and very loud) ban
androgynous angel presides over all, stretching its da Vinci-esque flying
wings across an exposed brick wall. If you turn your attention away from
roundings, however, you'll notice that the inventive food is what really tal
here. That's apparent as soon as you spread a piece of feather-light focacci
delectable basil- and olive-infused tapenade. Under executive chef Brad Kra
food has taken a decidedly American turn. Look for offerings such as a chees
on a house-made focaccia roll with applewood-smoked bacon and white
cheese. Eclectic combinations continue to reign on this inspired menu, with
ranging from spicy tuna tartare to delicate English pea-filled ravioli, fron
burning pot stickers to comfort food like garlic mashed potatoes. Portions a
erous, but try to save room for dessert; choices that seem passé on paper, s
chocolate mud pie and crème caramel, turn out to be retro revelations. Ser
savvy but a bit slow, which gives you a chance to soak up the scene and consi
rest of the evening. $$; AE, DC, MC, V; *no checks; dinner Tues–Sat; full bar;
vations recommended; at San Salvador St.*

Chez Sovan Restaurant / ★★

923 OLD OAKLAND RD, SAN JOSE (AND BRANCHES); 408/287-7619 This re
rant specializes in Cambodian cuisine and exceptionally friendly service. For a
review, see the Restaurants section of Campbell. $; AE, MC, V; *no checks; l*

bowl filled with fat wheat noodles, loads of tender strips of chicken, ribbons of egg, green onion, and a sheaf of dried seaweed. Be sure to check the specials board for such irresistible nibbles as deep-fried oysters or cold chicken salad served on buckwheat noodles. *$; cash only; lunch, dinner Mon–Sat; beer and wine; reservations recommended; between 4th and 5th Sts.*

La Forêt French Restaurant / ★★★

21747 BERTRAM RD, SAN JOSE; 408/997-3458 Located in an old two-story hotel overlooking Los Alamedos Creek, this picturesque and pricey restaurant offers unusual wild game that's flown in daily. Chef Vazgen "Ken" Davoudi can always be counted on to create superb sauces for the day's special, which might be tender medallions of wild boar marinated in shallots, balsamic vinegar, brandy, and cumin and topped with an outstanding pink peppercorn sauce, paired with medallions of elk in an equally masterful tarragon cream sauce. Davoudi's prowess isn't limited to game; he also works well with seafood, including a perfectly poached salmon served with a port wine sauce. Appetizers might feature fusilli with olive oil, herbs, garlic, wild mushrooms, and Gouda cheese or escargot with garlic butter and Pernod. The dessert list features a selection of cakes, cheesecakes, and exotic soufflés. *$$$; AE, DC, DIS, MC, V; no checks; dinner Tues–Sun, brunch Sun; full bar; reservations recommended; www.laforetrestaurant.com; from the Almaden Expwy, take the Almaden Rd exit, go S for 3 miles, turn left at Almaden Wy, and cross the small bridge to Bertram Rd.*

Orlo's / ★★★

200 EDENVALE AVE, SAN JOSE; 408/226-3200 Faith healer Mary Hayes Chynoweth built a gorgeous 41,000-square-foot Mediterranean Revival-style mansion in 1905 as a base of operations for her ministry. Unfortunately, the wealthy do-gooder passed away four months before the house was completed, and the grand estate fell into disrepair years later. These days, the restored and sensitively modernized mansion is a home-away-from-home for Silicon Valley professionals attending meetings at the Hayes Conference Center. Most of the healing going on here now takes place in the health spa, but one might also reap salubrious benefits from a meal at Orlo's, an innovative restaurant open to the public. Housed in the former family dining room, the elegant space has floral-fabric-and-wood-covered walls, green and maroon carpeting, ornate metal table bases, and built-in Mission-style furniture. Service is a bit formal, which seems right for the setting, and the seasonal menu, which stresses fresh, first-rate ingredients, stops just short of fussy. Appetizers include the classic oysters Rockefeller and a splendid salad of baby greens with a walnut-balsamic vinaigrette and Danish blue cheese. Entrees are notable for unusual renderings of traditional fare, such as a charbroiled top sirloin with a honey and chipotle glaze; or the roasted rack of lamb with a port wine and fig sauce served with truffle-whipped potatoes. Some of the bewitching items on the dessert tray look better than they taste (try the chocolate opera cake, which is ethereally light and boasts a liquory bite). *$$$; AE, DC, DIS, MC, V; no checks; lunch Mon–Fri, dinner every day; full bar; reservations recommended; www.hayesmansion.com; from Hwy 101 turn W on Blossom Hill Rd, then right on Lean Ave, which turns into Edenvale Ave.*

Paolo's / ★★★

333 W SAN CARLOS ST, SAN JOSE; 408/294-2558 A longtime San Jose institution, Paolo's moved to expensive new digs in 1991, and while the handsome facility may have a bit of a corporate America feel, the flavorful food remains authentically Italian. Look for unexpected little flourishes that give even the most tried-and-true dishes an interesting twist: osso buco, for example, is served on a bed of saffron-infused farro, while Paolo's gnocchi is baked with black truffle butter. Other outstanding items include *ravioli con formaggi di pecora* (pasta stuffed with sheep's-milk ricotta, fava beans, and heirloom tomatoes); roasted quail with white raisins and grappa; and an intriguing appetizer of pan-seared foie gras with caramelized fennel, grilled strawberries, and a chestnut honey–infused duck sauce. Service can be a little brusque at times, especially if you're not a silver-haired CEO on his or her lunch hour, but it's always efficient. The wine list could bring a tear of joy to Bacchus's eye—the 50-page tome encompasses an outstanding variety of domestic and European selections. *$$$; AE, DC, DIS, MC, V; no checks; lunch Mon–Fri, dinner Mon–Sat; full bar; reservations recommended; www.paolos restaurant.com; between Woz Wy and Almaden Blvd.* ♿

71 Saint Peter / ★★

71 N SAN PEDRO ST, SAN JOSE; 408/971-8523 Chef/co-owner Mark Tabak has attracted a loyal following with this tiny and romantic Mediterranean bistro. The Spanish floor tiles, flowers, exposed brick walls, and crisp linens help create a feeling of rustic elegance, a theme echoed by Tabak's robust yet refined cuisine. Outstanding starters include steamed New Zealand clams simply seasoned with tomato, basil, and garlic, and a bevy of interesting salads. For your entree, you'd do well to consider the roasted hazelnut pork loin cloaked in a Zinfandel-mango au jus with pear chutney and spinach mashed potatoes, the seafood linguine in a spicy tomato broth, or any of the fresh fish dishes. Tabak is justly proud of his crème brûlée, which was once voted the best in Santa Clara Valley. The sensibly priced wine list includes French and Italian selections as well as the usual California suspects. *$$; AE, DC, DIS, MC, V; local checks only; lunch Mon–Fri, dinner Tues–Sat; beer and wine; reservations recommended; www.71saintpeter.com; between St John and Santa Clara Sts.*

LODGINGS

The Fairmont / ★★★

170 S MARKET ST, SAN JOSE; 408/998-1900 OR 800/527-4727 President Clinton's done it. So have Al Gore, Luciano Pavarotti, Neil Diamond, Mike Wallace, the elder George Bush, and a host of other celebs—slipped between the Supercale cotton sheets of San Jose's Fairmont, that is. Twenty stories high in the heart of downtown, the city's most luxurious hostelry has become one of the best-known features of the skyline. After spending $67 million in 2003, the hotel now features a grand 13-story tower that boasts 264 additional rooms and 74 luxurious suites, bringing the total capacity to 805 rooms. The guest rooms (as well as the public areas) have been refurbished and feature such niceties as marble bathrooms, plush robes, electric shoe polishers, desks, walk-in closets, custom-made mattresses, minibars, and nightly turndown service. In keeping with the Silicon Valley setting, they also contain an arsenal of tech toys such as high-speed modem links for computers and fax machines and interactive TV sets that let a guest do everything from ordering up a movie to checking out of the hotel. During the summer months the cabana rooms that directly face the 58-foot-long swimming pool and feature small, private sun decks are especially popular. Three well-regarded restaurants stand ready to serve peckish travelers: the Pagoda serves Chinese food at lunch and dinner; the Fountain is a casual spot for breakfast, lunch, and dinner; the poolside Gazebo Bar and Grill offers cocktails and light fare in summer and fall, weather permitting. In addition, an elegant afternoon tea is served in the hotel's lobby on weekends. *$$$; AE, DC, DIS, V; checks OK; www.fairmonthotels.com; between San Fernando and San Carlos Sts.* &

The Hensley House / ★★

456 N 3RD ST, SAN JOSE; 408/298-3537 Close to museums, theaters, and restaurants, this stately Queen Anne is a haven for corporate visitors and child-weary couples. Proprietors Toni Contreras and Ron Evans restored the landmark building. They added four more rooms, including three units in the lovely Craftsman-style house across the street. Each of the guest rooms has a queen-size featherbed, private bath, TV with VCR, and telephone. If you're ready to splurge, try the Judge's Chambers, with its wet bar, whirlpool bath for two, hand-painted ceiling and walls, and fireplace. (By the way, the ghost of the room's namesake, Superior Court Judge Perley Gosbey, one of the home's original owners, is rumored to pay a friendly visit now and then.) Guests are treated to a full breakfast. High tea is available to guests and the public on Thursday and Saturday afternoons by appointment only. *$$–$$$; AE, DC, DIS, MC, V; checks OK; www.hensleyhouse.com; at Hensley St.*

Hotel De Anza / ★★★

233 W SANTA CLARA ST, SAN JOSE; 408/286-1000 OR 800/843-3700 Renovations that took 10 months and $10 million brought this 1931 grande dame back to life after years of decay. The richly colored Moorish ceilings in the De Anza Room and the Hedley Club are art deco jewels, and the same design influence can be felt in the guest rooms. Each of the 101 rooms has a multiple-line desk phone with a dedicated data line and fax port, high-speed Internet access, an armoire with an honor bar, and a TV with a VCR (you can check out movies gratis from the video library downstairs). Ask for one of the south-facing rooms to enjoy a sweeping view of downtown. The hotel's flagship restaurant, La Pastaia, serves some of the best Italian food in town, and the place is always packed with locals as well as hungry travelers. The stately Palm Court Terrace is a favorite place to meet for drinks in the warmer months, and a live jazz band performs in the Hedley Club on Wednesday through Saturday nights. *$$$; AE, DC, MC, V; checks OK; www.hoteldeanza.com; at Almaden Blvd.*

Hyatt Sainte Claire / ★★★

302 S MARKET ST, SAN JOSE; 408/298-1234 OR 800/233-1234 This gracious Spanish Revival–style hostelry was built in 1926 by the same architectural firm responsible for the design of the Mark Hopkins Hotel in San Francisco. The 170 refurbished guest rooms (including 14 one-bedroom suites and 1 grand suite boasting 2 fireplaces and a library) feature featherbeds, dual phone lines with high-speed modems, safes, and minibars among the other usual first-class amenities. In addition, some of the rooms have whirlpool tubs and fireplaces, and 80 percent are equipped with laser printers and IBM-compatible computers with Internet access. A small exercise room with a treadmill and an exercise bike stands ready to help guests work out any knots or kinks resulting from sessions at those computers. And the Hyatt has a pleasant coffee shop, the Panetteria, serving Italian sandwiches and pastries, as well as a top-rated branch of Il Fornaio restaurant. *$$$; AE, DC, DIS, MC, V; checks OK; www.sanjose.hyatt.com; at San Carlos St.*

Santa Clara

RESTAURANTS

Birk's / ★★

3955 FREEDOM CIRCLE, SANTA CLARA; 408/980-6400 Despite its office-park setting and rather stern exterior, Birk's is a handsome American grill with a spirited atmosphere. Design features mark Birk's as a Pat Kuleto creation, and the hearty food reflects the vaguely men's-club feel of the place. Appetizers might include steak bits with béarnaise sauce, a grilled artichoke with garlic-lemon aioli, or oysters Rockefeller. For a main course, you can choose from all manner of grilled and smoked meat, fish, and fowl. Standouts include the popular smoked prime rib, peppered filet mignon topped with a Cognac–green peppercorn sauce, and grilled lamb chops marinated in oregano, lemon, garlic, and olive oil. Probably the most surprising item on the menu is a pasta paella loaded with prawns, crab, mussels, fresh fish, and sausage in a steaming saffron cream sauce. If you still have room for dessert, Birk's offers a dynamite chocolate cake, berry crisp à la mode, and other oh-I'll-diet-tomorrow temptations. The wine list reflects a good range of California vintners, and you'll find an excellent selection of single-malt scotches and beers on tap, many from local microbreweries. *$$$; AE, DC, DIS, MC, V; no checks; lunch Mon–Fri, dinner every day; full bar; reservations recommended; www.birksrestaurant.com; at Hwy 101 and Great America Pkwy.*

Campbell

RESTAURANTS

Chez Sovan Restaurant / ★★

2425 S BASCOM AVE, CAMPBELL; 408/371-7711 An upscale cousin of the San Jose original, Chez Sovan's Campbell branch features the same authentic Cambodian cuisine and exceptionally friendly service. The stars of the menu are the *samlaws*, Cambodian stews. *Samlaw korko* is a brothy concoction that combines tender chicken with an exotic array of vegetables. Several catfish dishes are offered, too, including a dynamite version with black beans, green onions, vinegar, and loads of fresh ginger.

Skip the house specialty, *amok*—chicken or fish marinated in coconut milk and wrapped in a banana leaf (it may be a little too authentic for untutored Western palates). The fresh salads are packed with cilantro, mint, shredded Napa cabbage, bell peppers, and carrots, plus your choice of chicken, pork, or beef. *$; AE, DIS, MC, V; no checks; lunch, dinner Mon–Sat; beer and wine; reservations recommended; www.chezsovan.comnear; Dry Creek Rd.*

Los Gatos

RESTAURANTS

Cafe Marcella / ★★★

368 VILLAGE LN, LOS GATOS; 408/354-8006 This sophisticated little side-street bistro's flavorful California-Mediterranean cuisine has won a loyal following. The small but provocative menu features individual pastas and a handful of entrees, all supplemented by an ever-changing list of daily specials. Starters range from wild mushroom risotto to foie gras with candied pecans and a fig-port wine compote. Entrees include such interesting fare as pork medallions with sun-dried cherries, swordfish steaks with bok choy, Yukon gold potatoes with a citrus-coconut chili sauce, and rabbit with orange-mustard sauce. And no matter how full you are, order dessert—many locals would argue that Cafe Marcella's are the best around (how about the classic crème brûlée for a taste of the real thing, or perhaps warm bread pudding drizzled with a rich bourbon sauce?). The cafe is also known for its wine list, which offers a host of selections from both local vineyards and European boutique wineries. *$$$; AE, MC, V; no checks; lunch Tues–Sat, dinner Tues–Sun; beer and wine; reservations recommended; www.cafemarcella.com; between Santa Cruz and University Aves.* &

I Gatti / ★★★

25 E MAIN ST, LOS GATOS; 408/399-5180 With its sponge-painted mustard and red-brown walls, weathered wooden shutters, and terra-cotta floor tiles, I Gatti (the Italian counterpart to Los Gatos, Spanish for "the cats"—get it?) evokes a Tuscan patio on a sunny afternoon. Terrific appetizers are *scampi al vino blanco,* goat-cheese ravioli with a rich Chianti-wine glaze, and gnocchi (which can be a little doughy) with a first-rate creamy tomato-vodka sauce. There's a selection of both traditional and unusual salads (try the mixed greens with roasted walnuts, goat cheese, and caramelized onions drizzled with a balsamic pancetta dressing) and *secondi piatti* that include roasted filet mignon with a Barolo wine and wild mushroom sauce, braised lamb shank, and *pollo modo mio* (lightly breaded breast of chicken served with a champagne, lemon-herb, and caper sauce). *$$$; AE, MC, V; checks OK; dinner every day; beer and wine; reservations recommended; near University Ave.*

Los Gatos Brewing Company / ★

130-G N SANTA CRUZ AVE, LOS GATOS; 408/395-9929 This cheery, upscale techno-barn of a restaurant has something for everyone: good, house-made beers and ales for the thirsty, a lively singles scene for the action-oriented, crayons and coloring books for the wee ones, and, most important, good pub fare for the hungry. Executive chef Jim Stump (who formerly graced Birk's in Santa Clara) has created an ambitious menu encompassing everything from pizzas and fresh oysters on the half shell to roasted chicken. You can indulge in a dainty seared ahi tuna salad or give your arteries a workout with the generously portioned pot roast accompanied by hearty root vegetables and mashed potatoes. In-house brewskis include special seasonal brews ranging from nut-brown ale to a German-style wheat beer. *$$; AE, DC, DIS, MC, V; no checks; lunch, dinner every day, brunch Sun; beer and wine; reservations recommended; www.lgbrewingco.com; at Grays Ln.* &

Manresa / ★★★★

320 VILLAGE LANE, LOS GATOS; 408/354-4330 Despite the dot-com collapse in Silicon Valley, a handful of restaurants continue to serve exquisite food at exquisitely high prices. Manresa is one of them. Chef-owner David Kinch, who sold the highly regarded Sent Sovi in Saratoga, has turned his full attention to this year-old restaurant and has already earned a devoted following who swoon over his contemporary American cuisine. Blond wood, muted walls, and cement floors covered with Oriental rugs give the dining room a modern sensibility. But it is evident from the first bite of lychee nut, mint, and condensed-milk granita that it is all about the food here. The unusual combinations of savory and sweet in a less qualified chef's hands could be disastrous, but with Kinch it works—magically. Select from one of three prix-fixe menu options, or try the "seasonal and spontaneous" chef's tasting menu for the ultimate splurge. A recent menu included a remarkable egg dish with fleur de sel and a soft egg topped with maple syrup and sherry vinegar; black olive madeleines sweetened with molasses were equally surprising and tasty. The strawberry gazpacho topped with chives was a bit of a stretch, but a perfectly grilled duck breast surrounded by gold beets and plums was unforgettable. The surprising combinations continue through the dessert menu with Earl Grey ice cream filled with a tart lemon curd; plum polenta cake served with rosemary ice cream; and the more traditional chocolate fondant with cherry compote. The 17-page wine list can be intimidating, but a knowledgeable wait staff is eager to make recommendations. Don't be in a hurry—dinner can easily be a three-hour event here; just relax and savor every bite. *$$$$; MC, V; no checks; dinner daily; beer and wine; reservations recommended; www.manresarestaurant.com; near Santa Cruz Ave.* &

Pigalle / ★★

27 N SANTA CRUZ AVE, LOS GATOS; 408/395-7924 Playing off its name, some Los Gatos residents have affectionately dubbed this French bistro "Pig Alley" because of the generous, reasonably priced portions served here. Although the owners probably wouldn't appreciate that version of their moniker, they can't quibble with the loyalty their top-notch French country cuisine inspires. Named after Paris's red-light district (a mural of a Parisian street scene sets the mood), Pigalle offers a small, interesting menu that changes seasonally. Lunch offerings may range from a seafood fettuccine with scallops and prawns to a chicken pie made with artichoke hearts, mushrooms, and cream sauce. For dinner, tempting entrees may include crisp roast duck in a caramelized orange sauce, braised rabbit with a red wine reduction, or the more unusual grilled fillet of boar served with a rosemary Madeira sauce. Dessert specialties include soufflés and fruit concoctions such as poached pears drenched in a port wine sauce. Reasonably priced prix-fixe menus are available for both lunch and dinner. *$$; MC, V; local checks only; lunch, dinner every day; beer and wine; reservations recommended; www.pigallerestaurant.com; near Main St.*

LODGINGS

Hotel Los Gatos / ★★

210 E MAIN ST, LOS GATOS; 408/335-1700 OR 866/355-1700 Joie de Vivre Hospitality, known for its stylish boutique hotels, has finally come to Los Gatos. Unlike many of this company's ventures, Hotel Los Gatos was built from the ground up and was clearly tailor-made for this upscale suburb. The eclectic decor of Old World baroque–meets–sun-splashed Mediterranean works surprisingly well at this 72-room luxury hotel. Rich, deep-colored fabrics and custom furnishings adorn all of the rooms; a stone-tiled bathroom adjoins each room. The usual amenities are offered along with a heated pool, business services, high-speed Internet access (this is Silicon Valley), and a full-service day spa. Everything is clean and new, and the sophisticated courtyard design features fountains, gardens, and decorative ceramic tile that make you feel like you're in a private villa. Kuleto's Italian restaurant on the ground floor offers well-prepared northern Italian fare and boasts a spacious court-yard ideal for eating alfresco in the summer months. *$$$$; AE, DC, DIS, MC, V; checks OK; www.jdvhospitality.com; between Fiesta Wy and Jackson St.*

Sunnyvale

RESTAURANTS

Il Postale / ★★

127 WASHINGTON ST, SUNNYVALE; 408/733-9600 Set in Sunnyvale's old post office (hence the name), Il Postale is an airy, attractive trattoria with brick walls hung with large framed prints of Italian postal stamps, dark wood bistro furniture set with white linens, and an open kitchen. Although owner Joe Antuzzi insists that his welcoming little restaurant serves Italian-American bistro food, that designation doesn't begin to describe the ambitious menu. Sure, there are plenty of Italian classics (spaghetti puttanesca, linguine with clams, veal braciola, cheese pizza), but the kitchen seems to delight in putting its own twist on some of the standards, tossing grilled boar sausage in wild mushroom risotto; serving veal scaloppini with a sun-dried tomato, caper, and black-olive sauce; even stuffing agnolotti with garlic mashed potatoes (yikes!). And then there are dishes like grilled prawns with soba noodles, defying inclusion on any Italian-American menu we've ever seen. Most of the time this iconoclastic approach works, resulting in a satisfying, interesting meal at a reasonable price. *$$; AE, DC, DIS, MC, V; no checks; lunch Mon–Fri, dinner every day; beer and wine; reservations recommended; www.ilpostale.com; near Murphy Ave.*

Kabul Afghan Cuisine / ★★

833 W EL CAMINO REAL, SUNNYVALE; 408/245-4350 This family-run establishment re-creates the Mediterranean to Southeast Asian tastes of Afghanistan's national cuisine. For a full review, see the Restaurants section of San Carlos. *$$; AE, MC, V; checks OK; lunch Mon–Fri, dinner every day; beer and wine; reservations recommended; at Pastoira St.* &

Mountain View

RESTAURANTS

Amber India Restaurant / ★★

2290 EL CAMINO REAL, MOUNTAIN VIEW; 650/968-7511 Opened in 1995 in a small, unprepossessing shopping center on busy El Camino Real, Amber India offers an escape into a serene, exotic realm. Soft light from brass sconces reflects off rough-textured white stucco walls, partitions and archways divide the space into a series of cozy areas, and wood-and-fabric awnings jut over the central dining room. The staff is solicitous and welcoming, and the food is a cut above the fare typically found in Bay Area Indian restaurants, in terms of both quality and variety. The menu derives its inspiration from several regions of India, resulting in an adventurous selection of exceptionally flavorful yet well-balanced dishes. Appetizers include deep-fried fish pakora, *shami kabab* (lamb patties mixed with lentils and onions), and *reshmi tikka* (marinated and barbecued chicken morsels seasoned with saffron and topped with mint). A large variety of distinctively spiced curries, tandoori selections, and rice dishes rounds out the menu; come with a group so you can order enough items to sample the kitchen's impressive breadth. Intrepid diners can top off their meal with *kulfi* (saffron-flavored ice cream with pistachios) or *gulab jamun* (deep-fried cheese balls drizzled with honey). *$$; AE, DC, DIS, MC, V; no checks; lunch, dinner every day; full bar; reservations recommended; www.amber-india. com; between Rengstorff and Ortega Aves.*

Hangen / ★★

134 CASTRO ST, MOUNTAIN VIEW; 650/964-8881 Mountain View's Castro Street is undeniably saturated with Asian restaurants of all descriptions, but chef Neng Wang's delicate and tasty Sichuan fare still has managed to carve out a distinctive niche. At lunch, Hangen caters to its workday crowd by offering multicourse menus entitled the Executive Lunch and the Business Lunch, both of which provide several choices. At dinner the chef spreads his culinary wings, and the far-ranging menu includes delights such as Emerald Shrimp (shrimp with a spinach-wine sauce perched on a bed of orange slices and lettuce), deep-fried whole fish in a spicy sauce, beef satay, conch salad, tea-smoked duck, and mushrooms in a tangerine zest sauce. Some non-Asian customers grumble about being given a different, smaller menu than their Chinese counterparts, but they're still assured plenty of delicious options. *$$; AE, DC, MC, V; no checks; lunch, dinner every day; beer and wine; reservations recommended; just W of the Central Expwy.*

PARAMOUNT'S GREAT AMERICA

Once the gleaming high-tech, dot-com center of the universe, Santa Clara and other cities in the Silicon Valley are still reeling from one of the most spectacular boom-bust economic cycles in history. With the dot-com meltdown, a steady stream of cutbacks in the high-tech industry, and massive job losses, the landscape has changed dramatically in this once high-powered tech universe. Alongside empty office buildings, though, is one of California's largest and most popular theme parks—**PARAMOUNT'S GREAT AMERICA** (Great America Pkwy between Hwys 101 and 237; 408/988-1776; www.pgathrills.com). If you have kids, it's a must visit. With more than 50 rides, this park has some of the most thrilling roller coasters anywhere (with names like Delirium and Soar on Stealth). For the younger non-thrillseeking set there is also the Nickelodeon park at Great America, filled with favorite characters from the network's popular television shows. A new Australian-themed water park, Boomerang Bay (the size of five football fields!), is in the works and will feature a variety of slides and kiddie splash areas. Be forewarned: It gets very hot during the summer, so pack the sunscreen, hats, and lots of water.

Los Altos

RESTAURANTS

Beauséjour / ★★★

170 STATE ST, LOS ALTOS; 650/948-1382 A downtown gem, Beauséjour (bow-zay-ZHUR, French for "a beautiful visit") presents French cuisine in a charming old building with a European country-house feel. The atmosphere may be a little prim, but the food is executed with rare skill and precision. Traditional favorites are well covered, including escargots in puff pastry and sautéed sweetbreads, but the menu also branches out into unusual, lighter fare. Starters might include pan-seared prawns on a bed of Parmesan mashed potatoes or duck mousse pâté with truffles. The soups are excellent, and the salads range from a very simple medley of mixed baby greens to a tiger prawn salad with grapefruit and red potatoes. The inviting entrees include roasted chicken served on marsala risotto and herbed carrots, calamari steak in a lemon-caper sauce, and filet mignon with a mushroom herb sauce. Beauséjour is also known for its duck with raspberry sauce and lamb with mint sauce and potato timbale. A reasonably priced prix-fixe dinner is offered daily and includes soup or salad, entree, and dessert. *$$$; AE, DIS, MC, V; no checks; lunch Mon–Fri, dinner every day; full bar; reservations recommended; between 3rd and 4th Sts.*

Chef Chu's / ★★

1067 N SAN ANTONIO RD, LOS ALTOS; 650/948-2696 Take a culinary tour of Mainland China without ever leaving your table. Feast on dim sum from

Guangzhou, banquet dishes from Shanghai and Beijing, dumplings and stretched noodles from Xian, and spicy favorites from Sichuan and Hunan—all from the kitchen of Lawrence Chu, the chef-owner who's been expanding the culinary horizons of Los Altos for more than three decades. Chef Chu does all the standards well and offers some delicious innovations of his own, such as wok-seared scallops served in a spicy garlic sauce. Munch on jumbo prawns with candied pecans in a mild mustard sauce. The Peking duck, which must be ordered in advance, is crisp and flawless, with virtually all the fat melted away. *$$; AE, DC, DIS, MC, V; no checks; lunch, dinner every day; full bar; reservations recommended; at El Camino Real.* &

The Peninsula

The Peninsula Q&A:
Q: Are there houses for sale on the Peninsula under $700,000?
A: Not unless you're looking for a one-bedroom fixer-upper barely standing on its last leg.
Q: Will I see one of those artsy, hand-painted VW vans driving the streets of the Peninsula?
A: Only if one is visiting from Berkeley.
Q: Will I be able to fly down Highway 101 at the speed limit anytime I like?
A: Not unless you're driving at midnight.

The Peninsula enjoys a prime location between cosmopolitan San Francisco and the Silicon Valley. As a result, living, eating, and playing there all come at a premium. From the stately mansions on University Avenue in Palo Alto to the sprawling ranch-style homes of Los Altos and the hillside estates of Woodside, the Peninsula wears its prosperity sometimes with restraint, other times with abandon, but always with pride.

With the tech explosion, the Peninsula catapulted past its already posh aura to an almost astronomical exclusivity. Since the dot-com collapse, housing prices have become slightly less prohibitive, but for most remain exorbitant. A television news feature captured the Peninsula's air of privilege best; when viewers were asked to share their most outrageous real estate stories, this one came to the fore. A man was sitting in his house. A real estate agent rang the doorbell, introduced himself, and said, "I have a client in my car. He wants to buy your house. He's willing to offer you $20 million for it." The homeowner, understandably flabbergasted, said, "Sorry, I'm not selling my house," or something to that effect. A few days later the real estate agent returned, telling the man, "My client is now willing to offer you $45 million." Escrow ensued shortly thereafter. That's the Peninsula for ya.

ACCESS AND INFORMATION

SAN FRANCISCO INTERNATIONAL AIRPORT (SFO; 650/876-2377) services both the Peninsula and San Francisco (of course) handily. Well, as handily as can be expected with traffic being what it is. Plan your appointments to allow for jockeying through traffic delays to your final destination. In fact, if at all possible, it would be best not to plan anything of importance to attend to for several hours after you arrive.

Sometimes—OK, frequently—SFO can be blanketed in fog as thick and heavy as a down comforter, so don't be surprised if your takeoff or landing at SFO is delayed, especially if you're arriving on a morning when the white stuff is spilling over the Peninsula hills. Once you've landed, though, you'll find a user-friendly airport layout and plenty of **TAXIS** to spare. **SHUTTLE SERVICES** include Bayporter Express (415/467-1800), Bay Shuttle (415/564-3400), and Super Shuttle (800/258-3826). **CALTRAIN** (800/660-4287) runs train service the length of the Peninsula from Silicon Valley to San Francisco.

TEMPERATURES on the Peninsula are among the coolest in the Bay Area, often by several degrees, due to its close proximity to the chilly Pacific Ocean, so it's advisable to bring a midweight jacket, even in summer; evenings can be on the cool side.

Palo Alto

The home of **STANFORD UNIVERSITY,** notable restaurants, fine-art galleries, foreign-movie houses, great bookstores, a thriving theater troupe, and some of the best shopping this side of heaven, Palo Alto is a beacon of cosmopolitan energy shining on the suburban sea. In spite of the fact that many of the Bay Area's rich-and-maybe-famous call Palo Alto home, much of the fuel for this cultural lighthouse comes from the university, which offers tours of its attractive campus on a fairly regular basis. Highlights of the university include the Main Quad, Hoover Tower (there are great views from its observation platform), the huge bookstore, and gorgeous Memorial Church; call the campus (650/723-2560) for more tour information. If you'd like to try to glimpse some atom smashing, visit the nearby **STANFORD LINEAR ACCELERATOR CENTER;** call 650/926-3300 to arrange a tour.

Moviegoers have a broad range of choices. The beautifully restored **STANFORD THEATER** (221 University Ave; 650/324-3700), which showcases classic flicks, is especially worth a visit. If you prefer your performances live, check out the local **THEATREWORKS** troupe (650/463-1950), the **LIVELY ARTS** series at Stanford University (650/725-2787), or the top-name talents currently appearing at the **SHORELINE AMPHITHEATER** (1 Amphitheater Pkwy, Mountain View; 650/967-3000).

If you have nothing to wear for the show (or, indeed, if you have any other shopping need), Palo Alto won't let you down. **UNIVERSITY AVENUE** and its side streets contain a plethora of interesting stores. The **STANFORD SHOPPING CENTER** (N of downtown on El Camino Real; 650/617-8585) is a sprawling, beautifully landscaped temple of consumerism (stores include Bloomingdales, Macy's, Nordstrom, Ralph Lauren, the Gap, Crate & Barrel, and many more). Good places to eat in this shoppers' paradise include Bravo Fono, Oakville Grocery, Max's Opera Cafe, and LongLife Noodle Company (avoid the handsome but substandard branch of Piatti).

Although several locally owned bookstores have closed their doors, Palo Alto and its neighbors still offer some good outlets for bibliophiles. **KEPLER'S BOOKS AND MAGAZINES** (1010 El Camino Real, Menlo Park; 650/324-4321) is a wonderland for serious bookworms, and you'll find a healthy selection of mind food at

BORDERS BOOKS (456 University Ave; 650/326-3670) and **BOOKS INC.** (at the Stanford Shopping Center, on El Camino Real near University Ave; 650/321-0600).

You'll probably need to follow that literary excursion with a cup of joe. Some of the bookstores, such as Borders, serve coffee and light snacks, but for authentic coffeehouse atmosphere and great espresso try **CAFFE VERONA** (236 Hamilton Ave; 650/326-9942) or **CAFE BORRONE** (1010 El Camino Real, Menlo Park; 650/327-0830), located right next to Kepler's.

RESTAURANTS

Bistro Elan / ★★★

448 CALIFORNIA AVE, PALO ALTO; 650/327-0284 This natty little bistro, open since 1995, is one of the best and brightest to emerge in the California Avenue area. Although many of the offerings would be at home in any classic French bistro (duck confit, grilled pork tenderloin, lamb ragout), chef/co-owner Ambjörn Lindskog is not averse to taking cues from California cuisine. You'll find such seemingly disparate appetizers as sautéed Sonoma foie gras on brioche with oranges and arugula in hazelnut oil or fresh Maine crab with cucumber, mango, avocado, and a honey-and-coriander vinaigrette. Entrees might range from duck with English pea and Parmesan risotto to sautéed California swordfish with sweet corn, okra, and Yukon gold potatoes. Desserts include such diverse creations as a stellar warm orange chocolate cake with whipped cream, a trio of tropical fruit ice creams topped with vanilla-butter sauce, and fresh-baked cookies and cupcakes. *$$$; AE, DC, MC, V; no checks; lunch Tues–Fri, dinner Tues–Sat; beer and wine; reservations recommended; just off El Camino Real.* &

Evvia / ★★★

420 EMERSON ST, PALO ALTO; 650/326-0983 This warm and welcoming restaurant has a sun-drenched, Mediterranean feel. Colored bottles, ceramic plates, and copper pots line the walls and the mantel of an imposing fireplace; beaded light fixtures cast a golden glow; and wooden beams and a planked oak floor add handsome rustic accents. Traditional Greek dishes have succumbed to California's culinary charms here, resulting in an emphasis on fresh produce and interesting twists on traditional dishes such as moussaka and Greek salad. Fish and pasta dishes are other good choices, and if leg of lamb is offered as a special, order it—the meat is exceptionally tender and juicy and comes flanked by some fine roasted potatoes and vegetables. Good desserts include the baklava and the chocolate torte. Order a traditional Greek coffee to top off your meal. *$$$; AE, DC, DIS, MC, V; no checks; lunch Mon–Fri, dinner every day; full bar; reservations recommended; www.evvia.net; between Lytton and University Aves.* &

Higashi West / ★★

636 EMERSON ST, PALO ALTO; 650/323-9378 It's East meets West at this small, slick restaurant, where lamb chops are marinated in shallots and plum wine and mashed potatoes are infused with wasabi. Some people will delight in the experimentation (the success of the wasabi mashed potatoes is an especially happy surprise); others might wonder what the heck they're smoking in the kitchen. The space

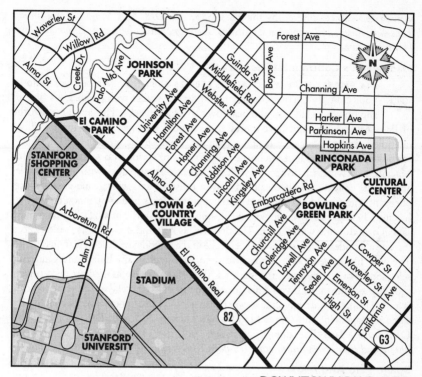

DOWNTOWN PALO ALTO

is a bit loud and cramped and service can be slow, but adventuresome eaters will forgive all that. The murmur of the wall-mounted sculptural fountain, the stands of black bamboo, and the modern paintings help create a pleasing, sophisticated setting for the unusual fare. There's an excellent but expensive sushi bar and about 30 varieties of sake to sip. *$$$; AE, DC, DIS, MC, V; no checks; dinner Mon–Sat; full bar; reservations recommended; between Hamilton and Forest Aves.*

L'Amie Donia / ★★★

530 BRYANT ST, PALO ALTO; 650/323-7614 One of the first superstar chefs to desert San Francisco for the Peninsula, Donia Bijan, whose résumé includes the Sherman House and Brasserie Savoy, opened this amiable, bustling French bistro and wine bar in the summer of 1994. Expect traditional favorites from her seasonally changing menu such as onion soup, galantine of duck, and steak bordelaise with pommes frites, dished up in a pleasant space dominated by a zinc bar and a battery of banquettes covered in burgundy and green fabric reminiscent of a wine-country harvest. In keeping with her reputation, Bijan renders her traditional fare with a light touch, allowing diners to save room for one of her superb desserts, such as the celebrated tarte Tatin with vanilla ice cream. She has instituted an imaginative wine list, equally divided between California and French varietals, with several of the

139

well-priced choices offered by the glass. *$$$; AE, DIS, MC, V; no checks; dinner Tues–Sat; beer and wine; reservations recommended; between University and Hamilton Aves.*

Maddalena's Continental Restaurant / ★★★

544 EMERSON ST, PALO ALTO; 650/326-6082 If your mood is romantic, your culinary craving continental, and your wallet well padded, it's time to slip on your glad rags and head over to Maddalena's. This longtime favorite of Palo Alto's haves and have-mores is a splendid example of a dying breed: an unapologetically classic continental restaurant. The lush decor exudes an Old World formality, and waiters in tuxes hover about, ready to spring into service. Chef Jaime Maciel excels with veal dishes and such opulent fare as crisp duck with juniper berries and cassis, delicate poached salmon with a mustard-and-white-wine cream sauce, pheasant with Grand Marnier, and steak au poivre. If it's pasta you fancy, try the Fettuccine Chef Maciel (with smoked duck, spinach, and garlic in a light Roma tomato sauce) or fettuccine with lobster. The desserts, as rich and decadent as you'd expect, include a wonderful house-made cheesecake and a three-layer chocolate mousse cake. The wine list, tipped toward expensive vintages, offers mostly Italian and California selections. For a romantic surprise, book the beautifully appointed art deco private room for two upstairs. If you'd like to sample this Palo Alto classic but your bankroll is a little thin, try Cafe Fino, the less-expensive Italian bistro next door, which has the same management and shares Maddalena's kitchen. *$$$; AE, DC, MC, V; checks OK; lunch Tues–Fri, dinner Mon–Sat; full bar; reservations recommended; www.maddelenasrestaurant.com; between University and Hamilton Aves.*

Spago Palo Alto / ★★★

265 LYTTON AVE, PALO ALTO; 650/833-1000 When Jeremiah Tower and his business partners opened Stars Palo Alto in 1995, it was an undeniable signal that the increasingly sophisticated Peninsula/South Bay restaurant scene had truly come of age. But plagued by management problems, poor service, uneven food, and a dizzying succession of short-lived head chefs (Tower left after just a few months), Stars Palo Alto never quite caught on. Enter Wolfgang Puck. Puck took one look at the dazzling restaurant—and declared that he at last had found the perfect site for his first Northern California outpost since unveiling the highly regarded Postrio in San Francisco in 1989. Spago Palo Alto opened in December 1997, boasting an exhibition kitchen, a remodeled formal dining room, a separate casual cafe and bar area, and a menu featuring American cuisine with European and Asian influences. And, as at most Puck enterprises, you won't see the celebrity chef in the kitchen very often. Instead, you'll find chef Aram Mardigian, who has worked at several of Puck's restaurants in Los Angeles and Chicago. Mardigian stays the California-Asian course, but he adds a healthy dose of Mediterranean to the menu: some of his standouts include duck spring rolls with plum chutney and toasted brioche, sautéed shrimp with spicy pad thai noodles in a coconut curry sauce, and pan-roasted chicken with goat cheese pasta, smoked tomatoes, and broccoli rabe. Be sure to top off the memorable meal with a superb chocolate-filled crepe topped with vanilla ice cream. *$$$; AE, DC, DIS, MC, V; no checks; lunch Mon–Fri, dinner every day; full bar; reservations recommended; between Bryant and Ramona Sts.*

Tamarine / ★★★

546 UNIVERSITY AVE, PALO ALTO; 650/325-8500 If you think the only way to enjoy Vietnamese food is at your favorite hole-in-the wall where you resort to pointing to menu items because you don't speak Vietnamese, think again. Upscale Vietnamese restaurants are popping up everywhere, and one of the best is the stylish and hip Tamarine in downtown Palo Alto. Owners Anne Le and Tammy Huyhn learned the trade at their family business, Vung Tau in San Jose and Milpitas, and have created an exciting concept that includes everything from a stunningly designed space showcasing the works of Vietnamese artists to exquisitely fresh, inventive food. The small plates are meant to be shared; some of the best include shrimp cupcakes made with crispy rice flour and coconut milk; juicy shaking beef served on a mound of watercress; perfectly seared ahi tuna salad over green papaya; and spicy mango and noodles topped with lemongrass sea bass. Several infused rices, such as a ginger and garlic, coconut, or coriander, are available to mix and match with the wide range of flavors. For an unconventional dessert, try the chocolate-filled wontons. *$$; AE, DC, DIS, MC, V; no checks; lunch Mon–Fri, dinner every day; full bar; reservations recommended; www.tamarinerestaurant.com; between Webster and Cowper Sts.*

LODGINGS

The Garden Court Hotel / ★★★

520 COWPER ST, PALO ALTO; 650/322-9000 OR 800/824-9028 If you like elegance, pampering, and a happening location (well, some people may not), this is a darn good place to stay. A flower-laden courtyard, providing the balcony view for most of the 62 rooms, is surrounded by Italianate architecture draped with arches and studded with colorful tile work and hand-wrought iron fixtures. The Mediterranean modern rooms are tinted in pastel shades of green, peach, and violet; most have four-poster beds, white faux-marble furniture, and thickly cushioned couches. The suites approach decadence; the penthouse, for example, has a fireplace, a whirlpool bath, and a wet bar. All the little details are covered in style, from an exercise room to terry-cloth robes to complimentary copies of the *Wall Street Journal*. Complimentary fresh Bing cherries and iced tea are offered to guests in the summer, and hot apple cider takes the chill off weary travelers in the winter. The hotel is in a good shopping and nightlife area, just off University Avenue, and room service is available from Il Fornaio restaurant, which shares the building. *$$$$; AE, DC, MC, V; checks OK; www.gardencourt.com; between University and Hamilton Aves.* &

Menlo Park

RESTAURANTS

Carpaccio / ★★

1120 CRANE ST, MENLO PARK; 650/322-1211 Carpaccio was started by the same folks responsible for the wildly successful Osteria in Palo Alto, but a parting of the ways has left this restaurant to evolve along its own lines. Carpaccio holds tightly to its northern Italian roots, as evidenced by such dishes as the grilled polenta with tomatoes and pesto and the restaurant's namesake dish, served with onions, capers, lemon, and mustard, plus a grating of grana cheese and a drizzle of olive oil. The real treat here is the free-range veal: the scaloppine features veal medallions and mushrooms, but those in search of the platonic veal ideal should choose the simple grilled chop. Also keep an eye out for the prosciutto-wrapped grilled prawns with garlic and shallots in a smooth lemon-cream sauce. The wood-burning oven (with bricks imported from Italy) turns out divine pizzas with premium toppings laced together with fresh mozzarella, Gorgonzola, and fennel sausage on wonderful smoke-flavored crusts. *$$; AE, DC, MC, V; no checks; lunch Mon–Fri, dinner every day; full bar; reservations recommended; www.carpaccios.com; between Oak Grove and Santa Cruz Aves.*

Dal Baffo / ★★

878 SANTA CRUZ AVE, MENLO PARK; 650/325-1588 A dignified fixture on the Peninsula dining scene for more than 20 years, Dal Baffo serves classic continental cuisine in a plush, old-fashioned setting. This is the type of place where tuxedo-clad waiters whip up Caesar salads tableside while the kitchen delights traditionalists with its competent renderings of classic French and Italian dishes. The pasta, lamb, and beef entrees tend to be especially good; if you're in the mood for a magnificent hunk of meat, knife into the filet mignon served over grilled portobello mushrooms with a cabernet wine sauce. The award-winning wine list is four inches thick and contains rare (not to mention incredibly expensive) selections that will make a connoisseur's heart go pitter-pat. *$$$; AE, DC, DIS, MC, V; no checks; lunch Mon–Sat, dinner ever day; full bar; reservations recommended; www.dalbaffo.com; at University Ave.*

Marché / ★★★

898 SANTA CRUZ AVE, MENLO PARK; 650/324-9092 If you are looking for bizarre flights of food fancy, you won't find them here; Marché ("market" in French) offers refined, straightforward French-inspired food in a sophisticated and elegant setting. The modern dining room with its pale yellow walls, burgundy banquettes, and dark wainscoting is formal but inviting. Chef-owner Howard Bulka's confident cooking style shines in his weekly-changing menu that relies heavily on whatever is fresh at the market. Recent starters included a crispy soft-shell crab with citrus slaw and chile dipping sauce; a very rich sweet corn soup with lobster garnish; and an heirloom tomato salad with house-made pita bread and hummus. Competent wait staff seem to magically appear with impeccably prepared entrees, such as a juicy pan-roasted pork chop served with colorful spiced peach chutney; a guinea hen sautéed with bacon, pearl onions, and mushrooms; and a nine-spice lamb sirloin simply cooked in a red wine sauce and served with grilled polenta and rosemary-glazed carrots. Bulka began his culinary career as a pastry chef—which explains why his classic Paris-Brest of cream puff pastry and almond praline custard is downright dreamy, and the lemon tart is made with the sweetest, freshest lemon curd you will ever taste. Prices are high, but that doesn't seem to faze the predominately older clientele who frequent this upscale establishment. *$$$$; AE, DC, DIS, MC, V; no checks; dinner Tues–Sat; full bar; reservations recommended; at University Ave.*

LODGINGS

Stanford Park Hotel / ★★★

100 EL CAMINO REAL, MENLO PARK; 650/322-1234 OR 800/368-2468 Cedar shingles, dormer windows, serene courtyards, and a copper-clad gabled roof distinguish this gracious low-rise hotel near Stanford University, just a credit card's throw from the wonderful Stanford Shopping Center. Some of the 163 rooms have fireplaces, balconies, vaulted ceilings, courtyard views, or parlors, and all are appointed with handsome English-style furniture and splashed with accents of green and mauve— a pleasant change from the timid beige-and-pastel color schemes found in so many other executive-class hotels. The Stanford Park provides a fitness room, a sauna, a heated pool, and a spa for its guests, as well as complimentary newspapers, morning coffee, turndown service, fresh-baked cookies, and shuttle service within the Menlo Park–Palo Alto area. For business travelers, high-speed Internet access is available. The Duck Club restaurant serves good American regional cuisine and, appropriately enough, duck is the specialty of the house. Guests can dine or enjoy an evening cocktail outside in the serene courtyard. *$$$$; AE, DC, DIS, MC, V; checks OK; www.stanfordparkhotel.com; just N of University Ave.* &

Woodside

RESTAURANTS

Buck's / ★★

3062 WOODSIDE RD, WOODSIDE; 650/851-8010 Since it opened in 1991, Jamis MacNiven's cheery and eccentric restaurant has become one of the most unlikely spots for power breakfasts in all of Silicon Valley and the Peninsula. Where else can you find high-profile execs, entrepreneurs, and venture capitalists cutting deals as they chow down on huevos rancheros and silver-dollar pancakes under brightly painted cowboy hat lamps, while life-size marlin figurines, a 6-foot plaster Statue of Liberty, and a flying horse look on? Most of the design touches—including palomino-colored walls, rows of natty cowboy boots, and a portrait of Mona Lisa decked out in a Stetson and bandanna—play into a tongue-in-cheek Western motif, a good fit in this wealthy, horsey community. The food, however, is a cut above chuckwagon fare. Breakfast includes tasty and well-prepared renditions of the usual muffins, waffles, egg dishes, and the like; lunch ranges from chili to hot Dungeness crab sandwiches; and dinner features a freewheeling menu that has everything from Yankee pot roast to chicken piccata "so tender it will sing you to sleep" (it says so right on the mock-newspaper-style menu). *$$; AE, DIS, MC, V; no checks; breakfast, lunch, dinner every day; full bar; reservations recommended; www.buckswoodside. com; near Canada Rd.*

John Bentley's Restaurant / ★★★

2991 WOODSIDE RD, WOODSIDE; 650/851-4988 Housed in Woodside's first firehouse, John Bentley's resembles a snug cabin inside and out. But this is a classy kind of rustic, with wood paneling on the ceiling and walls, a potbellied stove, dangling light fixtures with ribbed-glass shades, chair backs fashioned out of verdigris wrought-iron leaves, and a brown-and-green color scheme that heightens the mountain-retreat mood. In keeping with the atmosphere of backwoods elegance, chef-owner Bentley serves fare that's bold yet refined and generously laced with rarefied ingredients: lobster-ginger wontons in a delicate broth, ravioli stuffed with artichokes and caramelized onions, medallions of venison with shiitakes and braised red cabbage. With options like apple tart with sun-dried-cherry ice cream and a milk chocolate crème brûlée so smooth it seemingly lacks molecules, desserts are a must here. *$$$; AE, MC, V; local checks only; lunch Tues–Sat, dinner Tues–Sun; beer and wine; reservations recommended; www.johnbentleys.com; between Hwy 280 and Canada Rd.* &

The Village Pub / ★★★

2967 WOODSIDE RD, WOODSIDE; 650/851-1294 Don't let the name mislead you: this pub in the hills of Woodside is hardly typical of the genre—unless you're used to encountering a parking lot full of Mercedeses, Jaguars, and BMWs in front of your favorite watering hole. You won't exactly find bangers and mash on the menu either—think refined American cuisine served in a modern, elegant setting. A couple of years ago this longtime neighborhood haunt closed and reopened in its new downstairs location. The refurbished room with dark wainscoting and Bordeaux-colored booths and chairs has a warm and luxurious feel to it. Even the bar with its limestone fireplace is homey and inviting. Chef Mark Sullivan has created an inspired menu with starters that include a selection of house-cured charcuterie, decadent sweetbreads inventively prepared with poached eggs and a brown-butter vinaigrette, and a smooth-as-silk gazpacho. Only a handful of entrees are offered nightly; some intriguing choices include seared rare ahi with Provençal vegetables and toasted almonds or roasted duck breast with a rich demi-glace sauce and zucchini blossom beignets. Or you can share sorrel roasted chicken served over a fragrant saffron risotto and field greens prepared for two. A number of good California and European wines are offered by the glass, and the expert sommelier is ready to assist. Living up to its name, the Village offers a pub menu with an $11 burger, duck confit, and other not-so standard pub fare. *$$$; AE, DC, DIS, MC, V; no checks; lunch Mon–Fri, dinner every day; full bar; reservations recommended; 1 mile W of Hwy 280.*

Redwood City

LODGINGS

Hotel Sofitel San Francisco Bay / ★★★

223 TWIN DOLPHIN DR, REDWOOD CITY; 650/598-9000 OR 800/763-4835 This gray behemoth perched in a corporate park is distinguished by its pretty setting on a man-made lagoon and Gallic touches provided by the French management: filigreed ironwork above the entrance, old-fashioned Parisian street lamps scattered throughout the property, and a staff endowed with charming accents. The 319 spacious guest rooms are decorated in a French country motif and feature blond-wood furniture and amenities like desks, TVs, voice mail, imported toiletries, minibars, and turndown service. The lobby and restaurants boast a large sweep of windows that take full advantage of the Sofitel's waterfront location, and the hotel is equipped with a workout room, a par course, a health and beauty spa, and an outdoor pool. French regional food is served all day at the casual Gigi Brasserie, while the formal and well-regarded Baccarat restaurant specializes in classic French cuisine. *$$$$; AE, DC, MC, V; checks OK; www.hotelsofitelsfbay.com; turn on Shoreline Dr to reach the hotel's entrance.* &

San Carlos

RESTAURANTS

Creo La. / ★★★

344 EL CAMINO REAL, SAN CARLOS; 650/654-0882 It took awhile for this restaurant serving terrific New Orleans–style food to catch on in San Carlos, but now that the food-savvy know to ignore its inauspicious El Camino Real location and humble facade, Creo La. has come into its own. After working six years in the kitchen, chefs Edwin Caba and Robin Simmons bought the restaurant from original owner Bud Deslatte. This team knows how to craft a menu that ably represents the new, lighter side of Creole and Cajun cooking. They go right to the source for many of their dishes, flying out andouille sausage, Gulf shrimp, and several other top-notch ingredients from Louisiana. For appetizers, try the Shrimp Bourbon Street (lightly battered, flash-fried prawns served with a tangy orange marmalade–horseradish sauce), Satchmo's Special (red beans and rice with andouille sausage rings), or the crawfish hush puppies with rémoulade. Interesting salads are served, too, including a Caesar topped with bacon-wrapped fried oysters. The list of entrees includes everything from alligator piccata and pan-blackened catfish to chicken with corn-bread stuffing and crawfish étouffée. Creo La.'s lineup of desserts includes a not-to-be-missed silky Cajun Velvet Pie with a light-as-air peanut butter mousse filling. *$$; AE, DC, DIS, MC, V; no checks; dinner every day; beer and wine; reservations recommended; just N of Holly St.* &

Kabul Afghan Cuisine / ★★

135 EL CAMINO REAL, SAN CARLOS; 650/594-2840 Afghanistan's national cuisine has roots ranging from the Mediterranean to Southeast Asia. This family-run establishment re-creates these tastes for Northern California with the highest-quality ingredients, including well-marbled meats along with spices the owners procure on trips to Asia and the Middle East. Set in a corner of a small shopping center, Kabul's spacious interior is unexpectedly atmospheric, with glimmering, candlelit, whitewashed stucco walls studded with bright Afghani tapestries and costumes; pink and white tablecloths; and the low whine of sitar music discreetly in the background. The management and servers are charming and attentive (even when you wander in with children—the true test of a place's friendliness quotient). A few dishes shouldn't be missed: the fragrant charbroiled lamb chops marinated in yogurt, olive oil, fresh garlic, and black and white pepper; the splendid sautéed pumpkin topped with yogurt and a tomato-based ground-beef sauce; and *aushak* (leek-and-onion-filled dumplings topped with yogurt and a meat sauce). First-timers might enjoy Kabul's combination platter for lunch—a generous sampler of three popular appetizers. Another Kabul restaurant run by the same family is located in Sunnyvale. *$$; AE, DC, MC, V; checks OK; lunch Mon–Fri, dinner every day; beer and wine; reservations recommended; in the San Carlos Plaza, between Holly St and Harbor Blvd.*

San Mateo

RESTAURANTS

Lark Creek Cafe / ★★

50 E 3RD AVE, SAN MATEO; 650/344-9444 In 1996, uber-chef Bradley Ogden expanded his Lark Creek Inn empire by opening this inviting, casual-chic cafe on San Mateo's main drag. The Lark Creek has continued the tradition of serving what Ogden likes to call "seasonal farm-fresh American fare," a concept that translates into updated versions of such stick-to-your-ribs dishes as fried chicken, pot roast and mashed potatoes, and spiral pasta with green beans, pesto, and goat-cheese ricotta. You'll also find burgers, pizza, sandwiches, salads, and Ogden's justly celebrated onion rings with blue-cheese dipping sauce. Lark Creek prides itself on scouring the local produce markets for the best raw ingredients. The smartly designed dining room, with its whimsical collection of gaily painted birdhouses, lark-bedecked light fixtures, roomy booths, and long bar counter, sports an inviting country-sophisticate look, and service is polished and friendly. The wine list is carefully chosen and concentrates on California selections. Another branch of this cafe is located in Walnut Creek. *$$; AE, DC, DIS, MC, V; no checks; lunch, dinner every day; full bar; reservations recommended; www.larkcreek.com; near El Camino Real, in the Benjamin Franklin Hotel.*

Ristorante Capellini / ★★

310 BALDWIN AVE, SAN MATEO; 650/348-2296 Opened in 1990, this dapper trilevel restaurant designed by (who else?) Pat Kuleto was one of the first to bring big-city sophistication to San Mateo's dining scene. The antipasto, fried calamari, and *insalata con pera* (a seasonal salad of pears, endive, radicchio, arugula, pine nuts, and Gorgonzola in a champagne-shallot vinaigrette) make excellent starters. You might move on to one of the imaginative thin-crust pizzas or to entrees such as sole piccata, veal Milanese, or steak with a merlot-mushroom sauce. The pasta is usually excellent here, light and cooked al dente; the long lineup includes linguine with assorted seafood; four-cheese ravioli in a lemon-pesto cream sauce; and penne with pancetta, tomatoes, garlic, mushrooms, and smoked mozzarella. The creamy tiramisu ranks as the most popular dessert, but the *torta di limone* and the warm bread pudding served with brandy hard sauce and a scoop of vanilla gelato are also winners. *$$$; AE, DC, MC, V; no checks; lunch Mon–Fri, dinner every day; full bar; reservations recommended; www.capellinis.com; at the corner of South B St.*

Spiedo Ristorante / ★★

233 4TH AVE, SAN MATEO; 650/375-0818 Good Italian regional fare is served in an attractive, modern setting at this family-friendly restaurant. The owners are justly proud of their mesquite-fired rotisserie, from which emerge herb-kissed and succulent chicken, game hen, rabbit, and duck. Savvy choices from the grill include the salmon, lamb chops, and pork cutlets. The kitchen also has a pleasant way with pasta, turning out delicate noodles flavored by interesting sauces; the fettuccine with prawns, green peas, and basil and the *tortelloni di ànitra* (hat-shaped pasta filled with duck and zucchini in a sun-dried tomato and wild mushroom cream sauce) are two winners. Pizzas are quite good here, too. When it's time for dessert, forsake the unremarkable gelato and opt for the tiramisu—the raspberry sauce gives this old standard an unexpected twist. *$$; AE, DC, DIS, MC, V; no checks; lunch Mon–Sat, dinner every day; full bar; reservations recommended; www.spiedo.com; between Ellsworth and B Sts.*

231 Ellsworth / ★★★

231 S ELLSWORTH, SAN MATEO; 650/347-7231 In 2000, this upscale restaurant that caters to the refined palates of old-money Peninsulites from Hillsborough and other tony suburbs endured a major overhaul—everything from new ownership to an entire remodel. The 20-year-old pink and aqua color scheme gave way to beautiful custom built-in cabinetry, soft lighting, and a dramatic blue vaulted ceiling. The food also changed; fortunately, the mostly American menu continues to feature fresh seasonal produce and inspired offerings like marinated baby beets with ricotta salata and house-made potato gnocchi. A duck breast served with foie gras and rhubarb; roasted halibut with English pea and leek stew and caviar; and pork tenderloin with Walla Walla onion purée and summer truffles are typical of the complex, compelling entrees. Primo desserts include light and airy sugar-and-spice brioche doughnuts with rhubarb marmalade and buttermilk *panna cotta,* and a delicate warm chocolate fondant bathed in an unusual caramel and fleur de sel sauce—heaven on a plate. The prodigious cellar offers more than 800 fine wines from Europe and California. Service is usually impeccable, although when the restaurant gets packed, the pace of the meal can sometimes be measured in geologic time. You'll also find three-, five- or seven-course prix-fixe dinner menus that are not outrageously priced. *$$$; AE,*

DC, DIS, MC, V; checks OK; lunch Mon–Fri, dinner Mon–Sat; full bar; reservations recommended; www.231ellsworth.com; between 2nd and 3rd Aves.

Burlingame

RESTAURANTS

Kuleto's / ★★

1095 ROLLINS RD, BURLINGAME; 650/342-4922 A spin-off of the popular San Francisco restaurant that bears the same name, this Burlingame branch immediately became one of the area's see-and-be-seen places when it opened in 1993. The sophisticated decor (which isn't, believe it or not, a product of the restaurant's namesake, designer Pat Kuleto) is bright and lively, with expanses of polished wood, a smattering of booths swathed in handsome fabrics, a large wood-burning oven, and a multilevel dining area. Alas, the northern Italian food is not always as winning as the environment—it's not uncommon to see a diner swooning with ecstasy over a meal while her companion complains about his disappointing dish. Reliable selections include baby spinach salad with crispy pancetta and goat cheese; penne with house-made lamb sausage; or roasted duck with soft polenta, braised cabbage, and grappa-soaked cherry sauce. However, the staff is often helpful about steering you through the menu's shoals, and the pizzas, salads, and many of the roast meats and pasta selections are noteworthy. *$$; AE, DC, DIS, MC, V; no checks; lunch Mon–Fri, dinner every day; full bar; reservations recommended; www.kuletos trattoria.com; just W of Hwy 101.*

LODGINGS

Embassy Suites San Francisco Airport–Burlingame / ★★★

150 ANZA BLVD, BURLINGAME; 650/342-4600 OR 800/EMBASSY This hotel's a towering pink-and-aqua spectacle more typical of the sunny Southland than Northern California. In front, a cobblestone drive encircles a Spanish-style fountain; just inside, another fountain gurgles in front of the junglelike atrium. Each of the 340 suites has a private bedroom and a separate living room complete with a refrigerator, a wet bar, a coffeemaker, a microwave, two color televisions, two telephones, and a pullout sofa bed. Ask for a room overlooking San Francisco Bay. You can amuse yourself by lounging in the indoor swimming pool or by checking out the action at R Rings, a popular singles bar and restaurant specializing in hearty fare like steaks, ribs, and chops. *$$$; AE, DC, DIS, MC, V; no checks; www.embassy burlingame.com; just off Hwy 101.* &

Millbrae

RESTAURANTS

Hong Kong Flower Lounge / ★★★

51 MILLBRAE AVE, MILLBRAE; 650/878-8108 Hong Kong, probably the world's most competitive culinary arena, has hundreds of excellent restaurants vying to produce the freshest, subtlest, and most exciting flavors. In 1987 Alice Wong, whose family owns four Flower Lounges in and around that city, expanded their empire to California with a small restaurant on Millbrae's main drag (which was recently sold). Its success prompted her to open another, fancier branch on Millbrae Avenue. Fortunately, the food at the Millbrae location has remained legendary, thanks largely to the Hong Kong chefs, who continue to produce cuisine according to the stringent standards of their home city. The red, gold, and jade decor is pure Kowloon glitz (although the patrons are comfortably informal), and the service is outstanding. Among the best dishes on the vast menu are the exquisite minced squab in lettuce cups, the delicate crystal scallops in shrimp sauce, the fried prawns with walnuts, and any fish fresh from the live tank. An excellent Peking duck is served at a moderate price. *$$; AE, DC, DIS, MC, V; no checks; lunch, dinner every day; full bar; reservations recommended; at El Camino Real (Millbrae Ave).*

LODGINGS

Inn at Oyster Point / ★★

425 MARINA BLVD, MILLBRAE; 650/737-7633 This small, pleasant hotel works hard to accentuate the positive (attractive, well-appointed rooms, a spectacular bay setting) and diminish the negative (the fact that you have to wade through an industrial park to get here). In keeping with its marina setting, the modern, Cape Cod–style inn is decked out in a snappy nautical-looking blue-and-white color scheme, and the 30 guest rooms have bay views, featherbeds, and tile fireplaces. A continental breakfast is included in the price of the room, and there's free shuttle service to nearby San Francisco International Airport (by prior arrangement). A branch of Dominic's Italian restaurant occupies part of the first floor, and its deck overlooks the marina and is a great place for lunch on a warm day. *$$$; AE, DC, DIS, MC, V; no checks; www.innatoysterpoint.com; take the Oyster Pt Blvd exit off Hwy 101, head toward the bay, and turn right at Marina Blvd.*

CENTRAL COAST

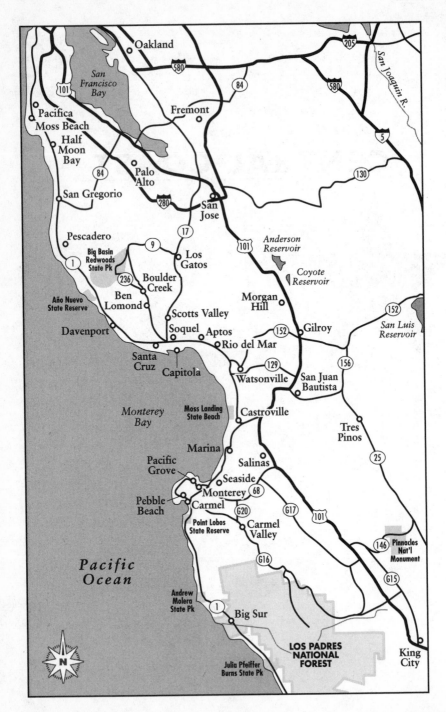

CENTRAL COAST

With its dramatic coastlines, farmlands, forests, and unique small towns, Northern California's Central Coast offers up breathtaking beauty with laid-back style. Even though it's easily accessible from either San Francisco or Southern California, the Central Coast feels as though it's taken a time-out from the rush and noise of the rest of the world. It's the perfect place to spend hours collecting seashells or listening to the silence of the redwood trees, and you won't have to worry about bumping elbows with anyone. With 16 state and national parks, there's more than enough nature to go around.

The largest park on the Central Coast is one you might not see up close, unless you take a fishing or whale-watching excursion from Half Moon Bay, Santa Cruz, or Monterey, but its influence and importance is felt everywhere here. The **MON-TEREY BAY MARINE SANCTUARY,** established in 1992, is a vast biologic conservatory that stretches from the mouth of the San Francisco Bay in the north to the tip of Big Sur in the south, encompassing one-fifth of California's coastline and covering 5,300 square miles. Monterey Canyon, the most dramatic submarine feature of the sanctuary, is more than 10,000 feet deep and rivals the Grand Canyon in size and topographic complexity. The nutrient-enriched seawater that upwells from its steep walls draws in more than 30 species of marine mammals, making it one of the Northern Hemisphere's most diversified underwater areas. On land, the Central Coast is dotted with beach towns, farm communities, and vacation destinations; underwater, it's an international hub.

ACCESS AND INFORMATION

Northern California's Central Coast includes nearly 400 miles of shoreline, from Pacifica in the north to Big Sur in the south. **HIGHWAY 1,** also named the **CABRILLO HIGHWAY** after the first Spanish explorer to lay claim to the land, is a scenic two-lane highway that meanders all along the coast, connecting with **HIGHWAY 92** at Half Moon Bay, **HIGHWAY 17** at Santa Cruz, and **HIGHWAY 101** near Monterey. The Central Coast's inland valleys are served by Highway 101, but anyone traveling the inland route from San Francisco will want to take **HIGHWAY 280** to avoid commuter traffic on the 101 San Francisco–San Jose stretch.

SAN FRANCISCO INTERNATIONAL AIRPORT (SFO) (650/821-8211; www.flysfo.com) offers passengers the largest international terminal in the nation, while visitors to points south—Santa Cruz to Big Sur—will appreciate the convenience of **SAN JOSE INTERNATIONAL AIRPORT** (408/277-4759; www.sjc.org). It's smaller than SFO and less congested but offers many of the same flights as its larger cousin to the north. **CAR RENTALS** are available at both airports and in the larger cities, such as Santa Cruz and Monterey.

With a rainy season that lasts from November through March, and an average daily temperature of 60°F—that's year-round—no one's ever going to confuse the Central Coast with Malibu. During spring and summer, offshore breezes strip away the warm surface waters of the Pacific and bring frigid waters to the top. The result is a heavy marine layer (a.k.a. fog) that settles over the coast morning and evening. It's always wise to carry a sweater, as summer can be just as blustery as winter. This might not be everyone's idea of perfect beach weather, but when summer temps scorch the valleys there's a massive influx of cool-ocean-breeze worshippers. The best months are September and October, when the crowds disappear along with the fog.

Half Moon Bay Region

With the exception of Half Moon Bay, the picturesque stretch of shore between Moss Beach and Año Nuevo has been left undisturbed by development (thanks in part to the often blustery weather hereabouts). This lack of super-luxe lodgings is a boon to nature lovers, as many of the beaches are open to the public. Check out the marine life at Moss Beach's Fitzgerald Reserve, or pay a visit to the elephant seals' breeding ground at Año Nuevo.

ACCESS AND INFORMATION

The fastest way to the Half Moon Bay region from San Francisco is to take the Highway 92 exit off Interstate 280, which leads straight into town. Far more scenic, however, is the drive along Highway 1, which, aside from the section known as Devils Slide, moves right along at a 50mph clip. The entrance to Half Moon Bay's Main Street is located about two blocks up (east) Highway 92 from the Highway 1 intersection. Head toward the Shell station, then turn right (south) onto Main Street until you cross a small bridge.

The **HALF MOON BAY VISITORS BUREAU** (520 Kelly Ave at Hwy 1; 650/726-8380; www.halfmoonbaychamber.org or www.coastsidelive.com) is open Monday though Friday 9am to 4pm, Saturday 10am to 3pm.

Moss Beach

Don't take it personally if you've never heard of Moss Beach; this tiny town between Pacifica and Half Moon Bay has had a long history of being discreet. During the Prohibition years, bootleggers stored their illegal wares along the hollowed-out seacliffs below and depleted them at the Moss Beach Distillery above. Today, despite the excellent selection of beaches and tide pools in the area, Moss Beach is anything but a tourist town—for shopping, dining, and such, a short drive down to Half Moon Bay is a requisite.

The highlight of Moss Beach is the **JAMES V. FITZGERALD MARINE RESERVE** (415/728-3584). At high tide, one wonders what all the excitement is about, but come back at low tide and wow! Thirty-five acres of tidal reef house more than 200 species of marine animals—sea anemones, urchins, snails, hermit and rock crabs, starfish, sponges—making it one of the most diverse tidal basins on the West Coast (and one of the safest, thanks to a wave-buffering rock terrace 50 yards from the beach). It's OK to touch the marine life as long as you don't pick it up, but nothing—not even a rock—is available as a souvenir. Call the reserve before coming to find out about the tide and the docent-led tour schedules (tours are usually on Saturdays). No dogs are allowed, and rubber-soled shoes are recommended. It's located at the west end of California Avenue off Highway 1 in Moss Beach.

RESTAURANTS

Moss Beach Distillery / ★★

140 BEACH WY AT OCEAN BLVD, MOSS BEACH; 650/728-5595 Used by bootleggers during Prohibition to store their illicit wares, this coastal grande dame was treated to a $2 million face-lift back in 1997, and the old gal's better for it. With its blue-painted walls, cozy dining alcoves, and massive patio and windows affording magnificent ocean views, the cliff-side landmark still has its beguiling 1920s beach-house atmosphere. The food has gotten considerably better, too. Gone is the pedestrian surf-and-turf fare; in its place are creative California–Mediterranean dishes such as grilled portobello mushrooms with cabernet sauce, shrimp tempura with a ginger vinaigrette, and a fork-tender pork chop enlivened by a mustard-shallot sauce and leek-buttermilk mashed potatoes. As if the views, historical setting, and good food weren't enough, the Distillery also lays claim to a couple of resident ghosts, including the famous Blue Lady, a flapper-era beauty who's said to haunt the place searching for her faithless lover. *$$; DC, DIS, MC, V; no checks; lunch Mon–Sat, dinner every day, brunch Sun (patio menu available all day); full bar; reservations recommended; www.mossbeachdistillery.com; from Hwy 1, take the Cypress Ave turnoff and turn right on Marine Blvd, which turns into Beach Wy.*

LODGINGS

Seal Cove Inn / ★★★

221 CYPRESS AVE, MOSS BEACH; 650/728-4114 OR 800/995-9987 Karen Brown Herbert (of *Country Inns* guidebook fame) knows what makes a superior bed-and-breakfast, and she didn't miss a trick when she and her husband, Rick, set up their own. The result is a gracious, sophisticated B&B that somehow manages to harmoniously blend California, New England, and European influences in a spectacular seacoast setting. The large, vaguely English-style country manor has 10 bedrooms that overlook a colorful half-acre wildflower garden dotted with birdhouses. All the rooms have fireplaces, fresh flowers, antique furnishings, original watercolors, grandfather clocks, hidden televisions with VCRs, and refrigerators stocked with free beverages. One thing's for sure: you won't starve here. Early in the morning, you'll find coffee and a newspaper outside your door, and a full breakfast is served wherever you prefer to eat. In the afternoon, wine and hors d'oeuvres are offered in the dining room. The inn's extravagant backyard garden fronts open parkland with seaside meadows and a miniforest of cypress trees. On the other side of the park is the Fitzgerald Marine Reserve, one of the area's best spots for exploring tide pools. Nearby are some interesting local restaurants, horseback riding on the beach, and a seaside bike trail. *$$$$; AE, DIS, MC, V; checks OK; sealcove@coastside.net; www.sealcoveinn.com; 6 miles N of Half Moon Bay on Hwy 1, then W on Cypress Ave.* &

Princeton-by-the-Sea

At the north end of Half Moon Bay is the small, quiet community of Princeton-by-the-Sea, anchored by the industrial-strength **PILLAR POINT HARBOR**, a major supplier to San Francisco's seafood market. Until recently it was a one-hotel town, but within the last couple of years Princeton has beefed up its tourism market by adding several new hotels and restaurants.

RESTAURANTS

Barbara's Fish Trap / ★

281 CAPISTRANO RD, PRINCETON-BY-THE-SEA; 650/728-7049 To get any closer to the ocean than Barbara's Fish Trap, you'd have to get your feet wet. Situated on stilts above the beach, Barbara's has indoor and outdoor dining with panoramic views of Half Moon Bay. The decor is classic fish 'n' chips (complete with checkered plastic tablecloths, fishnets on the ceilings, and a wooden fisherman by the door), but the food is a cut above. Barbara's offers a large selection of deep-fried seafood as well as daily fresh fish specials such as tangy Cajun-spiced snapper. The garlic prawns, clam chowder, calimari tempura, and steamed mussels are all local favorites, as is the ever-important beer selection. Lunch is a far better deal than the inflated dinner prices; better yet, order some fried clams from the walkaway counter and go for a stroll down the wharf. *$$; no credit cards; checks OK; lunch, dinner every day; beer and wine; no reservations; 4 miles north of Half Moon Bay on Hwy 1, west on Capistrano Rd to Pillar Point Harbor.*

LODGINGS

Pillar Point Inn / ★★

380 CAPISTRANO RD, PRINCETON-BY-THE-SEA; 650/728-7377 OR 800/400-8281 Located on a bustling harbor with a commercial fishing fleet, sportfishing and whale-watching charters, a few popular restaurants, and a busy pier, this modern inn is surprisingly quiet. Cheery and reminiscent of Cape Cod, the inn's 11 sunny, smallish rooms have harbor views, private baths, gas fireplaces, featherbeds, televisions with VCRs, and video libraries. Breakfast, served in the common room, includes coffee, tea, juice, house-made granola, fresh fruit, and a daily hot entree such as cheese-potato pie, quiche, or Belgian waffles. *$$$–$$$$; AE, MC, V; checks OK; info@pillar-point.com; www.pillarpointinn.com; 4 miles N of Half Moon Bay on Hwy 1, then W on Capistrano Rd.* &

Half Moon Bay

Victorian houses and boutiques line downtown Half Moon Bay, the oldest city in San Mateo County, while produce stands, U-pick farms, well-stocked nurseries, and flower farms ring its perimeter. Once a sleepy town whose main attraction was its annual Pumpkin Festival, Half Moon Bay has become a satellite city for neighboring Silicon Valley—and seen its real estate prices rise right along with the sale of microchips. At once chichi and funky, it has an old-time Americana ambiance that residents and visitors love; anyone witnessing its Fourth of July parade or annual Civil War Reenactment will get a kick out of the low-key, small-town hoopla. Half Moon Bay also has a history as a hippie haven: rocker Neil Young lives in the mountains off Highway 92, and tie-dyed establishments such as Mystic Gifts and the Center for Contemporary Shamanism somehow fit right in with the flag-waving elders and cell-phoning commuters. Even though there's plenty to do and see, and enough good restaurants to keep you well fed from dawn to dusk, Half Moon Bay is the antithesis of bright lights, big city. From all indications it plans to stay that way—good news for those looking for a peaceful getaway.

Since 1970 the **HALF MOON BAY ART & PUMPKIN FESTIVAL** has featured all manner of squash cuisine and crafts, as well as the Giant Pumpkin weigh-in contest, won recently by a 974-pound monster. A Great Pumpkin Parade, pumpkin-carving competitions, pie-eating contests, and piles of great food pretty much assure a good time for all; for more information call the Pumpkin Hotline at 650/726-9652; www.miramarevents.com.

The best way to explore the small, flat town of Half Moon Bay and its beaches is on a beach cruiser–style bicycle, available for rent at the **BICYCLERY** (101 B Main St at Hwy 1; 650/726-6000). Prices range from $8–$12 an hour to $25–$30 all day. Be sure to ask one of the staffers about the best biking trails in the area, particularly the wonderful beach trail from Kelly Avenue to Pillar Point Harbor.

Once you have explored the town, spend some time hiking through **PURISIMA CREEK REDWOODS** (650/691-1200), a little-known sanctuary frequented mostly by locals. Located on the western slopes of the Santa Cruz Mountains, the preserve is filled with fern-lined creek banks, lush redwood forests, and fields of wildflowers and berries that are accessible to hikers, mountain bikers, and equestrians along miles of trails. From the Highway 1/Highway 92 intersection in Half Moon Bay, drive 1 mile south on Highway 1 to Higgins Purisima Creek Road and turn left, then continue 4½ miles to a small gravel parking lot—that's the trailhead.

Another popular Half Moon Bay activity is **DEEP-SEA FISHING**. Even if you don't fish, it's worth a trip to **PILLAR POINT HARBOR** to take in the pungent aroma of the sea; the rows of rusty trawlers and the salty men and women tending to endless chores evoke a sort of Hemingwayish sense of romance. Pillar Point Harbor (4 miles north of Half Moon Bay off Highway 1) is just that sort of big ol' fishing harbor. Visitors are encouraged to walk along the pier and even partake in a fishing trip. **CAPTAIN JOHN'S FISHING TRIPS** (650/726-2913 or 800/391-8787) and **HUCK FINN SPORTFISHING** (650/726-7133 or 800/572-2934) each charge around $65, including rod and reel, for a day's outing—a small price to pay for 30 pounds of fresh snapper or salmon. Between January and March, whale-watching trips also depart daily.

Near the harbor is one of the most infamous surf beaches in California: **MAVERICK BEACH**. If the name sounds familiar, that may be because this local Half Moon Bay surf spot made national headlines in 1995 when famed Hawaiian surfer Mark Foo drowned here after being thrown from his board by a 20-foot wave. On calmer days, though, secluded Maverick Beach is still a good place to escape the weekend crowds because, although everyone's heard about the beach, few know where it is (and it's not on any map). Here's the dope: From Capistrano Road at Pillar Point Harbor, turn left on Prospect Way, left on Broadway, right on Princeton, then right on Westpoint to the West Shoreline Access parking lot (on your left). Park here, then continue up Westpoint on foot toward the Pillar Point Satellite Tracking Station. Take about 77 steps, and on your right will be a trailhead leading to legendary Maverick Beach a short distance away.

If surfing isn't your thing, how about ocean kayaking? If you're one of those Type A people who can't just lie on the beach and relax, **CALIFORNIA CANOE & KAYAK** (Pillar Point Harbor at the Half Moon Bay Yacht Club; 800/366-9804; www.calkayak.com) has the answer: for $49 they'll take you out on the bay for a half-day tour of Pillar Point Harbor, allowing you to get up close and personal with harbor seals, marine birds, and other wildlife; rentals are also available.

Back on land is the **ANDREOTTI FAMILY FARM** (227 Kelly Ave, halfway between Hwy 1 and the beach; 650/726-9461). If you like vegetables, you'll love this place. Every Friday, Saturday, and Sunday one of the family members slides open the old barn door at 10am sharp to reveal a cornucopia of just-picked artichokes, peas, brussels sprouts, beans, strawberries, and whatever else is growing in their adjacent fields. The Andreotti enterprise has been in operation since 1926, so it's a sure bet they know their veggies (open until 6pm year-round).

If you're a golfer, be sure to reserve a tee time at one of the two ocean-side 18-hole courses at **HALF MOON BAY GOLF LINKS** (2000 Fairway Dr, next to the Half Moon Bay Lodge; 650/726-4438; www.halfmoonbaygolf.com). The Old Course (still our favorite) was designed by Arnold Palmer and is rated among the top 100 courses in the country. The newer Ocean Course was designed by award-winning golf architect Arthur Hills in the tradition of Scotland's finest "links" courses, with challenges to rival those in Scotland. Reserve for both courses as far in advance as possible.

On your way out of town, be sure to stop at **OBESTER WINERY**'s Wine-Tasting and Sales Room (12341 San Mateo Rd; 650/726-9463; www.obester winery.com), which is only a few miles from Half Moon Bay up Highway 92. It's a pleasant drive—passing numerous fields of flowers, Christmas tree farms, and pumpkin patches—to this wood shack filled with award-winning wines. Behind the tasting room is a small picnic area that's perfect for an afternoon lunch break (open every day, 10am–5pm).

RESTAURANTS

Pasta Moon / ★★

315 MAIN ST, HALF MOON BAY; 650/726-5125 Executive chef Matthew Kurze, formerly chef de cuisine at San Francisco's One Market, has updated Pasta Moon's traditional Italian-style menu with lighter, more creative fare. Kurze's new approach features lots of locally grown organic produce and fresh fish. Start with an appetizer of Half Moon Bay artichokes "à la grecque," served with Italian butter beans, arugula, and lemon vinaigrette, or house-smoked salmon with pickled pearl onions and parsley salad. *Secondi piatti* include wood-oven-roasted veal chop stuffed with portobello mushrooms, Parmesan polenta, and endive with thyme-infused olive oil, and pan-seared sea bass with asparagus and risotto with lemon, garlic, and shrimp vinaigrette. The focaccia is heavenly, the house-made pasta seldom disappoints, and pizza lovers can select from a wide range of thin-crust creations. Pastas, breads, and pastries are all made on the premises. *$$; AE, DC, DIS, MC, V; local checks only; lunch, dinner every day, brunch Sun; full bar; reservations recommended; www.pasta moon.com; in the Tin Palace, at the N end of Main St, near Hwy 92.*

San Benito House / ★★

356 MAIN ST, HALF MOON BAY; 650/726-3425 A pastel blue Victorian on Half Moon Bay's Main Street, San Benito House has a candlelit dining room that's one of the prettiest on the Central Coast, decorated with country antiques, vases of fresh flowers, and paintings by local turn-of-the-century artists. At lunch, the deli cafe turns out top-notch sandwiches on fresh house-made bread, perfect for a repast in the garden or on one of the nearby beaches. At dinnertime the kitchen prepares such interesting European fare as homemade ravioli stuffed with fennel, fontina, and toasted almonds with creamy leek sauce; fillet of beef with Gorgonzola and herb butter; and salmon topped with a lemon-caper vinaigrette on a bed of lentil ragout. Desserts are terrific here, and may include a strawberry-rhubarb crepe served with crème anglaise and strawberry sauce, chocolate-espresso custard with Chantilly cream, and a pear poached with ginger and port wine. Thursday night is "Casual Menu" night; all entrees are only $9 or less. Too stuffed to move? Consider spending the night upstairs in one of the dozen modest but cheerful guest rooms (the one above the garden is the best). Arrive a bit early for a predinner cocktail at the cozy old-fashioned saloon. *$$; AE, DC, MC, V; no checks in the restaurant, advance checks OK in the hotel; lunch (deli cafe only) every day, dinner (main restaurant only) Thurs–Sun; full bar; reservations recommended; www.sanbenito house.com.* &

Sushi Main Street / ★★

696 MILL ST, HALF MOON BAY; 650/726-6336 The food is Japanese, the decor is Balinese, and the background music might be anything from up-tempo Latin to bebop American. Hard to envision, yes, but these elements come together beautifully at Sushi Main Street, a funky yet tranquil oasis in the heart of town. The alluringly offbeat ambiance blends Eastern elements with contemporary Western details like spot lighting and towering flower arrangements. Grab a seat at the L-shaped sushi bar, pull up a chair at one of the rust-colored asymmetrical slate tables, or, if you're feeling limber, plunk yourself down at the large, low table designed for traditional cross-legged dining. You might want to tickle your tonsils with a drop of the special sake (served room temperature in a traditional wooden box) or nosh on a kelp salad (a crisp, sesame-laden mixture of Japanese seaweeds) before diving into your main course. You can choose from a wide range of sushi and sashimi, from arctic surf clams to marinated mackerel. For a Zen sense of wholeness, top off your meal with green-tea ice cream or a dessert roll with papaya, plum paste, sesame seeds, and teriyaki sauce. *$$; MC, V; checks OK; lunch Mon–Sat, dinner every day; beer and wine; reservations recommended; www.sushimainst.com; just off Main St.*

LODGINGS

Beach House Inn at Half Moon Bay / ★★★

4100 COAST HWY 1, HALF MOON BAY; 650/712-0220 OR 800/315-9366 This three-story Cape Cod–style building overlooking Pillar Point Harbor offers 54 deluxe suites with enough amenities to make you feel right at home. Each guest room features a separate sleeping area, step-down living room with fireplace, private patio or balcony, wet bar, refrigerator, microwave, two TVs, and five-CD player. Oversize baths offer deep soaking tubs and separate showers. A small swimming pool and roomy Jacuzzi spa on the south-facing terrace afford views of Surfer's Beach and local surfers—a perfect place to warm up on a foggy morning. If the spa and the calming sound of surf aren't enough to work out those stress-related kinks, make an appointment with the Beach House Day Spa for a massage or aromatherapy wrap; for a small extra charge, the massage therapists will perform their healing ministrations in your room. A complimentary continental breakfast is served in the lobby. *$$$$; AE, DC, DIS, MC, V; checks OK; view@beach-house.com; www.beach-house.com; 3 miles N of Half Moon Bay.*

Cypress Inn on Miramar Beach / ★★★

407 MIRADA RD, HALF MOON BAY; 650/726-6002 OR 800/832-3224 With Miramar Beach literally 10 steps away, this wonderful modern inn is the place to commune with the ocean along the Peninsula coast. From each of its 12 rooms you not only see the ocean but also hear it, smell it, even feel it when a fine mist drifts in with the morning fog. The cheerful wooden building, set at the end of a residential block, has beamed ceilings, skylights, terra-cotta tiles, colorful folk art, and warm, rustic furniture made of pine, heavy wicker, and leather: sort of a Santa-Fe-meets-California effect. All of the guest rooms in both the main Beach House building and the newer Lighthouse annex across the street are romantically outfitted with featherbeds, gas fireplaces, private baths, and ocean views. Most have private balconies, and the enormous penthouse also boasts a two-person soaking tub. Breakfast is far above the standard B&B fare; expect fresh juices, croissants, a fruit parfait, and made-to-order entrees such as eggs Benedict and the inn's signature peaches-and-cream French toast. In the afternoon you'll find an elaborate feast of wine and hors d'oeuvres (perhaps prosciutto and melon, freshly baked quiche, and fresh fruit pie) in the common room. And if the proximity to the sea, engaging decor, great food, and flawless service aren't enough to relax you, make a reservation with the in-house masseuse. *$$$$; AE, MC, V; checks OK; CypressInn@Innsbythesea.com; www.cypressinn.com; 3 miles N of the junction of Hwys 92 and 1, turn W on Medio Rd, and follow it to the end.* &

Mill Rose Inn / ★★

615 MILL ST, HALF MOON BAY; 650/726-8750 OR 800/900-7673 One of the oldest bed-and-breakfasts on the Peninsula coast, the Mill Rose Inn fancies itself an old-fashioned English country house, with an extravagant garden and flower boxes as well as all the requisite lace curtains, antique beds, and nightstands. Romantics may love it here, but the inn's profusion of fabric flowers and slightly garish wallpapers (think William Morris on LSD) take it over the top for many folks; frankly, the overall effect is more Harlequin romance than authentic British country manor. But the rooms are spacious and chock-full of creature comforts, hosts Terry and Eve Baldwin are very friendly, and the Jacuzzi, tucked inside a frosted-glass gazebo, is quite enjoyable on a chilly coastal evening. The six guest rooms have private entrances and private baths, king- or queen-size featherbeds, fireplaces (with the exception of the Baroque Rose Room), and views of the garden. They also have telephones, televisions with cable and VCRs, well-stocked refrigerators, fresh flowers, chocolates, and liqueurs. Two rooms, the Bordeaux and Renaissance Suites, have sitting rooms as well. In the morning, you'll find a newspaper outside your door and a full breakfast that you can enjoy in the dining area or in the privacy of your room. *$$$–$$$$; AE, DIS, MC, V; checks OK; info@millroseinn.com; www.millroseinn.com; 1 block N of Main St.*

Old Thyme Inn / ★★

779 MAIN ST, HALF MOON BAY; 650/726-1616 OR 800/720-4277 Located on the quiet southern end of Main Street, this 1898 B&B is the epitome of Victorian style and grace. Each of the seven guest rooms—named after the herbs that grow in the inn's English garden—are painted in restful colors and decorated with well-chosen antiques. All offer private baths, TVs and VCRs, and sumptuous queen-size featherbeds topped with down comforters and imported linens. The Garden Room and the Thyme Room feature double whirlpool tubs and fireplaces. Every morning, innkeepers Rick and Kathy Ellis serve gourmet breakfasts with delectable entrees such as lemon-rosemary or banana-coconut crumb cake, quiche du jour, lemon-cheese pancakes with strawberry syrup, chiles rellenos, zucchini soufflé, or eggs Benedict. Wine and hors d'oeuvres are served daily in the parlor. *$$$–$$$$; AE, DC, DIS, MC, V; checks OK; innkeeper@oldthymeinn.com; www.oldthymeinn.com; near Filbert St.*

The Zaballa House / ★★

324 MAIN ST, HALF MOON BAY; 650/726-9123 The oldest building in Half Moon Bay, this 1859 pastel blue Victorian offers a few amenities that go beyond the usual B&B offerings. Homey, pretty, and unpretentious, the nine guest rooms in the main house are decorated with understated wallpaper and country furniture. Some have fireplaces, vaulted ceilings, or garden views. None have telephones, but three rooms have TVs. A more recent addition that was designed and painted to mimic this historic structure houses three attractive (and costlier) private-entrance suites that feature kitchenettes, double Jacuzzis, large bathrooms, fireplaces, VCRs, and private decks. Each is decorated differently: Casablanca-inspired number 10 is a charming, airy room with skylights, ceiling fans, and light wood-and-wicker furniture; number 11 has a French country look; and number 12—the most opulent—uses red velvet and plaster pillars, busts, and cornices to create an over-the-top classical look that will thrill some and be Greek to others. Whether you're staying in the suites or in the original structure, in the evening you may partake of wine, hors d'oeuvres, and cookies by the fireplace in the main house's snug, antique-filled living room. Come morning, guests are treated to a lavish buffet breakfast. Pets are welcome as well. *$$–$$$; AE, DIS, MC, V; checks OK; zaballahouse@earthlink.net; www.zaballa house.net; at the N end of town.*

Pescadero

Were it not for the near-mythical status of Duarte's Tavern, Pescadero would probably enjoy the sane, simple small-town life in relative obscurity. Instead, you can pretty much count on the town's population tripling on weekends as everyone piles into the bar and restaurant to see what all the hubbub is about. Whether it's worth the visit depends mostly on your interest in seeking out Duarte's holy recipe for cream-of-artichoke soup.

A few miles east of Duarte's Tavern on Pescadero Road is **PHIPPS RANCH** (2700 Pescadero Rd; 415/879-0787; www.phippscountry.com), a sort of Knott's Berry Farm back when it was a farm. Kids can play with the animals in the barnyard while Mom and Dad load up on the huge assortment of fresh, organically grown fruits and vegetables (including an amazing selection of dried beans) or browse the nursery and gardens. In the early summer, pick your own strawberries, olallieberries, and boysenberries in the adjacent fields. It's open daily 10am to 7pm (winter 10am–6pm). About 7 miles north of Pescadero on Highway 1 is the turnoff to Highway 84 and the legendary **SAN GREGORIO GENERAL STORE** (Hwy 84 at Stage Rd; 415/726-0565). Since 1889 this funky old place has been providing the nearby ranching and farming community with a bewildering assortment of "shoat rings, hardware, tack, bullshit, lanterns," and just about everything else a country boy needs to survive. It's truly worth a gander, particularly on Saturday and Sunday afternoons when the Irish R&B or Bulgarian bluegrass bands are in full swing. It's located 1 mile up Highway 84 from the Highway 1 intersection and is open daily 9am to 6pm.

At the turnoff to Pescadero is one of the few remaining natural marshes left on the central California coast, the **PESCADERO MARSH NATURAL PRESERVE**. The 600 acres of wetlands—part of the Pacific flyway—are a refuge for more than 160 bird species, including great blue herons that nest in the northern row of eucalyptus trees. Passing through the marsh is the mile-long Sequoia Audubon Trail, accessible from the parking lot at Pescadero State Beach on Highway 1 (the trail starts below the Pescadero Creek Bridge).

RESTAURANTS

Duarte's Tavern / ★

 202 STAGE RD, PESCADERO; 415/879-0464 Duarte's (pronounced "doo-arts") is a rustic gem, still owned and operated by the family that built it in 1894. Back then it was the place to buy a 10-cent shot of whiskey on the stagecoach ride from San Francisco to Santa Cruz. Nowadays Duarte's is half bar, half restaurant (when Duarte's tavern caught fire in 1927, local firefighters examined their priorities and sacrificed the restaurant to save the bar), but it's still set in an Old West–style wood-and-stucco building near Pescadero's general store. The dimly lit bar is typically filled with locals drinking a few beers after work. The unassuming wood-paneled restaurant next door serves steak, prime rib, and plenty of fresh coastal fare such as red snapper, halibut, sole, sand dabs, and salmon in season. Most of the fruits and vegetables come from the Duartes' own gardens behind the restaurant (be sure to go take a peek after lunch). It's sort of a county misdemeanor if you don't start dinner with a bowl of cream-of-artichoke soup and finish with a slice of Lynn Duarte's famous melt-in-your mouth olallieberry pie. Reservations are recommended for dinner. *$–$$; AE, MC, V; local checks only; breakfast, lunch, dinner every day; full bar; reservations recommended; downtown.*

LODGINGS

Costanoa / ★★☆

 2001 ROSSI RD, PESCADERO; 650/879-1100 OR 800/738-7477 Ever dream of communing with the great outdoors without all the packing and unpacking, tent collapsing in the middle of the night, or pesky critters in your sleeping bag? Costanoa's lodge, cabins, and tent bungalows provide an ideal alternative. Set in a pristine wilderness bordering four state parks and 30,000 acres of hiking trails, Costanoa is a perfect place to get away from it all in grand style. With its wide variety of accommodations, you can choose exactly how rough you want to rough it. If you're a tenderfoot, stay in the lodge, a striking cabinlike structure with 40 superlative guest rooms. In keeping with Costanoa's eco-sensibilities, the rooms are decorated with a well-designed mix of natural materials: polished wood, slate tile, and pale, earth-toned hues. Room amenities include private baths, Bose stereo systems, refrigerators, robes, private decks, and access to the lodge's spa facilities and outdoor hot tub. Many rooms have fireplaces and soaking tubs. One step lower on the luxury ladder are the six duplex cabins. Each of the 12 cabin rooms features a vaulted ceiling, fireplace, and deck with porch swing that overlooks wild, lush terrain. The cabins don't have private baths, but one of six "comfort stations" (sleek and upscale, with heated floors, large showers, and dry saunas) is only a short walk away. Reserve one of the deluxe tent bungalows for Costanoa's most unique lodging experience. Their queen-size beds, down comforters, heated mattress pads, and retro-style furnishings will make you feel like Meryl Streep in *Out of Africa.* As with Costanoa's other accommodations, daily maid service and continental breakfast are part of the deal. A variety of less luxurious tent bungalows are also available, as is a small area for pitching your own tent or parking your RV. The General Store on the premises offers a coffee bar and deli with all the makings for a gourmet picnic; the small spa offers Swedish, deep tissue, or shiatsu massage, aromatherapy, a sauna, and a steam room. Activities include hiking, on-site mountain bike rentals and horseback riding, and a children's play area. *$–$$$$; AE, DC, DIS, MC, V; no checks; www.costanoa.com; Hwy 1 between Pigeon Point Lighthouse and the Año Nuevo State Reserve, 9 miles S of Pescadero.*

Santa Cruz and the Monterey Bay Area

Although the Santa Cruz Boardwalk and Monterey Bay Aquarium get the lion's share of visitors, there's much more to do in this mountains-meets-the-sea region than ride the country's oldest roller coaster or gawk at fish. For adventures off the beaten track, explore the redwood-studded valley setting of Ben Lomond, the historic mission at San Juan Bautista, or the bucolic little farming towns of Tres Pinos, Castroville, and Moss Landing.

CENTRAL COAST THREE-DAY TOUR

DAY ONE: Marine magic. Get up early and grab a latte and a bagel to go, and start the day by exploring the teeming tide pools of the **FITZGERALD MARINE RESERVE** at Moss Beach. Enjoy lunch at **MOSS BEACH DISTILLERY**, then browse the shops along Half Moon Bay's quaint **MAIN STREET** or rent a beach cruiser and take a leisurely **BIKE RIDE** along the shoreline. Drive south on Highway 1 to check into your deluxe tent bungalow at **COSTANOA** in Pescadero. For an ocean view of the setting sun, take a hike on the **PAMPAS HEAVEN LOOP TRAIL**. Start at the main trailhead at Costanoa, cross Whitehouse Creek Bridge, and follow Whitehouse Creek Trail to the loop. Try **DUARTE'S TAVERN** in Pescadero for dinner, or bring your own fixins and fire up one of the barbecues in the camp.

DAY TWO: Sweet nature and spas. Rise early and walk the **REDWOOD NATURE TRAIL** to commune with the flora and fauna in **BIG BASIN REDWOODS STATE PARK** (21600 Big Basin Wy; 831/338-8860). Return to Costanoa for continental breakfast, a shower, and a sauna; don't forget to stock up on gourmet goodies for the road at Costanoa's General Store. Take Highway 1 south and follow the signs to Pacific Grove and **17-MILE DRIVE** for a tour of some of the world's most expensive real estate.

ACCESS AND INFORMATION

HIGHWAY 1 and scenic but highly trafficked **HIGHWAY 17** lead right into the center of Santa Cruz. Just "over the hill" is **SAN JOSE INTERNATIONAL AIRPORT**, with plenty of major airlines and **CAR RENTAL COMPANIES**. **GREYHOUND** (800/231-2222; www.greyhound.com) provides service to Santa Cruz's downtown bus terminal (425 Front St, Santa Cruz; 831/423-1800). The excellent **VISITORS INFORMATION CENTER** (1211 Ocean St, Santa Cruz; 831/425-1234 or 800/833-3494; www.santacruzca.org) boasts a friendly staff and lots of info about area attractions and events.

Highway 1 continues on with direct access to Monterey. From **HIGHWAY 101**, take the **HIGHWAY 156–MONTEREY EXIT**, which merges with Highway 1. The **MONTEREY PENINSULA AIRPORT** (831/648-7000; www.montereyairport.com; Hwy 68 off Holsted Rd, 4 miles from Monterey) has nearly 100 arrivals and departures daily, with connections to all domestic and foreign airlines. **CAR RENTAL** offices of Avis, Budget, and National are located here. **AMTRAK**'s (800/USA-RAIL; www.amtrak.com) Coast Starlight route stops in Salinas; free bus service is provided for the 30-minute ride into downtown Monterey. The **MONTEREY PENINSULA VISITORS AND CONVENTION BUREAU** (831/649-1770 or 888/221-1010; www.monterey.com) has two visitor centers: one located in the lobby of the Maritime Museum at Custom House Plaza near Fisherman's Wharf, and the other at Lake El Estero on Camino El Estero. Both locations are open daily and offer an array of maps, free pamphlets, and visitors' guides. Another good on-line source for Monterey information is **MONTEREY-CARMEL.COM** (www.monterey-carmel.com).

Exiting 17-Mile Drive at Ocean Avenue will put you right in the center of Carmel's many boutiques and restaurants. After lunch at **CASANOVA RESTAURANT,** you can opt for a little **SHOPPING** or a walk along glorious **CARMEL BEACH.** Head to Carmel Valley to spend the night at **BERNARDUS LODGE.** Before dinner at the lodge's **MARINUS** restaurant, freshen up with a dip in the pool, or indulge in a massage or facial at the luxurious on-site spa.

DAY THREE: Big Sur-prises. After breakfasting on your private terrace, enjoy a game of tennis, boccie ball, or croquet at Bernardus, or a round of golf at one of Carmel Valley's championship courses. Travel south on Highway 1 for a look at literary memorabilia in the **HENRY MILLER LIBRARY** and lunch at Big Sur's **NEPENTHE RESTUARANT.** Browse the **PHOENIX GIFT SHOP** at Nepenthe for imported treasures and locally made jewelry, soaps, and aromatic oils before driving a few miles north to the **POST RANCH INN.** After checking in to your mountain- or ocean-view cabin, take the walking trail down to the inn's Olympic-size pool for a late afternoon swim, or drink in an amazing view of the Pacific (and predinner cocktails, if you like) while relaxing in the giant hot tub known as the Basking Pool. End the day with dinner at Post Ranch's romantic **SIERRA MAR** restaurant and some stargazing from the restaurant patio.

Ben Lomond

RESTAURANTS

Ciao! Bella!! / ★★

9217 HWY 9, BEN LOMOND; 831/336-9221 Ciao! Bella!! is a restaurant with a sense of humor: mannequin legs wearing fishnet stockings and platform shoes stick out of the ground by the entrance, a parking slot is marked "Reserved for Elvis," and a Rapunzel-like sister mannequin leans out of a dormer above, letting down her hair, a perfect metaphor. Nestled in a mountain redwood grove in the San Lorenzo Valley, the roadhouse restaurant serves what owner Tad Morgan describes as "new California-Italian" cuisine. In addition to nightly specials, Ciao! Bella!! serves up hefty portions of pasta dishes, ranging from Tutto Mare (prawns, clams, calamari, and fresh fish sautéed in cream and white wine) to Penne alla Napoletana (penne with tomatoes, basil, garlic, and mozzarella tossed in a marinara sauce). *Secondi piatti* include scampi as well as chicken with prosciutto, mozzarella, and spinach, topped with a sauce of basil, tomatoes, and garlic. Be sure to start with the Tuscan steamed clams and save room for the house-made desserts: zabaglione, tiramisu, and bread pudding. *$$; AE, DIS, MC, V; no checks; dinner every day; beer and wine; reservations recommended; just S of town.*

Santa Cruz

Long regarded as a seaside nirvana for hippies and anyone else eschewing the conventional lifestyle, the Santa Cruz coast simply ain't what it used to be—spend a day on the boardwalk and you'll see more bike locks than dreadlocks. It all comes down to money, of course. Tourism is the big draw here: some 3 million annual visitors are the major source of income for the city, which in turn is doing everything possible to make Santa Cruz a respectable and safe place to bring the family. The result? A little of everything. Walk down gilded Pacific Avenue and you're bound to see the homeless mix it up with the alternative lifestylers as they hang out in front of a sea of yuppie shops and shiny cafes. The cultural dichotomy is glaringly manifest, but nobody seems to mind; rather, most locals are pleased with the turnout. As one resident put it, "Anything but Carmel."

The half-mile-long, 100-year-old **SANTA CRUZ BEACH BOARDWALK** (400 Beach St; 831/426-7433; www.beachboardwalk.com) is the last remaining beachfront amusement park on the West Coast. Take a spin on the famous Giant Dipper, one of the best and oldest wooden roller coasters in the country (with a great view at the top), then grab a seat on one of the intricately hand-carved horses on the 1911 Looff Carousel, the last bona fide brass ring merry-go-round in North America (both rides are listed on the National Register of Historic Places). Of course, the Boardwalk (now a cement walk) also caters to hard-core thrill-seekers who yearn for those whirl-and-twirl rides that do their best to make you lose your lunch. Newer rides and attractions include a 3D Fun House, where you wear 3D glasses and walk through a space filled with optical illusions, and Ghost Busters, an interactive "dark ride" where you can zap ghosts with phasers as they zip by. Also part of the boardwalk is **NEPTUNE'S KINGDOM,** an enormous indoor family recreation center whose main feature is a two-story miniature golf course. If you're among the crowds here on a Friday night in the summer, don't miss the Boardwalk's free concerts, which feature retro rock 'n' roll from groups such as the Shirelles, the Drifters, and the Coasters.

Beaches are Santa Cruz's other crowning glory. On the north end of West Cliff Drive is **NATURAL BRIDGES STATE BEACH** (831/423-4609; www.scpark friends.org/natbrdges), named after archways carved into the rock formations here by the ocean waves (only one of the three original arches still stands). The beach is popular with surfers, windsurfers, tide-pool trekkers, and sunbathers, as well as fans of the migrating monarch butterflies that roost in the nearby eucalyptus grove from late October through February. On the south end of West Cliff Drive is **LIGHTHOUSE FIELD STATE BEACH** (831/420-5270; www.santacruzparksandrec.com), the reputed birthplace of American surfing. This beach has several benches for sitting and gazing, a jogging and bicycling path, and a park with picnic tables, showers, and even plastic-bag dispensers for cleaning up after your dog (it's one of the few public places in town where canines are allowed). The nearby brick lighthouse is now home to the tiny **SANTA CRUZ SURFING MUSEUM** (West Cliff Dr at Lighthouse Point; 831/420-6289; www.santacruzparksandrec.com), the first of its kind in the world and built in memory of Mark Abbott, a young local surfer who died doing what he loved most: surfing. Old photographs, a surfboard bitten by a shark, vintage boards, and piles of other memorabilia depict the history and evolution of surfing around the world (open from noon–4pm Wednesday through Monday; admission is free).

Between the lighthouse and the Boardwalk is that famous strip of the sea known as **STEAMERS LANE,** the summa cum laude of California surfing spots (savvy surfers say this—not Southern California—is the place to catch the best breaks in the state). Watch some of the nation's best surfers ride the breaks, then head over to the marvelous (but often crowded) white-sand Santa Cruz Beach fronting the Boardwalk. The breakers are tamer here, and free volleyball courts and barbecue pits make this a favorite spot for sunbathing, swimming, picnicking, and playing volleyball on the sand courts. In the center of the action is the 85-year-old **MUNICIPAL WHARF** (831/420-6025), where you can drive your car out to the shops, fish markets, and seafood restaurants.

VISION QUEST KAYAKING (831/427-2267; www.kayaksantacruz.com), located on the northeast end of the wharf, rents single-, double-, and triple-seater kayaks for exploring the nearby cliffs and kelp beds, where a multitude of sea otters, seals, sea lions, and other marine animals congregate. No experience is necessary, and all ages are welcome. Guided tours and moonlight paddles are also available.

Even if you can't paddle, the view of the Santa Cruz coast from the water shouldn't be missed. **STAGNARO FISHING TRIPS AND BAY TOURS** has a one-hour tour of the bay that cruises the harbor, swoops around the wharf, and passes by Seal Rock and back (831/427-2334; www.stagnaros.com). They also offer sport fishing and whale-watching trips in season. For a more elegant tour, sign up for the **CHARDONNAY,** a 70-foot luxury yacht that sails year-round on sunset, ecology, wine-tasting, and whale-watching tours (831/423-1213; www.chardonnay.com). Better yet, sign up for some surfing lessons. Both **COWELL'S BEACH 'N' BIKINI SURF SHOP** (109 Beach St; 831/427-2355) and **CLUB ED SURF SCHOOL** (831/464-0177 or 800/287-SURF; www.club-ed.com) offer surf lessons on Cowell Beach. Whether you take the two-hour group session, a private lesson, or a seven-day surf camp, they guarantee you'll get up.

The **PACIFIC GARDEN MALL** (a.k.a. Pacific Avenue), Santa Cruz's main shopping district, was hit hard by the Loma Prieta earthquake in 1989, but the entire area has been rebuilt, and it's shinier and spiffier than before. Major retailers such as the Gap and Starbucks have settled in alongside book, antique, and vintage clothing stores; movie theaters; and sidewalk cafes. As you make your way down the mall, look for the **OCTAGON BUILDING,** an ornate, eight-sided Victorian brick edifice built in 1882. The building once served as the city's Hall of Records and is now part of the **MUSEUM OF ART AND HISTORY** (705 Front St at Cooper St; 831/429-1964).

The nearby **BOOKSHOP SANTA CRUZ** (1520 Pacific Ave; 831/423-0900) has an inventory worthy of any university town, with a particularly good children's section, an adjacent coffeehouse, and plenty of places to sit, sip, and read a bit of your prospective purchase. For great organically grown produce and other picnic-basket goodies, shop at the **FARMERS' MARKET** (Lincoln St, between Pacific Ave and Cedar St), held year-round on Wednesdays from 2:30 to 6:30pm.

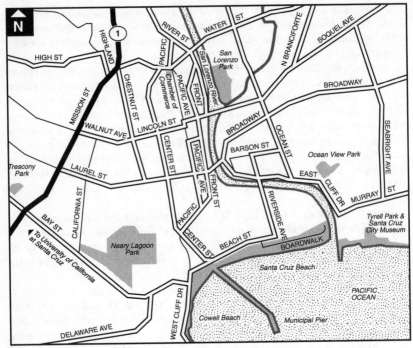

SANTA CRUZ

Secrets of the sea are revealed at the **SEYMOUR MARINE DISCOVERY CENTER** (100 Shaffer Rd, at the end of Delaware Ave; 831/459-4308; www2.ucsc.edu/seymourcenter). The center's exhibit galleries, aquariums, and teaching laboratories provide an inside look at UC Santa Cruz's Institute of Marine Sciences marine research laboratory, as well as explaining the part that marine scientific research plays in the conservation of the world's oceans. Children love the tide-pool touch tanks that allow visitors to handle—and learn about—sea stars, anemones, sea cucumbers, and other slimy marine life. Behind the gift shop are the skeletal remains of an 85-foot blue whale.

For some serious hiking and mountain biking, drive about 23 miles north to the 18,000-acre **BIG BASIN REDWOODS STATE PARK** (21600 Big Basin Wy, off Hwy 236, 9 miles N of Boulder Creek; 831/338-8860; www.bigbasin.org), California's first state park and its second-largest redwood preserve. Big Basin is home to black-tailed deer and mountain lions, and 80 miles of trails wind past 300-foot-high redwoods and many waterfalls.

Locomotive lovers, kids, and fans of Mother Nature should hop aboard one of the trains at **ROARING CAMP RAILROADS** (5355 Graham Hill Rd, Felton; 831/335-4484; www.roaringcamp.com). The Roaring Camp Train is a narrow-gauge, steam-powered train that was originally used to haul redwood logs out of the mountains. It now takes passengers for a s-l-o-w 6-mile round-trip excursion up one of the steepest narrow-gauge grades in North America, passing through stately redwood groves as it winds its way to the summit of Bear Mountain. A second Beach Train route offers an 8-mile ride through mountain tunnels and along the scenic San Lorenzo River before stopping at the Santa Cruz Beach Boardwalk. Both trains are located on Graham Hill Road off Highway 17 in Felton (follow the signs); the Beach Train Railroad can also be boarded at the east end of the Santa Cruz boardwalk.

RESTAURANTS

El Palomar / ★★

1336 PACIFIC AVE, SANTA CRUZ; 831/425-7575 El Palomar, Mexican restaurant extraordinaire, is a Santa Cruz institution. You have two choices: sit inside in the shadowy, dramatic dining room with a vaulted ceiling that was the lobby of a '30s hotel, featuring its beams painted in the Spanish manner and a huge mural depicting a Mexican waterfront village scene, or sit out in the happy, glassed-roof conservatory-patio, where the sun always seems to shine and you might squint and think you are in Mexico itself. If you need further convincing, have an Ultimate Margarita and munch on tortilla chips still warm from the oven. El Palomar is known for its seafood dishes, which are topped with exotic sauces, but traditional Mexican favorites such as burritos and tacos are also outstanding. A casual sister restaurant, Cafe El Palomar (2222 E Cliff Dr; 831/462-4248), serves breakfast, lunch, and "taco cafe" fare beside the Santa Cruz harbor from 7am to 7pm. *$$; AE, DIS, MC, V; local checks only; lunch, dinner every day, brunch Sun; full bar; no reservations; www.elpalomarrestaurant.com; in the Pacific Garden Mall, near Soquel Ave.* ও

O'mei Restaurant / ★★★

2316 MISSION ST, SANTA CRUZ; 831/425-8458 Named after a mountain in the Sichuan province of China, this acclaimed Chinese restaurant is a wondrous little paradox tucked into one of Santa Cruz's many strip malls. Chef-owner Roger Grigsby is not Chinese, nor are any of his cooks, but his food caters less to American sensibilities than do most Chinese restaurants. While you may order predictable northern Chinese offerings such as Mongolian beef and mu shu pork, those with adventurous palates are better served if they forgo the old standbys. Pushing the envelope of Chinese cuisine, O'mei (pronounced "oh-MAY") offers wonderful provincial curiosities such as Chengdu-bean-curd sea bass in a spicy *dou-ban* sauce (a rich wine-chile sauce), lychee *pi-pa* bean-curd balls, and an enchanting black sesame ice cream. The most popular dish is *gang pung* chicken—battered chicken with wood ear mushrooms, ginger, and cilantro, served with a sweet and slightly spicy sauce. We also really enjoyed the rock cod in black-bean and sweet-pepper sauce. Another plus: O'mei boasts a limited but well-chosen wine list, with most wines available by the glass. O'mei is so popular with locals that, even with reservations, you may wait a while to be seated, especially on weekends. *$$; AE, MC, V; no checks; lunch Mon–Fri, dinner every day; beer and wine; reservations recommended; near Fair Ave.*

Oswald / ★★☆

1547 PACIFIC AVE, SANTA CRUZ; 831/423-7427 This small California-French bistro has a lot in common with Berkeley's celebrated Chez Panisse—a reverence for fresh produce and restrained spicing and saucing that let the flavors of the principal ingredients sing out loud and clear. The dining room has a spare, arty look, with bold still-life paintings on the brick and pale-yellow-painted walls, high ceilings, wooden banquettes, and a petite wrought-iron-railed balcony set with a couple of tables. The small seasonal menu is supplemented nightly by a roster of specials that take good advantage of the best meats and veggies in the markets that day (organic whenever possible). Good options are the sherry-steamed mussels with fried garlic and parsley; poached foie gras with port wine reduction and toasted hazelnuts; and a butter lettuce salad with citrus and creamy herb dressing. Entrees include the crispy and moist "chicken under a brick" served with sweet pepper and potato hash. There's always a very reasonably priced entree of carefully cooked vegetables for vegetarians. The dessert list includes a seasonal fruit choice as well as a chocolate soufflé, a classic crème brûlée, and a Basque almond custard torte. Sweet wines are recommended for each dessert—with the chocolate soufflé a 1987 Graham's Malvedos Vineyard Porto, with the crème brûlée the NV Broadbent Terrantez (40 to 50 years old). The servers are knowledgeable and solicitous, and the wine list features a good lineup of both California and French offerings. *$$; AE, DC, MC, V; local checks OK; dinner Tues–Sun; beer and wine; reservations recommended; near Water St (use parking lot on Cedar St and enter through courtyard).* ዿ

Ristorante Avanti / ★★★

1711 MISSION ST, SANTA CRUZ; 831/427-0135 Most tourists who take one look at this unpretentious restaurant set in a humble strip mall keep on driving. The locals, however, are hip to Ristorante Avanti's fantastic food and considerate, professional service. In keeping with the Santa Cruz lifestyle, Avanti prides itself on serving "the healthiest meal possible" (think fresh, organic produce and free-range chicken, veal, and lamb). The modern, casual decor, with a long wooden counter dominating one of the small rooms and Italian ceramics scattered throughout, provides a welcome setting for aromatic, seasonal dishes such as sweet squash ravioli with sage butter, lasagne al forno, spaghetti with wild-mushroom and shallot duxelles, and orecchiette with salmon, Italian greens, mushrooms, and sun-dried tomatoes. The grilled lemon chicken and balsamic vinegar–marinated lamb chops also demonstrate the kitchen's skillful and delicate touch, and you simply can't go wrong with the daily specials. Menu items change with the seasons, and anything with wild mushrooms is prepared with locally gathered varieties. The ample and reasonably priced wine list contains selections from California, France, Spain, and Italy. *$$; AE, MC, V; local checks only; breakfast, lunch, dinner every day; beer and wine; reservations recommended; near Bay St.* ዿ

LODGINGS

The Babbling Brook Inn / ★★

1025 LAUREL ST, SANTA CRUZ; 831/427-2437 OR 800/866-1131 Ensconced in a fantastical garden with waterfalls, gazebos, and, of course, the babbling brook, Santa Cruz's oldest B&B offers 13 rooms, most named after famous artists. The original building was a gristmill, and the 200-year-old working mill wheel still churns water from a creek that flows through the property from high above town. The mauve-and-blue Van Gogh Room has a private deck, a fireplace, a beamed ceiling, and a whirlpool tub for two. Peach and ivory predominate in the Cézanne Room, with its generous bath and canopy bed. The blue-and-white Monet Room has a corner fireplace, a private deck, and a view of the waterfall and footbridge. Breakfast is served in the comfortable lobby, and wine and snacks are also served there from 5:30pm to 7:30pm. *$$$; AE, DC, DIS, MC, V; checks OK; babblingbrook@innsbythesea.com; www.babblingbrookinn.com; near California St.*

Casa Blanca Inn / ★

101 MAIN ST, SANTA CRUZ; 831/423-1570 OR 800/644-1570; 831/426-9063 (RESTAURANT) Right across the street from the beach and wharf, the Casablanca Inn has a close-up view of the ongoing street carnival that is the Santa Cruz Boardwalk. The 39 rooms are divided between the four buildings of the Cerf Mansion, a multilevel Spanish-style structure with a red-tile roof. Because the Cerf Mansion is a historic building, each room has a slightly different configuration, and rooms on the upper end of the rate scale have decidedly more personality. All guest rooms come with telephones, cable TVs, microwaves, and refrigerators; a good number feature fireplaces, kitchens, or private terraces; and 33 of the 39 have ocean views. If you're in the mood for a party, reserve a room facing Beach Street; if you'd rather stay in a less boisterous environment, opt for a room in the Guest House or Carriage House. There's nothing very Moroccan about the hotel's Casablanca Restaurant, a boardwalk bastion of California-continental cuisine, except, perhaps, the palpable air of romance. Starters include fried calamari with a spicy lime dipping sauce and Blue Point oysters on the half shell. Entrees range from grilled salmon with citrus vin blanc to filet mignon with wild mushroom whole grain demi-glace. Local wines share a book-length wine list with selections from Italy, Germany, France, and Australia. *$$$; AE, DC, DIS, MC, V; checks OK; www.casablanca-santacruz.com; at Beach St, on the waterfront.*

Cliff Crest Bed and Breakfast Inn / ★★

407 CLIFF ST, SANTA CRUZ; 831/427-2609 From its perch on Beach Hill high above the boardwalk, this antique-laden Victorian B&B offers five highly decorated rooms. The more casual lobby and solarium/sitting room/breakfast nook features a fireplace, antique furniture, and displays of old-time family photos from the original owners. The entire house has carved woodwork, bright square panes of stained glass, intriguing nooks, claw-footed tubs, and converted gaslight fixtures. The Empire Room downstairs has a four-poster king bed (all the rooms have four-posters) and a fireplace, and the Rose Room upstairs boasts bay views, a sitting area, and an Eastlake bed, with a private bath across the hall containing a claw-footed bathtub and a profusion of lace. Two other guest rooms have fireplaces, all the rooms are equipped with telephones, and TVs are available upon request. The complimentary full breakfast is served downstairs in the solarium, or you can take it to your room. There is off-street parking, and you can walk to the wharf or boardwalk or to town. *$$$–$$$$; AE, DIS, MC, V; checks OK; innkpr@cliffcrestinn.com; www.cliffcrestinn.com; near 3rd St.*

The Darling House—a Bed-and-Breakfast Inn by the Sea / ★★

314 W CLIFF DR, SANTA CRUZ; 831/458-1958 Location, location, location. There are probably no better views in all of Santa Cruz than those you'll find at the Darling House, a Spanish Revival mansion built as a summer home for a Colorado cattle baron in 1910. From its vantage point a few yards from the water, you can see endless miles of gray-blue sea, boats, seagulls, and the lights of faraway towns. On chilly days a fire crackles in the living room's glorious art deco fireplace. The downstairs has not been gentrified, and the beautiful Craftsman-style living room has carved oak pillars and beveled glass windows. Upstairs, the large Pacific Ocean Room is decorated like a sea captain's quarters, with a crown Victorian bed, a fireplace, and a telescope to spy ships at sea. Across the hall, the Chinese Room features an exotic canopied, carved, and gilded Chinese rosewood wedding bed. The cottage out back has a kitchenette, a wood-burning stove, and two bedrooms—each with a double bed, a claw-footed tub, and a kitchenette. Owners Darrell and Karen Darling have worked hard to preserve the house's beautiful woodwork and have outfitted all eight guest rooms with mostly American Victorian antiques; there are also fluffy robes in every closet. Karen's breakfasts include fresh fruit, homemade granola with walnuts, and oven-fresh breads and pastries. *$$$; AE, DIS, MC, V; checks OK; ddarling@darlinghouse.com; www.darlinghouse.com; on W Cliff Dr between the pier and the lighthouse.*

Capitola-by-the-Sea

Just east of Santa Cruz sits Capitola-by-the-Sea, a tiny, very popular resort town nestled around a small bay. The Mediterranean-style buildings, curved streets, white-sand beaches, outdoor cafes, and perpetually festive atmosphere seem more akin to the French or Italian Riviera than Monterey Bay. If you're staying on the coast for more than a day, and especially if you're around during the week, a visit to this ultra-quaint hamlet is highly recommended. Park the car anywhere you can, feed the meter (bring quarters), spend an hour browsing the dozens of boutiques along the esplanade, then rest your bones at Zelda's sunny beachside patio with a pitcher of margaritas. As in any upscale beach town, the ambiance is breezy and informal, and you can go anywhere in a bathing suit with a cover-up.

At the west end of town is the bustling 867-foot-long **CAPITOLA PIER**—a great place to hang out, admire the view of the town, and, on weekends, listen to live music. Many anglers come here to try their luck at reeling in the big one (and you don't need a license to fish from a pier in California). If you'd rather try your luck out at sea, visit **CAPITOLA BOAT & BAIT** (1400 Wharf Rd; 831/462-2208;

www.santacruzboatrentals.net; closed Jan–mid-Feb) at the end of the pier. Rates are reasonable and include fuel, safety equipment, and a map of the hot fishing spots. You can also rent fishing gear and purchase one-day licenses, so there's no excuse not to brave the open ocean—if only just for the halibut.

RESTAURANTS

Gayle's Bakery & Rosticceria / ★★

504 BAY AVE, CAPITOLA-BY-THE-SEA; 831/462-1200 Take a number and stand in line; it's worth the wait. A self-service bakery and deli, Gayle's offers numerous imaginative sandwiches, pastas, casseroles, roasted and barbecued meats, salads, cheeses, appetizers, breads, and treats. The variety is staggering and the quality top-notch. There's a good selection of wine, beer, bottled water, and espresso drinks, too. Once you've fought your way to the counter, you'll have the makings of a first-class picnic to take to one of the nearby parks or beaches. Daily specials range from carrot ginger soup to braised meatballs with red wine gravy. You can also eat your feast in the cafe's small dining area or on the heated patio. Gayle's Web site lists hot items and the next day's specials. *$; MC, V; checks OK; breakfast, lunch, dinner every day; beer and wine; no reservations; www.gaylesbakery.com; by Capitola Ave.*

Shadowbrook Restaurant / ★★

1750 WHARF RD, CAPITOLA; 813/475-1511 OR 800/975-1511 Known for years as the most romantic restaurant in the county, Shadowbrook is everyone's favorite place for proposals, birthdays, and anniversaries: the fun starts with the ride aboard the restaurant's funicular, a small cable railway that runs down through the ferny woods, past a waterfall, to the multistoried, woodsy restaurant bedecked in white lights. Now people are also beginning to come for the food on the seasonal California–Mediterranean menu. Starters might include the signature crab cakes, artichoke hearts with lime-cilantro sauce, or tender calamari strips served with a Creole rémoulade. Some of the more popular entrees are blackened lamb with roasted root vegetables, tender braised lamb shank, bacon-wrapped prawns with creamy polenta, and swordfish. Jack Daniels mud pie and New York–style cheesecake remain the most requested desserts. The best seats in the house are at the alfresco tables on the brickwork terraces, nestled romantically among rock gardens and rhododendrons; otherwise, opt for dining at the informal bar area with a view of the waterfalls and gardens. *$$$; AE, DC, DIS, MC, V; local checks only; lunch Mon–Fri (served only in the Rock Room Lounge May–Sept), dinner every day, brunch Sun; full bar; reservations recommended; www.shadowbrook-capitola.com; near the end of Capitola Rd.*

LODGINGS

The Inn at Depot Hill / ★★★

250 MONTEREY AVE, CAPITOLA-BY-THE-SEA; 831/462-3376 OR 800/572-2632 When Martha Stewart stayed here a few years ago, she enthused about the Delft Room, with its antique Dutch tile fireplace, featherbed decked out in white Belgian lace, and collectible Dutch blue and white porcelains. Located in a

STEINBECK COUNTRY

John Steinbeck's novel *Cannery Row*, set amid the sardine canneries of Monterey in the 1940s, begins with the line "Cannery Row is a stink, a poem, a grating noise." This doesn't exactly hold true anymore; the smell left when the canneries closed down in the 1950s. However, a few of Cannery Row's monuments remain, most notably the Wing Chong Grocery, which now houses Alicia's Antiques (835 Cannery Row, Monterey; 831/372-1423). Stand across the street to see its vintage facade and imagine the Chinese immigrants who lived upstairs in its 22 hotel rooms; inside, be sure to check out the Steinbeck memorabilia room and the collection of authentic Chinese lanterns.

One of the best places to get a feel for Steinbeck's life and work is at Salinas's fascinating National Steinbeck Center (1 Main St, Monterey; 831/796-3833; www.steinbeck.org). Opened in 1998, the center contains a theater that shows a short biographical film, multimedia exhibits, and a gallery with Steinbeck-themed art. This fun, family-oriented museum is no dusty shrine: kids (especially those who can read) will have a blast exploring the colorful interactive exhibits, which allow them to touch clothing and tools in a replica of the bunkhouse from *Of Mice and Men*, smell the sardines at a Monterey cannery, and try washing laundry as the Joads did in *The Grapes of Wrath*. If they get too rowdy, have them chill out in the refrigerated boxcar à la *East of Eden*. The on-site gift shop has a comprehensive collection of Steinbeck's works, and the museum's One Main Street Cafe offers breakfast and lunch with regionally inspired dishes such as Gilroy Garlic Fries, Chicken Castroville, and Tortilla Flat Black Bean Soup.

1910-era former Southern Pacific train depot, the Inn at Depot Hill sits on a bluff overlooking Capitola, but its selection of rooms will take you around the world. Decorated with passionate attention to detail, the 12 guest rooms, lavishly designed to evoke international ports of call, seem to have sprung directly from the pages of *Architectural Digest*. The terra-cotta-walled Portofino Room, patterned after a coastal Italian villa, sports a stone cherub, ivy, frescoes, and a brick patio. No less charming is the Stratford-upon-Avon, a faux English cottage with a cozy window seat. The Railroad Baron Room has sumptuous red fabric walls, heavy gold silk drapes, and formal gilt mirrors. Every room has a TV and a VCR, a built-in stereo system, a gas fireplace, and a marble-appointed bathroom complete with a mini-TV and a coffee machine. In the morning, there's a buffet of pastries, cereal, and quiche, as well as a hot dish such as French toast or a spinach omelet. In the evening, you'll find sweets and wine in the downstairs parlor. You may also browse along the massive wall-length bookcase for a tome or videotape to borrow. *$$$$; AE, DIS, MC, V; checks OK; depothill@innsbythesea.com; www.innatdepothill.com; near Park Ave, next to railroad tracks.*

Aptos

Most of Aptos's appeal is of the outdoor variety: beyond its handful of B&Bs, people come for the good hiking trails, state beaches, and state parks. Aptos has little in the way of tourist entertainment, leaving that up to neighboring Capitola and Santa Cruz. The focus here is on quality lodgings in quiet surroundings. The only drawback is that the beaches are too far to walk to from town, but if you don't mind the short drive, Aptos is the ideal place for a peaceful vacation on the coast. Seacliff State Park Beach has picnic tables with shade covers as well as the infamous Concrete Ship, built by the Navy to sail the coast but now permanently moored (it later became a dance hall) and looking very much like a concrete wharf. In the spring the local park in Aptos Village is home to a fun and funky blues festival.

RESTAURANTS

Cafe Sparrow / ★★

8042 SOQUEL DR, APTOS; 831/688-6238 Chef-owner Bob Montague and his wife, Julie, opened this quaint French country restaurant in June 1989. Then along came the October 17 Loma Prieta earthquake, reducing the cafe to little more than a pile of rubble. Fortunately, the couple didn't throw in the towel, and their remodeled restaurant is now a gem of a dining spot and a magnet for local gourmets. Two dining rooms, decorated with country furniture and a tentlike expanse of French printed fabric, provide a romantic backdrop for Montague's spirited culinary creations. Lunch may include a croissant layered with shrimp in lemon, fresh dill, and crème fraîche, or a bowl of creamed spinach with a vinaigrette salad and bread. Dinner, however, is when Montague puts on the Ritz. Start with a pâté of fresh chicken livers seasoned with herbs and Cognac, or a fondue of white wine, herbs, and cheeses served in a puff pastry with fresh fruits and vegetables. Then progress to such entrees as an Yvette salad—grilled chicken breast with pears topped with Brie; or lamb chops in a rich red-wine and mint sauce. Favorite desserts are profiteroles—puff pastries filled with custard or vanilla ice cream and smothered in Ghirardelli chocolate sauce. The wine list is far-ranging and agreeably priced, and the service is amiable. *$$; MC, V; checks OK; breakfast Sat, lunch Mon–Sat, dinner every day, brunch Sun; beer and wine; reservations recommended; www.cafe sparrow.com; near Trout Gulch Rd.*

LODGINGS

Historic Sand Rock Farm / ★★★

6901 FREEDOM BLVD, APTOS; 831/688-8005 The word "nestled" was made for this inn, positioned on a woodsy knoll under a grove of redwoods. It originally was a 1,000-acre ranch and winery built in the 1880s by a doctor's family, who also built the Craftsman-style shingled mansion in 1910 from virgin redwood growing on the site. Lynn Sheehan, formerly chef at several of San Francisco's finest restaurants, and her mother, Kris Sheehan, who previously was innkeeper at the Wild Rose Inn in Sonoma, have teamed up to create this inn, bringing the home back to its original glory with European antiques and an obvious love for light, airy rooms. The living room features redwood box beams, leaded glass, and a mantel made of rare curly redwood. The Sun Porch Suite, a large, open room in the lower wing of the house, has a private enclosed sunporch sitting area and access to a large outdoor hot tub. The Hidden Garden Suite opens onto a rose garden framed by a stone wall. The Morning Glory Room has rugs blooming with morning glories and faces east; as the sun rises, the Eastlake-style brass queen bed glows with reflected light. Breakfast is a gourmet experience, usually served outdoors on the redwood deck under the trees. There are many nooks, crannies, hidden gardens, and old winery buildings to explore at this historic country retreat. *$$; AE, MC, V; no checks; reservations@sandrockfarm.com; www.sandrockfarm.com; on Freedom Blvd, ½ mile from Hwy 1.*

Seascape Resort / ★★

I SEASCAPE RESORT DR, APTOS; 408/688-6800 OR 800/929-7727 This attractive condo-resort complex on 64 cliff-side acres offers spacious accommodations and plenty of creature comforts. The 285 guest suites and villas are arranged in a cluster of three-story stucco buildings and are available in studio or one- or two-bedroom configurations. Each suite and beach villa is outfitted with identical beach house–style furnishings in light colors of sand and blue and comes with a fireplace, a private balcony or patio, a TV, and a kitchenette. The studios are quite large, with minikitchens, and the one- and two-bedroom villas are larger still, with complete kitchens, sitting areas, and, in the two-bedroom units, washer-dryers. All rooms and villas have balconies or patios. Largely given over to corporate functions during the week, the complex turns into a haven for couples and families on the weekend. For a fee you can have the staff provide wood and build a private bonfire on the beach, or you can just buy a bundle of wood from the resort and do it yourself. A paved path leads down through a small canyon to the beautiful beach, and guests enjoy member privileges at a nearby PGA-rated golf course and the Seascape Sports Club, which offers tennis, swimming, and a fully equipped gym. The resort also provides 24-hour room service, a children's program during the summer, and a spa offering massage and beautician services. Fresh seafood is the specialty at Sanderlings, the resort's airy restaurant, with curvy light wood dividers and a mega-aquarium. You can sit inside or on the patio; either way you'll see gorgeous ocean vistas. Rates come down in the winter months. *$$$$; AE, DC, MC, V; checks OK; info@seascaperesort.com; www.seascaperesort.com; at Sumner Blvd 9 miles S of Santa Cruz.* &

Rio Del Mar

Located on the ocean side of Highway 1 near Aptos, Rio Del Mar is a wide strip of welcoming sand, a jetty, and an upscale residential neighborhood, but the palisades of Rio Del Mar were once the site of the first crop of sugar beets in California, planted by sugar magnate Claus Spreckels.

RESTAURANTS

Bittersweet Bistro / ★★

787 RIO DEL MAR BLVD, RIO DEL MAR; 831/662-9799 Local gourmets love "the Bittersweet," a sleek American bistro-style restaurant and wine bar featuring a patio for dining alfresco and a stylish mahogany, lacquer, and black granite bar area. Chef-owner Thomas Vinolus is at the kitchen's helm, creating appetizers such as grilled shrimp martini with mesclun and cocktail sauce or Monterey Bay calamari. Pasta offerings include seafood puttanesca and five-cheese ravioli. For a main course, order the oak-roasted pork tenderloin with apple Calvados jus; the fresh fish of the day in parchment paper over spinach, squash, tomatoes, and eggplant; or the Bittersweet paella. The seasonal menu also features a range of pizzas from the wood-fired oven. The pretty-as-a-picture desserts range from lemon napoleon to ricotta cheesecake and chocolate mousse in a florentine cookie cup, to name just a few. That's no surprise, given that the chef's last gig involved whipping up pastries at Carmel's Casanova restaurant. The wine list is extensive and varied, with some interesting if pricey older vintages among its treasures. *$$$; AE, MC, V; local checks only; late lunch 3pm–6pm, dinner every day, brunch Sun; full bar; reservations recommended; www.bittersweetbistro.com; take Hwy 1 south of Santa Cruz to the Rio Del Mar exit.* &

Gilroy

Will Rogers called Gilroy the only town in America where you can marinate a steak just by hanging it out on the line—and, yes, when the wind's blowing in the right direction, the aroma from the area's garlic fields is just about that strong. So it only made sense that the people of Gilroy decided in 1979 to celebrate their odoriferous claim to fame with the now-famous **GARLIC FESTIVAL** (408/842-1625; www.gilroygarlicfestival.com), held the last weekend in July. The three-day-long festivities attract throngs of people eager to try such oddities as garlic ice cream and garlic chocolate, and to enter their own stinking-rose recipes in the Great Garlic Cook-Off. You can also buy any number of garlic-based foodstuffs and doodads. To find out about Gilroy before the age of garlic, visit the **GILROY HISTORICAL MUSEUM** (5th and Church Sts; 408/848-0470). If bargain hunting, not garlic, happens to set your heart aflutter, be sure to stop at the **GILROY PREMIUM OUTLETS** center (Leavesley Rd, just east of Hwy 101; 408/847-4155), with 150 outlets for big-name retailers.

San Juan Bautista

This sunny little town is home to one of the most beautifully restored missions in California. Built just 2 feet away from the main trace of the San Andreas Fault, **MISSION SAN JUAN BAUTISTA** (831/623-2127; www.san-juan-bautista.ca.us) was nearly destroyed by the 1906 quake, but locals raised the money to rebuild it. With its pretty chapel and gardens, the mission sits on a broad plaza surrounded by other well-preserved Spanish colonial buildings. Several rooms in the mission are preserved as well, such as the library for the priests, full of old leather-bound books and maps. Fans of Alfred Hitchcock's *Vertigo* will want to explore the bell tower from which Kim Novak's character fell to her death. San Juan Bautista is also home to the world-famous theater troupe **EL TEATRO CAMPESINO** (705 4th St; 831/623-2444; www.elteatrocampesino.com). Director Luis Valdez left the San Francisco Mime Troupe in the '60s to form this political theater group composed of migrant farmworkers. The group puts on plays throughout the year and is most famous for its Christmas plays, *La Virgen del Tepeyac* and *La Pastorela,* presented at the mission. Hikers, rock climbers, bird-watchers, and other nature lovers will want to explore the cliffs and caves of nearby **PINNACLES NATIONAL MONUMENT** (831/389-4485), a glorious 16,000-acre volcanic park located high in the hills above the Salinas Valley off Highway 101. The dark red contorted rock shapes and crumbling terraces sit on top of a still-active earthquake fault. If you can stay only a short while, visit the park's east side, which has the most dramatic rock formations and caves. Of the four self-guided trails, the favorite (and the easiest) is Moses Spring Trail.

RESTAURANTS

Felipe's California & Mexican Cuisine / ★

313 3RD ST, SAN JUAN BAUTISTA; 831/623-2161 One of several Mexican places on San Juan Bautista's main street, this crowded storefront restaurant serves all the standard Mexican fare—good chicken mole, pork burritos, and light, freshly made tortilla chips—but its Salvadoran dishes are what set it apart. Especially delicious are the handmade *pupusas* (fat corn tortillas stuffed with cheese) and the *plátanos fritos* (fried plantains) served on a bed of rich, nicely textured refried pinto beans. The Salvadoran entrees are served with an appropriately tangy pickled-cabbage dish called *curtido*. Felipe's also has several good Mexican beers. Don't leave without trying the fried ice cream, a house specialty. Vegetarians take note: Felipe's uses no lard. *$; MC, V; no checks; lunch, dinner Wed–Mon; beer and wine; no reservations; between Mariposa and Polk Sts.*

Tres Pinos

If you blink, you'll miss Tres Pinos, located on Highway 25 south of Hollister. There's not much of a town, just an intersection; most people blast through here on the way to Pinnacles National Monument. It once was home to an agricultural community, but now migrant workers are being replaced by high-tech commuters and well-off retirees who live in the new housing developments that have spread outward from Hollister.

RESTAURANTS

Inn at Tres Pinos / ★★

6991 AIRLINE HWY, TRES PINOS; 831/628-3320 This dark, romantic restaurant in a former bordello built in 1880 makes for a surprising find in the tiny town of Tres Pinos outside Hollister. "Keep it fresh and keep it simple" is the credo here. Popular dishes include filet mignon with green peppercorn sauce, Fettuccine Fantasia (chicken, artichoke hearts, sun-dried tomatoes, olives, herbs, and garlic with a white-wine and cream sauce), and calamari sautéed in chardonnay and butter. Rustic but surprisingly elegant, the inn wins high praise for its desserts, from New York–style cheesecake with fresh raspberries and mango to a Granny Smith apple crisp. *$$$; AE, MC, V; local checks only; dinner Tues–Sun; full bar; reservations recommended; 5 miles S of Hollister.* &

Moss Landing

Nature lovers have long revered Moss Landing's **ELKHORN SLOUGH** as a prime spot to study egrets, pelicans, cormorants, terns, great blue herons, and many other types of aquatic birds, not to mention packs of frolicking harbor seals and otters. Besides hiking or kayaking, one of the best ways to explore this scenic coastal wetland is to embark on an **ELKHORN SLOUGH SAFARI** (831/633-5555; www.elkhorn slough.com). Naturalist guides provide expert and enthusiastic commentary aboard a 27-foot-long pontoon boat, and special activities (such as Bird Bingo) are provided for children. Binoculars are available for rent, and coffee, soda, and cookies are served on the way back. The two-hour tours operate every day, year-round.

RESTAURANTS

Phil's Fish Market / ★★

 7600 SANDHOLDT RD, MOSS LANDING; 831/633-2152 Turn at the Whole Enchilada, keep driving inland on Sandholdt Road, over the short one-lane bridge and past fishing boats, and you'll come to Phil's Fish Market, a local institution owned by the eternally cheerful Phil DiGirolamo. It's much more than a fish market—it's a kind of community center, joke central, and indoor picnic spot as well as a restaurant and takeout place. And of course there are the fresh fish, lying in state on ice like sculptures in a museum. Beautiful fish, most of it caught that morning. If you like your fish still moving, there are banks of tanks full of undulating catfish, clunky lobsters, and mussels. Phil's most famous dish is cioppino-to-go, but he also offers lunch items including albacore salad and pizzas with shrimp and sun-dried tomatoes. For dinner there's fettuccine with lobster meat, bay scallops in saffron cream sauce, or a blackened scallops Alfredo. Should you get addicted to Phil's grub, you can have his chowder base with clams and red potatoes (just add milk or cream) or his Lazy Man's Cioppino shipped overnight in a frozen vacuum gel pack to any place in the country. Just open and heat! Phil even provides a kids' menu and live bluegrass music on Monday and Thursday nights. *$; AE, DC, DIS, MC, V; local checks only; lunch, dinner every day; beer and wine; no reservations; www.philsfishmarket.com; off Hwy 1 at the end of Sandholdt Rd.* &

The Whole Enchilada / ★

7902 HWY 1, MOSS LANDING; 831/633-3038 Fresh seafood is the focus of this upbeat Mexican restaurant on Highway 1. Gaily painted walls, folk-art decorations, and leather basket chairs lend an engaging south-of-the-border ambiance. Voted "Best Mexican Restaurant" in a local readers' poll, the Whole Enchilada offers the usual lineup of burritos, tacos, chiles rellenos, and enchiladas on the comprehensive menu. But hold out for one of the more exotic regional specialties, such as Oaxacan tamales filled with fresh albacore or chicken, wrapped in a banana leaf and drenched in a rich, dark mole salsa. The catch of the day is right off the local fishing boats and prepared in the authentic Mexican coastal style. Wash it all down with a *muy bueno* Cadillac margarita. Service is warm and efficient, and little touches like crayons and plastic mermaids clinging to the drink cups make this a place your kids will like, too. *$$; AE, DC, DIS, MC, V; no checks; lunch, dinner every day; full bar; reservations recommended; www.wenchilada.com; at Moss Landing Rd.*

Castroville

Gilroy made history with garlic; Castroville chose the artichoke. The undisputed Artichoke Capital of the World, tiny Castroville celebrates its choke-hold on the artichoke market during the annual Artichoke Festival, held every third weekend in September. It's mostly small-town stuff: the crowning of the Artichoke Queen, a 10K run, artichoke cook-offs, and the Firefighters' Pancake Breakfast. The town's most famous queen of the thistle was Marilyn Monroe. The best souvenir in town is the postcard with an (apparently) nude model lying in a sea of artichokes. If that's too racy for you, you can still get deep-fried artichokes at almost every quick-food place.

RESTAURANTS

Restaurant La Scuola / ★★

10700 MERRITT ST, CASTROVILLE; 831/633-3200 This *buonissimo* Italian restaurant on the main street of Castroville is a real find. Tucked away in a tall schoolhouse that's more than a century old, it's an elegant little place serving up classic Italian staples such as veal parmigiana, lasagne, and chicken Toscana. The most popular appetizer is a giant artichoke (naturally), prepared five different ways. The fettuccine with fresh Manila clams is very good (the house-made pasta comes perfectly al dente, and the fresh clams explode with flavor), as is roasted garlic chicken in a mushroom and white wine sauce. The vegetable side dishes are cooked just enough to bring out their flavor and color, and the buttery, oven-roasted potatoes are delicately crisp on the outside and creamy-smooth within. *$$; AE, DIS, MC, V; no checks; lunch Tues–Fri, dinner Tues–Sat; full bar; no reservations; at Preston Rd, downtown.* &

Monterey

Monterey is really two towns: Old Monterey (the historic part, including colonial buildings and Fisherman's Wharf) and New Monterey, home to Monterey Bay Aquarium and Cannery Row. If you're looking for the romantically gritty, working-class fishing village of John Steinbeck's novel *Cannery Row,* you won't find it here. Even though Monterey was the sardine capital of the Western Hemisphere during World War II, overfishing (among other factors) forced most of the canneries to close in the early '50s. Resigned to trawling for tourist dollars instead, the city converted its low-slung sardine factories along Cannery Row (831/649-6690; www.cannery row.com) into a rather tacky array of boutiques, knickknack stores, yogurt shops, and—the Row's only saving grace—the world-famous Monterey Bay Aquarium. As you distance yourself from Cannery Row, however, you'll soon see that Monterey also has its share of pluses that help even the score: dazzling seacoast vistas, stately Victorian houses, wonderfully preserved historic architecture, and a number of quality lodgings and restaurants. More importantly, Monterey is only minutes away from Pacific Grove, Carmel, Pebble Beach, and Big Sur, which makes it a great place to set up base while exploring the innumerable attractions lining the Monterey coast.

Attracting nearly 2 million visitors each year, the **MONTEREY BAY AQUARIUM** (866 Cannery Row; 831/648-4888 or 800/756-3737; www.montereybay aquarium.org) is Monterey's jewel in the crown and a must-see experience. It's the largest aquarium in the United States, with more than 350,000 marine animals, birds, and plants on display in over 200 galleries and exhibits. One of the aquarium's main exhibits is a three-story, 335,000-gallon tank with clear acrylic walls that offers a stunning view of leopard sharks, sardines, anchovies, and other sea creatures swimming through a towering kelp forest. Even more impressive, however, is the Outer Bay, a million-gallon exhibit that showcases aquatic life living in the outer reaches of Monterey Bay. Schools of sharks, barracuda, yellowfin tuna, sea turtles, ocean sunfish, and bonito can be seen through one of the largest windows on earth: a 78,000-pound acrylic panel that measures 15 feet high, 13 inches thick, and 54 feet long. The Deep Sea exhibit is the largest collection of live deep-sea species in the world, many of which have never been part of an exhibit before. Another popular exhibit is the sea otter "playground": be sure to stop by for the daily feedings. The Splash Zone caters to the little ones, with hands-on interactive tours through two shoreline habitats. Tip: You can avoid lines at the gate by ordering tickets in advance. Also, go in the early afternoon—by 2pm the crowds have thinned out and you'll have a much easier time getting an unobstructed view of the exhibits.

To get the flavor of Monterey's heritage, follow the 2-mile **PATH OF HISTORY,** a walking tour of the former state capital's most important historic sites and splendidly preserved old buildings—remember, this city was thriving under Spanish and Mexican flags when San Francisco was still a crude village. Free tour maps are available at various locations, including the **CUSTOM HOUSE** (at the foot of Alvarado St, near Fisherman's Wharf), California's oldest public building, and **COLTON HALL** (on Pacific St, between Madison and Jefferson Sts), where the California State

Constitution was written and signed in 1849. Call **MONTEREY STATE HISTORIC PARK** (831/649-7118) for more information.

Nautical history buffs should visit the **MARITIME MUSEUM OF MONTEREY** (5 Custom House Plaza, near Fisherman's Wharf; 831/372-2608), which houses ship models, whaling relics, and the two-story-high, 10,000-pound Fresnel lens used for nearly 80 years at the Point Sur lighthouse to warn mariners away from the treacherous Big Sur coast.

One of the most enjoyable ways to spend a sunny day on the Monterey coast is paddling a sea kayak among the thousands of seals, sea lions, sea otters, and shorebirds that live within the Monterey Bay National Marine Sanctuary. Another thrill is seeing the Monterey Bay Aquarium from the water. No kayaking experience is necessary—just follow behind the instructor for an interpretive tour of the bay. For reservations contact **MONTEREY BAY KAYAKS** (831/373-5357 or 800/649-5357; www.montereybaykayaks.com). Prices start at about $55 per person for a three-hour tour.

The landmark **FISHERMAN'S WHARF** (831/649-6544; www.montereywharf.com), the former center of Monterey's cargo and whaling industry, is awash in mediocre restaurants and souvenir shops—although, with its seaside-carnival ambiance, it's a place the kids might like. The best time to visit is in the winter or spring, when **WHALE-WATCHING TRIPS** sail regularly from the wharf. You'll have a number of tour companies to choose from; a popular choice is **CHRIS' FISHING TRIPS & WHALE WATCHING**, 48 Fisherman's Wharf (831/375-5951; www.chriss fishing.com), which offers whale-watching tours in season, as well as fishing excursions for cod, salmon, and whatever else is running. Serious shoppers will be better off strolling **ALVARADO STREET,** a pleasantly low-key, attractive downtown area with a much less touristy mix of art galleries, bookstores, and restaurants. Alvarado Street is also the site of the popular **OLD MONTEREY FARMERS' MARKET AND MARKETPLACE.** Held every Tuesday year-round from 4pm to 8pm in the summer and 4pm to 7pm in the winter, it's a real hoot, with more than 100 vegetable, fruits, and crafts vendors plus musicians and performers.

Children will love the **DENNIS THE MENACE PLAYGROUND** (Camino El Estero and Del Monte Ave, near Lake El Estero). Designed by cartoonist Hank Ketcham, it has enough climbing apparatuses to please a monkey. For fun on the water, take your Curious Georges on a paddleboat and pedal around **LAKE EL ESTERO** (831/375-1484). You can rent bicycles and inline skates at the **MONTEREY BAY RECREATION TRAIL,** which runs along the Monterey shore for 18 miles to Lovers Point in Pacific Grove. For a self-guided tour of area's wineries, stop in at the **MONTEREY COUNTY VINTNERS ASSOCIATION** (831/375-9400; www.monterey wines.org), where you can get a wine-tasting and touring map of Monterey County's excellent vineyards and wineries, many of which have public tasting rooms and picnic grounds.

On the third weekend in September top jazz talents such as Wynton Marsalis, Etta James, and Ornette Coleman perform at the **MONTEREY JAZZ FESTIVAL** (925/275-9255 for tickets; 831/373-3366 for information; www.montereyjazz festival.org), one of the country's best jazz jubilees and the oldest continuous jazz celebration in the world. Tickets and hotel rooms sell out fast, so plan early—die-hard jazz fans make reservations at least six months before show time. Monterey also hosts a **BLUES FESTIVAL** (831/394-2652; www.montereyblues.com) in late June, which attracts a respectable but smaller crowd.

RESTAURANTS

Cafe Fina / ★★

47 FISHERMAN'S WHARF, MONTEREY; 831/372-5200 OR 800/THE-FINA It's a surprise to find a fine restaurant in the carnival atmosphere of Fisherman's Wharf, but Cafe Fina certainly fits the bill. Owner Dominic Mercurio cooks with a wood broiler and wood-fired brick oven and offers fresh fish, mesquite-grilled chicken and beef, salads, house-made pasta with inventive herb sauces, salmon burgers, and pizzettes—little pizzas hot from the brick oven. Specialties are the seafood and pasta dishes, including clams with garlic butter, prawns and Pernod, and the flavorful Pasta Fina (linguine with baby shrimp, white wine, olives, clam juice, olive oil, tomatoes, and green onions). The food is delicious and carefully prepared, the atmosphere is casual and fun, and the vista is a maritime dream when the sea otters and sea lions are playing within view. Be sure to pick up a business card, which has a recipe for roasted garlic printed on the back. You can sit inside—request a window-side table—or walk up to the window and get a pizza or deep-fried artichoke hearts to go. *$$; AE, DC, DIS, MC, V; no checks; lunch, dinner every day; full bar; reservations accepted; info@cafefina.com; www.cafefina.com; on Fisherman's Wharf.*

Fresh Cream / ★★★

99 PACIFIC ST, MONTEREY; 831/375-9798 At this upstairs aerie perched on a knoll, you can dine and have a bird's-eye view of Monterey Bay and Fisherman's Wharf. Specializing in French cuisine with hints of California influence, Fresh Cream thrills the eye and the palate all the way through dessert. Appetizers range from lobster ravioli with gold caviar to escargots in garlic butter with Pernod to a smooth-as-silk goose liver pâté with capers and onions. Executive chef Gregory Lizza's luscious entrees include roasted duck with black currant sauce, the definitive rack of lamb dijonnaise, and a delicate poached salmon in saffron-thyme sauce. Vegetarians needn't feel left out; the tasty grilled seasonal vegetable plate is a cut above most veggie entrees. For dessert try the Grand Marnier soufflé or the amazing *sac au chocolat,* a dark chocolate bag filled with a mocha milk shake. Service tends to be a bit on the formal side; the wine list is extensive and expensive. *$$$; AE, DC, DIS, MC, V; checks OK; dinner every day; full bar; reservations recommended; dining@freshcream.com; www.freshcream.com; Ste 100C in the Heritage Harbor complex, across from Fisherman's Wharf.* &

Montrio / ★★★

414 CALLE PRINCIPAL, MONTEREY; 831/648-8880 Curved lines, stools of woven branches, and soft-sculpture clouds overhead punch up the decor of this converted 1910 firehouse, and the wait staff are cordial and insightful. The only edgy element here is the food, which has the lusty, rough-yet-refined flavors characteristic of Rio Grill and Tarpy's, two other local favorites founded by Montrio co-owners Tony Tollner and Bill Cox. An oak-fired rotisserie grill in the open kitchen lets you watch the action. Try such dishes as grilled salmon over beans and black rice in a citrus-cumin broth, or duck with wild rice and a dried plum–juniper reduction. The wine list, which received *Wine Spectator* magazine's Award of Excellence, includes many fine vintages by the glass. Or you can opt to sample a wee dram of single-malt Scotch or small-batch bourbon—and if it's a thrill you seek, try a Tombstone Martini, described on the menu as "soooo smooth it's scary." Desserts are worth the calories, particularly the white nectarine pecan crisp with vanilla-bean ice cream. Surprisingly for such a stylish place, a kids' menu and crayons are available, which should keep junior diners as contented as their parents. *$$$; AE, DIS, MC, V; no checks; dinner every day; full bar; reservations recommended; www.montrio.com; near Franklin St.* ♿

Stokes Restaurant and Bar / ★★★

500 HARTNELL ST, MONTEREY; 831/373-1110 Formerly Stokes Adobe, the name was changed because too many people assumed the restaurant served basic Mexican food. Not likely in this sophisticated place. An inspired redesign has literally gilded the lily at the historic peach-colored adobe built in 1833 for the town doctor. Co-proprietors Dorothea and Kirk Probasco didn't miss a trick when they opened Stokes in 1996, snagging Brandon Miller as head chef and assembling a staff that is both well trained and friendly. The two-story adobe and board-and-batten house is surrounded by attractive gardens and reflects the Spanish character of Old Monterey. Inside, using hand-cut stencils, interior designer Daniel Peterson has applied intricate gold leaf panels and friezes of elaborate Renaissance design. The large space has been divided into several airy dining rooms with terra-cotta floors, bleached-wood plank ceilings, and Mediterranean-inspired wooden chairs and tables. The main dining room is airy, with walls of small-paned windows and seating covered in blue, teal, and tan fabrics. It's a soothing showcase for Miller's terrific food, which he describes as contemporary rustic. That means, for example, when he takes a pizza out of his pizza oven, it won't always be perfectly round. You can come just for tapas such as fava bean crostini or crispy potatoes with aioli, or for a full meal. Popular items include grilled lavender pork chop with leek-lemon bread pudding and pear chutney, and a roasted half chicken on currant-candied pecan and crouton salad. Don't let the "rustic" label fool you; this is extremely refined cooking that respects the individual flavors of the high-quality ingredients. Desserts are wonderful here, especially the chocolate lava cake (as in volcano). *$$; AE, MC, V; no checks; lunch Mon–Sat, dinner every day; full bar; reservations recommended; www.stokesrestaurant.com; at Madison St.* ♿

Tarpy's Roadhouse / ★★★

2999 MONTEREY–SALINAS HWY, MONTEREY; 831/647-1444 Tarpy's may single-handedly give the word roadhouse a good name. Worth a hop in the car for a spin on Highway 68, this exuberant 1917 roadhouse restaurant set on 5 landscaped acres features a broad, sunny patio shaded by market umbrellas and a handsome Southwestern decor inside with rustic, bleached-wood furniture, golden

ESALEN: A BIG SUR RETREAT FOR MIND, BODY, AND SPIRIT

To Esalen we can give thanks—or blame—for bringing terms like self-actualization, peak experience, encounter group, and Gestalt therapy into the popular lexicon, and for that essential contribution to instant enlightenment, the hot tub. Originally located at the ocean's edge, the baths were a source of controversy during Esalen's first two decades, generating rumors of drug use and public sex. In the early '60s, founders Michael Murphy and Richard Price tried to keep the lid on, so to speak, by declaring the baths chastely separate-sex, but the demand for co-ed nudity eventually over rode them. In 1998, *El Niño* storms caused extensive damage to the baths and the towering slope that rises above them. The baths were moved to the top of the bluff, where they'll remain until the hillside and the baths are repaired. They're still co-ed and clothing-optional and continue to be popular with Esalen guests, but the wild antics are long gone. Hey, it's not the '60s anymore.

Almost 40 years have passed since the heady days when Alan Watts and Joseph Campbell debated the mysteries of the universe, Joan Baez gave impromptu concerts, and George and Ringo flew in with the Maharishi in tow, but Esalen continues to be a countercultural enclave for spiritual seekers. A smorgasbord of more than 400 annual workshops dealing with trauma, art and creativity, massage, yoga, martial arts, and relationships offer enough options to keep anyone's body, mind, and spirit in proper working order. Workshops are either two-day (Fri–Sun) or five-day (Sun–Fri), and reservations are essential. Shared lodgings and all meals are included. For more information, call 831/667-3000 or visit www.esalen.org. General questions can also be e-mailed to info@esalen.org.

stone walls, and whimsical art. Lunch emphasizes well-prepared sandwiches and salads, but dinner is when Tarpy's really shines. Appetizers might include grilled polenta with mushrooms and Madeira, fire-roasted artichokes with lemon-herb vinaigrette, and Pacific oysters with red wine–jalapeño mignonette. Entrees, cooked on a wood-burning grill, run the gamut from a bourbon-molasses pork chop or a Dijon-crusted lamb loin to sea scallops with saffron penne or a grilled vegetable plate with succotash. Desserts include lemon and fresh ginger crème brûlée, a triple-layer chocolate cake, and olallieberry pie. The wine list is thoughtfully selected, though skewed toward the expensive side. Tarpy's offers a kids' menu as well, with everything at or under $5. $$$; AE, DIS, MC, V; no checks; lunch, dinner every day, brunch Sun; full bar; reservations recommended; www.tarpys.com; at Hwy 68 and Canyon Del Rey.

LODGINGS

Tip: If you're having trouble finding a vacancy, try calling Resort 2 Me (800/757-5646; www.resort2me.com), a local reservation service that offers free recommendations on Monterey Bay Peninsula hotels in all price ranges.

Hotel Pacific / ★★★

300 PACIFIC ST, MONTEREY; 831/373-5700 OR 800/554-5542 The Hotel Pacific is a modern neo-hacienda hotel that blends in well with the authentic old Monterey adobes it stands amid. A sparkling fountain burbles beside the entrance; inside you'll find handwoven rugs, muted Southwestern colors, terra-cotta tiles, and beamed ceilings soaring above rounded walls. Connected by tiled courtyards with hand-carved fountains, arches, and flowered pathways, a scattering of low-rise buildings holds 105 small suites. All rooms have private patios or terraces overlooking the gardens, fireplaces, hardwood floors, goose-down feather beds, three telephones, and two TVs (one in the bathroom). Ask for a room on the fourth level with a panoramic view of the bay, or a room facing the inner courtyard with its large fountain. A deluxe continental breakfast is provided in the morning, and guests may indulge in afternoon tea. Complimentary underground parking is available, too. *$$$$; AE, DC, DIS, MC, V; checks OK; reservations@innsofmonterey.com; www.hotel pacific.com; between Scott St and Del Monte Blvd.* &

Monterey Plaza Hotel & Spa / ★★★

400 CANNERY ROW, MONTEREY; 831/646-1700 OR 800/368-2468 Situated right at the edge of Monterey Bay, the Monterey Plaza Hotel brings big-city style and services to Cannery Row. In contrast to the California beach-house decor often found in waterfront hotels, this place strikes a note of classic, sleek traditionalism, with a spacious lobby that gleams with Brazilian teakwood walls, Italian marble, and red, Oriental-style carpeting. Beidermeier-style armoires and writing desks, cozy duvet bedspreads, and sumptuous marble baths carry the classic look into the hotel's 290 guest rooms and suites. And 24-hour in-room dining, a well-stocked honor bar, pay-per-view videos, and nightly turndown on request make guest rooms especially nice to cocoon in. Many of the rooms face the bay and feature sliding glass doors and private balconies that place you right above the lapping surf. The addition of the Plaza's 11,000-square-foot European-style spa has transformed it from simply a nice place to stay into something of a destination. Although the spa services are extra, use of the well-equipped fitness room is complimentary with any spa treatment. The hotel's Duck Club Restaurant enjoys an enviable location right on the water and serves American regional cuisine with an emphasis on wood-roasted specialties, including duck, beef, lamb, chicken, and fresh seafood. The adjacent Schooner's Bistro serves lighter fare, with a tasty range of starters, salads, sandwiches, and pastas. *$$$$; AE, DIS, MC, V; checks OK; www.wood sidehotels.com; at Drake St.*

Old Monterey Inn / ★★★

500 MARTIN ST, MONTEREY; 831/375-8284 OR 800/350-2344 When was the last time you paid $300 for a room and felt you had underpaid? You may feel that way after a night at this elegantly appointed inn. Nestled among giant oak trees and gardens filled with rhododendrons, begonias, fuchsias, and ferns, this Tudor-style country inn built as a home in 1929 positively gleams with natural wood, skylights, and stained-glass windows. The 10 beautifully decorated guest rooms, each with a private bath, are filled with charming antiques and comfortable beds with plump down comforters and huge, fluffy pillows. Nine of the ten accommodations have fireplaces, and all rooms have TVs with VCRs and telephones for outgoing calls only, to preserve guest privacy; hosts Ann and Gene Swett and their staff will happily take incoming calls and deliver messages to your room. For the utmost privacy, request the lacy Garden Cottage, which has a private patio, skylights, and a fireplace sitting room, but book it many months ahead because it is a favorite with honeymooners. The deluxe Ashford Suite is the largest, in a wing all its own, and was the master suite of the house. It has a sitting area with a fireplace, a separate dressing room, a king-size bed, an antique daybed, a very large "gentleman's tub," and a panoramic garden view. Another standout: the handsome Library guest room, with its book-lined walls, stone fireplace, and private sun deck. Breakfast, taken in the formal dining room or en suite, might include orange blossom French toast, crepes, artichoke strata, or waffles. The next day's breakfast menu is posted in the evening, or you can inform the staff of your specific diet needs and they will prepare something special for you. You'll also find a delightful afternoon tea and evening hors d'oeuvres. There are plenty of low-key ways to pamper yourself around here, such as lounging at the picnic tables in the rose garden or strolling around the acre-plus grounds. *$$$$; MC, V; checks OK; omi@oldmontereyinn.com; www.old montereyinn.com; near Pacific St.*

Spindrift Inn / ★★★

652 CANNERY ROW, MONTEREY; 831/646-8900 OR 800/841-1879 With its soaring four-story atrium and rooftop garden, the Spindrift is an unexpected and elegant refuge amid the hurly-burly tourist world of Cannery Row. Downstairs in this former bordello, plush Oriental carpets muffle your footsteps, and a tall pair of attractive if politically questionable Italian blackamoor statues keep you company in the fireside sitting room. Upstairs, all 42 rooms have feather beds (many with canopies) with down comforters, fireplaces, hardwood floors, telephones, and tiled bathrooms with marble appointments. You'll also discover terrycloth robes, cable TVs, and nightly turndown service. The corner rooms, with their cushioned window seats and breathtaking ocean views, are the best in the house. In the morning there will be a newspaper and a breakfast of fruit, orange juice, croissants, and sweet rolls waiting outside your door on a silver tray. In the afternoon you are invited to partake of tea, pastries, wine, and cheese. *$$$$; AE, DC, DIS, MC, V; checks OK; reservations@innsofmonterey.com; www.spindriftinn.com; at Hawthorne St.*

Pacific Grove

In 1875, Methodists set up a summer retreat, pitching tents near what is now Lovers Point. Before long, board-and-batten cottages were built right over the tents, and in some of those former cottages current residents still find scraps of the original tent material in the eaves. As one might suppose, things were pretty buttoned up for a while, and Pacific Grove once even had an ordinance that residents' curtains must be open during the day so no hanky-panky could transpire. The town was incorporated in 1889, just about the time Robert Louis Stevenson visited and said, "I have never been in a place that seemed so dreamlike." This beautiful Victorian seacoast village is still a bit dreamlike and retains its decorous old-town character, though it's loosened its collar a bit since the early days, when dancing, alcohol, and even the Sunday newspaper were banned. Less tourist-oriented than Carmel, less commercial than Monterey, P.G. (as locals call it) exudes peace and tranquillity.

Geographically, Pacific Grove begins at the Monterey Bay Aquarium and ends at the 17-Mile Drive gate. Introduce yourself to the town by strolling the 4 miles of trails that meander between the white-sand beaches and rocky tide-pool-dotted coves at **LOVERS POINT BEACH** (off Ocean View Blvd on the east side of Point Piños) and **ASILOMAR STATE BEACH** (off Sunset Dr on the west side of Point Piños). Be sure to sit and enjoy the view from the landmark Lovers Point (named for lovers of Jesus Christ, not the more carnal kind) and keep an eye out for sea otters sleeping atop the kelp beds—there are tons of them here.

At the tip of Point Piños (Spanish for "Point of the Pines") stands the Cape Cod–style **POINT PIÑOS LIGHTHOUSE** (Asilomar Blvd at Lighthouse Ave; 831/648-5716), the oldest continuously operating lighthouse on the West Coast, built in February 1855. This National Historic Landmark is open to the public Thursday through Sunday, from 1pm to 4pm, and admission is free.

P.G. is famous for its Victorian houses, inns, and churches, and hundreds of them have been declared historically significant by the Pacific Grove Heritage Society. Every October, some of the most artfully restored are opened to the public on the **VICTORIAN HOME TOUR**. If you can't make the tour, you can at least admire the ornate facades clustered along Lighthouse Avenue, Central Avenue, and Ocean View Boulevard.

Pacific Grove bills itself as Butterfly Town, USA, in honor of the thousands of monarchs that migrate here from late October to mid-March. Two popular places to view the alighting lepidoptera are the **MONARCH GROVE SANCTUARY** (at Lighthouse Ave and Ridge Rd) and **GEORGE WASHINGTON PARK** (at Sinex Ave and Alder St). To learn more about the monarchs, visit the charmingly informal and kid-friendly **PACIFIC GROVE MUSEUM OF NATURAL HISTORY** (Forest and Central Aves; 831/648-5716; www.pgmuseum.org), which has a video and display on the butterfly's life cycle, as well as exhibits of other insects, local birds, mammals, and reptiles (admission is free). For good books and international gifts, amble over to **BOOKWORKS** (667 Lighthouse Ave; 831/372-2242), where yellow crime tape festoons the mystery section and there's an easy chair for reading, along with an extensive array of magazines and newspapers.

Around the corner from the Monterey Bay Aquarium is the **AMERICAN TIN CANNERY PREMIUM OUTLETS** center (125 Ocean View Blvd; 831/372-1442), where more than 40 high-quality clothing, shoes, and accessories stores—including Anne Klein, Bass, London Fog, Reebok, Big Dog, OshKosh B'Gosh, Samsonite, and

Izod—sell their wares for up to half of what you'd normally pay. Particularly worth a look are the amazing deals at the Woolrich outlet, where many items are 50 percent off.

For more information about P.G., call or visit the Pacific Grove Chamber of Commerce, located at the corner of Forest and Central Avenues (831/373-3304 or 800/656-6650; www.pacificgrove.org).

RESTAURANTS

Fandango / ★★★

223 17TH ST, PACIFIC GROVE; 831/372-3456 Fandango, the name of a lively Spanish dance, is the perfect moniker for this kick-up-your-heels restaurant specializing in Mediterranean country cuisine. It's a big, sprawling, colorful place with textured adobe walls and a spirited crowd filling six separate dining rooms; the glass-domed terrace in back, with its stone fireplace and open mesquite grill, is especially pleasant. Start with a few tapas—perhaps spicy sausage, roasted red peppers, or a potato-and-onion frittata. If you're feeling adventurous, order the Velouté Bongo Bongo, an exotic creamy soup with oysters, spinach, and Cognac. For the main course, choose from the flavorful Paella Fandango (served at your table in a huge skillet), pasta puttanesca (tomatoes, basil, garlic, capers, and olives), bouillabaisse Marseillaise, osso buco, or the 26-ounce porterhouse steak, with tarragon and Cognac herbed butter. For dessert, try the profiteroles filled with chocolate ice cream and topped with hot fudge sauce. *Olé! $$$; AE, DC, DIS, MC, V; no checks; lunch Mon–Sat, dinner every day, brunch Sun; full bar; reservations recommended; www.fandangorestaurant.com; near Lighthouse Ave.*

Old Bath House Restaurant / ★★★

620 OCEAN VIEW BLVD, PACIFIC GROVE; 831/375-5195 Although many locals are quick to dismiss the Old Bath House as a pricey tourist restaurant (and it is indeed guilty on both counts), the food is meticulously prepared and the setting is undeniably romantic. This former bathhouse at Lovers Point has a fine view of the rocky coast and a wonderful wood interior with a low, carved ceiling. The continental menu offers such starters such as grilled prawns and wild boar sausage, and artichoke and Gorgonzola cheese ravioli with a lemon-nutmeg cream sauce. Entrees may feature an oak-grilled lavender-thyme pork porterhouse with grilled nectarines and chive mashed potatoes; a Muscovy duck breast with a tart dried cherry–merlot reduction and risotto with hazelnuts; or Beef Bindel, a filet mignon baked in a puff pastry with Black Forest ham and mushrooms. Tempting desserts include hot pecan ice-cream fritters and the aptly named Oceans of Chocolate (a bittersweet chocolate brownie with espresso cream cheese, vanilla or chocolate ice cream, and warm chocolate sauce). The service is impeccable and the wine list extensive. There's a children's menu as well. *$$$; AE, DC, DIS, MC, V; no checks; dinner every day; full bar; reservations recommended; www.oldbathhouse.com; at Lovers Point Park.*

Pasta Mia Trattoria / ★★

481 LIGHTHOUSE AVE, PACIFIC GROVE; 831/375-7709 A small, century-old Victorian house provides a homey backdrop for Pasta Mia's hearty Italian fare. The soup and appetizers tend to be tried-and-true standards, such as minestrone, mozzarella fresca, and carpaccio, but the house-made pastas include some intriguing choices, such as a black-and-white linguine with scallops, caviar, cream, and chives, or half-moon pasta stuffed with pesto in a lemon-zest cream sauce dotted with chicken and sun-dried tomatoes. The corkscrew pasta with sausage and chicken in a pink sauce is satisfying and flavorful, as is the scampi in a light champagne cream sauce. *Secondi piatti* include veal marsala; breast of chicken with a garlic, wine, and rosemary sauce; and a daily fresh-fish preparation. Portions are generous in this friendly, informal restaurant, though service can be slow at times. *$$; AE, MC, V; no checks; dinner every day; beer and wine; reservations recommended; near 14th St.*

Red House Cafe / ★★

662 LIGHTHOUSE AVE, PACIFIC GROVE; 831/643-1060 A trim, 103-year-old, red brick house in downtown Pacific Grove is the deceptively modest setting for some of the most adroit cooking on the Monterey Peninsula. It offers a handful of humble-sounding dishes at breakfast and lunch—items such as Irish oatmeal, Belgian waffles, pastries, a mixed green salad, roast beef on sourdough, a BLT, and eggs any way you like them as long as they're scrambled. Sit in one of the snug, country cottage–style dining rooms or enjoy the ocean breezes on the porch with its smattering of wicker chairs and tables for two. Often local salmon or other Monterey Bay seafood is on the menu, and the crab cakes are to die for, full of succulent crab and not much else. Locals love it here, and often have a favorite menu item they always order. Perfectly cooked, every dish demonstrates the kitchen's insistence on first-rate ingredients—heck, even the toast and jam tastes like a gourmet treat. On the sidewalk outside there is a large, round embedded stone engraved with the word JOY. When you take your first bite you will see why. *$; cash only; breakfast, lunch Tues–Sun, dinner Thurs–Sat; beer and wine; reservations recommended; info@red housecafe.com; www.redhousecafe.com; at 19th St.*

Taste Cafe & Bistro / ★★★

1199 FOREST AVE, PACIFIC GROVE; 831/655-0324 Although it's a bit hard to see on Forest Avenue, in a small mini-mall with only one entry, food lovers seek out Taste Cafe. You'll be hard-pressed to find higher-quality food for the same price anywhere else on the coast. The menu combines rustic French, Italian, and California cuisines made from the best and freshest produce, seafood, and meats from local suppliers. Lunch could be a grilled eggplant sandwich with smoked Gouda cheese and caramelized onion on toasted focaccia, or chicken-apple sausages with au gratin potatoes. At dinner, start your meal with house-cured salmon carpaccio with a mustard-dill dressing, butternut squash agnolotti, or an organic red Oakleaf salad with crumbled blue cheese, balsamic dressing, sliced pears, and glazed pecans. Move on to entrees such as tortellini Florentine, marinated rabbit with braised red cabbage, and lean pork medallions with sautéed napa cabbage, onions, celery, and apples. Be sure to save room for one of the wonderful desserts: warm brioche pudding with apricot coulis and crème fraîche, or a bittersweet chocolate torte. The interior is simple, airy, high-ceilinged, and graced with beautiful flower arrangments. The word is out on this terrific restaurant, so be sure to call well ahead for reservations, especially for weekend dinners. *$$; AE, MC, V; checks OK; lunch, dinner Tues–Sun; beer and wine; reservations recommended; www.tastecafebistro.com; at Prescott Ave.* &

LODGINGS

Gatehouse Inn / ★★

225 CENTRAL AVE, PACIFIC GROVE; 831/649-8436 OR 800/753-1881 This big yellow Victorian looks a bit like the haunted house at Disneyland, but much cheerier. When State Senator Benjamin Langford built the ocean-view mansion in 1884, Pacific Grove was less a town than a pious Methodist meeting ground, separated from wicked, worldly Monterey by a white picket fence. Langford's domain is now an enticingly eccentric B&B, where each of the nine individually decorated guest rooms range in style from Victoriana to Persia to Beach House. All guest rooms have private baths and queen-size beds, with the exception of the Cannery Row Room, which has a king-size bed. The Langford Room ranks as the inn's most luxurious, with an ocean-view sitting room, a potbellied stove, and a claw-footed bathtub that's just a step away from the bed and commands a stunning view of the coast (talk about soaking it all in). In the morning, the sun just streams in. Looking for something more exotic? You might try the Turkish Room. You'll find hors d'oeuvres, tea, and wine in the lobby every evening and a full breakfast buffet with house-baked breads every morning, and you can even help yourself to cookies and beverages from the kitchen any time of day or night. *$$$; AE, DIS, MC, V; checks OK; 2-night minimum stay on weekends May–Oct; lew@sueandlewinns.com; www.sueandlewinns.com/gate house; at 2nd St.*

Grand View Inn / ★★★☆

557 OCEAN VIEW BLVD, PACIFIC GROVE; 831/372-4341 Even in a town as rich in resplendent Victorians as Pacific Grove, this pristine and romantic inn within a few feet of the water on Ocean View Boulevard stands out. Built in 1910 as the residence of Dr. Julia Platt, a marine biologist who became Pacific Grove's first female mayor, the inn is owned by the family who also owns the Seven Gables Inn next door (see review, below). A bit more casual and restrained in decor than its ornate sister, this charmer with the cheerful blue exterior has 10 guest rooms and a separate cottage, all with bay views, high plaster ceilings with decorative detailing, eclectic antique furniture and light fixtures, queen-size beds, Gilchrist & Soames bath amenities, sitting areas, and beautifully appointed marble bathrooms; most have views of the ocean. A full breakfast is served in the elegant first-floor dining room with its breathtaking view of Lovers Point; later in the day the same room is the setting for an elaborate spread, modestly called afternoon tea. These two sister inns have their own chef, who cooks up savories as well as sweets for the afternoon tea. Complimentary off-street parking is available, too. *$$$$; MC, V; checks OK; www.7gables-grandview.com; at Grand Ave.*

Lighthouse Lodge and Suites / ★★

1150 AND 1249 LIGHTHOUSE AVE, PACIFIC GROVE; 831/655-2111 OR 800/858-1249 Less than a block from the ocean, the Lighthouse Lodge and Suites is really two entities with rather distinct personalities. The lodge consists of 64 motel-like rooms and suites—complete with large TVs, minibars, refrigerators, and microwaves—that are ideally suited for families, particularly when booked as part of the hotel's discount vacation package. Those seeking more luxurious accommodations should spring for one of the 31 newer suites down the hill and across the road. The Cape Cod–style suites—all with beamed ceilings, plush carpeting, fireplaces, wing chairs, vast bathrooms with marble whirlpool tubs, large-screen TVs, mini-kitchens, and king-size beds—glow in peacock hues of purple, green, and fuchsia. The overall effect is a bit nouveau riche, but riche all the same. A full breakfast and afternoon poolside barbecue are included in the room rate. After breakfast take a morning stroll around the grounds, cleverly landscaped with fountains and native plants, or go for a swim in the outdoor heated pool. *$$ (lodge), $$$–$$$$ (suites); AE, DC, DIS, MC, V; no checks; reservations@lhls.com; www.lhls.com; at Asilomar Blvd.*

The Martine Inn / ★★★☆

255 OCEAN VIEW BLVD, PACIFIC GROVE; 831/373-3388 OR 800/852-5588 Perched like a vast pink wedding cake on a cliff above Monterey Bay, this villa with a Mediterranean exterior and a Victorian interior is one of Pacific Grove's most elegant bed-and-breakfasts. Built in 1899 for James and Laura Parke (of Parke-Davis Pharmaceuticals fame), the inn has two dozen spacious guest rooms, all with private baths and high-quality antiques, including lamps with interesting shades. Owner Dan Martine has accumulated the best collection of ornately carved armoires on the planet. Most rooms have wood-burning fireplaces; all have views of the water or the garden courtyard with its delightful dragon fountain. If you feel like splurging, the Parke Room at the very top of the house is outstanding. Originally the master bedroom, it has three walls of windows with views of the waves crashing against the rocks, an 1860s Chippendale Revival bedroom set complete with four-poster canopy bed, a sitting area, a claw-footed tub, and a massive, white-brick corner fireplace. No matter which room you choose, you'll find a silver basket of fruit and a rose waiting for you upon arrival, and a newspaper at your door in the morning. Several intimate sitting rooms offset three large common areas: the library, the main dining room (with a dazzling view of the bay), and the breakfast parlor. The personable Mr. Martine is your host and will be happy to show you his collection of five vintage roadsters, including a 1925 MG, which he races. Martine serves an elaborate and well-prepared breakfast at a table set with old Sheffield silver, crystal, and lace, and offers wine and hors d'oeuvres in the late afternoon in the formal parlor with its baby grand piano. *$$$–$$$$; AE, DIS, MC, V; checks OK; don@martineinn.com; www.martineinn.com; 4 blocks from Cannery Row.*

Seven Gables Inn / ★★★☆

555 OCEAN VIEW BLVD, PACIFIC GROVE; 831/372-4341 Set in an immaculate yellow Victorian mansion built in 1886 and surrounded by gardens, this family-run inn—they also own the Grand View Inn next door (see review, above)—commands a magnificent view of Monterey Bay. Chock-full of formal European antiques, Seven Gables will seem like paradise to those who revel in things Victorian. Once you're ensconced in one of the 14 guest rooms, which are divided among the main house, a guest house, and a smattering of cottages, the warm and welcoming Flatley family will see to your every comfort. The uniquely appointed rooms feature gorgeous ocean views, private baths with Gilchrist & Soames bath amenities, and queen-size beds with down comforters. A pull-out-all-the-stops breakfast is served by the house chef in the imposing dining room, and tea service is set out every afternoon. *$$$$; MC, V; checks OK; www.7gables-grand view.com; at Fountain Ave.*

Pebble Beach and the 17-Mile Drive

How much are a room and a round of golf at Pebble Beach these days? Let's put it this way: If you have to ask, you can't afford it. If the 6,000-or-so residents of this exclusive gated community had their way, Pebble Beach would probably be off-limits to mere commoners. Perhaps more of an indignity, though, is the $8-per-car levy required to trespass on their gilded avenues and wallow in envy at how the ruling class recreates. If you have no strong desire to tour corporate-owned hideaways and redundant—albeit gorgeous—seascapes along the famous **17-MILE DRIVE**, save your lunch money; you're not really missing anything that can't be seen elsewhere along the Monterey coast (just drive along the coast on Ocean View Boulevard in Pacific Grove and you'll see pretty much the same views). Then again, some folks swear that cruising past Pebble Beach's mansions and manicured golf courses is worth the admission just to contemplate the lifestyles of the very rich.

If you decide to pay the toll, you'll see everything from a spectacular Byzantine castle with a private beach—the **CROCKER MANSION** near the Carmel gate—to several tastefully bland California Nouvelle country-club establishments in perfectly maintained forest settings. Other highlights include the often-photographed gnarled **LONE CYPRESS** clinging to its rocky precipice above the sea; miles of hiking and equestrian trails winding through groves of native pines and wildflowers, with glorious views of Monterey Bay; and **BIRD ROCK**, a small offshore isle covered with hundreds of seals and sea lions (bring binoculars). Self-guided nature tours are outlined in a variety of brochures, available for free at the gate entrances and at **THE INN AT SPANISH BAY** and **THE LODGE AT PEBBLE BEACH** (see reviews, below).

There are five entrances to the 17-Mile Drive, each manned by spiffy security guards, and the entire drive takes about one to two hours (though you can whiz by the highlights in 30 minutes). Your best bet is to avoid the busy summer weekends and come midweek. Visitors may enter the 17-Mile Drive for free on foot or bike, although **CYCLISTS** are required to use the Pacific Grove gate on weekends and holidays. For more information, call the **PEBBLE BEACH RESORT** at 831/624-3811 or log onto www.pebblebeach.com/17miledrive.html.

LODGINGS

The Inn at Spanish Bay / ★★★★

2700 17-MILE DR, PEBBLE BEACH; 831/647-7500 OR 800/654-9300 Set on the privately owned 17-Mile Drive, this sprawling modern inn defines deluxe. Consistantly ranked among the top resorts in the world, its 270 luxuriously appointed rooms and suites perched on a cypress-dotted bluff have gas fireplaces, quilted down comforters, and elegant sitting areas. Most have private patios or balconies with gorgeous views of the rocky coast or the Del Monte Forest. Three of the most deluxe suites even come with grand pianos. The bathrooms, equipped with all the modern conveniences you could want, are appropriately regal. Hotel guests have access to eight tennis courts, an outdoor swimming pool, a 22,000-square-foot full-service spa and salon, and miles of hiking and equestrian trails. Along with the well-respected Roy's at Pebble Beach, the resort recently added an Italian restaurant, Peppoli, which serves rich Tuscan fare. *$$$$; AE, DC, MC, V; checks OK; www.pebblebeach.com; near the Pacific Grove entrance.* ₺

The Lodge at Pebble Beach / ★★★½

17-MILE DR, PEBBLE BEACH; 831/647-7500 OR 800/654-9300 Despite greens fees of $380 (hey, it *includes* a cart), Pebble Beach remains the mecca of American golf courses, and avid golfers feel they have to play it at least once before retiring to that Big Clubhouse in the Sky. The guest rooms are tastefully decorated, swathed in soothing earth tones and outfitted with a sophisticated, modern decor. There are 161 suites and rooms, most with private balconies or patios, brick fireplaces, sitting areas, and gorgeous views. All the usual upscale amenities are provided, from phones by the commode and honor-bar refrigerators to robes and cable TVs. The whole effect is very East Coast country club. Four restaurants cater to visitors, most notably Club XIX, where chef Philip Baker features his elegant mix of French and Californian cuisine, and the Stillwater Bar and Grill, with a menu that offers seafood, steak, and even hamburgers. Jackets for men are required at Club XIX. Hotel guests have preferred tee times at the world-famous Pebble Beach, Spanish Bay, and Spyglass Hill golf courses, as well as access to the oceanside Beach & Tennis Club, an outdoor swimming pool, a 22,000-square-foot full-service spa and salon, and miles of hiking and equestrian trails. *$$$$; AE, DC, DIS, MC, V; checks OK; www.pebblebeach.com; near the Carmel Gate.* ₺

Carmel

In the not-so-distant past, Carmel was regarded as a reclusive little seaside town with the sort of relaxed Mediterranean atmosphere conducive to such pursuits as photography, painting, and writing. Robert Louis Stevenson, Upton Sinclair, and Ansel Adams all found Carmel peaceful and intellectually inspiring enough to settle down here. They wanted to be left alone, and fought street improvements and numbered

AÑO NUEVO STATE RESERVE

You're not the only one having fun in the sun. For a seaside sex show, pull off Highway 1 between the coastal towns of Pescadero and Davenport (22 miles north of Santa Cruz) at Año Nuevo State Reserve (800/444-4445, tickets; 650/879-0227, information; www.anonuevo.org), a unique and fascinating breeding ground for **NORTHERN ELEPHANT SEALS**. A close encounter with a 16-foot-long, 2-ton male elephant seal waving his humongous schnoz is an unforgettable event. The seals are named after the male's dangling proboscis, which can grow up to a couple of feet long. The reserve is open year-round, but you'll see hundreds of these marine mammals during their mating season, which starts in December and continues through March. To access the reserve during the mating season, you must have a reservation for one of the 2½-hour naturalist-led tours (offered Dec 15–Mar 31). The tours are terrific and tickets are cheap, but they sell out fast, so plan about two months ahead (and don't forget to bring a jacket).

house addresses to ensure their seclusion. The charmingly ragtag bohemian village of yesteryear has long since given way to a major tourist hot spot brimming with chichi inns, art galleries, and house-and-garden shops offering $300 ceramic geese and other essentials. Traffic—both vehicular and pedestrian—can be maddeningly congested during the summer and on weekends, and prices in the shops, hotels, and restaurants tend to be high. The funny thing is, no matter how crowded or expensive Carmel gets, nobody seems to mind. Enamored of the village's eclectic dwellings, expensive boutiques, quaint cafes, and silky white beaches, tourists arrive in droves during the summer to lighten their wallets and darken their complexions. In fact, most lodgings are booked solid from May to October, so make your reservations far in advance and leave plenty of room on the credit cards—you'll need it. And bring your dog if you have one; many inns welcome them with doggy biscuits at the desk and pet beds in the rooms, and in many shops it's perfectly OK to bring Fido in to browse.

Without doubt, the best way to see Carmel is on foot. **CARMEL WALKS** (831/642-2700; www.carmelwalks.com) offers a two-hour guided walk of the town's most interesting paths and courtyards, including Hugh Comstock's storybook cottages and the homes of famous former denizens such as feminist Mary Austin, photographer Edward Weston, and poet Robinson Jeffers. Tours cost $20 and are offered Tuesday through Friday at 10am, Saturday at 10am and 2pm; meet in the courtyard of the Pine Inn (Lincoln St at Ocean Ave).

The restored Mission San Carlos Borromeo del Río Carmelo, better known as the **CARMEL MISSION** (3080 Rio Rd, at Lasuén Dr, several blocks W of Hwy 1; 831/624-3600; www.carmelmission.org) is located next to **MISSION TRAILS PARK**, with 5 miles of winding paths dotted by wildflowers, willows, deer, and redwoods. Established in 1770, the Carmel Mission was the headquarters of Father Junípero Serra's famous chain of California missions—and his favorite (Serra is buried in front of the altar in the sanctuary, which is marked with a plaque). The vine-covered baroque church with its 11-bell Moorish tower, completed in 1797, is one of California's architectural treasures. Be sure to see the main altar, with its Gothic arch and elaborate decorations, and Serra's restored cell, where he died in 1784. The mission houses three extensive museums, and its surrounding 14 acres are planted with native flowers and trees. The cemetery has more than 3,000 graves of Native Americans who worked and lived in the mission; in place of a gravestone, many plots are marked by a solitary abalone shell.

TOR HOUSE (26304 Ocean View Ave, at Stewart Wy; 831/624-1813; www.tor house.org), the former home of poet Robinson Jeffers, is a rustic granite building that looks as though it were transplanted from the British Isles. Constructed over several years beginning in 1914, today it's the residence of one of Jeffers's descendants. Even more intriguing is the nearby four-story **HAWK TOWER**, which Jeffers built for his wife, Una, with huge rocks he hauled up from the beach below. Guided tours of the house and tower are available for a fee on Friday and Saturday by reservation only (no children under 12 admitted).

Are you ready for a good dose of Mother Nature's great wonders? Then visit one of the town's two beautiful beaches. **CARMEL CITY BEACH,** at the foot of Ocean Avenue and the town's shopping district, tends to be overcrowded in the summer (though its chilly aquamarine water is unsafe for swimming), but the gorgeous white sand and towering cypresses are worth the price of sunbathing among the hordes. Or head a mile south on Scenic Drive to spectacular **CARMEL RIVER STATE BEACH,** where the locals go to hide from the tourists (though swimming is unsafe here, too). The Carmel River enters the Pacific at this point, and you'll see a bird sanctuary frequented by pelicans, hawks, sandpipers, kingfishers, willets, and the occasional goose. **MIDDLE BEACH** and **MONASTERY BEACH** lie beyond. These areas are remarkably scenic, but Mother Nature saved her best efforts for the 1,276-acre **POINT LOBOS STATE RESERVE** (831/624-4909 for park information; 831/624-8413 for scuba-diving reservations; pt-lobos.parks.state.ca.us/; on Hwy 1 approximately 3 miles S of Carmel). More than a dozen Point Lobos trails lead to ocean coves, where you might spy sea otters, harbor seals, California sea lions, large colonies of seabirds and, between December and May, migrating California gray whales. Some trails will even take you to one of the two naturally growing stands of Monterey cypress remaining on earth (the other stand is in Pebble Beach on the 17-Mile Drive). For more nearby hiking recommendations, see the Big Sur section in the following pages.

Shopping is a popular pastime in Carmel—at least for those who don't blanch at astronomical price tags. Not only is its downtown packed with interesting little boutiques, but also just outside of town lie two luxe suburban malls: **THE BARNYARD** (on Hwy 1 at Carmel Valley Rd; 831/624-8886) and **THE CROSSROADS** (on Hwy 1 at Rio Rd; 831/624-9492). **OCEAN AVENUE** between Junipero and San Antonio avenues has its share of tourist-schlock shops, it's true, but hit the side streets for some fine adventures in consumerland. Numerous quality art galleries are located between Lincoln and San Carlos Streets and Fifth and Sixth Avenues. Particularly noteworthy is the **WESTON GALLERY** (6th Ave, at Dolores St; 831/624-4453), which showcases 19th- and 20th-century photographers' works, including a permanent display featuring such famous Carmelites as Edward Weston, Ansel Adams, and Imogen Cunningham. If you want to tour the galleries, pick up a copy of the Carmel Gallery Guide from the Carmel Visitor Information Center (see below).

Carmel has an active theater scene, perhaps best represented by the **PACIFIC REPERTORY THEATRE COMPANY** (831/622-0100; www.pacrep.org), which puts on an outdoor musical and Shakespeare festival each summer and performs other classics such as *The Madness of George III* and *Death of a Salesman* in its indoor theater year-round.

The annual monthlong **CARMEL BACH FESTIVAL** (831/624-2046; www.bach festival.com) offers numerous concerts, recitals, lectures, and discussion groups—some are even free. In addition to Bach masterpieces, you'll hear scores by Vivaldi, Scarlatti, Beethoven, and Chopin. The most sought-after ticket of the event is the formal concert in the mission (book far ahead for that one). The classical music celebration begins in mid-July; series tickets are sold starting in January, and single-event tickets (ranging from $10 to $50) go on sale in April.

For more information about Carmel, call or visit the **CARMEL VISITOR INFOR-MATION CENTER** (831/624-2522; www.carmelcalifornia.org), located on San Carlos Street between 5th and 6th Avenues, which is amply stocked with maps, brochures, and publications on area attractions and lodgings. It's open Monday through Friday from 9am to 5pm. There's also a Visitor Information kiosk at Carmel Plaza, on Ocean Avenue between Junipero and San Carlos streets. It's open from 11am to 5pm year-round on Saturday, and Wednesday through Sunday Memorial Day through Labor Day.

RESTAURANTS

Anton & Michel / ★★

MISSION ST, CARMEL; 831/624-2406 OR 866/244-0645 This longtime Carmel favorite overlooks the Court of the Fountains with its Louis XV lions and verdigris garden pavilions. Anton & Michel's elegant dining room has pink walls, white wainscoting, and tall, slender pillars adorned with curlicue cornices. Despite the interesting decor, the continental cuisine isn't exactly daring, but it's extremely well prepared. Standouts include the rack of lamb with an herb-Dijon mustard au jus, grilled veal with a spinach-Madeira sauce, and medallions of ahi tuna with a black-pepper-and-sesame-seed crust and a wasabi-cilantro sauce. Anton & Michel also offers traditional French desserts such as crepes suzette, cherries jubilee, and chocolate mousse cake with sauce anglaise. Service is courtly, and the extensive wine list has garnered many *Wine Spectator* magazine awards. *$$$; AE, DC, DIS, MC, V; no checks; lunch, dinner every day; full bar; reservations recommended; www.carmelsbest.com; between Ocean and 7th Aves.*

Casanova Restaurant / ★★

5TH AVE, CARMEL; 831/625-0501 The former home of Charlie Chaplin's cook, this sunny cottage with a Mediterranean feel attracts happy throngs of locals and tourists alike. Casanova specializes in Italian and French country–style dishes; the pasta creations, such as linguine with seafood served in a big copper pot, are particularly fetching. At dinner, there is a required three-course prix-fixe menu, so don't come just to graze on appetizers. Lunch on the big patio out back is informal and fun, with heaters keeping patrons warm on chilly afternoons. Inside, the cottage is a jumble of nooks and crannies decked out in rustic European decor. Casanova prides itself on its extensive and reasonably priced wine list, including the well-received Georis merlot and cabernet, produced by one of the restaurant's owners. Cap off your meal with one of Casanova's superb desserts; the many choices include a Basque-style pear tart and a chocolate custard pie with whipped cream, nuts, and shaved dark and white Belgian chocolates. *$$; MC, V; no checks; lunch, dinner every day, brunch Sun; full bar; reservations recommended; www.casanovarestaurant.com; between San Carlos and Mission Sts.* &

Flying Fish Grill / ★★

MISSION ST, CARMEL; 831/625-1962 Hidden on the ground level of the Carmel Plaza shopping center, this ebullient newcomer is worth seeking out for its fun, stylish atmosphere and superb seafood. The interior is a maze of booths and tables flanked by an expanse of warm, polished wood and crisp blue-and-white banners. Chef-owner Kenny Fukumoto offers such creative East-West fusion dishes as Yin-Yan Salmon (roast salmon on angel hair pasta sprinkled with sesame seeds and served with a soy-lime cream sauce); catfish fillets with fermented Chinese black beans, ginger, and scallions steamed in paper pouches; pan-fried Chilean sea bass with almonds, whipped potatoes, and a Chinese cabbage and rock shrimp stir-fry; and his specialty, rare peppered ahi tuna on angel hair pasta. New York steak and a couple of flavorful Japanese clay pot dishes (seafood or beef) that you cook at your own table round out the menu. There's also a tempting lineup of desserts, including Chocolate Decadence, a warm banana sundae, and an assortment of delicate sorbets. *$$; AE, DIS, MC, V; no checks; dinner Wed–Mon; beer and wine; reservations recommended; between Ocean and 7th Aves, in Carmel Plaza.*

Grasing's Coastal Cuisine / ★★★

6TH AVE, CARMEL; 831/624-6562 Noted chefs Kurt Grasing and Narsai David teamed up to open this eponymous restaurant (formerly the Sixth Avenue Grill), which serves a more casual version of the contemporary California-Mediterranean cuisine Grasing previously turned out at tony eateries like San Mateo's 231 Ellsworth. At lunch, you'll find superb pastas, salads, sandwiches, and entrees such as bronzed salmon with grilled portobellos, roasted potatoes, and garlic. Dinner starters might include potato, wild rice, and zucchini pancakes with house-cured salmon and crème fraîche, or a savory three-onion tart with a fennel sauce and balsamic syrup. Main courses range from wild-mushroom stew with creamy polenta to roast duck with an orange-port glaze and local swordfish over orzo pasta with snow peas, bok choy, and ponzu sauce. The dining room is a cheerful stage for Grasing's inspired cooking, with Milano-modern furnishings, textured ocher walls, cathedral ceilings, and witty sculptures and art. The wine list is ample and thoughtfully selected, desserts are diet-busting delights, and there's a small patio for dining alfresco. *$$; AE, DC, MC, V; local checks only; lunch, dinner every day; beer and wine; reservations recommended; www.grasings.com; at Mission St.* &

Katy's Place / ★

MISSION ST, CARMEL; 831/624-0199 A few steps from the city library is Katy's Place, the locals' favorite spot in Carmel for breakfast. The country kitchen–style restaurant specializes in comfort food: big helpings and endless variations of pancakes, waffles, and eggs, including a dynamite eggs Benedict. Eat in the pretty dining room or on the patio under the redwood trees. This is a great place to bring the kids. *$; no credit cards; local checks only; breakfast, lunch every day; beer and wine; no reservations; between 5th and 6th Aves.* &

La Bohème / ★★

DOLORES ST, CARMEL; 831/624-7500 If you tend to have trouble choosing what to have for dinner, head for La Bohème. You won't have to make a choice at all in this small, romantic restaurant where the walls are painted a pale blue and dotted with cream puff clouds. La Bohème serves only one prix-fixe menu for about $30 per person, and the selection changes nightly. How do you know if it's something you'll like? Calendars posted outside the restaurant list the entrees for an entire month, and patrons in the know make it a point to pick up this schedule as soon as they hit town (or simply look on the Web site). The three courses include a salad, a bowl of soup, and a main course—perhaps lamb with mint, garlic, and wine; beef bourguignon; or filet mignon with Madeira wine sauce. The soups, such as salmon bisque, and the salads, with Carmel Valley organic greens, are universally wonderful. Two of the most sought-after tables are tucked inside a topsy-turvy little toy house—part of the whimsical street scene mural. While this restaurant is not always consistent, when everything works, La Bohème's cuisine ranks among the best in Carmel, at bargain prices to boot. *$$; MC, V; no checks; dinner every day; beer and wine; reservations recommended; www.laboheme.com; at 7th Ave.*

La Dolce Vita / ★★

SAN CARLOS ST, CARMEL; 831/624-3667 Those in the mood for authentic Italian food in a casual atmosphere will enjoy this restaurant, a local favorite. The terrace, which overlooks the street, is popular for both sunny lunches and moonlit dinners (heaters take the chill off when necessary). Decorated in an Italian-flag color scheme—green chairs, Astroturf, and plastic red-and-white tablecloths—it's a wonderfully unassuming place to sit back, sip a glass of wine, and revel in *la dolce di far niente* ("the joy of doing nothing"). The main dining room is a bit more gussied up; it resembles a cozy trattoria with slate floors, light wood furniture, and peach-toned walls bedecked with garlic braids. Specialties include the transporting Ravioli alla Rachele (homemade spinach ravioli stuffed with crab and cheese in a champagne cream sauce, topped with scallops and sun-dried tomatoes) and Gnocchi della Nonna (fresh potato dumplings with choice of a tomato or Gorgonzola-sage-cream sauce—ask for a little of both). A range of individual-size pizzas is also available, along with *secondi piatti* ranging from traditional osso buco to calamari steak drizzled with sun-dried tomato pesto, lemon juice, and crisp Orvieto wine. The wait staff can be a bit cheeky at times, but hey, with food this *bellissima*, you're not likely to get your feathers ruffled. *$$; MC, V; local checks only; lunch, dinner every day; beer and wine; reservations recommended; between 7th and 8th Aves.* &

Pacific's Edge / ★★★★

HWY 1 (HIGHLANDS INN); 831/622-5445 OR 800/682-4811 Perched on an eyebrow cliff over Highway 1 in the Highlands area is Pacific's Edge, the Highlands Inn Park Hyatt Hotel's flagship restaurant and named one of America's best restaurants by *Wine Spectator* magazine. If you are going to break the bank for one special evening, this is the place, as it serves inspired California cuisine in a gorgeous setting—the rich earth tones, natural woods, and stone blend seamlessly with the surroundings—with panoramic 180-degree views of the coastline (reserve well in advance for a table at sunset). Starters might include farm-fresh artichokes with basil mayonnaise, potato-wrapped ahi tuna, or grilled quail with creamy rosemary polenta. Entrees on the three- to five-course menu range from grilled Monterey Bay salmon in an onion-rosemary sauce to roasted rack of lamb with white truffle potatoes. While you're dining, enjoy the view right down the rocks to the water—at night it is magical. Choosing the appropriate wine shouldn't be a problem—the inn's wine cellar has consistently won *Wine Spectator*'s Grand Award. *$$$; AE, DC, DIS, MC, V; checks OK; lunch, dinner every day, brunch Sun; full bar; reservations recommended; www.highlands-inn.com; 4 miles S of Carmel.*

Rio Grill / ★★

101 CROSSROADS BLVD, CARMEL; 831/625-5436 This noisy Southwestern-style grill is packed with a lively crowd from opening till closing. The salads, such as organic mixed greens with aged goat cheese, seasoned walnuts, and curry vinaigrette, are wonderfully fresh, and appetizers, like the ever-popular onion rings and fried Monterey Bay squid with orange-sesame dipping sauce, draw raves. The tasty barbecued baby back ribs and the herb-crusted chicken with crispy broccoli-corn risotto cakes are good bets for the main course, as is the pumpkin-seed-crusted salmon with chipotle-lime vinaigrette and roasted red pepper–potato cakes. Don't miss the French fries with rosemary aioli. Desserts include a killer olallieberry pie and caramel-apple bread pudding. While the atmosphere may be chaotic, the service isn't, and the grill boasts a large wine list, with many selections available by the glass. They also have a kids' menu with all items under $5. *$$; AE, DIS, MC, V; no checks; lunch, dinner every day, brunch Sun; full bar; reservations recommended; www.riogrill.com; in the Crossroads Shopping Village, at Hwy 1 and Rio Rd.* ♿

LODGINGS

Cypress Inn / ★★

LINCOLN ST, CARMEL; 831/624-3871 OR 800/443-7443 One of the more elegant hotels in Carmel, this Spanish Colonial–style inn in the center of town is owned by movie star and animal-rights activist Doris Day. Pets, naturally, are more than welcome. In fact, the immaculate hotel even provides dog beds for its four-footed guests. The 34 guest rooms come in a wide variety of sizes, shapes, and locations. Try to book a tower suite, with the bedroom reached by a winding stair, plus whirlpool tub, arched windows, and bookshelves complete with books. All rooms contain some thoughtful touches: fresh fruit, bottles of spring water, chocolates left on the pillow at night, and a decanter of sherry. Some have sitting rooms, wet bars, private verandas, and ocean views; all have marble bathrooms, fruit baskets, nightly turndown service, and special blankets for pets. Light sleepers should ask for a room on the second floor. Downstairs there's a spacious Spanish-style open-beam living room with a comforting fire and a friendly bar that dishes out coffee and a continental breakfast in the morning, as well as libations of a more spirited kind at night. Posters of Doris Day movies add a touch of glamour and fun to the decor. *$$$–$$$$; AE, DIS, MC, V; checks OK; www.cypress-inn.com; at 7th Ave.*

Highlands Inn / ★★★

HWY 1, CARMEL; 831/620-1234 OR 800/682-4811 Set high above the rocky coastline south of Carmel with fine views of Yankee Point, the Highlands Inn, a Park Hyatt property, is a sprawling modern complex of glowing redwood and soaring glass. In the main lodge, a skylit promenade leads to a series of glass-walled salons built for watching sunsets. In the fireside lobby you'll find deep leather settees, a granite fireplace, a grand piano, and elaborate floral displays. Outside, flower-lined walkways connect the cottagelike collection of rooms and suites. Every suite and townhouse unit comes with a full parlor, kitchen, and bath with a massive spa tub. The 142 guest rooms are furnished with jewel-toned accents and fabrics and carpeting with earth tones. Most rooms have fireplaces, private decks, and fabulous views of the ocean, landscaped grounds, and evergreen-draped hills. Another perk is the inn's elegant restaurant, Pacific's Edge (see review, above), and the less formal California Market, which boasts wonderful coastline views and serves casual, well-prepared California fare. *$$$$; AE, DC, DIS, MC, V; checks OK; www.highlands-inn.com; 4 miles S of town.* &

La Playa Hotel / ★★★

CAMINO REAL, CARMEL; 831/624-6476 OR 800/582-8900 Originally built in 1904 as a wedding gift for a member of the Ghirardelli chocolate family, this Mediterranean villa–style luxury hotel spills down a terraced, bougainvillea-and-jasmine-strewn hillside toward the sea. The classic and subdued lobby sets the tone, with Greek caryatid priestess figures holding up the fireplace mantel. Paths lit by gas street lamps wind among lush gardens with cast-iron gazebos and past a heated swimming pool festooned with mermaids, La Playa's mythical mascots. The 75 guest rooms and suites are comfortable, with hand-carved furniture, color TVs, and nightly turndown service. Many overlook the gorgeous courtyard. To do La Playa right, invest in one of the five cottages, some of which are nestled in the gardens. These have varying numbers of rooms, and four of them offer full kitchens, fireplaces, and private patios. The hotel's restaurant, the Terrace Grill, has a fine view of the gardens and serves such seasonal fare as artichoke ravioli, grilled shrimp risotto, and chicken breast stuffed with dried cherries, cranberries, and walnuts. To reserve a massage, facial, or other services at the hotel's Garden Spa, call 831/227-3279. *$$$–$$$$; AE, DC, MC, V; checks OK; info@laplayahotel.com; www.laplayahotel.com; at 8th Ave.* &

Lincoln Green Inn / ★★

CARMELO ST, CARMEL; 831/624-7738 OR 800/262-1262 (VAGABOND'S HOUSE INN) If you're looking for a place to pop the question and promise a rose garden in a cottage built for two, you could do worse than make your pitch in one of Lincoln Green Inn's four cottages. Located at Carmel Point just across the road from picturesque River Beach, the white, green-shuttered cottages (named Robin Hood, Maid Marian, Friar Tuck, and Little John) occupy a bucolic English garden setting. Each storybook cottage features a living room with cathedral ceiling and stone fireplace; three have full-size kitchens. The Lincoln Green Inn is about as close as you can get to your own Carmel summer house without spending a fortune; it's a nice place for families or groups, affording closeness and privacy in equal measure. Antiques and sailing ship images accent a clean, elegant East Coast/Hamptons–style decor. There is no proprietor on site; just step into the tiny wooden phone booth to call the management at the Vagabond's House Inn. *$$$–$$$$; AE, DIS, MC, V; checks OK; innkeeper@vagabondshouse inn.com; www.vagabondshouseinn.com/cottages.html; at 15th Ave.*

Mission Ranch / ★★★

26270 DOLORES ST, CARMEL; 831/624-6436 OR 800/538-8221; 831/625-9040 (RESTAURANT) Actor and former Carmel mayor Clint Eastwood owns this inn located on a former dairy farm. Nestled in back of the Carmel Mission, the Ranch overlooks a carpet of pastureland that gives way to a dramatic view of Carmel River Beach, with the craggy splendor of Point Lobos stretching just beyond. When Eastwood bought the property in the late 1980s, he poured a ton of money and a lot of love into restoring the Victorian farmhouse, cottages, bunkhouse, and other buildings, determined to be true to the original spirit of the place. The result is simply wonderful. The peaceful, Western-style spread offers everything a guest needs to feel comfortable—without a single silly frill. Most of the 31 rooms are housed in Western ranchlike buildings with slight porch overhangs like those we used to see on *Bonanza*. They are sparsely but tastefully appointed, with props from Eastwood's films, such as the clock from *Unforgiven*, nonchalantly scattered among the furnishings. Handmade quilts grace the custom-made country-style wooden beds that are so large you literally have to climb into them, and each guest room has its own phone, TV, and bathroom. Rates include a continental breakfast served in the tennis clubhouse. The informal and Western-themed Restaurant at Mission Ranch, which operates under separate management, serves hearty American-style fare. The place's only flaw is that the piano bar can get a little rowdy, and guests in the structures closest to the restaurant may find themselves reaching for earplugs in the middle of the night. Otherwise, Stetsons off to Clint. *$$–$$$$; AE, MC, V; checks OK; at 15th Ave.* &

Carmel Valley

Carmel Valley is a relaxed, ranchlike enclave where horses and wine are the main draw for those who need wide-open spaces. There's no coastal fog here, so prepare for sunny skies for your outing. Some of California's most luxurious golf resorts lie in this valley, and it's also studded with interesting specialty nurseries and wine-tasting rooms. Some believe the valley's growing conditions are similar to those of the Bordeaux wine area of France. From Carmel, take Highway 1 to Carmel Valley Road.

Approximately 3½ miles after entering the valley you will approach **EARTH-BOUND FARM** (7250 Carmel Valley Rd; 831/625-6219; www.ebfarm.com), an organic farm that operates a large Farm Stand along with daily educational programs such as classes on growing and cooking organic foods, bug walks, garlic-braiding demonstrations, compost workshops, flower-arranging workshops, and chef walks though the gardens (check the website for a calendar of events). Any day of the week you can buy products such as figs, strawberries, baked breads, honey, and tomatoes. At the Farm Stand's Organic Kitchen—the first certified organic deli, bakery, and juice bar in California—you can grab a light lunch from the wide array of soups, salads, sandwiches, desserts, juices, smoothies, baked goods, coffees, teas, and prepared foods, all made fresh daily with organic ingredients (naturally). Earthbound Farm is open 7am to 7pm Monday–Saturday, 9am to 6pm Sunday and holidays.

About 5½ miles into the valley you'll see a French-style château. It's the **CHATEAU JULIEN WINE ESTATES** (8940 Carmel Valley Rd; 831/624-2600; www.chateau julien.com), open for tastings and picnics Monday–Friday 8am to 5pm, Saturday–Sunday 11am to 5pm. Each of its wines is produced from 100 percent Monterey County grapes. Taste estate wines such as the 1999 chardonnay, the 1998 cabernet sauvignon, and the 1998 merlot. In the cool, high-ceilinged tasting room, pick up copies of recipes such as Pears in Port with Juniper and Ginger.

Roughly 9 miles into the valley, pull into the parking lot for the **GARLAND RANCH,** a park with acres of open space. Follow the trail sign down the steps into the woods, across a wooden bridge over the murmuring Carmel River, strewn with mossy stones, and on into an open valley with the Santa Lucia Mountains rising ahead. Many people walk their dogs here or hike the scenic trails, or do bird-watching—pick up a "Checklist of Birds" brochure at the usually unstaffed visitor center to mark those you've seen. The center also provides hiking maps: try the 1¼-mile Lupine Loop or the 1½-mile Rancho Loop. The park has an area set aside for mountain biking, too, plus picnic tables in the lower area just beyond the Carmel River.

LODGINGS

Bernardus Lodge / ★★★★

415 CARMEL VALLEY RD, CARMEL VALLEY; 831/659-3131 OR 888/648-9463 You'll sigh with satisfaction the moment you enter Bernardus Lodge, Carmel Valley's newest boutique resort, where check-in is seamless from the time you drive up; you're offered a glass of chilled white wine upon entering the lobby. The simple, elegant colonial-flavor lodge is the vision of Bernardus Vineyard and Winery owner Ben Pon, who spared no expense getting everything just right. Situated on a terraced hillside dotted with ancient oaks and pines and affording grand vistas of the surrounding Santa Lucia Mountains, the lodge offers terra-cotta- and lemon-colored buildings that hold 57 guest rooms and suites, two restaurants, two tennis courts, boccie and croquet courts, a swimming pool, and a full-service spa and salon. Understated elegance is a key theme here; Pon has mercifully deleted the nouveau from the riche. Generously sized guest rooms feature stone fireplaces, antique wardrobe armoires, a sitting area with sofa and chairs, vaulted ceilings, French doors, private patios, and king-size featherbeds with

LEARN TO SURF, SANTA CRUZ STYLE

If you've always wanted to ride the waves hanging ten (toes), it's not too late to learn. Club Ed Surf School, located on Cowell Beach in front of the West Coast Santa Cruz Hotel, is one of the most respected surfing schools in the world. Most days owner Ed Guzman and his staff teach a two-hour small group lesson for $80 that includes rental of a wet suit, surfboard, and water booties. The class starts with yoga stretches on the surfboard on shore, and goes on to include how to read waves, how to position yourself on the board, how to paddle, and of course how to stand up and actually surf. Guzman has designed special surfboards that are extra wide and thick, so they catch waves well and are easy to stand up on, and he has taught wishful surfers from 4 years old up to 71 how to do it. Ed can also take paraplegics and quadriplegics out on his tandem board to experience the sensation of surfing. Classes are offered spring through fall. Call 831/464-0177 or 800/287-7873, or log onto www.club-ed.com for more information or reservations, or e-mail Ed at clubed@sbcglobal.net.

down comforters and soft-as-silk Frette linens. The spa is a restorative haven; be sure to reserve spa treatments when you make your room reservation—weekend appointments fill up far in advance. Under the direction of award-winning chef Cal Stamenov, formerly of Highlands Inn and, before that, Domaine Chandon in Yountville, Marinus restaurant offers French-inspired Wine Country cuisine. Wickets Bistro, a less formal environment, also draws upon Bernardus's extensive wine list and penchant for local, fresh ingredients. Although jacket and tie are optional in both establishments, a slightly snooty wait staff may make you wish you'd worn your Sunday best. *$$$$; AE, DC, DIS, MC, V; no checks; www.bernardus.com; at Los Laureles Grade.* &

Carmel Valley Ranch / ★★★

1 OLD RANCH RD, CARMEL VALLEY; 831/625-9500 OR 800/422-7635 Nestled on a 400-acre spread, this haven for golf and tennis enthusiasts (and corporate retreaters) is about as plush a ranch as you're ever likely to encounter. Outfitted in earth tones, burgundies, and greens, the 144 guest suites are arranged in low-lying, condo-like clusters on the rolling hills; each comes equipped with cathedral ceilings, a wood-burning fireplace, a well-stocked refreshment center, two TVs, a trio of phones, a private deck, and a richly appointed bathroom. Some of the pricier suites come with a dining area, a kitchenette, and a private outdoor whirlpool tub (discreetly enclosed, of course). You might need that whirlpool after partaking of the ranch's activities: golf at the Pete Dye 18-hole course, tennis on one of a dozen clay and hard-surface courts, guided nature hikes, biking, horseback riding, workouts with a personal trainer at the fitness club, or a dip in one of two swimming pools. When you're ready to relax, you can also indulge in a facial or a manicure, a soak in one of the fitness center's six whirlpool spas, or perhaps a couple's massage followed by champagne and chocolate-covered strawberries. The ranch has three

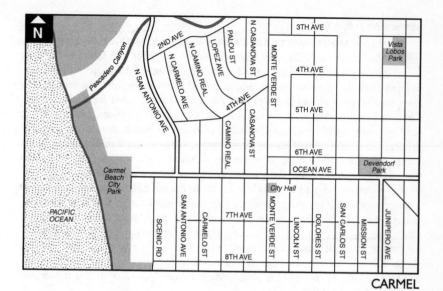

restaurants, including the elegant Oaks, which serves refined American regional cooking in a formal room graced by Old California antiques, a towering stone fireplace, and a phalanx of windows affording a panoramic view of the oak-covered hills. *$$$$; AE, MC, V; checks OK; www.wyndham.com; off Carmel Valley Rd.* &

Quail Lodge Resort and Golf Club / ★★★

8205 VALLEY GREENS DR, CARMEL VALLEY; 831/624-2888 OR 888/828-8787 This posh resort catering to golfers and tennis players has 100 guest rooms set along winding paths flanking a meticulously kept 18-hole course and a series of pretty little ponds. Comfort, not ostentatious luxury, is the byword here, and Quail Lodge does comfort very well indeed. Decorated in nature-inspired shades of green, yellow, and red, even the least expensive rooms are spacious and have private balconies or patios. Higher-priced units feature fireplaces, whirlpool tubs, and separate living rooms. Nice touches abound: all rooms have a coffeemaker, robes, room service, a minibar, a refrigerator, cable TV, and a bathroom equipped with every amenity. Ask for one of the rooms in the 100s building, which have two fireplaces, two TVs, a minibar, Asian cabinets, and lush draperies dividing the living room and bedroom. Many have views of the lake as well. The resort has a European-style spa with steam rooms, two outdoor pools, a fitness center, and a large hot tub for your dipping pleasure. The Covey Restaurant offers Wine Country cuisine, such as venison osso buco, sweetbread salad, crab-crusted halibut, and other fare that reflects an emphasis on fresh local products. Well-prepared California cuisine is served at Edgar's, the clubhouse's restaurant and sports bar that overlooks the course. *$$$$; AE, DC, MC, V; checks OK; info@quaillodge.com; www.quaillodge.com; 3½ miles E of Hwy 1, just off Carmel Valley Rd.* &

Stonepine / ★★★★

150 E CARMEL VALLEY RD, CARMEL VALLEY; 831/659-2245 This exquisite Mediterranean villa (the former country home of the Crocker banking family) rises in terraced splendor among 330 acres of Carmel Valley's oak-covered hills. Surrounded by cypress, imported stone pines, and wisteria trailing from hand-carved Italian stone pillars, the inn has eight guest suites throughout Château Noel (named after owner Noel Hentschel), three houses, and the idyllic (and astronomically expensive) Briar Rose Cottage, a two-bedroom affair with a private rose garden, living room, dining room, kitchen, and bar. The suites in the main house are studies in formal splendor; all have French antique furnishings, spa tubs, down comforters, and fluffy robes, and five of them feature fireplaces. The cost of your room includes a big breakfast; for an additional charge you may partake of a wine reception followed by an elegant five-course estate dinner in the dining room. During the day, float in the jewel-like swimming pool, play tennis, explore the ranch's trails, or horse around at the Stonepine Equestrian Center. Beware: The equestrian staff takes horseback riding mighty seriously, and more than one city slicker has suffered a bruised ego as well as a sore derriere after a turn on the trails. *$$$$; AE, MC, V; checks OK; director@stonepinecalifornia.com; www.stonepine california.com; 13 miles E of Hwy 1.* &

Big Sur

Originally *el pais grande del sur* (Spanish for "the big country to the south"), Big Sur encompasses 90 miles of rugged, spectacular coastline that stretches south from Carmel to San Simeon. A narrow, twisting segment of **HIGHWAY 1** (built with convict labor in the 1930s) snakes through this coastal area, and the mist-shrouded forests, plunging cliffs, and cobalt sea bordering the road make the drive one of the most beautiful in the country, if not the world. The region is so scenic that some folks favor giving it national park status; others, however, recoil in horror at the thought of involving the federal government in the preservation of this untamed land and have coined the expression "Don't Yosemitecate Big Sur."

Keeping your Big Sur visit low-stress is challenging since driving Big Sur can be a bit confusing. Some of the park names sound so similar (too many Pfeiffers!), and it's hard to watch the road, take in the scenery, and still be ready to stop in time when you come to a park or gallery of interest. It will help if you can come either off-season or midweek, when traffic along Highway 1 is fairly light. Another tip: Come in the spring, April through early June, when the golden California poppies, yellow mustard, and purple lupines brighten the windswept landscape.

Whether you're cruising through for the day or have booked a few nights at a resort, be sure to spend some time hiking in the gorgeous **POINT LOBOS STATE RESERVE** (for more details on the reserve, see the Carmel section). Farther south, Highway 1 crosses Bixby Creek via the 268-foot-high, 739-foot-long **BIXBY BRIDGE** (also known as the Rainbow Bridge), a solitary, majestic arch built in 1932 that attracts lots of snap-happy photographers. Nearby is the automated **POINT SUR LIGHTHOUSE** (off Hwy 1; 831/625-4419; www.lighthouse-pointsur-ca.org; 19

miles S of Carmel), situated 360 feet above the surf on **POINT SUR**, a giant volcanic-rock island. The lighthouse was built in 1889 and is the only complete turn-of-the-century light station open to the public in California. Inexpensive (though physically taxing) three-hour guided lighthouse tours are offered on Saturday and Sunday year-round, with additional tours on Wednesday and Thursday during the summer and full-moon tours every month (be sure to take a jacket, even in the summer months).

Hikers and bicyclists often head farther south to navigate the many trails zigzagging through the sycamores and maples in 4,800-acre **ANDREW MOLERA STATE PARK** (831/667-2315; www.bigsurcalifornia.org), the largest state park on the Big Sur coast. A mile-long walk through a meadow laced with wildflowers leads to the park's 2-mile-long beach harboring the area's best tide pools. A few miles down Highway 1 on the inland side is one of California's most popular parks, **PFEIFFER–BIG SUR STATE PARK** (800/444-7275; www.bigsurcalifornia.org). Here, 810 acres of madrona and oak woodlands and misty redwood canyons are criss-crossed with hiking trails, and many paths provide panoramic views of the sea. The **BIG SUR RIVER** meanders through the park, too, attracting anglers and swimmers who brave the chilly waters. Nearby, the unmarked **SYCAMORE CANYON ROAD** (the only paved, ungated road west of Hwy 1 between the Big Sur Post Office and Pfeiffer–Big Sur State Park) leads to beautiful but blustery **PFEIFFER BEACH** (follow the road until it ends at a parking lot, about 2 miles from Hwy 1) with its white-and-mauve sands and enormous sea caves.

If your idea of communing with nature is a comfy chair in the shade, grab a seat on the upper deck of the fabled Nepenthe bar and restaurant (see review, below), perched 800 feet above the roiling Pacific. Four miles south of Nepenthe is the **COAST GALLERY** (831/667-2301), a showplace for local artists and craftspeople featuring pottery, jewelry, and paintings, including watercolors by author Henry Miller, who lived nearby for more than 15 years. The author's fans will also want to seek out the **HENRY MILLER LIBRARY** (just beyond Nepenthe restaurant on the E side of Hwy 1; 831/667-2574; www.henrymiller.org). In addition to a great collection of Miller's books and art, the library serves as one of Big Sur's cultural centers and features the art, poetry, prose, and music of locals; it's open Thursday through Sunday in the summer, Friday through Sunday in the winter. Seekers of other sorts flock to **ESALEN INSTITUTE** (831/667-3000), the world-famous New Age retreat and home of heavenly massages and hot springs that overlook the ocean.

At the southern end of Big Sur is beautiful **JULIA PFEIFFER BURNS STATE PARK** (800/444-7275; www.bigsurcalifornia.org), with 4,000 acres to roam. You'll find some excellent day hikes here, but if you just want to get out of the car and stretch your legs, take the quarter-mile **WATERFALL TRAIL** to 80-foot-high McWay Waterfall, one of the few falls in California that plunges directly into the sea. Keep an eye open for the sea otters that play in **MCWAY COVE**. But wherever you trek through Big Sur, beware of the poison oak—it's as ubiquitous as the seagulls hovering over the coast.

RESTAURANTS

Big Sur River Inn / ★

HWY 1, BIG SUR; 831/667-2700 OR 800/548-3610 The Big Sur River Inn is exactly the kind of restaurant you would expect to find in a mountain community—a large, rustic cabin (circa 1934), built and furnished entirely with rough-hewn woods, warmed by a large fireplace surrounded by comfy chairs, and occupied by jeans-clad locals sharing the day's news over beers at the corner bar. In the summer most everyone requests a table on the shaded back deck, which overlooks a picturesque stretch of the Big Sur River. Since the restaurant caters to the inn's guests, it's open morning till nightfall. Breakfast is all-American (eggs, pancakes, bacon, omelets, and such), as are lunch and dinner. The menu offers a wide range of choices: pasta, burgers, chicken sandwiches, salads, fish 'n' chips, and a whole lot more. Recommended plates are the Black Angus Burger with a side of beer-battered onion rings, or a big platter of the Roadhouse Ribs served with cowboy beans. Wash either down with a cool glass of Carmel Brewing Co. Amber Ale, and you're ready to roll. *$; AE, DC, DIS, MC, V; no checks; breakfast, lunch, dinner every day; beer and wine; no reservations; www.bigsurriverinn.com; on Hwy 1 at Pheneger Creek, 2 miles N of Pfeiffer–Big Sur State Park.*

Nepenthe Restaurant / ★

HWY 1, BIG SUR; 831/667-2345 This venerable Big Sur institution has been operating for more than half a century and still draws in the crowds. Located 800 feet above the ocean, Nepenthe commands views of the Big Sur coastline that will make you gasp. It is a friendly, family-owned and managed place, and therein lies part of its appeal. Originally a log cabin that housed Lolly and Bill Fassett and their five children, it became Nepenthe when they realized that the only way to keep their family amply fed was to open a restaurant. The log cabin remains, but over the years Nepenthe has grown to encompass the entire bluff it rests upon. The restaurant boasts a full bar, and two outdoor areas offer lots of room for alfresco dining. Even after warnings about overpriced meals, locals insist visitors to Big Sur should try Nepenthe at least once. The fare tends toward standard American with a twist. Starters include Cajun poached shrimp and Castroville artichoke; entrees include a choice of fresh fish, steaks, and broiled or roast chicken. Burgers and salads should keep kids and vegetarians happy. Be sure to check out Nepenthe's **PHOENIX GIFT SHOP** on your way out. This upscale store harbors a hodgepodge of imported treasures, indoor fountains, garden sculpture, elegant women's clothes, books, jewelry, kids' toys, and locally made soaps, lotions, and body oils. Located one flight of stairs below Nepenthe Restaurant is the far less expensive **CAFE KEVAH** (831/667-2344), an order-at-the-counter cafe where breakfast is served all day (omelets, burritos, huevos rancheros) and lunch offers a spicy chicken brochette, a grilled salmon with salsa verde, quesadillas, and a Caesar salad. *$$; AE, MC, V; no checks; lunch, dinner every day; full bar; reservations required for parties of 5 or more; www.nepenthebigsur.com; 27 miles S of Carmel.*

RIDE THE WAVE: MONTEREY'S
FREE SHUTTLE SERVICE

Eliminate the hassle and high price of parking on Monterey's crowded streets by catching a ride on the WAVE (Waterfront Area Visitor Express) shuttle, which operates from May 24 to September 1 and takes passengers to and from all the major waterfront attractions, including Fisherman's Wharf, Cannery Row, and the Monterey Bay Aquarium. The free shuttle departs from the downtown parking garages at Tyler Street and Del Monte Avenue every 10 to 12 minutes and operates all day, 10am–7pm. Other WAVE stops include many hotels and motels in Monterey and Pacific Grove. For more information call Monterey–Salinas Transit at 831/899-2555.

Sierra Mar / ★★★

HWY 1 AT BIG SUR (POST RANCH INN); 831/667-2800 Situated high on the ridge, the Sierra Mar Restaurant at Post Ranch Inn is a gorgeous, cliff-hugging restaurant that has been hailed as one of the best on the Central Coast. It serves a sophisticated brand of California cuisine in a serene expanse of wood, brushed metal, and glass that lets you drink in the incredible views along with the costly wine. When you can wrest your eyes from the ocean and focus on the four-course prix-fixe dinner menu, which changes daily, you might see such sumptuous starters as pine-smoked squab with ginger and cilantro; mussel soup with saffron and potatoes; and perhaps a salad of lettuces (organic, of course) mixed with shaved fennel, oranges, Parmesan, and a Campari vinaigrette. Main courses include such bounty as roast rack of venison with glazed chestnuts and huckleberries, truffled fettuccine with asparagus and English peas, and roasted guinea fowl with potato gnocchi and pearl onions. Finish off your feast with a plate of assorted house-made sweets. *$$$; AE, MC, V; local checks only; lunch, dinner every day; full bar; reservations recommended; www.postranchinn.com; 30 miles S of Carmel.* ♿

LODGINGS

Deetjen's Big Sur Inn / ★

48865 HWY 1, BIG SUR; 831/667-2377 Don't blink or you'll miss this charming cluster of ramshackle cabins as you head around the curve on Highway 1 just south of Ventana. During the '30s and '40s, travelers making the long journey up or down the coast used to drop in and stay the night with Grandpa Deetjen, a Norwegian immigrant. No doubt weary of houseguests, he constructed a cluster of redwood buildings nestled in Castro Canyon with 20 rooms to accommodate them. Grandpa's idea of comfort was a bit austere, but then again, he never expected to charge $75 to $195 per night. Located in a redwood canyon, most cabins are divided into two units, each with dark wood interiors, hand-hewn doors without locks or keys (they can be secured with the hook and eye from within, though), and nonexistent insulation. Some have shared baths, and many are cozy in a rustic sort of way, but they're definitely not for everyone. If you stay in one of the two-story units (some with fireplaces or wood-burning stoves), be sure to request the quieter upstairs rooms. The cabins near the river offer the most privacy. Grandpa's Room #13 has a bed built just under a large window overlooking the creek, and also has a pedal organ that belonged to the old gentleman. Deetjen's **BIG SUR INN RESTAURANT**, which has garnered a loyal following, serves good Euro-California cuisine that takes advantage of local produce and seafood. The setting is rustic-romantic, with white walls, dimly lit old-fashioned lamps, and antiques in every nook. A wood-burning stove provides heat on chilly winter nights. The most robust fare includes coq au vin, roasted rack of lamb with a panko crust, and a prime New York steak with macadamia-nut risotto. *$–$$$; MC, V; checks OK; www. deetjens.com; on Hwy 1, 4 miles south of Pfeiffer–Big Sur State Park.*

Post Ranch Inn / ★★★★

HWY 1, BIG SUR; 831/667-2200 OR 800/527-2200; 831/667-2800 (RESTAURANT) Discreetly hidden on a ridge in the Santa Lucia Mountains, architect Mickey Muennig's redwood complex was completed in April 1992. Muennig supposedly camped out on the property for five months before setting pencil to paper for his design, which had to conform to the strict Big Sur Coastal Land Use Plan. He propped up six of the inn's units (known as the Tree Houses) on stilts to avoid disturbing the surrounding redwoods' root systems and sank others into the earth, roofing them with sod. The inn's deceptively simple exteriors are meant to harmonize with the forested slopes, while windows, windows everywhere celebrate the breathtaking vista of sky and sea that is Big Sur's birthright. Inside, the lodgepole construction and wealth of warm woods lend a rough-hewn luxury to the rooms. Earth tones, blues, and greens predominate, extending the link between the buildings and their environment. "Environment," in fact, is a word you'll hear a lot around this place, which was named after William Post, one of the area's early settlers. The Post Ranch Inn is one of the orginal eco-hotels, where the affluent can indulge in sumptuous luxury and still feel politically correct. The water is filtered; visitors are encouraged to sort their paper, glass, and plastic garbage; and the paper upon which guests' rather staggering bills are printed is recycled. Despite this ecologically correct attitude, the folks behind the Post Ranch Inn haven't forgotten about the niceties of life. The 30 rooms have spare—but by no means spartan—decor, including fireplaces, massage tables, king-size beds, and sideboards made of African hardwoods (nonendangered, naturally). Designer robes hang in the closets and whirlpool tubs for two adorn the well-equipped bathrooms. In the lobby and public areas, stereo systems fill the air with ethereal New Age music. A continental breakfast and guided nature hikes are included in the room rates; the massages, facials, herbal wraps, and yoga classes are not. The inn's restaurant, **SIERRA MAR**, serves a sophisticated brand of California cuisine in a stunning setting (see review, above). *$$$$; AE, MC, V; checks OK; www.postranchinn.com; 30 miles S of Carmel.*

Ventana Inn & Spa / ★★★★

HWY 1, BIG SUR; 831/667-2331 OR 800/628-6500 Set 1,200 feet above the Pacific Ocean on the brow of a chaparral-covered hill in the Santa Lucia Mountains, this modern, weathered cedar inn is serene, contemplative, and very discreet, which explains why celebrities such as Goldie Hawn, Barbra Streisand, and Francis Ford Coppola have been vacationing here since 1975. Its 60 spacious rooms, decorated in an upscale country style and divided among 12 low-rise buildings, look out over the plunging forested hillsides, wildflower-laced meadows, or roiling waters of the Big Sur coast. Since you're already splurging, go ahead and book one of the cedar-lined Vista Suites, which come with an ocean-view deck with a private outdoor spa, a fireplace, and an oversized bathroom with an open-slate shower. The inn's other big draw is Cielo Restaurant ("heaven" in Spanish), which delivers panoramic patio views of 50 miles of coastline at prices that can be equally breathtaking. Although critics have been unanimous in praising its aesthetics, a revolving-door parade of chefs has kept them uncertain about the quality of the food since Jeremiah Tower's star turn here many years ago. The current menu offers "New American"–style dishes such as caramelized Maine Diver scallops with baby carrots, asparagus, basmati rice, and red Thai curry coconut milk broth; summer vegetable risotto with English peas, sweet corn, summer squash, and asparagus; and oak-grilled Kansas City steak au Poivre with a side of grilled Castroville artichoke and mashed potatoes. $$$$; AE, DC, DIS, MC, V; checks OK; www.ventanainn.com; 28 miles S of Carmel, 2 miles S of Pfeiffer–Big Sur State Park.

WINE COUNTRY

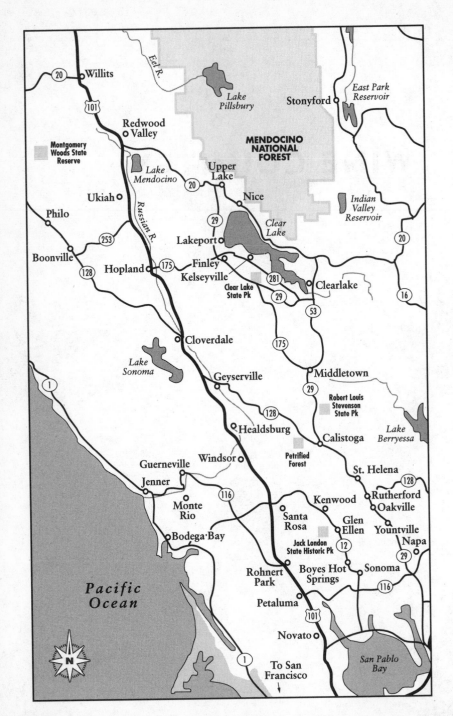

WINE COUNTRY

Napa and Sonoma are two of the top tourist attractions in the United States, with little wonder. When you combine supernatural scenic beauty with nearly year-round excellent weather, top-notch restaurants, and world-class wines, what's not to like? These qualities have made the region, which includes pastoral Anderson Valley and its fringe of Mendocino County towns, a popular destination for oenophiles and gourmets alike. And for the nature lover who comes along for the ride, Wine Country delivers some of America's most stunning vistas. Like competitive siblings of the same robust family, these areas contain many similarities, but each also retains its individual personality.

ACCESS AND INFORMATION

There are two main options for those arriving in the Wine Country **BY AIR**. Fly into **SAN FRANCISCO INTERNATIONAL AIRPORT (SFO)** (located off Hwy 101, just S of San Francisco; 650/821-8211) or **OAKLAND INTERNATIONAL AIRPORT (OAK)** (1 Airport Dr; 510/577-4000), and then rent a car, since that is by far the best way to tour this largely rural area.

Driving from San Francisco, you will likely hit more traffic, and the route can be tricky: from the airport, head north on Highway 101 toward San Francisco. Take the 101 North/Duboce/Mission Street exit, stay right, then turn right onto Mission Street/US 101 North. Turn left onto South Van Ness, which will take you north across the city. Turn left onto Lombard and follow signs to the Golden Gate Bridge. Cross the bridge (there's a toll), then continue on Highway 101 North.

In Novato, exit onto Highway 37. For the town of Sonoma, head east on 37 for about 8 miles. Take a left onto Highway 121 North (Sears Point Raceway will be on your left). You are now in the Sonoma Valley. Stay on 121 and take Highway 12 North.

For Napa, follow the directions above but stay on 121, following signs for Napa until you reach Highway 29, which will then take you the length of the valley to your destination. Travel time to Napa from SFO is approximately 2 hours (1½ hours to Sonoma); add an extra hour or more during rush hour. For other Sonoma County destinations, stay on 101 and continue north.

Napa is easily accessible from the East Bay side of the Bay Area, and that makes the **OAKLAND AIRPORT** a good choice (Oakland flights can also be cheaper and less inclined to be delayed by fog than flights to and from SFO). From Oakland, take Highway 80 North to Vallejo, then take the Highway 37/Marine World exit going west. This will take you to Highway 29, where you will go right (north) to Napa. As you approach Napa, the road will split; for downtown Napa, stay to the right and follow the signs that say Lake Berryessa/Downtown Napa. (You can also take one of four downtown Napa exits off of Highway 29.) For the rest of the Napa Valley, stay to the left and follow signs for 29 North.

If you want to rent a car but would rather skip the Bay Area traffic, you can take a **SHUTTLE BUS TO NAPA, SONOMA, OR SANTA ROSA** and rent a car there. Evans Airport Shuttle (707/255-1559) has scheduled shuttles to and from both airports to Napa. You'll need to take a short taxi ride to downtown Napa's rental car companies. Sonoma Airporter (800/611-4246; www.sonomaairporter.com) connects all of Sonoma Valley's towns with SFO. Sonoma County Airport Express (707/837-8700; www.airportexpressinc.com) has scheduled rides to and from Santa Rosa and both airports. **CAR RENTALS** available in Napa and Santa Rosa include Avis, Budget, Enterprise, and Hertz.

If driving is simply not an option, your choices are limited. The Wine Country doesn't have the best public transportation, so you'll need to either set up camp in a walkable city such as downtown Napa or downtown Sonoma or hire someone to drive you to the attractions. The **NAPA VALLEY CONFERENCE AND VISITORS BUREAU** can arrange bicycle, van, and limousine tours of the wineries.

The **SONOMA VALLEY VISITORS BUREAU** (453 1st St E, Sonoma; 707/996-1090; www.sonomavalley.com) has winery tour information. Both the Napa and the Sonoma Valley Visitors Bureaus can connect you with group and private-tour services.

Napa Valley

Given that Napa Valley is the country's most extensive adult playground for food, wine, and luxury lovers, it's almost fitting that the 35-mile-long stretch of grape-strewn real estate surrounding rural Highway 29 is right up there with kid-oriented Disneyland as one of the most-visited destinations in California. More than 4.9 million visitors annually make the grape escape to the valley's towns and world-renowned wineries, resorts, and restaurants, which means roads and attractions can be more tightly packed than a cluster of heavy-hanging chardonnay fruit—especially in high season (March through November). During this time the traffic on Highway 29 that gets you to your next winery can be as loathsome as big-city gridlock. But no matter. When spring displays vibrant green hills and bright yellow mustard blossoms, summer brings everyday sunshine and hillsides fat with fruit, fall explodes with brilliant autumnal colors and the excitement of harvest, and winter makes for even more excuses to indulge in some of the world's best food and wine, you're quick to realize road congestion is a small price to pay for paradise.

There are other costs to the visitor, too. Popularity has resulted in most wineries charging a tasting fee—which can range from $5 for sips of three or more current releases to $25 for a single glass at Opus One—and most hotels jacking up rates, so break open the piggy bank before you come.

Lodging information, winery maps, and details about parks, hot-air balloon rides, and other recreational pastimes like the **NAPA VALLEY WINE TRAIN** (707/253-2111), a dining train that traverses the valley floor, are available at the **NAPA VALLEY CONFERENCE AND VISITORS BUREAU** (1310 Town Center Mall, off 1st St, Napa; 707/226-7459; www.napavalley.com).

Napa Wineries

Staff at most wineries assume that the folks who walk through their doors are not wine connoisseurs, and they welcome questions. During the congenial process of touring their facilities and sampling various vintages, they try to show visitors what makes their product unique. So if you've ever dreamed of entering a fine restaurant and confidently describing the exact style of wine you like and want, this is the place to learn how to do it—and what fun the learning is!

Although most vintners now charge you to taste their wines, tours are usually free. Some require reservations, but don't let that deter you: many establishments, especially those in residential areas, are required to limit the number of guests at any one time.

Since Napa has more than 280 wineries, it's safe to say you won't see them all in a weekend. A good plan of attack is to choose the ones you most want to visit and then tour three or four a day—with a leisurely lunch break somewhere in between. Leave room in your schedule for the serendipitous detour, because this is the best way to make new discoveries. Napa's wineries are mainly clustered along Highway 29 and the Silverado Trail, two parallel roads running the length of the valley. On summer weekends, the traffic on 29 slows to a standstill, so the wise traveler will look for alternatives. But even when the coast is clear for putting the pedal to the metal, *don't speed along these roads!* Local law enforcement officers have little to do other than making sure tourists aren't cruising the area after one too many sips of chardonnay.

When planning your winery visits, keep in mind that most open around 10am and close by 5pm. Some summer hours are extended, but it's a good idea to confirm open hours before you hit the road. Here's a roster of some of the Napa Valley's most popular wineries, many of which offer free tours of their facilities.

BEAULIEU VINEYARDS (1960 St. Helena Hwy, Rutherford; 707/963-2411; www.bvwines.com). Nicknamed "BV," this winery housed in a historic estate is the third-oldest continuously operating winery in Napa Valley and is famous for its cabernet sauvignon. Tastings cost $5.

BERINGER VINEYARDS (2000 Main St, St. Helena; 707/963-7115; www.beringervineyards.com). The Napa Valley's oldest continuously operating winery features a stately old Rhineland-style mansion and good tours of the vineyards and caves. It's well known for its chardonnay, cabernet sauvignon, and white zinfandel. You can taste current vintages for $5.

CHÂTEAU MONTELENA WINERY (1429 Tubbs Ln, Calistoga; 707/942-5105; www.montelena.com). This stunning French château-style winery is built of stone and is celebrated for its chardonnay. The beautiful setting includes a lake with two islands and wonderful gazebos. Tastings will set you back $10.

CLIFF LEDE & S. ANDERSON VINEYARDS (1473 Yountville Crossroad, Yountville; 707/944-8642; www.4bubbly.com). Previously S. Anderson, the new owners added their last name to the marquee, but they still produce sparkling and still wines. Lively candlelight tours of the caves (scheduled twice daily) educate the visitor on the *méthode champenoise*—the method for making premium sparkling wines—and include a tasting of four wines. The cost is $10 per person.

CLOS PEGASE (1060 Dunaweal Ln, Calistoga; 707/942-4981; www.clos pegase.com). Designed by architect Michael Graves, this stunning, modern facility offers grand outdoor sculpture, a "Wine in Art" slide show, and good guided tours of the winery, caves, and art collection. Sample three wines for $7.50.

DOMAINE CHANDON (1 California Dr, Yountville; 707/944-2280; www.chandon.com). Excellent sparkling wines as well as chardonnay, pinot noir, and its rustic cousin pinot meunier (say "muh-NYAY") come from this winery's handsome building and its stunning landscaped grounds. There's a four-star dining room (see the restaurant's review, below), fantastic guided tours, and a "salon" where you can sip bubbly ($9 to $14 per glass) and order snacks inside or on the terrace.

THE HESS COLLECTION WINERY (4411 Redwood Rd, Napa; 707/255-1144; www.hesscollection.com). A stone winery in a remote and scenic mountainside location, the Hess Collection is well known for its cabernet sauvignon and chardonnay. But art lovers are equally smitten with the Contemporary American and European art gallery showcased in a dramatic building, part of an informative self-guided tour. Tastings are $3.

MERRYVALE VINEYARDS (1000 Main St, St. Helena; 707/963-7777; www.merryvale.com). Merryvale's romantic, historic stone winery offers daily tastings for $3 and, by appointment only, informative, thorough tasting classes on Saturday and Sunday mornings. The winery is best known for its cabernet, but it's got loads of other tasty varietals to sample, too.

NIEBAUM-COPPOLA ESTATE WINERY (1991 St. Helena Hwy, Rutherford; 707/968-1100; www.niebaum-coppola.com). Filmmaker Francis Ford Coppola now owns the former Inglenook grand château, built in the 1880s. The stunning estate and winery features displays on Coppola's film career and Inglenook's history, plus an enormous gift shop stocked with wine, gifts, books, gourmet foods, and even Coppola's favorite cigars. Daily wine tastings are $10; tours of the extensive grounds by appointment only are $20 and include tastings.

OPUS ONE (7900 St. Helena Hwy, Oakville; 707/944-9442; www.opusonewinery.com). Robert Mondavi started this extraordinary venture in collaboration with France's Baron Rothschild. In a dramatic bermed neoclassical building, tours and expensive wine tastings ($25 for a 4-ounce glass of wine) are offered by appointment.

ROBERT MONDAVI WINERY (7801 St. Helena Hwy, Oakville; 707/963-9611; www.robertmondaviwinery.com). This huge, world-famous winery, housed in a Mission-style building, offers $5 tastings, excellent tours of the facilities and specialty tours, a famous cooking school, and numerous special events.

SCHRAMSBERG VINEYARDS (1400 Schramsberg Rd, Calistoga; 707/942-4558; www.schramsberg.com). Schramsberg's first-rate sparkling wines are showcased in attractive, historic facilities and extensive caves. Enchanting, free guided tours are available by appointment only and include, if desired, a $20 tasting that's not offered without the tour.

STERLING VINEYARDS (1111 Dunaweal Ln, Calistoga; 707/942-3300; www.sterlingvineyards.com). Sterling offers an excellent self-guided tour through its sleek, white Mediterranean-style complex perched on a hill. Access is via an aerial tramway ($10, including a tasting) offering splendid views, and there's a vast tasting room with panoramic vistas.

Napa

At the southernmost end of Napa Valley is the sprawling part-pretty, part-industrial city of Napa, where about half of the county's 73,000-plus residents live. Although its name is synonymous with wine, most of the valley's wineries are actually several miles north of town. Though most tourists previously zoomed past the city for the more pastoral Wine Country towns to the north, Napa, founded in 1848 and boasting stunning Victorian structures, is coming into its own. Thanks to ridiculous housing prices to the south, ongoing restorations, and new restaurants and attractions, downtown Napa is getting hot, hot, hot and offers plenty of reasons to pull off the highway before heading north.

The new $70 million **COPIA: THE AMERICAN CENTER FOR WINE, FOOD & THE ARTS** (500 1st St; 707/257-3606; www.copia.org) is a cultural museum with offerings ranging from cooking demonstrations and wine-tasting classes to art lectures, an exhibition organic garden, movies, and live musical performances.

After a glorious restoration, the Napa Valley Opera House (1030 Main St; 707/226-7372; www.nvoh.org), where Jack London once gave readings, reopened in 2003 with its first performance since 1914. The principal theater in the 116-year-old structure is known as the **MARGRIT BIEVER MONDAVI THEATER** due to the winemaking family's restoration leadership. Nearby, the riverfront historic **HATT BUILDING** (500 Main St; 707/251-8500) features a boutique hotel, shops, restaurants, and an adorable bakery.

For the traffic-weary traveler, downtown Napa provides a base from which a plethora of Victorian bed-and-breakfasts and nearby restaurants, as well as the attractions listed above, can all be accessed on foot. Lodging reservations and walking tour maps are available through the **NAPA VALLEY CONFERENCE AND VISITORS BUREAU** (1310 Town Center Mall, Napa; 707/226-7459; www.napavalley.com). For a break from seeing the sights, stop at **ABC BAKING COMPANY** (1517 3rd St; 707/258-1827) and enjoy goodies like espresso, killer breakfasts, sandwiches, and chocolate-caramel cake. Or browse the large selection of books on the Wine Country at **COPPERFIELD'S** (1303 1st St; 707/252-8002), then walk down to **NAPA VALLEY ROASTING COMPANY** (948 Main St; 707/224-2233) to read your selections over a latte. Around the corner drop into **BOUNTY HUNTER RARE WINE AND PROVISIONS** (975 1st St; 707/255-0622; www.bounty hunterwine.com), a sleek and sexy place to saddle up to the sophisticated Western-inspired bar, sip or buy wines, and snack on gourmet appetizers anytime of day or late into the evening.

RESTAURANTS

Angèle / ★★☆

540 MAIN ST, NAPA; 707-252-8115 Pronounced "AHN-zhel," this family effort by Claude Rouas (Auberge du Soleil and Piatti founder) and daughters Bettina and Claudia is a wonderful combination of truly captivating surroundings and cozy and classic country French cuisine. It's the wood beam ceiling, candlelight, sleek bar, and heated riverfront patio seating that set the stage. Then the ovation-worthy

WINE COUNTRY THREE-DAY TOUR

DAY ONE: Glamorous Napa. The ultimate Napa experience begins at **AUBERGE DU SOLEIL** hotel with a leisurely breakfast on the patio overlooking the valley (also available to nonguests). Drive your convertible south down the **SILVERADO TRAIL**—taking in the vineyard views—and make a right onto Yountville Crossroad to catch the morning tour at **CLIFF LEDE & S. ANDERSON VINEYARDS**. Buy a bottle of Diva to take home. Cruise west along Yountville Crossroad to downtown Yountville for a 12:30pm lunch reservation at **BISTRO JEANTY**. Next, head north on Highway 29 to the **NIEBAUM-COPPOLA ESTATE WINERY**. Try the claret, buy wine paraphernalia in the gift shop, and peruse Francis Ford Coppola's movie memorabilia collection upstairs. Continue north along 29 to **BERINGER VINEYARDS** and investigate the lovely Rhine House, then visit the tasting room. Stroll along St. Helena's **MAIN STREET** before heading on to have a Tuscan-inspired dinner down the road on the patio at **TRA VIGNE**. Then head back to your room at Auberge du Soleil for a good night's rest.

DAY TWO: Scenic Sonoma. From Napa, begin your day with a woodsy drive along the hairpin curves of **OAKVILLE GRADE** (which, closer to Sonoma, will become first Dry Creek Road, then Trinity Road). At Glen Ellen, turn left and follow Highway 12 south to the town of Sonoma. Grab a cappuccino and pastry at **CUCINA VIANSA**, then begin shopping in the gourmet deli for the day's picnic lunch. Walk around the plaza and continue gathering goodies from the **SONOMA CHEESE FACTORY** and whatever else strikes your fancy. Drive north of town to **RAVENSWOOD WINERY** for some of the best zinfandels around. Take your picnic to **BARTHOLOMEW PARK WINERY**, and after tasting the wines and visiting the museum, lunch on the 400-acre grounds and walk the trails. Next stop is historic **BUENA VISTA WINERY** (try the cream sherry), followed by a visit to **GUNDLACH BUNDSCHU WINERY**, where you can hike up the hill to view the valley below. Drive back into Sonoma for dinner on the vine-covered patio at **DELLA SANTINA'S** before heading back to the hotel.

DAY THREE: Calistoga mud baths. Breakfast again at **AUBERGE DU SOLEIL**, then begin the day with the breathtakingly beautiful tram ride up the mountain to **STERLING VINEYARDS**, where you can taste wines on the patio. Next head south to **WINE SPECTATOR RESTAURANT AT GREYSTONE** and while away a couple of hours eating lunch, touring the building, watching a cooking demo, and the visiting the basement cookware marketplace. Head back to Calistoga for an afternoon of sybaritic pleasures at **INDIAN SPRINGS**, the region's historic Victorian spa. Have a mud bath or facial, then soak up the sun in the enormous mineral springs–fed swimming pool. Enjoy a relaxed dinner at **ALL SEASONS CAFE** before heading out of town. Drive south along the Silverado Trail, savoring the final vineyard views in the last dying rays of the sun.

performance begins with attentive service, decadent oxtail and lentil salad with tangy *ravigote* dressing, steamed mussels in braised fennel broth, and the town's best gourmet hamburger, and ends with finales of sorbet and coffee pot de crème. Despite the chic environs, kids are welcomed and accommodated here, which—along with yummy French fries—is one reason wine industry heavyweights make this the spot for family night out. *$$; AE, MC, V; local checks only; lunch, dinner every day; full bar; reservation recommended; www.angele.us; at the Napa River.*

Bistro Don Giovanni / ★★★

4110 ST. HELENA HWY, NAPA; 707/224-3300 An absolute favorite for locals, Bistro Don Giovanni manages to be all things to all people. The bar is a preferred perch for gathering and chatting over a glass of wine or a complete dinner. The bright dining room is comfortable and bustling, and the heated patio overlooking a fountain and vineyards is perfect year-round. Donna and Giovanni Scala are the masterminds behind the perfectly al dente pasta (try it with rich duck ragout); superb thin-crust, crisp pizzas with exotic toppings like fig, proscuitto, and balsamic; and the beet and *haricot vert* salad, which is as vibrant as it is flavorful. Meat dishes are also fantastic. The wine list, although skewed toward expensive California vintages, is extensive and imaginative, and dessert beckons with such offerings as watermelon granita and textbook tiramisu. *$$; AE, DC, DIS, MC, V; local checks only; lunch, dinner every day; full bar; reservations recommended; www.bistrodongiovanni.com; on Hwy 29, just N of Salvador Ave.*

Cole's Chop House / ★★

1122 MAIN ST, NAPA; 707/224-6328 Some may have considered opening an expensive American steak house in predominantly blue-collar Napa a raw idea, but from the beginning owner Greg Cole has welcomed brisk business to this bright, airy restored historic building, built in 1886. Apparently meat lovers don't hesitate to pay close to $30 for aged steak without accompaniments served in downtown's most upscale environment. Whether you mosey up to the bar, dine alfresco on the charming courtyard patio, or soak in the old-meets-new ambiance of stone walls, hardwood floors, cushy booths, and beamed ceilings, you need not stick with steak: additional menu classics include a tangy Caesar salad, rich oysters Rockefeller, veal, lamb, and a few vegetarian dishes thrown in for modern measure. Old-school side dishes, such as creamed spinach, are ordered à la carte, the wine list emphasizes expensive reds, and a city-smart cocktail menu rounds out the retro drinking and dining options. *$$$; AE, DC, MC, V; local checks only; dinner Tues–Sun; full bar; reservations recommended; www.coleschophouse.citysearch.com; behind the big pink movie theater on Soscol Ave, just N of 1st St.* &

Foothill Cafe / ★★★

2766 OLD SONOMA RD, NAPA; 707/252-6178 This hidden gem is favored by locals who know to turn off the main streets and into the eastern Napa neighborhood for great food at amazingly low prices. Despite the ongoing attention to chef-owner Jerry Shaffer's (of San Francisco's Masa's and St. Helena's original Miramonte) American restaurant, the space maintains its sense of whimsy; even decorative items, such as wrought-iron artwork by a local artist, are fanciful.

Virtually anything from the big oak oven is a sure thing, such as oak-roasted baby back ribs, which come in snack and fill-'er-up sizes, or eight-hour-smoked prime rib with potato Stilton gratin, homemade horseradish, and a melange of seasonal vegetables. Then again, it's hard to go wrong with sautéed salmon fillet with cracked black pepper, ginger, and cabernet balsamic reduction, served with garlic mashed potatoes. Dessert favorites include classic vanilla-bean and Cognac crème brûlée. Like the rest of the menu, wines are affordably priced. *$$; AE, MC, V; local checks only; dinner Wed–Sun; beer and wine; reservations recommended; from Hwy 29 go W on Imola Ave, right at Foster Rd, left on Old Sonoma Rd; in J&P Center.* &

Pearl / ★★

1339 PEARL ST, STE 104, NAPA; 707/224-9161 This homey establishment is a favorite with locals, mainly because it's been one of the few places in town where you can count on friendly—albeit woefully slow—service and consistently good fare. Owners Nickie and Pete Zeller divide duties; Nickie presides over the kitchen, and Pete runs the front of the house. The menu offers something for all tastes and budgets, running the gamut from an array of raw and prepared oyster appetizers to goat cheese pizzas to an Asian-inspired ahi tuna sandwich with red cabbage coleslaw to a hearty triple pork chop with mashed potatoes. Pearl is located in a terra-cotta-colored stucco building, with a cute patio on the street and live music on the patio on summer weekends. *$$; MC, V; local checks only; lunch, dinner Tues–Sat; beer and wine; reservations recommended; www.therestaurantpearl.com; at Franklin.*

Villa Corona / ★

3614 BEL AIRE PLAZA (TRANCAS ST), NAPA; 707/257-8685 This low-key Mexican restaurant in a mall serves such clean, delicious, authentic cuisine that local chefs come here on days off. Stand in line, order from the counter, grab a number, and settle down at one of the tables amid brightly colored walls or at one of the few patio tables outside. After a short wait, huge plates will come your way. Classic burritos—especially *carnitas* (pork)—are outstanding, but the homemade corn tortillas and delicious red sauce make the tacos and enchiladas other favorites. Prawns are flavor-packed with garlic butter or spicy hot sauce, and all the usual suspects—chimichangas, chiles rellenos, tamales, tostadas—are just as good. Breakfast includes a concise list of items: *chilaquiles* (scrambled eggs with tortilla strips and salsa), huevos rancheros, and *machaca* (eggs and roasted pork scramble). *$; MC, V; no checks; breakfast, lunch, dinner Tues–Sun; beer and wine; no reservations; off Trancas St hidden in the SE corner of the mall.*

Zuzu / ★★★

829 MAIN ST, NAPA; 707/224-8555 Downtown Napa's favorite neighborhood restaurant is this comfy, rustic-chic come-as-you-are joint serving tapas and tasty wines at great prices. A no-reservation policy means you might have to wait for a table in the small downstairs dining room, along the compact wine bar, or upstairs in the quieter loft. But chef Charles Webber's Moroccan barbecued lamb chops with a sweet-spicy sauce; tangy paella topped with braised meats, shellfish, and a dollop of aioli; and apple empanadas are worth it—especially when practically every dish is less than $10 and comes with convivial atmosphere, an eclectic wine list, and a good time that often costs three times the price in these parts. *$; AE, MC, V; no checks; lunch Mon–Fri, dinner every day; beer and wine; no reservations; info@zuzunapa.com; www.zuzunapa.com; at Third St.*

LODGINGS

Cedar Gables Inn / ★★

486 COOMBS ST, NAPA; 707/224-7969 OR 800/309-7969 Beautiful Cedar Gables may be a B&B, but its attention to decor and service puts many of the valley's upscale hotels to shame. Innkeepers Margaret and Craig Snasdell have worked wonders with their 1892 Victorian and its nine rooms. The historic theme extends from the large and cozy family room, where guests meet each night to enjoy wine and cheese or watch TV in front of a blazing fire, to the breakfast room, where a full hot morning meal might include homemade breads, in-season fruit, French toast soufflé with strawberries and walnuts, or a Southwest casserole. Rooms are lavishly and appropriately adorned with tapestries, gilded antiques, and, in five rooms, fireplaces and/or whirlpool tubs. Bonuses uncommon to B&Bs include a decanter of port in each room, robes, irons and ironing boards, CD players, and hair dryers. *$$$; AE, DIS, MC, V; checks OK; info@cedargablesinn.com; www.cedargablesinn.com; from*

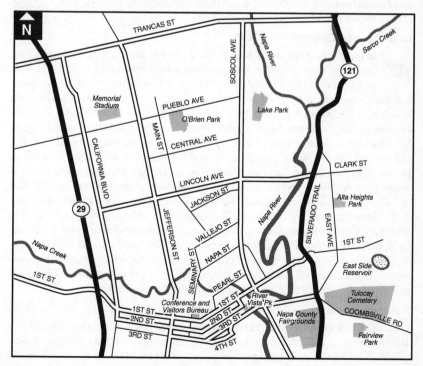

Hwy 29 exit onto 1st St, follow signs to downtown, turn right on Coombs St, and proceed to corner of Oak St.

Churchill Manor / ★★

485 BROWN ST, NAPA; 707/253-7733 Churchill Manor is an elegant, meticulously maintained mansion, incongruously set in a modest neighborhood. Built in 1889 by a local banker, it is listed on the National Register of Historic Places. The Colonial Revival house, which rises three stories above an expanse of beautiful gardens, is graced by stately pillars and a large, inviting veranda. Each of the 10 immaculate guest rooms features antique furnishings, ultra-plush carpeting, a fireplace, and an elegant private bath; among the favorites are Victoria's Room (imposing and spacious, with a king-size bed and a claw-footed tub perched by the fireplace), Rose's Room (with a scattering of French antiques including a carved-wood king-size bed), and Edward's Room (the largest room, Mr. Churchill's former sanctuary also boasts magnificent French antiques and a lavish bath with hand-painted tiles). Rates include a full breakfast served in the marble-floored sun room, fresh-baked cookies and coffee or tea in the afternoon, and a wine-and-cheese reception in the evening. When you're not out touring the local wineries, you may tickle the ivories of the grand piano in the parlor, play croquet on the lovely side lawn, or tour Old Town Napa on the inn's tandem bicycles. Owners Brian Jensen and Joanna Guidotti are attentive and welcoming hosts. *$$; AE, DIS, MC, V; checks OK; www.churchillmanor.com; at Oak St.*

La Résidence Country Inn / ★★

4066 ST. HELENA HWY, NAPA; 707/253-0337 Set back in the trees along busy Highway 29, this multimillion-dollar creation of partners David Jackson and Craig Claussen has 23 guest rooms scattered throughout three buildings separated by a heated swimming pool and an elaborate gazebo. The main house, a Gothic Revival mansion built in 1870 by a former New Orleans riverboat captain, contains nine comfortable guest rooms beautifully decorated with designer fabrics and American antiques. Most have sitting rooms and fireplaces; all have CD players and private baths. Airier accommodations can be found in the modern French-style barn across the plaza. Filled with simple pine antiques, these spacious rooms have fireplaces, private baths, and French doors that open onto small patios or balconies. The most recent addition is the Cellar House, where three suite-type rooms have king-size beds, cable TV, fireplaces, and wet bars. A delicious gourmet breakfast is served downstairs in the barn in a cheery, sunny dining room. Although La Résidence is undeniably one of the region's loveliest small inns, its location next to the highway detracts from the away-from-it-all feel that B&Bs usually try to cultivate. *$$$$; AE, DC, DIS, MC, V; no checks; reservations@laresidence.com; www.laresidence.com; on Hwy 29, next to Bistro Don Giovanni.*

Silverado Country Club & Resort / ★★

1600 ATLAS PEAK RD, NAPA; 707/257-0200 Golfers and tennis players flock to this 1,200-acre estate, and it's easy to see why. The Silverado boasts two perfectly maintained 18-hole golf courses designed by Robert Trent Jones Jr. and the largest tennis complex in North America, with 17 championship courts rimmed with flowered walkways. If you're not into golf or tennis, however, there's little reason to stay here; the 280 unprepossessing rooms seem to have been designed for people who don't plan to spend much time indoors. The standard rooms are individually decorated in a condo-like warren. One- and two-bedroom suites overlooking the golf course are prettier but tend to be equally soul-less and gleamingly modern with black-marble fireplaces and well-appointed kitchens. A few minutes' drive from the main complex are the more secluded Oak Creek East accommodations, street after street of mind-numbingly similar houses and condominiums owned by country-club members and rented out to guests. Numerous swimming pools dot the extensive grounds—popular spots to cool off on the valley's sweltering summer days. The resort's clubhouse and restaurants are located in the magnificent colonnaded Southern Gothic mansion at the heart of the main complex. Vintners Court, a formal dining room dominated by a glittering chandelier and a white grand piano, is open only on Friday nights for a seafood buffet. The fancy Royal Oak serves steak and seafood nightly. For a more casual meal, order a club sandwich or a hamburger at the Silverado Bar & Grill. Though the restaurants are unmemorable, the property's full-service spa is definitely worth visiting. *$$$$; AE, DC, DIS, MC, V; checks OK; resv@silveradoresort.com; www.silveradoresort.com; from Hwy 29, turn right onto Trancas St (Trancas St will become Hwy 121), then turn left onto Atlas Peak Rd.*

Yountville

Given that the commercial hub is about three blocks long, sleepy little Yountville, located 9 miles north of Napa off Highway 29 and founded in the mid-19th century by pioneer George Clavert Yount (reportedly the first American to settle in Napa Valley), has developed quite a reputation as a top-notch destination. The hullabaloo began with the **FRENCH LAUNDRY,** which has been touted as the best restaurant in the United States—and the most impossible to get into. But on the heels of its success came two glorious French bistros, **BOUCHON** and **BISTRO JEANTY;** a handful of expensive inns; more foot traffic to the small collection of boutiques; and, most recently, the 2003 additions of new destination eateries **BOUCHON BAKERY** (6528 Washington St, Yountville; 707/944-BAKE), famed chef Thomas Keller's takeout spot selling stunning fresh-from-the-oven French breads, sandwiches, and pastries, and Philippe Jeanty's latest restaurant, **PÈRE JEANTY** (see review, below).

RESTAURANTS

Bistro Jeanty / ★★★

6510 WASHINGTON ST, YOUNTVILLE; 707/944-0103 Philippe Jeanty was a culinary pioneer in Napa. He came from France to head Domaine Chandon's now-legendary kitchen back when the region was known more for cattle and prunes than for four-star wines. After 20 years at Chandon, he left to open his own place in Yountville, and it's been a success ever since, with the James Beard Foundation nominating it for recognition as the best new restaurant in the United States. Bistro Jeanty represents the rare perfect marriage of setting and cuisine, perhaps because Jeanty designed the whole thing himself, modeled on the small French bistros from his childhood. The details are flawless—from the window boxes with geraniums outside to the antiques and specials chalkboard inside. A large "community table" by the front door seats the diners without partners or reservations and is a favorite of locals who drop by. The food remains true to Jeanty's heritage: lamb tongue salad, *haricots verts*, sole meunière, steak tartare, and a dreamy coq au vin—all of which are well followed by a sinfully luxurious crème brûlée, which includes a surprise layer of chocolate mousse. *$$$; MC, V; no checks; lunch, dinner every day; full bar; reservations recommended; www.bistrojeanty.com; at Mulberry St.*

Bouchon / ★★½

6534 WASHINGTON ST, YOUNTVILLE; 707/944-8037 Thomas Keller opened this small bistro to handle the overflow business from the French Laundry and as a late-night gathering place for the valley. Bouchon looks like a miniature Paris bistro—one with such a sophisticated, elegant atmosphere that you immediately feel stylish simply by walking through the door. A zinc bar is put to good use serving raw seafood specialties such as oysters, mussels, and langoustines. The fare is traditional *bistro français*: foie gras, quiche du jour, charcuterie plates, onion soup gratin, steak frites, mussels marinières, and for dessert, tarte Tatin and profiteroles with ice cream and chocolate sauce. Don't miss the French fries—they're the best in the valley—or the pristine and oh-so-pretty butter lettuce salad. The short menu of appetizers, entrees, and desserts served until 12:45am daily lures the post-work restaurant crowd. *$$$; AE, MC, V; local checks only; lunch, dinner every day; full bar; reservations recommended; www.frenchlaundry.com; across from the Vintage 1870 shopping center.*

The French Laundry / ★★★★

6640 WASHINGTON ST, YOUNTVILLE; 707/944-2380 A serious dining affair awaits those who are fortunate (or persistent) enough to snare a reservation at the French Laundry, the top-ranked restaurant in the country. Draped in ivy, surrounded by herb gardens, and bearing the most incognito sign announcing its purpose, the discreet restaurant is occupied by brilliant chef Thomas Keller, who designs unbelievably intricate meals accompanied by stellar wines, and faultless (and yes, formal) service. Here it's all about edible artistry and everything is coddled, sculpted, ornamented, and coaxed to beyond perfection. The prix-fixe tasting menu—always lavish, extraordinary, and very precious—offers a choice of five or nine courses that change daily and invariably are accompanied by more than one *amuse-bouche*. Think rich scrambled duck eggs with truffle sauce; a velvety sabayon of pearl tapioca with Bagaduce oysters and osetra caviar; fresh fava bean agnolotti with roasted abalone mushrooms and Madras curry emulsion; perfectly grilled prime beef with shiitake mushrooms; and to-die-for butterscotch pot de crème. There's also a multicourse lunch, which is best enjoyed on the patio next to the flower and herb gardens. Reservations are accepted up to two months in advance. Good luck getting through to a receptionist, though. *$$$$; AE, MC, V; local checks only; lunch Fri–Sun, dinner every day; beer and wine; reservations required; www.frenchlaundry.com; at Creek St.*

ROBERT LOUIS STEVENSON'S TIME IN NAPA

The Scottish author Robert Louis Stevenson came to California in search of Fanny, a married woman 10 years his senior whom he'd met and fallen in love with in France. By the time he arrived by ship in San Francisco, he was half dead from bronchitis, his condition worsening as he waited for Fanny to obtain a divorce. By then he was penniless and critically ill.

The couple married in May 1880 and, in an attempt to restore the groom's health, spent their last $10 on a honeymoon cabin at a hot springs resort in Calistoga—a region even then famed for its restorative powers. With their money gone, they spent the summer in the old bunkhouse of an abandoned silver mine on **MOUNT ST. HELENA**. Their neighbors were grizzly bears, mountain lions, and rattlesnakes.

Dry weather and sunshine did, in fact, restore Stevenson's health. He describes his adopted home in a memoir, *Silverado Squatters:*

> The house, after we had repaired the worst of the damages, and filled in some of the doors and windows with white cotton cloth, became a healthy and a pleasant dwelling-place, always airy and dry, and haunted by the outdoor perfumes of the glen. Within, it had the look of habitation, the human look. . . . And yet our house was everywhere so wrecked and shattered, the air came and went so freely, the sun found so many portholes, the golden outdoor glow shone in so many open chinks, that we enjoyed, at the same time, some of the comforts of a roof and much of the gaiety and brightness of alfresco life. A single shower of rain, to be sure, and we should have been drowned out like mice. But ours was a California summer, and an earthquake was a far likelier accident than a shower of rain.

The writer admits more than the weather was a draw to Napa: "I was interested in California wine. Indeed, I am interested in all wines, and have been all my life. . . ." To this end, he spent time with Jacob Schram, who founded **SCHRAMSBERG VINEYARDS**.

While Stevenson idled on the mountain with Fanny, his family accepted the news of his marriage. The couple returned to Scotland, where Stevenson wrote *Treasure Island.* Mount St. Helena is said to be the inspiration for *Spyglass Hill.*

Today, at **ROBERT LOUIS STEVENSON STATE PARK**, you can hike up rugged, solitary Mount St. Helena to the site where the newlyweds squatted; a stone monument of a book marks the spot. In St. Helena, the **SILVERADO MUSEUM** (1490 Library Ln, St. Helena; 707/963-3757) houses one of the world's largest collections of Stevenson memorabilia. Documentary filmmakers from Scotland have, ironically, made the pilgrimage to Napa to research one of their most distinguished native sons.

Mustards Grill / ★★☆

7399 ST. HELENA HWY, YOUNTVILLE; 707/944-2424 Some critics call Mustards' feisty American regional cuisine comfort food, but that's too complacent a description for the vigorous, spicy, vaguely Asian-influenced bistro fare served here. Chef Cindy Pawlcyn's popular restaurant keeps it casual with a big open kitchen, white walls, dark wood wainscoting, and a black-and-white checkerboard floor. Appetizers range from seared ahi with wasabi cream and sesame crackers to Caesar salad with Parmesan croutons. The menu changes frequently, but might include tea-smoked Peking duck with almond-onion sauce, lemon and garlic chicken with garlic mashed potatoes, and chipotle-rubbed quail with wild mushroom tamale and jicama-radish slaw. *$$; AE, DC, MC, V; no checks; lunch, dinner every day; full bar; reservations recommended; www.mustardsgrill.com; S of the Vintage 1870 shopping center.*

Père Jeanty / ★★☆

6735 WASHINGTON ST, YOUNTVILLE; 707/945-1000 Chef Philippe Jeanty of Bistro Jeanty furthers his local fame with this stunning Provençal restaurant, which opened at the end of 2003. One look at the country French cottage oasis and it's obvious Jeanty's a man who relishes the details. Every nook and cranny, from the open kitchen with a wood-fired oven, cartoonish murals, lace curtains, and butcher paper–covered tables to the exterior's 100-year-old olive trees and 200-year-old roof tiles proves Jeanty was uncompromising in his efforts to make this restaurant embody the kind of place that would become everyone's *père*, or "old friend." The menu diverts from the butter, cream, and meats standbys of Bistro Jeanty to a more generous use of olive oil and fish, pizza *pissaladière* (anchovies, onions, olives), and mesquite-grilled items. The wine list focuses on Napa Valley, but gives a wink to Italy, Spain, and southern France. *$$$; AE, MC, V; no checks; lunch, dinner every day; full bar; reservations recommended; www.perejeanty.com; at Pedroni St* &

LODGINGS

Maison Fleurie / ★★

6529 YOUNT ST, YOUNTVILLE; 707/944-2056 OR 800/788-0369 Built in 1873, this beautiful, ivy-covered brick-and-fieldstone hotel was a bordello and later a 4-H clubhouse before it opened in 1971 as the Napa Valley's first bed-and-breakfast inn. Purchased by the owners of the Four Sisters Inns company (who also run the charming Petite Auberge in San Francisco and Pacific Grove's Gosbey House), the old Magnolia Hotel was reborn as Maison Fleurie in 1994 and endowed with a French country feel. Seven of the guest rooms are located in the main house, with its thick brick walls, terra-cotta tiles, and vineyard views; the remaining six are divided between the old bakery building and the carriage house. All have private baths, and some feature fireplaces, private balconies, sitting areas, and patios. After a long day of wine tasting, unwind at the pool or soak your tired dogs in the outdoor spa tub. The inn also provides bicycles for tooling around town. *$$$; AE, MC, V; no checks; www.foursisters.com; at Washington St.*

Vintage Inn / ★★

6541 WASHINGTON ST, YOUNTVILLE; 707/944-1112 OR 800/351-1133 Spread throughout a 23-acre estate, the Vintage Inn provides the Napa Valley traveler with a host of creature comforts in a modern setting. The 80 large, cheery rooms, bathed in soothing earth tones and wood accents, are all equipped with fireplaces, Jacuzzi tubs, refrigerators, patios or verandas, ceiling fans, and plush private baths. Guests may take a dip in the heated pool or outdoor spa, play a game of tennis, order room service, sip a spirit at the bar, or rent the inn's bikes or private limo for a tour of the Wine Country. You'll also be treated to a buffet breakfast served with glasses of bubbly, complimentary wine on arrival, afternoon tea, and access to the heated outdoor pool and hot tub, and spa services at their sister property Villagio, which is a Tuscan village–style resort located down the block. *$$$$; AE, DC, DIS, MC, V; no checks; www.vintageinn.com; just E of Hwy 29.*

Oakville

Other than several world-class wineries, Oakville's main claim to fame is the **OAKVILLE GROCERY CO.** (7856 St. Helena Hwy, at Oakville Cross Rd, 707/944-8802; www.oakvillegrocery.com), a local icon and old-fashioned country market complete with a fading "Drink Coca-Cola" sign outside. It's not a scene for the claustrophobic; any given noontime will find this homey establishment clogged with tourists lined up to buy gourmet deli treats. But those who brave the scene will find a fine variety of local wines, a small espresso bar tucked in the corner, and pricey but delicious picnic supplies ranging from pâté and caviar to sliced-turkey sandwiches and freshly made sweets.

Rutherford

LODGINGS

Auberge du Soleil / ★★★★

180 RUTHERFORD HILL RD, RUTHERFORD; 707/963-1211 OR 800/348-5406 The exclusive 33-acre, 50-unit resort, inspired by the sunny architecture of southern France, is nestled in an olive grove on a wooded hillside above the Napa Valley. Here it's all about exclusivity in the form of cottages and suites you could get lost in, complete with rough-textured adobe-style walls, white French doors and windows, and shocking pink textiles that are whimsical upon first encounter and old hat by the second or third visit. Each cottage has four guest rooms. Suites have very private entrances and patios or balconies. Upstairs rooms, which boast vaulted, exposed-beam ceilings, are particularly posh, but even the humblest accommodations here are sinfully hedonistic, with fireplaces, CD players, original artwork, comfortable furnishings, candles, sitting areas, tiled floors, and to-die-for bathrooms. Two rooms lack fireplaces but have king-size beds and French doors that open onto private terraces. Tack on the pool, the valley's best spa, a gym, and the restaurant serving excellent Wine Country cuisine (go for terrace seating!) and there's little reason to leave. *$$$$; AE, DIS, MC, V; checks OK; www.aubergedusoleil.com; N of Yountville—from the Silverado Trail, turn right on Rutherford Hill Rd.*

St. Helena

For many years St. Helena has been entrenched in a never-ending battle to preserve its exclusive, small-town way of life—instead of becoming one more tourist haven for Wine Country visitors. Citizens have filed injunctions against everything from the Napa Valley Wine Train (forbidding it to stop in town) to Safeway (the grocery giant wanted to build a supermarket larger than the one that already exists). Needless to say, Wal-Mart was out of the question.

As a result, **MAIN STREET** has retained its Victorian Old West feel, and historic structures like **STEVE'S HARDWARE** (1370 Main St; 707/963-3423) coexist with the trendy live music and bar venue **1351 LOUNGE** (1351 Main St; 707/963-1969), located in a former bank complete with vault. Just off the main drag you can find more down-home pleasures at the **NAPA VALLEY OLIVE OIL MANUFACTURING COMPANY** (835 Charter Oak Ave; 707/963-4173), an authentic and ramshackle Italian deli and general store stuffed to the rafters with goodies like dried fava beans, biscotti, salami, and fresh mozzarella. For great gifts, be sure to pick up a bottle or two of the top-notch extra-virgin olive oil or the olive oil soap. Just south of town, the New York gourmet superstore **DEAN & DELUCA** (607 S St. Helena Hwy; 707/967-9980; www.deananddeluca.com) sells a mind-boggling array of cheeses, wines, deli items, specialty foods, and cookware. An excellent way to rub elbows with locals and find great edibles is to attend the **ST. HELENA FARMERS MARKET** (Crane Park, off Hwy. 29, east on Sulphur Springs Ave, right on Crane Ave; 707/265-8602), held every Friday from 7:30am to noon May through October. For a picnic, take your treats to **LYMAN PARK** (on Main St between Adams and Pine) and sit on the grass or in the beautiful little white gazebo where bands sometimes perform summer concerts. A more bucolic picnic spot is **BALE GRIST MILL STATE HISTORIC PARK** (Hwy 29, 3 miles N of St. Helena).

RESTAURANTS

Taylor's Automatic Refresher / ★★

933 MAIN ST, ST. HELENA; 707/963-3486 Anyone who knows how tiresome fancy food can get might understand why Taylor's Refresher, a classic burger stand straight out of the 1950s, is a favorite among even the region's top chefs and the nation's best-regarded food editors. Sure, the 1949-built outdoor diner is a looker, with its yesteryear fast-food-shack design and outdoor seating. But more important, it doles out some darned good burgers and fries—juicy, thick, and served with all the toppings. Wine Country living doesn't get much better than a patty smothered with cheese, accompanied by a creamy shake or fizzy root beer float or a nice glass of wine. Those who beg to differ can always belly up for a good old-fashioned corn dog; steak, fish, or chicken taco; or veggie burger. *$; AE, MC, V; local checks only; lunch, dinner every day; beer and wine; no reservations; right on the highway, you can't miss it.* &

Terra / ★★★★

1345 RAILROAD AVE, ST. HELENA; 707/963-8931 If you can have only one dinner out while visiting Napa Valley, have it at Terra. Housed in a historic stone building with high ceilings and arched windows, Terra's subdued dining rooms have an ineffable sense of intimacy about them. Fervid tête-à-têtes, however, are more likely to revolve around Terra's fine southern French/northern Italian food than around *amore*. Yet this isn't the sort of food that screams to be noticed; chef Hiro Sone, who won the James Beard Foundation's Best California Chef award in 2003, creates incredible food that never grandstands. Though the menu changes with the seasons, tried-and-true standbys include fried rock shrimp with organic greens and chive mustard sauce; broiled sake-marinated rock cod with shrimp dumplings; spaghettini with tripe, tomato, and butter beans; and grilled, dry-aged New York strip steak with sautéed vegetables and anchovy garlic sauce. Sone's wife and business partner, Lissa Doumani, is behind the outstanding desserts, which might include strawberries drenched in a cabernet-and-black-peppercorn sauce served with vanilla ice cream or a sculptural tiramisu. Service is formal yet friendly, and the wine list highlights local producers. *$$$$; DC, MC, V; local checks only; dinner Wed–Mon; beer and wine; reservations recommended; www.terrarestaurant.com; between Adams and Hunt Sts, 1 block E of Main St.*

Tra Vigne & Cantinetta / ★★★½

1050 CHARTER OAK AVE, ST. HELENA; 707/963-4444 (RESTAURANT) OR 707/963-8888 (CANTINETTA) The Italian-style courtyard dining is pure heaven, the Tuscan-inspired food at Tra Vigne is exceptionally fresh, and almost everything is made on the premises. Unfortunately, chefs changed a few times over the past two years, and as of late food can range from simply good to great. The menu is seasonal, but you can usually find excellent *fritti* of fried prawns and vegetables in arborio rice flour served with mustard vinegar, or expert wood-fired pizza specials such as a classic Margherita. Pastas run the gamut from traditional to outrageous—such as rigatoni with tomatoes, pecorino, and basil; or ravioli with eggplant, ricotta, mozzarella, tomato conserva, and warm oregano crumbs. Entrees might include grilled wild king salmon with fresh chickpeas, Blue Lake beans, and Meyer lemon sauce; roasted organic chicken breast with roasted carrots, potatoes, escarole, and garlic-lemon jus; and a savory grilled lamb sirloin with rapini and olive jus. Servers are knowledgeable, witty, and efficient. The wine list, though not large, includes a carefully chosen array of Italian and Napa Valley bottles. The vast, swank dining room has soaring ceilings and taupe walls covered with big, bright Italian poster art. For a lighter lunch, food to-go, or wine tastings, amble over to the less-expensive Cantinetta Tra Vigne. The cantinetta sells several varieties of focaccia pizza, gourmet sandwiches, interesting soups and salads, pastas topped with smoked salmon and other delights, a variety of sweets, and around 100 wines by the glass. *$$$; CB, DC, DIS, MC, V; no checks; lunch, dinner* *every day (restaurant); lunch every day (cantinetta); full bar; reservations recommended; www.travignerestaurant.com; off Hwy 29.*

Wine Spectator Restaurant at Greystone / ★★

2555 MAIN ST, ST. HELENA; 707/967-1010 When you first spot Greystone perched high atop a hill, you'll catch your breath, as it's the closest thing to a castle you'll find in the United States. The building, which formerly housed the Christian Brothers winery, was constructed in 1889 out of local tufa stone. The restaurant is on the first floor of the Culinary Institute of America (it's named for *Wine Spectator* magazine, which donated $1 million to the school's scholarship fund) and is in a large, noisy room with a fireplace and a display kitchen surrounded by a bar. The CIA's cooking students play an integral role in restaurant preparations that tend to trot the globe in their inspiration. Appetizers nod to the East with curried cauliflower soup with turmeric oil and bow to Spain with steamed mussels with chorizo, romesco sauce, and grilled bread. Entrees say *olé!* with fire-roasted poblano peppers stuffed with fresh corn polenta, ricotta cheese, and black bean sauce and accentuate the local bounty with filet of beef with original Point Reyes blue cheese, heirloom tomatoes, shoestring potatoes, and red wine sauce. The wine list is extensive, offering something for every taste and price range. Tours of the building are also available, as are weekend cooking demonstrations (707/967-2320). The basement houses a decent cookware emporium, complete with great gadgets and cookbooks. *$$$$; AE, DC, MC, V; local checks only; lunch, dinner every day; full bar; reservations recommended; www.ciachef.edu; at Deer Park Rd.*

LODGINGS

El Bonita Motel / ★

195 MAIN ST, ST. HELENA; 707/963-3216 OR 800/541-3284 Thanks to an extensive remodeling, El Bonita is indeed *bonita*. Hand-painted grapevines grace many of the room entrances, and inside the walls are colored a faint pink, with floor-length baby blue drapes and pink-and-baby-blue floral bedspreads. Each of the 41 rooms has a private bath, cable TV, refrigerator, microwave, coffeemaker, phone, and—for a little more money—whirlpool bath. Huge oak trees surround the motel, a heated kidney-shaped swimming pool sits in front, and a sauna and an outdoor whirlpool are on the premises; massages are available by appointment. The rates vary from month to month (depending on business), but in general you (and your pet) can get a reasonably priced room. El Bonita fronts Highway 29, so try to reserve a room as far from the street as possible. *$$; AE, DC, DIS, MC, V; no checks; elbonita1@aol.com; www.elbonita.com; just S of downtown St. Helena on Hwy 29.*

The Ink House Bed and Breakfast / ★

1575 ST. HELENA HWY, ST. HELENA; 707/963-3890 This gorgeous Italianate Victorian inn, built in the shape of an ink bottle by Napa settler Theron Ink in 1884, would merit three stars if it weren't for its no-star location along a busy, noisy stretch of Highway 29. The three-story yellow-and-white home has seven sumptuously decorated guest rooms, plus a lavish living room and three parlors, one with an old-fashioned pump organ. The B&B's most interesting architectural feature is the glass-walled cupola observatory that sits atop the house like the stopper of an inkwell and offers a sweeping 360-degree view of the Napa Valley hills and vineyards. The best (and quietest) room is the spacious, high-ceilinged French Room, with its richly carved French oak bed graced by an elegant quarter-canopy. The rooms at the front of the house are for sound sleepers only. Innkeeper Diane De Filipi is incredibly friendly and helpful, and she'll keep you nourished with a full country breakfast, plus wine and appetizers in the afternoon. *$$$; MC, V; checks OK; inkhousebb@aol.com; www.inkhouse.com; at Whitehall Ln.*

Inn at Southbridge / ★★★☆

1020 MAIN ST, ST. HELENA; 707/967-9400 OR 800/520-6800 This sister to the swanky Meadowood Napa Valley resort fills the gap between Napa's ultra-luxe digs and its ubiquitous bed-and-breakfast inns. Designed by the late William Turnbull Jr., the 21-room inn is part of a terra-cotta-hued complex that dominates a long block on St. Helena's main drag. Inside, there's not much in the way of common areas, but the guest rooms are almost Shaker in their elegant simplicity, with white piqué cotton comforters, candles, fireplaces, vaulted ceilings, and French doors opening onto private balconies. Guest privileges are available at the exclusive Meadowood Napa Valley resort, though the on-site Health Spa Napa Valley offers a plethora of spa services, a swimming pool, and exercise equipment. In the courtyard, a sign boasting a big red tomato sets the mood at Pizzeria Tra Vigne, the stylish pizzeria neighboring the inn. Sit on one of the bar stools facing the open kitchen and order the clam pie, a winning pizza combo. *$$$$; DC, MC, V; checks OK; www.slh.com; between Charter Oak Ave and Pope St.*

Meadowood Napa Valley / ★★★★

900 MEADOWOOD LN, ST. HELENA; 707/963-3646 OR 800/458-8080 Rising out of a surreal green sea of fairways and croquet lawns, Meadowood's pearl-gray, New England–style mansions are resolutely East Coast. Winding landscaped paths and roads connect the central buildings with smaller lodges scattered over 256 acres; the lodges are strategically situated near an immaculately maintained nine-hole golf course, two croquet lawns (with a full-time croquet pro on hand), seven championship tennis courts, and a 25-yard lap pool. The 85 exorbitantly priced accommodations range from one-room studios to four-room suites, each with a private porch and a wet bar. The suites tucked back in the woods are the most private, but the Lawnview Terrace rooms are the best, with their vaulted ceilings, massive stone fireplaces, and French doors opening onto balconies that overlook the croquet green. The vast bathrooms have hair dryers, magnified makeup mirrors, thick bathrobes, and floors inset with radiant heating to keep your toes cozy as you pad to the cavernous shower. All guests have access to the swimming pool, the outdoor whirlpool, and the well-equipped health spa that offers a weight room, aerobics classes, massages, and numerous other ways to pamper your body. The octagonal Restaurant at Meadowood, which serves California Wine Country cuisine, has a high ceiling and a beautiful balcony overlooking the golf course. The more informal Grill at Meadowood offers breakfast, lunch, and dinner daily. *$$$$; AE, DC, DIS, MC; checks OK; reservations@meadowood.com; www.meadowood.com; off the Silverado Trail.*

White Sulphur Springs Inn & Spa / ★★

3100 WHITE SULPHUR SPRINGS RD, ST. HELENA; 707/963-8588 OR 800/593-8873 (IN CA) Pastoral surroundings and an uncommonly casual St. Helena atmosphere are all yours at this rustic property with 330 acres of wilderness and natural springs that inspired the resort's original construction in 1852. Today the 9 cozy creek-side cabins and 28 rooms, which were renovated in 1999, are dispersed among three structures, including the old Carriage House. Rooms are adorned with country-style furnishings; some have fireplaces or wood-burning stoves and/or kitchenettes. Cottages have picnic tables and barbecues and modern touches like air conditioning and heaters. Rooms at the "inn" have private entrances and showers (no tubs), and the two-story Carriage House boasts shared bathrooms for each floor (men's and women's are separate, but bring a bathrobe for the dash to the shower and back). There are no TVs, phones, or Internet access, so it's easy to forget the dramas of everyday life. Equally stress-free is the cost, which is far better than what you'd pay at most properties in the area. The best perk is easy access to nature and the spa, which offers everything from rock therapy and salt scrubs to massage and use of the heated outdoor pool and natural hot springs. *$$; MC, V; no checks; www.whitesulphursprings.com; turn W at Exxon gas station (Spring St) and continue 3 miles.*

Calistoga

Mud baths, mineral pools, and massages are still the main attractions of this charming little spa town, founded in the mid-19th century by California's first millionaire, Sam Brannan. Savvy Brannan made a bundle of cash supplying miners in the Gold Rush and quickly recognized the value of Calistoga's mineral-rich **HOT SPRINGS.** In 1859 he purchased 2,000 acres of the Wappo Indians' hot springs land, built a first-class hotel and spa, and named the region Calistoga (a combination of the words California and Saratoga). He then watched his fortunes grow as affluent San Franciscans paraded into town for a relaxing respite from city life.

Generations later, city slickers are still making the pilgrimage to this strip of spas. These days, however, more than a dozen enterprises touting the magical restorative powers of mineral baths line the town's Old West–style streets. You'll see an odd combo of stressed-out CEOs and earthier types shelling out dough for a chance to soak away their worries and get the kinks rubbed out of their necks. While Calistoga's spas and resorts are less glamorous than the Fairmont Sonoma Mission Inn & Spa (see review in Lodgings section of Sonoma), many offer body treatments and mud baths you won't find anywhere else in this part of the state. Among the most popular spas are **DR. WILKINSON'S HOT SPRINGS** (1507 Lincoln Ave; 707/942-4102; www.drwilkinson.com), where you'll get a great massage and numerous other body treatments in a rather drab setting; **CALISTOGA SPA HOT SPRINGS** (1006 Washington St; 707/942-6269; www.calistogaspa.com), a favorite for families with young children that boasts four mineral pools in addition to several body-pampering services; **INDIAN SPRINGS** (1712 Lincoln Ave; 707/942-4913; www.indian springsnapa.com) for pricey spa treatments in a historic setting and the best (and largest) mineral pool in the area (you can even see—and hear—the steam from one of the geysers feeding hot mineral water into the pool); and **LAVENDER HILL SPA** (1015 Foothill Blvd/Hwy 29; 707/942-4495; www.lavenderhillspa.com), which provides aromatherapy facials, seaweed wraps, mud baths, and other sybaritic delights in one of the most attractive settings in town.

After you've steamed or soaked away all your tensions, head over to the **CALIS-TOGA INN**'s (1250 Lincoln Ave; 707/942-4101; www.calistogainn.com) pretty out-door patio for a tall, cool drink. Try one of the house-brewed beers or ales, but save your appetite for one of the better restaurants in town. Once you're rejuvenated, stroll down the main street and browse through the many quaint shops marketing everything from French soaps and antique armoires to silk-screened T-shirts and saltwater taffy. For a trip back in time to Calistoga's pioneer past, stop by the **SHARPSTEEN MUSEUM AND BRANNAN COTTAGE** (1311 Washington St; 707/942-5911; www.sharpensteen-museum.org). Just outside of town you can marvel at **OLD FAITHFUL GEYSER** (1299 Tubbs Ln, 2 miles N of Calistoga; 707/942-6463; www.oldfaithfulgeyser.com), which faithfully shoots a plume of 350°F mineral water 60 feet into the air at regular intervals.

Other natural wonders abound at the **PETRIFIED FOREST** (4100 Petrified Forest Rd, off Hwy 128, 6 miles N of town; 707/942-6667; www.petrifiedforest.org), though if you aren't a trained geologist, it might be hard to appreciate those tow-ering redwoods turned to stone when Mount St. Helena erupted 3 million years ago. For a splendid view of the entire valley, hike through the beautiful redwood canyons and oak-madrona woodlands in **ROBERT LOUIS STEVENSON STATE PARK** (off Hwy 29, 8 miles N of Calistoga; 707/942-4575) to the top of Mount St. Helena.

RESTAURANTS

All Seasons Cafe / ★★☆

1400 LINCOLN AVE, CALISTOGA; 707/942-9111 Many restaurants in the Napa Valley have elaborate wine lists, but none compare to this cafe's award-winning roster. The rear of the restaurant—a retail wine store with a tasting bar—stocks hundreds of first-rate foreign and domestic selections at remarkably reasonable prices. If nothing catches your fancy on the restaurant's regular wine list, ask to see the shop's enormous computerized catalog. The All Seasons menu is structured around wine as well as the seasons: the appetizers, such as salmon tartare with crispy taro root chips and wasabi emulsion, are recommended to accompany sparklers, chardonnay, and sauvignon blanc; entrees such as braised short ribs with polenta cake, wild mushrooms, and red wine sauce are paired with zinfandel and Rhône wines; and oven-roasted Colorado lamb sirloin with port-roasted figs or gratin of potato and turnip are matched with merlot or cabernet. The enthusiastic and opin-ionated servers can usually steer you safely to the better choices on the changing menu. *$$; DIS, MC, V; local checks only; lunch Fri–Sun, dinner every day; beer and wine; reservations recommended; www.allseasonsnapavalley.com; at Washington St.*

Wappo Bar & Bistro / ★★

1226-B WASHINGTON ST, CALISTOGA; 707/942-4712 Husband-and-wife chefs Aaron Bauman and Michelle Matrux opened this zesty bistro in 1993 and immediately began collecting accolades for what Bauman describes as "regional global cuisine." Confused? Well, even Bauman admits the cuisine is hard to pinpoint, merrily skipping as it does from the Middle East to Europe to Asia to South America to the good old USA. The small menu changes often, but this culinary United Nations has embraced such diverse dishes as Thai noodle and green papaya salad with shredded vegetables, herbs, peanuts, marinated chicken, and ginger-lime dressing; and yogurt-lemon marinated chicken skewers with orzo pasta and Greek salad. One dish that turns up often due to popular demand: chiles rellenos stuffed with basmati rice, crème fraîche, currants, and fresh herbs, dipped in a blue cornmeal batter, deep-fried, and served on a bed of walnut-pomegranate sauce. This is ambitious, imaginative cooking, and the talented chefs usually pull it off with aplomb. Unfortunately, service was lacking during recent visits. *$$; AE, MC, V; local checks only; lunch, dinner Wed–Mon; beer and wine; reservations recommended; www.wappobar.com; off Lincoln Ave.*

LODGINGS

Cottage Grove Inn / ★★

1711 LINCOLN AVE, CALISTOGA; 707/942-8400 OR 800/799-2284 If B&B quarters are a little too cozy for comfort, you can't beat the privacy of your very own cottage tucked in a grove of elm trees. Too bad Calistoga's busiest street is a little too close to some of the cottages at this resort along Lincoln Avenue (though the walls have double layers of Sheetrock to cut down on noise). Still, the 16 gray clapboard structures are storybook sweet, with white wicker rockers and firewood on the porches, two-person Jacuzzi tubs, fireplaces, hardwood floors, TVs with VCRs, CD players, and quaint quilts on the beds. An expanded continental breakfast of pastries, fresh fruit, cereal, coffee, and juice (included in the rate) is served in the guest lounge, and wine and cheese are offered in the evening. *$$$$; AE, DC, DIS, MC, V; checks OK; innkeeper@cottagegrove.com; www.cottage grove.com; at Wappo Ave.*

Indian Springs Resort / ★

1712 LINCOLN AVE, CALISTOGA; 707/942-4913 This historic inn was built in 1860 by Sam Brannan, the founder of Calistoga, on a site where Native Americans used to erect sweat lodges to harness the region's thermal waters. A procession of palm trees leads to the accommodations—17 rustic and casually furnished wooden cottages with partial kitchens, which appeal to families eager to cavort in the resort's huge hot-springs-fed swimming pool. Indian Springs also offers a playground and the full gamut of spa services (massages, facials, mud baths, and more). The spa is open to the public, but the wonderful pool is now restricted to spa and hotel guests. *$$$; DIS, MC, V; checks OK; www.indianspringscalistoga.com; between Wappo Ave and Brannan St.*

Clear Lake Area

California's largest freshwater lake, Clear Lake once had more than 30 wineries ringing its shore. Prohibition put an end to all that in 1919. The land was converted to walnut and Bartlett pear orchards, and only in the past few decades have the grapes (and the wineries) been making a comeback. This area may one day become as celebrated as Napa and Sonoma, but unlike these trendy stepsisters to the south, there ain't nothin' nouveau about Clear Lake. Country music wafts from pickup trucks, bored (and bared) youths wander the roads aimlessly (perhaps in search of their shirts), and there's generally not a whole lot going on until the weekend boaters and anglers arrive.

Middletown

If you're traveling north from the Napa Valley to Clear Lake, stop at the well-regarded **GUENOC WINERY** (21000 Butts Canyon Rd, 6 miles E of Middletown; 707/987-2385; www.guenoc.com), a 23,000-acre estate owned by British actress **LILLIE LANGTRY** in the 1880s. In Langtry's memory, the current owners grace their wine labels with her portrait. Take a tour of the winery and taste the buttery chardonnays and the trendy blend of reds called Meritage. For the lowdown on what to expect up ahead in the Clear Lake region, contact the county-run **LAKE COUNTY VISITORS CENTER** (6110 E Hwy 20, Lucerne; 707/274-5652 or 800/525-3743; www.lakecounty.com), open daily from 9am to 5pm.

Clear Lake

Clear Lake's informal annual blowout is on the Fourth of July weekend (contact the **CLEAR LAKE CHAMBER OF COMMERCE**, 707/994-3600; www.clear-lakechamber.com), when thousands of born-again patriots amass (and timorous locals split) for a three-day sunburnt orgy of flag-waving, fireworks, waterskiing, and a parade. If you want to dive into the aquatic activities on boats of all shapes and sizes, contact **FUNTIME WATERSPORTS** (6035 Old Hwy 53, Clear Lake; 707/994-6267) or **ON THE WATERFRONT** (60 3rd St, Lakeport; 707/263-6789), which also rents jet skis and Sea-Doos.

Clear Lake also draws crowds eager to snag some of its largemouth bass, catfish, perch, and crappie. Although the lake has earned the title of **BASS CAPITAL OF THE WEST**, there aren't any shops renting fishing equipment, so you'll have to tote your own. For a stunning view of the lake and the surrounding mountain peaks, hop aboard a **GLIDER PLANE**; flights are available through **CRAZY CREEK GLIDERS** (18896 Grange Rd, 3 miles N of Middletown; 707/987-9112; www.crazy-creekgliders.com). For more information on Clear Lake and its surrounding towns and wineries, call or drop by the **LAKE COUNTY VISITOR INFORMATION CENTER** (875 Lakeport Blvd, Vista Point, Lakeport; 707/274-5652 or 800/LAKESIDE; www.lakecounty.com).

Lakeport

With its small, old-fashioned downtown, Lakeport is the prettiest town on Clear Lake. Formerly known as Forbestown (after early settler William Forbes), the area is usually very peaceful until summer, when people from outlying cities pack up their Jeeps and station wagons and caravan out here for fishing, camping, swimming, and wine tasting. **CLEAR LAKE STATE PARK** (off Soda Bay Rd, S of Lakeport; 707/279-4293; www.parks.ca.gov) is one of the area's main draws, with its campgrounds (no reservations available during off-season), miles of hiking trails, and a beach. Folks also flock to Lakeport every Labor Day weekend for the **LAKE COUNTY FAIR**, featuring 4-H exhibits, livestock auctions, horse shows, and a carnival; it's held at the fairgrounds (401 Martin St; 707/263-6181; www.lakecountyfair.com).

RESTAURANTS

Park Place / ★★

50 3RD ST, LAKEPORT; 707/263-0444 Ever since the Loon's Nest restaurant in nearby Kelseyville closed, there hasn't been much debate over Lake County's best restaurant. It's Park Place—a small lakeside cafe serving very good Italian and California-inspired food. Owners Barbara Morris and Nancy Zabel make fettuccine every day and serve it with simple, fresh sauces such as creamy alfredo, zingy marinara, pesto, or *quattro formaggi*. Also highly recommended are Nancy's made-from-scratch soups (particularly the chunky Italian vegetable) and house-made focaccia sandwiches. Save room for the superb cheesecake. *$$; MC, V; checks OK; lunch, dinner every day; beer and wine; reservations recommended; off Main St, near the lake.*

Nice

LODGINGS

Featherbed Railroad Company / ★

2870 LAKESHORE BLVD, NICE; 707/274-8378 OR 800/966-6322 Nine cabooses that look as though they would be right at home in Disneyland are spread out underneath a grove of oak trees at this gimmicky but fun bed-and-breakfast. The freight-train cars are burdened with cutesy names, but they're equipped with featherbeds, private baths (some with Jacuzzi tubs), and other amenities that make up for the silliness. Favorite train cars include two newer cabooses, the Orient Express (with a private deck) and the Casablanca (complete with a piano and bar), but it's the black-and-maroon La Loose Caboose (tackiest of them all, with a bordello decor, a deck, and a mirror over the bed) that's always booked. The Rosebud Caboose has a Jacuzzi tub for two. Breakfast is served at the Main Station, a century-old ranch house, in front of a cozy fire or on the porch overlooking the lake. A small pool and spa adjoin the house. *$$; AE, DIS, MC, V; no checks; www.featherbedrailroad.com; off Hwy 20, at the SW end of town.*

Sonoma County

Many would argue that when it comes to comparing Sonoma Valley's Wine Country with Napa's, less is definitely more: Sonoma is less congested, less developed, less commercial, and less glitzy than its rival. Smitten with the bucolic charm of the region, oenophiles delight in wandering the area's backroads, leisurely hopping from winery to winery and exploring the quaint towns along the way. There are moments when—sitting in the sunshine at some of the beautifully landscaped wineries, inhaling the hot camphor smell of the eucalyptus trees, listening to a gurgling brook and the serenade of songbirds as you sip a glass of chilled sauvignon blanc—you think that even Eden would be a disappointment after Sonoma.

Sonoma Wine Country is informally divided into two regions: Sonoma Valley and northern Sonoma County. The valley is relatively condensed: about 40 wineries and a modest countrified social life revolve around downtown Sonoma and its historic plaza. Santa Rosa is the gateway to northern Sonoma County, where wineries are discovered along winding one-lane country roads, and famous growing areas such as Dry Creek promise killer zinfandel and intimate winery experiences.

Before setting out for this verdant vineyard-laced region, stop at the **SONOMA VALLEY VISITORS BUREAU** (453 1st St E; 707/996-1090; www.sonomavalley.com) for lots of free, helpful information about the area's wineries, farmers markets, historic sites, walking tours, recreational facilities, and seasonal events. If you're exploring northern Sonoma County, contact the **SONOMA COUNTY TOURIST PROGRAM** (800/576-6662) to order a free brochure, or visit their Web site at www.sonomacounty.com for every possible thing you might want to know about the area.

Sonoma Wineries

California's world-renowned wine industry was born in the Sonoma Valley. Franciscan fathers planted the state's first vineyards at the Mission San Francisco Solano de Sonoma in 1823 and harvested the grapes to make their sacramental wines. Thirty-four years later, California's first major vineyard was planted with European grape varietals by Hungarian Count Agoston Haraszthy at Sonoma's revered Buena Vista Winery. Little did the count know that one day he would become widely hailed as the father of California wine. Today nearly 40 wineries dot the Sonoma Valley, most offering pretty picnic areas and free tours of their winemaking facilities. Alas, free tastings used to be the norm, but like Napa wineries, Sonoma wineries have also begun charging fees (usually around $5) to sample. Here's a roundup of some of Sonoma's best:

BARTHOLOMEW PARK WINERY (1000 Vineyard Ln, Sonoma; 707/935-9511; www.bartholomewparkwinery.com). The winery sits in the midst of 400-acre Bartholomew Memorial Park, making it one of the most beautiful settings in the valley and an exceptional picnic spot, complete with hiking trails. A museum displays photos by Victorian photographer Eadweard Muybridge, who documented viticulture practices from the 19th century. Tastings are $5.

BENZIGER FAMILY WINERY (1883 London Ranch Rd, Glen Ellen; 707/935-3000 or 800/989-8890; www.benziger.com). Tram ride tours ($10) take visitors through the vineyards here, and $5 tastings of their extensive portfolio are held in the wine shop.

BUENA VISTA WINERY (18000 Old Winery Rd, Sonoma; 707/938-1266). California's oldest premium winery (founded in 1857) is a large estate set in a forest with picnic grounds. Tours of the stone winery and the hillside tunnels are available, and a gallery features locals' artwork. Tastings start at $5.

CHÂTEAU ST. JEAN (8555 Sonoma Hwy/Hwy 12, Kenwood; 707/833-4134; www.chateaustjean.com). Beringer purchased Château St. Jean in 1996; since that time the mansion and 250-acre estate have undergone a dramatic renovation. So did the tasting room, which is now reminiscent of a Napa corporate winery, as opposed to its previous intimate atmosphere. Still, the place is beautiful with great picnic grounds.

FERRARI-CARANO VINEYARDS AND WINERY (8761 Dry Creek Rd, Healdsburg; 707/433-6700; www.ferrari-carano.com). This cutting-edge facility features 5 acres of spectacular gardens. Ferrari-Carano made its reputation with its chardonnay but also offers top-notch fumé blanc and cabernet sauvignon, which you can sample for $3.

GLORIA FERRER CHAMPAGNE CAVES (23555 Hwy 121, Sonoma; 707/996-7256; www.gloriaferrer.com). This champagne house's subterranean cellars make for an excellent tour.

GUNDLACH BUNDSCHU WINERY (2000 Denmark St, Sonoma; 707/938-5277; www.gunbun.com). Located in a grand, historic building set on impressive grounds, Gundlach Bundschu is known primarily for its zinfandel but also makes several interesting German-style whites. Picnic facilities are available and tastings are $5.

KENWOOD VINEYARDS (9592 Sonoma Hwy/Hwy 12, Kenwood; 707/833-5891; www.kenwoodvineyards.com). Kenwood is renowned for its quaint wooden barns and red wines. The best of its zinfandel and cabernet grapes come from Jack London's old vineyard on Sonoma Mountain. Tastings start at $2.

KORBEL CHAMPAGNE CELLARS (13250 River Rd, Guerneville; 707/824-7000; www.korbel.com). In an ivy-covered brick building set in a redwood forest with a view of the Russian River, Korbel hosts informative tours and free tastings. The extensive and beautiful flower gardens are open for tours from May through mid-October, and a deli offers great picnic items.

KUNDE ESTATE WINERY (10155 Sonoma Hwy/Hwy 12, Kenwood; 707/833-5501; www.kunde.com). The Kunde family has been growing grapes for more than five generations, and today they're one of Sonoma County's largest suppliers. Their century-old winery sits in the middle of this lovely 2,000-acre setting.

LEDSON WINERY & VINEYARDS (7335 Sonoma Hwy, Santa Rosa; 707/833-2330; www.ledson.com). Located in a modern-day castle complete with formal gardens and fountains, the winery offers a large array of wines for tasting ($5) and a well-stocked deli.

MATANZAS CREEK WINERY (6097 Bennett Valley Rd, Santa Rosa; 707/528-6464; www.matanzascreek.com). A beautiful drive leads to this winery's attractive facilities surrounded by lavender. Matanzas offers outstanding chardonnay and merlot as well as guided tours and picnic tables. Tastings $5.

QUIVIRA VINEYARDS (4900 W Dry Creek Rd, Healdsburg; 707/431-8333; www.quivirawine.com). Quivira is housed in a postmodern barn in a quiet vineyard setting. The winery is known for its zinfandel, but the superbly spicy Sauvignon Blanc Fig Tree Vineyard is worth trying as well. Free tastings.

RAVENSWOOD WINERY (18701 Gehricke Rd, Sonoma; 800/NO-WIMPY or 707/938-1960; www.ravenswoodwinery.com). Home of some of the tastiest zinfandels made, Ravenswood offers vintages that run the full range of styles from jammy to peppery. Along with a $5 tasting, the winery offers the perfect accompaniment—barbecue—on weekends, Memorial Day through Labor Day.

SEBASTIANI VINEYARDS & WINERY (389 4th St E, Sonoma; 707/938-5532 or 800/888-5532; www.sebastiani.com). Sonoma's largest premium-variety winery, Sebastiani Vineyards provides tours of its fermentation room and aging cellar, which includes an interesting collection of carved-oak cask heads. There's also a slick, enormous tasting room-cum-gift shop where you can taste for free.

VIANSA WINERY AND ITALIAN MARKETPLACE (25200 Hwy 121, Sonoma; 707/935-4700; www.viansa.com). Modeled after a Tuscan village, these buildings and grounds are owned by the Sebastiani family. They produce several fine Italian-style wines, like dolcetto and nebbiolo. Grilled meats, gourmet Italian picnic fare, and local delicacies are available for enjoying on the beautiful hillside picnic grounds.

Sonoma

Sonoma, one of the most historic towns in Northern California, is a good place to experience the region's Mexican heritage. Designed by General Mariano Vallejo in 1835, Sonoma is set up like a Mexican town, with an 8-acre parklike plaza in the center—complete with a meandering flock of chickens and crowing roosters. Several authentic adobe buildings hug the perimeter; most now house an assortment of boutiques, restaurants, and also the vintage **SEBASTIANI THEATRE** (476 1st St E; 707/996-2020; www.sebastianitheatre.com). **MISSION SAN FRANCISCO SOLANO DE SONOMA** (on the corner of 1st St E and E Spain St; 707/938-1519; www.california missions.com), a.k.a. the Sonoma Mission, is the northernmost and last of the 21 missions built by the Spanish fathers.

A stroll around the plaza area offers interesting shopping and an excellent bookstore, **READER'S BOOKS** (127 Napa St E; 707/939-1779; www.readersbooks.com). Or find everything for a Wine Country feast: cheeses and deli fare galore from the **SONOMA CHEESE FACTORY** (2 W Spain St; 707/996-1931; www.sonomajack.com). If you didn't have time to hit all the wineries you wanted, or if you're ready for a beer instead, stop by the **WINE EXCHANGE** (452 1st St E; 800/938-1794; www.wine exsonoma.com). Wine and beer tastings are available in the rear, and you can choose from an enormous selection of each to complete your picnic. **CUCINA VIANSA** (400 1st St E; 707/935-5656) has takeout gourmet fare and also features wine tasting, an espresso bar, and ice cream. Listen to acoustic music on Thursday through Sunday nights at **MURPHY'S IRISH PUB** (435 1st St E; 707/935-0660), hidden in the court-yard behind the Sebastiani Theatre. Late-night wine tasting, live jazz, and tasty "small plates" are available at the new and extremely elegant **LEDSON HOTEL AND HARMONY CLUB** (480 1st St E; 707/996-9779; www.ledson.com), which serves breakfast, lunch, and dinner daily.

RESTAURANTS

Cafe La Haye / ★★★

140 NAPA ST E, SONOMA; 707/935-5994 Located just off the main plaza, this light-filled cafe blends two sensual pleasures: art and food. Paintings in the bold California Colorist style cover the walls, and larger-than-life fantasy nudes float across the bathroom walls. Not to be outdone, the food is also a unique work of art. Brunch dishes offer surprising twists, like a poached egg with ham bobbing in a sea of white cheddar grits. Or try the ubiquitous eggs Benedict, updated here with roasted red peppers and shiitake mushrooms, served on an herb biscuit. Dinner offers a short menu of rustic European dishes, like seared black pepper–lavender fillet of beef with Gorgonzola potato gratin, or risotto and fish specials that change daily. The wine list is three times as long as the menu and, in keeping with the theme, offers some unusual Sonoma specialties. *$$; MC, V; local checks only; dinner Tues–Sat, brunch Sun; beer and wine; no reservations for brunch, reservations recommended for dinner; just E of the Plaza.*

Della Santina's / ★★

133 NAPA ST E, SONOMA; 707/935-0576 A fixture on the plaza for years, this popular and traditionally Italian dining room has a homey interior and a wonderful vine-laced brick patio tucked in back that's *the* place to dine when the weather is warm. The menu includes a good selection of light to heavy house-made pastas (the Gnocchi della Nonna with a tomato, basil, and garlic sauce would impress any Italian grandmother) and wonderful meats from the *rosticceria* (the chicken with fresh herbs is tender and perfectly spiced). Be sure to inquire about the *pasticceria*— and if *panna cotta* (a vanilla cream custard flavored with Italian rum) is among the offerings, nab it. Paired with an espresso, it's the perfect finale to a fine meal. *$$; AE, DIS, MC, V; local checks only; lunch, dinner every day; beer and wine; reservations recommended; off 2nd St.*

the girl & the fig / ★★

110 W SPAIN ST (IN THE SONOMA HOTEL), SONOMA; 707/938-3634 "Country food with French passion" doesn't get more inviting than at cozy the girl & the fig. Owner Sondra Bernstein's restaurant, which celebrates among other things the decadent fig, is a cozy spot where tables in the cheery yellow dining room with wood paneling are a wee bit tight, but all the better to get a sneak preview from your neighbor's plate. Patio Seating is prime country dining when the weather's right. Chef John Toulze prepares dishes such as fig salad with arugula, dried figs, pecans, chèvre, pancetta, and a fig-port vinaigrette; aromatic steamed mussels with Pernod, garlic, leeks, fresh herbs, and croutons; or savory pan-seared striped bass with roasted shallot and chive vinaigrette and mashed potatoes. Cheese lovers should splurge on the cheese menu featuring local productions. If nothing else, forks should stand at attention for the sensuous lavender crème brûlée or delicate chilled Meyer lemon soufflé with whipped cream and fruit compote. Just as exciting as the food is the trend-setting wine list, which goes against the Sonoma grain with Rhône-style California wines. *$$; AE, MC, V; checks OK; lunch, dinner every day; full bar; reservations recommended; www.thegirlandthefig.com; on Sonoma Plaza, on the ground floor of the Sonoma Hotel.* &

Juanita Juanita / ★★☆

19114 ARNOLD DR, SONOMA; 707/935-3981 For the occasions when heaven is a roadside shack, cold beer, and a heaping plate of nachos, Juanita Juanita is your savior. Locals are loyal to this spray-painted-mural box of a restaurant, and no wonder. It's not every day that you can play Trivial Pursuit or admire customers' artwork while digging into a plastic bucket of thick, crisp tortilla chips and zesty salsa and waiting for your grilled chicken quesadilla, beef enchilada, or fish taco. The intentionally ramshackle decor with clustered tables, Formica counter seating, and convivial dinnertime crowd is half the fun; the other half is the dependable fare, which is fresh, hearty, and served with a sarcastic wink. Hint: Come at off-hours to avoid the wait. *$; no credit cards; local checks only; lunch, dinner every day; beer and*

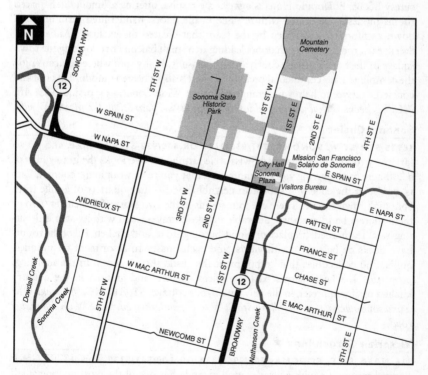

wine; no reservations; from Sonoma Plaza head W on W Napa St, turn right on Arnold Dr, and continue until you see the shack on the left side of the street.

La Poste / ★★☆

599 BROADWAY, SONOMA; 707-939-3663 This tiny restaurant a few blocks off Sonoma Plaza evokes the inviting and informal bistros of Paris with its cramped seating, pressed-tin ceiling, sidewalk tables, and rich homey cuisine of chef Rob Larman. Dining here is a friendly affair where you're bound to get to know your neighbors since they're practically sitting at your table. But when the room's cast in a warm glow and chef Larman starts sending out welcome *gougères* (tasty little cheese puffs), generous helpings of fried pheasant with potato gratin, decadent braised veal cheeks with cream, Calvados, English peas, and chanterelles, and good old profiteroles, all you can say is *"Magnifique!"* *$$$; AE, MC, V; no checks; lunch, dinner Wed–Sun; beer and wine; reservations recommended; www.bistrotlaposte.com; at Patten St.*

LODGINGS

El Dorado Hotel / ★★

405 1ST ST W, SONOMA; 707/996-3030 OR 800/289-3031 If you've had it with cutesy B&Bs, El Dorado Hotel is a welcome respite, offering 27 moderately priced rooms modestly decorated with terra-cotta tile floors, handcrafted furniture, and down comforters. Renovated by the team that created the exclusive Auberge du Soleil, each room has French doors leading to a small balcony overlooking the town square or the hotel's private courtyard—a pleasant, sunny spot where you can enjoy the complimentary continental breakfast. There's also a heated outdoor lap pool and concierge service to help you arrange your next Wine Country excursion. *$$$; AE, MC, V; checks OK; www.hoteleldorado.com; at W Spain St, on the plaza's W side.*

Sonoma Chalet / ★★

18935 5TH ST W, SONOMA; 707/938-3129 OR 800/938-3129 So close, and yet so far: every room in this secluded Swiss-style farmhouse overlooks the grassy hills of a 200-acre ranch, giving you the impression that you're way out in the country. Fact is, you're at the edge of a suburban neighborhood—three-quarters of a mile from Sonoma's town square. There are four rooms in the two-story 1940s chalet (two of them share a bath) and three adorable private cottages, each with its own little sitting area, featherbed, fireplace or wood-burning stove, and kitchen. All of the rooms have decks or balconies with views, and each boasts an assortment of antiques, quilts, and collectibles that complement the rustic surroundings. In the morning, proprietor Joe Leese serves pastries, juices, yogurt, and granola in the country kitchen or, if you prefer, in the privacy of your cottage. *$$; AE, MC, V; checks OK; www.sonomachalet.com; follow 5th St W to the end, then continue W on the gravel road.*

Victorian Garden Inn / ★

316 NAPA ST E, SONOMA; 707/996-5339 OR 800/543-5339 This 1870s Greek Revival farmhouse with a wraparound veranda has one of the most inviting small gardens you'll ever see: lush bowers of roses, azaleas, and camellias encircle wonderful little tables and chairs, while flowering fruit trees bend low over Victorian benches. The inn's four guest rooms, decorated in white wicker and florals, are pretty, if a bit cloying. The most requested room is the Woodcutter's Cottage, favored for its comfy sofa and armchairs facing the fireplace and its private entrance and bath. In the evening, owner Donna Lewis pours glasses of wine and sherry for guests to enjoy in front of the parlor fireplace. Breakfast, served at the dining table, in the garden, or in your room, consists of granola, croissants, gourmet coffee, and fruit picked right from the garden. A big bonus is the large swimming pool in the backyard—a blessing during Sonoma's typically hot summer days—and a therapeutic hot tub located in the gardens. *$$$; AE, DC, MC, V; checks OK; info@victoriangardeninn.com; www.victoriangardeninn.com; between 3rd St E and 4th St E, 2 blocks from the plaza.*

Boyes Hot Springs

LODGINGS

Fairmont Sonoma Mission Inn & Spa / ★★★

18140 SONOMA HWY, BOYES HOT SPRINGS; 707/938-9000 OR 800/862-4945
With its ethereal, serene grounds and elegant pink stucco buildings, the Sonoma Mission Inn feels a bit like a convent—except that novitiates wear white terry-cloth bathrobes or colorful running suits instead of nuns' habits. And that indulgence, in body and spirit, is the order of the day. The recently renovated European-style spa offers everything from aerobics classes and Swedish massages to aromatherapy facials, seaweed wraps, and tarot card readings in perfectly groomed surroundings (the likes of Barbra Streisand, Tom Cruise, and Harrison Ford come here to get pampered). You'll also find exercise rooms, saunas, Jacuzzis, a salon, yoga and meditation classes, and two swimming pools, one of which is filled with artesian mineral water. While the luxurious spa is the main draw, the inn also recently reacquired its historic golf course, which had been sold during the Depression. Thirty new suites were added in 2000; they offer every amenity, including Mission-style decor and views of the gardens and fountain. Bathed in shades of light peach and pink, each of the more than 230 rooms features plantation-style shutters, ceiling fans, and down comforters. Some units have wood-burning fireplaces and luxe granite or marble bathrooms big enough for an impromptu tango. Also pleasing are the rooms overlooking the inn's swimming pool (a favorite, room 232, is in a turret), which are in the historic building. The inn's two restaurants, Sante and the Big 3 Diner, are both Californian. Sante is one of the most expensive restaurants in Sonoma; the less-expensive Big 3 Diner offers California-Mediterranean fare such as light pastas, pizzas, and grilled items, as well as hearty breakfasts. *$$$$; AE, DC, DIS, MC, V; checks OK; smi.reservations@fairmont.com; www.sonomamission.com; just west of Hwy 12, at Boyes Blvd.*

Glen Ellen

There are more places and things named after Jack London in Sonoma County than there are women named María in Mexico. This cult reaches its apex in Glen Ellen, where the writer built his aptly named Beauty Ranch, an 800-acre spread now known as **JACK LONDON STATE HISTORIC PARK** (2400 London Ranch Rd, off Hwy 12; 707/938-5216; www.jacklondonpark.com). London's vineyards, piggery, and other ranch buildings are here, as well as a house-turned-museum containing his art collection and mementos (including a series of rejection letters London received from several publishers, who must have fallen over backward in their cushy chairs the day they learned London had become the highest-paid author of his time). Ten miles of trails lead through oaks, madrones, and redwoods, including a grove of oaks shading London's grave. If you'd rather ride than walk through London's land, let the friendly folks at the **TRIPLE CREEK HORSE OUTFIT** (located in Jack London State Historic Park; 707/933-1600; www.triplecreekhorseoutfit.com) saddle up a horse for you. Call for the lowdown on their **GUIDED HORSEBACK TRIPS** (reservations are required).

The tiny town of Glen Ellen was also the longtime home of the late celebrated food writer **M. F. K. FISHER**. It offers a couple of good restaurants, plus wine-tasting and antiquing excursions. The **WINE COUNTRY FILM FESTIVAL** (707/935-FILM or www.winecountryfilmfest.com), a three-week summer splurge of screenings and parties throughout Napa and Sonoma, is headquartered here.

RESTAURANTS

Glen Ellen Inn Restaurant / ★★★

13670 ARNOLD DR, GLEN ELLEN; 707/996-6409 If you're staying in Glen Ellen, it's nice to know you don't have to go far to find a good meal. In fact, Christian and Karen Bertrand's tiny, romantic restaurant is worth a drive from farther afield. The menu changes frequently but always features local cuisine at its freshest and in beautiful preparations. Dinner might include spinach, mission figs, walnuts, and chèvre in a chilled crepe, with port dressing; expertly seared ahi tuna in a wasabi cream sauce and port reduction; or grilled pork tenderloin with pineapple-mango chutney and smoked Sonoma Jack cheese polenta. The award-winning wine list features an excellent selection of varietals from near and far. With just 15 white-clothed tables in the dining room and 15 more outside in the herb garden, service is personal and attentive, almost as if you've been invited into the Bertrands' home. $$; AE, MC, V; local checks only; lunch Fri–Tues, dinner every day; beer and wine; reservations recommended; www.glenelleninn.com; at O'Donnell Ln.

LODGINGS

Beltane Ranch / ★★★

11775 SONOMA HWY, GLEN ELLEN; 707/996-6501 Surrounded by vineyards at the foot of the Mayacamas Mountains, this century-old buttercup yellow and white clapboard farmhouse was a bunkhouse long before it was a bed-and-breakfast—but certainly the cowhands of old never had it so good. Each of the inn's five rooms is uniquely decorated; all have sitting areas, private baths, separate entrances, and a family antique or two. Ask for one of the upstairs rooms that opens onto the huge wraparound doubledecker porch equipped with hammocks and a swing. Or if a little extra privacy is on your itinerary, go for the two-room Garden Cottage, which lies a few yards from the main house and has French doors that open onto a private garden and patio. All guests are welcome to the full country breakfast served in the garden or on the porch, which overlooks Sonoma's hillsides. Blissfully calm and beautiful, the whole place makes you feel as though you should be wearing a wide-brimmed hat and sipping a mint julep. Should you tire of lolling Southern belle–style, knock a few balls around the tennis court near the house, pitch horseshoes in the garden, or hike the trails through the estate's 1,600 acres of vineyards and hills. *$$; no credit cards; checks OK; www.beltane ranch.com; on Hwy 12, 2.2 miles past the Glen Ellen turnoff.*

Gaige House Inn / ★★★★

13540 ARNOLD DR, GLEN ELLEN; 707/935-0237 OR 800/935-0237
From the outside, the Gaige House looks like yet another spiffed-up Victorian mansion, inevitably filled with the ubiquitous dusty antiques and family heirlooms. Inside, however, the Victorian theme comes to a screeching halt. All 15 rooms are spectacular, and each is individually decorated in an Indonesian plantation style with an eclectic mix of modern art. Owners Ken Burnet Jr. and Greg Nemrow have a discerning sense of style that's evident from one secluded room with a private Japanese garden and waterfall to the Gaige Suite, which features a king-size four-poster canopy bed and an unbelievably large and luxe bathroom with a whirlpool tub that could easily fit a party of six (and probably has), as well as a huge wraparound balcony. The three Garden Rooms, slightly smaller and less expensive, open onto a shaded deck and are within steps of a beautiful brick-lined 40-foot swimming pool surrounded by a large, perfectly manicured lawn. Included in the room rate—which is surprisingly affordable considering the caliber of the accommodations—is a two-course gourmet breakfast served at individual tables in the dining room and superb evening appetizers and wine. *$$$; AE, DIS, MC, V; checks OK; gaige@sprynet.com; www.gaige.com; from Hwy 12, take the Glen Ellen exit.*

Kenwood

LODGINGS

Kenwood Inn & Spa / ★★★

10400 SONOMA HWY, KENWOOD; 707/833-1293 OR 800/353-6966 This posh inn resembles a centuries-old Italian pensione with freestanding accommodations around a garden court and pool. The 28 guest rooms are beautifully decorated, each with a fluffy featherbed, a fireplace, and a sitting area. Room 3, bathed in shades of gold, has a pleasant private balcony, and room 6 is a suite sporting a sitting room with a stereo, Jacuzzi, and balcony overlooking the vineyards and the swimming pool. The additional 18 rooms and two-bedroom villa added in

2003 also come with all the exclusivity this property is known for. The six-room, full-service spa pampers guests with Caudalie Vinotherapie treatments, which employ vine and grape-seed extracts that are known to combat the free radicals that contribute to aging. Breakfast, served in the new dining room, is an impressive spread that may include fresh fruit, polenta with poached eggs, and buttery house-made croissants. $$$$; AE, MC, V; checks OK; www.kenwoodinn.com; on Hwy 12, 3 miles past Glen Ellen.

Santa Rosa

Santa Rosa is the closest thing Sonoma County has to a big city, but it's more like a countrified suburb. Oddly enough, it's got more than its share of offbeat museums. Botanists, gardeners, and other plant lovers will want to make a beeline for the popular gardens and greenhouse at the **LUTHER BURBANK HOME & GARDENS** (corner of Santa Rosa and Sonoma Ave; 707/524-5445; www.lutherburbank.org). Burbank was a world-renowned horticulturist who created 800 new strains of plants, fruits, and vegetables at the turn of the century. Pop culture fans will get a kick out of **SNOOPY'S GALLERY & GIFT SHOP** (1665 W Steel Ln; 707/546-3385; www.snoopygift.com), a "Peanuts" cartoon museum with the world's largest collection of Snoopy memorabilia, thanks to donations by the beagle's creator, the late Charles Schulz, who lived in Santa Rosa.

For music, magicians, and a plethora of fresh-from-the-farm food, head over to the wildly successful **SANTA ROSA DOWNTOWN MARKET** on downtown Santa Rosa's Fourth Street from B Street to D Street, which is closed to traffic every Thursday night from 5pm to 8:30pm for this festive event that draws folks from far and near, from Memorial Day through Labor Day (707/542-2123; www.srdowntownmarket.com). Another local crowd-pleaser is the annual **SONOMA COUNTY HARVEST FAIR** (1350 Bennett Valley Rd; 707/545-4200; www.harvestfair.org), a wine-tasting, food-gobbling orgy held at the fairgrounds from late July to early August.

RESTAURANTS

Hana Japanese Restaurant / ★★★

101 GOLF COURSE DR, ROHNERT PARK; 707/586-0270 Unbeknownst to most visitors, this Japanese restaurant, located in a strip mall in Santa Rosa suburb Rohnert Park, is *the* place for sushi in Northern California. What it lacks in its almost motel-style decor it more than makes up for with mind-blowing raw and cooked fish dishes and astoundingly beautiful presentations created by chef-owner Ken Tominaga. Try tuna, salmon, albacore, and yellowtail; choose rolls that range from California or spicy salmon to tuna-belly-and-green-onion or soft-shell crab. But it's Ken's specials that really shine—foie gras with *unagi* (eel), sea-urchin egg custard, ahi poke, octopus salad, and everything else that Ken designs. For the sushi experience of your life, ask him to lead the way. But be sure to tell him up front how much you want to spend. Folks who aren't raw fish fans can choose from the huge lunch and dinner menu including light and crisp tempura, juicy grilled steak (perhaps with shiitake

248

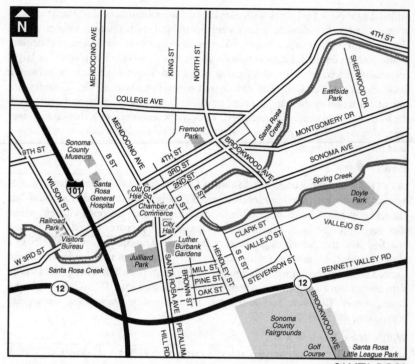

SANTA ROSA

mushrooms and soy-cabernet sauce), grilled Atlantic salmon with creamy potatoes and saffron cream sauce, or chicken teriyaki. Wash it down with one of the great premium sakes or a Japanese beer. At lunch, the bento boxes, donburi, and udon meals (complete with miso soup, Japanese pickles, salad, and rice) are great deals. *$$$; AE, DC, DIS, MC, V; no checks; lunch Tues–Sat, dinner Tues–Sun; beer and wine; reservations recommended; call for directions.* &

John Ash & Co. / ★★★

4330 BARNES RD (IN THE VINTNERS INN), SANTA ROSA 707/527-7687 This casually elegant restaurant, founded by Wine Country cuisine guru John Ash, has topped the list of Santa Rosa's best restaurants for many years. It's pricey, but the service is expert, the food is fabulous, and the serene dining room with cream-colored walls, tall French windows, and a crackling fire will entice you to settle in for a good long time. The menu, under the direction of executive chef Jeffrey Madura, is a classic California hybrid of French, Italian, Asian, and Southwestern cuisines. A meal might begin with such glorious dishes as rich house-made porcini ravioli with porcini cream and Italian parsley, followed by moist grilled local king salmon with sun-dried tomato vinaigrette, white bean, and arugula sauté; juicy roasted pork chop with cinnamon couscous, gingered applesauce, and cider cream sauce; or an expertly grilled Angus New York steak with blue cheese butter, basil béarnaise, tomatoes, and pommes frites. For dessert, pastry chef Scott Noll makes diners swoon with a Vanilla-Mint Melt Down, a warm, flourless chocolate cake with a gooey chocolate truffle center, vibrant Tahitian vanilla syrup, mint oil, and crème anglaise. The large, reasonably priced wine list, showcasing Napa and Sonoma wines, also includes a good selection of ports, sherries, and dessert wines. For a taste of Wine Country cuisine at a fraction of the regular price, sit at the bar or on the patio and order from the Vineyard Cafe menu. *$$$; AE, MC, V; local checks only; lunch Tues–Sun, dinner every day, brunch Sun; full bar; reservations recommended; www.johnashco.com; next to Vintners Inn, off River Rd, at Hwy 101.*

Syrah / ★★★

205 5TH ST, SANTA ROSA; 707/568-4002 Owners Josh and Regina Silvers preside over a local favorite, serving French-inspired American cuisine within a casual-chic historic building. Choose your table on the patio or near the open kitchen, where chef Josh (previously of Mustards in Napa Valley) prepares baked brioche and poached foie gras, which might be accompanied by marinated dried cherries in a terra-cotta pot, or sautéed crab cakes tenderly placed on an arugula salad with roasted beets and horseradish vinaigrette. Other starters include a moist duck confit with beluga lentil salad and succulent pork tenderloin. *$$$; DIS, MC, V; no checks; lunch, dinner Tues–Sat; beer and wine; reservations recommended; www.syrah bistro.com; at Davis St.*

Willi's Wine Bar / ★★★

4104 OLD REDWOOD HWY, SANTA ROSA; 707/526-3096 Locals slink into this dark, low-slung, and laid-back spot for wine and a whimsical global dining adventure. Chef Mark Stark (from Gordon Biersch and the California Cafe) and wife Terri (from Restaurant LuLu's catering division in San Francisco) oversee the exhaustive menu of internationally influenced small plates. Each dish bucks the expected—from artfully presented brandade spring rolls with herb salad and romesco to wonton-paper-wrapped scallop dumplings seasoned with lemongrass butter and pancetta. Pairing's not a problem thanks to 40 wines by the 2-ounce pour, glass, or half bottle. *$$; AE, MC, V; no checks; lunch, dinner Wed–Sat and Mon; beer and wine; reservations recommended; near River Rd.*

Zazu / ★★★

3535 GUERNEVILLE RD, SANTA ROSA; 707/523-4814 Hiding out in a funky roadhouse a few miles from downtown Santa Rosa, rustic-chic Zazu has railroad-apartment-meets-clapboard-shack ambiance—the perfect match for chef/co-owners Duskie Estes and John Stewart's Americana/Italian/farmers market–influenced comfort food. It's not uncommon to spot winemakers huddling around one of the copper-topped tables and devouring a crisp poppyseed-crusted soft-shell crab with ruby grapefruit, avocado, and poppyseed dressing; a robust star-anise rubbed duck with apricot sambal, crispy rice cake, and bok choy; a juicy, naturally raised flat-iron steak with Point Reyes blue cheese ravioli and roasted garlic; or the legendary slow-roasted balsamic pork shoulder with caramelized onions and mashed potatoes. No one can resist the retro-inspired dessert of homemade nutter-butter cookies with Scharffen Berger chocolate fondue. Wines focus on varietals made within a 50-mile radius and include lots of affordable options. *$$$; MC, V; local checks only; dinner Wed–Sun; beer and wine; reservations recommended; at Willowside Rd.*

LODGINGS
Vintners Inn / ★★

4350 BARNES RD, SANTA ROSA; 707/575-7350 OR 800/421-2584 The Vintners Inn combines the charm of a country inn with the conveniences of a modern hotel. Its four Provençal-style buildings are clustered around a central courtyard set amid vineyards. The inn's 44 rooms were renovated in 2002 to reflect a European sensibility with king-size beds, plush carpets, armoires and desks, and separate sitting areas; many have wood-burning fireplaces, too. The old-world antics don't extend to smoking, which is not allowed. French doors open onto a balcony or patio with a view of the vineyards or the landscaped grounds (ask for a room with a vineyard view facing away from Highway 101). The young, courteous staff is very attentive, providing first-class room service. A complimentary full breakfast is served in the main building's sunny dining room until 10am on weekdays and 10:30am on weekends. Though there's also a fine deck for sunning and a Jacuzzi, the inn's best feature is its adjoining restaurant, John Ash & Co. (see review, above). *$$$$; AE, DC, MC, V; checks OK; www.vintnersinn.com; off River Rd, at Hwy 101.*

Healdsburg

This is one tourist town whose charm seems completely unforced. Boutiques and bakeries surround a pretty, tree-lined plaza where you can sit and read the newspaper while munching on pastries from the marvelous **DOWNTOWN BAKERY & CREAMERY** (308-A Center St; 707/431-2719; www.downtownbakery.net). In the summer, nothing beats paddling down the glorious **RUSSIAN RIVER** past vineyards and secret swimming holes in a canoe rented from W. C. "Bob" Trowbridge Canoe Trips (20 Healdsburg Ave; 707/433-7247 or 800/640-1386; www.trowbridge canoe.com). If you're in need of a respite from your activity-packed day trips, catch a flick at the **RAVEN THEATER** (115 North St, 707/433-5448; www.raven theater.com), the area's best movie house for new releases and art films.

RESTAURANTS
Bistro Ralph / ★★☆

109 PLAZA ST E, HEALDSBURG; 707/433-1380 In a town where restaurants have been afflicted with the revolving door syndrome, simple yet stylish Bistro Ralph continues to thrive. Housed in a slender storefront on the square, Ralph Tingle's intimate bistro serves consistently excellent food, with a focus on local ingredients. Choice starters include grilled portobello mushrooms with white truffle oil and crispy Sichuan pepper calamari. The lamb dishes are always good, particularly the hearty spring lamb stew à la provençal, and the lamb shanks with crème fraîche–horseradish mashed potatoes. The lunch menu sticks to upscale salads and sandwiches, such as the grilled ahi or salmon sandwich and the popular lamb burger on a fresh roll, all three served with a pile of irresistible shoestring fries. The decor has a cozy, slightly industrial feel, with a dozen or so linen-topped tables, white brick walls, and a long concrete counter where you can watch chef Tingle perform culinary magic in the small open kitchen. *$$; MC, V; local checks only; lunch, dinner Mon–Sat; beer, wine, and martinis; reservations recommended; on the plaza.*

Zin / ★★

344 CENTER ST, HEALDSBURG; 707/473-0946 Located just off Healdsburg's main plaza, Zin specializes in updated versions of American classics, and each day features a blue plate special, such as meat loaf or St. Louis–style barbecued ribs. The dishes are particularly well-suited to pairing with zinfandels, and the wine list features a whole page of them—a fitting tribute, considering Sonoma is prime zin country. The hush puppies with red pepper make a great starter—a mountain of them served hot and fluffy and grease-free. Entrees include a succulent sliced duck breast served on a bed of garlic mashed potatoes topped by sautéed spinach. Grilled lamb chops come with asparagus and a giant helping of roasted new potatoes. This is a great place for those with hearty appetites, because portions are huge. Zin's architecture is Postmodern California Bomb Shelter—a concrete bunker trimmed in redwood—which, thankfully, has little to do with the aesthetic of the food. *$$$; AE, MC, V; local checks only; lunch, dinner every day; beer and wine; reservations recommended; 1 block from the plaza.*

LODGINGS

Belle de Jour Inn / ★★★

16276 HEALDSBURG AVE, HEALDSBURG; 707/431-9777 In a region where rampant Victoriana is all the rage, Belle de Jour's four romantic hillside cottages and large carriage house have a refreshingly spare, uncluttered feel. From the bedroom of the cottage called the Terrace Room, you can savor a fine view of the valley from the comfort of a giant Jacuzzi. Also recommended is the Caretaker's Suite with its lace-canopied four-poster bed, private deck with a vine-covered trellis, and blue-tiled whirlpool tub. All of the accommodations have fireplaces, ceiling fans, and refrigerators and are air-conditioned—a big plus around here in the summer. Innkeepers Tom and Brenda Hearn whip up a bountiful country breakfast in their beautiful state-of-the-art kitchen and serve it on the deck of the main house. Also available to guests for an hourly fee is a chauffeured backroads winery tour in the Hearns' 1925 Star touring car—something to consider if wine tasting makes you tipsy. *$$$; AE, MC, V; no checks; belledejourinn.com; 1 mile N of Dry Creek Rd, across from Simi Winery.*

Haydon Street Inn / ★★

321 HAYDON ST, HEALDSBURG; 707/433-5228 OR 800/528-3703 This pretty blue 1912 Queen Anne Victorian inn with a large veranda set behind a white picket fence offers eight cheery guest rooms, all with private baths. But your best bet is to rent one of the two larger rooms in the Victorian Cottage tucked behind the main house. The first floor of the cottage is not for rent, but the upstairs has been turned into two spacious rooms with vaulted ceilings, queen-size beds, high dormer windows, big whirlpool tubs, and loads of charm. In the morning you'll find a full country breakfast featuring such treats as green chile frittatas with basil and cilantro, fresh fruit or baked apples, and plenty of house-made muffins and croissants. *$$$; AE, DIS, MC, V; checks OK; www.haydon.com; at Fitch St.*

Healdsburg Inn on the Plaza / ★★★

110 MATHESON ST, HEALDSBURG; 707/433-6991 OR 800/431-8663 Originally built as a Wells Fargo Express office in 1900, this surprisingly quiet inn on the plaza has high ceilings and a lovely old staircase leading from the ground-floor art gallery to the nine attractive guest rooms upstairs, one downstairs, and one carriage house. The four rooms facing the plaza have beautiful bay windows; particularly engaging is the spacious pale yellow and white Song of the Rose Room, which has a king-size white iron and brass bed, a whirlpool tub, and a fireplace. One of the largest rooms is the Garden Suite, with its Jacuzzi, king-size bed, and private patio bedecked with flowers. All rooms have private baths with showers, TVs with VCRs, and air conditioning; all but one have gas-log fireplaces and five have claw-footed bathtubs. A full breakfast and afternoon wine and snacks are served at tables for two in the glass-enclosed solarium. *$$$; MC, V; no checks; www.healdsburginn.com; on the plaza's S side.*

Hotel Healdsburg / ★★★

317 HEALDSBURG AVE, HEALDSBURG; 707/431-2800 OR 800/889-7188 Healdsburg's latest, greatest, and only full-service luxury hotel offers plush rooms, spa services, and instant access to downtown's adorable old-fashioned square. Upscale perks abound within the 55 sunny Pottery Barn–chic rooms, elegantly ornamented with Tibetan rugs, dark wood furnishings, goose-down duvets, CD players, Frette bathrobes, large glittering bathrooms that beckon with walk-in showers and two-person tubs, and French doors opening to private balconies overlooking the plaza. Though plaza shopping and dining is outside the front door, there's plenty of reason to hang around, specifically a grappa bar, an enormous garden pool, a full-service spa, a fitness room, and famed chef Charlie Palmer's excellent and expensive Dry Creek Kitchen, which serves seasonal cuisine accentuating pure flavors and local ingredients. Continental breakfast, included in the rates, is served in the hotel lobby. *$$$$; AE, DC, MC, V; checks OK; frontoffice@hotelhealdsburg.com; www.hotel healdsburg.com; on the plaza.* &

Geyserville

LODGINGS

Hope-Bosworth House / ★★

21238 GEYSERVILLE AVE, GEYSERVILLE; 707/857-3356 OR 800/825-4233 Across the street from its showier cousin, the Hope-Merrill House, the 1904 Hope-Bosworth House provides a cheery, informal, and less expensive place to stay. This Queen Anne–style Victorian inn has four bedrooms, all of which have full baths,

NAPA VALLEY'S WINE HISTORY

Napa's famous wine region began with a bang. **MOUNT ST. HELENA** was once an active volcano, and its eruptions left the valley with the loamy soil in which grapes thrive. The first person to take advantage of this development was also Napa's first American settler; George Yount planted vineyards in 1838 and shared the fruits of his labor with other thirsty pioneers.

By the latter half of the 19th century, European immigrants began making their mark, establishing a wine industry in the valley. Many of their names can still be seen on today's vintages: Charles Krug (**CHARLES KRUG WINERY**); Jacob Schram (**SCHRAMSBERG VINEYARDS**); Gustave Niebaum (**NIEBAUM-COPPOLA ESTATE WINERY**); and Frederick and Jacob Beringer (**BERINGER VINEYARDS**).

By the 1890s, the industry was thriving, with more than 140 wineries in operation, when disaster struck in the form of phylloxera, a louse that destroys the grapes' roots. (A hundred years later, phylloxera would strike again—forcing grape growers to replant the majority of their vineyards.) Then, in 1919, a plague more deadly than any parasite finished off Napa's wine industry: Prohibition. Only a handful of wineries survived—by making blessed sacramental altar wine.

By 1960, only 25 wineries remained in Napa Valley. Instead of grapes, the sleepy farming community raised cattle, walnuts, and prunes. But the next three decades would witness an amazing resurrection of Napa's wine industry.

including one with a Jacuzzi tub. The downstairs Sun Porch Room has the dry, woody fragrance of a summer cottage, and it reverberates each morning with bird-song from the backyard. Everyone's favorite, however, is the sunny and spacious Wicker Room with its old-fashioned white and pink flowered wallpaper. Guests are treated to the same elaborate breakfast as their neighbors, and they have access to the pool and other facilities at the Hope-Merrill House. $$$; AE, DIS, MC, V; checks OK; from Hwy 101, take the Geyserville exit.

Hope-Merrill House / ★★★

21253 GEYSERVILLE AVE, GEYSERVILLE; 707/857-3356 OR 800/825-4233 Since nearly every mediocre shack built in the late 19th century gets dubbed "Victorian," it's easy to forget the dizzying architectural and design heights reached during that period. This beautifully restored 1870 Eastlake Stick will remind you: the two-story brown and cream Hope-Merrill House has expansive bay windows and a back veranda furnished with comfortable cane chairs. The landscaping is formal and strictly symmetrical, with box hedges and weeping mulberries. The inn offers eight individually decorated guest rooms with private baths and queen-size beds. The fairest is the Peacock Room: images of gold, rose, and gray-blue peacocks strut around a ceiling border, a gas fireplace dominates one wall, and French doors open

Through a dedication to quality, a handful of winemakers gradually began to elevate the stature of Napa's wines, attracting international attention. Still, California vintages were always considered second-rate to France until a landmark event occurred in 1976, known as the Paris Tasting. Organized to coincide with the American Bicentennial, the blind tasting was held in Paris, with French judges. And to every Napa Valleyite's joy and amazement, Napa Valley wines won—in both the white and red categories. The French judges cried foul and demanded to see their tasting notes again. But when they dried their eyes, the facts remained: a **CHÂTEAU MONTELANA** chardonnay and a **STAG'S LEAP** cabernet sauvignon had beaten all the grand crus from France. *Time* magazine immediately dispatched a team of journalists to Napa to cover the story, and winemakers and oenophiles alike headed to the valley to find out what all the fuss was about.

Today the region boasts more than 280 wineries, and no one is surprised anymore when Napa vintages garner international awards. A fitting monument to local accomplishments was unveiled in 2001 when the $70 million **COPIA: THE AMERICAN CENTER FOR WINE, FOOD & THE ARTS** opened in downtown Napa. This museum and cultural institute celebrates America's unique contributions to food and wine; its board of directors features some of the key players who helped shape the nation's appetites: Robert Mondavi, Julia Child, and Alice Waters. At the center, visitors can dine in **JULIA'S KITCHEN,** learn how to taste wine, or examine a demonstration vineyard—because, after all, that's where the valley's fame and fortune began.

into a bathroom with an immense marble-topped two-person whirlpool tub. For the best views, ask for the Vineyard View Room or the Bradbury Room, which have fireplaces, two-person showers, and views of the property's swimming pool (closed in winter) and the pretty gardens. A hearty breakfast is included in the rates. *$$$; AE, DIS, MC, V; checks OK; from Hwy 101, take the Geyserville exit.*

Cloverdale

LODGINGS

Vintage Towers Bed and Breakfast Inn / ★★

302 N MAIN ST, CLOVERDALE; 707/894-4535 OR 888/886-9377 Listed on the National Register of Historic Places, this beautiful mauve mansion located on a quiet residential street has seven air-conditioned guest rooms. The three corner suites have tower sitting rooms (one round, one square, and one octagonal), sleeping quarters, and private baths. Particularly unique is the Vintage Tower Suite, which has its own private porch complete with a telescope for stargazing and a spiral staircase that descends to the yard. Downstairs you'll find a large dining room with a fireplace, a parlor, and a library. In the morning, friendly owner Polly Grant serves a full gourmet breakfast in the dining room; the veranda is the spot to relax and snack on ever-available cookies, sodas, and other treats. *$$$; AE, DIS, MC, V; checks OK; www.vintagetowers.com; at 3rd St, off Cloverdale Blvd.*

Anderson Valley and Mendocino County Wine Region

For a glimpse of what Napa Valley looked like 30 years ago, visit the quiet, bucolic Anderson Valley. Once noted only for sheep, apples, and timber, the Anderson Valley has become the premier producer of cool-climate California wines such as chardonnay, gewürztraminer, and Riesling. The enological future of this valley, whose climate is almost identical to that of the Champagne region of France, may also reside in the production of sparkling wine, now that some of France's best champagne makers have successfully set up shop here.

Anderson Wineries

Most of the Anderson Valley's wineries line the narrow stretch of Highway 128 that winds through this gorgeous, verdant 25-mile-long valley before it reaches the Pacific Coast. Here are some of Anderson's premier wineries:

GREENWOOD RIDGE (5501 Hwy 128, Philo; 707/895-2002; www.green woodridge.com). Known for its white Riesling (and cabernet and zinfandel produced in another region), Greenwood is the site of the annual California Wine Tasting Championships (for novices and pros) held on the last weekend of July; it also has a picnic area by a pond and a tasting room.

HANDLEY CELLARS (3151 Hwy 128, Philo; 707/895-3876; www.handley cellars.com). Popular for its chardonnay, which is free to taste, Handley has a tasting room full of exotic artifacts from around the world, and a picnic area in a garden courtyard.

HUSCH VINEYARDS (4400 Hwy 128, Philo; 707/895-3216; www.huschvine yards.com). The oldest winery in the Anderson Valley (founded in 1971), Husch produces chardonnay, pinot noir, and gewürztraminer, along with wines from its Ukiah vineyards. It offers free samples in a small, rustic redwood tasting room and also has picnic tables.

NAVARRO VINEYARDS (5601 Hwy 128, Philo; 707/895-3686; www.navarro wine.com). This small, family-owned winery pioneered the region's trademark wine (dry, fruity, spicy Alsatian-style gewürztraminer) and produces outstanding chardonnay, pinot noir, white riesling, and sexy straight-up grape juice. Navarro wines are sold only by mail order, at the winery, and in restaurants; the winery has a surprisingly large—and free—tasting menu.

PACIFIC ECHO CELLARS (8501 Hwy 128, Philo; 707/895-2957; www.clic quot.com). In 1991 Scharffenberger Cellars was sold to Moët Hennessey, which has since begun bottling its traditional French sparkling wine under the generic-sounding label "Pacific Echo Cellars." The company still produces excellent brut, blanc de blancs, brut rosé, and crémant. The tasting room is in a remodeled farmhouse. Tours are available.

ROEDERER ESTATE (4501 Hwy 128, Philo; 707/895-2288; www.roeder erestate.net). This winery was established by one of France's most prestigious champagne producers. Inside the quietly elegant hillside facility, visitors can take tours by appointment to learn about the sparkling wine–making process. Inside the tasting room you can sample high-quality sparkling wines ($3 tastings).

Boonville

This speck of a town in the heart of the Anderson Valley is best known for a regional dialect called Boontling, developed by townsfolk at the beginning of the century. No one really speaks Boontling anymore, though a few old-timers remember the lingo. As in most private languages, a large percentage of the words refer to sex, a fact glossed over in most touristy brochures on the topic. Most people don't know what the Boontling word for beer is, but the folks at the **ANDERSON VALLEY BREWING COMPANY** (17700 Boonville Rd; 707/895-BEER; www.avbc.com) definitely do and will tell you during brewery tours daily at 1:30pm and 4pm. If you simply want to sample their suds, you can mosey up to the **BUCKHORN SALOON** (14081 Hwy 128; 707/895-3369), a fine little microbrewery across from the Boonville Hotel. While you're in town, grab a copy of the *Anderson Valley Advertiser,* a rollicking, crusading (some say muckraking) small-town paper with avid readers from as far away as San Francisco and the Oregon border. **BOONT BERRY FARM** (13981 Hwy 128; 707/895-3576), an organic-produce market and deli in a small, weathered-wood building, turns out terrific treats.

LODGINGS

The Boonville Hotel and Restaurant / ★★★

14050 HWY 128, BOONVILLE; 707/895-2210 After a roller-coaster history of highs and lows, the Boonville Hotel languished for a few years until current owner John Schmitt brought it back to life as a small restaurant and inn. The decor of the Old West–style hotel is pleasantly austere, but feels more modern Shaker these days. Half of the rooms have private balconies, although two of them overlook the busy highway. Two newer suites and two cottages offer spacious separate sitting areas, making them well suited to those with kids in tow. (The staff hasn't seemed to figure out that the bare hardwood floors of the old hotel are not suited to the clomping of small children, a fact that can make sleeping near-impossible for the other guests.) The smaller rooms at the back of the hotel are quieter and less expensive. Medium-size room 3, with its unique iron bed, is a good compromise between affordability, spaciousness, and peacefulness. Guests are treated to breakfast beverages in the sunny dining room. A deck overlooks the beautiful 2-acre vegetable and herb garden behind the hotel. The restaurant, a gathering spot for local wine makers, is still one of the best north of the Napa Valley. Chef Schmitt (who for years cooked with his mother when she owned the French Laundry restaurant in Yountville) offers a fresh mix of California, Southwestern, and backwoods regional cuisine, such as sliced pork tenderloin with cumin, cilantro, and oranges, and chicken breast with roasted tomato–mint salsa. From May through October, the hotel parking lot becomes the site of the festive Boonville Farmers Market, held every Saturday from 9:45am to noon; here you can purchase wonderful produce, handmade soaps, wool, and even the occasional billy goat. Reservations are recommended for the restaurant, especially in summer. *$$$; MC, V; checks OK; usually closed Jan; www.boonevillehotel.com; at Lambert Ln, in the center of town.*

Philo

There's not much to see in this hamlet, but about 2 miles west you'll find **GOWAN'S OAK TREE** (6350 Hwy 128; 707/895-3353), a great family-run roadside fruit-and-vegetable stand with a few picnic tables in back and a swing for road-weary tots.

LODGINGS

Philo Pottery Inn / ★★

8550 HWY 128, PHILO; 707/895-3069 This 1886 redwood farmhouse and former Wells Fargo stagecoach stop is pure and authentic country—no frilly ruffles, no overdressed dolls, just a lavender-filled English garden in the front yard and bright handmade quilts and turn-of-the-century antiques in each of the five guest rooms. You may linger in the library downstairs or snooze in the bent-willow loungers on the rustic front porch. Evaline's and Donna's Rooms are the lightest and most spacious, but the favored unit is the cozy one-room cottage with a detached private bath, a woodburning stove, and a back porch. Owners Monika Fuchs and Beverley Bennett will direct you to all the best hiking and biking trails (ask about the great 12-mile mountain bike route) and will happily arrange private tastings at the valley's many small private wineries. They also serve a full organic breakfast, featuring many homemade treats, in the dining room and provide chocolates and port free for the taking. *$$; MC, V; checks OK; info@philopotteryinn.com; www.philopotteryinn.com; in town.*

Hopland

This small town's name originated from hops, an herb used to flavor beer. Hop vines once covered the region from the 1860s until mildew wiped out the crop in the 1940s. The only legacy left of that era today is the hops growing in the beer garden of Mendocino Brewing Company, a location that's also home to several award-winning microbrews. Today, Hopland's rich alluvial soil is dedicated to the production of wine grapes and Bartlett pears.

LODGINGS

The Hopland Inn / ★

13401 HWY 101, HOPLAND; 707/744-1890 OR 800/266-1891 Built as a stage stop in 1890, this haughty cream-colored combination of Gothic spires and gabled windows still looks like a luxurious frontier saloon-hotel, thanks to an $800,000 restoration in 1990. The lobby is dominated by a long, mirrored, polished wood bar; and the gorgeous dark wood–paneled library is filled with interesting old books, velvet settees, shiny brass reading lamps, and a fireplace. A wide, curving wood stairway leads from the lobby to 21 charmingly decorated guest rooms on the second and third stories—all with private baths. The quietest rooms with the best views are on the south side of the hotel overlooking the backyard patio with a fountain, wrought-iron lampposts, and a giant oak tree. A continental breakfast is included in the rate. The hotel's restaurant, The Bar & Bistro at the Hopland Inn, serves acceptable but uninspired California cuisine. *$$$; AE, MC, V; checks OK; info@hopland inn.com; www.hoplandinn.com; downtown.*

Ukiah

Located in the upper reaches of the California Wine Country, Ukiah is still what Napa, Sonoma, and Healdsburg used to be—a sleepy little agricultural town surrounded by vineyards and apple and pear orchards. Peopled by an odd mix of farmers, loggers, and back-to-the-landers, Ukiah is a down-to-earth little burg with few traces of Wine Country gentrification. That doesn't mean there isn't any wine, however. **JEPSON VINEYARDS** (10400 Hwy 101; 707/468-8936; www.jepson wine.com) produces a wide variety of wines, including chardonnay, sauvignon blanc, sparkling wine, and brandy, which is distilled in a copper alembic. Mendocino County's oldest winery, founded in 1932, is **PARDUCCI WINE ESTATES** (501 Parducci Rd; 707/462-WINE or 888/362-9463; www.parducci.com), an enterprise that produces a variety of reds and whites. And if you continue up the road a bit to the Redwood Valley, you'll find **FREY VINEYARDS** (14000 Tomki Rd, off Hwy 101, Redwood Valley; 707/485-5177 or 800/760-3739; www.freywine.com), one of the few wineries in the state that doesn't add sulfites to its wines and uses certified organically grown grapes. Sample the Frey family's petite syrah, cabernet, sauvignon blanc, and more.

Soak away the aches and pains of your long drive (Ukiah is a long drive from almost anywhere) at the clothing-optional **ORR HOT SPRINGS** (13201 Orr Springs Rd; 707/462-6277), or in North America's only warm and naturally carbonated mineral baths at **VICHY SPRINGS RESORT** (see review, below). Hikers will want to stretch their legs at **MONTGOMERY WOODS STATE RESERVE** (on Orr Springs Rd, off Hwy 101, 15 miles NW of Ukiah; www.parks.ca.gov); it features 1,142 acres of coastal redwoods with a self-guided nature trail along Montgomery Creek. In town, the main attraction is the **GRACE HUDSON MUSEUM AND SUN HOUSE** (431 S Main St; 707/467-2836; www.gracehudsonmuseum.org), housing Hudson's paintings of Pomo Indians and a collection of beautiful Pomo baskets.

RESTAURANTS

Schat's Courthouse Bakery and Cafe / ★

113 W PERKINS ST, UKIAH; 707/462-1670 Schat's Courthouse Bakery has been open in Ukiah since 1990, but its history dates back to Holland in the early 1800s—which is as far back as the fifth-generation baker brothers Zach and Brian Schat can trace the roots of a very long line of Schat bakers. In 1948, the Schat clan emigrated to California, bringing with them the hallowed family recipe for their signature Sheepherder's Bread, a semisour, dairy- and sugar-free round loaf that's so popular it's been featured in *Sunset* magazine's "Best of the West" column. What really separates Schat's Courthouse Bakery from the rest are the huge, more-than-you-can-possibly-eat lunch items: made-to-order sandwiches, build-your-own baked potatoes, house-made soups, tangy Caesar salad, and huge slices of vegetarian quiche (served with bread and a salad), all for around five bucks. Dinner's also a deal with the likes of grilled salmon or filet mignon—at palatable prices. Located just off Highway 101, this is a great spot to load up on munchies while exploring the local wine country. *$$; MC, V; local checks only; breakfast, lunch, dinner Mon–Sat; beer and wine; reservations recommended; from Hwy 101 take the Perkins St exit W; ½ block W of State St, across from the courthouse.*

LODGINGS

Sanford House Bed and Breakfast / ★★

306 PINE ST S, UKIAH; 707/462-1653 There's something indisputably small-town about this tall, yellow Victorian inn on a tree-lined street just west of Ukiah's Mayberry-like downtown. Peaceful, unhurried, and bucolic, Sanford House boasts only one Gothic turret, but it does have a big front porch dotted with white wicker chairs and an old-fashioned baby buggy, plus an English garden complete with a koi pond. Inside, antiques grace every room and everything is freshly painted, but it's far too comfortable and unpretentious to be called a showplace. The five guest rooms are named after turn-of-the-century presidents; the Taft Room, with its dark four-poster bed, floral fabrics, and a sort of spooky Princess Di doll in a wedding dress, is the most elegant, but equally pleasant is the spacious cream-and-green Wilson Room with its floral wallpaper, beautiful armoire, and sunny turret sitting area. Innkeeper Dorsey Manogue serves a breakfast feast every morning in the dining room using fresh, mostly organic ingredients, and in the evening she offers homemade biscotti (dipped in white and dark chocolate) and wine in the parlor. *$$; MC, V; checks OK; www.sanfordhouse.com; from Hwy 101, take the Perkins St exit, head W, and turn left on Pine.*

Vichy Springs Resort / ★

2605 VICHY SPRINGS RD, UKIAH; 707/462-9515 Although the rejuvenating effect of the naturally carbonated mineral pools at Vichy Springs had been known by the Pomo Indians for hundreds of years, it wasn't until the mid-1800s that others caught on to the idea. Since then, this California Historic Landmark has attracted the likes of Ulysses S. Grant, Teddy Roosevelt, Mark Twain, and Jack London to the famed baths that have a mineral content identical to the famed pools in Vichy, France. With such a remarkable distinction and luminous history, one would expect the four-star resort with fancy bathhouses. Ironically, the estate was practically a disaster area for years until proprietors Gilbert and Marjorie Ashoff refurbished the 700-acre property and reopened it in 1989. Even with its face-lift, the resort is far from posh, though five creek-side rooms, all with private baths, and the two-bedroom Jack London Cottage bring the accommodations up a notch. Twelve more small, simply decorated guest rooms—all with private baths and most with queen-size beds—line a long ranch house–style building. If you're visiting with children, consider staying at one of the eight private cottages, each fully equipped with a kitchen, a wood-burning stove, and a shaded porch. Built more than 130 years ago, the eight indoor and outdoor baths remain basically unchanged (bathing suits required). Also on the grounds are a nonchlorinated Olympic-size pool filled with the therapeutic bubbly, a modern whirlpool bath, a small cabin where Swedish massages are administered, and 6 miles of ranch roads available to hikers and mountain bikers. Room rates include an expanded continental breakfast and unlimited use of the pools, which are rarely crowded. The baths are available for day use, too, and the resort has basic services for business travelers. *$$$; AE, DC, DIS, MC, V; checks OK; info@vichysprings.com; www.vichysprings.com; from Hwy 101, take the Vichy Springs Rd exit and head W.*

Redwood Valley

RESTAURANTS

Broiler Steak House / ★★

8400 UVA DR, REDWOOD VALLEY; 707/485-7301 The Broiler is more than a steak house—it's a temple to meat. If you arrive without a reservation, expect to wait awhile in the giant cocktail lounge—a good place to catch up on the latest Western fashions. Eventually you'll be ushered into the inner sanctum, where, if you're a true believer, you'll order a juicy steak grilled (to your exact specifications, of course) over an oak wood pit. All entrees include a mammoth baked potato with butter, sour cream, and chives, plus a garden-fresh dinner salad the size of your head. *$$; AE, DIS, MC, V; no checks; dinner every day; full bar; reservations recommended; from Ukiah, drive 7 miles N on Hwy 101, take the West Rd exit, and turn left.* &

NORTH COAST

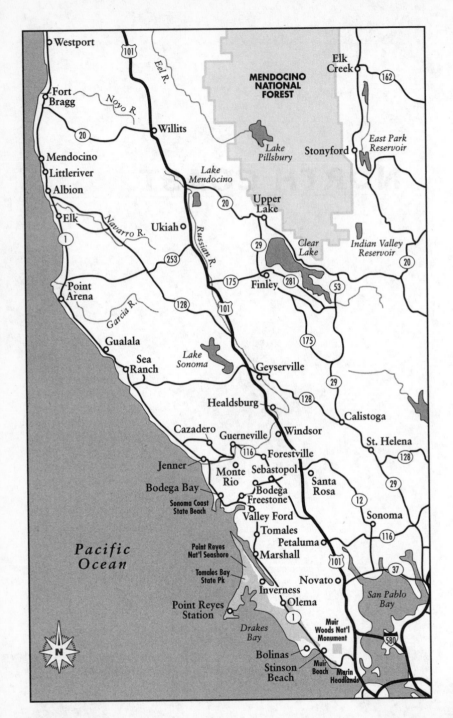

NORTH COAST

From the point where the Golden Gate Bridge touches the sunny shores of Marin County to the ruggedly beautiful timber- and trawler-dotted land and seascapes of Fort Bragg, the North Coast offers some of the most beautiful scenery on California's coastline. You can leave your ties and high heels at home, because informality reigns supreme in these parts. It's all about walks on the beach, farm-fresh cuisine, spectacular vistas, and forgetting your worries for a while.

ACCESS AND INFORMATION

Two major highways provide access to the North Coast: **HIGHWAY 1**, the only route that runs along the coast, and **HIGHWAY 101**, the central artery that connects to Highway 1 via three main scenic roads. To enjoy the full-blown coast experience, take the Stinson Beach/Highway 1 exit from Highway 101 north and head west. Driving is always slow along the coast; on a good day it'll take you five hours to reach Mendocino. Here are four alternative Highway 1/Highway 101 combo routes to consider, depending on time constraints and how far north you want to travel. First: From Highway 101 take the Highway 1/Stinson Beach exit about 7 miles north of the Golden Gate Bridge. This is the quickest route to Muir Woods and Stinson Beach. Second: Exit from Highway 101 at Sir Francis Drake Boulevard, which will take you through West Marin to Olema, where Highway 1 and Sir Francis Drake Boulevard intersect (the quickest route to Point Reyes and Tomales Bay). Third: Traveling north on Highway 101, exit at Petaluma/Highway 116 west. Follow Bodega Avenue to Petaluma Valley Ford Road and continue on to Bodega Highway (the easiest route to Bodega Bay and Jenner). Fourth: Traveling north on Highway 101, exit at Highway 128 *West* (don't take the first "East" exit) just past Cloverdale, which will take you to Highway 1 just below Mendocino. This is by far the fastest route to Mendocino and Fort Bragg.

Once you exit Highway 101—avoid commute hours like the plague—you will be rewarded with scenic drives through idyllic pastoral settings and little traffic aside from the occasional moving house (a.k.a. motor home).

Expect more fog, wind, and cold weather as you travel north along the coast. The **NATIONAL WEATHER SERVICE** (831/656-1725) provides updated weather reports, or log onto www.weather.com. Call **CALTRANS** (800/427-7623) for **HIGHWAY CONDITIONS**. Stock up on provisions for the drive, bring Dramamine if you're prone to carsickness (which you will be on these roads), and bring layers of clothing. Oh yes, and don't forget the binoculars and wide-angle camera lens.

The **MARIN COUNTY CONVENTION & VISITORS BUREAU** (1013 Larkspur Landing Circle, Larkspur, CA 94939; 415/499-5000; www.visitmarin.org) is an excellent Marin County information resource. Contact the **FORT BRAGG–MENDOCINO COAST CHAMBER OF COMMERCE** (332 N Main St, Fort Bragg, CA 95437; 707/961-6300 or 800/726-2780; www.mendocinocoast.com) for information about the Mendocino area.

The Marin Coast

Although Marin County has one of the highest per-capita incomes in the nation, you won't find even a Motel 6 along the entire Marin coast, due partly to very restrictive zoning laws but mostly to the inaccessibly rugged, heavily forested terrain (it may look like a 15-minute drive from San Francisco on the map, but 90 minutes later you'll probably still be negotiating hairpin curves down the side of Mount Tamalpais). The only downside to the Marin coast's underdevelopment is the scarcity of affordable lodgings; expensive B&Bs reign supreme, which is fine if you don't mind spending $200 a night or more (with a two-night minimum, of course) for a bed and a bagel. Otherwise, the Marin coast is just short of Eden, a veritable organic playground for weary commuters and adventure-bound tourists.

Marin Headlands

On a sunny San Francisco day, there's no better place to spend time outdoors than in the Marin Headlands. For more than a century following the Civil War, this vast expanse of grass-covered hills and rocky shore was off-limits to the public, appropriated by the U.S. Army as a strategic base for defending the bay against invaders. Remnants of obsolete and untested defense facilities—dozens of thick concrete bunkers and batteries recessed into the bluffs—now serve as viewing and picnic sites for the millions of tourists who visit each year.

There's a wealth of scheduled activities offered daily within the 15-square-mile **GOLDEN GATE NATIONAL RECREATION AREA (GGNRA)**, including birding clinics, bunker tours, wildflower hunts, and geology hikes. The **MARIN HEADLANDS VISITOR CENTER** (415/331-1540; www.nps.gov/goga/mahe) houses plenty of information, including maps and pertinent facts about all the locations listed below. The center, located within the Headlands, is open daily from 9:30am to 4:30pm. To get here, take the Alexander Avenue exit (second exit after crossing the Golden Gate Bridge) off Highway 101 and follow the signs.

The **MARINE MAMMAL CENTER** (415/289-SEAL; www.tmmc.org), a popular Marin Headlands attraction, is a volunteer-run hospital for injured and abandoned mammals of the sea. Signs list each animal's adopted name, species, stranding site, and injury—the latter of which is usually human-caused. The center, located at the east end of Fort Cronkhite near Rodeo Lagoon, is open daily from 10am to 4pm. Admission is free (donations appreciated).

Closed to the public for several years due to storm damage, the precariously perched 1877 **POINT BONITA LIGHTHOUSE** (415/331-1540; www.nps.gov/goga/mahe/pobo) is once again thrilling those tourists brave enough to traverse the long, dark tunnel and seven small footbridges leading to the beacon. The reward for such bravery is, among other things, a rare and sensational view of the entrance to the bay. The story goes that one 19th-century lighthouse keeper rigged ropes around his children to prevent them from slipping into the raging sea below. It's open Saturday, Sunday, and Monday 12:30pm to 3:30pm.

Also within the Marin Headlands is **HAWK HILL** (located above Battery 129, where Conzelman Rd becomes one-way), one of the most remarkable avian sites in the western United States and the biggest hawk lookout in western North America. Record count in 1992 was more than 20,000 birds, including 21 species of hawk. The best time to visit is during September and October, when thousands of birds of prey soar over the hill each day.

Muir Woods

When you stand in the middle of Muir Woods (from Hwy 101 in Sausalito, take the Stinson Beach/Hwy 1 exit heading W and follow the signs; 415/388-2595; www.nps.gov/muwo) surrounded by a canopy of ancient redwoods towering hundreds of feet skyward, it's hard to fathom that San Francisco is less than 6 miles away. It's a den of wooden giants; tourists speak in hushed tones as they crane their necks in disbelief, snapping photographs that don't begin to capture the immensity of these living titans.

Muir Woods can get absurdly crowded on summer weekends. Admission is $3 per person, 17 years and older. Picnicking is not allowed, but there is a snack bar and gift shop at the entrance. It's typically cool and damp, so dress appropriately. Open 8am to sunset.

Three miles west of Muir Woods, along Highway 1, is a small crescent-shaped cove called **MUIR BEACH**. Strewn with bits of driftwood and numerous tide pools, Muir Beach is a more sedate alternative to the beer 'n' bikini crowds at the ever-popular Stinson Beach up north. If all you're looking for is a sandy, quiet place for some R&R, park your car right here and skip the trip to Stinson.

RESTAURANTS

The Pelican Inn / ★☆

10 PACIFIC WY, MUIR BEACH; 415/383-6000 One of the better ways to spend a Sunday afternoon in the Bay Area is to take a leisurely drive to this homey little English pub, grab a table at the glassed-in patio or by the fireplace, and gorge yourself proper on a steaming shepherd's pie. Rack of lamb, prime rib, and a few fish dishes are also on the menu, and in the bar you'll find a goodly number of British, Irish, and Scottish beers on tap. After lunch, burn a few calories with a stroll down Muir Beach. Note: We used to recommend the inn's quaint-looking lodgings as well, but after several complaints of shoddy furnishings and fixtures, we yanked it. *$$; MC, V; no checks; lunch, dinner every day May–Oct and holidays year-round (lunch, dinner Tues–Sun Nov–Apr); beer and wine; reservations recommended; www.pelicaninn.com; at the entrance to Muir Beach.* &

Stinson Beach

On those treasured weekend days when the fog has lifted and the sun is scorching the Northern California coast, blurry-eyed Bay Area residents grab their morning paper and beach chairs, pile into their SUVs, and scramble to the sandy shores of popular Stinson Beach—the North Coast's nice-try answer to the fabled beaches of Southern California.

A 3½-mile stretch of beige sand provides elbow room for everyone to spread out beach blankets, picnic baskets, and toys. Swimming is allowed, and lifeguards are on duty from May through mid-September, though notices about riptides (plus the sea's toe-numbing temperatures and the threat of sharks) tend to discourage folks from venturing too far into the water. Call 415/868-1922 for recorded **WEATHER AND SURF CONDITIONS.**

Joined at the hip with *la playa* is a village filled with art galleries, specialty shops, and informal cafes. There are plenty of adventurous things to do in the area. For example, **OFF THE BEACH BOATS** (15 Calle del Mar, next to the Stinson Beach Post Office; 415/868-9445) offers three-hour lessons on the basics of sea and surf kayaking. They also rent sea and surf kayaks, surfboards, bodyboards, and wetsuits.

The most famous of all bards livens up weekend evenings May through October. Dress warmly, grab your blanket, and head for **SHAKESPEARE AT STINSON** (Hwy 1 at Calle del Mar; 415/868-9500; www.shakespeareatstinson.org). Enjoy *Much Ado About Nothing, Twelfth Night,* or *Macbeth* in the damp sea breeze beneath the stars.

Skinny-dipping is the trend at **RED ROCK** (www.redrockbeach.com), one of the few nude beaches on the Marin coast. Located about 1 mile south of Stinson Beach on Highway 1, it's easy to miss since you can't see it from the road. Park at the first dirt pull-off on your right after leaving Stinson and look for a steep path leading down to the water.

RESTAURANTS

The Parkside Cafe / ★★

43 ARENAL AVE, STINSON BEACH; 415/868-1272 During the day this popular neighborhood cafe bustles with locals and Bay Area beachgoers who stop for an inexpensive breakfast or lunch before shoving off to Stinson Beach around the corner. Morning favorites are the omelets, blueberry pancakes, and the not-to-be-missed raisin-walnut bread. For lunch there are basics like burgers, grilled sandwiches, and soups, as well as daily specials. Once the beach crowd departs, the kitchen starts preparing the seasonal evening menu, which might include oven-roasted Sonoma squab, pan-seared Alaskan halibut, or grilled filet mignon. On sunny days dine alfresco on the brick patio; otherwise, cozy up to the fire. For a quick bite to go, the cafe's snack bar sells great burgers, fries, and shakes daily from March through September, and on weekends from October through February. *$–$$; AE, MC, V; local checks only; breakfast, lunch, dinner every day; beer and wine; reservations recommended for dinner; www.parksidecafe.com; off Calle del Mar.* &

LODGINGS

Stinson Beach Motel / ★

3416 HWY 1, STINSON BEACH; 415/868-1712 This vintage beach lodging—it's more than 70 years old—is a real charmer. As you walk into the courtyard, you're surrounded by colorful flowering plants—bright red bougainvillea, pink fuchsias, yellow African daisies, purple morning glories. The individually decorated cottages have been completely remodeled in shades of soothing blues, and all have garden views, queen beds with expensive sheets and goose-down comforters, and new TVs. Which cottage you'll want depends on your needs: Unit 2 has a large living room with sofa bed and is best for families, while units 1, 2, and 7 have small kitchens. Spacious unit 7 is our favorite, with flower views from each window and plenty of privacy. Guests can relax in reclining padded deck chairs on the three courtyards paved with bright white stone blocks. The beach and restaurants are a short walk away. *$$–$$$; MC, V; checks OK; www.stinsonbeachmotel.com; at the S end of Stinson Beach near the fire station.*

Bolinas

The beach town of Bolinas, a tight-knit community of free-spirited individuals, is one of the most reclusive towns in Northern California. Residents regularly take down highway signs pointing the way to their rural enclave, an act of rebellion that ironically has created more publicity for Bolinas than any road sign ever did. As a tourist, you don't have to worry about being chased out of town by a band of machete-wielding Bolinistas, but don't expect anyone to roll out the welcome mat, either. The trick is not to look like a tourist, but more like a Bay Area resident who's only here to buy some peaches at the **PEOPLE'S STORE** (14 Wharf Rd; 415/868-1433; open every day 8:30am–6:30pm).

What's the People's Store, you ask? It's a town landmark that's well known for its locally grown organic produce and exceptional service—the antithesis of the corporate supermarket. It's a little hard to find, hidden at the end of a gravel driveway next to the Bolinas Bakery (don't confuse it with the much larger general store down the street), but it's worth searching out just to see—and taste—the difference between Safeway and the Bolinas way.

Three side trips offer plenty of entertainment. Just before entering downtown Bolinas, turn right (west) on Mesa Road, left on Overlook Road, and right on Elm Road, and you'll dead-end at the **DUXBURY REEF NATURE RESERVE** (415/499-6387), the largest intertidal reef in North America. Rich tide pools harbor an array of starfish, lacy purple plants, sea anemones, and kelp. Check the tide conditions and wear appropriate shoes; the rocks are slippery. If you continue west on Mesa Road you'll reach the **POINT REYES BIRD OBSERVATORY** (415/868-1221; www.prbo.org), where ornithologists keep an eye on more than 400 feathered species. Admission to the visitors center and nature trail is free, and visitors are welcome to observe the tricky process of catching and banding the birds. It's open daily from dawn to dusk. Banding hours vary seasonally; call 415/868-0655 for exact times. At the very end of Mesa Road is the **PALOMARIN TRAILHEAD,** which accesses beautiful coast and inland trails that stretch for more than 12 miles. The 6-mile round-trip trek passes several small lakes and meadows before it reaches **ALAMERE FALLS,** a freshwater stream that cascades down a 40-foot bluff onto **WILDCAT BEACH.**

BOLINAS LAGOON, a placid saltwater expanse that serves as refuge for numerous shorebirds and harbor seals, is just south of the town of Bolinas on Highway 1. Across from the lagoon is the **AUDUBON CANYON RANCH'S BOLINAS LAGOON PRESERVE** (415/868-9244; www.egret.org), a 1,014-acre wildlife sanctuary that supports a major population of **GREAT BLUE HERONS** and **WHITE GREAT EGRETS.** This is the premier spot along the Pacific Coast to watch these immense, graceful seabirds as they court, mate, and build huge nests at the top of towering redwoods. Baby birds are usually in the nests by late April. The trails leading to the overlook are steep and often slippery. Wear sturdy shoes or boots. Admission is free; donations are appreciated. It's open mid-March through mid-July on Saturdays, Sundays, and holidays, 10am to 4pm, and by appointment for groups.

LODGINGS

Thomas' White House Inn / ★★

118 KALE RD, BOLINAS; 415/868-0279 This inn is Bolinas personified—charming, offbeat (e.g., the bathroom doubles as an aviary), peaceful, and surrounded by incredible vistas. Lounging on the immense and beautifully landscaped front lawn—it alone is worth the room rate—you get a sweeping view of the Bay Area coastline from Marin to Half Moon Bay. The two guest rooms are located on the top floor of a two-story Cape Cod–style home and boast cathedral ceilings, window seats that are ideal for gazing out at the sea, and an array of antiques and country accents. The larger room (our favorite) has a more rustic feel, with old pine furnishings and an antique steamer trunk, while the smaller room is decorated in softer tones with lace and white wicker. Owner Jackie Thomas serves a simple continental breakfast. *$$; No credit cards; checks OK; jackiesinn@earthlink.net; www.thomaswhitehouseinn.com; call for directions.*

Point Reyes National Seashore

Hiking, biking, swimming, sailing, windsurfing, sunbathing, camping, fishing, horseback riding, bird-watching, kayaking—all are fair game at this 71,000-acre sanctuary of forested hills, deep green pastures, and undisturbed beaches. Point Reyes is hardly a secret anymore—more than 2 million visitors arrive each year—but the land is so vast and varied that crowds are a rarity.

There are four towns in and around the Point Reyes National Seashore boundary: **OLEMA, POINT REYES STATION, INVERNESS PARK,** and **INVERNESS.** Choose one and you'll be within a stone's throw of the park. While the selection of lodging in Point Reyes is excellent, it's also expensive, with most rooms well over $150 per night. Be sure to make your reservation far in advance for the summer and holidays, and bring layers of clothing: Point Reyes gets chilly at night regardless of the season. If you're having trouble finding a vacancy, call the **INNS OF MARIN** (415/663-2000 or 800/887-2880; www.innsofmarin.com) or **WEST MARIN NETWORK** (415/663-9543) for information on available lodgings. The **WEST MARIN CHAMBER OF COMMERCE** (415/663-9232; www.pointreyes.org) is also a good source for lodging and visitor information.

Your first stop is the **BEAR VALLEY VISITOR CENTER** (Bear Valley Rd; 415/464-5100; www.nps.gov/pore/), located at the entrance to the Point Reyes National Seashore; follow the signs from Highway 1 in Olema. Pick up a free map and trail guide and chat with a friendly ranger about overnight campsites, weather forecasts, tide conditions, and special programs. The center is open weekdays 9am to 5pm and weekends 8am to 5pm. Drive out to the **POINT REYES LIGHTHOUSE** (415/669-1534; open 10am–4:30pm Thurs–Mon, weather permitting) at the westernmost tip of the Point Reyes Peninsula. It's a 45-minute scenic excursion through windswept meadows and working dairy ranches—watch out for cows on the road. When the fog burns off, the lighthouse and the headlands provide a fantastic lookout point for spying **GRAY WHALES** and thousands of **COMMON MURES** that inundate the rocks below. Visitors have free access to the lighthouse via a windy 0.4-mile walk with a thigh-burning 308-step staircase.

If bivalves are your thing, stop off at **JOHNSON'S OYSTER FARM** (off Sir Francis Drake Blvd, about 6 miles W of Inverness; 415/669-1149). It may not look like much—a cluster of trailer homes, shacks, and oyster tanks surrounded by huge piles of oyster shells—but that certainly doesn't detract from the taste of fresh-out-of-the-water oysters dipped in Johnson's special sauce. Eat 'em on the spot, or buy a bag for the road—either way, you're not likely to find California oysters as fresh or as cheap anywhere else. The oyster farm resides within Drakes Estero, a large saltwater lagoon on the Point Reyes peninsula that produces nearly 20 percent of California's commercial oyster yield. It's open 8am to 4pm Tuesday through Sunday.

A popular Point Reyes pastime is **OCEAN KAYAKING**. Don't worry, the kayaks are very stable and there are no waves to contend with because you'll be paddling through placid Tomales Bay, a haven for migrating birds and marine mammals. Rental prices at **TOMALES BAY SEA KAYAKING** (415/663-1743; www.tamalsaka.com) start at about $35 for a half-day. You can sign up for a guided day trip, a sunset cruise, or a romantic full-moon outing. Instruction, clinics, and boat delivery are available; all ages and levels welcome. The launching point is located on Highway 1 at the **MARSHALL BOATWORKS**, 8 miles north of Point Reyes Station.

As most ardent Bay Area mountain bikers know, Point Reyes National Seashore boasts some of the finest **MOUNTAIN BIKE TRAILS** in the state. Narrow dirt paths wind through densely forested knolls and end with spectacular ocean views. A map is a must (available for free at the Bear Valley Visitor Center) since many of the park trails are off-limits to bikes. To rent a bike, call David Barnett at **CYCLE ANALYSIS** (415/663-9164 or 415/663-1645; www.cyclepointreyes.com).

Olema

RESTAURANTS

Olema Inn Restaurant / ★★★

10000 SIR FRANCIS DRAKE BLVD, OLEMA; 415/663-9559 A favorite destination restaurant of Marinites, the whitewashed, airy restaurant inn (see review, below) retains the elegance of a stage stop for upscale Victorian travelers and prides itself on its beautifully prepared fresh food. The dining rooms are bright, courtesy of big mullioned windows; the original woodwork has been refinished in pastels; and the floor is pine, refashioned from a 19th-century tobacco warehouse. In the evening, candles decorate the tables and flicker in antique wall sconces. In balmy weather, guests may dine outdoors on the back patio. The menu is small but consistent in quality; one evening's choice may include cassoulet, Niman Ranch sirloin (hormone-free), and side dishes such as ramps (a crunchy green vegetable), fava beans, morel mushrooms, and red potatoes. The goal of the kitchen is to help people savor the bounty of the Marin coast; menus are planned around seasonal local produce and meats. In fact, much of the restaurant's produce is grown in an organic garden and an orchard on the premises. *$$$; AE, MC, V; checks OK; lunch Fri–Sun, dinner Wed–Mon, brunch Sun; beer and wine; reservations recommended; info@theolema inn.com; www.theolemainn.com; corner of Sir Francis Drake Blvd and Hwy 1.* &

LODGINGS

An English Oak / ★★

88 BEAR VALLEY RD, OLEMA; 415/663-1777 In the shadow of Inverness Ridge, the quiet that pervades the grounds of this lovely farmhouse reduces guests to whispers. Formerly known as the Bear Valley Inn, this B&B is decorated in a comfortable English country style. The two-story Victorian home, built in 1899, has three guest rooms and a shared bath (though a detached private bath is available during the week) and a private cottage with a fully equipped kitchen and two futon couches in the living area that are suitable for children. When you return from your day of exploring, plop yourself onto one of the overstuffed chairs and relax in front of the old wood-burning stove. A hearty breakfast is served in the farmhouse-style dining room. It's a peaceful place for rest and recreation. *$$–$$$; MC, V; checks OK; 2-night minimum stay on weekends; sharyn@anenglishoak.com; www.anenglishoak.com; at intersection of Hwy 1 and Bear Valley Rd.* &

Olema Inn / ★★★

10000 SIR FRANCIS DRAKE BLVD, OLEMA; 415/663-9559 This 1876 building, a former stagecoach stop, is loaded with modern luxuries yet still manages to retain its period charm. It features six rooms with European Sleepworks mattresses, down comforters, Ralph Lauren linens, and antique furniture. Four of the rooms have showers and baths, and two have showers only. The decor is simple and elegant, in keeping with the style and era of the building: high ceilings, antique light fixtures, baths in Victorian-style white porcelain and chrome, and roomy armoires. Soft-colored pastels and florals and beige wool carpeting enhance the clean, crisp look. Views are of the back garden and Olema Valley beyond. Try to reserve room 3, which overlooks the garden and is the quietest of the six. Guests are encouraged to stroll behind the inn to the orchard, and on the stone pathways of the vegetable gardens; the property is landscaped with pink roses, violets, hostas, and large mature maples, oaks, and elms. A complimentary breakfast of croissants, local cheeses, seasonal fruit, coffee, and juice is served in the dining room. *$$$; AE, MC, V; checks OK; info@theolemainn.com; www.theolemainn.com; corner of Sir Francis Drake Blvd and Hwy 1.*

Point Reyes Station

It feels like time stood still in this West Marin community (population 675) that was a rail town in the 1890s and is steeped in dairy-farming tradition. Maybe that's why so many weary Bay Area commuters flock to Point Reyes Station on weekends. The three blocks everyone calls **MAIN STREET** are actually on Highway 1. It's worth waiting in line to sample the breads and pastries at the renowned **BOVINE BAKERY** (415/663-9420); if gourmet picnic goodies are on your list, head for **TOMALES BAY FOODS** (415/663-9335)—also home of the **COWGIRL CREAMERY**. Those Western gals sure know how to make ice cream and cheeses. **TOBY'S FEED BARN** (415/663-1223) is the place to buy farm-fresh fruits and vegetables, seeds, sunbonnets, local arts and crafts, and souvenir postcards. The **PINE CONE DINER** (415/663-1536) rustles up made-from-scratch biscuits and gravy every morning.

RESTAURANTS

The Station House Cafe / ★★

11180 SHORELINE HWY, POINT REYES STATION; 415/663-1515 For more than two decades the Station House has been a favorite stop for West Marin residents and San Francisco day-trippers. The menu changes weekly, but you can count on the kitchen creating daily wonders with local produce, seafood, and organic beef from Niman Ranch. Breakfast items range from French toast made with Il Fornaio bakery's sweet challah to buckwheat pancakes and roasted vegetable frittatas. For dinner, start with a platter of local oysters and mussels, followed by a braised lamb shank (made with Guinness Stout), salmon with roasted yellow pepper sauce, or one of the Station House's old standbys such as fish-and-chips with country fries and coleslaw. There's a good selection of wines, too. When the weather's warm, sit outside in the shaded garden area—particularly if you're eating breakfast here on a sunny day. In the summer, barbecued oysters are often served on the patio. $$; DIS, MC, V; local checks only; breakfast, lunch, dinner every day; full bar; reservations recommended; on Main St. &

Inverness Park

LODGINGS

Blackthorne Inn / ★★★

266 VALLEJO AVE, INVERNESS PARK; 415/663-8621 With its four levels, five rooms, multiple decks, spiral staircase, skybridge, and fire pole, the Blackthorne Inn is more like a treehouse for grown-ups than a B&B. The octagonal Eagle's Nest, perched on the top level, has its own sundeck and a 360-degree view of the forest (the bath, however, is located across the skybridge—a bit of an adventure on blustery nights); the spacious Forest View and Hideaway Rooms, which share a bath, have sitting areas facing the woods; the outdoor treetop-level hot tub offers a great view of the stars. All have private bathrooms. The main sitting room in the house features a large stone fireplace, skylight, and beautiful

NORTH COAST THREE-DAY TOUR

DAY ONE: Meet the giants. Fuel up at the **DIPSEA CAFE** (200 Shoreline Hwy, Mill Valley; 415/381-0298). Follow the curves on Highway 1 to **MUIR WOODS**, home of the giant redwoods. Grab your jacket, pick up a trail guide at the entrance, and look up in awe. Take the 1-mile main trail loop to **CATHEDRAL GROVE**, where you might be inspired to grow a tree of your own. Live redwood burls are sold at the gift shop. Back on Highway 1, expect winding roads aplenty and gorgeous views as you wind down to **STINSON BEACH**. Get your toes wet in the sand or search for an elusive sand dollar. Refuel at the **PARKSIDE CAFE**, then move on to the **POINT REYES NATIONAL SEASHORE**. Check in at the **OLEMA INN** and enjoy a refreshing respite. Round 'em up and head for Main Street at Point Reyes Station. Dinner's served at the **STATION HOUSE CAFE**. Be sure to mosey across the street to the **OLD WESTERN SALOON** for a nightcap before you hit the hay.

DAY TWO: Earth-shaking events. Time to see what's shaking at the **BEAR VALLEY VISITOR CENTER**: Stop at the seismograph station and check out the status of "the big one." Walk through the large picnic area in back of the visitor center and follow the signs to the half-mile-long **EARTHQUAKE TRAIL**. Walk along the San Andreas fault and examine the epicenter of the 1906 San Francisco earthquake. Then check out the **MORGAN HORSE FARM** and drop into the sweat house at Kule Loko, a re-created **COAST MIWOK INDIAN VILLAGE**. For a great picnic, buy your provisions at

stained-glass windows, and is surrounded by a huge deck. A country buffet breakfast, included in the room rate, is served on the upper deck when the sun is shining. *$$$$; MC, V; checks OK; susan@blackthorneinn.com; www.blackthorneinn.com; from Inverness Park, go 1¼ mile up Vallejo Ave.*

Holly Tree Inn / ★★★

3 SILVERHILLS RD, INVERNESS PARK; 415/663-1554 OR 800/286-4655 Hidden within a 19-acre valley with a meandering creek and wooded hillsides is the blissfully quiet Holly Tree Inn. This family-owned B&B has four cozy guest rooms, each with a private bath (one with a fireplace) and decorated with Laura Ashley prints and country antiques. The large, airy living room has a fireplace and comfortable chairs where guests converse over afternoon tea. If privacy is what you're after, tucked in a far corner of the estate is the Cottage-in-the-Woods, a two-room hideaway with a small fireplace, a king-size bed, and an old-fashioned bathtub from which you can gaze at the garden. Families or honeymooners should inquire about the separate Sea Star Cottage—built on stilts over Tomales Bay—and the two-bedroom Vision Cottage: both have hot tubs. In the morning, enjoy a bountiful country breakfast included in the room rate. *$$$–$$$$;*

TOMALES BAY FOODS and set out on Highway 1, bound for **TOMALES** and **DILLON BEACH.** Spread out your blanket and soak up the fresh air and sweet sound of the surf. You'll be camping tonight, Tuscan style, at the **SONOMA COAST VILLA.** Hang up your gear and prepare to be pampered. If you're still raring to go after watching the sunset, have dinner at the **DUCK CLUB,** or call it a day with a 90-minute massage.

DAY THREE: Damme it all! Let the fog burn off while you linger over a full breakfast at the Villa. Set your compass north; take it easy on the curves. Cruise through **BODEGA BAY** and pick up a quart of crab cioppino and some sodas at the **LUCAS WHARF DELI.** The second pit stop is **JENNER,** home of **GOAT ROCK BEACH.** You can stand on the cliffs by the road and, with the aid of binoculars, get close-up views of the harbor seals congregated on the sandbar below. Dig into that cioppino while you're at it. Back in the car, hug the curves to **POINT ARENA.** Find out about those ships of the night and mysterious lights when you tour the **POINT ARENA LIGHTHOUSE AND MUSEUM.** On to **MENDOCINO.** Fortified with a sugar rush from the **TOTE FÊTE BAKERY,** stroll through the galleries and shops before making your way to **VAN DAMME STATE PARK** to hike the **FERN CANYON TRAIL.** Check into the **MENDOCINO FARMHOUSE,** play with Molly for a while on the front lawn, then head back to Mendocino for dinner at the **MOOSSE CAFE** followed by a nightcap at **DICK'S PLACE** before settling in for the night with one of the cats at the Farmhouse.

AE, MC, V; checks OK; info@hollytreeinn.com; www.hollytreeinn.com; off Bear Valley Rd.

Inverness

Affluent San Franciscans built summer homes in Inverness at the turn of the century; sailors have always been attracted to the misty waters. Today expensive B&Bs are hidden in the wooded hillsides, kayaks glide on Tomales Bay, and it's as serene and peaceful as ever. If you want to paddle around for yourself, check in at **BLUE WATERS KAYAKING** (415/669-2600; www.bwkayak.com).

RESTAURANTS

Manka's Inverness Lodge / ★★★★

ARGYLE ST, INVERNESS; 415/669-1034 OR 800/58-LODGE Dining at Manka's is like being in a Jack London novel. Sit in the lobby's plush high-backed chairs, warm your toes by the small wood-burning fireplace, and watch in fascination as one of the cooks kneels beside you to grill the house-made wild boar sausages over the fire. To complement the hunting-lodge ambience, the restaurant serves "unusual game"—from the aforementioned wild boar to pan-seared elk tenderloin, black buck antelope chops, and Canadian pheasant—as well as local seafood. Appetizers range from grilled California quail with wild mushroom sauce to fire-roasted figs with black-pepper syrup. The divine desserts—such as the cinnamon-croissant pudding with warm caramel sauce—are made from scratch, and the wine list is longer than the drive to get here. There's no standard menu—all dinners are prix fixe, and the selection changes daily. In fact, the restaurant's boast is that the majority of the fish, fruits, and vegetables it serves are grown, raised, or caught within 15 minutes of its kitchen. A five-course meal is offered Thursday, Friday, and Sunday for about $50; the dinner on Saturday is about $70, while Monday is about $35. $$$$; MC, V; checks OK; dinner Thurs–Mon; beer and wine; reservations recommended; www.mankas.com; on Argyle St, off Sir Francis Drake Blvd.

LODGINGS

Manka's Inverness Lodge / ★★★★

ARGYLE ST, INVERNESS; 415/669-1034 OR 800/58-LODGE What a difference a Grade makes. For years Manka's was a mediocre Czech restaurant, but when Margaret Grade and family took over in 1989, things changed. This former hunting and fishing lodge soon became one of the most romantic places to stay in California, as well as a wonderful place to eat (see review, above). Manka's offers a dozen accommodations, including four upstairs guest rooms that look as though they came out of a Hans Christian Andersen fairy tale—small and cozy, with tree-limb bedsteads, down comforters, high ceilings, and old-fashioned bathrooms. Rooms 1 and 2 extend out to large private decks overlooking Tomales Bay and have fireplaces and double tubs with showers open to the sky. Manka's also offers four handsome rooms in its Redwood Annex, and two spacious one-bedroom cabins with living rooms, fireplaces, and hot tubs. Friendly and refreshingly unpretentious, Manka's Inverness Lodge is an idyllic weekend getaway. $$$$; MC, V; checks OK; www.mankas.com; on Argyle St off Sir Francis Drake Blvd.

Tomales

Most people don't even know the town of Tomales exists. Consisting of not much more than a general store, two churches, and a superb little bakery, the tiny ranching community looks pretty much as it did a hundred years ago. It's in a prime location, though—only 30 minutes' drive from **POINT REYES NATIONAL SEASHORE,** yet far enough away to avoid the traffic and commotion. The 4-mile drive from Tomales to **DILLON BEACH** (via Dillon Beach Rd) is one of the most scenic routes on the Marin coast. There is a $5 day-use fee at the beach. The fishing pier and dune campgrounds at **LAWSON'S LANDING** (707/878-2443) also attract visitors.

Tomales is a popular stop for fresh raw and barbecued oysters. The **TOMALES BAY OYSTER COMPANY** (15479 Hwy 1; 415/663-1242; open daily 9am–5pm) has been in business since 1909. They sell them by the dozen or in a sack of 100. Those in the know bring their own knives, lemons, cocktail sauce, and even bags of charcoal for the nearby barbecue pits.

The Sonoma Coast

Mention Sonoma and everyone's immediate association is "wine country." What few Californians seem to know, however, is that Sonoma County gerrymanders a hefty chunk of the coast as well—more than 50 miles of mostly undeveloped shoreline from Bodega Bay to Gualala. And judging from the mostly vacant state parks and beaches, even fewer Californians seem to know what a good thing they're missing as they migrate lemming-like to Mendocino or Carmel. The Sonoma coast isn't for everyone, though; there's little in the way of shopping, sightseeing, and such. It's more of a place where inlanders return annually to bury themselves in a book, wiggle their toes in the sand, and forget about work for a while.

Valley Ford

This sleepy little community is just a charming bend in the road for most coastal travelers. The Northern Pacific Railroad steamed through here in 1876, potato farming flourished in the 1920s, and today most of the 126 residents are ranchers of cows or sheep. There were traffic jams in 1976 when the artist Christo installed his Running Fence, 18 feet high and 24½ miles long, through Valley Ford. Created from pure white silk, the undulating fence snaked over green rolling hills straight into the Pacific.

LODGINGS

Valley Ford Hotel / ★

14415 HWY 1, VALLEY FORD; 707/876-3600 The pleasant, old-fashioned Valley Ford Hotel, built in 1864 and well-maintained ever since, is a good choice for travelers who prefer the privacy of a hotel to the more social aspect of a B&B. The seven rooms are clean, spacious, and simply furnished. Each has a private bath; bed sizes range from queen to king. The Bernardoni Suite is the most luxurious accommodation, with a sitting room, a gas fireplace, a satellite TV, and videos. For those who crave sports and company, there is a full bar with satellite TV in the cocktail lounge. Many move into the adjoining restaurant after the game, choosing dinner entrees like chicken saltimbocco or filet Madagascar, served Wednesday through Sunday. The restaurant also serves weekend brunches on the patio, making it a good place to take a break on your way to the coast. *$$$; AE, MC, V; checks OK; info@valley fordhotel.com; www.valleyfordhotel.com; downtown.* &

Bodega Bay

When it comes to fancy restaurants, accommodations, and boutiques, Bodega Bay has a long way to go. There is only one three-star lodge and restaurant, and the town's most venerable store sells taffy and kites. This is odd, considering that Bodega Bay is only a few hours' drive from the Bay Area, a good two to three hours closer than Mendocino, and has all the beautiful scenery and golden beaches you could possibly hope for. Spend a few hours meandering through town and it becomes apparent that Bodega Bay is, for the most part, still a working-class fishing village. Most people start their day before dawn—mending nets, rigging fishing poles, and talking shop. But if all you want to do is breathe in some salty air and you couldn't care less about Gucci boutiques and dancing till dawn, come to Bodega Bay—ain't much here, which is precisely the point.

The **SONOMA COAST VISITORS CENTER** (850 Hwy 1; 707/875-3866; www.bodegabay.com or www.visitsonomacoast.com) is a good place to load up on free maps, guides, and brochures, including the "Bodega Bay Area Map & Guide." The latter gives the exact locations of all the town's attractions, including nearby **BODEGA HEAD** (from downtown Bodega Bay, turn W on Eastshore Rd, go right at the stop sign onto Bay Flat Rd, and follow it to the end), the small peninsula that shelters Bodega Bay. You'll discover two superb **WALKING TRAILS** that follow the ocean at the Head. The first, a 4-mile round-trip trail, starts from the west parking lot, leads past the **BODEGA BAY MARINE LABORATORY** (707/875-2211; www.bml.ucdavis.edu), which conducts guided tours of its lab projects on Friday afternoons between 2pm and 4pm, and ends at the sand dunes of **SALMON CREEK BEACH.** An easier, 1½-mile round-trip walk begins in the east parking lot and encircles the edge of Bodega Head. From December through April, Bodega Head also doubles as one of the premier **WHALE-WATCHING** points along the California coast.

A great way to spend a lazy afternoon in Bodega Bay is at the **DOCKS,** watching the rusty fishing boats unload their catches. **TIDES WHARF RESTAURANT** (835 Hwy 1 in Bodega Bay; 707/875-3652) has the most active dock scene, including a viewing room near the processing plant that allows you to witness a fish's ultimate fate—a swift and merciless gutting by deft hands, followed by a quick burial in ice (kids are mesmerized by this). Just outside, sea lions linger by the dock hoping for a handout.

Linking Bodega Bay and the nearby town of Jenner are the **SONOMA COAST STATE AND COUNTY BEACHES,** 16 miles of pristine sand and gravel beaches, tide pools, rocky bluffs, hiking trails, and one heck of a gorgeous drive along Highway 1. Although all the beaches are pretty much the same, the safest for kids is **DORAN PARK BEACH,** located just south of Bodega Bay. When the water's rough everywhere else, Doran is still calm enough for swimming, clamming, and crabbing (an added bonus: the adjacent Doran mud flats are a favorite haunt of egrets, pelicans, and other seabirds). The best tide pools are at the north end of **SALMON CREEK BEACH** (off Bean Ave, 2 miles N of town) or **SHELL BEACH,** a small low-tide treasure trove 10 miles north of Bodega Bay. If all you want to do is get horizontal in the sand, deciding which of the 14 beaches along Highway 1 looks the best will drive you nuts; just pick one and park.

RESTAURANTS

The Duck Club / ★★★

103 HWY 1 (BODEGA BAY LODGE & SPA), BODEGA BAY; 707/875-3525 OR 800/368-2468 Bodega Bay sure took its sweet time coaxing a premier chef to the coast, but now that Jeff Reilly (formerly the executive chef at Lafayette

Park in Walnut Creek) is in town, gastronomes up and down the coast are coming to the Bodega Bay Lodge & Spa to sample his wares. "Sonoma County cuisine" best describes Reilly's penchant for local yields, with creations such as roasted Petaluma duck with Valencia orange sauce or a Sonoma farm-fresh asparagus strudel bathed in a mild curry sauce. *Le poisson du jour* comes straight from the docks down the street. Large windows overlook the bay, so be sure to beg for a table-with-a-view when making the required reservations. The Duck Club offers a lengthy wine list with an extensive selection of Sonoma County labels. Picnic lunches are available upon request. *$$$; AE, DC, DIS, MC, V; no checks; breakfast, dinner every day; beer and wine; reservations required; www.bodegabaylodge.com; S end of town.* &

The Tides Wharf & Restaurant / ★

835 HWY 1, BODEGA BAY; 707/875-3652 Few tourists come to Bodega Bay just for the seafood, as you'll soon discover if you spend more than a day here. There are only two "seafood" restaurants in town, Tides Wharf and Lucas Wharf, and both do little to excite the palate. Yes, the fish is fresh off the boats, but the preparations are basic and uninspired (though the hundreds of people who dine here daily in the summer don't seem to mind). Also, don't expect the weather-beaten luncheonette you may remember from Hitchcock's film *The Birds*—a $6 million renovation has transmogrified the place beyond recognition. The best tables offer views overlooking the ocean, and the bill of fare is seafood standard: oysters on the half shell, clam chowder, and fish caught from the restaurant's own boat. Prime rib, pasta, and poultry dishes are available as well. Your best bet, however, is to skip the full service and go down the street to the **LUCAS WHARF DELI** (595 Hwy 1; 707/875-3562), pick up a $6 pint of crab cioppino or a big ol' basket of fresh fish 'n' chips, and make a picnic of it on the dock. *$$; AE, DIS, MC, V; checks OK; lunch, dinner every day; full bar; www.innatthetides.com/tideswharf.html; at the south end of town.* &

LODGINGS

Bodega Bay Lodge & Spa / ★★★

103 HWY 1, BODEGA BAY; 707/875-3252 OR 800/368-2468 Granted, the competition isn't very fierce, but it's safe to say that the Bodega Bay Lodge & Spa provides some of the Sonoma coast's finest accommodations. It's the view that clinches it: all 78 rooms—swathed in handsome hues of cardinal red and forest green, with fireplaces and stocked minibars—have private balconies with a wonderful panorama of Bodega Bay and its bird-filled wetlands. The lodge also offers six deee-lux Ocean Club suites featuring Jacuzzi tubs for two, a black granite fireplace, and a romantic ocean view. Should you ever leave your balcony, a short walk through elaborate flower gardens leads to an outdoor fieldstone spa and heated swimming pool overlooking the bay. A fitness center, sauna, and complimentary morning newspaper are part of the package, as is a complimentary wine hour from 5pm to 6pm. Ask about the on-site facials, massages, and body treatments that are among the extra offerings. More proof of Bodega Bay Lodge & Spa's top standing is its Duck Club restaurant (see review, above), easily the Sonoma Coast's best. *$$$$; AE, DC, DIS, MC, V; checks OK; reservations@bodegabaylodge.com; www.bodega baylodge.com; S end of town.* &

279

Inn at the Tides / ★★

800 HWY 1, BODEGA BAY; 707/875-2751 OR 800/541-7788 In Bodega Bay the architectural style of most structures is nouveau Californian—wood-shingled boxes with lots of glass—and the Inn at the Tides is no exception. Perched on a hillside overlooking Bodega Bay, it offers 86 units with bay views, spacious interiors, contemporary (albeit *dated* contemporary) decor, and all the usual amenities of an expensive resort: terry-cloth robes, coffeemakers, hair dryers, cable TVs, refrigerators, minibars, fresh flowers, continental breakfasts, and access to the indoor/outdoor pool, sauna, and whirlpool tubs. A few of the rooms have king-size beds, and most have fireplaces. The Inn at the Tides's restaurant, the Bay View, is open for dinner only Wednesday through Saturday. It offers ocean views and has a romantic, somewhat formal ambiance. *$$$; AE, DIS, MC, V; checks OK; iatt@monitor.net; www.innatthetides.com; across from the Tides Wharf.* &

Bodega

A quick trip to the town of Bodega, a few miles southeast of Bodega Bay off Highway 1, is a must for any Hitchcock fan. The attraction is a bird's-eye view of the hauntingly familiar **POTTER SCHOOL HOUSE** and **ST. TERESA'S CHURCH**, both immortalized in Hitchcock's *The Birds*, filmed here in 1961. The two or three boutiques in downtown Bodega manage to entice a few visitors to park and browse, but most people seem content with a little rubbernecking and finger-pointing as they flip U-turns through the tiny town.

LODGINGS

Sonoma Coast Villa / ★★★☆

16702 COAST HWY 1, BODEGA; 707/876-9818 OR 888/404-2255 If your idea of a vacation is a Mediterranean footbath, rejuvenating body massage, and soothing facial in a beautiful Tuscan setting, you're in luck. Susan and Cyrus Griffin purchased the Sonoma Coast Villa in 1992, spent a year refurbishing every inch of the country estate and courtyard spa, and settled into the role of innkeepers with a zestful hospitality. Along with the spa, an outdoor swimming pool, and an indoor whirlpool spa, the estate houses 12 spacious guest rooms featuring exposed wooden beams, wood-burning fireplaces, Italian slate floors, large marble walk-in showers or jetted tubs, well-stocked mini-refrigerators, TVs with VCRs, and private patios. Phones are not featured in this quiet refuge, but there are board games aplenty and a nine-hole putting green. Ask to take a peek in the all-glass Tower Library Room perched at the top of the winding wrought-iron staircase. Cyrus will have been busy in the kitchen long before you rise, rustling up a hot country breakfast accompanied by fresh baked goods, served in the dining room with its vaulted wood-beamed ceiling, fireplace, and windows overlooking the lush gardens. *$$$$; AE, MC, V; checks OK; reservations@scvilla.com; www.scvilla.com; 2 miles past Valley Ford.* &

Occidental

LODGINGS

The Inn at Occidental / ★★★

3657 CHURCH ST, OCCIDENTAL; 707/874-1047 OR 800/522-6324
Innkeeper Jack Bullard has remodeled this stately 1887 Victorian into one of
the finest country inns anywhere. Covered porches, wainscoted hallways,
antique wicker furniture, walled-in English gardens, and a comfortable sitting parlor
are all elegant reminders of the historic days when Occidental was a stopping point
on the railroad between San Francisco and the Northwest. The 16 individually decorated rooms have private baths, beds topped with overstuffed down comforters,
comfortable sitting areas, and fireplaces, and are furnished with the innkeeper's vast
collection of heirlooms, antiques, and original artwork. Most rooms also offer spa
tubs for two and private decks. Overlooking the courtyard is the Marble Suite,
sumptuously furnished with an antique pine queen bed, a large separate sitting area
with a fireplace, comfortable chairs, and a spa tub for two overlooking the hill and
woods behind the inn. For the ultimate Sonoma escape pad, inquire about the separate Sonoma Cottage. Guests are treated to a full gourmet breakfast of fresh fruit,
juices, homemade granola, freshly baked pastries, and hot entrees such as orange-
thyme pancakes or French toast with jam—all served in the dining room or outdoors. Inquire about the inn's six-course winemaker dinners with preferred seating
for guests. *$$$$; AE, DIS, MC, V; checks OK; innkeeper@innatoccidental.com;
www.innatoccidental.com; off the Bohemian Hwy.* &

Sebastopol

Situated at the crossroads of Highway 116 and Highway 12, Sebastopol is the
gateway between western Sonoma County and the North Coast. Gravenstein
apples, the area's greatest claim to fame, were introduced in the late 1800s. The
APPLE BLOSSOM FESTIVAL is held every April, and **CHRISTMAS TREE FARMS**
bustle during the holidays. Antique shopping is a popular pastime year-round. Gardeners will enjoy a walking tour of **GOLD RIDGE FARM** (7781 Bodega Ave; 707/829-
6711; www.wschs-grf.pon.net/bef.htm). This is where **LUTHER BURBANK,** the
world-renowned horticulturist, conducted plant-breeding experiments at the turn of
the century. For more information, contact the Sebastopol Visitor Center (265 S
Main St; 707/823-3032 or 877/828-4748; www.sebastopol.org).

RESTAURANTS

Chez Peyo / ★★

2295 GRAVENSTEIN HWY, SEBASTOPOL; 707/823-1223 Pierre and Rose Marie
Lagourgue, chef and hosts of this homey restaurant, have been serving savory French
California cuisine to satisfied diners since 1977. Pierre (Peyo is the Basque form of
his name) is well-known for the fare he dishes up, like the braised lamb shanks
dressed in a pinot noir sauce. Another favorite is the baked salmon coated in an

almond-and-black-pepper crust and topped with a citrus beurre blanc. The restaurant's Sunday champagne brunches, featuring the likes of eggs basquaise and vegetarian Benedict, are a popular tradition in Sebastopol. *$$; MC, V; local checks OK; lunch, dinner Wed–Sun, brunch Sun; beer and wine; reservations recommended; chezpeyo@sonic.net; www.sterba.com/chezpeyo; on Hwy 116, 2 miles S of town.* &

Stella's Cafe / ★★★

4550 GRAVENSTEIN HWY N, SEBASTOPOL; 707/823-6637 Foodies will think they have died and gone to heaven when they discover this little gem. Located in a structure built for the 1930s World Trade Fair, the small restaurant—it seats 50, including the bar space—opened in October 1999. Gregory Hallihan, the gregarious owner, graduated from the California Culinary Academy in 1992. He brings years of experience, including a stint with the Ritz-Carlton in Hawaii, to Stella's Cafe. There is something for everyone on the ever-changing menu, from vegan, vegetarian, and seafood selections to old-fashioned rib-eye steak and pan-roasted chicken with Dijon and truffled mashed potatoes. Try the likes of coconut lentil soup or spicy grilled prawns with red jalapeño mango purée and pineapple couscous salad. You'll soon know why locals fill the place night after night and scoring a reservation can be difficult. Wine connoisseurs will also be pleased with the excellent choices, many from nearby vineyards. If you're still hankering for a sweet road treat after the divine strawberry shortcake, try Mom's Apple Pie, located next door. *$$; MC, V; checks OK; dinner Wed–Mon; beer and wine; reservations recommended; just before Forestville, adjacent to Mom's Apple Pie (look for the green awning imprinted with "Stella's Cafe").* &

LODGINGS

Avalon / ★★★

11910 GRATON RD, SEBASTOPOL; 707/824-0880 OR 877/3AVALON The secluded entrance to Avalon, a luxury bed-and-breakfast, conjures up images of a magical forest reminiscent of the knights of the round table. And yes, soft mists often hug the old bay trees and towering redwoods. Hilary and Gary McCalla, the engaging owners and hosts, fulfilled a cherished dream when they opened this charming Tudor-style B&B in early 2000. Avalon, a family name, coupled with a love of old English legends, inspired the themes and unique decor of the three beautifully decorated (and very spacious) suites. Try the Magician's Suite, featuring a spacious steam room shower, sleek three-sided fireplace, bright-blue-glass vessel sinks, and a tranquil forest view. Sweet dreams are yours in the Enchanted Forest Suite: soak in the full-size outdoor hot tub before sinking into the elegant king-size bed and being lulled to sleep by a splashing creek. Honeymooners should choose Guenevere's Tower, complete with a spacious sitting area, antique clawfooted soaking tub, and two Romeo and Juliet–style balconies. Each suite features a separate entrance, gas fireplaces with thermostats, king-size beds, fine linens, large private baths, and local handmade soaps. Indoor exercise facilities are available for those who miss the gym, while the brave of heart might enjoy an invigorating plunge in the nearby swimming hole. Tea is an afternoon ritual, and Hilary whips up a bountiful breakfast every morning. "French Babies," scalloped puff pastries filled

POINT REYES NATIONAL SEASHORE RULES AND REGULATIONS

You will find no gates or tollbooths on the roads leading in and out of Point Reyes; access is free and relatively unlimited, but you won't be allowed to park your car overnight here since car camping is prohibited (although the rangers won't stop you from taking an innocent midnight stroll on a clear night, they may stop by to check to see if you're all right). Most of the rules here are aimed at one of two goals: protecting park visitors from injuring themselves, and protecting rare and endangered wildlife from being trampled or otherwise disturbed by their admirers. Here are the basics: Dogs are allowed only on Kehoe Beach, Palomarin Beach, North Beach, South Beach, and southern Limantour Beach, but must be kept on leashes at all times. Don't take your dog on any hiking trails within the seashore boundaries. Camping is limited and very closely regulated. If you don't have a reservation and a permit for one of the four small backpacking camps in the park, you will not be allowed to spend the night. Permits are required for all fires, including beach fires. Bicycles are allowed on just 35 miles of the park's more than 140 miles of trails, and cyclists are required to yield right-of-way to every other class of trail user (especially equestrians). The 15mph bicycle speed limit is strictly enforced. Finally, disturbing or harassing any wildlife in the park is prohibited. Observe seasonal beach closures and trail restrictions that may become necessary to protect nesting, breeding, or molting animals. To plan your visits, contact one of three visitor centers: Bear Valley Visitors Center, Bear Valley Road, 415/464-5100; the Ken Patrick Visitors Center, mile 14, Sir Francis Drake Boulevard, 415/669-1250; or the Lighthouse Visitors Center, end of Sir Francis Drake Boulevard, 415/669-1534.

with Brie and fresh strawberries, are a specialty, along with baked pears or apples and homemade scones. $$$$; AE, DC, MC, V; checks OK; 2-night minimum stay on weekends, 3-night minimum stay on holiday weekends; info@avalonluxury inn.com; www.avalonluxuryinn.com; 3.3 miles off Graton Rd.

The Sebastopol Inn / ★★

6751 SEBASTOPOL AVE, SEBASTOPOL; 707/829-2500 Guests at the Sebastopol Inn enjoy comfortable accommodations in a historic setting. Located behind the restored vintage Gravenstein Railroad Station in downtown Sebastopol, the inn exudes country charm. Constructed with vertical board-and-batten siding and topped with a verdigris copper roof, it has 31 rooms and suites to choose from. You can expect all the amenities of a boutique hotel, including queen- or king-size beds, coffeemakers, TVs, and full concierge service. Some rooms have fireplaces, whirlpool tubs, microwaves, and refrigerators. Ask about the balcony rooms looking out on pristine wetland preserves, and bring a bathing suit for the heated pool and Jacuzzi in the garden courtyard. Right next door is the

New Dawn Day Spa, offering Sebastopol Inn guests a variety of massage, spa body, facial skin care, and waxing treatments. $$–$$$; AE, DC, MC, V; checks OK; info@sebastopolinn.com; www.thesebastopolinn.com; downtown, look for the old train barn. &

Vine Hill Inn / ★★

3949 VINE HILL RD, SEBASTOPOL; 707/823-8832 The rolling vineyards will remind you of bella Tuscany, but this beautifully restored 1897 Victorian farmhouse and its rambling country gardens belong in western Sonoma. You'll feel right at home, too, when you snuggle up in one of the four upstairs bedrooms. Furnished with charming antiques, each has a private bath; choose from a whirlpool tub or claw-footed bath with shower. An inviting porch or deck, with comfortable seating and glorious views, is never far away. How about a cool dip in the pool, nap in the hammock, or an amusing game of table tennis? Wake up to the clucking of hens and the aroma of a hearty country breakfast coming from the kitchen. $$$; AE, DIS, MC, V; checks OK; innkeeper@vine-hill-inn.com; www.vine-hill-inn.com; follow Hwy 116 W to Vine Hill Rd.

Forestville

From this tiny hamlet surrounded by redwoods you can launch an all-day **CANOE TRIP** down the gentle Russian River. Set forth from **BURKE'S CANOE TRIPS** (707/887-1222; www.burkescanoetrips.com) from May through September, and someone there will pick you up 10 miles down the scenic river—a haven for turtles, river otters, egrets, and great blue herons—and take you back to your car. Also worth a detour is **KOSLOWSKI FARMS** (5566 Gravenstein Hwy; 707/887-1587), a family farm that has turned into a gourmet-food business. The Koslowskis' apple butter, jams, and vinegars are sold in specialty shops throughout Sonoma County and beyond.

RESTAURANTS

Topolos Russian River Vineyards Restaurant & Winery / ★

5700 GRAVENSTEIN HWY, FORESTVILLE; 707/887-1562 Greek food on the Russian River may be an oxymoron, but that hasn't stopped folks from lining up for Bob Engel and Christine Topolos's Mediterranean cuisine made from generations of Topolos recipes. Every meal at this family-owned restaurant—spartanly decorated, as most cafes are along the Aegean—comes with tzatziki, a garlic-laden cucumber-yogurt dip for bread, and a tomato stuffed with aromatic ratatouille. Follow that with an order of mezes: a plate of dolmas, tiropita (a cheese-and-egg pie wrapped in flaky filo pastry), marinated eggplant, and feta. Then choose from such main courses as roast Petaluma duckling with a black currant–Madeira wine sauce, roast rack of baby lamb, or prawns Santorini, prepared with tomato, feta, and dill. Both Topolos wines (made here) and other local wines are served with dinner. Dessert, naturally, is a hunk of honey-drenched baklava. $$$; AE, DC, MC, V; checks OK; lunch, dinner every day, brunch Sun (call ahead in winter); wine only; reservations recommended; topolos@topolos.net; www.topolos.net; on Hwy 116, ¼ mile S of town.

LODGINGS

Farmhouse Inn / ★★★

7871 RIVER RD, FORESTVILLE; 707/887-3300 OR 800/464-6642 Don't let the outside of the Farmhouse Inn's eight guest cottages fool you. At first glance these buildings tucked within a grove of trees look like roadside motel cabins. But step inside and you'll see that these little lodges are actually quite luxurious, with plush carpets, wood-burning fireplaces, CD players, saunas, thick robes, featherbeds with down comforters and fine linens, European "rain" showerheads, and jumbo two-person Jacuzzis—all the toys you need for a romantic weekend in the Wine Country. The grounds, 6 acres of hills and redwoods, include a large swimming pool, a croquet course, and formal English gardens. Spa services—massages and facials—are also available. Guests gather for a hearty breakfast in the conservatory-style dining room or outdoors on the terrace. Expect to be treated to fruit, cereal, and hot dishes such as huevos rancheros or eggs Florentine. The inn's restaurant is also open to the public for dinner Thursday through Sunday. *$$$–$$$$; AE, MC, V; checks OK; innkeep@farmhouseinn.com; www.farmhouseinn.com; River Rd (at Wohler Rd).* &

Guerneville

The longtime residents of Guerneville—one of the busiest logging centers in the West during the 1880s—have seen their town undergo a significant change of face in every recent decade. Once it was a haven for bikers—the leather, not the Lycra, sort—then it became a hangout for hippies. Now it's a summer mecca for the Bay Area gay community and for naturalists attracted by the beauty of the redwoods and the **RUSSIAN RIVER**. The town is a good launching spot for nature expeditions and touring the area's wineries. **KORBEL CHAMPAGNE CELLARS** (13250 River Rd; 707/824-7000; www.korbel.com), overlooking the vineyards and the Russian River, is one of the region's most popular wineries and offers free tastings of its bubbly. **ARMSTRONG WOODS STATE RESERVE** (17000 Armstrong Woods Rd; 707/869-2015) is a peaceful grove of spectacular ancient redwoods with a variety of hiking trails. Equestrians should saddle up at **ARMSTRONG WOODS PACK STATION** (707/887-2939; www.redwoodhorses.com), which offers 1½-hour and half- and full-day horseback rides with gourmet lunches as well as overnight camping rides. From May through October, you can rent canoes, kayaks, and paddleboats at **JOHNSON'S BEACH & RESORT** (707/869-2022; www.johnsonsbeach.com) just under the main bridge. Johnson's Beach is also home to the wildly popular **RUSSIAN RIVER JAZZ FESTIVAL** (707/869-2022; www.jazzontheriver.com), held every September. For more information, check out the Russian River Chamber of Commerce & Visitors Center (16209 1st St, Guerneville; 707/869-9000 or 800/823-8800; www.russianriver.com).

RESTAURANTS

Applewood Restaurant / ★★★

13555 HWY 116 (APPLEWOOD INN), GUERNEVILLE; 707/869-9093 OR 800/555-8509 Folks at the nearby inn are apt to describe the Applewood Restaurant's design as rustic-barn architecture, but don't be fooled. When was the last time you saw a barn with lofty beam ceilings, two river-rock fireplaces, and spacious windows looking out to towering redwoods? Guests are invited to arrive in casual attire and linger over a romantic candlelit dinner impeccably prepared by executive chef Brian Gerritsen. Formally trained at the New England Culinary Institute, he also brings his enriching experiences in the French countryside to the Russian River Valley. In keeping with Applewood's culinary history, Brian uses only the freshest ingredients, with a strong focus on the organic bounty from the inn's own 2-acre garden and fruit orchard. For starters you'll find treats like the lightly curried cauliflower soup with duck prosciutto or hazelnut-crusted sweetbreads on a celery root and Asian pear rémoulade. Entrees range from a hearty veal osso buco braised in cabernet with white beans and Spanish olives, to grilled Pacific swordfish on a warm cabbage, watercress, and citrus salad. Save room for the warm roasted pear fritters with ginger and vanilla cream, or chocolate graham pound cake with cocoa hazelnuts and cinnamon ice cream. Wine lovers will be in heaven: there are more than 250 selections—many from local vineyards—to choose from. *$$$; AE, MC, V; no checks; dinner Tues–Sun; beer and wine; reservations recommended; www.applewoodinn.com; 1 mile S of Guerneville.* ⅙

LODGINGS

Applewood Inn / ★★★★⅙

13555 HWY 116, GUERNEVILLE; 707/869-9093 OR 800/555-8509 A grand old 1922 California Mission Revival mansion, formerly the country home of a wealthy banker, is the centerpiece of this tranquil inn and restaurant (see review, above). The 19 secluded rooms and suites, each individually decorated with stylish antiques and attractive artwork, are located in three Mediterranean-style villas that surround a terraced garden courtyard and look out onto the surrounding redwoods, apple trees, and vineyards. All rooms have TVs, fresh flowers, and private baths, and many come with either a spa tub or shower-for-two. Everyone feels pampered with lush Turkish cotton towels, European down comforters, and hand-pressed linens. Room 1, decorated in soothing forest green colors and English oak, features French doors that open onto a private patio and garden; room 4 has a Louis Philippe cherry-wood sleigh bed and a sitting room framed by huge, curved bay windows. The Gate House, completed in 1999, offers three contemporary deluxe suites featuring bedside fireplaces, whirlpool baths, couples' showers, and private decks. You'll discover cozy sitting areas, some with fireplaces, throughout the inn. The Mediterranean-style garden is always beckoning. There's a large outdoor swimming pool and spa beyond the stone courtyard and bubbling lion's-head fountain. Guests welcome the day with a breakfast of eggs Florentine, French toast, or other well-prepared dishes, served in the airy Applewood Restaurant. *$$$–$$$$; AE, MC, V; no checks; inninfo@applewoodinn.com; www.applewoodinn.com; 1 mile S of Guerneville.* ⅙

Jenner

About 16 miles north of Bodega Bay on Highway 1 is what seems to be every Northern Californian's "secret" getaway spot: Jenner. Built on a bluff rising from the mouth of the Russian River, the tiny seaside town consists of little more than a gas station, three restaurants, two inns, and a deli, which means the only thing to do in town is eat, sleep, and lie on the beach—not a bad vacation plan. It is also two hours closer to the Bay Area than Mendocino, yet offers the same spectacular coastal scenery and a far better selection of beaches.

The sandbar at beautiful **GOAT ROCK BEACH** (707/875-3483), a breeding ground for **HARBOR SEALS,** becomes a major seasonal attraction during pupping season—March through May. Seals give birth on land, and orange-vested volunteers are usually around to protect the playful mammals, answer questions, and even lend binoculars for a closer look.

A serpentine 12-mile drive north of Jenner on Highway 1 takes you to the **FORT ROSS STATE HISTORIC PARK** (707/847-3286; www.parks.sonoma.net/ fortross.html), a fortress built by Russian fur traders in 1812. The fort's distinctive structures, including a stockade, a Russian Orthodox chapel, and the commandant's house, have been replicated and restored. Short history lessons are offered in the Fort Compound (11:30am, 1:30pm, and 3:30pm from Memorial Day to Labor Day, and noon and 2pm the rest of the year, but call ahead to make sure).

A great day trip from Jenner is the scenic drive along Highway 101 to **SALT POINT STATE PARK** (707/847-3221). There are 3,500 acres to explore and all kinds of things to do, including **FREE DIVING** off rocky beaches, **TIDE POOLING,** and **HIKING** through coastal woodlands. Simply pull the car over anywhere along Highway 1 and start walking. At the north end of the park on Kruse Ranch Road is the 317-acre **KRUSE RHODODENDRON PRESERVE** (707/847-3221), a forested grove of plants that grow up to 18 feet tall under a vast canopy of redwoods. Masses of vivid pink and purple flowers appear in early spring. Peak blooming time varies, but April is usually the month to see the world's tallest *Rhododendron californicum.*

RESTAURANTS

River's End / ★★☆

1104A HWY 1, JENNER; 707/865-2484 Longtime fans of this popular restaurant and former chef-owner Wolfgang Gramatzki will be glad to know that the place is still bustling. The menu, which changes monthly, is still decidedly eclectic, with entrees ranging from Indian curries to racklets of elk, coconut shrimp, pheasant breast, and locally harvested seafood. Lunch is more down to earth, with reasonably priced burgers and sandwiches. Local Sonoma meats, poultry, and organic vegetables are used whenever possible, including Sonoma microbrews and wines. Most tables have a wonderful view of the ocean, as does the small outside deck—the perfect spot for a glass of Sonoma County wine. The hours tend to vary as much as the menu, so be sure to call ahead if you're planning to dine here. *$$; MC, V; no checks; lunch, dinner Thur–Mon (Fri–Sun Nov–Apr); full bar; reservations recommended; just N of town.* &

> ## RIDING THE RIDGE
>
> North and just east of Point Reyes National Seashore is Bolinas Ridge Trail, a moderate 22-mile round-trip mountain bike ride through beautiful vistas overlooking Kent Lake and Olema Valley. With no switchbacks or difficult climbs, and sparse use on weekdays, this is a good bike ride for beginners who have the strength for the climb but lack the technical skills necessary to keep from wiping out on steep downhill grades and tricky corners. Access is from the town of Fairfax or from Shoreline Highway/Highway 1. From Broadway in Fairfax, turn left at the stop sign onto Bolinas–Fairfax Road and follow it past Alpine Dam to the intersection with West Ridgecrest Boulevard. Backtrack on Bolinas–Fairfax Road for a tenth of a mile and look for the Bolinas Ridge trailhead on the north side of the road. Or from Shoreline Highway/Highway 1, look for Bolinas–Fairfax Road on the right approximately a tenth of a mile north of Audubon Canyon Ranch. Drive up a tenth of a mile past the intersection with West Ridgecrest Boulevard and look for the trailhead. Before setting out on this adventure, however, check with the Olema Valley ranger station (415/464-5100) for updated trail condition information; both the road and trail are particularly vulnerable to inclement weather and are sometimes closed. If you need to rent a mountain bike, call David Barnett at **CYCLE ANALYSIS** (415/663-9164 or 415/663-1645; www.cyclepointreyes.com).

Sizzling Tandoor / ★

9960 HWY 1, JENNER; 707/865-0625 When the weather is warm and sunny, Sizzling Tandoor is the best place on the Sonoma coast to have lunch. This Indian restaurant is perched high above the placid Russian River, and the view, particularly from the outside patio, is fantastic. Equally great are the inexpensive lunch specials: huge portions of curries and kebabs served with vegetables, soup, pilau rice, and superb naan (Indian bread). Even if you don't have time for a meal, drop by and order some warm naan to go. *$; AE, DIS, MC, V; no checks; lunch, dinner every day; beer and wine; reservations recommended; at S end of the Russian River Bridge, S of Jenner.* &

Sea Ranch

Sea Ranch is undoubtedly one of the most beautiful seaside communities in the nation, due mostly to rigid adherence to environmentally harmonious architectural standards. Approximately 300 homes, some quite grand, are available as **VACATION RENTALS**. There are eight or nine rental companies, charging prices ranging from as low as $200 to as high as $700 for two nights—rates are generally lower on the east side of Highway 1. The **SEA RANCH LODGE AND RESTAURANT** (707/785-2371 or 800/732-7262; www.searanchlodge.com) offers the only hotel accommodations. Return visitors often sample different locations—woods, meadows, ocean bluffs. For rentals contact **SEA RANCH RENTALS** (888/732-7262; www.sea ranchvillage.com) or **RAMS HEAD REALTY** (800/785-3455; www.ramshead-realty.com). Rentals also include use of the community's three outdoor heated swimming pools, tennis courts, and recreation center. The award-winning **SEA RANCH GOLF LINKS** (located along Sea Ranch's northern boundary at the entrance to Gualala Point Regional Park; 707/785-2468), a challenging Scottish-style 18-hole course, was designed by Robert Muir Graves and is open daily to the public.

The Mendocino Coast

There are four things first-time visitors should know before heading to the Mendocino coast. First, be prepared for a long, beautiful drive; there are no quick and easy routes to this part of California, and there's no public transportation, so traveling by car is your only option. Second, make your hotel and restaurant reservations as far in advance as possible because everything involving tourism books up solid during summers and holidays. Third, bring warm clothing. A windless, sunny, 80-degree day on the Mendocino coast is about as rare as affordable real estate. Fourth and finally, bring a lot of money and your checkbook. Cheap sleeps, eats, and even banks are few and far between along this stretch of shoreline, and many places don't take credit cards (though personal checks are widely accepted).

So where exactly is the Mendocino coast? Well, it starts at the county line in the town of Gualala and ends a hundred or so miles north at the sparsely populated stretch known as the Lost Coast. The focal point is the town of Mendocino, but the main center of commerce—and the region's only McDonald's (if you can believe it)—is in Fort Bragg, 15 miles up the coast. Compared with these two towns, every other part of the Mendocino coast is relatively deserted—something to consider if you're looking to escape the masses. Spring is the best time to visit, when the wildflowers are in full bloom and the crowds are still sparse. Then again, nothing on this planet is more romantic than cuddling next to the fireplace on a winter night, listening to the rain and thunder pound against your little cottage. For more information on visiting the area, contact the **FORT BRAGG–MENDOCINO COAST CHAMBER OF COMMERCE** in Fort Bragg (332 N Main St; 800/726-2780 or 707/961-6300; www.mendocinocoast.com).

Gualala

The southernmost town in Mendocino County, Gualala also happens to have the most mispronounced name in Mendocino County. Keep the G soft and you end up with "wah-LAL-ah," the Spanish version of *walali,* which is Pomo Indian patois for "water coming down place." The water in question is the nearby Gualala River, a placid year-round playground for kayakers, canoers, and swimmers.

Once a lively logging town, Gualala has tamed considerably since the days loggers literally climbed the saloon walls with their spiked boots. Though a few real-life lumberjacks still end their day at the Gualala Hotel's saloon, the coastal town's main function these days is providing gas, groceries, and hardware for area residents. On the outskirts, however, are several excellent parks, beaches, and hiking trails; combine this with the region's glorious seascapes, and suddenly little mispronounced Gualala emerges as a serious contender among the better vacation spots on the North Coast.

One of the most enjoyable activities on the California coast is river and sea kayaking, and the **GUALALA RIVER** is ideal for beginner kayakers. **ADVENTURE RENTS** (downtown Gualala in the Cantamare Center; 707/884-4386 or 888/881-4386; www.adventurerents.com) provides the necessary gear, instruction, and transportation of the kayaks and canoes to and from the river.

Of the six public beach access points along Highway 1 between Sea Ranch and Gualala, the one that offers the most bang for the $3 parking fee is the 195-acre **GUALALA POINT REGIONAL PARK** (707/785-2377). The park has 10 miles of trails through coastal grasslands, redwood forests, and river canyons, as well as picnic sites, camping areas, and excellent bird- and whale-watching along the mostly deserted beaches.

RESTAURANTS

The Food Company / ★★☆

38411 HWY 1, GUALALA; 707/884-1800 For fine dining in Gualala, go to St. Orres. For every other kind of dining, come here. Open from 8:30am to 6:30pm Thursday through Monday, the Food Company is a cross between a deli, bakery, and cafe, serving fresh-baked breads, pastries, and sandwiches alongside an ever-changing menu of meat pies, pastas, quiches, tarts, meat loafs, stuffed bell peppers, moussaka, enchiladas, and lord knows what else. It's sort of like coming home from school for dinner—you never know what's going to be on the table, but you know it's probably going to be good. On sunny afternoons, the cafe's garden doubles as a picnic area; throw in a bottle of wine from their modest rack, and you have the makings for a romantic—and inexpensive—lunch. *$; MC, V; checks OK; breakfast, lunch, dinner Thur–Mon; beer and wine; no reservations; ½ mile N of Gualala at the corner of Hwy 1 and Robinsons Reef Rd.*

St. Orres Restaurant / ★★★

36601 HWY 1 (ST. ORRES INN), GUALALA; 707/884-3335 St. Orres Restaurant is one of Gualala's star attractions and one of the main reasons people keep coming back to this region. Situated below one of the main building's onion domes, the restaurant's constantly changing prix-fixe dinner menu focuses on North Coast cuisine, including a fair amount of wild game. Self-taught chef Rosemary Campiformio's dark and fruity sauces and sublime soups are perfectly suited to the flavorful game, resulting in a distinctly Northern California rendition of French country cuisine. It's an adventuresome menu she's put together: fresh wild salmon with zucchini cakes; grilled veal chop with garlic mashed potaotes, foie gras, and truffle Madeira sauce; rack of wild boar with Rosemary's spicy applesauce and apple pancakes. St. Orres's wine cellar stores a sizable selection of rich California reds that are well-suited for such hearty entrees. *$$$; MC, V; checks OK; breakfast (inn guests only), dinner every day (call ahead in winter); beer and wine; reservations recommended; dine@saintorres.com; www.saintorres.com; 2 miles N of Gualala on the E side of Hwy 1.* &

LODGINGS

The Old Milano / ★★★

38300 HWY 1, GUALALA; 707/884-3256 Overlooking the rugged coastline above Castle Rock Cove are five ultra-romantic, Victorian-rich cottages and a kick-ass caboose situated throughout a 3-acre estate brimming with flower gardens and the soothing sounds of crashing waves. Each cottage is decked out with queen-size canopied European featherbeds, private baths, and original antique furnishings; some come with elevated spas and stained-glass windows. We adore the secluded Vine Cottage with its sleeping alcove and reading loft, but our favorite is the Caboose, a genuine railroad caboose converted into the coolest and coziest lodging on the coast. Inside you'll find a wood-burning stove and two upstairs brakeman's seats for enjoying the sunsets. Breakfast is delivered to your cottage each morning and is included in the rate. The clincher is the sprawling bluff-top lawn and cliff-side Jacuzzi. *$$$; MC, V; checks OK; coast@oldmilanohotel.com; www.old milanohotel.com; 1 mile N of town, just N of the Food Company.* &

St. Orres / ★★★

36601 HWY 1, GUALALA; 707/884-3303 In the early '70s, a group of young architects and builders, inspired by the Russian architecture of the early Northern California settlers, took their back-to-the-land dreams to Gualala and created this dazzling copper-domed inn from redwood timbers scrounged from old logging mills and dilapidated bridges. Located just off Highway 1 and within walking distance of a sheltered, sandy cove, St. Orres consists of 8 small, less expensive rooms with three shared baths in the main lodge (the 2 front rooms with ocean views are the best) and 13 private cottages scattered throughout the 50 acres of wooded grounds. The best cottage is the ultra-rustic Wild Flower Cabin, a former logging-crew shelter furnished with a cozy sleeping loft, a wood-burning stove (topped with cast-iron skillets), an adorable outside shower over-looking the woods, and even a gaggle of wild turkeys waiting for handouts at your doorstep. Another top choice is the gorgeous Sequoia Cottage, a solid-timbered charmer tucked into the edge of the forest. Then again, all the cottages are pretty darn romantic. All guests start the day with a complimentary full breakfast (delivered to the cottages in baskets); spend the rest of the day lolling around the nearby beaches, then have dinner at St. Orres's superb restaurant (see review, above). Reserve a table for dinner (cost not included in room rate) when you make your room reservation; the restaurant is almost always booked. *$$$–$$$$; MC, V; checks OK; stay@saintorres.com; www.saintorres.com; 2 miles N of Gualala on the E side of Hwy 1.* &

Point Arena

Fifteen miles north of Gualala is one of the smallest incorporated cities in California, Point Arena. This former bustling shipping port now has a population of 400; many residents are transplants from larger cities, and some have set up shop along the three-block **MAIN STREET**.

The **POINT ARENA LIGHTHOUSE** (707/882-2777; www.mcn.org/1/palight) is the biggest attraction in the area. Built in 1870 after 10 ships ran aground here on a single stormy night, the fully operational lighthouse had to be rebuilt after the 1906 earthquake. But now it's solid enough for visitors to trudge up the six-story tower's 145 steps for a standout view of the coast—*if* the fog has lifted. A look through the dazzling 6-foot-wide, lead-crystal lens is worth the hike alone. The lighthouse is open 10am to 4:30pm April–September and 10am to 3:30pm October–March. You'll find it at the end of scenic Lighthouse Road, about 5 miles northwest of downtown Point Arena off Highway 1. The parking/tour/museum fee is about $5.

Virtually isolated is the 5-mile sweep of shore, dunes, and meadows of **MANCHESTER STATE BEACH** (707/882-2463). Though several access roads off Highway 1 lead to the shore, the closest one to Point Arena also happens to be the best—the 15-minute walk across the dunes from the parking lot is a leg-burner, but it's a small price to pay for your own private beach. Take the Stoneboro Road exit west off Highway 1; the beach is 2 miles north of the turnoff to Point Arena Lighthouse.

Elk

Once known as Greenwood, this tiny former logging town was renamed Elk by the postal service when someone realized there was another town in California called Greenwood. For such a small community (population 250), it sure has a booming tourist trade: six inns, four restaurants, and one authentic Irish pub. Its close proximity to the big tourist town of Mendocino, a mere 30-minute drive up the coast, is one reason for its popularity. Elk's paramount appeal, however, is its dramatic shoreline; the series of immense sea stacks here creates one of the most awesome seascapes on the California coast.

RESTAURANTS

The Harbor House Restaurant / ★★★

5600 S HWY 1 (HARBOR HOUSE INN), ELK; 707/877-3203 OR 800/720-7474 The four-course prix-fixe dinners served at the Harbor House Restaurant change nightly, but they always begin with a small, hot-from-the-oven loaf of bread that's perfect for sopping up the chef's delicious soups, such as the tomato-basil or Indian spice-spinach. The salad, made from homegrown vegetables, might be a combination of greens tossed with an herb vinaigrette or sprouts mixed with olives, water chestnuts, and a toasted sesame-seed dressing. The seafood is harvested from local waters, and the meats and cheeses come from nearby farms. Expect to find entrees such as ravioli stuffed with crab, fennel, and shiitakes in a Pernod cream sauce, or seared sea scallops on roasted-yellow-pepper rouille with Spanish basmati rice pilaf. Many of the fine wines offered are locally produced. To take full advantage of the restaurant's spectacular view, beg for a window table (alas, you can't reserve a particular table). The only seating (which is very limited when the inn is full) is at 7pm. *$$$$; AE, MC, V; checks OK; dinner every day; beer and wine; reservations required; www.theharborhouseinn.com; in the Harbor House Inn, at the N end of Elk.*

LODGINGS

Greenwood Pier Inn / ★★★

5928 HWY 1, ELK; 707/877-9997 What separates this cliff-top wonder from the dozens of other precariously perched inns along Highway 1 are its rooms' fantastic interiors and the brilliant flower gardens gracing the property. The inn offers 14 guest rooms, including 3 detached cliff-hanging suites (Cliffhouse and the two Sea Castles) and the separate Garden Cottage. All the units have private decks with stunning views of Greenwood Cove, and all guests have access to a hot tub on the cliff's edge. The whimsical avant-garde decor and tile and marble detailing in most rooms are the work of artist Kendrick Petty, who owns and operates this quartet of cafe, country store, garden shop, and seaside inn. Some units also feature Petty's colorful airbrush collages, and all the rooms have private baths, fireplaces or wood-burning stoves, ocean views, private decks, and CD players. The elegantly rustic Cliffhouse is a favorite, with its expansive deck, marble fireplace, whirlpool tub, and Oriental carpets. While the suites and Sea Castles are rather expensive, the rooms in the main house are moderately priced. Room rates include a continental breakfast delivered to your doorstep, and you can even have a cafe dinner brought to your room. In-room therapeutic massage and herbal facial massage are available as well. *$$$–$$$$; AE, MC, V; local checks only; gwpier@mcn.org; www.green woodpierinn.com; center of town.* &

The Harbor House Inn / ★★★

5600 S HWY 1, ELK; 707/877-3203 OR 800/720-7474 Constructed in 1916 in the classic Craftsman style, the majestic redwood-sided, two-story Harbor House was originally an executive lodge for Goodyear Redwood Lumber Co. executives. There are six regally appointed rooms in the main house, all with classic and antique furnishings, fireplaces, decks, and private baths throughout. The names of the rooms, such as Cypress, Harbor, and Lookout, reflect the inn's soothing natural setting. And should you want a cottage nestled among the 3 acres of redwoods, there are four to choose from, intimate and tastefully appointed. Down comforters, featherbeds, luxurious robes, and CD players come with each of the 10 rooms. Fine dining is a tradition at the Harbor House Inn; a full breakfast and four-course dinner for two are included in the rates (see review, above). *$$$$; MC, V; checks OK; innkeeper@theharborhouseinn.com; www.theharborhouseinn.com; N end of Elk.*

Albion

A renowned haven for pot growers until an increase in police surveillance and property taxes drove most of them away, Albion is more a free-spirited ideal community than an actual town. A white wooden bridge, the last of its kind on Highway 1, marks the entrance to town.

THE SECRETS OF MENDOCINO

LITTLE RIVER'S SECRET SINKHOLE: Known by locals as the Little River Cemetery Sinkhole, this almost perfectly circular sinkhole is simply amazing. At low tide you can walk through the wave-cut tunnel to the tide pools at the bottom of the bluff; at high tide, you can sit on the tiny sandy beach and look at the tunnel as the waves blast through. Either way, the feeling of being within this natural phenomenon is borderline sacred. To get here, park across from the Little River Cemetery on Highway 1, walk to the southwest corner of the cemetery, and look for a small opening in the chain-link fence. The sinkhole is only a few dozen yards down the trail, but be prepared to enter and exit the hole on all fours or you might end up buried alongside it.

MENDOCINO'S SECRET BEACH: There couldn't possibly be a cuter, more secluded little beach on the California coast than this one. Naturally, there are no signs pointing the way and it requires a little effort to get there, but my-oh-my is it worth the walk. First you need to find the Pine Beach Inn along Highway 1 between Fort Bragg and Mendocino. Take the Ocean Drive exit next to the hotel's giant sign, park in the small dirt parking lot near the tennis courts, walk toward the ocean, and you'll see the trailhead leading into a small forest. A five-minute walk through scrub pines and

RESTAURANTS

Albion River Inn Restaurant / ★★

3790 HWY 1, ALBION; 707/937-1919 OR 800/479-7944 Chef Stephen Smith has presided over the Albion Inn's ocean-view dining room for nearly a decade, and contented diners keep coming back for more of his consistently good coastal cuisine. Fresh local produce complements such dishes as braised Sonoma rabbit, grilled sea bass, fennel-crusted ahi tuna, oven-roasted quail, and rock shrimp pasta. The extensive, award-winning wine list—more than 500 choices—includes hard-to-find North Coast labels. Arrive before nightfall to ooh and aah over the view. *$$$; AE, DIS, MC, V; checks OK; dinner every day; beer and wine; reservations recommended; www.albionriverinn.com; on the NW side of the Albion bridge.* &

The Ledford House Restaurant / ★★★

3000 HWY 1, ALBION; 707/937-0282 It's rare when an ocean-view restaurant's food is as good as the view, but owners Lisa and Tony Geer manage to pull it off, serving Provençal-style cuisine in a wonderfully romantic cliff-top setting. One part of chef Lisa's menu is reserved primarily for hearty bone-warming bistro dishes such as Antoine's Cassoulet (lamb, pork, garlic sausage, and duck confit slowly cooked with white beans), potato gnocchi with a rosemary Gorgonzola cream sauce, and fresh fish stew in a white wine, tomato, fennel, and saffron broth. The other half is dedicated to the classics: rack of lamb, Pacific salmon, roast duckling, and New York steak. Vegetarian entrees and soups are always featured as well. With a view like meadows rewards you with a billion-dollar view of the coast. At the bluff's edge, head south toward the green-roofed house, and you'll come to a small creek that provides easy access to the beach.

THE SECRET GORDON: Here's a little-known walk for people who love to sit alone for hours and watch the waves pound against stone. About a mile south of Mendocino along Highway 1, look for the Gordon Lane turnoff heading inland. Park on the raised dirt shoulder across from the Gordon Lane turnoff and look for a small opening in the barbed-wire fence. The unmarked half-mile trail through Chapman Point's meadows ends at an enormous rocky outcropping with a letter-box view of Mendocino far across the bay.

THE SECRET SUNSHINE: When the fog refuses to lift for days—even weeks—at a time during Mendocino summers, locals are sure to be found a few miles inland at the perpetually sunny "3.66 Beach" on the Navarro River. The small golden-sand beach fronts a placid pool of cool green river water that's ideal for swimming. To get here, head south from Mendocino on Highway 1, turn inland at the Highway 128 junction, and look for the 3.66 mile marker. Park along the road and take the short, well-worn path down to the beach.

this, a window table at sunset is a must. After dinner, sidle up to the bar and listen to the live music, featured nightly. *$$$; AE, MC, V; checks OK; dinner Wed–Sun (closed 3 weeks in Feb); full bar; reservations recommended; ledford@ledfordhouse.com; www.ledfordhouse.com; exit W off Hwy 1 at Spring Grove Rd.* &

LODGINGS

Albion River Inn / ★★★

3790 HWY 1, ALBION; 707/937-1919 OR 800/479-7944 This seaside inn, poised 90 feet above Albion Cove where the Albion River meets the sea, is one of the finest on the California coast—the kind of place where guests return again and again. Under the same ownership for more than 20 years, each of the 22 individually decorated New England–style cottages—situated right along the bluff—feature distinctive antique and contemporary furnishings, king- or queen-size beds, fireplaces, and lots of potted plants. Additional perks for each room include binoculars for wildlife viewing, robes, a bottle of wine, fresh ground coffee, a refrigerator, the daily newspaper, and private decks with cozy wooden Adirondack-style lounging chairs. If you really want to impress your partner, reserve one of the rooms with a spa tub for two set right next to a large picture window with postcard views of the coast. A full country breakfast, served in the restaurant (see review, above), is included in the rates. *$$$–$$$$; AE, DIS, MC, V; checks OK; innkeepers@albionriverinn.com; www.albionriverinn.com; on the NW side of the Albion bridge.* &

Little River

Once a bustling logging and shipbuilding community, Little River is now more like a suburb of Mendocino. The town does a brisk business handling the tourist overflow from its neighbor 2 miles up the coast; vacationers in the know reserve a room in serene Little River and make forays into Mendocino only for dining and shopping.

The town is near **VAN DAMME STATE PARK** (707/937-5804), a 2,337-acre preserve blanketed with ferns and second-growth redwoods. One of the finest state parks on the Mendocino coast, it has a small beach, visitor center, and campground, but its main attraction is the 15 miles of spectacularly lush trails—ideal for a stroll or a jog—that start at the beach and wind through the redwood-covered hills. **FERN CANYON TRAIL** is the park's most popular, an easy and incredibly scenic 2½-mile hiking and bicycling path that crosses over the Little River. You can also hike or drive (most of the way) to Van Damme's peculiar **PYGMY FOREST**, an eerie scrub forest of waist-high stunted trees. To reach the Pygmy Forest by car, follow Highway 1 south of the park and turn up Little River Airport Road, then head uphill 2¾ miles.

LODGINGS

Glendeven Inn / ★★★

8221 HWY 1, LITTLE RIVER; 707/937-0083 OR 800/822-4536 The Glendeven Inn was named one of the 10 best inns in America by *Country Inns* magazine, and rightly so. This stately 1867 farmhouse resides among 2½ acres of well-tended gardens and heather-covered headlands that extend all the way to the blue Pacific. The 10 spacious rooms and suites feature an uncluttered mix of country antiques and contemporary art. Most have ocean views, fireplaces, and porches, and all have wireless Internet access. For the ultimate in luxury, stay in the Pinewood or Bayloft Suites in the Stevenscroft Annex—each has a sitting parlor, a fireplace, and a partial ocean view. The cozy East Farmington Room, with its private garden deck and fireplace, is another good choice. Above the Glendeven Gallery, the inn's fine-arts boutique, sits the fabulous Carriage House Suite, a two-story, redwood-paneled house ideal for families or two couples. The La Bella Vista vacation rental house is also a great choice for familes: it has two bedrooms, two bathrooms, a kitchen, a gas barbecue grill, and a Jacuzzi. After a gourmet hot country breakfast in bed—brought to your room in a basket—walk to the beautiful fern-rimmed canyon trails in nearby Van Damme State Park. *$$$–$$$$; AE, DIS, MC, V; checks OK; innkeeper@glendeven.com; www. glendeven.com; 2 miles S of Mendocino.*

Heritage House Inn & Restaurant / ★★★

5200 HWY 1, LITTLE RIVER; 707/937-5885 OR 800/235-5885 Immortalized as the ultimate bed-and-breakfast lodge in the movie *Same Time, Next Year*, the Heritage House estate has a history well suited to Hollywood melodrama: its secluded farmhouse was used as a safe house for smugglers of Chinese laborers during the 19th century, for rumrunners during Prohibition, and for the notorious bandit "Baby Face" Nelson during the '30s. Since 1949, however, the hotel has catered to a considerably tamer crowd. The country club–style estate is situated on a bluff overlooking a rocky cove and is surrounded by 37 acres of cypress trees, bountiful flower and vegetable gardens, and expansive green lawns. Lodging consists of three guest rooms in the ivy-covered New England–style main building; the rest of the accommodations are in cottages grouped two to four under one common roof. All rooms are individually decorated with original antiques and locally made furnishings; amenities include bathrobes, umbrellas, and newspaper delivery. Most have wood-burning fireplaces or stoves, private decks, sitting areas, and ocean views; several of the suites come with wet bars and Jacuzzis. The best units are the cliff-hanging cottages such as Same Time and Next Year with their king-size beds and extraordinary ocean views. The Heritage House Restaurant offers high-quality cuisine served in several dining rooms, with alfresco seating on sunny days. The menu, which changes seasonally, may include such selections as braised lamb shank with Basque white beans, pan-roasted pork chops, grilled salmon, and roast Peking duck breast. The extensive wine list ranks among the highest-rated in the country. *$$$–$$$$; AE, MC, V; checks OK; info@heritagehouseinn.com; www.heritage houseinn.com; just S of Van Damme State Park.* &

The Inn at Schoolhouse Creek / ★★

7051 N HWY 1, LITTLE RIVER; 707/937-5525 OR 800/731-5525 Whereas most small inns located along the Mendocino coast have to make do with an acre or less, the Inn at Schoolhouse Creek has the luxury of spreading its cadre of adorable cottages amid 8 acres of beautiful flower gardens, lush meadows, and cypress groves. Most of the cottages are designed for couples, though a few can comfortably fit kids in as well; our favorite is the secluded Cypress Cottage, with its private yard graced by an inviting pair of Adirondack chairs. All are luxuriously loaded with fireplaces, TVs with VCRs, CD players, phones, private baths, private entrances, and decks or adjoining garden seating areas. Rates include a bountiful buffet breakfast and evening wine and hors d'oeuvres, served on the front porch of the inn's 1862 Ledford Farmhouse. Perhaps the best indulgence, however, is the inn's hot tub, perched at the top of a meadow overlooking the ocean. *$$$; MC, V; checks OK; innkeeper@schoolhousecreek.com; www.innatschoolhousecreek.com; just S of Little River.* &

Little River Inn & Restaurant / ★★

7750 HWY 1, LITTLE RIVER; 707/937-5942 OR 888/466-5683 Set on a 225-acre parcel of oceanfront land, the Little River Inn is an ideal retreat for those North Coast travelers who simply can't leave their golf clubs or tennis rackets at home. The family-owned and -operated resort is often jokingly referred to as the poor man's Pebble Beach, complete with a nine-hole golf course, driving range, putting green, full-service salon and day spa, restaurant, and two lighted tennis courts. All the estate's 65 rooms and cottages offer ocean views, many feature fireplaces, and some also have whirlpool tubs (if you prefer to relax indoors, check out the inn's extensive video library). The antique-filled rooms in the main Victorian house are preferable to the north wing's motel-style units, which suffer from uninspired decor. The Little River Inn Restaurant is a casual place for breakfast, dinner, and weekend brunch. Dishes are made from mostly local products: fresh fish from nearby Noyo

Harbor; lamb, beef, and potatoes from the town of Comptche; and greens and vegetables from local gardens. For breakfast try the popular Ole's Swedish Hotcakes. *$$–$$$$; AE, MC, V; checks OK; info@littleriverinn.com; www.littleriverinn.com; across from the Little River Market and Post Office.* &

Rachel's Inn / ★★★

8200 N HWY 1, LITTLE RIVER; 707/937-0088 OR 800/347-9252 Strategically situated between Van Damme State Park and the Mendocino headlands is Rachel Binah's 1860s Victorian farmhouse and barn, one of the finest bed-and-breakfasts on the Mendocino coast. Each of the nine beautifully decorated rooms and suites has a queen or king bed with a fluffy comforter and a private bath; many of the rooms also have fireplaces. Gardeners will especially appreciate the Blue Room, complete with a balcony overlooking the back garden, meadow, and trees. The Parkside Cottage, nestled in a stand of cypress trees, comes with a private back porch, wet bar with coffeemaker and refrigerator, whirlpool bathtub, gas fireplace, and window seat. Families or honeymooners should ask about Rachel's Little River Cottage, an adorable Victorian home built more than 150 years ago. The inn's main attraction, however, is Rachel, a vivacious innkeeper who spends her time campaigning to protect our nation's coastline from offshore oil drilling when she's not busy welcoming guests or preparing one of her grand breakfasts. *$$$$; MC, V; checks OK; innkeeper@rachelsinn.com; www.rachelsinn.com; 1½ miles S of Mendocino.* &

Stevenswood Lodge / ★★★

8211 HWY 1, LITTLE RIVER; 707/937-2810 OR 800/421-2810 Stevenswood Lodge is for people who want the comforts of a modern hotel—cable television, telephone, refrigerator, honor bar—without feeling like they're staying at a Holiday Inn. As it works out, not many Holiday Inns are surrounded on three sides by a verdant 2,400-acre forest, or located just a quarter of a mile from the Mendocino shoreline, or embellished with sculpture gardens and contemporary art displays throughout the grounds. Built in 1988, the lodge's rooms and suites are outfitted with handcrafted burl-maple furniture, large windows with striking vistas (some with a partial ocean view), private bathrooms, wood-burning fireplaces, and access to several shared decks. The lodge also has two spas set within the forest canyon, as well as a restaurant offering upscale coastal cuisine. Rates include a full breakfast. *$$$–$$$$; AE, DC, DIS, MC, V; checks OK; info@stevenswood.com; www.stevenswood.com; 2 miles S of Mendocino.* &

Mendocino

The grande dame of Northern California's coastal tourist towns, this refurbished replica of a New England–style fishing village—complete with a white-spired church—has managed to retain more of its charm and allure than most North Coast vacation spots. Motels, fast-food chains, and anything hinting of development are strictly forbidden here (even the town's only automated teller is subtly recessed into the historic Masonic Building), resulting in the almost-passable illusion that Mendocino is just another quaint little coastal community. Try to find a parking space on a summer weekend, however, and the illusion quickly fades; even the four-hour drive fails to deter hordes of Bay Area residents.

Founded in 1852, Mendocino is still home to a few anglers and loggers, although writers, artists, actors, and other urban transplants now far outnumber the natives. Spring is the best time to visit, when parking spaces are plentiful and the climbing tea roses and wisteria are in full bloom. Start with a casual tour of the town, and end with a stroll around Mendocino's celebrated headlands. Suddenly the long drive and inflated room rates seem a trivial price to pay for visiting one of the most beautiful places on earth.

To tour Mendocino proper, lose the car and head out on foot to the **TOTE FÊTE BAKERY** (10450 Lansing St; 707/937-3383). Fuel up with a double cappuccino and cinnamon bun, then throw away your map of the town and start walking—the **SHOPPING DISTRICT** of Mendocino is so small it can be covered in less than an hour, so why bother planning your attack? One must-see shop is the **GALLERY BOOKSHOP & BOOKWINKLE'S CHILDREN'S BOOKS** (45098 Main St; 707/937-BOOK; www.gallerybooks.com), one of the best independent bookstores in Northern California, with a wonderful selection of books for kids, cooks, and local-history buffs. Another is **MENDOCINO JAMS & PRESERVES** (440 Main St; 707/937-1037 or 800/708-1196; www.mendojams.com), a town landmark that offers free tastings—à la bread chips—of its luscious marmalades, dessert toppings, mustards, chutneys, and other spreads.

As with many towns that hug the Northern California coast, Mendocino's premier attractions are provided by Mother Nature and the Department of Parks and Recreation, which means they're free (or nearly free). **MENDOCINO HEADLANDS STATE PARK,** the grassy stretch of land between the village of Mendocino and the ocean, is one of the town's most popular sites. The park's flat, 3-mile trail winds along the edge of a heather-covered bluff, providing spectacular sunset views and good lookout points for spotting seabirds and California gray whales. The headlands' main access point is at the west end of Main Street—or skip the footwork altogether and take the scenic motorist's route along Heeser Drive off Lansing Street. **MENDOCINO STATE PARK VISITOR CENTER** is located at Ford House (735 Main St; 707/937-5397).

About 2 miles north of Mendocino, off Highway 1, is the worst-kept secret on the coast: **RUSSIAN GULCH STATE PARK** (707/937-5804), a veritable paradise for campers, hikers, and abalone divers. After paying a small entry fee, pick up a trail map at the park entrance and find the path to **DEVIL'S PUNCH BOWL**—a 200-foot-long, sea-carved tunnel that has partially collapsed in the center, creating an immense blowhole that's particularly spectacular during a storm. Even better is the 5½-mile round-trip hike along **FALLS LOOP TRAIL** to the **RUSSIAN GULCH FALLS**, a misty 35-foot waterfall secluded in the deep old-growth forest.

If you have a passion for plants and flowers, spend a few bucks on the admission fee to the **MENDOCINO COAST BOTANICAL GARDENS** (18220 Hwy 1; 707/964-4352; www.gardenbythesea.org), located 2 miles south of Fort Bragg. The nonprofit gardens feature 47 acres of plants—ranging from azaleas and rhododendrons to dwarf conifers and ferns—as well as a picnic area, retail nursery, and gift store.

The black sheep of Mendocino's hiking trails is **JUG HANDLE STATE RESERVE'S ECOLOGICAL STAIRCASE TRAIL** (707/937-5804). This 5-mile round-trip trail is a wonderful hike and gets surprisingly little traffic. The attraction is a series of naturally formed, staircase-like bluffs—each about 100 feet higher and 100,000 years older than the one below it—that differ dramatically in ecological formation: from beaches to headlands to an amazing pygmy forest filled with waist-high, century-old trees. The trail entrance is located on Highway 1, 1½ miles north of the town of Caspar, between Mendocino and Fort Bragg.

After a full day of adventuring, why not top off the evening with a little nightcap and music? If you appreciate classical tunes and warm snifters of brandy, take a stroll down Mendocino's Main Street to the elegant bar and lounge at the **MENDOCINO HOTEL AND RESTAURANT** (see review, below). If blue jeans and baseball caps are more your style, hang out with the guys at **DICK'S PLACE** (45080 Main St; 707/937-5643), which has the cheapest drinks in town and the sort of jukebox 'n' jiggers atmosphere you'd expect from this former logging town's oldest bar. For a rowdy night of dancing and drinking, head a few miles up Highway 1 to **CASPAR INN** (Caspar Rd exit off Hwy 1, ¼ mile N of Mendocino and 4 miles S of Fort Bragg; 707/964-5565; www.casparinn.com), the last true roadhouse in California, where everything from rock and jazz to reggae and blues is played live Thursday through Saturday nights starting at 9:30pm (check their Web site calendar for upcoming shows).

RESTAURANTS

Cafe Beaujolais / ★★★

961 UKIAH ST, MENDOCINO; 707/937-5614 Cafe Beaujolais started out as the finest little breakfast and lunch place in Mendocino. Then, over the years, renowned chef Margaret Fox (author of two best-selling cookbooks, *Cafe Beaujolais* and *Morning Food*) and her husband, Chris Kump, managed to turn this modest 1893 Victorian farmhouse into one of the most celebrated restaurants in Northern California. Over time the cafe has lost much of its illustrious status, but the tradition of featuring locally grown organic produce, meat from humanely raised animals, and fresh, locally caught seafood continues. Carnival-glass chandeliers, oak floors, and heavy oak tables adorned with flowers add to the intimate country atmosphere. The menu changes weekly and usually lists about five main courses. A typical dinner may start with a warm free-range duck confit salad in raspberry vinaigrette, with fresh raspberries and toasted walnuts on mixed greens, followed by fresh Alaskan halibut, pan roasted with fresh chanterelles, local sweet peppers, and red onions, served with sautéed chard and oven-roasted eggplant, or perhaps, the Washington sturgeon fillet, pan roasted with truffle emulsion sauce and served with house-made tagliatelle, wild mushrooms, beets, and snap peas. For dessert it's a no-brainer: choose the lemon-glazed persimmon cake with vanilla-bean *panna cotta* and red currant sauce. Try to avoid sitting in the bustling bench section, which has itsy-bitsy tables; rather, opt for the enclosed atrium overlooking the garden. For a take-home treat, Cafe Beaujolais's renowned "brickery breads" are sold daily from 11am to around 5pm at their bakery on Ukiah Street, just east of the restaurant. Note: The restaurant usually closes for a winter break during most of December and January. *$$$$; AE, DIS, MC, V; checks OK; dinner every day; beer and wine; reservations recommended; www.cafebeaujolais.com; at Evergreen St.* ᵭ

MacCallum House Restaurant / ★★★

45020 ALBION ST, MENDOCINO; 707/937-5763 Using the freshest ingredients—seafood straight from the coast and organic meats and produce from neighboring farms and ranches—chef-owner Alan Kantor, a graduate of the Culinary Institute of America, whips up some wonderful North Coast cuisine. Situated within an 1882 Victorian mansion and warmed by a crackling fire in the stone fireplace, this intimate restaurant is the ideal setting for Kantor's sophisticated North Coast cuisine. Entrees on the seasonally changing menu may range from roasted Pacific salmon with saffron-pistachio risotto and arugula pesto to pan-seared Sonoma duck breast with huckleberry-honey vinegar sauce and grilled Niman Ranch pork chops with walnut bread pudding and pear chutney. After dinner stroll over to the Grey Whale bar for a martini. *$$$; MC, V; no checks; dinner every day; full bar; reservations recommended; macmendo@mcn.org; www.maccallumhousedining.com; between Kasten and Lansing Sts.* ᵭ

The Moosse Cafe / ★★☆

390 KASTEN ST, MENDOCINO; 707/937-4323 One of the most popular restaurants in Mendocino is this petite cafe set in a New England–style home. The rather unorthodox modern interior is due partly to a 1995 fire—after burning to the ground, the entire place had to be rebuilt and redecorated. The menu changes seasonally and often includes locally grown herbs and vegetables. A popular combo is the superb Caesar salad and Rocky Range roast chicken with garlic mashed potatoes. Seafood specials range from crab cakes served over basmati rice with a roasted red pepper rémoulade to fresh grilled swordfish. The lavender-smoked double-thick pork chop served with roasted yam and apple purée is also quite good. Save room for the decadent house-made desserts. *$$$; MC, V; checks OK; lunch, dinner every day; beer and wine; reservations recommended; www.theblueheron.com; at the corner of Kasten and Albion Sts.* ᵭ

955 Ukiah Street Restaurant / ★★★

955 UKIAH ST, MENDOCINO; 707/937-1955 This relatively unknown Mendocino restaurant is described by local epicureans as "the sleeper restaurant on the coast." Shortly after this building's construction in the 1960s, the region's most famous painter, Emmy Lou Packard, commandeered its premises as an art studio for the creation of a series of giant murals. The dramatic interior, with its split-level dining room, massive wood beams, 20-foot ceilings, rustic wood-trimmed walls, and elegant table settings create the proper mood for the North Coast cuisine, which might include seared pork loin stuffed with prosciutto, crispy duck served with ginger-apple brandy sauce, and a thick swordfish steak resting in a red chile–tomatillo sauce. The upstairs section can get cramped and a little noisy, so try to sit downstairs—preferably at the corner window table—where the vaulted ceiling imparts a

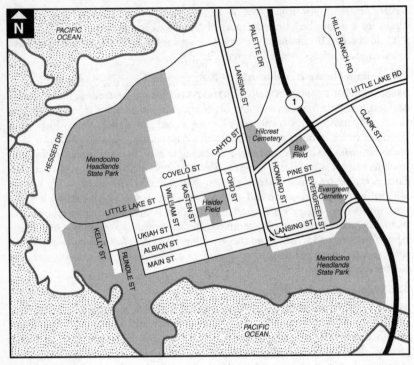

MENDOCINO

comfortable sense of space. *$$$; MC, V; checks OK; dinner Wed–Sun; beer and wine; reservations recommended; Ukiah and Evergreen Sts, E end of town.* &

The Raven's Restaurant / ★★

HWY I AND COMPTCHE-UKIAH RD (THE STANFORD INN BY THE SEA), MENDOCINO; 707/937-5615 OR 800/331-8884 To complement their environmentally friendly lodge (see review, below), Joan and Jeff Stanford have taken a huge gamble and opened the region's only fine-dining vegetarian/vegan restaurant. The menu varies monthly to take advantage of seasonal organic produce, some of which derives from the lodge's own gardens. Dishes range from lighter fare—herbed Asiago polenta cakes sautéed in a roasted garlic–chardonnay sauce with local organic shiitake mushrooms (fantastic)—to hearty entrees such as tarragon roasted acorn squash filled with wild rice, shiitake mushrooms, roasted garlic, and caramelized apples. These are masterfully crafted dishes that explode the myth that it takes meat to make a meal. Though the dining room exudes a rustic elegance, dining attire is anything but formal. *$$; AE, DC, DIS, MC, V; checks OK; breakfast Mon–Sat, dinner every day, brunch Sun; full bar; reservations recommended; 1 mile S of Mendocino.*

LODGINGS

Agate Cove Inn / ★★★

11201 N LANSING ST, MENDOCINO; 707/937-0551 OR 800/527-3111 If there's a more beautiful coastal setting than the one at Agate Cove Inn, we've yet to discover it. The view from the inn's front lawn is so stunningly pretty— a sweeping vista of the sea and its surging waves crashing onto the rocky bluffs— you can't help but stare in silence as you sit on the inn's weathered wooden bench under the cypress tree. This well-run inn consists of a main house trimmed in blue and white surrounded by several single and duplex cottages; it offers seclusion, privacy, and views that in-town B&Bs just can't match. All cottages have light pine furnishings, a "casual country" decor, king- or queen-size featherbeds with Scandia Down comforters, CD players, TVs with VCRs (and a free video and CD library), and private decks, and all but one room have ocean views and a fireplace. In the morning on your doorstep you'll find the *San Francisco Chronicle,* which you can peruse at your leisure over a bountiful country breakfast in the main house's enclosed porch. *$$$$; AE, MC, V; checks OK; info@agatecove.com; www.agatecove.com; ½ mile N of downtown.*

John Dougherty House / ★★★

571 UKIAH ST, MENDOCINO; 707/937-5266 OR 800/486-2104 This classic saltbox is a wonderful example of why so many movies supposedly set in New England (*The Russians Are Coming, Summer of '42*) are actually filmed in Mendocino. The John Dougherty House features authentic Early Americana throughout: stenciled walls, Early American furniture, and all-cotton linens on the beds. Innkeepers Marion and David Wells have given each of the eight rooms touches of individual charm, but your first choice should be either the Osprey Room or the Raven Room, which feature beautiful ocean views, jet tubs for two, fire stoves, and king-size four-poster beds. Another favorite is Kit's Cabin—a cozy two-room cottage hidden in the flower garden that comes with a wood-burning stove and four-poster bed. All the rooms have private baths, wood-burning fireplaces, and queen beds; most have TVs (the Starboard and Port Cottages have new jet tubs for two as well). An expansive breakfast including homemade bread and scones is served next to a crackling fire. *$$$–$$$$; DIS, MC, V; checks OK; jdhbmw@mcn.org; www.jdhouse.com; Ukiah St just W of Kasten St.*

Joshua Grindle Inn / ★★★

44800 LITTLE LAKE RD, MENDOCINO; 707/937-4143 OR 800/GRINDLE The most authentic of Mendocino's many New England–style B&Bs, this masterpiece was built in 1879 by the town's banker, Joshua Grindle. Startlingly white against a backdrop of wind-whipped cypress trees, the two-story beauty has lovely bay windows and a wraparound front porch trimmed with gingerbread arches. There are five Early American rooms in the clapboard house (including one with a whirlpool tub and fireplace), two in the saltbox cottage, and three in an old-fashioned water tower set back in the trees. Top picks are any of the cute water-tower rooms or the Library Room with its four-poster bed, deep soaking tub, and 19th-century hand-decorated tiles encircling the wood-burning fireplace.

All of the rooms have sitting areas and private baths. The large front lawn and garden, equipped with a pair of Adirondack chairs and a redwood picnic table, is an ideal place to relax in the sun. Sherry, snacks, and tea are offered in the afternoon, while a complimentary full breakfast is served in the dining room. In addition to the inn, the proprietors also offer a two-bedroom, two-bathroom ocean-view rental home with floor-to-ceiling windows, a large kitchen, and a wood-burning fireplace. *$$$$; MC, V; no checks; stay@joshgrin.com; www.joshgrin.com; E end of Little Lake Rd.*

Mendocino Farmhouse / ★★☆

43410 COMPTCHE RD, MENDOCINO; 707/937-0241 OR 800/475-1536 Once you emerge from deep within the redwood forest surrounding Marge Kamb's secluded estate, you know you're going to be very happy here. First to greet you is Marge's friendly farm dog, Molly, followed by her can't-pet-me-enough cats, and finally the instantly likable Marge herself. All six rooms—four in the farmhouse and two in the adjacent Barn Cottage—are filled with antique furnishings and fresh flowers from the surrounding English gardens and come with private baths, queen- or king-size beds, and, if you listen carefully, echoes of the nearby ocean; all but two have fireplaces as well. Each morning in the sitting room, Marge serves up a real country breakfast, after which the dog gives free lessons in the meadow on how to loll around in the sunshine. *$$–$$$; MC, V; checks OK; innkeeper@mendocinofarm house.com; www.mendocinofarmhouse.com; off Olson Ln.*

Mendocino Hotel & Garden Suites / ★★☆

45080 MAIN ST, MENDOCINO; 707/937-0511 OR 800/548-0513 The Mendocino Hotel, built in 1878, combines modern amenities—telephones, full bathrooms, room service—with turn-of-the-century Victorian furnishings to create a romantic yesteryear setting with today's creature comforts. The hotel's 51 rooms—all decorated with quality antiques, patterned wallpapers, and old prints and photos—range from inexpensive European-style rooms with shared baths to elaborate garden suites with fireplaces, king-size beds, balconies, and parlors. The Ocean View Suites on the hotel's third floor have wonderful views of Mendocino Bay from their private balconies. Other favorites are the deluxe rooms with private baths, particularly rooms facing the sea. Breakfast and lunch are served downstairs in the verdant Garden Cafe. The hotel's intimate Victorian Dining Room serves California-style cuisine such as pan-seared ahi tuna, double-baked pork chops, and prime rib au jus. Budding sommeliers should inquire about the hotel's popular winemaker dinners. *$$–$$$$; AE, MC, V; checks OK; info@mendocinohotel.com; www.mendocino hotel.com; between Lansing and Kasten Sts.* &

The Stanford Inn by the Sea / ★★★★

HWY 1 AND COMPTCHE-UKIAH RD, MENDOCINO; 707/937-5615 OR 800/331-8884 Hats off to Joan and Jeff Stanford, the environmentally conscious couple who turned this parcel of prime coastal property and the former Big River Lodge into something more than a magnificent resort. It's a true ecosystem, a place where plants, animals, and people coexist in one of the most unforgettable lodging experiences in California. Upon entering the estate you'll see

TICK TALK

After a walk through coastal forests or meadows, it's always a good idea to check for hitchhikers on your pant legs and socks. The western black-legged tick, bearer of the dreaded Lyme disease, awaits its prey at the tips of knee-high vegetation, then burrows its head into the victim's skin.

While there are dozens of old wives' tales on how to remove a tick (from dousing it in peanut butter to "unscrewing" it counterclockwise), the only real solution is to pull it straight out—without twisting or jerking—with tweezers. Grab the tick as close to the skin as possible and gently pull. If you have to use your fingers, be sure to use a tissue; afterward, wash your hands and the bite with warm, soapy water and apply an antiseptic.

Symptoms of Lyme disease include a bull's-eye marking or other rash around the bite, often accompanied by a fever or flulike feeling anywhere from a week to months after the encounter. Since Lyme disease can be fatal, it's a good idea to call your doctor or the Infectious Diseases branch of the California Department of Health Services in Berkeley (510/540-2566) if symptoms start to occur.

several tiers of raised garden beds, where a wide variety of vegetables, herbs, spices, and edible flowers are organically grown for local grocers and restaurants. Watching your every move as you proceed up the driveway are the Stanfords' extended family of curious llamas, which, besides providing an endless source of entertainment, do their part in fertilizing the gardens. Guests may also bring along their own menagerie of critters, be they pet dogs, cats, parrots, or iguanas. Also on the grounds is a beautiful plant-filled greenhouse that encloses a grand swimming pool, sauna, and spa. And if all this doesn't provide you with enough diversions, there's also a mountain bike and canoe shop on the property. The inn's 23 rooms and 10 suites display a mixture of styles, from units with dark wood walls, deep burgundy furnishings, and four-poster beds to sun-streaked suites with pine interiors, country antiques, and sleigh beds topped with down comforters. All of the rooms feature decks with ocean views, fireplaces or Waterford stoves, TVs with VCRs, telephones, and sitting areas. The isolated, utterly romantic River Cottage sits right on the water's edge—an ideal honeymooners' hideaway. A cooked-to-order full breakfast, served in the Raven's Restaurant (see review, above), afternoon snacks, and evening wine and hors d'oeuvres are included in the price. $$$$; AE, DC, DIS, MC, V; checks OK; stanford@stanfordinn.com; www.stanfordinn.com; ½ mile S of Mendocino. &

Whitegate Inn / ★★★

499 HOWARD ST, MENDOCINO; 707/937-4892 OR 800/531-7282 During their movie shoots Julia Roberts, Mel Gibson, Bette Davis, and Angela Lansbury preferred to stay at the Whitegate Inn, one of the finest B&Bs in Mendocino. This beautifully restored 1883 Victorian mansion offers six rooms individually decorated with classic antiques, fireplaces, immaculate private baths,

European featherbeds with soft down comforters, European toiletries, TVs, and garden or ocean views. Our favorite is the Enchanted Cottage; secluded in the Victorian garden, it has a private entrance and deck, king-size bed, claw-footed tub, and shower. In the morning a full breakfast is served in the dining room. *$$$–$$$$; MC, V; checks OK; staff@whitegateinn.com; www.whitegateinn.com; corner of Howard and Ukiah Sts.*

Fort Bragg

Originally built in 1855 as a military outpost to supervise the Pomo Indian Reservation, Fort Bragg is still primarily a logging and fishing town proud of its century-old timber-and-trawler heritage.

Two popular festivals are celebrated annually: **PAUL BUNYAN DAYS** on Labor Day weekend features a big Labor Day parade and log-cutting races, and the annual **WHALE FESTIVAL,** held the third Saturday of March, includes ranger-led talks about the cetaceans, a Whale Run, and a beer and chowder tasting.

If you've visited all of Mendocino's boutiques and still haven't shrugged the shopping bug, head over to **HISTORIC DOWNTOWN** Fort Bragg. The facades of buildings have been restored to their early 1900s look; inside you'll find shops, galleries, and restaurants—all within walking distance of each other. Two dangerous places for a credit card are the **UNION LUMBER COMPANY STORE** (corner of Main and Redwood Sts) and **ANTIQUE ROW** (Franklin St between Laurel and Redwood).

One of the prettiest—and largest—public beaches on the Mendocino coast is **MACKERRICHER STATE PARK** (707/937-5804), located 3 miles north of Fort Bragg off Highway 1. The 8-mile shoreline is the perfect place to while away an afternoon, and it's free-admission to boot. The highlight of the park is the **LAGUNA POINT SEAL WATCHING STATION,** a fancy name for a small wooden deck that overlooks the harbor seals sunning themselves on the rocks below.

One of the most popular attractions in Fort Bragg is the **SKUNK TRAIN** (100 Laurel St, Fort Bragg; 800/77-SKUNK or 707/964-6371; www.skunktrain.com). The unusual name is derived from the odoriferous mix of diesel fuel and gasoline once used to power the train—you could smell it coming. Depending on which day you depart, a steam-, diesel-, or electric-engine train will take you on a scenic six- to seven-hour round-trip journey through the magnificent redwoods to the city of Willits and back again, crossing 31 bridges and trestles and cutting through two deep tunnels (half-day trips are offered daily from March 1 through the end of November). Reservations are recommended, especially in summer.

If you're passing through between December and April, be sure to watch the migrating California gray whales and humpback whales make their annual appearances along the North Coast. Although they're visible from the bluffs, you can practically meet the 40-ton cetaceans face to face by boarding one of the **WHALE-WATCHING** boats in Fort Bragg. Just south of town, Noyo Fishing Center (32440 N Harbor, Noyo; 707/964-3000; www.fortbraggfishing.com) is the best source of information on whale-watching tours and **SPORT FISHING** excursions.

RESTAURANTS

North Coast Brewing Company / ★★

444 N MAIN ST, FORT BRAGG; 707/964-3400 If Norm Peterson of *Cheers* died and went to heaven, he'd end up here, permanently hunched over the bar within easy reach of his own ever-flowing tap of the North Coast Brewing Company's Scrimshaw Pilsner (a Gold Medal winner at the Great American Beer Fest, the Super Bowl of beer tastings). To his right would be a bowl of the brewery's tangy Route 66 Chili, on his left a hearty plate of beef Romanov (made with braised sirloin tips, fresh mushrooms, and Russian Imperial Stout), and in front of his brewski would be a big platter of fresh Pacific oysters. This homey brew pub is the most happening place in town, especially at happy hour, when the bar and dark wood tables are occupied by boisterous locals. The pub is housed in a dignified, century-old redwood structure, and the beer is brewed on the premises in large copper vats displayed behind plate glass. A pale ale, wheat beer, stout, pilsner, and a seasonal brew are always available, though first-timers should opt for the inexpensive four-beer sampler—or, heck, why not indulge in the eight-beer sampler?—to learn the ropes. You'll like the menu, too, which offers above-average pub grub such as roast Cornish game hen with a raspberry-balsamic glaze or sautéed sole with lemon, wine, and capers. After your meal, browse the retail shop or take a free tour of the brewery. *$$; DIS, MC, V; checks OK; lunch, dinner every day; beer and wine; reservations not accepted; www.northcoastbrewing.com; on the corner of Pine and Main Sts.* &

Viraporn's Thai Cafe / ★☆

500 S MAIN ST, FORT BRAGG; 707/964-7931 When Viraporn Lobell opened this tiny Thai cafe in 1991, Asian-food aficionados on the North Coast breathed a communal sigh of relief. Born in northern Thailand, Viraporn attended cooking school and apprenticed in restaurants there before coming to the United States. After moving to the North Coast with her husband, Paul, she worked for a while at Mendocino's renowned Cafe Beaujolais. A master at balancing the five traditional Thai flavors of hot, bitter, tart, sweet, and salty, Viraporn works wonders with refreshing Thai classics such as spring rolls, satays, pad thai, lemongrass soup, and a

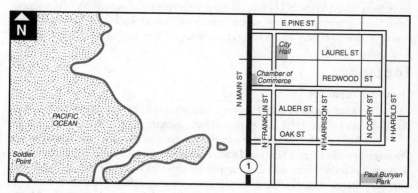

FORT BRAGG

wide range of spicy curry dishes that are best cooled down with a super-sweet Thai iced tea. *$; no credit cards; checks OK; lunch, dinner Wed–Mon; beer and wine; reservations recommended for parties of 4 or more; across from RiteAid off Hwy 1.* &

LODGINGS

Grey Whale Inn / ★★

615 N MAIN ST, FORT BRAGG; 707/964-0640 OR 800/382-7244 Wide doorways and sloped halls are the only vestiges of this popular inn's previous life as the town hospital, built in 1915. In 1978 this stately four-story redwood building was converted into one of the more comfortable and distinctive inns on the coast. Decorated with handmade quilts, heirlooms, and antiques, the 13 large guest rooms have private baths, TVs, and views of town or sea. The best guest rooms are the two penthouse rooms: Sunrise offers a view of the town, pretty wicker furniture, and a double whirlpool bath, while Sunset opens onto a private deck overlooking the ocean. Another good choice for romatically bent couples is the spacious and elegant Campbell Suite, which comes with a king bed, TV with VCR, and marble gas-log fireplace. The full buffet breakfast is served in the Craftsman-style breakfast room (with trays for carrying your food back to bed, if you prefer) and is included in the rates. There's even a game room with a pool table and foosball table. *$$$; AE, DIS, MC, V; checks OK; stay@greywhaleinn.com; www.greywhaleinn.com; corner of Main and 1st Sts.* &

Willits

RESTAURANTS

Purple Thistle / ★★☆

50 S MAIN ST, WILLITS; 707/459-4750 If you're looking for a good restaurant in the Willits area, head to the Purple Thistle, where you'll find the freshest fish around. It's a homey spot with a loyal following, good food, and friendly faces. Red snapper, prawns, chicken breast, or tofu can be served up grilled, Cajun-style, or in a tempura batter. In deference to unrepentant carnivores, however, Harris Ranch steaks have been added to the bill of fare. There are also plenty of vegetarian options made from almost entirely organic produce. *$; no credit cards; checks OK; lunch Mon–Fri, dinner every day; beer and wine; reservations recommended; on Hwy 101, near Commercial St.* &

LODGINGS

Emandal Farm / ★

16500 HEARST POST OFFICE RD, WILLITS; 707/459-5439 OR 800/262-9597 Since 1908 this thousand-acre working farm situated along the Eel River has been a popular summer getaway for Bay Area families who long for a stint on the farm. The second and third generations of the Adams family own and run Emandal Farm, and they happily let children and their parents assist with the daily chores, such as feeding the pigs, milking the goats, tending the garden, and gathering eggs in the chicken coop. The fruits of their labor are often presented hours later at meals. In addition to helping out on the farm, guests may enjoy the Adamses' private sandy beach on the river or explore trails meandering through the valley. At night a campfire circle inevitably forms, where parents struggle to remember old skits, ghost stories, and campfire songs. The 17 rustic redwood cabins are nestled under a grove of oak and fir trees. They're not equipped with much—just single and queen-size beds, cold spring water, and electricity (and that's it). The bathrooms and showers are housed in a separate, communal facility. The Adamses prepare a healthy, hearty breakfast, lunch, and dinner (two meals on Sunday), all included in the room price. Expect fare like omelets stuffed with garden-fresh vegetables, garden lasagne with homemade noodles, barbecued chicken (most likely the bird your child befriended earlier in the day), and homemade bread that's baked fresh daily. Although no alcohol is permitted at tables, guests may bring beer and wine into the cabins. The farm is usually open to guests for weeklong stays in August and for weekend trips only in September; the schedule occasionally changes, so call for an update. *$$; MC, V; checks OK; open late July–late Sept; emandal@pacific.net; www.emandal.com; 16 miles E of town (call for directions).*

Westport

If you've made it this far north, you're either lost or determined to drive the full length of Highway 1. If it's the latter, then you'd best stock up on a sandwich or two at the **WESTPORT COMMUNITY STORE & DELI** (37001 N Hwy 1; 707/964-2872) because this is the northernmost town on the Mendocino coast, and you still have a loooong way to go.

LODGINGS

DeHaven Valley Farm & Country Inn / ★★★

39247 HWY 1, WESTPORT; 707/961-1660 OR 877-DEHAVEN This remote 1875 Victorian farmhouse, with its sublime rural setting and access to a secluded beach, comes complete with a barnyard menagerie of horses, sheep, goats, and donkeys. If the animals aren't enough to keep you amused, try a game of croquet or horseshoes, do a little bird-watching or horseback riding, or take a meditative soak in the hot tub set high on a hill overlooking the ocean. The inviting parlor has deep, comfortable couches, while the six guest rooms in the house and the three nearby cottages are decorated with colorful comforters and rustic antiques; some even have fireplaces. In the morning, you'll wake to such complimentary treats as apple pancakes or potato-artichoke frittata. The small DeHaven Valley Farm Restaurant offers a commendable prix-fixe multicourse dinner menu Wednesday through Sunday that might go like this: cucumber salad, asparagus soup, freshly baked sweet French bread, entrees such as roasted pork tenderloin with apple horseradish or freshly caught salmon, and a killer apple strudel for dessert. Reservations are required. A $5 box lunch can be assembled upon request, just the thing for a picnic at the beach. *$$–$$$; AE, MC, V; checks OK; info@dehavenvalleyfarm.com; www.dehaven-valley-farm.com; 1.7 miles N of Westport.*

Howard Creek Ranch / ★★★

40501 N HWY 1, WESTPORT; 707/964-6725 Located off a remote stretch of Highway 1 near the tiny town of Westport, this isolated 40-acre ranch appeals to travelers who want to *really* get away from it all. You'll revel in the peace and quiet of this rustic retreat, which Mendocino County has designated a historic site. For more than two decades, proprietors Sally and Charles (a.k.a. Sunny) Grigg have been renting out three cabins, four guest rooms in the 1871 Farmhouse, and six rooms in the renovated 1880s Carriage Barn. Set back just a few hundred yards from an ocean beach, the farmhouse and barn are on opposite sides of Howard Creek, connected by (among other routes) a 75-foot-long swinging footbridge. The rooms in the farmhouse feature separate sitting areas, antiques, and homemade quilts, while the barn units—each one handcrafted by Charles, a master builder with a penchant for skylights—have curly-grain redwood walls and Early American collectibles. The separate Beach House, with its freestanding fireplace, skylights, king-size bed, large deck, and whirlpool tub, is a great romantic getaway. A hot tub and sauna are perched on the side of a hill, as are Sally's guardian cows, sheep, llama, and horses. In the morning, Sally rings the breakfast bell to alert her guests that it's eatin' time—and the hearty country fare is definitely worth getting out of bed for. Note: Pet dogs are welcome with prior approval. *$$$; AE, MC, V; checks OK; www.howardcreekranch.com; 3 miles N of Westport.*

REDWOOD EMPIRE

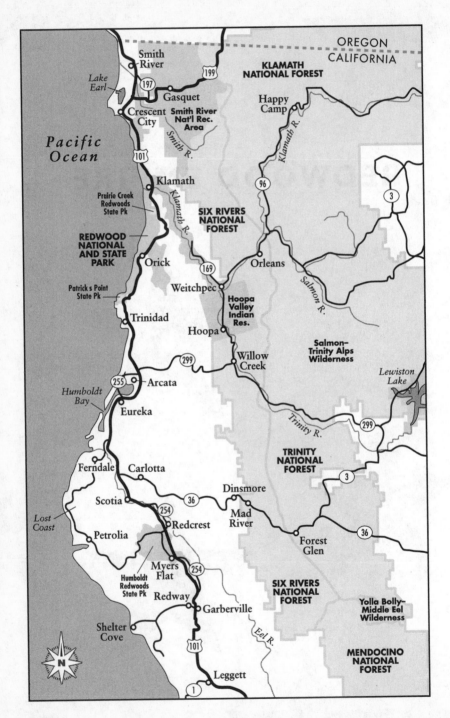

REDWOOD EMPIRE

Considering that California's Redwood Coast contains the most spectacular coastal forests in the world—including the world's tallest tree—it's surprising how few tourists care to venture north of Mendocino to get there. Perhaps it's the myth that the upper coast is permanently socked in with rain and fog, and that the only places to stay or eat are cheap motels and greasy diners.

Like most myths, of course, this isn't true (at least it's no longer true). Granted, the coastal weather can be miserable, but the fog usually burns off by the afternoon, and the rain—well, bring an umbrella; it's the price you pay for vacationing among the thirsty redwood giants. And while there are no Hyatts or Hiltons this far north, the Redwood Coast offers something even better: a wealth of small, personable inns and bed-and-breakfasts run by proprietors who bend over backward to make your stay as enjoyable as possible. The food? Combine the northern region's penchant for organic gardening with a year-round supply of just-off-the-boat seafood, and you have the ingredients for remarkably fresh and healthy gourmet cuisine.

The reason for the Redwood Coast's recent upswing in fine dining and accommodations is that an increasing number of Bay Area baby boomers are migrating northward for a little more elbow room. Among the pilgrims are a number of noted chefs and innkeepers who have pulled up their big-city stakes and relocated in small towns such as Eureka and Arcata to open their own restaurants or inns. This, combined with the region's beautiful scenery and absence of crowds, has made the Redwood Coast one of the premier—and relatively unknown—tourist destinations in California. You can camp, hike, fish, cycle, kayak, beachcomb, whale watch, and bird-watch, or just enjoy having a magnificent forest practically to yourself.

For those who can't survive without good restaurants, interesting boutiques, and a few bookstores to browse, Eureka, the largest town in northwestern California (population 27,000), has all those hallmarks of civilization in and around its picturesque Old Town. Located on historic Humboldt Bay, it also has a number of bed-and-breakfast inns that are as fine as any in far more expensive locales. Just 16 miles away, the entire village of Ferndale has been designated a State Historical Landmark for its well-preserved Victorian architecture. If your perfect bliss is the total absence of civilization, however, the romantically named Lost Coast is as remote and empty as the most confirmed misanthrope could desire. This 850-square-mile area south of Ferndale and north of Westport, with more than 75 miles of coastline, has few roads, and though several towns are shown on maps, it is almost uninhabited. Backpackers love the beaches with their pristine tide pools, abundant wildlife, remnants of legendary shipwrecks, and miles and miles of solitude.

ACCESS AND INFORMATION

US Highway 101 stretches north from Willits in northern Mendocino County to Humboldt County and Eureka on the coast, then farther north to Crescent City and into Oregon. The seldom-visited **LOST COAST** can be reached by the **MATTOLE ROAD**, which starts just north of Weott at the southern boundary of the Avenue of the Giants, runs north and west to the hamlets of Honeydew and Petrolia, and reaches the coast just south of Cape Mendocino. From there it continues north to Ferndale.

Three other roads for the adventuresome lead east over the mountains: California 36 runs from Fortuna along the Van Duzen River to Dinsmore and Mad River, ending at Interstate 5 in Red Bluff (past Mad River the going gets really rough, and the road is sometimes closed in winter); California 299 follows the Klamath and Trinity Rivers to Weaverville and Lewiston, then continues on to Interstate 5 in Redding; and California 199 parallels the Smith River (nationally designated a wild and scenic river, and California's only undammed river system) north and east to Oregon and Interstate 5 at Grants Pass. Travel tip: A popular option among families and groups is to rent a small motor home for transportation and book a series of inns and motels for sleeping; look in the phone directory under "Motor Home—Renting and Leasing" for the nearest motor home rental outfit or contact Cruise America (480/464-7300; www.cruiseamerica.com), the largest RV rental company in the nation.

The **ARCATA/EUREKA AIRPORT** in McKinleyville (11 miles N of Eureka) is served by Alaska Airlines/Horizon Air (800/252-7522; http://horizon air.alaskaair.com) and United Express (800/241-6522; www.united.com). **RENTAL CARS** are available there. **GREYHOUND BUS** (800/231-2222; www.grey hound.com) offers service along Highway 101; there are two buses each way daily for travelers from San Francisco and Oregon.

Tourism is the area's number-two revenue generator, gaining fast on timber, and information about tourist destinations is plentiful. Contact the **HUMBOLDT COUNTY CONVENTION AND VISITORS BUREAU** (1034 2nd St, Eureka; 707/443-5097 or 800/346-3482; www.redwoodvisitor.org) or the **CRESCENT CITY–DEL NORTE COUNTY CHAMBER OF COMMERCE** (1001 Front St, Crescent City; 707/464-3174 or 800/343-8300; www.northerncalifornia.net) for information.

The Lost Coast

The Lost Coast is proof that if you don't build it, they won't come. What wasn't built between Ferndale and Rockport was a coastal road: the geography of the 90-mile stretch—steep mountain ranges abutting rocky shore—wouldn't allow it. The result is the last untamed and undeveloped region of the California coast, a place where two cars following each other are considered a convoy and where more cows than people lie on the beach (seriously). Popular with campers, backpackers, and fishers, the Lost Coast is beginning to see a hint of gentrification at its only seaside town, Shelter Cove. Otherwise, the land is inhabited mainly by ranchers, retirees, and alternative lifestylers (a.k.a. hippies), the latter of which have made the Lost Coast one of the most productive pot-growing regions in the world.

The Lost Coast also makes for a fantastic day trip by car. Of the three entrance points into the region—Garberville, Humboldt Redwoods State Park, and Ferndale—the most scenic route is through the state park. From Highway 101 take the State Park turnoff and follow the Mattole Road all the way to Ferndale and back onto Highway 101. The three- to four-hour, 75-mile drive transports you through lush redwood forests, across golden meadows, and along miles of deserted beaches (well, if you don't count the cows). Be sure to fill up your gas tank, and bring a jacket if you plan to venture anywhere on foot.

Garberville

RESTAURANTS

Woodrose Cafe / ★

911 REDWOOD DR, GARBERVILLE; 707/923-3191 This homey small-town coffee shop is the social center of Garberville and a good place to break your fast with their renowned green chilie omelet before heading deep into the Lost Coast. Black-and-white prints by local artists hang on the textured peach walls with dark redwood trim, and in back there's a small outdoor patio perfect for basking in the sun and wolfing down healthy fare such as tofu scramble, granola, vegetarian garden burgers, organic-fruit shakes, and chunky vegetable-based soups served with sourdough garlic bread. Organic produce is used whenever possible. Everything is skillfully and tastefully prepared, and you'll certainly leave feeling well nourished. *$; no credit cards; checks OK; breakfast, lunch every day (open Sat–Sun until 1pm); beer and wine; no reservations; from Hwy 101, take the Garberville exit.*

LODGINGS

Benbow Inn / ★★

445 LAKE BENBOW DR, GARBERVILLE; 707/923-2124 OR 800/355-3301 From its sophisticated afternoon tea to its beautifully cultivated gardens of primroses, narcissus, tulips, and roses, this elegant Tudor-style inn built in 1926 is a little slice of England nestled in the redwoods. A National Historic Landmark, the inn (named after the family who built it) has hosted such luminaries as Herbert Hoover, Eleanor Roosevelt, and Charles Laughton, and caters mostly to a older clientele. The 55 guest rooms vary in size and amenities; the priciest accommodations such as the Honeymoon Cottage include private patios overlooking the river, Jacuzzis, fireplaces readied with kindling, and VCRs (there's a large movie library at the front desk). The least expensive rooms are small but comfortable, and while they don't have the frills of the other rooms, they are tastefully decorated with antiques. The aristocratic (and expensive) dining room is lined with carved-wood and marble sideboards, and the large-paned windows provide a great view of the river and gardens. The menu changes frequently but always features seafood, beef, pasta, and poultry dishes. Dinner entrees might include fresh salmon, grilled chicken breast marinated in lime and herbs, and honey-miso-roasted pork loin served with black-eyed peas. Breakfast and lunch are served daily, and on Sunday the Benbow offers a sumptuous champagne brunch. Of course, as British etiquette dictates, complimentary afternoon tea and scones are served in the lobby at 3pm, hors d'oeuvres in the lounge at 5pm, and port wine in the lounge at 9pm. Beautiful Benbow Lake State Park is right out the front door, and a golf course is across the highway. The inn hosts many special events throughout the year, including a Nutcracker Christmas celebration, a New Year's dinner dance, a summer Shakespeare on the Lake festival, and a fall Murder Mystery Weekend. Note: Be sure to request that the housekeeping staff go light on the "air freshener," which smells anything but fresh. *$$–$$$$; AE, DIS, MC, V; checks OK; breakfast, lunch Mon–Sat,* *dinner every day, brunch Sun (lunch is not served mid-Sept–mid-May, except on holidays); open mid-Apr–Dec 31; full bar; reservations recommended; www.benbow inn.com; from Hwy 101, take the Benbow Dr exit.*

Redway

RESTAURANTS

The Mateel Cafe / ★★

3342 AND 3344 REDWOOD DR, REDWAY; 707/923-2030 With its fresh, healthful food and lively atmosphere, the Mateel has become a social and cultural magnet for the southern Humboldt region (SoHum to the natives). Lunch and dinner are served in three areas: the main dining room, which has high-backed wooden booths and a modest collection of watercolors by local artists; the African-style Jazzbo Room, decked out in giraffe decor; and the covered patio, the preferred spot on warm days and nights. A worldly selection of food is served here, ranging from roast rack of lamb to seafood linguine, Louisiana tiger prawns, Thai tofu, and fresh seafood specials of the day. All entrees are served with appetizers, soup or salad, and house-made pita bread. If you're not up to one of the full meals, try a stone-baked pizza (there are more than 20 toppings to choose from) or an organic salad such as the napa cabbage, spinach, and chicken salad topped with tomatoes and almonds and a curry dressing. *$; MC, V; checks OK; lunch, dinner Mon–Sat; beer and wine; no reservations; from Hwy 101, take the Redway exit to downtown.* ♿

Shelter Cove

RESTAURANTS

Cove Restaurant / ★

10 SEAL COURT, SHELTER COVE; 707/986-1197 At the north end of a small runway for private planes, this rather remote restaurant—selected by *Private Pilot* magazine as one of the nation's premier fly-in lunch spots—is situated in an A-frame beach house with two-story-high picture windows, an outdoor dining area, and a spectacular view of this untamed region of California known as the Lost Coast. The menu's offerings are wide ranging and well prepared: charbroiled steak cut to order, Cajun-style fish (we're talking right out of the water), grilled chicken, juicy hamburgers, and piles of fresh shellfish. All meals are served with a choice of a creamy clam chowder; shrimp salad or green salad; and house-made bread. Desserts range from fresh fruit pies (snatch a slice of the wonderfully tart wild blackberry if it's available) to chocolate mousse and cheesecake. *$$; MC, V; checks OK; lunch, dinner Thurs–Sun; full bar; reservations recommended; off Lower Pacific Dr.*

LODGINGS

Shelter Cove Ocean Inn / ★★

148 DOLPHIN DR, SHELTER COVE; 707/986-7161 Snoozing seals, grazing deer, and migrating whales are just some of the sights you'll see in Shelter Cove, the Lost Coast's only oceanside community. Once you leave Highway 101 in Garberville, prepare to navigate along 24 miles of steep, twisting tarmac that passes through rocky grasslands and patches of forest before reaching the cove (good brakes are a must). At the end of the journey you'll reach the Shelter Cove Ocean Inn, a handsome Victorian-style building built smack-dab on the shoreline. The inn, which is popular with recreational pilots because they can park their planes within walking distance, offers two spacious suites with sitting rooms and Jacuzzi tubs. Two smaller rooms upstairs have private baths and balconies. All rooms have an ocean view, but the panorama from the suites is definitely worth the extra expense. Serious R&R is the theme here: lie on the sundeck overlooking the ocean, play a round of golf across the street, or walk to the nearby black sand beach, 'cause there ain't nothin' to do around here except relax. Note: The inn was recently renovated and scheduled to reopen in the spring of 2004. *$$; AE, MC, V; checks OK; turn right off Lower Pacific Dr.* &

Myers Flat

LODGINGS

Myers Country Inn / ★

12913 OLD REDWOOD HWY/AVE OF THE GIANTS, MYERS FLAT; 707/943-3259 OR 800/500-6464 The two-story, wood-framed Myers Inn, constructed in 1860 and restored in 1906, sits just outside Humboldt Redwoods State Park in Myers Flat, a hamlet reminiscent of a cardboard-cutout saloon town. Ten comfortable, sparkling clean guest rooms—all individually decorated and with private baths—have been renovated with an eye toward upscale country charm. Verandas encircle the building on both floors, providing every room with a balcony that has a view of the town, mountains, and forest. A large wood-burning fireplace in the common room keeps guests warm at night. Although the inn is close to the highway—it was once a stage stop—the nearby Eel River and redwoods seem to absorb most of the noise. The forest also provides plenty of superb hiking and biking trails. *$$; AE, MC, V; no checks; innkeeper@myersinn.com; www.myersinn.com; in the center of town.*

REDWOOD EMPIRE THREE-DAY TOUR

DAY ONE: Bagels to beaches. Start things off with a bagel and coffee at **LOS BAGELS** in Arcata, followed by a stroll around **ARCATA PLAZA**. Then hop in your car and head 20 miles north of Eureka to **TRINIDAD**, a tiny fishing village of white clapboard houses overlooking Trinidad Bay. Admire the view, then purchase a few pounds of smoked salmon at **KATY'S SMOKEHOUSE**. Continue north on Highway 101 along the coast through Orick, the burl capital of the world. Keep an eye peeled for burl artists deftly wielding small chain saws. About 5 miles farther, take the **NEWTON B. DRURY SCENIC PARKWAY**—a 10-mile trip through the unspoiled scenery of **PRAIRIE CREEK REDWOODS STATE PARK**, with herds of Roosevelt elk, giant trees, fern canyons, and beaches along the way. As beautiful as it is, you can't dawdle too long, because you have to go back the way you came, following the signs to **PATRICK'S POINT STATE PARK**, 5 miles north of Trinidad. Here you can look for whales, hunt for semiprecious stones on Agate Beach, and wander through Sumeg, a Yurok Indian village with redwood houses and a sweat lodge still used for traditional ceremonies. Another option—and hugely recommended in the fall—is a short hike into **TALL TREES GROVE** to see the tallest tree in the world, followed by a drive along **HOWLAND HILL ROAD** through **JEDEDIAH SMITH REDWOODS STATE PARK**. Head back to Trinidad, check into the **LOST WHALE BED AND BREAKFAST INN**, and enjoy a soak in the ocean-view hot tub at sunset before you finish the day with dinner at the nearby **LARRUPIN' CAFE**.

DAY TWO: All about town. After breakfast at the inn, head to Eureka, stroll the **OLD TOWN** with its restored Victorian shops, and take a few photos of the **CARSON**

Redcrest

RESTAURANTS

Eternal Treehouse Cafe / ★

26510 AVE OF THE GIANTS, REDCREST; 707/722-4247 OR 707/722-4262
Located in the tiny town of Redcrest on the scenic Avenue of the Giants, the Eternal Treehouse is an all-American cafe right down to the house-made pies and country-and-western music flowing out of the kitchen. This family-run cafe serves the best biscuits and gravy in the county, as well as wholesome daily specials such as corned beef and cabbage served with potatoes, carrots, and a choice of soup or salad—all for less than the price of a movie. *$; MC, V; checks OK; breakfast, lunch, dinner every day; no alcohol; no reservations; from Hwy 101, take the Redcrest exit.*

HOUSE MANSION, possibly the finest Victorian anywhere (but you can't go in, as it's privately owned). After having a sandwich and truffle at **RAMONE'S BAKERY & CAFE**, hop aboard the **MADAKET**, the oldest passenger vessel on the Pacific Coast, for a tour of Humboldt Bay. For dinner you can choose between gobs of basic, rib-stickin' food at the historic **SAMOA COOKHOUSE** or an elegant dinner at **RESTAURANT 301**, the best restaurant on the North Coast. Then it's off to the Victorian village of Ferndale, just a hop away, for a performance at the **FERNDALE REPERTORY THEATER**. Spend the night in the village's most elegant B&B, the fabled **GINGERBREAD MANSION**, where you can wind down with a soak in matching claw-footed tubs.

DAY THREE: Lumbering among the giants. After a lavish B&B breakfast, you're on the road to **SCOTIA** for a glimpse of a real company town, built entirely of redwood, and owned by the Pacific Lumber Company. It's so clean and tidy it's almost surreal. Take the self-guided tour through one of the last sawmills in the area (and the world's biggest). It will give you a perspective on your next destination, the **AVENUE OF THE GIANTS**. The Avenue was originally a stagecoach road, and it winds some 32 miles along the Eel River through stunning groves of coast redwoods. Be sure to take a walk through **FOUNDERS GROVE**. For lunch, grab a bite in the down-home **ETERNAL TREEHOUSE CAFE** in tiny Redcrest, complete with country or gospel music coming from the kitchen. Don't dally, though, because you're going to want to check into the historic **BENBOW INN** as early as possible so you can catch a few rays on its private beach before dinner in the restaurant. Afterward, see what's happening across the road at Lake Benbow's outdoor stage—jazz, pop, reggae, or Shakespeare—under the stars and the redwoods, with the lake as a backdrop.

Scotia

LODGINGS

Scotia Inn / ★★☆

100 MAIN ST, SCOTIA; 707/764-5683 OR 888/764-2248 This grand three-story hotel, constructed entirely of redwood, is the pride of Scotia, one of the last company-owned towns in America. In fact, the whole town is built of redwood—no surprise once you discover the town's owner is the Pacific Lumber Company. Built in 1923 during the Arts and Crafts period, the Scotia Inn has 2 guest rooms downstairs and 20 spacious rooms on the second floor, each gussied up with Arts and Crafts furnishings, period antiques, and an abundance of flowery patterns. The inn's private bathrooms are equipped with showers and claw-footed tubs. The elaborate Redwood Room restaurant, handsomely decorated in rust, green, and burgundy and lit by gas transition chandeliers, serves traditional American fare such as steak, prime rib, elk, and seafood featuring locally grown vegetables and berries. The wine list is excellent and the service always friendly. For classic, hearty steak-house grub in a less formal setting, you can also dine nightly at the inn's Steak and Potato Pub. *$$–$$$; AE, DIS, MC, V; checks OK; stay@scotiainn.com; www.scotiainn.com; at Mill St, directly across from the mill; from Hwy 101, take the Scotia exit.*

Bridgeport

RESTAURANTS

The Weekender Cafe / ★

HWY 36, BRIDGEPORT; 707/574-6521 All the proceeds of this homey, volunteer-run cafe support the local fire department and its four secondhand engines. Neighbors donate the homemade rolls, muffins, breads, pies, cakes, cookies, soups, relishes, salads, and even the fresh flowers decorating every table, and the fire chief answers the phone. Most of the ingredients come from local pastures, chicken coops, and gardens (including sun-ripened tomatoes and sweet, freshly picked carrots and celery) and are prepared in a family-size kitchen behind the eight-stool counter (newly expanded from five). For breakfast the staff whips up waffles, pancakes, freshly made Danish pastries, homemade biscuits and gravy, and a variety of egg dishes. This is the kind of place where you help yourself to the coffee, and if the vinyl chairs get too uncomfortable you can always take a seat on the couch in front of the fire. Note: Because it's volunteer run, the cafe's days and hours of operation may vary: be sure to call ahead first. *$; no credit cards; checks OK; breakfast, lunch Thurs–Sun; no alcohol; no reservations; 1½ miles E of Dinsmore, between Bridgeville and Mad River.*

Mad River

LODGINGS

Journey's End Resort / ★

200 MAD RIVER RD, MAD RIVER; 707/574-6441 This remote resort is settled on the edge of little-known Ruth Lake, a well-hidden man-made lake that's a 1½-hour winding drive from the coast. Created in 1962, the lake is frequented by serious anglers in search of its sizable trout and black bass, which explains why a good number of guests at Journey's End are fisher folk (and the rest are typically water-skiers and jet-skiers). The motel's no-frills guest rooms are clean and warm, equipped with two firm double beds and a bathroom with a shower. A cabin on the premises sleeps up to five people and is supplied with a dishwasher, stove, microwave, refrigerator, and a barbecue on the porch—all you need to bring is food. Evening entertainment is left to the imagination rather than the networks, and if that doesn't suffice, there's a game-filled saloon with a satellite TV. The resort also has a grocery store, a laundry, basic fishing and boating supplies, and a small restaurant

PLEASE, SIR, MAY I HAVE SAMOA?

Visiting the Eureka area without a stop at the **SAMOA COOKHOUSE** is like visiting Paris without seeing the Eiffel Tower. This enormous barnlike building is the last surviving cookhouse in the West (it's been in operation since 1893) and a Humboldt County institution. When logging was king in redwood country, every mill operation had a cookhouse that was the hub of life in the community. Lumbermen worked six days a week, 12 hours a day, and were served three hot meals a day. Appetites were enormous, and waitresses rushed back and forth from the kitchen to the tables trying to keep the platters filled. Today's cookhouse patrons are served in the exact same lumber-camp style, where everyone is seated elbow to elbow at long tables covered with checkered oilcloths. Few decisions are required—just sit down, and the food will come until you say "Uncle!" Breakfast typically features sausages, biscuits, scrambled eggs, and potatoes as well as a choice of French toast, hash browns, or pancakes (not to mention all the coffee and OJ you can drink). Lunch and dinner include soup, salad, potatoes, and the meat-of-the-day, which might be ham, fried chicken, pork chops, roast beef, barbecued chicken, or fish. Mind you, the food isn't haute cuisine (except for the delicious bread, which is baked on the premises), but there's plenty of it, and prices are modest. And just when you think you're about to burst, along comes the fresh-baked pie. After your meal, spend a few minutes waddling through the adjoining **LOGGING MUSEUM** to see a wonderful collection of logging tools and photographs of early lumber and shipping activities in Eureka. The cookhouse name, by the way, comes from the old company town of Samoa, so-called because Humboldt Bay resembles the harbor at Pago Pago. From Eureka on Highway 101, take the Samoa Bridge to the end, turn left on Samoa Road, then left on Cookhouse Road (707/442-1659; www.humboldtdining.com/cookhouse).

that specializes in made-from-scratch pizzas and range-fed, hand-cut rib eyes and New York steaks served with house-made fries, sautéed mushrooms, and grilled onions. *$$; AE, DIS, MC, V; no checks; www.thejourneysend.com; at the NE end of Ruth Lake, 9 miles S of Hwy 36.*

Ferndale

Even if Ferndale isn't on your itinerary, it's worth taking a detour off Highway 101 to stroll for an hour or two down the colorful Main Street, browsing through the art galleries, gift shops, and cafes strangely reminiscent of Disneyland's "old town." Ferndale, however, is for real, and hasn't changed much since it was the agricultural center of Northern California in the late 1800s. In fact, the entire town is a National Historic Landmark because of its abundance of well-preserved Victorian storefronts, farmhouses, and homes. What really distinguishes Ferndale from the likes of Eureka and Crescent City, however, is the fact that Highway 101 doesn't pass through it—which means no cheesy motels, liquor stores, or fast-food chains.

For a trip back in time, view the village's interesting memorabilia—working crank phones, logging equipment, and a blacksmith shop—at the **FERNDALE MUSEUM** (515 Shaw St at 3rd St; 707/786-4466). Not officially a museum, but close enough, is the **GOLDEN GATE MERCANTILE** (421 Main St). Part of this general store hasn't been remodeled (or restocked) in 50 years, giving you the feeling that you're walking through some sort of time capsule or movie set. Far less historic but equally engrossing are the pedal-powered, amphibious entries in the wacky three-day **WORLD CHAMPIONSHIP GREAT ARCATA TO FERNDALE CROSS-COUNTRY KINETIC SCULPTURE RACE** on display at the **KINETIC SCULPTURE MUSEUM** (580 Main St at Shaw St; no phone). The dusty, funky museum is unlike anything you've ever seen, but it seems a fitting tribute to a race that gives eccentricity new meaning.

Another worthy Ferndale attraction is the leisurely drive along scenic **CENTERVILLE ROAD**. The 5-mile excursion starts at the west end of Main Street downtown and passes by several ranches and dairy farms on the way to the **CENTERVILLE BEACH COUNTY PARK**. If you continue beyond the park and past the retired naval facility, you'll be rewarded with an incredible view of the Lost Coast to the south. On the way back, just outside of town on the north side of the road, keep an eye out for **FERN COTTAGE**, a restored 1865 Victorian farmhouse built by the late state senator Joseph Russ, one of the first Ferndale settlers. Tours of the farmhouse are by appointment only; call 707/786-4835 to make a reservation.

In keeping with its National Historic Landmark status, Ferndale has no movie theaters. It has something better: the **FERNDALE REPERTORY THEATRE** (447 Main St; 707/786-5483). Converted in 1972 from a movie theater, the 267-seat house hosts live performances by actors from all over Humboldt County. The revolving performances run pretty much year-round and range from musicals to comedies, dramas, and mysteries. Tickets are reasonably priced and, due to the popularity of the shows, reservations are advised. For more information on Ferndale's upcoming events and activities, visit the town's Web site (www.victorianferndale.org/chamber).

RESTAURANTS

Curley's Grill / ★★☆

400 OCEAN AVE (VICTORIAN INN), FERNDALE; 707/786-9696 Longtime restaurateur and Ferndale resident Curley Tait decided it was finally time to open his own business. So in April 1995 he opened Curley's Grill in a little hole-in-the-wall on Main Street, and it was a big hit—so much so that Curley recently relocated to fancy, spacious digs in the Victorian Inn several blocks down the street. The reason Curley's place is considered the best in town? He doesn't fool around: the prices are fair, the servings are generous, the food is good, and the atmosphere is bright and cheerful. Recommended starters are the grilled polenta with Italian sausage, fresh mushrooms, and sage-laden tomato sauce, and the moist tortilla-and-onion cake served with a tangy onion salsa. For the main course the meat loaf with garlic mashed potatoes or the fall-off-the-bone barbecued baby back ribs will leave you happily stuffed. Indulge in the house-made breads and desserts, and take a look at Curley's collection of Marilyn Monroe memorabilia, including Marilyn Merlot wine and martinis. On sunny afternoons, request a seat on the shaded back patio. *$$; DIS, MC, V; checks OK; breakfast Sat–Sun, lunch, dinner every day; beer and wine; reservations recommended; curley@foggy.net; www.restaurant.com/curleysgrill; corner of Ocean Ave and Main St.* &

LODGINGS

The Gingerbread Mansion / ★★★

400 BERDING ST, FERNDALE; 707/786-4000 OR 800/952-4136 The awe-inspiring grande dame of Ferndale, this peach-and-yellow Queen Anne inn is a lavish blowout for Victoriana buffs. Gables, turrets, English gardens, and architectural gingerbread galore have made it one of the most-photographed buildings in Northern California. The mansion has been through several reincarnations since 1899, including stints as a private residence, a hospital, a rest home, an apartment building, and even an American Legion hall before it was converted into a B&B in 1983. All 11 guest rooms have queen- or king-size beds and private baths. For the ultimate in luxury, though, reserve the Empire Suite, an orgy of marble and columns with twin fireplaces and a lavish bathing area. In the morning all guests awaken to a sumptuous breakfast in the formal dining room that overlooks the garden. An extravagant afternoon tea is served in one of five parlors, each handsomely furnished with Queen Anne, Eastlake, and Renaissance Revival antiques. Even if you're not staying in Ferndale, it's worth stopping by for a tour, scheduled from noon to 4pm daily. *$$$–$$$$; AE, MC, V; checks OK; innkeeper@gingerbread-mansion.com; www.gingerbread-mansion.com; at Brown St, 1 block S of Main St.*

Shaw House Inn Bed and Breakfast / ★★★

703 MAIN ST, FERNDALE; 707/786-9958 OR 800/557-SHAW This Carpenter Gothic beauty, the oldest structure in Ferndale and the oldest B&B in California, is modeled after the titular manse of Nathaniel Hawthorne's *House of the Seven Gables,* complete with numerous balconies, bay windows, and jutting gables. It was built in 1854 by Ferndale founder Seth Louis Shaw and is listed on the National Register of Historic Places. A gazebo and fish pond highlight the inn's well-tended 1-acre yard, verdantly graced with 25 varieties of mature trees. The B&B has been meticulously restored and filled with books, photographs, and all manner of memorabilia. Each of the eight individually decorated guest rooms—replete with antiques, luxurious fabrics, and period fixtures—has a private bath, and four have private entrances. Three rooms have balconies overlooking the tranquil cottage garden, and the Fountain Suite has its own fireplace (a romantic must on those chilly nights). Each morning guests feast on homemade breakfast fare such as mushroom-leek frittatas, quiches, crepes, and house-baked breads. *$$$; DIS, MC, V; checks OK; stay@shawhouse.com; www.shawhouse.com; on Main St, just E of downtown Ferndale.*

The Victorian Inn / ★★☆

400 OCEAN AVE, FERNDALE; 707/786-4949 OR 888/589-1808 If you can get your honey past the jewelry store on the first floor, you'll love the romantic rooms at this conveniently located bed-and-breakfast and country inn in the heart of Ferndale. Built in 1890 entirely of North Coast redwood, the inn is one of the most photographed buildings in Northern California. This ornately constructed and spacious inn has 12 guest rooms, all with private baths and some with fireplaces and sitting areas. The high-ceilinged rooms are individually decorated with charming wallpaper, antiques, formal draperies, and period fixtures, as well as TVs, CD players, telephones, and cable Internet access. If you're traveling with the family, request a room with an additional trundle bed. Included in the room rate is a full breakfast served at Curley's Grill, located in the inn. *$$–$$$; AE, DIS, MC, V; checks OK; innkeeper@a-victorian-inn.com; www.a-victorian-inn.com; corner of Ocean Ave and Main St.*

Eureka

Named after the popular gold-mining expression "Eureka!" (Greek for "I have found it"), the heart of Eureka is **OLD TOWN**, a 13-block stretch of shops, restaurants, and hotels, most of them housed in painstakingly preserved Victorian structures. It's bordered by First and Third Streets, between C and M Streets. One of the finest Victorian architectural masterpieces is the multigabled-and-turreted **CARSON MANSION** (on the corner of 2nd and M Sts), built of redwood in 1886 for lumber baron William Carson, who initiated the construction to keep mill workers occupied during a lull in the lumber business. Although the three-story, money-green mansion is closed to the public (it's now a snooty men's club), you can stand on the sidewalk and click your Kodak at one of the state's most-photographed houses. For more Old Town history, stroll through the **CLARKE MEMORIAL MUSEUM** (240 E St at 3rd St; 707/443-1947), which has one of the top Native American art displays in the state, showcasing more than 1,200 examples of Hupa, Yurok, and Karok basketry, dance regalia, and stonework. A block away, there's more Native American artwork, including quality silver jewelry, at the **INDIAN ART & GIFT SHOP** (241 F St at 3rd St; 707/445-8451), which sells many of its treasures at reasonable prices.

If you need a good book at a great price, stop by the **BOOKLEGGER** (402 2nd St at E St; 707/445-1344), a marvelous bookstore in Old Town with thousands of used paperbacks (especially mysteries, Westerns, and science fiction) as well as children's books and cookbooks. If purple potatoes, cylindra beets, and other fancy foods are on your shopping list, you're in luck, because you'll find them at the **FARMERS MARKETS** held weekly in Eureka and Arcata. Most of the produce is grown along the local Eel and Trinity Rivers and is sold at bargain prices. For more information call the **NORTH COAST GROWERS ASSOCIATION** at 707/441-9999.

Before you leave Eureka, be sure to take a bay cruise on skipper Leroy Zerlang's **MADAKET**, the oldest passenger vessel on the Pacific Coast. The 75-minute narrated tour—a surprisingly interesting and amusing perspective on the history of Humboldt Bay—departs daily from the foot of C Street in Eureka and gets progressively better

POOP GOES IN, PRIDE COMES OUT

The small town of Arcata, just north of Eureka, has garnered international praise for turning an abandoned industrial and landfill site into the beautiful, 154-acre **ARCATA MARSH AND WILDLIFE SANCTUARY**, with miles of trails, more than 100 varieties of plants, and more than 200 species of birds—including egrets, osprey, hummingbirds, and night herons. Not so unusual, you say? It wouldn't be, except that this natural splendor contains the 49 acres of oxidation ponds that treat Arcata's wastewater. Time, water, plants, bacteria, and fungi purify the wastewater that circulates through six marsh systems before it is finally released into Humboldt Bay. Natural processes in the marshes simultaneously purify the wastewater and feed marsh plants that attract birds, fish, and other wildlife. The community has received many awards and lots of press for the marsh, leading to its slogan, "Arcata residents flush with pride." Each Saturday at 8:30am and 2pm, local docents give free one-hour guided tours of the preserve—rain or shine—at the cul-de-sac at the foot of South I Street (reservations aren't required). Or just pick up a free self-guided walking tour map of the preserve, available at the Arcata Chamber of Commerce (1062 G St at 11th St; 707/822-3619).

after your second or third cocktail. For more information, call **HUMBOLDT BAY HARBOR CRUISE** (707/445-1910). Afterward, stroll over to the **LOST COAST BREWERY** (617 4th St, between G and H Sts; 707/445-4480) for a fresh pint of Alleycat Amber Ale and an order of buffalo wings.

RESTAURANTS

Los Bagels / ★

403 2ND ST, EUREKA; 707/442-8525 Simply put, this is Eureka's best bagel shop. For a full review of the original Los Bagels, see the Restaurants section of Arcata. *$; no credit cards; local checks only; breakfast, lunch Wed–Mon; no alcohol; no reservations; www.losbagels.com; at E St in Old Town.* &

Ramone's Bakery & Cafe / ★

209 E ST, EUREKA; 707/445-2923 Before you start exploring Old Town, start your day with an espresso and a cinnamon roll at Ramone's, Eureka's best bakery since 1986. Everything on the menu—pastries, breads, chocolate truffles, soups, salads, sandwiches—is made from scratch every morning without preservatives or dough conditioners. Along with huge sandwiches made with freshly baked breads, the cafe offers daily lunch specials such as lasagne and quiche. You can either order your goods to go—there's plenty of bench seating in Old Town—or dine in the cafe's small self-service dining room. At any time of the day it's a great place to stop in for a light, inexpensive meal. *$; no credit cards; local checks only; breakfast, lunch daily; no alcohol; no reservations; www.ramonesbakery.com; in Old Town.*

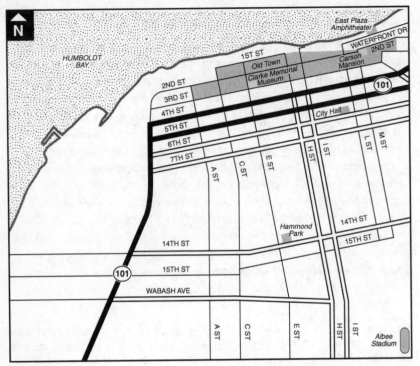

EUREKA

Restaurant 301 / ★★★

301 L ST (HOTEL CARTER), EUREKA; 707/444-8062 OR 800/404-1390
Seafood direct from local fisheries, one of the finest wine lists in the nation, and herbs, vegetables, and edible flowers from the hotel's extensive gardens are just a few of the highlights at Restaurant 301, Eureka's finest restaurant. Diners, seated at window-side tables overlooking the waterfront, may either order à la carte or splurge on the Discovery Menu, a prix-fixe five-course affair that pairs each course with suggested wines by the glass. A typical dinner may begin with an artichoke, green lentil, and fennel salad, followed by a warm chèvre cake appetizer or a savory satay of grilled marinated quail, then on to main entrees such as a grilled duck breast served with a seasonal fruit and zinfandel sauce, or tender grilled medallions of filet mignon served with smoked oyster dressing and a green peppercorn glaze. For dessert, the fresh rhubarb tart drizzled with lemon-curd sauce is superb. Restaurant 301's astounding wine list—courtesy of the 301 Wine Shop and Wine Bar within the hotel—is a recipient of the Grand Award from *Wine Spectator* magazine. $$–$$$; AE, DC, DIS, MC, V; checks OK; breakfast, dinner every day; full bar; reservations recommended; reserve@carterhouse.com; www.carterhouse.com; at 3rd St in Old Town. &

LODGINGS

Abigail's Elegant Victorian Mansion Bed & Breakfast / ★★

1406 C ST, EUREKA; 707/444-3144 This inn is a jewel—a National Historic Landmark built in 1888 and lovingly maintained by owners Doug "Jeeves" Vieyra and Lily Vieyra. If you're a fan of Victoriana, be prepared for a mind-blowing experience. Each of the four guest rooms upstairs has furnishings reflecting a different period, place, or personage. The light-filled Lillie Langtry Room, named for the famed 19th-century chanteuse who once sang at the local Ingomar Theatre, has an impressive four-poster oak bed and a private bath down the hall. The French country–style Governor's Room sleeps up to three, has a private bath, and offers a distant view of the bay. The Vieyras have a great array of old (1905–40) movies and a collection of popular music from the same era, which guests often enjoy in the common room. Then there's Doug's obsession with antique autos—he's frequently seen motoring around (with guests on board) in his 1928 Model A Ford. The Vieyras are incredibly attentive hosts: they'll lend you bicycles, serve ice-cream sodas and lemonade while you play croquet on the manicured lawn, show you the way to their Finnish sauna and Victorian flower garden, pore over road maps with you, and make your dinner reservations. Lily, trained as a French chef (and Swedish masseuse), prepares a morning feast. *$$–$$$; MC, V; no checks; www.eureka-california.com; at 14th St.*

Carter House, Hotel Carter, Bell Cottage, Carter Cottage / ★★★★

301 L ST, EUREKA; 707/444-8062 OR 800/404-1390 What is now one of the finest accommodation-and-restaurant complexes on the upper North Coast started serendipitously in 1982, the year Eureka resident Mark Carter converted his newly built dream home—a four-story, five-bedroom Victorian reproduction—into an inn. Not only did Mark turn out to be one of the area's best hosts, but he also actually reveled in his newfound innkeeper role. Once word got around that the Carter House was *the* place to vacation, he was flooded with folks who wanted a room. In 1986, Mark, a former builder, added the 23-room Hotel Carter across the street (its design is based on the blueprints of a historic 19th-century Eureka hotel), and four years later he refurbished the Bell Cottage, an adjacent three-bedroom Victorian home built in 1890. A year later, in 1991, next door to the other two, he added Carter Cottage, perhaps the most romantic of all—an entire house that's been lavishly furnished as a honeymoon getaway: a chef's kitchen, two fireplaces, a grand bathroom with a whirlpool tub for two, a private deck, and even a wine cellar. The foursome of inn, hotel, and two cottages offers a contrasting array of luxury accommodations, ranging from rooms with classic Victorian dark-wood antique furnishings in the house and cottage to a softer, brighter, more contemporary look in the hotel. Amenities include baskets filled with wine and specialty foods, concierge services, a videotape and CD library, tea-and-cookie bedtime service, and wine and hors d'oeuvres in the evening. Included in the room rate is a full breakfast featuring fresh-baked tarts, muffins, cinnamon buns, breads, fresh fruit, and an ever-changing array of entrees, juices, and strong coffee. The highly acclaimed Restaurant 301 (see review, above), is located on the first floor of Hotel Carter and is widely regarded as one of the North Coast's top spots for dining. *$$$–$$$$; AE, DC, DIS, MC, V; checks OK; reserve@carterhouse.com; www.carterhouse.com; at 3rd St in Old Town.* &

Arcata

Home to the **CALIFORNIA STATE UNIVERSITY AT HUMBOLDT,** a liberal arts school, Arcata is like most college towns in that everyone tends to lean toward the left. Environmentalism, artistry, good breads, and good bagels are indispensable elements of the Arcatian philosophy, as is a cordial disposition toward tourists, making it one of the most interesting and visitor-friendly towns along the North Coast.

The heart of this seaside community is **ARCATA PLAZA,** where a statue of President McKinley stands guard over numerous shops and cafes housed in historic buildings. A walk around the plaza—with its perfectly manicured lawns, hot dog vendor, and well-dressed retirees sitting on spotless benches—is enough to restore anyone's faith in small-town America. At the plaza's southwest end is its flagship structure, **JACOBY'S STOREHOUSE** (791 8th St at H St), a handsomely restored 1857 brick pack-train station that now holds shops, offices, and restaurants. If you need a new book, the **TIN CAN MAILMAN** (1000 H St at 10th St; 707/822-1307) is a terrific used-book store with 130,000 hard- and softcover titles, including a few collector's items.

You can see (and touch!) 3-billion-year-old fossils and view various California flora and fauna exhibits at Humboldt State University's **NATURAL HISTORY MUSEUM** (13th and G Sts, downtown; 707/826-4479). For a wide range of first-run and classic college flicks, queue up at the **MINOR THEATRE** (1013 H St at 10th St; 707/822-5171), which offers a wide range of films at starving-student prices (the daily matinees are particularly cheap). After the flick, savor a pitcher of Red Nectar Ale at the **HUMBOLDT BREWING COMPANY** (856 10th St at G St, next to the Minor Theatre; 707/826-1734); brewery tours are offered, too.

Once you've toured the downtown area, it's time to explore Arcata's numerous parks and preserves. A two-minute drive east of downtown on 11th Street will take you to Arcata's beloved **REDWOOD PARK,** a beautiful grassy expanse—ideal for a picnic—complemented by a fantastic playground that's guaranteed to entertain the tots. Surrounding the park is the **ARCATA COMMUNITY FOREST,** 600 acres of lush second-growth redwoods favored by hikers, mountain bikers, and equestrians; before you go, pick up a free guide to the forest's mountain-biking or hiking trails at the **ARCATA CHAMBER OF COMMERCE** (1635 Heindon Rd at Janes Rd; 707/822-3619; www.arcatachamber.com).

The best way to spend a summer Sunday afternoon in Arcata is at the **ARCATA BALLPARK** (707/822-3619), where only a few bucks buys you nine innings of America's favorite pastime hosted by the **HUMBOLDT CRABS** semipro baseball team. With the brass band blasting and the devoted fans cheering, you'd swear you were back in high school. Most games are played Wednesday, Friday, and Saturday (doubleheader) evenings and Sunday afternoons in June and July. The ballpark is located at the corner of Ninth and F Streets in downtown Arcata, but don't park your car anywhere near foul-ball territory.

RESTAURANTS

Abruzzi / ★★

791 8TH ST, ARCATA; 707/826-2345 Named after a region on the Italian Adriatic, Abruzzi is located on the bottom floor of the historic Jacoby Storehouse, a mid-19th-century brick complex that's been converted into the Arcata Plaza shopping and dining complex. If you have trouble finding the place, just follow your nose: the smell of garlic and fresh bread will soon steer you to this popular restaurant, where you'll be served an ample amount of artfully arranged food in a romantic setting of dark wood and dim lighting. Meals begin with a basket of warm breads from a local bakery, followed by such highly recommended dishes as sea scallops with langoustines tossed with cheese tortellini, *linguine pescara* (prawns, calamari, and clams tossed in a light Sicilian tomato sauce), range-fed veal piccata, or any of the fresh seafood specials. The standout dessert is the Chocolate Paradiso—a dense chocolate cake set in a pool of champagne mousseline. The restaurant's owners also run the Plaza Grill on the third floor of the same building—a great place to finish off the evening by sipping a glass of wine in front of the fireplace. *$$; AE, DIS, MC, V; checks OK; dinner every day; full bar; reservations recommended; www.abruzzicatering.com; at H St in the Arcata Plaza.* &

Folie Douce / ★★

1551 G ST, ARCATA; 707/822-1042 To say Folie Douce just serves pizza is like saying Tiffany's just sells jewelry. "Designer pizza" is a more apt description: molé chicken with tomatoes, roasted peppers, jalapeño, and queso fresco; green coconut curried prawns with fresh mango, jalapeño, and cilantro; salami and Brie with mozzarella and apricot jam—all made with fresh ingredients from local farmers and baked to perfection in a wood-fired oven. If the unorthodox pizzas don't set your heart aflutter, the appetizers and entrees will. Start with the artichoke-heart cheesecake

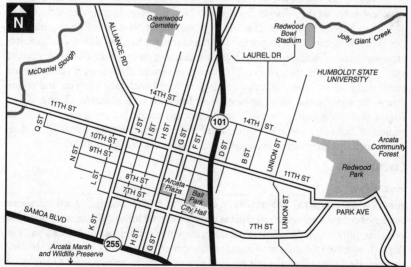

Arcata

HEAVEN ON EARTH VIA THE HOWLAND HILL ROAD

For car-bound cruisers who want to take a journey through an unbelievably spectacular old-growth redwood forest, there's a hidden, well-maintained gravel road called **HOWLAND HILL ROAD** that winds for about 12 miles through the misty, silent groves of Jedediah Smith Redwoods State Park. To get there from Highway 101, turn right on Elk Valley Road at the south end of Crescent City (at the "76" gas station) and follow it to Howland Hill Road, which will be on your right. After driving through the park, you'll end up near the town of Hiouchi, and from there it's a short jaunt northwest on Highway 199 to get back to Highway 101. Plan at least two to three hours for the 45-mile round-trip, or all day if you want to do some hiking among the world's tallest trees—in what many consider one of the most beautiful places in the world. Trailers and motor homes are not allowed.

appetizer, perhaps followed by a brandy-flambéed filet mignon topped with Roquefort cheese and green peppercorns, or the rosemary and mustard grilled lamb chops topped with a roasted garlic and red wine demi-glace. You'll appreciate the award-winning yet reasonably priced wine list as well. Locals love this festive, brightly painted bistro, so reservations, even for early birds, are strongly recommended. *$$; DIS, MC, V; checks OK; dinner Tues–Sat; beer and wine; reservations recommended; www.holyfolie.com; between 15th and 16th Sts.* &

Los Bagels / ★

1061 I ST, ARCATA; 707/822-3150 In 1987 bagel companies all over the country sent their doughy products to NBC's *Today* show to vie for the title of best bagel. The verdict: The best bagel outside of New York City was made by Los Bagels in Arcata. This emporium is a popular town hangout where you'll see lots of folks scanning the morning paper while munching on bagels layered with smoked salmon, smoked albacore, or lox. Try some fresh-baked challah or, if you're feeling particularly adventurous, a poppyseed bagel topped with jalapeño jam and cream cheese, or a multigrain bagel smeared with hummus or guacamole. Owing to Los Bagels' brisk business, the owners opened a second location in Eureka (see Restaurants section of Eureka). *$; no credit cards; local checks only; breakfast, lunch Wed–Mon; no alcohol; no reservations; www.losbagels.com; between 10th and 11th Sts.* &

LODGINGS

Hotel Arcata / ★

708 9TH ST, ARCATA; 707/826-0217 OR 800/344-1221 Located at the northeast corner of Arcata's winsome town plaza, this handsome turn-of-the-century hotel has been carefully restored to its original state, evoking an ambiance of Arcata's halcyon days. (It wouldn't take much to imagine Humphrey Bogart and Grace Kelly strolling through the lobby.) If you're not inclined to stay at the more sumptuous Lady Anne B&B (see review, below), this is definitely the next best choice. The 85 individually decorated rooms—many with claw-footed tubs—range from inexpensive small singles to quiet minisuites and a large Executive Suite that overlooks the plaza. A few modern amenities include cable TV, coffeemaker, data port, and shuttle service to the airport. Continental breakfast is complimentary, and on the premises—under different management—is a Japanese restaurant, Tomo. The hotel also offers its guests free passes to the health club and indoor pool just a few blocks down the street. Pets are accepted with a $5-per-day fee and a $50 deposit. *$$; AE, CB, DC, DIS, MC, V; no checks; www.hotelarcata.com; at the corner of 9th and G Sts.*

The Lady Anne / ★★

902 14TH ST, ARCATA; 707/822-2797 Just a few blocks from Arcata Plaza in a quiet residential neighborhood, this exquisite example of Queen Anne architecture has been painstakingly restored by innkeepers Sharon Ferrett and Sam Pennisi (who, by the way, was once Arcata's mayor). Five large and airy guest rooms are individually decorated with antiques, burnished woods, English stained glass, Oriental rugs, and lace curtains. The inn's two parlors are stocked with several games, as well as a grand piano and other musical instruments that you're welcome to play. Honeymooners should request the Lady Sarah Angela Room, with its cozy four-poster bed and pleasant bay view. When the weather is warm, relax on the Lady Anne's veranda or head out to the lawn for a game of croquet. Breakfast (beg for the Belgian waffles) is served in the grand dining room, which is warmed by a roaring fire in the winter. Several great restaurants are a short walk away at Arcata Plaza. *$$; MC, V; checks OK; ladyanne@humboldt1.com; www.arcataplaza.com/lodging; at I St.*

Trinidad

In the early 1850s Trinidad was a booming supply town with a population of 3,000; now it's one of the smallest incorporated cities in California, encompassing a little rocky bluff that a handful of anglers, artists, retirees, and shopkeepers call home. A sort of Mendocino-in-miniature, cute-as-a-button Trinidad is known mainly as a sportfishing town: trawlers and skiffs sit patiently in the bay, awaiting their owners or tourists eager to spend an afternoon salmon fishing. Scenery and silence, however, are the town's most desirable commodities; if all you're after is a little R&R on the coast, Trinidad is among the most peaceful and beautiful areas you'll find in California.

There's plenty to see and do in the Trinidad region. Five miles north of Trinidad, off Patrick's Point Drive, is **PATRICK'S POINT STATE PARK,** a 640-acre ocean-side peninsula with lush, fern-lined trails that wind through foggy forests of cedar, pine, and spruce. The park was once a seasonal fishing village of the Yurok Indians. Nowadays it's overrun with campers in the summer, but it's still worth a visit. Stroll down **AGATE BEACH** (keep an eye out for the semiprecious stones), climb the stone stairway up to the house-size **CEREMONIAL ROCK,** and admire the vistas from the **RIM TRAIL,** a 2-mile path along the cliffs where you can sometimes spot sea lions, harbor seals, and gray whales. In 1990 descendants of the original Native American settlers reconstructed an authentic Yurok village within the park, and visitors are welcome. A map and guide to all of the park's attractions are included in the $5-per-vehicle day-use fee; call 707/677-3570 for more details.

The **HUMBOLDT STATE UNIVERSITY MARINE LABORATORY** (570 Ewing St at Edwards St; 707/826-3671) features various live marine life displays, including a touch tank and tide pools; it's open to the public from 9am to 5pm Monday through Friday and 10am to 5pm Saturday and Sunday. Then again, why not catch your own sea critters? A day spent **SPORTFISHING** off Trinidad's bounteous coast is more fun and much easier than you probably think. You simply drop your prerigged line into the water, reel it in when something's tugging on the other end, and throw your catch in the burlap sack at your feet. The crew does all the dirty work of cleaning and cutting your fish, and **KATY'S SMOKEHOUSE** (740 Edwards St; 707/677-0151) will take care of the rest. Trinidad's two sportfishing charter boats—which operate seasonally—are the 36-foot **JUMPIN' JACK** (707/839-4743 or 800/839-4744 in CA) and the 45-foot **SHENANDOAH** (707/677-3625). Both charters offer morning and afternoon trips daily from Trinidad Pier, and walk-on customers are welcome. The five-hour salmon or rockfish hunt costs about $65 per person, which includes all fishing gear. One-day fishing licenses can be purchased on board the *Jumpin' Jack*. If you're lucky enough to reel in a lunker salmon, haul it to Katy's Smokehouse just up the road from the pier and have them smoke it up and wrap it to go—or even send it via UPS to your home. Katy's salmon jerky isn't bad, either.

RESTAURANTS

Larrupin' Cafe / ★★★

1658 PATRICK'S POINT DR, TRINIDAD; 707/677-0230 Situated on a quiet country road 2 miles north of Trinidad is the region's finest restaurant. You'll like this place from the moment you walk in the front door and admire the eclectic blend of Indonesian and African artifacts, colorful urns full of exotic flowers, and romantic candlelit tables. Dinner always starts with an appetizer board stocked with gravlax, pâté, dark pumpernickel, apple slices, and sauce, followed by a red-and green-leaf salad tossed with a Gorgonzola vinaigrette. The best menu items are the ones barbecued over mesquite fires, such as the pork ribs doused in a sweet-and-spicy barbecue sauce; the barbecued Cornish game hen served with an orange-and-brandy glaze; and a generous cut of fresh halibut, basted with lemon butter and served with mustard-flavored dill sauce. Often, oysters, mussels, and crab are served the same day they're plucked from Humboldt Bay. For dessert go with either the pecan-chocolate pie topped with hot buttered rum sauce, or the triple-layer chocolate cake layered with caramel and whipped cream. In winter the wood-burning fireplace gives off welcomed warmth; otherwise, request a table on the bamboo-fenced patio near the reflecting pool. Note: They don't take credit cards and the hours tend to vary seasonally, so be sure to call ahead and bring plenty of cash. *$$; no credit cards; checks OK; dinner Thurs–Mon; beer and wine; reservations recommended; from Hwy 101, take the Trinidad exit and head N on Patrick's Point Dr.* &

LODGINGS

The Lost Whale Bed and Breakfast Inn / ★★★

3452 PATRICK'S POINT DR, TRINIDAD; 707/677-3425 OR 800/677-7859 The Lost Whale isn't just a place to stay overnight; it's a destination in itself—particularly for families with small children. The traditional Cape Cod–style building, constructed in 1989, stands alone on a 4-acre grassy cliff overlooking the sea, with a private stairway leading down to miles of deserted rocky beach. The innkeepers manage to give romancing couples lots of space and solitude, yet they also have created one of the most family-friendly inns on the California coast. Five of the inn's eight soundproof rooms have private balconies or sitting alcoves with views of the Pacific, two rooms have separate sleeping lofts, and all have private baths and queen-size beds. After a day on the inn's private beach or at neighboring Patrick's Point State Park, relax in the outdoor hot tub while listening to the distant bark of sea lions or looking out for whales. Kids can romp around on the playground, which has a small playhouse with its own loft. You'll also enjoy the huge breakfasts—casseroles, quiches, home-baked muffins, fresh fruit, locally smoked salmon—and the profusion of snacks provided throughout the day and evening. *$$–$$$; AE, DIS, MC, V; checks OK; info@lostwhaleinn.com; www.lostwhaleinn.com; from Hwy 101, take the Seawood Dr exit and head N for 11 miles on Patrick's Point Dr.*

Trinidad Bay Bed and Breakfast / ★★

560 EDWARDS ST, TRINIDAD; 707/677-0840 Perched 175 feet above the ocean on a bluff overlooking Trinidad's quaint fishing harbor and the rugged California coast, this postcard-perfect Cape Cod–style inn is the dream house of innkeepers Cor and Don Blue (known to their friends as CorDon Bleu), Southern California transplants who fell in love with the area while vacationing here. The decor includes an eclectic mix of New England antiques and an impressive collection of antique clocks. There are four guest rooms—two standard rooms and two suites—all with private bathrooms. Both suites have private entrances, comfortable sitting rooms, spectacular views of Trinidad Bay, and breakfast-in-bed service. Guests love the Mauve Fireplace Suite because of its two comfy rockers situated in front of a wood-burning brick fireplace, the wraparound window with an amazing view, and the king-size bed. The full breakfast—served promptly at 8:30am—features entrees such as French toast puff and Italian egg pie accompanied by fresh and baked fruit and homemade breads. Note: The inn is open daily March through November, weekends only December through February. *$$$; MC, V; checks OK; info@trinidadbaybnb.com; www.trinidadbaybnb.com; from Hwy 101, take the Trinidad exit to Main St and turn left on Trinity St.*

Orick and Redwood National and State Parks

The burl art capital of the world, Orick looks more like a huge outdoor gift shop than a town. What's burl art, you ask? Well, take a sizable chunk of redwood, do a little carving here and there with a small chain saw, and when it resembles some sort of mammal or rodent, you have yourself a piece. There are thousands of burl pieces to choose from here, ranging from the Abominable Burlman to Sasquatch and the Seven Dwarfs. Several roadside stands have viewing booths where mesmerized tourists watch the redwood chips fly. Orick is also the southern entry to **REDWOOD NATIONAL AND STATE PARKS**; one mile south of town off Highway 101 is the **REDWOOD INFORMATION CENTER** (707/464-6101, ext. 5265; www.nps.gov/redw), where visitors can pick up a free park map and browse through geologic, wildlife, and Native American exhibits; open every day 9am to 5pm.

Of course, the best way to experience the parks and their magnificent redwoods is on foot. The short **FERN CANYON TRAIL** leads through an incredibly lush fern grotto. The **LADY BIRD JOHNSON GROVE LOOP** is an easy, one-hour self-guided tour that loops 1 mile around a gorgeous grove of redwoods. Closer to shore is the **YUROK LOOP NATURE TRAIL** at Lagoon Creek, located 6½ miles north of the Klamath River bridge on Highway 101; the 1-mile self-guided trail gradually climbs to the top of rugged sea bluffs—with wonderful panoramic views of the Pacific—and loops back to the parking lot. Perhaps the summa cum laude of trails is the **BOY SCOUT TREE TRAIL**, a 6-mile round-trip hike through a cool, damp forest brimming with giant ferns and majestic redwoods.

To see the world's tallest tree—we're talkin' 368 feet tall and 14 feet in diameter—you'll first have to go to the Redwood Information Center near Orick (see above) to obtain a free map and permit—only 50 issued per day—to drive to the trailhead of **TALL TREES GROVE**. Of course, you still have to walk a steep 1⅓ miles from the trailhead to the grove, but the reward is one of the most beautiful and awe-inspiring walks you'll ever take—particularly in the fall, when the brilliant yellow maple leaves blanket the ground.

RESTAURANTS

Rolf's Park Cafe / ★

HWY 101, ORICK; 707/488-3841 After decades of working as a chef in Switzerland, Austria, San Francisco, and even aboard the presidential ship SS Roosevelt, the trilingual Rolf Rheinschmidt decided it was time to semiretire. He wanted to move to a small town to cook, and towns don't get much smaller than Orick—population 650. So here, among the redwoods, Rheinschmidt serves up good bratwurst, Wiener schnitzel, and crepes suzette. His specialty is marinated rack of spring lamb, and he has some unusual offerings such as wild boar, buffalo, and elk steak (the truly adventurous should get the combo platter featuring all three). Each dinner entree includes lots of extras: hors d'oeuvres, salad, vegetables, farm-style potatoes, and bread. And ever since the debut of Rheinschmidt's German Farmer Omelet—an open-faced concoction of ham, bacon, sausage, mushrooms, cheese, potatoes, and pasta, topped with sour cream and salsa and garnished with a strawberry crepe—breakfast in Orick has never been the same. *$$; MC, V; local checks only; breakfast, lunch, dinner every day in summer (typically open Mar–Sept); beer and wine; no reservations; 2 miles N of Orick.* &

Klamath

From the looks of it, the town of Klamath hasn't recovered much since it was washed away in 1964, when 40 inches of rain fell within 24 hours. All that remains are a few cheap motels, trailer parks, tackle shops, and boat rental outlets, kept in business by the numerous anglers who line the mighty Klamath River, one of the finest salmon and steelhead streams in the world. The scenery around the river is extraordinary; **REDWOOD NATIONAL PARK** and **KLAMATH NATIONAL FOREST** have some incredible coastal drives and trails that even the timid and out-of-shape can handle with aplomb.

Stretch out your legs at the lofty **KLAMATH OVERLOOK,** which stands about 600 feet above an estuary at the mouth of the Klamath River. A short but steep trail leads down to a second overlook that's ideal for whale watching and taking photographs. To get there, take the Requa Road turnoff from Highway 101, north of the Klamath River bridge. For more hiking recommendations, read about Redwood National and State Parks in Orick (above).

One of the premier coastal drives on the Redwood Coast starts at the mouth of the Klamath River and runs 8 miles south toward **PRAIRIE CREEK REDWOODS STATE PARK.** If you're heading south on Highway 101, take the Alder Camp Road exit just south of the Klamath River bridge and follow the signs to the river mouth. North-bound travelers should take the Redwood National and State Parks Coastal Drive exit off the **NEWTON B. DRURY SCENIC PARKWAY.** Campers and cars with trailers are not advised. The narrow, partially paved road winds through stands of redwoods, with spectacular views of the sea and numerous turnouts for picture-taking (sea lions and pelicans abound) and short hikes. Keep an eye out for the World War II radar station disguised as a farmhouse and barn.

If you've never toured the mighty Klamath River aboard a giant jet boat, you're missing out on one heck of a thrill ride. These incredibly powerful and fast boats take visitors from the estuary upriver to view bear, deer, elk, osprey hawks, otters, and other wildlife along the riverbanks. They typically operate May through October. For more information and reservations, contact **KLAMATH RIVER JET BOAT TOURS** (707/482-5822 or 800/887-JETS; www.jetboattours.com).

LODGINGS

The Requa Inn / ★

451 REQUA RD, KLAMATH; 707/482-1425 OR 866/800-8777 The Requa Inn (pronounced "RECK-wah") was established in 1885, and despite going through several owners, four name changes, one relocation, and a major fire that burned it to the ground in 1914 (it was rebuilt the same year), this venerable riverside inn is still going strong. The slow pace, beautiful surroundings, and rustic simplicity give this boxy ol' inn its charm, and the inexpensive rates only add to the appeal. The 10 spacious guest rooms are modestly decorated with antique furnishings and have private baths with showers or claw-footed tubs. Four rooms offer views of the lower Klamath River, and all are refreshingly TV- and phone-free. Most guests, however, spend their time in the spacious sitting room, reading or doing jigsaw puzzles beside the wood-burning fireplace, or just sipping wine while admiring the view from the large picture window. Both breakfast and dinner are served in the inn's dining room, where guests feast on large portions of simple, straightforward dishes made with fresh ingredients. Excellent hiking trails through the Redwood National Park surround the lodge, and during salmon season you'll undoubtedly meet some ardent fishermen and dine on huge servings of the freshest possible salmon. *$–$$; DIS, MC, V; checks OK; breakfast (guests only) and dinner every day; beer and wine; www.requainn.com; from Hwy 101, take the Requa Rd exit and follow the signs.* ⅋

Crescent City

Because it's the northern gateway to the popular **REDWOOD NATIONAL AND STATE PARKS** (for park highlights, see Orick, above), one might assume Crescent City would be a major tourist mecca, rife with fine restaurants and hotels. Unfortunately, it's not. Cheap motels, fast-food chains, and mini-malls are the main attractions along this stretch of Highway 101, as if Crescent City exists only to serve travelers on their way someplace else. The city is trying, however, to enhance its image, and if you know where to go (which is anywhere off Highway 101), there are actually numerous sites worth visiting in the area and several outdoor-recreation options that are refreshingly nontouristy. You won't want to make Crescent City your primary destination, mind you, but don't be reluctant to spend a day lolling around here, either; you'd be surprised what the town has to offer besides gas and groceries.

For starters, take a side trip to the **NORTH COAST MARINE MAMMAL CENTER** (at the N end of Crescent City Harbor, at 424 Howe Dr in Beach Front Park; 707/465-MAML). This nonprofit organization was established in 1989 to rescue and rehabilitate stranded or injured marine mammals. Staffed by volunteers and funded by donations, the center is the only facility of its kind between San Francisco and Seattle, providing emergency response during environmental disasters and assisting marine researchers by collecting data on marine mammals. The center is open to the public every day year-round, and visitors are welcome to watch the volunteers in action, make a donation, and buy a nature book or two at the gift shop.

Other interesting local sites include the operational **BATTERY POINT LIGHTHOUSE** (707/464-3089), built in 1856 on a small island off the foot of A Street. Guided tours of the lighthouse and the light-keeper's living quarters are offered Wednesday through Sunday from 10am to 4pm, April through September, tide permitting (you have to cross a tide pool to get there). Next, head to the **B STREET PIER** (at the S foot of B St), rent a crab net ($5) and fishing pole ($5 including tackle) from

Popeye's bait shop, and do some fishing and crabbing off the city's 800-foot-long pier. Crabbing is simple: throw the prebaited net into the water (don't forget to tie the other end to the pier), wait about 10 minutes, then pull it up and see what's for supper. Because it's a public pier, you don't even need a fishing license.

If you're not one to get your hands dirty, take a shoreline tour along **PEBBLE BEACH DRIVE** from the west end of Sixth Street to Point St. George. You're bound to see a few seals and sea lions at the numerous pullouts. End the tour with a short walk though a sandy meadow to **POINT ST. GEORGE,** a relatively deserted bluff that's perfect for a picnic or beach stroll. On a clear day, look out on the ocean for the **ST. GEORGE REEF LIGHTHOUSE,** reportedly the tallest (146 feet above sea level), deadliest (several light-keepers died in rough seas while trying to dock), and most expensive ($704,000) lighthouse ever built.

One of the prettiest picnic sites on the California coast is along **ENDERTS ROAD** at the south end of town. Drive 3 miles south on Highway 101 from downtown, turn right on Enderts Road (across from the Ocean Way Motel), and continue 2⅓ miles. Park at the Crescent Beach Overlook, lay your blanket on the grass, and admire the ocean view. Type A personalities can drive to the end of Enderts Road and take the 1.2-mile round-trip hiking trail to **ENDERTS BEACH.** In the summer, free 1½- to 2-hour ranger-guided tide pool and seashore walks are offered when the tides are right, starting at the beach parking lot. For specific tour times, call 707/464-6101, ext. 5265.

Crescent City's best-kept secret, however, is the **LAKE EARL WILDLIFE AREA,** a gorgeous habitat replete with deer, rabbits, beavers, otters, red-tailed hawks, peregrine falcons, bald eagles, songbirds (some 80 species), shorebirds, and migratory waterfowl who share these 5,000 acres of pristine woodlands, grasslands, and ocean shore. Hiking and biking are permitted, but you'll want to make the trip on foot with binoculars in hand to get the full effect of this amazing patch of coastal land. To get there, take the Northcrest Drive exit off Highway 101 in downtown Crescent City and turn left on Old Mill Road. Proceed 1½ miles to the park headquarters at 2591 Old Mill Road (if it's open, ask for a map) and park in the gravel lot. Additional trails start at the end of Old Mill Road. For more information, call the Department of Fish and Game (707/464-2523).

And if you're planning to explore the Redwood National and State Parks, be sure to pick up a free map and guide at the **REDWOOD NATIONAL PARK HEADQUARTERS AND INFORMATION CENTER** (1111 2nd St at K St; 707/464-6101, ext. 5064).

RESTAURANTS

Beachcomber Restaurant / ★

1400 HWY 101 S, CRESCENT CITY; 707/464-2205 Although several trendy eateries have made a brave stand in Crescent City, they've all fallen by the wayside. Perched right on the beach a couple of miles south of Crescent City's center, the venerable Beachcomber Restaurant has been the locals' favorite for a reliably good meal since 1975. If you can live with the hokey nautical theme (scatterings of driftwood, fishnets, and buoys dangling above a dimly lit dining room), the restaurant does a commendable job of providing fresh seafood—halibut, red snapper, lingcod, shark, sturgeon, Pacific salmon—that is refreshingly free of heavy or complicated sauces. The Beachcomber also specializes in flame-broiled steaks, cooked to your specification on an open madrone-wood barbecue pit. Thick cuts of prime rib are the special every Saturday and Sunday. Ask for a booth by the window and start the evening with the steamer-clam appetizer: 1½ pounds of the North Coast's finest. *$$; MC, V; local checks only; dinner Thurs–Tues (closed Dec–Jan and part of Feb); beer and wine; reservations recommended; 2 miles S of downtown.* &

LODGINGS

Crescent Beach Motel / ★

1455 HWY 101 S, CRESCENT CITY; 707/464-5436 Crescent City has the dubious distinction of being the only city along the coast without a swanky hotel or B&B. There is, however, an armada of inexpensive accommodations, the best of which is the Crescent Beach Motel. A color scheme of brown, beige, and green has considerably improved the simply furnished interiors since our last visit, and all but 4 of the 27 rooms are within steps of the beach. Most units have queen-size beds and color TVs. The small lawn area and large sundecks overlooking the ocean are great venues for kicking back and enjoying some true R&R. Another perk: You can get a pretty good seafood dinner at the Beachcomber Restaurant (see review, above), which is right down the street. *$; AE, DIS, MC, V; no checks; www.crescent beachmotel.com; 2 miles S of downtown.* &

Curly Redwood Lodge / ★

701 HWY 101, CRESCENT CITY; 707/464-2137 Built in 1957 with lumber milled from a single ancient redwood, the Curly Redwood Lodge looks as if it's been preserved in a time capsule from the '60s, the kind of place where you might have stayed as a kid during one of those cross-country vacations in the family station wagon (with wood paneling, of course). Granted, it's not as fancy as the newer chain motels down the highway, but it's loaded with old-school charm (as well as the requisite TVs and telephones), lean on price, and generously spacious—particularly the two-room suites, which are perfect for families. As an added bonus, both the beach and the Beachcomber Restaurant (see review, above) are right across the highway. *$; AE, DC, MC, V; no checks; info@curlyredwood lodge.com; www.curlyredwoodlodge.com; 2 miles S of downtown on Hwy 101.*

NORTH MOUNTAINS

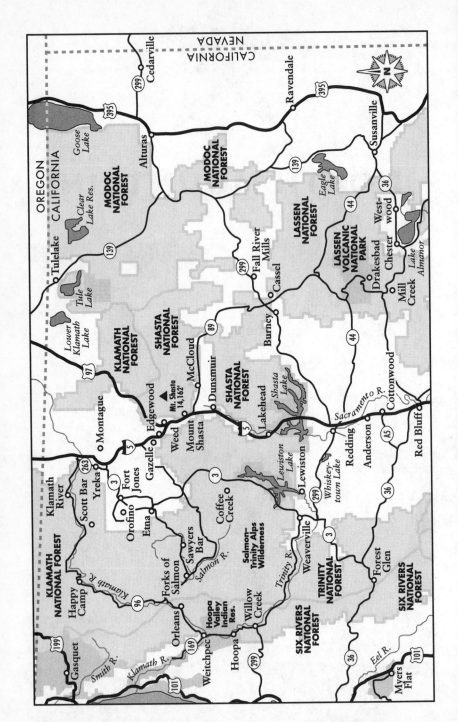

NORTH MOUNTAINS

As you drive north toward Redding up the flat, uninspiring Interstate 5 corridor, snow-topped Mount Shasta appears as a white smudge at the end of the highway. Venture a little closer and the imposing volcano soon dominates the horizon. This unforgettable sight heralds your approach to California's northern mountains. Step out of your car and you'll feel as though you've stepped back in time to a simpler (and, frequently, less expensive) way of life. This area offers everything a pleasure-seeking visitor could hope for: prime fishing, bird-watching, boating, waterskiing, mountain biking, rock climbing, camping, hiking, river rafting, kayaking, golfing, and, in winter, every kind of snow sport.

This little piece of California is nature's unspoiled, uncrowded playground. You can detoxify in one of the many gorgeous mineral springs; hang out on a houseboat on Shasta Lake; explore the tortured lava caves and steaming thermal vents in Lassen Volcanic National Park; take a scenic ride on the dinner train departing from the adorable little town of McCloud; bike or cross-country ski the 10-mile paved path at Lake Almanor; or, if you're in really good shape, climb the magic mountain itself.

Accommodations in this part of the state range from wonderful wood cabins lit by kerosene lanterns to luxurious bed-and-breakfasts. Some very good restaurants are tucked away in places you've probably never heard of—Weaverville, Dunsmuir, and Chester—which makes touring California's northern mountain towns a constant culinary adventure.

ACCESS AND INFORMATION

The region is predominantly medium-high mountain ranges (the Cascades, the Salmon and Siskiyou Mountains), with high desert and rangeland to the east. The three major highways run north-south. **INTERSTATE 5** from Los Angeles and Sacramento leaves the Central Valley at Redding (the largest town in the northern mountains region) and continues to Dunsmuir, Mount Shasta City, Weed, and Yreka, then on to Oregon. **US 395** heads north from Reno, Nevada, through high desert and not much else until it gets to Alturas, then leaves California via its lonely northeastern corner. **HIGHWAY 89**, the curviest of the three north-south routes, starts from **US 395** north of Reno and heads northwest to Lake Almanor and Chester. It winds its way through Lassen Volcanic National Park past Burney and McCloud, skirting the great mountain, then joins Interstate 5 just south of Mount Shasta City.

East-west roads through this country are mostly mountainous. **HIGHWAY 299** from Arcata to Redding via Weaverville is officially described as going "from the Redwood Coast to the Valley Oaks," neglecting any mention of the roller-coaster curves. From Redding it continues east to Alturas. **HIGHWAY 44** is the best route to Lassen Volcanic National Park from Redding.

The only airport in the region is the **REDDING MUNICIPAL AIRPORT**, served by two airlines, Alaska Airlines/Horizon Air (800/252-7522; http://horizonair.alaskaair.com) and United Express (800/241-6522; www.united.com). Car rentals are available there. The closest major airport is **SACRAMENTO INTERNATIONAL AIRPORT** (916/929-5411; 150 miles S of Redding; http://airports.saccounty.net).

GREYHOUND BUS (800/231-2222; www.greyhound.com) serves the towns along Interstate 5, and **AMTRAK'S COAST STARLIGHT** Train (800/USA-RAIL; www.amtrak.com) from Seattle to Los Angeles makes two stops a day (one each way) at Dunsmuir and Redding.

For more information, contact the **REDDING CONVENTION AND VISITORS BUREAU** (777 Auditorium Dr, Redding; 800/874-7562; www.visitredding.org) or the **SHASTA CASCADE WONDERLAND ASSOCIATION** (800/474-2782; www. shastacascade.org), which offers information on Lassen, Modoc, Plumas, Siskiyou, Shasta, and Trinity counties.

Redding and the Shasta Lake Area

About 20 minutes north of Redding, Shasta Lake, the largest reservoir in California and "Houseboat Capital of the World," is a perfect introduction to the pleasures of the region and the ideal place for fishing, waterskiing, or just lounging with a good book in the sun on a houseboat. Be sure to stop in Redding for homey pleasures and a bit of local history.

Redding

A popular attraction here is the new $15 million, 34,000-square-foot **TURTLE BAY EXPLORATION PARK** (530/243-8850; www.turtlebay.org), which provides a hands-on exploration of the natural world and explains how we all fit into it. On the banks of the Sacramento River, the park houses a museum, a river aquarium, the Butterfly House (May–September), live animals, a forest camp, several history and science exhibits, an art gallery, a museum store, a cafe, and activities for all ages. You can walk along an elevated boardwalk through a riparian forest and seasonal wetland or come face to face with white sturgeon, bull trout, and perch at the largest freshwater native fish aquarium in California. The art gallery displays a selection of original Ansel Adams photographs, and the Exploration Hall traces the historical path of the Wintu Indians. The museum is part of an $84 million complex now under way, which will eventually include a pedestrian bridge over the Sacramento River linking the museum to the north bank, with access to an arboretum, a wildlife center, and the existing Sacramento River trails.

The 10-mile long **SACRAMENTO RIVER TRAIL** meanders along the town's riverbanks and over a stress-ribbon concrete bridge—the only bridge of its kind in the country. This section of the river also offers good year-round urban fishing for steelhead, trout, and salmon; for information about where to cast your line, call Redding's world-class fly-fishing store, the **FLY SHOP** (800/669-3474). **WHISKEYTOWN LAKE**, west of Redding, offers great beaches, windsurfing, and sailings; for information, call the lake's visitors center (530/246-1225).

RESTAURANTS

Buz's Crab / ★

 2159 EAST ST, REDDING; 530/243-2120 Every day the bounty of the North Coast is hauled over the hills into California's parched interior to Buz's seafood market. With naugahyde booths and Formica tables, this ain't no pretty place for a romantic dinner for two, but Buz's earns its star for doing what it does perfectly. The seafood baskets offer much more than your standard fish-and-chips: you'll find everything here—from stuffed prawns, oysters, scallops, and clam strips to calamari, catfish, Cajun halibut, and crisp potato rounds. From December through May, order the fabulous crab (just plucked from the boiling crab pots on the patio), along with a slab of Buz's fresh-baked sourdough bread. Be sure to ask for a free copy of their excellent cioppino recipe. *$–$$; MC, V; local checks only; lunch, dinner every day; beer and wine; no reservations; N of W Cypress Ave and Pine St.*

Cheesecakes Unlimited & Cafe / ★★

1344 MARKET ST, REDDING; 530/244-6670 Cory Gabrielson and Nicholas Parker started Cheesecakes Unlimited as a wholesale cheesecake business, then opened a small cafe that offers light meals—so now you can have your cake and eat croissant sandwiches and freshly made salads, too. A couple of winners are the house-smoked salmon salad with tomatoes, cucumbers, asparagus, and oregano vinaigrette; and the prawn and pasta salad with a roasted garlic and herbed vinaigrette dressing. Of course, the New York–style cheesecakes (lemon, chocolate-chocolate, raspberry, almond amaretto, and mocha Baileys) are the kind you'd never want to pass up—or even share with your mate. *$; AE, DIS, MC, V; checks OK; lunch Mon–Fri; beer and wine; reservations recommended; just N of the downtown mall.* &

Jack's Grill / ★★

1743 CALIFORNIA ST, REDDING 530/241-9705 A 1930s tavern, Jack's Grill is a beloved institution in Redding—so beloved, in fact, that few even grumble over the typical two-hour wait for a table on the weekend. But be forewarned: this is a carnivores-only club, specializing in huge, juicy 1-pound steaks, tender brochettes, and thick steak sandwiches. The meaty meals are served with garlic bread, a green salad, a potato, and coffee. Jack starts cooking at 5pm, and hungry folks get there early. *$$; AE, DIS, MC, V; local checks only; dinner Mon–Sat; full bar; no reservations; S of the downtown mall, between Sacramento and Placer Sts.*

La Gondola / ★★

630 N MARKET ST, REDDING; 530/244-6321 La Gondola is so popular in Redding that when it moved to its current location, loans from loyal customers kept it going until the new place was up and running. The restaurant specializes in northern Italian cuisine, which features creamier, less spicy sauces than southern Italian food. Some of the most popular entrees are chicken stuffed with prosciutto cooked in white wine and cream; filet mignon topped with roasted garlic, caramelized onions, and Madeira; and spinach- and cheese-filled agnolotti. The restaurant's version of tiramisu, a

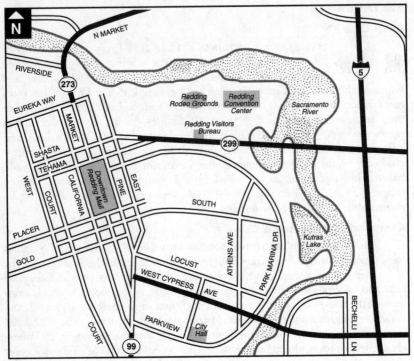

REDDING

layered confection of chocolate, mascarpone cheese, and Kahlua, is justifiably famous. *$$; AE, DIS, MC, V; local checks only; dinner Tues–Sat, brunch Sun; beer and wine; reservations recommended; a few blocks N of the Sacramento River.* &

LODGINGS

Tiffany House Bed and Breakfast Inn / ★★

1510 BARBARA RD, REDDING; 530/244-3225 Perched on a hill above town, Brady and Susan Stewart's beautifully refurbished Cape Cod–style home offers three guest rooms and a cottage, a swimming pool, and a fine view of Mount Lassen. The Victorian Rose Room, dressed in black-and-mauve rose-print walls, features charming cupola windows and a claw-footed bathtub. If you're an early bird, you'll appreciate the blue and white Tierra Room and the larger Oak Room, which both offer great sunrise views. Each room has a queen-size bed and a private bath. Guests are welcome to lounge in the antique-filled music parlor, where old-time sheet music is stacked on the piano. Another parlor houses a game table and a fireplace, an ideal retreat on cool nights. If you prefer total privacy (and can fork over a few more bucks), rent the attractive guest cottage, where you can bask in the luxurious indoor spa. *$$–$$$; AE, DIS, MC, V; checks OK; www.sylvia.com/tiffany.htm; off Benton Dr.*

Shasta Lake

To fully appreciate Shasta Lake's 370 miles of shoreline, view the lake by boat. And while you're at it, keep your eye on the sky for a glimpse of the mighty **BALD EAGLE**, the largest bird of prey in North America. Shasta Lake is currently the home of at least 18 pairs of the endangered bird—the largest nesting population of bald eagles in California. For information about other lake attractions and **HOUSEBOAT RENTALS**, contact the **REDDING CONVENTION AND VISITORS BUREAU** (800/874-7562; www.visitredding.org) or the **SHASTA CASCADE WONDERLAND ASSOCIATION** (800/474-2782; www.shastacascade.org).

If you're heading up to Shasta Lake on I-5, the monolithic 3,640-foot-long **SHASTA DAM** (from I-5, take the Shasta Dam Blvd exit and follow the signs; 530/275-4463) is a great place to pull over for a lengthy pit stop. Shasta is the second-largest and second-tallest concrete dam in the United States (it contains enough concrete to build a 3-foot-wide sidewalk around the world) and one of the most impressive civil engineering feats in the nation. The visitors center and viewing area are rather ho-hum, but the free 45-minute tour of the dam is outstanding. It kicks off with a speedy elevator ride into the chilly bowels of the 15-million-ton, 602-foot-high structure—definitely not recommended for claustrophobes. Dam tours are scheduled from 9am to 4pm every day; call for information and winter and holiday hours.

About 10 miles north of the dam is another popular attraction: guided tours of the impressive, crystal-studded stalagmites and stalactites in the **LAKE SHASTA CAVERNS** (from I-5, take the Shasta Caverns Rd exit and follow the signs; 530/238-2341). Getting there is an adventure in itself; after you pull off the highway and check in at cavern headquarters, you'll have to hop aboard a ferry for a 15-minute trip across Shasta Lake, then climb onto a bus for a white-knuckle ride up to the caverns (open every day, year-round). And anglers take note: The stretch of the **SACRAMENTO RIVER** between Shasta Lake and Mount Shasta is one of the top spots in the country for trout fishing, so don't forget to pack the rod and reel. For tips on touring the area north of Shasta Lake, see the Mount Shasta section in this chapter.

The Trinity Alps Region

National forest blankets 70 percent of Trinity County, which includes the stunning Trinity Alps north of Highway 299. The area is chock-full of good fishing spots, especially on the **TRINITY RIVER**, **TRINITY LAKE**, and **LEWISTON LAKE**. Mountain bikers, hikers, and horseback riders flock to the scenic 50-mile **WEAVER BASIN TRAIL**, which circles Weaverville.

NORTH MOUNTAINS THREE-DAY TOUR

DAY ONE: Trail and rail. Spend the first night in Chester. Have dinner under the aspens (and by the creek) on the deck of the **CYNTHIA'S** and stay at the **BIDWELL HOUSE BED AND BREAKFAST INN.** In the morning, grab breakfast at the B&B and then stop at one of the grocery stores downtown and get picnic fixings before you head out to **LASSEN VOLCANIC NATIONAL PARK**, where you can stretch your legs by walking the **BUMPASS HELL TRAIL** past wildflowers, hissing fumaroles, steam vents, and assorted mud pots. Back in the car, continue north on Highway 89 around Mount Lassen, briefly stopping at 129-foot-high **MCARTHUR-BURNEY FALLS** to watch some of the 200 million gallons of water that fall there daily. A short trip through the pines will get you to **MCCLOUD** to board the **SHASTA SUNSET DINNER TRAIN** for a fine dinner with **MOUNT SHASTA** as a backdrop. Repair to the **MCCLOUD BED AND BREAKFAST HOTEL** for the night.

DAY TWO: Up a mystic mountain. Fuel up at the B&B, then move on to Mount Shasta, stopping at **MOUNT SHASTA BOARD & SKI PARK** to rent a mountain bike and gear. Take the ski lift to the top (elevation: 6,600 feet) and bike back down to the lodge. Repeat this as many times as your nerves and muscles will allow. Then make the

Lewiston

LODGINGS

Old Lewiston Inn / ★★

DEADWOOD RD, LEWISTON; 530/778-3414 OR 800/286-4441 This B&B on the banks of the Trinity River's fly-fishing-only section caters—surprise—to fly fishermen (and women). It has seven guest rooms: three small rooms in the 1875 Baker House and four rooms in the adjoining inn. Most have private baths. A favorite is the Baker House's Herbert Hoover Room, where the 31st president once slept. The inn accommodations have less history but more elbow room, with private entrances and decks overlooking the Trinity River. The Old Lewiston Inn also has a hot tub for unwinding after a hard day of touring the area or fishing for trout. While you're having your hearty country breakfast, you can eat and keep an eye out the back door for fish rising in the river. $$; DIS, MC, V; checks OK; www.oldlewiston.com; ½ block from the bridge. ♿

Weaverville

Founded nearly 150 years ago by gold miners, the little rural town of Weaverville, population 4,000, is the largest town in Trinity County (an area the size of Rhode short drive to **MOUNT SHASTA CITY**, stopping at Lily's for lunch on the deck before you check in at the **MOUNT SHASTA RANCH BED AND BREAKFAST**. Do some serious lounging on the front lawn for late-afternoon views of America's most photogenic mountain before you get back in the car for a short jaunt to Dunsmuir for dinner at **CAFE MADDALENA**. Afterward, take a walk in the town's restored historic railroad section along Sacramento Avenue.

DAY THREE: Nature's temple. After a scrumptious breakfast at the inn, head for the beautiful **UPPER SACRAMENTO RIVER** (it's more of a stream here) down to **SHASTA LAKE**, stopping first for a ferry ride across the lake to visit the **LAKE SHASTA CAVERNS** with 20-foot-high stalactites/mites, followed by a stop at **SHASTA DAM**. Take the tour of the dam, descending 600 feet into its bowels to view its dynamos and turbines. Then it's on to **REDDING**, with a stop at **BUZ'S CRAB** for a quick Louie and a cold drink before heading west into the **TRINITY ALPS** to **WEAVERVILLE**. Walk around this 1850s gold-mining town that reeks of history, being sure to peek in at the old Chinese miners' **TAOIST TEMPLE** on Main Street. End your tour with one of Sharon Heryford's great dinners at the **LA GRANGE CAFE**, two short blocks from the temple, before heading to the **OLD LEWISTON INN** in Lewiston to unwind.

Island and Delaware combined). While cruising through the historic downtown district, keep your peepers open for the peculiar outdoor spiral staircases that grace many of the homes—they're remnants of the days when a different person owned each floor. For a bit of Gold Rush and Weaverville history, stroll down Main Street and visit the small **JAKE JACKSON MUSEUM** (508 Main St; 530/623-5211). Adjacent to the museum is **JOSS HOUSE STATE HISTORIC PARK**, site of the oldest **CHINESE TEMPLE** (530/623-5284) in the United States. The well-preserved temple was built by immigrant Chinese miners in 1874 and is worth a peek (and the nominal entrance fee); call for information on temple tours.

Another town highlight is the grueling **LA GRANGE CLASSIC MOUNTAIN BIKE RACE**, typically held the first weekend in June. To find out more about this mountain town's activities, call the **TRINITY COUNTY CHAMBER OF COMMERCE** (530/623-6101 or 800/487-4648). For information about fishing in the region, visit the helpful staff at **TRINITY FLY SHOP**, located at the bottom of Ohio Hill, Lewiston; 530/623-6757.

RESTAURANTS

La Grange Cafe / ★★★

226 MAIN ST, WEAVERVILLE; 530/623-5325 Named after a nearby mine, La Grange Cafe serves the best food in the county. Start your dinner with chef-owner Sharon Heryford's exceptionally fresh salad tossed with an Italian dressing and chunks of blue cheese. Then sink your teeth into her charbroiled

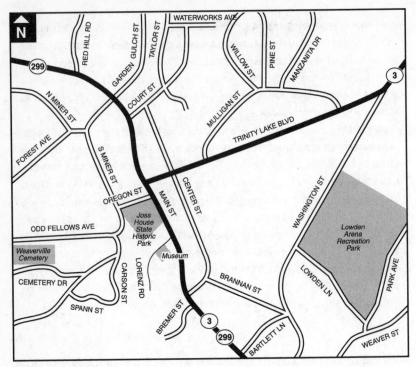

WEAVERVILLE

marinated steak served with black bean chili, or try one of the game dishes such as venison loin chops or buffalo burger steak. There are lots of choices of seafood, chicken, and pasta dishes, too. An excellent and moderately priced wine list boasts more than 100 selections. And then there's the sweet stuff: divine desserts—berry cobbler, banana cream pie, and old-fashioned bread pudding are made on the premises. La Grange is located in a big, airy brick building in the town's historic area, with lots of room for the folks who flock to the place. *$$; AE, DIS, MC, V; checks OK; breakfast Sun, lunch, dinner every day; full bar; reservations recommended; on Hwy 299.* &

Noelle's Garden Cafe / ★★

252 MAIN ST, WEAVERVILLE; 530/623-2058 This snug, cheerful cafe in an old two-story house has a phalanx of windows and a sunny outside deck. Proprietor Noelle Roget's specialties include Austrian strudel (a flaky puff pastry filled with shrimp, veggies, and cheeses) and a hefty veggie melt served with her home fries spiced with garlic and onion. The seasonal dinner menu may include such dishes as a perfectly cooked lime-marinated halibut or a stir-fry prepared with jumbo shrimp, chicken, or fresh vegetables. She also offers an array of baked desserts, and if the espresso cake is up for grabs, grab it. *$; no credit cards; checks OK; breakfast,*

lunch every day Memorial Day–Labor Day (Tues–Sat Labor Day–Memorial Day),
dinner Fri–Sat year-round; beer and wine; no reservations; 1 block W of Oregon St.

LODGINGS

Red Hill Motel / ★

RED HILL RD, WEAVERVILLE; 530/623-4331 The Red Hill's 14 well-maintained auto-court units (cabins with small covered garages) would have made a great set for a '40s film noir starring Ida Lupino and Humphrey Bogart. (If you've forgotten your film history lessons, auto-courts were a prominent feature of flicks in those days.) So put on your best Bogart fedora and step back in time by booking a night or two at these one- or two-bedroom cabins, decorated with authentic pre–World War II furnishings (except for the remote-control cable TVs and in-room phones, of course). Owners Patty Holder and her husband restored this jewel, surrounded by a rolling green lawn and ponderosa pines. Spend the day reeling in rainbow trout on the Trinity, then prepare your catch for supper at the Red Hill's fish-cleaning station. Or kick back in a lawn chair under the pines and think about the good ol' days, when life was simpler, the fish were bigger, and folks were named Claudette, Clark, Ida, and Humphrey. The friendly Red Hill folks permit pets, too. *$; AE, DIS, MC, V; no checks; across from the U.S. Forest Service station on Main St, at the W end of town.*

Weaverville Hotel

203 MAIN ST, WEAVERVILLE; 800/750-8920 This hotel has been in operation since 1861—a few fiery interruptions notwithstanding (it burned to the ground several times in the town's early days). Under new owners, Jeanne and Brian Muir, it has been totally restored and refurbished. Though the rooms are posh, they have no phones or TVs to ensure that guests slip into Weaverville's more relaxed tempo. Instead, there is a phone booth in the hall (restored of course), and a flat screen TV/VCR in a lounge behind the more formal lobby. Five of seven rooms have gas log fireplaces, and all have private showers as well as claw-foot tubs and spas. In colder seasons, the four-poster queen beds are converted to feather beds. Coffee, tea, and cookies are always available, and guests can use the gym across the street. Because of the antique furnishings, the hotel is not suitable for children under 12. *$$–$$$; AE, MC, V; checks OK; www.weavervillehotel.com; in the center of town.*

Willow Creek

RESTAURANTS

Cinnabar Sam's / ★

19 WILLOW WY, WILLOW CREEK; 530/629-3437 If you travel between the Pacific coastline and Redding, be sure to stop for a bite at Cinnabar Sam's. A popular hangout for rafters and kayakers, this restaurant is decked out in Western memorabilia: antique gas pumps, old photographs, and movie posters from the golden days—the salad bar is even in a claw-footed tub. A favorite breakfast dish is the Claim Jumper: ham, scrambled eggs, hash browns, onions, bell peppers, sausage, and cheese. For lunch or dinner, try the popular do-it-yourself fajitas, the behemoth burger, the sirloin steak, or the barbecued ribs. *$; AE, DIS, MC, V; checks OK; breakfast, lunch, dinner every day; no reservations; beer and wine; at Hwy 299, at the E end of town.* &

Forks of Salmon

LODGINGS

Otter Bar Lodge / ★★★

SALMON RIVER RD, FORKS OF SALMON; 530/462-4772 Surrounded by a pond and acres of mowed green grass, this seven-bedroom ranch-style lodge features oak floors, French doors, and lots of glass—all in an effort to bring the outdoors indoors. Two living rooms, two kitchens, a sauna, and a hot tub are also available to guests. The cedar-roofed, whitewashed rooms have private decks and down comforters on the beds, and some are stocked with good books. Reserve the romantic Tower Room, an upstairs retreat lined with windows offering views of the fir trees, or try one of the three cabins. Otter Bar Lodge doubles as a world-class kayaking school and offers some of the most beautiful mountain-biking trails in the state. The food is terrific—no ranch-style meat and potatoes here. Instead, look for paella, snapper Veracruz, and other sophisticated delights on the ever-changing menu. Breakfast offerings include veggie omelets, homemade granola, and berry pancakes. Weeklong stays are required. All meals are included in the weekly rate. *$$$$; MC, V; checks OK; open mid-Apr–Sept 30; www.otterbar.com; 15 miles E of Somes Bar.*

Coffee Creek

South of Etna on Highway 3 is the postage-stamp-size town of Coffee Creek, which supposedly got its name from a miner's pack train that spilled coffee into the town's creek, although some claim the name came from the spring runoff, which colors the creek brown. Whatever the case, this town dates back to the Gold Rush days of the 1850s. There aren't many places to dine around here, but your best bet is the **FOREST CAFE** (Hwy 3 at Coffee Creek Rd; 530/266-3575). Venture a little farther south, and you'll see **TRINITY LAKE** (also known as Clair Engle Lake in honor of an environmentally conscious local politician), a popular haunt of anglers and other lovers of the great outdoors.

LODGINGS

Ripple Creek Cabins / ★★

EAGLE CREEK LOOP, COFFEE CREEK; 530/266-3505 OR 510/531-5315 Set amid tall pines and cedars where Ripple Creek enters the Trinity River, all seven of Jim and Michele Coleman's well-furnished cabins have amply stocked kitchens (wow!—corkscrews and garlic presses!) and private baths. Most of the cabins accommodate two to six people. There's also a four-bedroom house for rent—ideal for a family reunion or group retreat. Diversions include table tennis, bicycles, a volleyball and badminton court, and a swimming hole. For a $10 fee, you can even bring your pooch along. *$–$$; no credit cards; checks OK; www.ripplecreek.com; off Hwy 3.*

Mount Shasta and the Yreka Area

Magnificent, snowcapped Mount Shasta, soaring 14,162 feet into the sky, is the largest volcano (by mass) in the contiguous 48 states. Shasta is a dormant volcano; it's not dead, just sleeping until it decides to blow its snowy stack—something it hasn't done since the late 1700s. Nestled about the peak are the railroad, mill, and lumber towns of Dunsmuir, McCloud, and Weed, along with Mount Shasta City. Traveling north toward the Oregon border, you'll discover the rustic treasures and rough-and-tumble pleasures of more small towns set in the great outdoors.

Dunsmuir

When a Southern Pacific train ran off the tracks in 1991 and spilled an herbicide in the Sacramento River, it killed all aquatic life for 45 miles along the river. And it darn near killed Dunsmuir. But this pretty, historic railroad town has a population of 2,300 resilient residents who have brought the town back with a vengeance. Using a financial settlement from Southern Pacific, the townsfolk have gussied up their community and hope to make Dunsmuir a major California tourist destination. They may just succeed. In addition to the beautiful natural surroundings, stylish gift shops and restaurants have sprung up on the city's streets (particularly on Dunsmuir and Sacramento avenues). Furthermore, **TROPHY-SIZE WILD TROUT** now abound in the Sacramento River, and the community slogan is "Home of the best water on earth." Fortunately, not all of the tourists are coming to Dunsmuir by car, thanks to the Amtrak train that stops here daily. Call the **DUNSMUIR CHAMBER OF COMMERCE AND VISITORS CENTER** (800/DUNSMUIR) for the nitty-gritty.

RESTAURANTS

Cafe Maddalena / ★★★

5801 SACRAMENTO AVE, DUNSMUIR; 530/235-2725 The new owners of Cafe Maddalena, chef Brett LaMott and his wife, Nancy, came here after establishing the wildly popular Trinity Cafe in Mount Shasta. They have expanded the previous menu, which was predominantly Sardinian, to include authentic dishes from southern France, Spain, and North Africa. Offerings may include *zarzuela* (a Spanish shellfish stew in a tomato-saffron broth); herb-roasted lamb rack with ratatouille; an exotic couscous with a tagine of yam, carrots, and prunes; or a pan-seared filet mignon with sauce *vin de minervois*. The menu changes seasonally, and everything is made fresh daily, including the bread and desserts. The wine list includes Italian, French, and Spanish labels to complement the entrees. During the summer months, request a table outside under the grape arbor. *$$; DIS, MC, V; checks OK; dinner Thurs–Sun (open March–Dec); beer and wine; reservations recommended; one block W of Dunsmuir Ave across from the Amtrak station and the Sacramento River.*

LODGINGS

Railroad Park Resort/The Caboose Motel

100 RAILROAD PARK RD, DUNSMUIR; 530/235-4440 A must for railroad buffs but a maybe for everyone else, the Railroad Park Resort's funky Caboose Motel offers quiet, comfortable lodgings in a boxcar and 23 refurbished cabooses (cabeese?) from the Southern Pacific, Santa Fe, and Great Northern railroads. Most have king- or queen-size beds with small bay windows or rooftop cupolas. The Boxcar (room 20) is decorated in country antiques and has a small private patio. Motel management also rents out four cabins. All guests have access to the pool and Jacuzzi—not to mention a great view of nearby Castle Crags. Guests may bring along their small pets for an extra $10. And if you're a big prime rib fan, you're in luck: that's the specialty of the Railroad Park Resort Restaurant. *$–$$; MC, V; checks OK; www.rrpark.com; 1 mile S of town.* &

McCloud

A company-built mill town, McCloud bills itself as "the quiet side of Mount Shasta." And true to its motto, this is a relatively sleepy place, but its many sumptuous B&Bs attract a lot of anglers, hikers, and other nature lovers who spend their waking hours outdoors, as well as those bleary-eyed city folk who long for little more than a warm bed and some solitude. Whatever your attraction to this neck of the woods, you can introduce yourself to the area in style by hopping aboard the **SHASTA SUNSET DINNER TRAIN** (530/964-2142 or 800/733-2141; www.shasta sunset.com), which follows a historic turn-of-the-century logging route. Now, as then, the steep grades, sharp curves, and a unique switchback at Signal Butte are still part of the route, though today's passengers ride in cars handsomely restored in wood and brass. As you nosh on a very good dinner in your railcar, you'll be treated to views of Mount Shasta, Castle Crags, and the Trinity Alps. The 40-mile, three-hour journey is run by the McCloud Railway Company year-round and costs $79.95 per person plus tax and gratuity, including dinner. Special-event train trips are scheduled throughout the year.

In the summer, you can watch—or, better yet, join—the McCloud locals as they kick up their heels every night from May to September in the town's air-conditioned dance hall. **DANCING**—especially square dancing—is a favorite pastime here, so if you want to promenade your partner or swing to the beat, call 530/964-2578 for the latest schedule. This part of the North Mountains is also extraordinarily rich in outdoor-recreational opportunities; see the Mount Shasta section for details.

LODGINGS

Hogin House / ★★★

424 LAWNDALE CT, MCCLOUD; 530/964-2882 OR 877-964-2882 Many innkeepers try, but few have managed to create the relaxing ambiance and charm of a country B&B as well as Angie and Rich Toreson have. Located just outside downtown McCloud, their small, delightfully cluttered two-story Victorian house was built in 1904 for the town doctor. The four guest bedrooms are decorated with antique toys, colorful quilts, calico fabrics, and country-style wallpaper. An expanded continental breakfast of fresh fruit, cereal, homemade breads and muffins, juice, coffee, and tea may be served in the dining room, on the porch, or on the lush lawn that sweeps down toward the center of town. It's just a short one-block walk from here to the popular Sunset Dinner Train. *$; AE, DIS, MC, V; checks OK; www.hoginhouse.com; at W Colombero Dr.*

McCloud Bed and Breakfast Hotel / ★★★★

408 MAIN ST, MCCLOUD; 530/964-2822 OR 800/964-2823 Built in 1916, the McCloud Bed and Breakfast Hotel has earned a highly coveted spot on the National Register of Historic Places. Its meticulous restoration was completed in 1995, and now the hotel offers 16 beautiful guest rooms gussied up with antiques, decorator fabrics, and, in many cases, tall four-poster beds. Each room also has a private bath. Gourmet breakfasts of fresh fruit, house-made bread, and a hot dish are served in the lobby area (though if you're staying in a suite, you can have the meal delivered to your room). Lunch and dinner are also available for guests. If you happen to tire of McCloud's numerous outdoor attractions, kick back in the hotel lobby's comfortable chairs and sofas and borrow one of the many books, games, and puzzles stashed here. *$$–$$$; AE, DIS, MC, V; checks OK; www.mccloudhotel.com; from exit off Hwy 89, follow signs to the historic district.* &

The Guest House / ★★★

606 W COLOMBERO DR, MCCLOUD; 530/964-3160 Built in 1907 for McCloud timber baron J. H. Queal, this stately, two-story mansion became the McCloud River Lumber Company's guest house after Queal's death in 1921. Herbert Hoover, Jean Harlow, and various members of the Hearst family dallied here in the '20s and '30s, but soon afterward the house fell into disrepair. Restored as a country inn and restaurant, McCloud Guest House reopened its doors in 1984. In 2003, new ownership brought new life to this wonderful inn. Downstairs in the lobby and dining room are delicately wrought cabinetry, beveled glass, antique wallpaper, and a massive stone fireplace. The inn's five spacious guest rooms have four-poster beds and antique furnishings. A multicourse spa breakfast is served with offerings like fresh fruit smoothies, Belgian waffles, potato pancakes, and, sometimes, freshly baked scones with Devonshire cream. *$$; MC, V; checks OK; www.themccloudguesthouse.com; at the W end of town.*

BIGFOOT STEPPED HERE

Consider yourself forewarned: California's North Mountains are Sasquatch territory. Also known as Bigfoot, this huge, hairy, apelike mammal has been the subject of hundreds of reports in and around Trinity County, including three sightings within 10 miles of each other (by different people) in the Shasta-Trinity National Forest in 1999. There's a Bigfoot Wing in the **WILLOW CREEK/CHINA FLAT MUSEUM** (corner of Hwys 299 and 96 in Willow Creek; 530/629-2653) that commemorates the elusive creature. You'll know you're in the right place when you see the 23-foot redwood carving of Bigfoot out front. The museum contains dozens of plaster casts of large footprints discovered in the Northern California wilderness as well as a Bigfoot research center.

The legend of the man-beast has been around forever, known in many countries and by many names: as Yeti, the abominable snowman; as one of the Mound People; as Sasquatch, a name that comes from an ancient tribal language in British Columbia; and as Bigfoot. Information compiled from thousands of reputed sightings in North America has been organized into a composite description. Bigfoot is typically described as

McCloud River Inn / ★★★

325 LAWNDALE CT, MCCLOUD; 530/964-2130 OR 800/261-7831 At this inn, yet another of the delightful bed-and-breakfasts in charming McCloud, the innkeepers knock themselves out to make sure their guests have a good time. Built at the turn of the century as headquarters for the McCloud River Lumber Company, the inn has been beautifully restored, and its five guest rooms are filled with period-style furnishings. All have private bathrooms (one with a spa tub and one with a claw-footed soaking tub). Breakfast is a big attraction, with fresh fruit, pastries, and frittata. The inn has massage therapists on call and a flower and gift shop. *$–$$$; AE, DIS, MC, V; checks OK; www.mccloudriverinn.com; at the N end of town.*

Mount Shasta

Mount Shasta is only the fifth-highest peak in the state, but unlike its taller cousins, which are clustered with other large mountains, this volcano stands alone, a position that seems to intensify its grandeur. "Lonely as God and white as a winter moon" is how author Joaquin Miller described this solitary peak in the 1870s. The mountain dominates the horizon from every angle, and on clear days it's visible from as far away as 150 miles.

Some Native Americans who lived in its shadow believed Mount Shasta was the home of the Great Spirit and vowed never to climb its sacred slopes, which they viewed as an act of disrespect. Today, men and women from around the world pay tribute to the volcano by making the spectacular trek to the top. This is not a mountain for novice hikers, but with some **BASIC MOUNTAIN CLIMBING** instruction and standing 7 to 12 feet tall and as weighing 250 to 400 pounds. Experts on the subject maintain that there are 133 such creatures living in 16 family groups in North America, and that an average family group consists of 8 members. Bigfoot is nocturnal, lives in caves, and has enhanced night vision, smell, and hearing. You will be relieved to know that the California Sasquatch is a vegetarian, while in the southern part of the United States, Bigfoot is a carnivore. This creature swims well, runs fast, is painfully shy— although curious—and apparently smells really, really bad.

The search for Sasquatch has gone high-tech in recent years, with investigators carrying tape recorders, motion detectors, infrared cameras, and night scopes into the wild. Sharing information on the Internet has enabled searchers to pursue patterns and similarities among the reported encounters. In spite of the footprints, sightings, blurry photographs, and tapes, however, no verifiable physical remains of Sasquatch have been found. A California Department of Fish and Game spokesperson in Redding declared that while Bigfoot sightings do occur in Trinity County, the agency probably won't investigate the most recent ones. "We don't have a management plan for Bigfoot," he explained.

a good study of Shasta's various routes, physically fit adventurers can safely reach its stunning summit ("It's just like climbing stairs nonstop from 9 to 5," says one veteran climber). You can buy a good map of the mountain and rent crampons, an ice ax, and sturdy, insulated climbing boots at the **FIFTH SEASON** (300 N Mount Shasta Blvd at Lake St; 530/926-3606 store, 530/926-5555 mountain report), staffed by experienced and helpful mountaineers. Beginners eager to climb Mount Shasta can take an all-day lesson in basic mountain-climbing skills from the folks at **SHASTA MOUNTAIN GUIDES** (530/926-3117), who also lead three- and four-day guided climbs. And whether you're a beginner or an expert climber, visit the **MOUNT SHASTA RANGER DISTRICT OFFICE** (204 W Alma St off N Mount Shasta Blvd; 530/926-4511), which provides up-to-date climbing literature as well as friendly advice. Get your free (and mandatory) **HIKING PERMIT** while you're there, so the rangers will know how long you'll be on the mountain. Permits are located in a small booth outside the front door. You also must sign off on your permit after you return from your climb so a rescue team won't be sent out to find you.

If all this climbing sounds a wee bit intimidating, there is an easier way. For the past decade, many folks have made their way up Mount Shasta via a chairlift (though it doesn't reach the peak) and down on skis. **MOUNT SHASTA BOARD & SKI PARK** (at the end of Ski Park Hwy, off Hwy 89, 10 miles E of I-5; 530/926-8610 ski resort, 530/926-8686 snow report) offers mostly intermediate runs with nary a mogul in sight, and the cost of the lift ticket won't require taking out a second mortgage on your home. Ski Park also has a ski and snowboard rental/repair shop, restaurant, snack bar, and ski school. In the summer, the resort provides naturalist-led walks, mountain-biking trails accessible by chairlift (bike rentals are available, too), and an indoor recreational climbing wall for people of all ages and abilities.

About a quarter-mile down the highway is the **NORDIC LODGE** (on Ski Park Hwy; 530/926-8610), a cross-country ski center with several miles of groomed tracks.

If you prefer to admire Mount Shasta from afar, visit **CASTLE CRAGS STATE PARK** (from I-5, take the Castle Crags State Park exit, about 13 miles S of Mount Shasta; 530/235-2684), one of California's geologic wonders. The park's enormous 6,500-foot spires of ancient granite are visible from the highway, but they deserve a much closer look. If you're anxious to really stretch your legs, hike up the park's moderately strenuous 2.7-mile **SUMMIT DOME TRAIL** to the base of the crags—the view of Mount Shasta alone is worth the trip. Less adventurous souls can stroll along the 1-mile **ROOT CREEK OR INDIAN CREEK TRAILS** or picnic among the pines and wildflowers.

For another unforgettable experience, why not splurge on a guided **WHITE-WATER-RAFTING** trip down the mighty **KLAMATH RIVER**. Daredevils can soar down the narrow, steep chutes appropriately called Hells Corner and Caldera, while saner souls (including children) can navigate the much-less-perilous forks. Trips are also available on the upper Sacramento, the Trinity, and other nearby rivers. Prices for one-day trips range from $85 to $120 (multiday trips are also available). Call the **TURTLE RIVER RAFTING COMPANY** (530/926-3223) for more details.

The town of Mount Shasta offers two good (and safe) attractions that won't even make a dent in your billfold: the free **SISSON MUSEUM** (530/926-5508) showcases changing exhibits on local history, nature, geology, and Native American life, and its adjacent **MOUNT SHASTA FISH HATCHERY** (take Lake St across the freeway, turn left on Hatchery Rd, and head to 3 N Old Stage Rd; 530/926-2215), the oldest hatchery in the West, keeps thousands of rainbow and brown trout, including a few biggies, in the holding ponds. For only a quarter you can get some fish food and incite a fish-feeding frenzy. For more information, contact the **MOUNT SHASTA VISITORS BUREAU** (300 Pine St at Lake St; 530/926-4865).

RESTAURANTS

Lily's / ★★

1013 S MOUNT SHASTA BLVD, MOUNT SHASTA; 530/926-3372 This popular place offers very good California cuisine with an ethnic flair. Start your dinner with spicy jalapeño pasta or baked Brie and follow that with an entree of prime rib, Chicken Rosie (a chicken breast browned in butter and simmered with raspberries, hazelnut liqueur, and a hint of cream), or the terrific enchiladas *suizas*, stuffed with crab, shrimp, and fresh spinach. Lunch offerings are equally varied and imaginative, and if you're looking for something a little different from the usual breakfast fare, try Lily's cheesy polenta fritters. *$; AE, DIS, MC, V; local checks only; breakfast, lunch Mon–Fri, dinner every day, brunch Sat–Sun and holidays; beer and wine; reservations recommended; www.lilyrestaurant.com; from I-5, take the Central Mount Shasta exit.*

Michael's Restaurant / ★

313 MOUNT SHASTA BLVD, MOUNT SHASTA; 530/926-5288 Michael and Lynn Kobseff have been running this estimable little restaurant since 1980, which makes them old-timers on the ever-changing Mount Shasta restaurant scene. Some of their best lunchtime offerings are the crisp, greaseless fried zucchini appetizer, the French fries, and a terrific Cajun turkey melt. Their Italian dinners will satisfy those with lumberjack-size appetites, especially the combination ravioli and linguine plate. Lynn makes all the desserts in-house. The small but varied wine list features several bargains. *$; AE, DIS, MC, V; local checks only; lunch Tues–Fri, dinner Tues–Sat; full bar; reservations recommended; from I-5, take the Central Mount Shasta exit.* &

Trinity Cafe / ★★★

622 N MOUNT SHASTA BLVD, MOUNT SHASTA; 530/926-6200 When Bill and Crystal Truby moved here recently, they brought the best aspects of their Napa Valley roots to Mount Shasta. They may have traded vineyards for snowy peaks, but when you settle in for dinner at the Trinity Cafe, you could easily believe you were in Napa. The menu combines the flair and eclecticism of Wine Country cooking with the Mount Shasta penchant for healthy dishes, using fresh produce from the local farmers' market and locally raised game. Try the cabernet braised lamb with mint pesto, grilled Pacific king salmon on panzanella salad, whole roasted tilapia with saffron risotto, or grilled vegetables stacked with polenta and fresh mozzarella. The wine list is predominantly California, with featured wines to complement the nightly specials. Desserts are all made in-house. *$$; AE, MC, V; checks OK; dinner Tues–Sat; beer and wine; reservations recommended; www.trinitycafe.net; between Jessie and Ivy Sts.* &

LODGINGS

Mount Shasta Ranch Bed and Breakfast / ★★

1008 W. A. BARR RD, MOUNT SHASTA; 530/926-3870 This comfortable 70-year-old bed-and-breakfast inn with gabled windows and hip roofs offers large rooms, large baths, large views, and even large breakfasts. In addition to five guest rooms in the main building, the Mount Shasta Ranch B&B has five rooms in a carriage house and a two-bedroom cottage. The main house, decorated with antiques and Oriental rugs, has the largest guest rooms (four of them sleep up to four people each), plus huge private bathrooms sporting original 1920s fixtures. The carriage house's five units are smaller and share two bathrooms but have great views of Mount Shasta and the rugged Siskiyous. Come morning, indulge in a hearty breakfast that might include cream-cheese-filled waffles with fresh fruit toppings, crepes bursting with local blackberries, plump sausages, a fresh fruit salad, and good strong coffee. Afterward, curl up with a book in front of the main lodge's gargantuan stone fireplace, or work off those waffles by hiking, swimming, playing a few rounds of table tennis or pool, or soaking in the inn's hot springs spa. And unlike most B&Bs, children are always welcome. *$–$$; AE, DIS, MC, V; checks OK; www.stayinshasta.com; S of the fish hatchery.* &

Mount Shasta Resort / ★★★

1000 SISKIYOU LAKE BLVD, MOUNT SHASTA; 530/926-3030 OR 800/958-3363 If you think people who live to hit little golf balls should get a life, you'll have second thoughts when you see the incredibly scenic Mount Shasta Resort. The prospect of spending all day on a rolling green lawn and breathing in clean air under the towering presence of Mount Shasta is alluring—even to those who have never heard of Tiger Woods. The 50 one- and two-bedroom Craftsman-style chalets have all the creature comforts, and they're located on the forested shore of Lake Siskiyou, where you can swim, fish, sailboard, kayak, canoe, or rent paddleboats. What? Left your putter at home? Don't despair. You can buy a new one here or consider such pastimes as fishing, hiking, mountain biking, or skiing—they're all within putting distance of the resort. Two-night minimum stays are required for Friday and Saturday in the summer and on major holidays. Chalet rentals vary seasonally. Ask about the special golf packages offered from May through September (weather permitting), the ski packages in the winter, or the romantic getaway deals year-round. The clubhouse restaurant serves good California cuisine, and there are several great restaurants nearby, in town and in Dunsmuir. *$$–$$$; AE, DC, DIS, MC, V; local checks only; www.mountshastaresort.com; from I-5, take the Central Mount Shasta exit, go W, turn left on Old Stage Rd, veer onto W. A. Barr Rd, and turn left on Siskiyou Lake Blvd.* &

Strawberry Valley Inn / ★★

1142 S MOUNT SHASTA BLVD, MOUNT SHASTA; 530/926-2052 Hosts Chuck and Susie Ryan have combined the privacy of a motel and the personal touches of a B&B to create this terrific 14-room inn surrounded by a lush garden and towering oaks. Guest rooms are individually decorated with color-coordinated fabrics; if you prefer lots of room to romp, ask for a two-room suite. A buffet breakfast featuring fresh fruit, granola, oatmeal, waffles, and pastries is set up next to the inn's stone fireplace (those who want to dine in private may take a tray to their room). Complimentary wine is poured at the cocktail hour every evening. *$; AE, DIS, MC, V; no checks; from I-5, take the Central Mount Shasta exit.* &

Weed

Nestled on the north flank of Mount Shasta, this little lumber town doesn't offer much to the tourist, except, perhaps, the popular "I got high on Weed, California" T-shirt.

LODGINGS

Stewart Mineral Springs / ★

4617 STEWART SPRINGS RD, WEED; 530/938-2222 Hidden in a forested canyon at the end of a twisting country road, Stewart Mineral Springs is a great place to commune with nature and unwind from the rigors of daily life. To ensure that you get the R&R you deserve, start off with a visit to the bathhouse, located across the creek at the end of the footbridge, for a detoxifying mineral bath, a sauna, and maybe even a plunge in the creek or the large pond. You can sleep in one of the two inexpensive but spiritually enriching tepees (bring your own bedding) or in one of the five more comfortable (though spartan) little cabins with kitchens. If you plan to cook in your cabin, buy food before you get to this remote locale—convenience stores and burger emporiums are, thankfully, not a part of the scenery here, though the resort does have a new restaurant now serving breakfast, lunch, and dinner. The five-bedroom A-frame is perfect for large groups of up to 10 people, and there are 10 modest motel rooms. Camping and RV sites are available as well. *$; DIS, MC, V; checks OK; www.stewartmineralsprings.com; about 7 miles NW of Weed; call for directions.*

Gazelle

LODGINGS

Edson-Foulke Guest Ranch / ★★★

🐷 **18705 OLD HWY 99, GAZELLE; 530/435-2627** Mount Shasta looms beyond this B&B's front yard like some giant ghostly apparition, giving Hollyhock Farm one of the most impressive views in the area. Though this 1902 Normandy-style stone farmhouse is easily overlooked, its charm and setting make it a required stop for visitors to the North Mountains. The upstairs suite includes a double bed, a daybed in the sunroom, and a private bath. For the ultimate in privacy, stay in the guesthouse behind the inn, equipped with a queen-size bed, twin bed, kitchenette, and private bath. The rooms have been tastefully furnished with antiques and lace curtains, and all have satellite TVs and VCRs. Hosts Britta and Terry Price will even house your canine companions in their kennel and your horses at the farm. Breakfast is served whenever you'd like it. *$–$$; MC, V; checks OK; www.efguestranch.com; just W of I-5; from Yreka, take the Grenada/Gazelle exit; from Weed, take the Edgewood/Gazelle exit.*

Etna

RESTAURANTS

Etna Brewing Company / ★

🐷 **131 CALLAHAN ST, ETNA; 530/467-5277** As Benjamin Franklin said, "Beer is proof that God loves us and wants us to be happy." Well, here's a little piece of happy. Originally established in 1872, the Etna Brewery was a thriving concern in the small town of Etna for 47 years before being shut down by Prohibition in 1919. In 1990, the brewery came back to life with the opening of the Etna Brewing Company, Siskiyou County's first microbrewery. The brewery changed hands again in 2001 and has been producing award-winning, all-natural beer ever since (including an outstanding root beer). To wash that beer down, you can choose from a full deli-style menu with sandwiches, wraps, salads, and standard pub fare—

burgers, hot dogs, chili, and such. Tours of the brewery are also available. *$; AE, DIS, MC, V; checks OK; lunch, appetizers Tues–Sun (open May–Dec); beer and wine; no reservations.*

Fort Jones

LODGINGS

The Wild Goose / ★★

11624 MAIN ST, FORT JONES; 530/468-2735 Furnished with family heirlooms and antiques, this 1890 country Victorian house has been rebuilt from the ground up by owners Terry and Cindy Hayes. The two rooms on the second floor were designed for the care and comfort of guests, and each has an antique double bed and a private bathroom. Step out onto the second-story veranda for a view of the village of Fort Jones and the distant Marble Mountains. The Wild Goose goes wild over breakfast, so bring your appetite to the table and prepare yourself for Belgian waffles with champagne and fruit sauté, homemade granola, and fresh-squeezed juice. *$; no credit cards; checks OK; off Hwy 3.*

Lassen Volcanic National Park and the Northeast

Surprisingly, many Californians have never even heard of Lassen Volcanic National Park, much less been there. In fact, it's one of the least crowded national parks in the country, forever destined to play second fiddle to its towering neighbor, Mount Shasta. This is reason enough to go, since the park's 108,000 acres (including 50 beautiful wilderness lakes) are practically deserted, even on weekends. But don't stop here. From Drakesbad to Mill Creek, this area of panoramic vistas, aspen-lined creeks, and popular lakes is worth exploring.

Lassen Volcanic National Park

The heart of the park is 10,457-foot **LASSEN PEAK**, the largest plug-dome volcano in the world (its last fiery eruption was in 1915, when it shot debris 7 miles into the stratosphere). For decades Lassen held the title of the most recently active volcano in the continental United States; it lost that distinction in 1980, when Washington's Mount St. Helens blew her top. The volcano also marks the southernmost end of the Cascade Range, which extends to Canada. A visitors' map calls the park "a compact laboratory of volcanic phenomena"—an apt description of this pretty but peculiar place. In addition to wildflower-laced hiking trails and lush forests typical of many national parks, parts of Lassen are covered with steaming thermal vents, boiling mud pots, stinky sulfur springs, and towering lava pinnacles—constant reminders that Mount Lassen is still active.

Lassen Park's premier attractions in the summer and fall are sightseeing, hiking, backpacking, and camping (sorry, no mountain bikes allowed). The $10-per-car entrance fee, valid for a week, gets you a copy of the "Lassen Park Guide," a handy little newsletter listing activities, hikes, and points of interest. Free naturalist programs are offered daily in the summer, highlighting everything from flora and fauna to geologic history and volcanic processes. If you have only a day here, spend it huffing up the mountain on the **LASSEN PEAK HIKE**, a spectacular 2½-mile zigzag to the top. Most hikers can make the steep trek in four to five hours—just don't forget to bring water, sunscreen, and a windbreaker. Another great—and much easier—trail is the 3-mile **BUMPASS HELL HIKE**, named after a mid-19th-century tour guide. Poor ol' Kendall Bumpass lost a leg on this one, but that was long before park rangers built wooden catwalks to safely guide visitors past the pyrite pools, steam vents, seething mud pots, and noisy fumaroles that line the trail.

Mount Lassen Park attracts a hardier breed of tourists in the winter, when the park's main thoroughfare is closed and the chief modes of transportation are snowshoes and cross-country skis. Smaller roads are plowed only from the north and south park entrances up to the ranger stations, and on sunny weekends parking lots are filled with families enjoying every kind of snow toy imaginable. On Saturday afternoons from January through March, a loquacious naturalist will take anyone who shows up at the **LASSEN CHALET** (at the park's S entrance, 5 miles N of the junction of Hwys 36 and 89) by 1:30pm on a free two-hour eco-adventure across the park's snowy dales. You must be at least eight years old, warmly dressed, and decked out in boots. Free snowshoes are provided (although a $1 donation for shoe upkeep is requested) on a first-come basis. Pack a picnic lunch. For more details, call park headquarters (530/595-4444).

For the best lodgings and restaurants near the park, see the Drakesbad, Chester, Lake Almanor, and Mill Creek sections in this chapter.

Drakesbad

LODGINGS

Drakesbad Guest Ranch / ★★★★

HWY 36, DRAKESBAD; 530/529-1512, EXT. 120 Hidden in a high mountain valley inside Lassen Volcanic National Park, the Drakesbad Guest Ranch is probably the worst-kept secret in California. Demand for this mountain retreat's 19 rooms is so high that it's often booked several months (and sometimes a year or two) in advance. Fortunately, plans made that far ahead often change, and February through June are good times to call to take advantage of cancellations. At night, kerosene lamps cast a warm yellow glow over the rustic accommodations; there's no electricity, except in the lodge. The tables, chairs, and

MYSTIC MOUNTAIN

Indigenous Native Americans have always considered Mount Shasta a holy mountain, the home of the Great Spirit. Over the years, spiritual seekers, New Age believers, and other metaphysical folk have also pronounced it one of the most powerful sacred sites in North America; organizations such as the Creative Harmonics Institute, the Ascended Master Teaching Foundation, the Temple of Cosmic Religion, I AM Activity, Planetary Citizens, and the Radiant School of Seekers and Servers have, at one time or another, made the base of the mountain their temporal home. And then there are the people *inside* the mountain. Lemurians, believed by some to be highly evolved beings descended from an ancient civilization called Lemuria, can supposedly materialize at will and may (it is said) occasionally show themselves to the faithful. Strange lights and noises on Mount Shasta are sometimes attributed to these folk. There is also an Indian legend that says ancient lizard people once built a city beneath the mountain. And, indeed, one visitor allegedly spotted a "lizard person" in 1972.

The most famous metaphysical assembly in recent years was the 1987 Harmonic

bedsteads are made of smooth-sanded logs and branches. There are a half-dozen pleasant rooms upstairs in the main lodge, but you might prefer one of the four quieter cabins at the edge of the woods, a good place to watch wildlife. The lodge's guest rooms and each of the cabins have their own sinks and toilets, but showers are in a shared facility. If you want a private bathroom, inquire about the two-room duplex (rented to a minimum of four people) or one of the six rooms in the bungalows at the edge of the meadow. One of the ranch's star attractions is the thermal swimming pool, fed by a natural hot spring and open 24 hours a day. Breakfast, lunch, and dinner (included in the price of lodging) are better than what you might expect in a national park. The breakfast buffet includes fresh fruit, hot and cold cereals, buttermilk pancakes, and excellent sausages. For lunch you can eat at the buffet or order a sack lunch. Dinner is a fancier affair, starting with soup or a fresh wild greens salad, followed by an entree such as roasted rosemary chicken with Monterey Jack polenta or vegetarian eggplant napoleon; dessert might be a white chocolate mousse cake. The popular Wednesday-night cookouts feature barbecued steak and chicken, plus pasta and an assortment of salads. *$$$$; DIS, MC, V; checks OK; closed mid-Oct–mid-June, depending on weather conditions; www.drakesbed.com; about 17 miles N of Chester, call for directions.* &

Convergence, a gathering of 5,000 people who met at Mount Shasta to create a cosmic consciousness providing "attunement to the planet and to higher galactic intelligences." Four UFOs and an angel announcing the beginning of heaven on earth reportedly appeared. The UFOs could be attributed to the saucer-shaped clouds that form around the mountain, emanating beams of light—a perfectly feasible explanation, scientists say. The angel remains a mystery.

Today around Mount Shasta you can take workshops employing sweat lodges, ceremonial circles, and Peruvian whistling vessels to awaken your inner warrior or to retrieve your soul. Locals not of the New Age persuasion have occasionally been heard to refer to their spiritual neighbors as "cosmic muffins," but for the most part, all is peace and harmony here. At the very least, you can get really good vegetarian food in town.

If you're interested in learning about the mountain's alleged mystical powers, visit the delightfully funky **GOLDEN BOUGH BOOKSTORE** (219 N Mount Shasta Blvd at Lake St, Mount Shasta City; 530/926-3228), where the staff can give you the lowdown and direct you to tapes, books, and all matter of spiritual info.

Cassel

LODGINGS

Clearwater House / ★★★

HAT CREEK AND CASSEL/FALL RIVER RDS, CASSEL; 415/381-1173 OR 530/335-5500 This fine turn-of-the-century farmhouse is nestled right next to some of the finest trout waters in the United States. Created by former wilderness and fishing guide Dick Galland, the inn features seven rooms (all with private baths) decorated in the style of an English angling lodge, with fish and game prints on the walls, Oriental rugs on the hardwood floors, and cherry-wood tables set for family-style meals. Pick up pointers on the art of fly-fishing at a five-day (Wed–Sun) fishing class. Meals are included in the room rate—and they're the best you'll find for miles around. Expect traditional breakfasts, picnic lunches, and well-prepared country-style dinners. A tackle shop and tennis courts round out the amenities. *$$$$; AE, MC, V; checks OK; open late Apr–mid-Nov; www.clearwatertrout.com; at the intersection of Hat Creek and Cassel/Fall River Rds.* &

Alturas

RESTAURANTS

Nipa's California Cuisine / ★

1001 N MAIN ST, ALTURAS; 530/233-2520 You won't find seared tuna in loquat sauce here. Nipa's version of California cuisine is actually spicy Thai food—and it's the finest fare of any kind in Modoc County. Located in an old drive-in burger joint that's been transformed into a contemporary cafe decorated with Thai artifacts, Nipa's serves such classic favorites as *tom yum kung,* a fragrant soup packed with prawns and mushrooms; pad thai, the satisfying pan-fried-noodle dish with prawns, chicken, egg, bean sprouts, green onions, and a sprinkling of ground peanuts; and a spicy, succulent red curry made with prawns, chicken, or beef simmered in coconut milk. Wash it all down with a deliciously sweet Thai iced tea. *$; MC, V; local checks only; lunch, dinner every day; beer and wine; no reservations; 1 block S of Hwys 299 and 395.*

LODGINGS

Dorris House / ★

COUNTY RD 57, ALTURAS; 530/233-3786 A room with a view is a standard feature of this two-story, turn-of-the-century ranch house, named for the brothers who founded Alturas in 1870. Set on a sage-covered plain at the edge of Dorris Lake, just below the towering Warner Mountains, the property is a favorite stop for migratory birds (not to mention patrons who migrate here for a respite). Hosts Mary Woodward has decorated their immaculate inn's four guest rooms with family antiques and comfortable furnishings, making the rooms a pleasant home-away-from-home. Longtime residents of Alturas, Mary know all the choice spots for hiking, fishing, bird-watching, and picnicking, so be sure to ask her for touring tips. Breakfast, served in the homey kitchen, is simple but very good, and might include moist zucchini nut bread, sweet bran muffins, or a dazzling fruit platter. *$; no credit cards; checks OK; 3 miles E of Hwy 395, on County Rd 56, turn right at County Rd 57 and drive 1 mile.*

Cedarville

North of Alturas, Highway 299 turns east and crosses the narrow, little-known, and seldom visited **WARNER MOUNTAINS**, where antelope often graze. Then the highway descends into the aptly named **SURPRISE VALLEY**, a onetime oasis for Overland Trail emigrants after the rigors of the Nevada desert, and Cedarville, a little old-fashioned town of a bygone time. As one local poet put it, Cedarville is "where the pavement ends, and the West begins."

Isolated by the Warner Mountains on one side and the western edge of the Great Basin on the other, Cedarville attracts an interesting mix of travelers: in addition to the usual hunters, fly fishers, history buffs, and bird and wildlife watchers, you'll find paleontologists and paleobiologists drawn to the plentiful animal and plant fossils found in this part of the Great Basin. Whatever lured you here, there are lots of hot springs to help rejuvenate those weary bones after a day of exploring.

RESTAURANTS

Country Hearth Restaurant & Bakery

551 MAIN ST, CEDARVILLE; 530/279-2280 The Country Hearth should be called the Country Heart for all the love owner Janet Irene puts into the meals served in her homey, pine-paneled dining room with its wood-burning stove. Bite into her good hamburgers served on toasted, fresh-baked rolls, or try the nightly special "country-cooked meal," which might feature pork chops or chicken-fried steak. Irene makes all the breads, rolls, pastries, and desserts, which are included in the price of dinner. You can also purchase baked goods for the trip home. *$; MC, V; checks OK; breakfast, lunch, dinner every day; beer and wine; reservations requested; S of Hwy 299.*

LODGINGS

J. K. Metzker House Bed and Breakfast / ★★

520 MAIN ST, CEDARVILLE; 530/279-2650 Built in 1860 by town founder William Cressler, this pretty clapboard house with its white picket fence and rose-lined walkway was the residence of Cressler's descendants until 1990, when Judy Metzker Topol acquired it. She named the B&B in honor of her great-great-great-grandfather, who followed the Oregon Trail and settled in the Surprise Valley. After that long trek, Mr. Metzker surely would have appreciated snoozing in the comfort of one of the three upstairs guest rooms. Each room has a private bath and a queen-size bed. Innkeeper Linda Naomi fixes a real country breakfast each morning with bacon and eggs, fruit and muffins, and special items for guests with particular dietary needs and desires. *$; no credit cards; checks OK; turn right onto Main St from Hwy 299.*

Susanville

RESTAURANTS

Grand Cafe / ★

730 MAIN ST, SUSANVILLE; 530/257-4713 The art deco light fixtures in this time warp of a restaurant are the real McCoy. Owned by the Sargent family since 1921, this green stucco building is furnished with green-and-black tiles, dark wooden booths, and a long Formica counter. There's also a nickel jukebox (it doesn't work, so save your nickel) and a small lamp with a pull chain in each booth. At the counter, wooden chairs on ornate iron bases have clips to hold diners' hats. The mounted deer staring from the walls were shot by a Sargent in the '30s—back when a tuna sandwich was a mere 35 cents (even now, they're not charging a whole lot more). For breakfast, try the sweet buckwheat hotcakes. At lunchtime, soup, house-baked bread, and a chocolate malt are your best bets. *$; no credit cards; checks OK; breakfast, lunch Mon–Sat; full bar; no reservations; near Gay St.*

St. Francis Champion Steakhouse / ★

830 MAIN ST (ST. FRANCIS HOTEL), SUSANVILLE; 530/257-4820 You won't hear anybody ask "Where's the beef?" in this cafe. Located in the 90-year-old St. Francis Hotel, the St. Francis Champion Steakhouse specializes in prime rib, indisputably the best (and the largest servings) in the area. If you're not at the door by 6pm on Friday and Saturday, you may be out of luck, because the prime rib can sell out quickly. There's also a hearty 10-ounce New York steak sandwich, and freshly made soups and salads. The adjacent hotel bar, the Round-Up Room, features Picon Punch on its list of spirits—a tasty Basque drink that transforms even the grumpiest cowboy into a very friendly dude. *$$; AE, DIS, MC, V; checks OK; lunch Mon–Fri, dinner Mon–Sat; full bar; reservations requested; at Union St.*

Chester

RESTAURANTS

Cynthia's / ★★★

278 MAIN ST, CHESTER; 530/258-1966 Formerly known as the Creekside Grill, Cynthia's is a pretty place with lots of natural wood and a great stone fireplace for winter dining. In warmer weather guests can dine outside on the cottonwood-shaded brick deck next to the creek where a every summer a mama wood duck raises her ducklings. Chef Cynthia Ware purchased the restaurant in 2001 and has enhanced its already glowing reputation—Sunset Magazine recently referred to it as a "rising star." Cynthia, a graduate of the prestigious California Culinary Academy in San Francisco, does the cooking (all dishes are prepared fresh daily) with the help of her son, Max, and daughter, Lydia. Lunches feature house-made soups, pot pies, and burgers on freshly baked French rolls. Kids love the children's menu with crusts cut off the sandwiches, no green stuff on the plate and root beer floats with house-made vanilla bean ice cream. Menus change to fit the season and feature items like Tuscan grilled steak drizzled with olive oil and lemon served with potato cakes and fresh vegetables, a grilled pork chop brushed with chipotle barbecue sauce and served with black beans, or fettucine with house-smoked chicken, sun dried tomatoes, and portabella mushrooms. The desserts, also made in-house, may include Champagne and fresh peach sorbet, warm chocolate cake and cherry-chocolate chunk ice cream with warm fudge sauce, and, on Valentine's Day, flaming baked Alaska. *$–$$; MC, V; local checks only; lunch Mon, Tues, Thurs–Sat, dinner Mon, Tues, Thurs–Sun in summer, Thurs–Sat in winter; beer and wine; reservations recommended.* ঙ

LODGINGS

The Bidwell House Bed and Breakfast Inn / ★★★

I MAIN ST, CHESTER; 530/258-3338 The beautifully restored Bidwell House, fronted by a yard of aspens and cottonwoods, looks out over mountain meadows and the broad expanse of Lake Almanor. The

former home of Chico pioneer John Bidwell, it opened as a B&B in 1991. The 14 guest rooms are furnished with antiques and a few have wood-burning stoves; most have private baths, and seven units are equipped with Jacuzzi tubs. A cottage that sleeps up to six makes an ideal family retreat. Be sure to show the kids the Bidwell House's pretty, enclosed downstairs porch fancied up with wicker furniture, a Gibson Girl sketchbook, and antique doll buggies and tricycles. The inn's manager is a creative pastry chef, so guests are treated to delicious breakfast dishes such as fresh fruit crepes washed down with frothy frappés, served in the airy dining room. If you're around in September, don't miss the popular cowboy poetry reading—it's a hoot. $$–$$$; MC, V; checks OK; www.bidwellhouse.com; E end of town.

Lake Almanor

RESTAURANTS

BJ's Bar-B-Que & Deli / ★

3881 HWY A-13, LAKE ALMANOR; 530/596-4210 Barbecue basics— beef, pork, and chicken—reign at this unassuming roadside spot. The baby back ribs are thick, tender, meaty, and slathered with a tangy sweet sauce, and the baked beans and barbecued pork sandwiches are good, too. Get plenty of napkins for this deliciously messy fare and eat it on the sunny, enclosed porch to the left of the front door. Prime rib takes a turn on the rotisserie Friday and Saturday nights, and it's so popular you'll need reservations. $; no credit cards; checks OK; lunch, dinner Tues–Sun (closed Nov–Mar); beer and wine; reservations recommended; Hamilton Branch.

Wilson's Camp Prattville & Carol's Cafe / ★

2932 ALMANOR DR W, LAKE ALMANOR; 530/259-2464 Certainly the oldest and funkiest place at Lake Almanor, Camp Prattville has been around since 1928, when it was founded by Frank and Nettie Wilson. Daughter-in-law Carol Wilson Franchetti, along with her new partner, Ken Wilson (one of four generations of Wilsons who have worked here), now runs the restaurant, which offers breakfast, lunch, and dinner in a small dining room crowded with knickknacks. The menu is prodigious, and breakfasts are served until 1pm. Sandwiches and French fries are among the better offerings, but save room for dessert, especially the terrific bread pudding with applejack hard sauce and the house-made pies with delicate, flaky crusts. When the weather is warm, eat lunch at one of the picnic tables on the deck overlooking the lake. $; MC, V; checks OK; breakfast, lunch, dinner every day (closed mid-Oct–Apr); beer and wine; reservations recommended; on the lake's W shore.

LODGINGS

Dorado Inn / ★★

4379 HWY 147, LAKE ALMANOR; 530/284-7790 What sets the Dorado apart from the other resorts along Lake Almanor's commercialized east shore are the spectacular Mount Lassen and lake views from the decks outside the cottages. All of the Dorado's six cottages (four two-bedroom cottages and two one-room units) are near the water's edge, and they have fully equipped kitchens, private bathrooms, electric heat, and wood-burning stoves. In addition to soaking in the view, most visitors spend their time either sunbathing and lounging lakeside, or boating, fishing, and swimming. *$$; no credit cards; checks OK; on the lake's E shore.* ♿

Mill Creek

RESTAURANTS

St. Bernard Lodge / ★★

44801 HWY 36 E, MILL CREEK; 530/258-3382 The St. Bernard Lodge was constructed in 1912 to house workers building the dam at Big Meadows (now known as Lake Almanor), and in 1929 it was picked up and moved to its present location, where it started a new life as a public lodge. Although there are seven comfortable rooms upstairs, most Mill Creek residents come here for the famous St. Bernard Burgers: a three-quarter-pound patty of lean chuck served on a fresh-baked bun (all breads are baked on site). You can also sink your teeth into prime rib, steak, fried chicken, and fried or sautéed fish. Before your meal, sip a cocktail in the antique bar with painted glass windows; afterward, head outside for a stroll along the deck and around the trout pond. *$$–$$$; AE, DIS, MC, V; checks OK; breakfast, lunch Sat–Sun, dinner Thurs–Mon; full bar; reservations required; www.stbernard lodge.com; on the S side of Hwy 36, 10 miles W of Chester.*

LODGINGS

Mill Creek Resort / ★★

1 HWY 172, MILL CREEK; 530/595-4449 If it's peace and solitude you're after, look no further. The Mill Creek Resort makes you feel as though you've stepped back in time to a quieter, gentler, and infinitely more affordable era (somewhere around 1925). A picture-postcard general store and coffee shop serve as the resort's center, and nine housekeeping cabins are rented on a daily or weekly basis. The units are clean and homey, with vintage '30s and '40s furniture. Seclusion is one of the main charms of the place, though it's not far from cross-country skiing trails and Lassen Volcanic National Park. Pets are welcome. *$; no credit cards; checks OK; www.millcreekresort.net; 3 miles S of Hwy 36.* ♿

SIERRA NEVADA

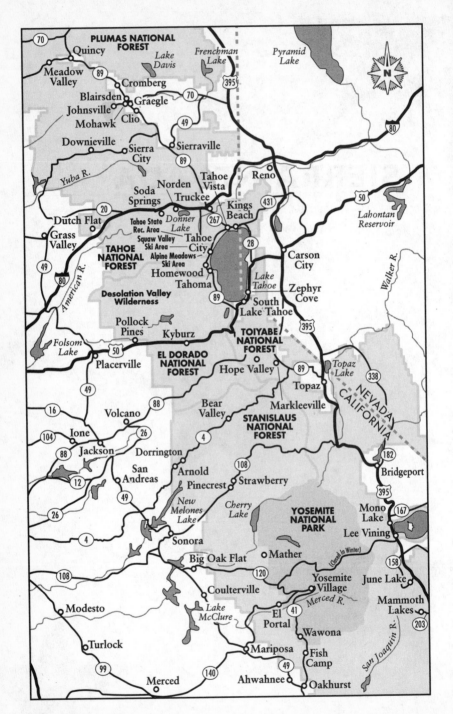

SIERRA NEVADA

The Sierra Nevada is home to two of the state's most popular destinations—Lake Tahoe and Yosemite. Keep in mind, however, that this mountain range is massive and offers dozens of other vacation destinations that are almost as gorgeous and far less crowded. If you have your heart set on the Lake or the Valley, remember, lots of other folks do, too.

In fact, Lake Tahoe and Yosemite are gradually being loved to death, although ambitious steps are being taken to slow the environmental damage to two of the most beautiful places on earth. Preservation of the water clarity of cobalt-blue Lake Tahoe and its crisp mountain air has become a priority for both the community and the state. A plan to drastically cut back the number of cars allowed in Yosemite Valley (using low-polluting or zero-emission motor coaches from outlying parking lots) is still being argued over, and is subject to change with each shift in prevailing political fortunes. In any case, try to plan your visit to either area for the spring or fall, when there are far fewer cars and people.

If you're after a more peaceful, but not primitive, communion with nature, take a peek at the Lakes Basin Area (about an hour's drive north of Truckee). This remote region has an assortment of lakeside lodges so sweetly simple and pleasant you'll remember them forever. On the eastern side of the Sierra Nevada, the haunting Mono Lake, a 60-square-mile desert salt lake with strangely beautiful limestone tufa spires, is like nothing you've ever seen before. Nearby Bodie is the most eerily authentic ghost town in California, kept in a state of "arrested decay" by park rangers. The Mammoth Lakes area, farther south, offers every kind of snow sport in winter, plus hiking, biking, and world-famous fishing in summer. It also has the Devils Postpile National Monument, eerie 60-foot-tall rock columns formed 100,000 years ago from molten lava. And if you're feeling frisky, the 211-mile John Muir Trail, which connects Yosemite with Kings Canyon and Sequoia national parks, is accessible here.

ACCESS AND INFORMATION

The 400-mile-long Sierra Nevada mountain range begins northwest of Quincy with 6,500-foot peaks, eventually rising to 14,494 feet at Mount Whitney, the highest summit in the continental United States. From there, going south, they decrease in height, ending in the desert near the town of Mojave.

The **HIGHWAY SYSTEM** through the Sierra looks like a ladder with two north-south, all-weather highways forming the legs—US 99 in the Central Valley just west of the foothills, and in the high desert to the east of the Sierra escarpment, US 395, one of the West's most beautiful scenic drives. The rungs are a series of east-west roads—highways in the north and increasingly narrow and twisting (though gorgeous) lanes as you progress south: **HIGHWAY 70,** from Oroville to Quincy; **HIGHWAY 49,** from Grass Valley to Sierraville; **INTERSTATE 80,** from Sacramento to Truckee and Reno; US 50, from Sacramento to South Lake Tahoe and Carson City; **HIGHWAY 88,** from Jackson to Kirkwood and the Hope Valley; **HIGHWAY 4,** from Stockton to Angels Camp to Markleeville; **HIGHWAY 108,** from Modesto to

Sonora to just north of Bridgeport; and **HIGHWAY 120**, from Manteca to Groveland. Some are closed in winter.

FRESNO–YOSEMITE INTERNATIONAL AIRPORT (559/251-7554; www.fly fresno.org) is approximately 65 miles from Yosemite and the southern Sierra. **MAMMOTH AIRPORT** is served by Mammoth Air Charter (760-934-4279). **RENO/TAHOE INTERNATIONAL AIRPORT** (www.renoairport.com) is approximately 45 miles from Lake Tahoe and 175 miles from Mammoth and the eastern Sierra. **SACRAMENTO INTERNATIONAL AIRPORT** (http://airports.saccounty.net) is approximately 100 miles from Lake Tahoe and the northern and central Sierra. **AMTRAK** (800/USA-RAIL; www.amtrak.com) **CALIFORNIA ZEPHYR** from San Francisco to Chicago stops at Truckee, with Amtrak bus service to South Lake Tahoe; the **SAN JOAQUIN TRAIN** from Oakland to Bakersfield stops at Merced, with Amtrak bus service to Yosemite.

GREYHOUND (800/229-9424; www.greyhound.com) has daily service from Sacramento to Lake Tahoe and Reno, and from Sacramento to Truckee and Reno. **VIA ADVENTURES** (Gray Line; 800/VIA-LINE; www.grayline.com) has four buses each day from Merced to Yosemite. The South Shore Chamber of Commerce's **TAHOE-CASINO EXPRESS** (800/446-6128) makes 14 round trips each day between Reno and South Lake Tahoe. **INYO-MONO TRANSIT** (800/922-1930) offers bus/van service along Highway 395 each day between Reno, Mammoth, Bishop, Lone Pine, and Ridgecrest.

YARTS (877/98-YARTS; www.yarts.com), the Yosemite Area Regional Transportation System, began running regional transit buses in 2000. YARTS offers an affordable, dependable alternative to travelers who would rather ride on a bus from outlying communities into Yosemite Valley than drive their vehicles into Yosemite and park. It provides service to and from Mariposa, Merced, and Mono counties.

Visitor information is available from a variety of locations: **JUNE LAKE CHAMBER OF COMMERCE** (760/648-7584; www.junelake.com), **LAKE TAHOE CENTRAL RESERVATIONS** (800/824-6348 or 530/583-3494; www.tahoefun.org), **LAKE TAHOE VISITORS AUTHORITY** (800/AT-TAHOE; www.virtualtahoe.com), **LEE VINING CHAMBER OF COMMERCE AND MONO LAKE VISITOR CENTER** (Hwy 395 and 3rd St, Lee Vining; 760/647-6629; www.leevining.com), **MARIPOSA COUNTY VISITORS BUREAU** (866/HALFDOME; http://mariposa.yosemite.net/visitor/), **TUOLUMNE COUNTY VISITORS BUREAU** (800/446-1333; www.thegreatunfenced.com), and **YOSEMITE AREA TRAVEL INFORMATION** (www.yosemite.com).

The Lake Tahoe region has dozens of other Web sites that are loaded with information, including www.skilaketahoe.com, www.laketahoeconcierge .com, www.vitualtahoe.com, www.tahoereservations.com, www.tahoesbest.com, and www.tahoevacationguide.com.

Lake Tahoe Area

Frontiersman Kit Carson was guiding General John Frémont's expedition across the Sierra Nevada in 1844 when he stumbled on an immense, deep-blue body of water, a lake so vast the native Washoe Indians were calling it tahoe ("big lake"). Carson was the first white man to see Tahoe, North America's largest alpine lake and the eighth deepest in the world (its deepest point is at 1,685 feet). If completely drained, Tahoe would cover the entire state of California with 14 inches of water.

Despite all its great ski resorts, Tahoe is actually most crowded in the summer, when thousands flock here to cool off at the lake (although what constitutes public shoreline versus private waterfront is still a matter of heated debate between home owners and county supervisors). Warm-weather activities abound: boating, water-skiing, bicycling, hiking, rock climbing, hot-air ballooning, horseback riding . . . you name it. Unfortunately, the area pays dearly for its myriad attractions in the form of tremendous traffic jams, water and air pollution, and a plethora of fast-food joints and condos erected before tough building restrictions were imposed. Despite these glaring scars, Lake Tahoe remains one of the premier outdoor playgrounds of the West, dazzling visitors with its soaring Sierra peaks and twinkling azure waters.

For a grand introduction to the area, take a leisurely 72-mile drive around the lake itself. **HIGHWAYS 50, 89,** and **28** hug the shore, providing gorgeous views from the car. Several stellar sights merit pulling over for a closer look, so be prepared to stop and haul out your camera (or camcorder) along the way. Topping the not-to-be-missed list are **EMERALD BAY** (off Hwy 89), one of the most photographed sights in the world; Cave Rock Tunnel, the 200-foot-long, drive-through granite tunnel along Highway 50 on the East Shore; and **SAND HARBOR STATE PARK** (off Hwy 28, on the East Shore), one of the lake's prettiest—and least visited—beaches. Allow about three hours to loop around the lake, or longer if you're traveling on a summer weekend, on a holiday, or when the road is covered with snow.

Dutch Flat

RESTAURANTS

Monte Vista Inn / ★

OFF I-80, DUTCH FLAT; 530/389-2333 For about 60 years, the Monte Vista has been a roadhouse catering to locals—and to travelers lucky enough to find it.

The comfortable inn is built of logs and indigenous stone, with a wood-burning stove in the bar and large sofas near the petrified-wood fireplace in the lounge. Kerosene lamps light the wooden dining tables, and old farm implements hang on the walls. The kitchen prepares generous portions of California cuisine, ranging from mesquite-grilled steaks to scampi sautéed with fresh mushrooms and garlic. They're famous for their prime rib, and smoke their own ribs using local fruit wood. Sitting neatly on the counter along the dining-room wall are a dozen or so freshly baked pies, which taste as good as they look (the blackberry pie is tangy with lemon). Live music livens up the bar on the weekend. *$$; MC, V; local checks only; dinner every day; full bar; reservations recommended; at the Dutch Flat exit, 9 miles E of Colfax.* &

Soda Springs

RESTAURANTS

Engadine Cafe / ★★★

RAINBOW RD (ROYAL GORGE'S RAINBOW LODGE), SODA SPRINGS; 530/426-3661 Within Royal Gorge's Rainbow Lodge (see review, below) is the charming and cozy Engadine Cafe, which boasts a large fireplace that's continuously ablaze on those freezing Sierra winter nights. Breakfasts are planned for folks with hearty let's-scale-a-mountain appetites and feature a wide range of choices, from a belly-packing stack of whole-wheat pancakes to three-egg omelets bursting with smoked ham, mushrooms, scallions, and Swiss cheese, accompanied by a pile of country fries. Lunches at the Engadine are simple and satisfying and might include pasta with fresh eggplant, tomato, and mushroom sauce; a juicy burger with all the fixins; and a luscious (and messy) sandwich Provençal with grilled vegetables, sun-dried tomatoes, artichoke hearts, and melted provolone on a toasted sourdough roll. In the evening the kitchen turns out an eclectic mix of terrific fare such as Swiss fondue for two, roast rack of lamb breaded with pistachio nuts and basted with Dijon mustard, and several daily seafood specials. The back deck looks out over the garden into the pines and is great for summer dining. *$$; MC, V; no checks; breakfast, lunch, dinner every day; full bar; reservations recommended; www.royalgorge.com; take Rainbow Rd exit off I-80 S and drive W.* ♿

LODGINGS

Ice Lakes Lodge / ★★

1111 SODA SPRINGS ROAD, SODA SPRINGS; 530/426-7660 If you want to avoid the ubiquitous Tahoe traffic and droves of holiday tourists, consider a stay at the Ice Lakes Lodge. Few people know that this beautiful lakeside lodge even exists. Constructed in 2000 by lifelong locals Matt and Vicki Williams—along with financial and moral support from more than 70 residents and property owners in the Serene Lakes region—this ideal family retreat replaces the old lodge that fell into ruin after 20 years of neglect. It's situated on the shore of Serene Lakes (the name was changed from Ice Lakes to attract more tourists), a small pair of lakes that are the summer playground of this quiet Soda Springs community. The three-level lodge is agleam with freshly milled knotty pine and new furnishings. Most of the 26 guest rooms—all with private baths, queen or king beds, telephones, and TVs—are situated on the third and ground floors; the upper-level rooms offer a private deck (book these rooms in the winter), while the ground rooms have small porches and instant access to the small sandy beach (summer only). The lake is ideal for swimming, sailing, and canoeing, and safe for small kids to play in. The lodge's restaurant serves breakfast, lunch, and dinner daily and has a bar and lounge that overlook the lake. They'll even make you a box lunch for your summer and winter outdoor adventures—the forest is right across the street, and the Sugar Bowl ski resort is only four minutes away via shuttle. *$$; AE, DIS, MC, V; local checks only; concierge@ice-lakeslodge.com; www.icelakeslodge.com; take Donner Pass Rd exit of I-80, then 4 miles S on Soda Springs Rd.* ♿

Royal Gorge's Rainbow Lodge and Wilderness Lodge / ★★

RAINBOW RD, SODA SPRINGS; 530/426-3871, 530/426-3661, OR 800/500-3871 (OUTSIDE NORTHERN CALIFORNIA ONLY) In 1922, the Rainbow Lodge was built of hand-hewn pine timbers and local granite at a bend in the Yuba River. The owner of the popular Royal Gorge cross-country ski resort, the largest cross-country center in the United States, bought this charming retreat several years ago. Each of the lodge's 32 simple, pine-paneled rooms comes with either a private bath, shower and sink, or just a sink (with a bath down the hall). Rooms 12, 14, 23, and 24 overlook the river. Within the lodge is the very pleasant Engadine Cafe (see review, above), which serves some of the best food in the region and is open to nonguests as well. Breakfast is included with a night's stay. Royal Gorge also offers cross-country skiers accommodations in its Wilderness Lodge, a handsome wood lodge with a huge stone fireplace that's tucked away in a remote part of the cross-country course. Guests arrive at the lodge by jumping aboard an open sleigh pulled by a Sno-Cat. The private knotty-pine guest rooms are equipped with bunks or double beds covered with floral-print comforters. *$$–$$$; MC, V; no checks; main lodge open year-round, Wilderness Lodge open during ski season only; www.royalgorge.com; take Rainbow Rd exit off I-80 S and drive W.* &

Norden

LODGINGS

Clair Tappaan Lodge / ★

19940 DONNER PASS RD, NORDEN; 530/426-3632 This is no place for wimps, but those hardy souls who want to meet new people and limit expenses and don't mind a few housekeeping tasks should pack their bags and hike on in. Built by Sierra Club volunteers in 1934, Clair Tappaan Lodge is a massive, rustic three-story structure near Donner Summit, 7,000 feet above sea level. Guests carry their own bedding and luggage 100 yards uphill from the road to a building that accommodates up to 140 people. Dorm-style rooms vary from two-person cubicles with thin walls to family bunk rooms and a men's and a women's dorm (psst . . . the romantically inclined should note that most beds are single bunk beds). The pine-paneled living room is warmed by a rock fireplace in the winter, and a library, a hot tub, and a resident masseuse help keep you relaxed. Breakfast, lunch, and dinner are included in the room rate, and you're expected to help with basic caretaking chores such as dishwashing or mopping the floors. Guests get a hot breakfast and sack lunches to take skiing or hiking (tracks, slopes, and trails are close by, and the area receives the highest average snowfall of the entire Sierra Nevada range). The dinners here are casual, healthy, and filling affairs served family-style. They might include chips and salsa, a tossed green salad, warm corn bread, chili con carne (there's a vegetarian version), and, for dessert, big melt-in-your-mouth brownies. *$; MC, V; checks OK; www.sierraclub.org/outings/lodges; from I-80, take the Soda Springs/Norden exit; it's 2.4 miles E of the highway.*

Donner Summit

A whirl of white in the winter, the Donner region was named after the 89 members of the ill-fated Donner party who journeyed by wagon train to the area in October 1846. They had come from the Midwest and were bound for the West Coast but were trapped here by an early winter storm. The **EMIGRANT TRAIL MUSEUM** in **DONNER MEMORIAL STATE PARK** (12593 Donner Pass Rd, S of I-80; 530/582-7892 for general park information, 800/444-7275 for camping reservations) tells their grim story of starvation, cannibalism, and (for some members) survival. Nowadays the snow-blanketed Donner region is a major downhill and cross-country ski destination in the winter, and in the summer the long fingers of its sparkling azure lake are dotted with sailboats, dwarfed by the imposing forested slopes and granite palisades. Donner Lake is a great fishing and boating retreat (a public boat ramp is on the west side), and a public beach rims the east end of the lake. The 350-acre state park, adjacent to the lake, also offers campsites, picnic tables, and hiking trails.

LODGINGS

Loch Leven Lodge / ★

13855 DONNER PASS RD, DONNER LAKE; 530/587-3773 OR 877/663-6637 If you want to get away from the crowds in Tahoe but would like easy access to the area's restaurants and shops, this quiet, simple year-round lodge has been satisfying guests for more than 50 years. Each of its eight small units faces beautiful Donner Lake, and all but one have a kitchen. You can bask in the sun on the 5,000-square-foot redwood deck or put on your lime-green pants and head over to the AstroTurf putting green (clubs and balls are provided). The lodge also has picnic tables, lawn and fishing chairs, a barbecue, a spa, and a rowboat. Although the lower-level rooms offer the best lake views, they don't offer the most privacy (passersby occasionally walk past the exposed windows). If you're traveling with the gang, reserve the two-level town house that sleeps eight and has a fireplace, a fully equipped kitchen, a living room with a queen-size hideaway bed, an upstairs bedroom, and an adjoining bunk room with four single beds. $$; MC, V; checks OK; www.lochlevenlodge.com; 1½ miles from I-80 (take the Donner Lake exit and turn left on Donner Pass Rd).

Truckee

This popular little city packed with appealing shops, restaurants, and some terrific bed-and-breakfast inns started out in the mid-1800s as a railroad-lumber town with the construction of the first transcontinental railroad over Donner Summit. Its transformation from a dirty, run-down, one-horse town to a bustling city began in the 1970s. Today visitors arrive by car, bus, or the eastbound or westbound Amtrak passenger trains that stop at the yellow depot. A notable shop is the **BOOKSHELF AT HOOLIGAN ROCKS** (11310 Donner Pass Rd, at the W end of the Safeway shopping center; 530/582-0515 or 800/959-5083), one of the Sierra Nevada's best bookstores (it's named after a nearby outcropping of rocks where miscreants were once tarred and feathered). The Bookshelf also has branches in Quincy (353 W Main St;

530/583-2665) and Tahoe City (in the Boatworks Mall; 530/581-1900). In the summer, popular Truckee attractions include the **CANNIBAL CAR CRUISE** in June, the **FOURTH OF JULY PARADE,** and the **TRUCKEE CHAMPIONSHIP RODEO** in August. The **TRUCKEE RIVER REGIONAL PARK** (½ mile S of town on Hwy 267) has softball diamonds, picnic tables, tennis courts, and an outdoor amphitheater offering music programs (many are free) throughout the summer.

In December, when snow blankets the town and bright little white lights twinkle in the windows of the century-old facades along **COMMERCIAL ROW,** Truckee truly looks like a picture from a fairy tale. All winter long the town swarms with skiers who take advantage of its proximity to many first-rate alpine and cross-country ski areas. Others brave the freezing temperatures to engage in the 10-day winter carnival called **SNOWFEST IN MARCH,** or take a ride over the river and through the woods in a sleigh drawn by Clydesdales or Percherons. For more information, call the **TRUCKEE CHAMBER OF COMMERCE** (530/587-2757; www.truckee.com).

RESTAURANTS

Cottonwood Restaurant & Bar / ★★

10142 RUE HILLTOP, TRUCKEE; 530/587-5711 The Cottonwood Restaurant stands high on a hill on the south side of Truckee at the base of what was once California's first ski jump. The ski jump is long gone, but the rustic and pleasantly weathered restaurant affords a great view of the bright lights of Truckee from its spacious dining room and deck (if it's warm, dining on the deck is a must). The eclectic seasonal menu ranges from Southwestern to Creole to Mediterranean fare. Begin the evening by sharing the Cottonwood's famous garlic-slathered whole-leaf Caesar salad meant to be eaten with your fingers—it's one of the best dishes on the menu. Entrees might include a braised free-range rabbit cassoulet with andouille sausage and white beans; a seafood stew of shellfish, prawns, scallops, and boudin sausage in a saffron-tomato broth served over linguine; or Denver leg of venison with a port wine and green peppercorn demi-glace. If available, the fresh berry-apple crisp à la mode makes a sweet finale. Local musicians often entertain guests Thursday through Saturday nights. *$$; DIS, MC, V; checks OK; dinner every day; full bar; reservations recommended; info@cottonwoodrestaurant.com; www.cotton woodrestaurant.com; above town, right off Hwy 267 at Hilltop Lodge, just beyond the railroad tracks.*

Dragonfly / ★★★

10118 DONNER PASS RD, TRUCKEE; 530/587-0557 After years of training with the Tahoe master of fusion cuisine, Douglas Dale of Wolfdale's restaurant in Tahoe City (see the review in the Restaurants section of Tahoe City), the bearded and talented Billy McCullough pleased the local epicureans by opening this small Old Town Truckee restaurant in 2001. His Asian/California cuisine is an eclectic blend of Thai, Japanese, Indian, and Malaysian influences. Combined with seasonally fresh ingredients and creative presentations, this blend results in quite the dining adventure. A typical dinner from the weekly-changing menu may start with Thai-style seared sea scallops with rice, vermicelli noodle salad, and red curry satay sauce, followed by Asian-style asparagus soup with lemongrass, coconut milk, wonton strips

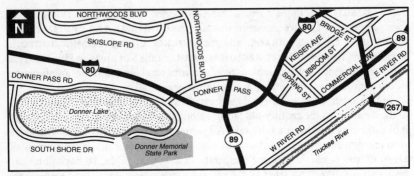

TRUCKEE

and ginger crème. The main entree may be an Asian noodle bowl with Australian lobster tail, prawn, smoked chicken, andouille, mussels, udon noodle, snap peas, and yellow Thai curry broth. (Truckee, you've come a long way, my friend.) Even the wine list is refreshingly eclectic. McCullough generously shares his recipes, so be sure to ask him if you're inclined. *$$; DIS, MC, V; local checks only; lunch, dinner every day; beer and wine; reservations recommended; billy@dragonflycuisine.com; www.dragonflycuisine.com; downtown.*

Moody's Bistro & Lounge / ★★★

10007 BRIDGE ST (THE TRUCKEE HOTEL), TRUCKEE; 530/550-8688 The owners of Moody's knew they were on the right track when, after finishing his meal, Paul McCartney sat down at the piano and sang a few tunes for the stunned staff and patrons. It was an understandable urge considering the atmosphere: a throwback to the 1950s, Moody's exudes a sort of an art deco–Ella Fitzgerald ambiance, particularly when the jazz combos are in full swing and the bartenders are pouring perfect Manhattans. The menu is equally hip and all over the place, with choices ranging from effete—seared Sonoma foie gras with Bing cherry compote and port-balsamic syrup—to meat-'n'-potatoes. Keep reading the menu and you may find "Big Ass" all-natural Salmon Creek Farms pork chops served with peach sauce, potato puree, and a crispy salad; Petaluma Poultry's Rocky Jr. half chicken, skillet fried and served with mashed taters, smoky country gravy, and Scotty's Slaw; or pepper-roasted venison loin topped with blackberry barbecue sauce and a side of mashed sweet potatoes. If you can't decide, opt for one of the tasting menus—great for family-style dining. If there aren't any superstars on stage, request a seat at the open-air patio, and be sure to arrive a bit early for a pre-dinner cocktail. *$$; AE, DC, DIS, MC, V; local checks OK; lunch, dinner every day, brunch Sat–Sun; full bar; reservations recommended; talktous@moodysbistro.com; www.moodysbistro.com; at Donner Pass Rd, in the Truckee Hotel.*

Truckee Trattoria / ★

11310-1 DONNER PASS RD, TRUCKEE; 530/582-1266 Conveniently located right off Interstate 80 within the Gateway Plaza, this popular and casual Italian cafe focuses primarily on pastas and roasted meats. Appetizers include garlic soup, portobello mushrooms stuffed with marinated goat cheese, and grilled artichokes. For a main course, try the fettuccine with tender strips of chicken and broccoli in a garlic cream sauce, or the capellini with plump shrimp, artichoke hearts, tomatoes, and spinach in a white wine and garlic sauce. Polish the meal off with gelato, tiramisu, biscotti, or strawberry napoleon, then hit the road again, well fed and ready for bed. *$–$$; DIS, MC, V; checks OK; dinner Wed–Mon; beer and wine; reservations recommended; at the W end of the Safeway shopping center. &*

LODGINGS

Hania's Bed & Breakfast Inn / ★★

10098 HIGH ST, TRUCKEE; 530/582-5775 OR 888/600-3735 Built in 1884, this pretty Victorian bed-and-breakfast has guest rooms decorated in Southwestern style with lodgepole pine furniture, colorful bedspreads, and original artwork. All the rooms have queen-size beds with down comforters, private baths, and TVs with VCRs. Located on a hillside within walking distance of downtown Truckee, the inn opened in 1997 and has rapidly gained a loyal clientele. There's a year-round hot tub with a mountain view, and a hearty breakfast is provided in the dining room, on the deck, or in your room. In the afternoon, wine is served in front of the wood-burning stove. Innkeeper Hania Davidson acquired her considerable innkeeping skills in Europe and can chat with you in English, Polish, German, or Russian. If you're coming to the area by train, plane, or bus, she'll even pick you up. *$$; AE, MC, V; checks OK; haniasbb@hotmail.com; downtown. &*

Richardson House / ★★★

10154 HIGH ST, TRUCKEE; 530/587-5388 OR 888/229-0365 Perched on a hill overlooking downtown Truckee and the Sierra Nevada, the lavishly restored Richardson House (built in 1886) sets the standard that other B&Bs in the area will have to strive for. Its eight beautiful guest rooms are elegantly appointed with plush carpeting, color-coordinated drapes and wallpaper, vintage fixtures, featherbeds and comforters, and claw-footed tubs. Six rooms have private bathrooms, and two adjoining suites share a bath. Some units have fireplaces, and Aunt Klara's Room offers every convenience for wheelchair-bound patrons. The vittles are first-rate, too. Soufflés, quiche, French toast, pancakes, hot cereal, and freshly baked scones are just some of the treats typically offered at the buffet breakfast. And if you ever manage to get hungry again, there's a 24-hour snack bar. Guests are welcome to lounge in the parlor, which has a player piano, a stereo with a CD player, and a cable TV with a VCR; or spend your time outdoors among the fountains, sundials, and native aspens on vintage wicker furniture. Discount plans for skiers include lift tickets and bus transportation to nearby ski resorts. *$$–$$$; AE, DIS, MC, V; checks OK; innkeeper@richardsonhouse.com; www.richardsonhouse.com; at Spring St. &*

The Truckee Hotel / ★★

10007 BRIDGE ST, TRUCKEE; 530/587-4444 OR 800/659-6921 Built in 1873, this handsome hotel is one of the oldest operating hotels in the Sierra Nevada. The original building was destroyed by a fire in 1909, and it was rebuilt with a steam heating system—the first hotel in the region to boast such a convenience. In 1992 and 1993 the owners hired skilled local craftsmen to renovate this former stagecoach stop, and their hard work was acknowledged by the California Heritage Council with an award for historic restoration. The hotel's showpiece is the Victorian-style parlor, a grand room with oak wainscoting, etched-glass doors, brass ceiling fans and light fixtures, and a marble fireplace. Upstairs there are 37 guest rooms with antique dressers, glass chandeliers, and full-, queen-, or king-size beds, many with elaborately carved wooden headboards; 8 rooms have private baths and the other 29 have basins and share bathrooms. The multiple configurations of rooms and suites can accommodate one to five people, and the units at the back of the hotel facing north—away from the railroad tracks and the bustling main street—are the quietest. Included in the rate is an expanded continental breakfast of hot and cold cereals, warm breads, and fresh fruit served in the parlor. Late-afternoon tea is served in the parlor on weekends. Skiers will appreciate the ski racks and lockers. The hotel also houses Moody's restaurant (see review, above), which serves lunch and dinner daily and brunch on weekends. $–$$; AE, MC, V; no checks; thetruckeehotel@sierra.net; www.thetruckeehotel.com; at Donner Pass Rd.

North Shore Lake Tahoe

Although the California–Nevada border basically bisects Lake Tahoe down the middle, leaving its west side in California and its east side in Nevada, the lake is more commonly referred to in terms of its north and south shores. The **SOUTH SHORE** area (see below) is the most populous and urban, where you'll hear all those slot machines ringing. If you'd rather steer clear of the one-armed bandits, head for the **NORTH SHORE**. There you'll find fewer casinos (and tourists) and more of everything else, including Tahoe's best alpine and cross-country ski resorts, first-rate restaurants, and luxurious lodgings. The best source for information about the North Shore is the **NORTH LAKE TAHOE RESORT ASSOCIATION VISITORS AND CONVENTION BUREAU** (530/583-3494 or 888/434-1262; www.tahoefun.org). This is also the place to call if you're having trouble finding a North Shore hotel room or campsite (a common problem during peak seasons) or need information on ski packages.

The hot summer weather brings a phenomenal array of lakeside activities, many of which don't cost a dime. Day hikers should head for the trails next to the **FOREST SERVICE VISITORS CENTER** (south shore of the lake, 5 miles S of Emerald Bay, just past Baldwin Beach; 530/573-2674; www.fs.fed.us/r5/ltbmu). It's the starting point for several well-marked trails, ranging from an easy half-mile stroll to a 10-mile leg-burning trek. Serious mountain bikers shouldn't miss huffing up and down the famous 24-mile **FLUME TRAIL**, which provides fantastic views of the lake; the trail-head begins at **NEVADA STATE PARK AT SPOONER LAKE** on the lake's eastern shore. Casual and asphalt-only pedalers can vie with in-line skaters, joggers, and strollers for room on North Tahoe's 15-mile-long paved trail, beginning at **SUGAR PINE POINT STATE PARK** on the West Shore and stretching north along the lake to Dollar Point on the North Shore. There's also a 3½-mile paved trail that parallels the

Truckee River and passes through Tahoe City; the trail starts at the turnoff to **ALPINE MEADOWS** ski resort on Highway 89. For the truly lazy (or crazy) rider, Northstar-at-Tahoe, Kirkwood, and Squaw Valley USA ski resorts offer miles of pedal-free trails accessible by chairlift or cable car—simply let the lifts tote you and your bike up the mountains, then spend the day cruising (or careening, if you wish) down the slopes.

If you weren't able to pack all your recreational toys, **PORTER'S SKI & SPORT** (501 N Lake Blvd, Tahoe City; 530/583-2314) has the best prices in town for outdoor rental equipment—everything from bikes to skates to rackets, as well as a full line of snow skis, water skis, and snowboards.

To try your luck at blackjack or craps, make the short drive to Nevada. Although the North Shore's casinos are more subdued and less glitzy than the South Shore's high-rolling high-rises, the dealers are still adept at taking your money. If you're a greenhorn, this is a good place to learn the ABCs of the games, especially during off-hours. North Shore casinos include the **TAHOE BILTMORE LODGE AND CASINO** (775/831-0660); **CAL-NEVA RESORT, SPA, AND CASINO** (800/225-6382); **HYATT REGENCY LAKE TAHOE** (775/832-1234 or 888/899-5019); and **CRYSTAL BAY CLUB CASINO** (775/831-0512).

North Lake Tahoe also offers a few nocturnal alternatives to the dice and the slots, but nightlife definitely isn't the North Shore's best attribute. You can dance any night of the week at **PIERCE STREET ANNEX** (850 N Lake Blvd, behind Safeway, Tahoe City; 530/583-5800; www.piercestreet.com), which caters primarily to a thirty-something crowd but attracts swingers of all ages. During the ski season, the lounge of the **RIVER RANCH LODGE** (see review in the Lodging section of Alpine Meadows) has a raging après-ski scene, with ski bums from all over kicking back and chowing down on cheap hors d'oeuvres. There's usually live music nightly at **BULLWHACKER'S PUB,** a popular locals' hangout located at the Resort at Squaw Creek (see review in the Lodgings section of Squaw Valley).

Tahoe Vista

RESTAURANTS

The Boulevard Cafe & Trattoria / ★★

6731 N LAKE BLVD, TAHOE VISTA; 530/546-7213 At the North Shore's most popular Italian restaurant, the breads, pastas, and just about everything else on the Boulevard's menu are made in-house. It's a small, casual roadside establishment with outdoor seating on the small patio among the pines. Start with a bottle of wine from the extensive, award-winning list and the butternut-squash gnocchi appetizer with walnuts and sage (ah heck,try the potato and white truffle ravioli appetizer as well). Then sink your fork into one of the delicious entrees, such as the osso buco (braised veal shank), rack of lamb with Gorgonzola and kalamata olives, honey-smoked pork loin with an apple-cranberry sauce, or one of the several seafood specials. Top it all off with a dish of the house-made ice cream. *$$;*

MC, V; no checks; dinner Tues–Sun; beer and wine; reservations recommended; on Hwy 28, 1½ miles W of Hwy 267.

Le Petit Pier / ★★★

7238 N LAKE BLVD, TAHOE VISTA; 530/546-4464 For more than 30 years Le Petit Pier has been North Lake Tahoe's finest French restaurant. It's fashioned after a cozy country inn, with three intimate dining rooms that are elevated just above the shore with a dazzling view, of the lake. Le Petit's menu features such mouthwatering appetizers as escargots in Roquefort butter, warm foie gras with truffle sauce, and oysters on the half shell. The exquisite entrees range from seafood (swordfish with ginger-raspberry sauce) and fowl (grilled breast of duck in a zinfandel sauce) to a superb rack of lamb. Also deservedly popular is the pheasant Souvaroff for two with foie gras and a rich demi-glace encrusted in puff pastry (but give the chef a 24 hours' notice). Le Petit Pier's wine list has won *Wine Spectator* magazine's Award of Excellence. When making a reservation, request a table by the window, and be sure to arrive before sunset—you don't want to miss this view, which extends clear across Lake Tahoe. *$$$; AE, DC, DIS, MC, V; local checks only; dinner Wed–Mon; full bar; reservations recommended; www.lepetitpier.com; on Hwy 28 at the W end of town.* &

Wild Goose / ★★★★

7320 N LAKE BLVD, TAHOE VISTA; 530/546-3640 It was inevitable: a true four-star restaurant on the shores of Lake Tahoe. Without a trace of fanfare or hint of pretension, executive chef John Tesar quietly opened what has already become Lake Tahoe's finest restaurant. As if the panoramic view of the lake wasn't stunning enough, the interior decor is fashioned after those classic lake cruisers of the 1920s, with subdued yet warmly textured modern design elements and a profusion of finely polished mahogany, metal, and granite—sleek, sexy, and very inviting. The cuisine is Contemporary American and on a par with the Bay Area's finest restaurants: fried squash blossom appetizer stuffed with herbed goat cheese, roasted tomato sauce, and tomato-basil sorbet; curried blue claw crab with sunflower sprouts, mango crème fraiche, and chili oil; wild mushroom-crusted halibut with purslane salad and creamy mashed potatoes; and hoisin-barbecued salmon with braised bok choy and shiitake mushroms, topped with a coconut–green curry sauce—all expertly prepared, beautifully arranged, and properly presented by a well-trained staff. In the winter, request a table near the custom-built fireplace; otherwise, you'll want a table at the terraced outdoor dining area overlooking the lake. *$$$–$$$$; AE, DC, DIS, MC, V; no checks; dinner Wed–Sun; full bar; reservations recommended; info@wildgoosetahoe.com; www.wildgoosetahoe.com; on Hwy 28 at the E end of town.* &

LODGINGS

Franciscan Lakeside Lodge / ★

6944 N LAKE BLVD, TAHOE VISTA; 530/546-6300 OR 800/564-6754 The best of the North Lake's motel scene, the Franciscan offers access to a private beach and pier, mooring buoys, a heated swimming pool, volleyball nets, a croquet set, horseshoe pits, a children's play area, and nearby tennis courts, ski areas, and a golf course. Its 54 plain but adequate units include studios, one- and two-bedrooms (and a four-bedroom house), full kitchens, private bathrooms, TVs, phones, and daily housekeeping service. The lakefront cottages have large porches overlooking the water (of course, they're the first to get booked, so make your reservations early). *$–$$; AE, MC, V; checks OK; franciscanlodge@aol.com; www.franciscanlodge.com; on Hwy 28, 1 mile W of Hwy 267.*

Kings Beach

RESTAURANTS

Log Cabin Caffe / ★

8692 N LAKE BLVD, KINGS BEACH; 530/546-7109 Originally a summer home, the funky Log Cabin Caffe is now the locals' favorite for breakfast in Lake Tahoe. The owner's penchant for freshness is what makes the Log Cabin such a hit: croissants and muffins are baked every morning, the orange juice is fresh-squeezed, and the fluffy Belgian waffles are topped with fresh fruit and nuts. The large lunch menu features everything from fresh vegetable soup and tofu burgers to pizza, pasta, and sliced turkey-breast sandwiches filled with cranberries and cream cheese. Behind the restaurant near the lakeshore is a picnic area where you can cool off with ice cream sundaes and sodas, served from 11am to 11pm throughout the summer. *$; MC, V; checks OK; breakfast, lunch every day; beer and wine; no reservations; on Hwy 28, ⅓ mile E of Hwy 267.* &

Squaw Valley

LODGINGS

PlumpJack Squaw Valley Inn / ★★★

1920 SQUAW VALLEY RD, SQUAW VALLEY; 530/583-1576 OR 800/323-7666 Restaurateurs Bill Getty (yes, those Gettys) and San Francisco Mayor Gavin Newsom, the dashing duo who own the highly regarded PlumpJack Cafe in San Francisco, teamed up in 1995 to create one of Tahoe's most stylish and sophisticated hotels and restaurants. Though it lacks the big-dollar toys offered by its competitor across the valley (the Resort at Squaw Creek), the PlumpJack Squaw Valley Inn is undeniably more chic; think of it as part ski chalet, part boutique hotel. The entire hotel bears a strong resemblance to the San Francisco restaurant, draped in muted tones of taupe and soft greens and highlighted with custom metalwork that imparts a handsome industrial-deco theme. Guest rooms are loaded with comforts, from plush hooded robes and terry-cloth slippers to thick down comforters atop expensive mattresses. The hotel boasts mountain views from each of its 61 rooms, as well as a swimming pool, two spas, a retail sports shop, ski rentals and storage, complimentary parking, and room service from the terrific cafe from 7am to 10pm. The adjoining **PLUMPJACK CAFE** and nearby **PLUMPJACK BALBOA CAFE** offer upscale cuisine and service regardless of your attire (this is, after all, a ski resort) and a tempting menu of modern American dishes: milk-brined double-cut pork chop with Yorkshire pudding and summer vegetables; spicy Maine soft-shell crab with pickled ginger vinaigrette and chili tobiko; duckling served two ways—roasted breast and confit leg with lime mashed sweet potatoes and huckleberry sauce. Those already familiar with PlumpJack in San Francisco know that the reasonably priced wine list is among the nation's best. *$$$; AE, DC, DIS, MC, V; svi@plumpjack.com; www.plumpjack.com; checks OK; off Hwy 89.* &

Resort at Squaw Creek / ★★★★

400 SQUAW CREEK RD, SQUAW VALLEY; 530/583-6300 OR 800/327-3353 Ranked among the top 50 resorts in North America by *Condé Nast Traveler*, the Resort at Squaw Creek—North Lake Tahoe's only superluxury resort hotel—is a paradise for skiers, golfers, and tennis players. Tucked away in an inconspicuous corner of Squaw Valley, the nine-story resort opened in 1990, offering a plethora of amenities—from parking valets, a concierge, and room service to children's activity programs, a shopping promenade, three swimming pools, a fitness center and spa, 20 miles of groomed cross-country ski trails, an equestrian center with stables, and even an ice-skating rink. Furthermore, it's only a stone's throw from the Squaw Creek chairlift, which accesses the entire Squaw Valley USA ski area. In the summer, golfers may tee off at the resort's 18-hole championship golf course designed by Robert Trent Jones Jr., while tennis buffs may rally at the resort's eight tennis courts. The 403 rooms, suites, and bilevel penthouses feature custom furnishings, original artwork, minibars, closed-circuit televisions, Nintendo, Starbucks in-room coffee and tea service, and telephones with speakerphones. In addition to a deli, a pub, a game lounge, and an outdoor cafe, the Resort at Squaw Creek offers three restaurants: the elegant Glissandi, which serves French-American cuisine; the continental restaurant Cascades; and the Ristorante Montagna, where you can dine alfresco on wood-oven-baked pizzas, rotisserie-grilled meats, and house specials such as the *agnello alla griglia*—oakwood-roasted rack of lamb with grilled vegetables. A $3 million refurbishment of the 10,000-square-foot spa added such state-of-the-art bliss inducers as a full-service salon, body wraps, and mud baths. Be sure to ask about the midweek package deals, which can knock a hefty amount off the normally exorbitant rates. *$$$$; AE, DC, DIS, MC, V; checks OK; info@squawcreek.com; www.squawcreek.com; off Hwy 89.* &

Alpine Meadows

LODGINGS

River Ranch Lodge / ★★

HWY 89, ALPINE MEADOWS; 530/583-4264 OR 800/535-9900 Established in 1888 as the Deer Park Inn, this historic lodge was a popular watering hole for passengers traveling by narrow-gauge railway. In 1950 the old building was replaced with the rustic, wood-shingled lodge that now stands on the banks of the picturesque Truckee River. The River Ranch's best rooms feature private balconies that overlook the river as it winds its way from Lake Tahoe to the town of Truckee, then east to Pyramid Lake in Nevada. All of the 19 rooms have private baths, antique or lodgepole pine furnishings, down comforters, TVs, and phones with data ports. Rooms 9 and 10, the farthest from the road, are the top choices because they're quiet and have the best river views from their private decks. In the winter, the lodge is a skier's paradise, a mere five-minute drive from both Squaw Valley USA and Alpine Meadows ski resorts (the Alpine Meadows stay-and-ski packages are outstanding); in the summer, guests relax under umbrellas on the huge patio overlooking the river, watching rafters float by while they munch on barbecued chicken and sip iced tea. A continental breakfast is included in the surprisingly reasonable rates. The River Ranch's spectacular circular cocktail lounge, which cantilevers over the river, has been a locals' haven for years and is an immensely popular après-ski spot for those who have been schussing the slopes of Alpine Meadows and Squaw Valley. Also a big hit is the handsome River Ranch Lodge Restaurant, which serves fresh fish, such as mountain rainbow trout sautéed with lemon butter, steaks, a full New Zealand rack of lamb, and something you probably don't cook at home: wood-oven-roasted Montana elk loin with a dried Bing cherry–port sauce. *$–$$$; AE, MC, V; no checks; info@riverranchlodge.com; www.riverranchlodge.com; at Alpine Meadows Rd, 3½ miles from Lake Tahoe and Tahoe City.* &

Tahoe City

RESTAURANTS

Bridgetender Tavern and Grill / ★

65 W LAKE BLVD, TAHOE CITY; 530/583-3342 Any bar that has Jaegermeister on tap is worth a visit. The fact that the Bridgetender has 20 other beers on tap and great burgers is icing on the cake. Despite being situated next to Tahoe City's most popular tourist attraction—Fanny Bridge—Tahoe's foremost tavern has always been a locals' hangout. The menu is basic—burgers, salads, sandwiches, and various appetizers like pork ribs, fish-and-chips, and deep-fried chicken strips—but the food is filling and cheap. Cholesterol-phobes will appreciate the healthy, low-fat chicken salad sandwich. In the summer the outside patio is always packed with giddy tourists unfamiliar with the effects of alcohol at high altitudes. *$; DIS, MC, V; no checks; lunch, dinner every day; full bar; no reservations; on Hwy 89 at Fanny Bridge, downtown.* &

Christy Hill / ★★★

115 GROVE ST, TAHOE CITY; 530/583-8551 Perched 100 feet above the lake in one of the most romantic fireside settings in Tahoe, the venerable Christy Hill restaurant has weathered more than two decades of droughts and recessions, yet still retains its title as one of the finest—and most expensive—restaurants in Tahoe City. The menu changes seasonally but always offers a wide selection of

SIERRA NEVADA THREE-DAY TOUR

Note: This itinerary is possible only from early summer to fall, when the High Sierra mountain passes are snow-free and open to traffic. It begins in Oakhurst in the foothills just south of Yosemite.

DAY ONE: Into the woods. Arrive the night before and check in at **CHÂTEAU DU SUREAU** (see review in the lodging section of Oakhurst, one of the most elegant inns in the West. Have dinner and breakfast at the château's four-star restaurant to fuel up for the mountaineering ahead. On the way to Yosemite, take a short detour to see the **MARIPOSA GROVE** of sequoias, including one of the world's largest trees, the **GRIZZLY GIANT**. Entering **YOSEMITE NATIONAL PARK** by the southern entrance, you'll see **TUNNEL VIEW**, one of the best scenic views of the park and the subject of a famous Ansel Adams photograph. Once you're in the valley, stop at the visitor center and take the two-hour open-air tram tour, or grab a map, rent bikes, and conduct your own tour. And don't worry if you don't get to see everything, because once you've been here, you're hooked; you'll return again and again. Finish your tour early enough to check into your room at the majestic **AHWAHNEE HOTEL** and have a drink in the granite-and-timbered Great Lounge before dinner in the hotel's legendary dining room.

DAY TWO: Summits and spooks. A big breakfast at the Ahwahnee, then cross the High Sierra on Highway 120. The road is barely two lanes, but the scenery is as breathtaking as the altitude, so take your time and enjoy the ride. Before you reach the 9,945-

fresh seafood—such as Fanny Bay oysters, broiled salmon, and Alaskan halibut oven-baked with garlic bread crumbs and served over endive with a shallot, garlic, and white wine butter sauce—plus choice-cut meats such as Australian lamb marinated in wine, honey, and herbs, broiled and served with a fresh peach, ginger, and garlic chutney. Christy Hill's experienced servers (most have been here at least 10 years) know the menu and extensive wine list well, so don't hesitate to seek their advice. Dessert is a wonderful excuse to extend your evening here; try the warm summer fruit cobbler with house-made vanilla ice cream or the chocolate pot de crème with crème Chantilly. Arrive before sunset to admire the spectacular view. *$$$; AE, MC, V; checks OK; dinner Tues–Sun; beer and wine; reservations recommended; www.christyhill.com; off Hwy 28/N Lake Blvd, behind the Village Store.*

Fire Sign Cafe / ★★

1785 W LAKE BLVD, TAHOE CITY; 530/583-0871 This converted old Tahoe home has been a favorite breakfast stop for locals since the late 1970s. Just about everything here is made from scratch, including the coffee cake and muffins that accompany generous servings of bacon and eggs. Even the savory, thinly sliced salmon used in the cafe's legendary eggs Benedict is smoked on the premises. Popular lunch items foot summit at **TIOGA PASS** (the highest motor-vehicle pass in California), stop and stretch your legs at beautiful **TUOLUMNE MEADOWS**, with the Tuolumne River on one side and soaring granite peaks on the other. Then drop down some 3,000 feet to Highway 395, and just north of the town of Lee Vining, stop at the **MONO BASIN SCENIC VISITORS CENTER** to get the scoop on the eerie lake and its otherworldly tufa towers of calcium. Next, take the lonely 12-mile detour to the magical mining town of **BODIE**. You'll swear this road doesn't go anywhere, but then you go over a rise and you're transported back in time to 1920. From here it's north on Highway 395 to Highway 89, over the Monitor Pass, and on to Markleeville for dinner at the small Italian restaurant **VILLA GIGLI**. After dinner it's a short trip to Hope Valley and a night in one of the rustic cabins at **SORENSEN'S RESORT**. Quite a change from the luxury of the Ahwanee and du Sureau, but it's just right for this side of the Sierra.

DAY THREE: By the big blue water. Enjoy your country breakfast at Sorensen's, because you're about to leave the simple, timeless charm of the remote High Sierra and head 15 miles north over the Luther Pass for the glitz, glamour, and gambling of **SOUTH LAKE TAHOE**. Drop your bags off at the **BLACK BEAR INN**, then take the two-hour lake cruise aboard the **TAHOE QUEEN**, an authentic Mississippi stern-wheeler. Pick up a picnic lunch at **SPROUTS**, then head across the state line to **ZEPHYR COVE** to indulge in some quality beach time on the beautiful golden sand beach. As the sun sets in the west, enjoy a romantic Italian dinner at **IVANO'S**, and after dinner head for the tables or slot machines at **CAESARS TAHOE** to try your luck.

include the garden burger, the chicken burrito, the grilled turkey sandwich with green chilies and cheese, and a wicked raspberry cobbler. In the summer, dine on the deck under the pines. Expect a long wait on weekends. *$; AE, MC, V; local checks only; breakfast, lunch every day; beer and wine; no reservations; on Hwy 89, 2 miles S of Tahoe City.* &

Jake's Lake Tahoe / ★★

780 LAKE BLVD, TAHOE CITY; 530/583-0188 If you're in the mood for steak and seafood, Jake's has been serving some of the best in Tahoe since 1978. One link in a wildly popular California and Hawaii chain, this handsome lakefront restaurant—the sweeping lake views are superb—offers consistently good food and service, provided in part by a candidate for California's most affable bartender, Montana. Specialties include rack of New Zealand lamb and fresh fish, such as the favored flame-broiled seven-spice ahi tuna with a saffron mustard sauce. And the terrific Hula Pie dessert (an Oreo cookie crust topped with mounds of macadamia-nut ice cream and smothered with fudge sauce and whipped cream) is worth the splurge. *$$; AE, DIS, MC, V; no checks; lunch every day June–Sept (lunch Sat only Oct–May), dinner every day; full bar; reservations recommended; www.jakestahoe.com; on Hwy 28, downtown.* &

Rosie's Cafe / ★★

571 N LAKE BLVD, TAHOE CITY; 530/583-8504 Most folks who spend a few days or more in North Lake Tahoe eventually wind up at Rosie's for breakfast, lunch, dinner, drinks, or all of the above. This humble Tahoe institution has served large portions of traditional American fare—sandwiches, steaks, burgers, salads—since 1980, but the dish that tourists always return for is the hearty Yankee pot roast (the perfect dish for those cold winter nights), served with mashed potatoes and gravy and a side of sautéed vegetables. Bring the kids; they get their own special menu and free balloons. *$$; AE, DC, DIS, MC, V; no checks; breakfast, lunch, dinner every day; full bar; no reservations for breakfast and lunch, reservations recommended for dinner; rosiescafe@aol.com; www.rosiescafe.com; downtown.*

Wolfdale's / ★★★

640 N LAKE BLVD, TAHOE CITY; 530/583-5700 Chef-owner Douglas Dale is well known for his innovative California cuisine that's often accented with Asian touches. His short, frequently changing menu offers an intriguing mix of truly one-of-a-kind, light, and beautifully arranged dishes that vary from very good to sublime. Everything served in this casually elegant restaurant—from the herb-kissed focaccia to the savory sausages, smoked fish, and divine desserts—is prepared on the premises. You might begin your meal with a soft-shell crab tempura or a vegetable spring roll with a Thai curry-ginger sauce, followed by grilled Columbia River sturgeon with mushroom duxelles and tomato coulis, barbecued ribs with white corn bisque, or roasted quail stuffed with fennel sausage and onions served on a bed of kale. Many of Wolfdale's regular patrons dine at the small bar, and in the summertime you can sit outdoors and enjoy the view of Lake Tahoe through the trees. *$$$; MC, V; no checks; dinner Wed–Mon (dinner every day July–Aug); full bar; reservations recommended; dale@wolfdales.com; www.wolfdales.com; on Hwy 28, downtown.* &

LODGINGS

The Cottage Inn / ★★

1690 W LAKE BLVD, TAHOE CITY; 530/581-4073 OR 800/581-4073 This is one of the more appealing places to stay in Tahoe City. Shaded by a grove of thick pine trees, each of the inn's unique country cottages—built in the "Old Tahoe" style with knotty pine paneling throughout—has Swedish-pine furniture, a stone fireplace, a private bath with a ceramic-tile shower, a thick and colorful quilt on the bed, and a TV with a VCR. A full country breakfast, included in the price, is served at the family-style tables in the main lodge's dining room or on the outside deck under umbrellas. After breakfast, read the morning paper in the comfortable sitting room in front of the large stone fireplace, take a steam in the Scandinavian sauna, or work on your tan at the nearby private beach and dock. *$$; MC, V; checks OK; cottage@ltol.com; www.thecottageinn.com; on Hwy 89, 2 miles S of town.*

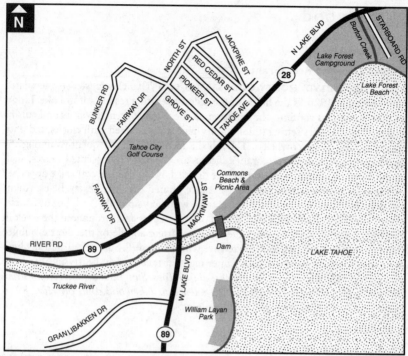

TAHOE CITY

Sunnyside Restaurant & Lodge / ★★

1850 W LAKE BLVD, TAHOE CITY; 530/583-7200 OR 800/822-2754 Built as a private lakeside home in 1908, this handsome mountain lodge and restaurant is one of the few grand old lodges left on the lakeshore. Replete with steep pitched roofs and natural-wood siding, it offers 23 guest rooms, each decorated in classic Tahoe lodge style complete with small decks, and all but four with an unobstructed view of Lake Tahoe. The best of the bunch are the bright and airy lakefront units (suites 30 and 31 and rooms 32 to 39). A complimentary continental breakfast buffet is served every morning, and in the afternoon locals and visitors assemble for lunch, dinner, or a drink on the huge redwood deck overlooking the lake, beach, and 25-boat marina. The Chris Craft Dining Room serves well-prepared California cuisine and specializes in fresh seafood, such as Hawaiian ahi and baked salmon with Roma tomatoes, fresh basil, and Gorgonzola. In the winter the lodge attracts a sizable après-ski crowd, that watches Sunnyside's ski flicks while munching on the inexpensive food at the bar. *$$$; AE, MC, V; no checks; lodgedesk@sunnysideresort.com; www.sunnysideresort.com; on Hwy 89, 2 miles S of town.*

Homewood

RESTAURANTS

Swiss Lakewood Restaurant / ★★

5055 W LAKE BLVD, HOMEWOOD; 530/525-5211 This classic Swiss-style chalet, first opened in 1920, is the home of the oldest operating restaurant in Lake Tahoe. Its current owners continue the tradition of offering fine French-continental cuisine in a traditional Swiss setting (think knotty-pine walls covered with clocks, old photographs, and Swiss cowbells). Though the menu changes frequently, among the secrets of this venerable restaurant's success are the perfectly executed sauces, such as the tangy caper-lemon-mustard sauce drizzled over a delicate crab cake appetizer or the tasty Madagascar green-pepper sauce poured over the hearty Black Angus pepper steak flambé, prepared at your table with fiery aplomb. And, but of course, there's the cheese fondue for two, served on weeknights and throughout the week in the winter. For dessert, consider the Grand Marnier soufflé or the cherries jubilee flambé for two. You'll enjoy the extensive wine list as well. Sure, it's all sinfully high in calories, but during those cold winter nights it takes a rich, hearty meal to keep you warm. *$$$; AE, MC, V; no checks; dinner Tues–Sun; full bar; reservations recommended; staff@swisslakewood.com; www.swisslakewood.com; on Hwy 89, 6 miles S of Tahoe City, next to Ski Homewood.* &

LODGINGS

Chaney House / ★★★

4725 W LAKE BLVD, HOMEWOOD; 530/525-7333 Built by Italian stone masons in the 1920s, the European-style Chaney House features 18-inch-thick stone walls, Gothic arches, and a massive stone fireplace that extends to a cathedral ceiling. Each of the four individually decorated rooms has a private bath and a queen- or king-size bed. The attractive Honeymoon Hideaway is a detached, very private unit with a fireplace and a granite Jacuzzi for two. Gary and Lori Chaney—two of Tahoe's more vivacious and friendly innkeepers—serve an elaborate breakfast on the patio (weather permitting) overlooking their private beach and pier. Lori likes to get creative in the kitchen—she often whips up such treats as French toast stuffed with cream cheese and topped with hot homemade blackberry sauce and crème fraîche, or a wonderful concoction of scrambled eggs mixed with artichokes, vermouth, and cheese. The Chaney House books up quickly, so make your reservations at least a month in advance. *$$; DIS, MC, V; checks OK; gary@chaneyhouse.com; www.chaneyhouse.com; on Hwy 89, 1 mile N of Ski Homewood.*

Rockwood Lodge / ★★★

5295 W LAKE BLVD, HOMEWOOD; 530/525-5273 OR 800/LE-TAHOE Situated on the West Shore is one of the prettiest B&Bs in Lake Tahoe. Built by a Vallejo valley dairyman in the 1930s using hand-hewn beams, pine paneling, and indigenous rock, the Rockwood Lodge was eventually converted into Tahoe's first B&B. Although you may be disconcerted by the innkeeper's requirement that you remove your shoes before entering (seasoned guests bring their own slippers), all is forgiven when your feet sink into the plush, cream-colored carpet. The lodge, located just across the street from the lake, has five rooms with lake or forest views, each furnished with antiques, featherbeds, and down comforters covered in Laura Ashley fabrics. Terry-cloth robes hang in the bedroom closets, and the extravagant private bathrooms feature brass fixtures, hand-painted tiles, and double showers or a tub for two. In the evening guests often play backgammon and sip cordials by the fireplace in the sitting room. A generous breakfast is served at 9am in the dining room or on the outdoor patio (early-rising skiers and golfers are also provided for). *$$–$$$; MC, V; checks OK; rockwood@inreach.com; www.rockwood lodge.com; on Hwy 89, next to Ski Homewood.*

Tahoma

LODGINGS

Tahoma Meadows Bed & Breakfast / ★★

6821 W LAKE BLVD, TAHOMA; 530/525-1553 OR 800/355-1596 Ulli and Dick White, owners of Tahoma Meadows Bed & Breakfast, are just the couple to run the finest moderately priced B&B in Lake Tahoe. Both are veterans of the hospitality industry and two of the nicest, most low-key people you're likely to meet on the lake. This popular B&B consists of 14 cabins perched on a gentle forest slope among sugar pines and flowers. The units are individually decorated; in each cozy little red cabin you'll find framed paintings of bucolic settings, a private bath, a discreetly placed TV, and a comfy king- or queen-size bed; four units have gas-log fireplaces. The largest cabins, Tree House and Sugar Pine, are ideal for families seeking privacy and plenty of elbow room. A full breakfast is served at the main lodge upstairs at independently owned Stoneyridge Cafe, which also serves dinner Thursday through Saturday. Nearby activities include skiing at Ski Homewood, fly-fishing at a private trout-stocked lake (Dick, an avid fly-fisherman, can give you tips), and sunbathing on the lakeshore just across the street. Tahoma Meadows is popular with the hiking and biking crowds, who like both the value and the superb trails nearby. *$$; AE, DIS, MC, V; checks OK; info@tahomameadows.com; www.tahomameadows.com; on Hwy 89, 8½ miles from Tahoe City.*

South Shore Lake Tahoe

Three premier attractions separate South Lake Tahoe from its more subdued northern counterpart: glitzy casinos with celebrity entertainers, long stretches of sandy beaches, and the massive **HEAVENLY SKI RESORT,** one of the largest ski resorts in North America. If skiing the slopes of Heavenly followed by gambling until 3am is your idea of paradise, then you're in for a treat.

Most of the weekend warriors who flock here on Friday afternoons book their favorite lodgings weeks—if not months—in advance. Follow their lead and plan early. For long-term stays, consider renting a condo with a group of friends. As soon as you roll into town, stop at the **SOUTH LAKE TAHOE CHAMBER OF COMMERCE** (3066 Lake Tahoe Blvd, 530/541-5255; www.tahoeinfo.com), where you'll find an entire room filled with free maps, brochures, and guidebooks to the South Lake region. And if you risked traveling to Tahoe without a hotel reservation, call **LAKE TAHOE VISITOR AUTHORITY** (800/210-3459; www.virtualtahoe.com). You can also log onto tahoereservations.com for help finding a vacancy.

In the summer, droves of tourists and locals arrive by bike, car, or boat at the **BEACON** (see review, below) to scope out the beach, babe, and bar scene—easily the best on the lake. In addition to **JAMISON BEACH,** the other popular public beaches are **NEVADA BEACH** (on Elk Point Rd, 1 mile E of Stateline, Nevada), which has spectacular views of Lake Tahoe and the Sierra Nevada, and **EL DORADO BEACH** (off Lakeview Ave in downtown S Lake Tahoe)—not as pretty but much closer to town.

Tahoe's brilliant-blue lake is so deep it never freezes, so it's navigable even in the dead of winter. One way to get on the water is to book a trip on the **TAHOE QUEEN** (530/541-3364 or 800/238-2463; www.laketahoecruises.com; reservations required), an authentic Mississippi stern-wheeler that regularly offers Emerald Bay sightseeing tours and dinner/dance cruises.

The latest big tourist attraction in South Lake is **GONDOLA AT HEAVENLY** (775/586-7000; www.skiheavenly.com). The $20 million state-of-the-art gondola consists of "cars" that transport you from the South Shore's downtown area up the steep mountainside to Heavenly Ski Resort's 14,000-square-foot observation deck. The 2½-mile ride rises to an elevation of 9,123 feet, offering passengers incredible views of Lake Tahoe, Carson Valley to the east, and Desolation Wilderness to the west. The gondola is located a half-block west of Stateline, a short walk from the downtown hotels.

The South Lake's number-one nighttime entertainment is, of course, the casinos. The top guns on this side of the lake are **HARRAH'S, CAESARS TAHOE, HARVEYS,** and the **HORIZON,** which are squeezed next to each other on Highway 50 in Nevada and burn enough bulbs to light a small city. Even if you can't afford to gamble your paycheck, stroll through the ruckus to watch the high rollers or gawk at those "just-one-more-try" players mesmerized by the flashy money machines. If you want to try your luck, a mere $10 can keep you entertained for quite a while on the nickel slots. Or spend the night on the dance floor at **NERO'S 2000 NIGHTCLUB** (55 Hwy 50, Stateline, Nevada; 702/588-3515) in Caesars, or visit **TURTLE'S SPORTS BAR AND DANCE EMPORIUM** (4130 Lake Tahoe Blvd, S Lake Tahoe; 530/544-5400) in the Embassy Suites.

For more than a century, **DAVID WALLEY'S RESORT, HOT SPRINGS & SPA** (2001 Foothill Blvd, 2 miles N of the E end of Kingsbury Grade, near Genoa, Nevada; 775/782-8155; www.davidwalleys.com) has been the place for South Lake residents to unwind after a hard day of skiing or mountain biking, even though it's about an hour-long drive from town. For $20 you can jump into the six open-air pools (each is set at a different temperature) and watch ducks and geese at the nearby wildlife area. If a good soak doesn't get all the kinks out, indulge in a rubdown at the resort's massage center.

South Lake Tahoe

RESTAURANTS

The Beacon Bar & Grill / ★★

1900 JAMISON BEACH RD, S LAKE TAHOE; 530/541-0630 On a warm summer afternoon there's no better place on the South Shore to sit outside on the deck, sip on a frosty Rum Runner (a blend of light and dark rums and seven juices), and say to yourself, "This is the life." Located right on Jamison Beach, the Beacon is where locals arrive by car, bike, or boat to bask in the sun, chow down on a bucket of steamed clams, and gawk at the tourist scene. The lunch fare favorites are the Beacon Suzette Salad, Beacon Burger, ribeye steak sandwich, and the Camp Richardson clam chowder, whereas dinner specialties range from fresh seafood such as macadamia-encrusted prawns served with Frangelico dipping butter to a New York Steak charbroiled and smothered in a green peppercorn sauce. In the summer the Beacon hosts jazz, reggae, country, and rock 'n' roll bands. Tip: Bring strong sunscreen—the alpine sun will cook you in minutes. *$$; AE, DIS, MC, V; no checks; lunch, dinner every day, brunch Sat–Sun; full bar; reservations recommended; www.camp rich.com; off Hwy 89, 2½ miles N of the Hwy 50 junction, at Camp Richardson.* &

Evan's American Gourmet Cafe / ★★★

536 EMERALD BAY RD, S LAKE TAHOE; 530/542-1990 You can tell from the rather dated decor that the food at this family-run establishment is its raison d'être. Entering the small, softly lit dining room of this 1930s vintage house, you'll be greeted by one of the owners, Candice or Evan Williams. The ever-changing menu features an eclectic and impressive blend of cuisine styles from around the world (these folks were doing the chic fusion-cuisine thing before it had a name). The philosophy here is to use only the finest, freshest ingredients and to not overwhelm them with heavy sauces or overstylized culinary technique. The wine list, with nearly 300 labels, is as engaging as the food. A recent repast featured seared Sonoma foie gras with curried ice cream and roast pineapple; loin of lamb, crusted with ginger, orange, and bread crumbs and served with coconut jasmine rice; and house-smoked duck breast salad with microgreens and papaya vinaigrette. After dinner, try one of Candice's lavish desserts. Seating is limited, so be sure to call ahead for reservations. *$$$; DIS, MC, V; no checks; dinner every day; beer and wine; reservations required; tahoewino@aol.com; www.evanstahoe.com; on Hwy 89, 1 mile N of the Hwy 50 junction, at 15th St.*

Ivano's / ★★★

605 HWY 50, #4, ZEPHYR COVE; 775/586-1070 His full name is Ivano Costantini, but to his legion of fans he's simply Ivano, the ebullient and charismatic owner and maitre d' of the best Italian restaurant in South Lake Tahoe. Located on the southeastern shoreline in Nevada, this small bistro is easy to miss, as it's recessed into a tiny business complex right off the highway. But as soon as you smell the aromas of garlic, olive oil, and fresh basil wafting through the front door, you know you've arrived. Guests are escorted past framed paintings of Italian coastal towns to the intimate dining room, which holds only about 10 tables, each bedecked with a white tablecloth and fresh flowers. Entrees range from reasonably priced pasta standards—linguine puttanesca, tortellini di Parma, fettuccine al bolognese—to *secondi* classics such as scaloppine parmigiana (veal with fresh tomato sauce, prosciutto, and mozzarella) and *filetto di Giovanni*—thinly sliced tenderloin marinated in olive oil, vinegar, and rosemary, then quickly seared to lock in the juices (no fusion confusion at *this* restaurant). The lengthy wine list offers more than 100 wines from Italy and California. *$$–$$$; AE, DIS, MC, V; no checks; dinner every day; beer and wine; reservations recommended; on Hwy 50 just S of the Zephyr Cove Resort.* &

The Naked Fish / ★★★

3940 LAKE TAHOE BLVD, S LAKE TAHOE; 530/541-3474 Yes, this sushi restaurant is a long way from the ocean, but the fish served here is as fresh as any you'll find in L.A. or San Francisco. But hey, who cares? All that's important is that the nigiri, maki, and sashimi served here are butter-soft and oh-so-flavorful. The colorful marine theme, with mermaids floating across the walls, adds to the laid-back atmosphere of this locally owned Japanese restaurant. In the spirit of a true sushi bar, the Japanese chefs are friendly and talkative, particularly if you buy them a beer. Pay close attention to the white "specials" board above the sushi bar—this is where the real action is. The live scallop sashimi special we ordered was so fresh the deftly shelled medallions were still moving, and the presentation was edible art. Full dinners such as sesame-crusted halibut, seared ahi steak, and the classic teriyaki standbys are available as well, but it's the outstanding nigiri (the fresh salmon rocks) and flavorful, inventive rolls that draw the locals in droves. *$$; AE, DC, DIS, MC, V; no checks; lunch Sat–Sun, dinner every day; beer and wine; reservations recommended for parties of 6 or more; at the junction of Hwy 50 and Pioneer Trail.* &

The Red Hut / ★

2749 HWY 50, S LAKE TAHOE; 530/541-9024 Satisfying South Lake locals and tourists since 1959, this all-American coffee shop, complete with an L-shaped Formica counter, red vinyl booths, and a bubble-gum machine, has become so popular the owners had to add a waiting room. The Red Hut's success is based primarily on its good coffee, hefty omelets with a variety of fillings, friendly waitresses, and, best of all, low prices. Lunch follows the same big-and-cheap all-American formula with a menu of mostly burgers and sandwiches (try the grilled cheese with fresh avocado). While the food isn't anything to swoon over, it beats the buns off the fast-food chains down the street. *$; cash only; breakfast, lunch every day; no alcohol; no reservations; ½ block S of Lake Tahoe Blvd, 4 miles E of Stateline, Nevada.*

Sprouts Natural Foods Cafe / ★★

3123 HARRISON AVE, S LAKE TAHOE; 530/541-6969 You don't have to be a granola-loving long-haired type to figure out that Sprouts is among the best places in town for a healthy, inexpensive meal. If the line out the door isn't a big enough hint, then perhaps a bite of the marvelous mayo-free tuna sandwich (made with yogurt and lots of fresh veggies) will make you a convert to feel-good food. As a premier vegetarian hangout, Sprouts fills a huge culinary hole in the South

Lake area. Almost everything is made on the premises, including the soups, tempeh burgers, sandwiches (try the Real Tahoe Turkey), huge burritos, muffins, fruit smoothies (a meal in themselves), coffee drinks, and fresh-squeezed juices. Order at the counter, then scramble for a vacant seat (outdoor tables are coveted) and listen for one of the buffed and beautiful servers to call out your name and deliver your tray of earthy delights. This is also an excellent place to pack a picnic lunch for a skiing, hiking, or mountain-biking expedition. *$; no credit cards; local checks only; breakfast, lunch, dinner every day; beer and wine; no reservations; on the corner of Hwy 50 and Alameda St.*

LODGINGS

Black Bear Inn Bed & Breakfast / ★★★

1202 SKI RUN BLVD, S LAKE TAHOE; 530/544-4451 OR 877/232-7466 The dream-come-true of a retired Texan defense attorney, the Black Bear Inn is a fine example of what a lot of money, excellent taste, and an incredible collection of early American antiques can produce. Everything about this neo-rustic B&B is designed to impress—from the towering three-story rock fireplace to the massive rough-hewn timbers, soaring ceiling, and artful blend of modern and authentic Old West furnishings. The inn consists of five rooms in the main lodge and three cabins of varying sizes set within a 1½-acre landscaped garden. Each of the spacious guest rooms has a king-size bed, a private bathroom, a TV/VCR/DVD player (with complimentary access to a DVD library), a gas fireplace, spa towels and robes for the trip to the gazebo spa, and very high-quality bedsheets. The cabins are popular with honeymooners, who prefer to have their breakfast—fresh-baked muffins, omelets, eggs Benedict, and other hearty dishes—delivered in bed. The cabins also have fully equipped kitchens or kitchenettes. One complaint: the location. Although this gorgeous B&B is just down the street from the Heavenly Ski Resort, it's also situated in one of the seediest parts of town, right next to a low-income apartment complex. *$$$–$$$$; MC, V; checks OK; info @ tahoeblackbear.com; www.tahoe blackbear.com; off Hwy 50.* &

Christiania Inn / ★★

3819 SADDLE RD, S LAKE TAHOE; 530/544-7337 Located only 50 yards from Heavenly Ski Resort's main chairlift, this European-style bed-and-breakfast inn, built in 1965 as a Scandinavian-style après-ski lodge, has two rooms and four suites that are frequently occupied by honeymooners. Why? Because this place is romance central: each cozy suite has a wood-burning fireplace, and all but one have king-size beds (but the room with the queen-size bed has an overhead mirror!). Room 6 comes with a dry sauna and whirlpool jet tub, the perfect remedy for a hard day's skiing. A continental breakfast (brought to your room every morning at your requested time) and an afternoon Cognac are included in the rates. The elegant and expensive Christiania Inn Restaurant offers continental cuisine, such as pan-seared spring venison with red currant cabernet sauce, boneless breast of Long Island duck with black currant sauce, and Chilean sea bass with fresh fruit salsa. Guests with lighter appetites may order from the appetizer menu in the lounge. During the winter season the inn hosts live jazz and blues on Friday and Saturday nights from 9pm to 1am. *$$; MC, V; local checks only; closed 3 weeks in May; thechris@sierra.net; www.christianiainn.com; off Ski Run Blvd, at the base of Heavenly Ski Resort.* &

Historic Camp Richardson Resort & Marina / ★

JAMISON BEACH RD AND HWY 89, S LAKE TAHOE; 530/541-1801 OR 800/544-1801 Richardson's, a popular family retreat, seems worlds away from the high-rise casinos and bustle of South Lake Tahoe, yet it's actually just a few miles outside town. Since the 150-acre resort was taken over from the Forest Service in 1985, the owners have restored the 65-year-old lodge, upgraded the inn and cabins, and added a large courtyard spa. The lodge, graced with a stately stone fireplace in the lobby, offers 28 sparsely furnished rooms with private baths and is only a five-minute walk from the lake. Even closer to the water are 39 homey cabins named after classic American cars and the small, 7-room Beach Inn (the rooms are slightly larger than the main lodge's and they have lake views, TVs, and telephones). The best cabins are near Jamison Beach and are usually reserved far in advance (only some of them are available to rent in the winter). In the summer the resort provides guests with an ice cream parlor, a general store (which includes beer and wine in its inventory), camping facilities, hiking and biking trails, volleyballs and nets, horseshoes and pits, and equipment rentals for almost anything that floats or rolls. Another perk: One of South Lake's best restaurants and bars, The Beacon Bar & Grill (see review, above) is just a short walk away. Staying at Richardson Resort is sort of like being at camp again, and it's a great place to take the kids. *$$; AE, MC, V; no checks; info@camprichardson.com; www.camprich.com; 2½ miles W of the Hwy 50 junction.*

Lakeland Village Beach & Ski Resort / ★★

3535 LAKE TAHOE BLVD, S LAKE TAHOE; 530/544-1685 OR 800/822-5969 Although a few of Lakeland Village's light-brown, two-story wood buildings are located on busy Highway 50, the 19-acre resort has more than 1,000 feet of beachfront property, two tennis courts, and two swimming pools—all beyond the sight and sound of the traffic. The condominium resort's 260 units, ranging from studios to five-bedroom town houses, are individually owned and best suited for families. Interior decor varies, but owners are required to meet or exceed AAA three-diamond standards. The most desirable town houses front the lake and get booked quickly during peak season—some also command hefty $600-per-night rates. The studio rooms in the main lodge and the one-bedroom suites are the least expensive, starting at about $100 per night. All units come with fireplaces, fully equipped kitchens, private balconies, and daily housekeeping service. Perks include free shuttle service to Heavenly and the casinos, children's activities in the summer, beach barbecues, and an underground parking garage. *$$–$$$; AE, DIS, MC, V; checks OK; stay@lakeland-village.com; www.lakeland-village.com; between Ski Run Blvd and Fairway Ave.* &

Marriott's Timber Lodge & Grand Residence Club / ★

4100 LAKE TAHOE BLVD, S LAKE TAHOE; 530/542-6600 OR 800/845-5279
The first phase of a massive redevelopment project slated for downtown South Lake Tahoe is this duo of colossal Marriott lodgings that, combined, offer a whopping 464 lodging units ranging from studios to three-bedroom condos. This "alpine village" consists of the two adjacent vacation ownership resorts (which also sell rooms on a per-night basis) and the Heavenly Village, a sort of alpine-style mall with shops, restaurants, bars, an ice skating rink, a movie theater, a ski gondola, an arcade, a . . . well, you get the picture. If you're into the whole corporate faux-village thing, you and your family will certainly enjoy the easy access to all the usual resort amenities, but don't expect a lick of originality, personalized service, or bargains. And although most of the well-appointed guest rooms are quite spacious and come with fully equipped kitchens, quality is lacking—our toilet didn't work, nor did the shower drain; the mattress was painfully firm; and the room lacked a high-speed Internet connection (an egregious oversight for a new resort). *$$$–$$$$; AE, DIS, MC, V; no checks; www.marriottvillarentals.com; downtown.* &

Zephyr Cove

LODGINGS

Zephyr Cove / ★★

HIGHWAY 50 AT ZEPHYR COVE, NEVADA; 775/589-4907 Along with Historic Camp Richardson Resort on the opposite side of the lake, Zephyr Cove is Lake Tahoe's best family destination (and not nearly as crowded). Situated amid a shady grove of tall pines, the resort's 28 cabins range in size from studios and cottages to four-bedroom cabins sleeping up to 10. Each cabin has a front porch with patio furniture, a cable TV with HBO, a telephone, Internet access, and a bathroom; each kitchen unit is equipped with refrigerator, oven, microwave, coffee maker, cookware, dishware, and utensils. OK, so it's not the Ritz, but the cabins are clean, inexpensive, and reasonably comfortable. Besides, you'll spend most of your time at the resort's beautiful gold-sand beach, catching a comfy buzz on mai tais at the Sunset Bar while the kids take turns on the rented jet ski. Pedal boats, kayaks, canoes, and ski boats are also available for rent, and the pier is the launching point for lake cruises on the *MS Dixie II* paddlewheeler and the *Woodwind II* catamaran. The Zephyr Cove Restaurant serves breakfast, lunch, and dinner daily, and it's a short drive to the restaurants and casinos in South Lake Tahoe (free shuttle service, even). Pets are allowed with a $10 charge per pet, per night. *$$; AE, DIS, MC, V; no checks; webmaster@zephyrcove.com; www.tahoedixie2.com; 4 miles N of Stateline on Hwy 5.*

Hope Valley

LODGINGS

Sorensen's Resort / ★★★

14255 HWY 88, HOPE VALLEY; 530/694-2203 OR 800/423-9949 Since 1926, Sorensen's cluster of 30 cabins—nestled among the meadows and aspen groves of alpine Hope Valley—have offered first-rate cross-country skiing in the winter, prime hiking, horseback riding, rafting, mountain biking, and llama treks in late spring and summer, and a terrific display of colors in the fall, when the aspens turn vibrant shades of yellow, gold, and red. There's good trout fishing here, too. Accommodations range from inexpensive, rustic-but-comfy cabins to grand, modern chalets. Norway House, a 13th-century Norwegian-style home with a hand-carved wooden facade and a sod roof, was actually built in Norway and transported here. It features a large open-loft bedroom, a kitchen, and a living/sleeping room, and is ideal for groups of up to eight people. The country decor, with quilts and vintage furniture, is attractive and unfussy. The cozy, creekside Waterfir Cabin, with its brass bed, kitchen, wood-burning stove, and natural-stone hearth, is the best choice for couples. If you rent one of the three smaller, less expensive cabins (Piñon, Lupine, and Larkspur), which, unlike the others, don't have kitchens, breakfast for two is included in the cost of your stay. There are also fully furnished homes for rent, which are ideal for families—kids can explore the log playhouse nearby and dip a fishing pole in the stocked fish pond. Sorensen's Country Cafe is open only to guests for breakfast, lunch, and dinner. The food is a cut above most mountain-resort fare, with good breakfasts of quiche, waffles, and fresh fruit, and your basic steak, pork chops, grilled salmon, and pasta for dinner. In snow season the resort rents cross-country skis and snowshoes. Sorensen's also runs the nearby Hope Valley Store and Cafe, which offers a modest menu of hot dogs, hamburgers, fries, and similar fare from Memorial Day through Labor Day—a good place for a quick, inexpensive meal. *$$; AE, MC, V; checks OK; info@sorensensresort.com; www.sorensens resort.com; 5 miles NW of Woodfords.* ♿

Markleeville

This tiny mountain town's claim to fame is the annual **DEATH RIDE TOUR OF THE CALIFORNIA ALPS**, a grueling 128-mile bike trek over five mountain passes (16,000 feet of climbing) that's renowned among bicyclists as one of the top-10 cycling challenges in the United States. The tour, limited to the first 2,500 prepaid applicants, is held the first Saturday after July 4; contact the **ALPINE CHAMBER OF COMMERCE** (530/694-2475; www.deathride.com) for more information.

The only place worth visiting in Markleeville besides the exceptional Villa Gigli Trattoria (see review, below) is the **CUTTHROAT BAR** (530/694-2150), located within the Wolf Creek Restaurant. (Alas, gone are the collection of brassieres hanging from the bar's ceiling.) Just outside of town is the popular **GROVER HOT SPRINGS STATE PARK** (4 miles W of Markleeville at the end of Hot Springs Rd;

530/694-2248; open 9am–9pm every day in summer, 2pm–9pm weekdays, and 9am–9pm weekends in winter), where you may soak in the plain but soothing cement mineral pools year-round (bathing suits are required).

RESTAURANTS

Villa Gigli Trattoria / ★★★

145 HOT SPRINGS RD, MARKLEEVILLE; 530/694-2253 Located on a remote hillside in this tiny Sierra town is Gina and Ruggero Gigli's Villa Gigli, a quintessential mom-and-pop cafe—it's situated alongside their modest home of nearly three decades. Every Saturday and Sunday morning Ruggero, who was raised in a small town in the hills of Tuscany, rolls pasta dough, bakes breads, and stuffs cannelloni in preparation for his two dozen or so nightly guests, most of whom have traveled hours to get here and made reservations weeks in advance—it's that special. The menu usually consists of four pasta dishes, two vegetarian and two with meat (such as lasagne al forno, tagliatelle with tomato sauce, or cannelloni), salad in the summer and soup in the winter, a dessert, and fresh-brewed coffee. Sparse, yes, but when you consider that Ruggero makes all the breads, pastas, sauces, and desserts by hand, without assistance in his tiny kitchen, it's amazing there are any choices. To find out what's on the menu before you arrive, just give him a call. Prices are surprisingly low: an entree with a bottle of the house red costs about half as much as you'd pay in other three-star establishments in the Sierra Nevada. Ruggero often cooks on his wood-burning barbecue on the deck, where guests dining alfresco can watch him prepare their main course. *$$; no credit cards; checks OK; dinner Sat–Sun (May–Oct); beer and wine; reservations required; trattoria@villagigli.com; www.villagigli.com; 2 blocks W of downtown, then W on Hot Springs Rd.* &

The Lakes Basin Area

The scenic **GOLD LAKE ROAD,** which starts at Highway 49 just east of Sierra City and ends several miles south of Graeagle, is a spectacular 14-mile stretch of tarmac that zigzags through verdant valleys dotted with farms, historic buildings, deer, cows, and horses, and passes nearly a dozen sky-blue lakes—there are 30 lakes within the Lakes Basin Area—most of them either visible from the highway or within easy walking distance. The **LAKES BASIN CAMPGROUND,** located right off the road, offers 24 sites on a first-come, first-served basis; call the Mohawk ranger station (530/836-2575) for details. Most of the lodges in the basin are quite rustic, and folks in the area like it that way. Whether you fancy horseback riding through meadows rife with wildflowers, fishing in roaring rivers, hiking through magnificent red-fir forests, or mountain biking on rugged, hilly trails, you'll find it here. The lakeside lodges book up quickly, so make reservations well ahead of time or try your luck at catching a last-minute cancellation. Bear in mind that the seasonal resorts tend to have a high turnover of chefs, so menus and the quality of the fare may change considerably from one season to the next. In the winter, the basin closes and the unplowed road becomes a haven for snowmobilers.

RESTAURANTS

Sardine Lake Resort

END OF SARDINE LAKE RD AT LOWER SARDINE LAKE, LAKES BASIN AREA; 530/862-1196 (SUMMER) OR 530/862-1363 (WINTER) When the stress of daily life begins to take its toll and you long for an escape to some peaceful, far-from-it-all retreat, some places quickly spring to mind. Sardine Lake is one of those places. The towering, craggy peaks of the Sierra Buttes are mirrored in this lake, where the tranquil forest is restorative for even the most frazzled city folk. The resort's proprietors, the Hunt family, take full advantage of the splendid setting, serving cocktails before dinner on a small gazebo that juts over the lake. The food is good, with a small but nicely rendered selection of meat, seafood, and poultry dishes. Restaurant reservations are a must—make them several weeks in advance. Unfortunately, the resort's nine cabins are often filled by a long list of returning clients, so the chance of getting a cabin reservation is, as one frustrated lad put it, "downright impossible." *$$; no credit cards; checks OK; dinner Fri–Wed (open mid-May–mid-Oct); full bar; reservations required; off Gold Lake Rd, 2 miles N of Hwy 49.*

LODGINGS

Gold Lake Lodge / ★

GOLD LAKE RD, LAKES BASIN AREA; 530/836-2350 Gold Lake Lodge sits in the heart of the Lakes Basin Area (elevation 6,620 feet) and within hiking distance of stunning High Sierra scenery, wildflower-filled meadows, and numerous lakes ideal for water play. Bear Lake is the closest (a one-third-mile hike), and Gold Lake is a five-minute drive by car. Nine tidy little cabins (and one tent cabin) line the edge of a pretty meadow and a stand of old-growth red fir trees. Most of the cabins sleep three to four people; each of the six standard cabins has a private bathroom, and the other three more rustic units share a detached bathing facility just a skip across the lawn. There is also one tent cabin for those who want to get closer to nature. Every cabin has electricity, a small front patio with a table and chairs, and housekeeping service. Breakfast and dinner are included in the rates, and meals are served in the lodge's dining room (open to nonguests, too), which is furnished with a nickel-plated Franklin stove, picnic tables, and wagon wheel chandeliers. The lodge prepares trail lunches for hikers. Dinner specials range from lasagne and pot roast to salmon and fried chicken, and the lodge's sun tea is the perfect antidote to a hot summer day. *$$$; MC, V; checks OK; open Father's Day–mid Sept; 7 miles S of Hwy 89.*

Gray Eagle Lodge / ★★★

ON GOLD LAKE RD, LAKES BASIN AREA; 530/836-2511 OR 800/635-8778 Gray Eagle Lodge is set in the heart of spectacular scenery at the northern edge of the Lakes Basin Area. Ironically, there isn't a lake nearby, but you will see a lovely stream, a waterfall, and Sierra trails trimmed with wildflowers. The resort's 18 refurbished cabins have small decks, private baths, wall-to-wall carpeting, mini-refrigerators, and queen- or king-size beds with electric blankets and comforters. Breakfast and dinner, included in the room rates, are served in the impressive lodge's dining room. Constructed of enormous sugar-pine beams, the light-filled, high-ceilinged inn, with its tall windows and rock fireplace, is all that a grand mountain hideaway ought to be. Dinner might include a carrot-curry soup with fresh ginger, a mixed baby greens salad with roasted walnuts and crumbled Roquefort cheese, and an entree of grilled salmon with a Mediterranean salsa accompanied by a garlic-polenta flan and baby green beans. The extensive wine list features primarily California labels and is the best in the Lakes Basin Area. If you're not staying at the lodge, dinner reservations are required. *$$–$$$; MC, V; checks OK; open May–Oct; www.grayeaglelodge.com; W of Gold Lake Rd.* &

Packer Lake Lodge / ★★

PACKER LAKE RD, LAKES BASIN AREA; 530/862-1221 (LATE MAY–OCT), 415/921-5943 (NOV–MID-MAY) Built in 1926, Packer Lake Lodge steadfastly maintains the combination of good food and—at a 6,218-foot elevation— great scenery. The tall pines, gently rippling waters, and profusion of wildflowers provide an atmosphere of serene seclusion. Accommodations are in 14 simply fur- nished cabins, ranging from rustic lakeside log cabins with shared bathrooms to three-room buildings with kitchens and private baths. Each cabin has its own row- boat, too. The single-room main lodge features a large stone fireplace, a tiny store that primarily sells candy bars and fishing supplies, a full bar, a reading and games nook, and a small dining room. Dinner fare includes fillet steaks, lamb, baby back ribs, pasta, and the "you-catch-it-and-clean-it-and-we'll-cook-it" trout special. Nonguests are welcome for dinner. *$–$$$; MC, V; checks OK; open May–Oct; reser- vations for dinner required; off Sardine Lake Rd, 4½ miles N of Hwy 49.*

Salmon Lake Lodge / ★

SALMON LAKE RD, LAKES BASIN AREA; 530/757-1825 You can't drive to this 1920s resort; instead, you have to drive to the north shore of Salmon Lake, telephone the lodge to send over a ferry, then hop aboard the boat to cross the lake (or you can hike a little less than a mile around the lake's splendid western rim). The 10 tent cabins offer canvas roofs, rough-wood walls, built-in double beds and single bunks, mini-refrigerators, and electric stoves; you need to bring a sleeping bag, towels, dishes, cooking gear, an ice chest, and groceries (showers and a washing machine—but no dryer—are available in a separate building). The three ridge-top cabins with their beautiful high-mountain views are the favorites, and each has a fully equipped kitchen (bring towels, bedding, and food). Also highly sought after is the lakeshore cabin, which has its own dock. Salmon Lake is great for swimming and boating, and rowboats, sailboats, canoes, and kayaks are provided to guests at no extra cost. You can also paddle a boat or take a barge to a lake island for a biweekly barbecue. *$$; no credit cards; checks OK; open June–mid-Oct, weather permitting; www.salmon-lake.net; 1 mile W of Gold Lake Hwy.* &

Clio

RESTAURANTS

The Wigwam Room / ★★★★

349 BEAR RUN, CLIO (NAKOMA RESORT AND SPA); 877/416-0880 Well, if that don't beat all . . . Frank Lloyd Wright's scions have bought themselves a major chunk of land in the sparsely populated, mountainous area above Graeagle and built a gated community with wooded, landscaped lots, fabulous homes, a world-class golf course, and the pièce de résistance, a sensational clubhouse, restaurant, and spa complex using an unbuilt Wright design. The development is called, appropriately, Gold Mountain. The restaurant serves very good food—Angus beef, fresh produce, baked goods from scratch, with an impressive array of menu choices for breakfast, lunch, and dinner. The cuisine changes with the seasons, featuring dinner entrees such as live Maine lobster with roasted shallot mashed potatoes, braised rabbit, and wild mushroom ragù with herb risotto, or oak-grilled elk chops with a dark rum sauce and apricot glaze. If you'd like to check out the place without busting the budget, come at lunchtime for good salads and sandwiches at remarkably reasonable prices. The nearby little railroad town of Portola—still reeling from the end of major logging in the area and the never-ending battle to eradicate pike in its legendary, trout-rich reservoir—is sprucing itself up a bit in case its glitzy neighbors wander down the hill. It's worth a gander, too, as is the Portola Railroad Museum (530/832-4131), where you can fulfill your lifetime fantasy and drive a train. *$$$; AE, MC, V; checks OK; breakfast, lunch, dinner every day (Apr–Oct); (Wed–Sun, Nov–Mar); full bar; reservations recommended; www.nakomaresort.com; County Rd A-15 between the towns of Clio and Portola.* &

Mohawk, Blairsden, and Graeagle

The tiny towns of Mohawk, Blairsden, and Graeagle sit cheek by jowl, so to speak—each is located less than a mile from the other. In Mohawk, an old lumber town at a crossroads on the middle fork of the Feather River, there's not much left except an old but well-maintained little cemetery, a deteriorating but interesting log cabin that was once the town's stage stop, a pleasant little deli-restaurant, and the funky little MOHAWK TAVERN (530/836-2610), a friendly watering hole adorned with signs labeling it the Mohawk Convention Center and City Hall. Blairsden boasts a nursery as well as a car-repair garage, a hardware store, several restaurants—including a cute little sandwich shop popular with the locals, the TIN ROOF (190 Bonta St, Blairsden; 530/836-1497)—and a truly great bakery (and coffee shop), the VILLAGE BAKER (340 Bonta St, Blairsden; 530/836-4064).

About a quarter mile south of Blairsden is the picturesque little city of Graeagle, a former company town of the California Fruit Growers Exchange. Fruit growers once had a lumber mill here that made wooden boxes for storing its produce, but the old mill is gone and the millpond has been converted into a family swimming area with grassy banks, gravel beaches, brown trout, and paddleboat rentals; in the winter, the pond is often a resting ground for gaggles of Canada geese. Graeagle modestly bills itself as the "Home of the World's Finest Golf Clubs" (there's a custom golf-club store here), and there are six golf courses in the area; for **GOLFING INFOR-MATION,** call or stop by Williamson Realty (Hwy 89; 530/836-0112) in the Graeagle Village Center. Other outdoor activities include tennis, hiking, and horseback riding. The rest of the town consists of a little grocery store, a tearoom, an antique shop, and a handful of other small businesses—most are located in former company houses painted barn-red with white trim. For more information and a brochure on the area, contact the **PLUMAS COUNTY VISITORS BUREAU** (800/326-2247; www.plumas.ca.us/visitors_bureau/). If you're looking for a place to stay, numerous condos that double as vacation homes are available for rent; call 530/836-0313 or 530/836-2525 for information.

RESTAURANTS

Grizzly Grill Restaurant and Bar / ★★★

250 BONTA ST, BLAIRSDEN; 530/836-1300 Owner Lynn Hagen is a true pioneer in this neck of the woods: she introduced baby greens, Muscovy duck, and Asiago cheese into this meat-and-potato belt. Next thing you know she'll be hosting martini and cigar nights. Her light, woodsy, and relaxed restaurant is a fine spot to have dinner or just a drink at the long bar staffed by a congenial crew. The Grizzly's menu will warm a yuppie's heart: a baby greens salad with walnuts, blue cheese, and a vinaigrette dressing; a portobello mushroom ravioli dish with fresh oregano beurre blanc and a marinara sauce; and a tasty Caesar salad. And that's just for starters. Among a number of very good pasta selections is a terrific linguine with wild mushrooms, sun-dried tomatoes, scallions, fresh basil, olive oil, and balsamic vinegar. Main courses range from a perfectly grilled Norwegian salmon with tomatoes, capers, and toasted garlic chips, to hearty lamb shanks with French white beans, caramelized onions, mushrooms, rosemary, and a merlot sauce. The small, daily dessert menu often holds some gems, and there is an extensive wine list. Many items are available in two sizes, and there are early-bird specials for those dining between 5:30 and 6:30pm. *$–$$; MC, V; checks OK; dinner every day; full bar; reservations recommended; www.grizzlygrill.com; near the junction of Hwys 70 and 89.*

LODGINGS

Feather River Inn / ★★

65899 HWY 70, BLAIRSDEN; 530/836-2623 OR 888/324-6400 Back in the '20s and '30s, when train-trip vacations were all the rage, the Feather River Inn was one of the prime destinations in the High Sierra, and it's working hard to make a comeback as a vacation destination. The palatial, rustic 1914 lodge is located off Highway 70 in a quiet woodland area. The lodge itself contains 26 recently remodeled rooms, and two suites with bedrooms and sleeper sofas in the sitting rooms. There are also a half-dozen chalets, which hold six to eight rooms each, and seven cabins with rustic but comfortable accommodations. Some of the rooms look out at the inn's nine-hole golf course and the surrounding mountains. The inn's broad veranda—its roof is supported by enormous tree-trunk columns and rafters—faces the ninth green and lovely pine trees. In addition to the golf course, guests can enjoy a swimming pool and volleyball, basketball, and tennis courts. The inn, owned and operated by the University of the Pacific in Stockton, offers daily breakfasts, holiday brunches, and conference space that accommodates up to 125 participants. *$–$$; AE, DIS, MC, V; checks OK; open Mar–Dec; www.featherriverinn.com; ½ mile NW of town.* ⅙

River Pines Resort / ★★

8296 HWY 89, GRAEAGLE; 530/836-0313 OR 800/696-2551 Set alongside the Feather River, a National Wild and Scenic River, the River Pines is a popular family retreat that folks return to year after year. It's fun and affordable, and it offers enough activities to keep any Type-A vacationer entertained. River Pines has a large pool and Jacuzzi with a poolside bar and snack bar, trout fishing, table tennis, shuffleboard, and horseshoes. It's also only a quarter mile from a stable with horseback riding excursions; nearby are several tennis courts and six golf courses. The resort has 63 units, including 18 one- and two-bedroom cabins constructed of stacked cedar. Each cabin has a fully stocked kitchen and a private bathroom; the one-room cabins have either a queen-size bed or two twins plus a futon that folds out into a double bed, while the two-room cabins have a queen, two twins, and a futon. The resort's other rooms are reminiscent of a standard motel, with knotty-pine walls and comfortable, albeit plain, furnishings; some rooms have kitchens and sitting areas, too. Lunches of hamburgers, hot dogs, and pizza are served poolside at the umbrella-topped tables or at the pool bar. Sharing the grounds is the popular **COYOTE BAR & GRILL** (530/836-2002), serving good Southwestern food, including a variety of steaks, blackened salmon, tequila-lime chicken, and seafood enchiladas. And they make a margarita that'll knock your huaraches off. *$$; DIS, MC, V; checks OK; www.riverpines.com; at the N end of town, on the S side of the Feather River.* ⅙

Johnsville

This tiny, charming town, established by the Sierra Buttes Mining Company in the 1870s, is a California treasure. It was built for the gold miners and their families, who didn't want to live next to the brothels and gambling centers in the nearby mining camps. Surrounded by the densely forested **PLUMAS-EUREKA STATE PARK**, Johnsville is a mix of old abandoned miner's shacks and restored ones that serve as private residences. In between the historic buildings are some new homes, most built to meet the Johnsville Historical Society's strict design guidelines. As you drive down Main Street, note the striking old barn-red **JOHNSVILLE HOTEL**, now a private home, and the toylike firehouse across the street with a bell in its steeple and a horse-drawn fire wagon inside. Among the many wonderful artifacts at the **PLUMAS-EUREKA STATE PARK MUSEUM** are a working blacksmith shop and a five-story 60-stamp mill where gold was processed. A nearby campground area straddles pretty Jamison Creek, and across the street from the museum is the diminutive **MORIARITY HOUSE**, a completely restored miner's home with furnishings and

IT TAKES GREEN TO KEEP TAHOE BLUE

By the time explorers Kit Carson and John Frémont ventured upon the brilliant blue waters of "Da-ow-wa-ga" (edge of the lake), what we now call Lake Tahoe for centuries had been a gathering place and spiritual site of the Washoe Indians. Fortune seekers soon followed the explorers, first for gold and silver, later for timber. Then wealthy San Franciscans in a quest for vacation sites fell in love with the lake, and hotels and gambling halls sprang up to shelter and entertain them. Tourism boomed. The 1960 Olympics at Squaw Valley revealed a first-class skiing area to the whole world. Today the lake is the focus of more than 20 million annual visitors—as many as 200,000 on fine summer weekends.

All this adoration has taken its toll. One of the clearest and deepest lakes in the world, Tahoe has seen its famous transparency drop from 105 feet to around 70 feet. Algae coats the shoreline rocks in the spring. Wood-burning fireplaces, automobile exhaust, outboard motors, golf course fertilizers—all these by-products of human activity have an impact on the lake. If current levels of pollution continue, scientists say, within 30 years the lake will have lost half its transparency, changing color from blue to green. Local wildlife and forests are also suffering from urbanization. That's the bad news.

The good news is that the pitched warfare between environmentalists and businesses/developers/property owners has abated, and a cooperative public-private partnership to preserve the lake and its environs seems to be genuinely under way. Up to $20 million in federal and state funds are being used for restoration and conservation efforts. In addition to the nature front, cooperative efforts are manifesting themselves in a cleanup of the tackier sections of urban areas. Low-rent motels, T-shirt stores, and souvenir shops in the commercial strip at the north end of South Lake Tahoe, for instance, are already being bulldozed out of existence and replaced by upscale hotels and restaurants, an ice skating rink, and a major shopping mall. While this may not seem like the stuff of a nature lover's dreams, the new development has a silver lining. Previously, 95 percent of the ground in the commercial areas was covered in concrete, allowing polluted snowmelt and rainwater to go straight into the lake. All newly redeveloped areas will have holding and treatment ponds to clean up the runoff, and must preserve the surrounding forests. Already in effect in South Lake is Heavenly's central ski gondola and a high-tech bus system, two eco-friendly modes of luring people out of their cars.

Perhaps the most visible sign of changing attitudes is the prevalence of Keep Tahoe Blue bumper stickers. At one time considered a symbol of environmentalist sympathies, like gang colors, the signs could get your car defaced. Now they are everywhere. Faced with the desecration of one of the world's natural wonders, admirers are at last united in efforts to save the lake—and it's working. The latest report is that the clarity of Lake Tahoe is improving.

equipment used by the 10-member Moriarity family in 1901. For museum and campground information, call 530/836-2380.

A mile up Johnsville's main road is a quaint, no-frills downhill ski resort for beginner to intermediate skiers. There are currently two historic poma lifts (rumored to be replaced soon by a more comfortable, if less challenging, chairlift), and hidden behind the historic ski lodge is a lift for snow-tubers.

RESTAURANTS

The Iron Door / ★★

5417 MAIN ST, JOHNSVILLE; 530/836-2376 Johnsville supports one business, and this is it. The Iron Door restaurant has occupied the century-old general store and post office building since 1961, and it hasn't changed much since then. The bar and dining room are decorated with antique farm equipment, lanterns, floral wreaths, and Gibson Girl–style hangings, and behind the bar is a drawing of the last miner in Johnsville, who worked his claim on Jamison Creek until the 1950s. The Iron Door's soups are thick and hearty, and the main bill of fare is heavy with beef, lobster, and fowl. And since the restaurant's owner is from Bavaria, you can also bite into several excellent and authentic schnitzels. A good selection of beer and wine rounds out the offerings. *$$; MC, V; local checks only; dinner Wed–Mon (open Apr–Nov); full bar; reservations required; in Plumas-Eureka State Park, 5 miles W of Graeagle.* &

Cromberg

RESTAURANTS

Mount Tomba Inn / ★

HWY 70, CROMBERG; 530/836-2359 Mount Tomba Inn is a genuine roadside dinner house that has managed to survive and thrive since 1936 in a sparsely populated area where businesses regularly go belly-up. The place is a hoot. It's not only a restaurant, it's also a shrine to John Wayne. The walls are papered with Wayne's mug, and every dish is named after one of the Duke's movies (well, except for the nameless vegetarian plate). Take a seat at the long bar, pardner, and order a tall one, or sit in front of the stone fireplace as you wait for a table. Mount Tomba's specialty is prawns—big, meaty, tender prawns, the way the Duke would have liked 'em. You can get them deep fried, boiled with drawn butter, or sautéed in garlic butter, olive oil, lemon, and white wine. And of course, no John Wayne shrine would be complete without every cut of beef, from filet mignon (named after *The Quiet Man* flick because the slabs of meat are "known for their tenderness") to prime rib (a.k.a. *True Grit,* a reference only the author of the menu understands). For those who like innards, there's calf's liver and onions. Diners also can choose from several chicken and fish dishes. Included in the price of every cowboy-size dinner is an excellent made-from-scratch soup (served in a large tureen), a nothing-special tossed green salad, a basket of warm bread, rice or a baked potato with all the trimmings, coffee, and a choice of sherbet, vanilla ice cream, or a chocolate sundae. *$–$$; DIS,*

MC, V; *checks OK; dinner Tues–Sun (Apr–Oct), Fri–Sun (Nov–Mar); full bar; reservations recommended; ½ mile E of town; 17 miles from both Quincy and Portola.* &

LODGINGS

Twenty Mile House / ★★★

OLD CROMBERG RD, CROMBERG; 530/836-0375 Take the Old Cromberg Road back in time to Twenty Mile House. Set on the middle fork of the Feather River, this inn has been a tranquil haven for travelers since 1854, when it served as a stagecoach stop. The two-story brick building is set amid 250 acres of wildflowers, evergreens, and wildlife, and only an occasional train rumbling by on the Feather River route disturbs the silence. The house has been carefully restored with New England pine paneling, decorative fretwork, and carved Victorian furnishings. It offers four guest bedrooms in the main house, all with private bathrooms. The Old Parlor Room has a private porch entrance, a brass Victorian double bed, and a wood-burning fireplace. Schoolroom is a two-room suite with a king bed and two twins, and the Old Trading Post Room, which also has its own entrance, boasts a queen-size and a single bed. Tucked into the nearby forest next to Jackson Creek are three housekeeping cabins; each sleeps four and has a kitchen, a bedroom, and a deck—the largest has three bedrooms and a fireplace. Anglers are particularly partial to Twenty Mile House since 2 miles of the Feather River—designated a National Wild and Scenic River—run through the inn's private property. Some years ago proprietor Barbara Gage stocked the river with wild and native trout, and their population is maintained by limiting the number of fly-fishers to four per day and restricting them to catch-and-release fishing. Breakfast for guests in the main house is served in the country kitchen or on the front porch of next door's Old General Store, recently restored and used as a local meeting and activities hall. *$$$; no credit cards; checks OK; www.graeagle.com/marketplace/twentymilehouse; 1 mile S of Hwy 70, 7 miles NW of Graeagle, and 18 miles SE of Quincy.* &

Quincy

Situated in a tranquil valley at the head of the beautiful Feather River Canyon, surrounded by national forest, Quincy is a pretty little mountain town struggling mightily to hang on to its small-town charm. The old town is centered around an imposing Victorian courthouse in a grassy plaza. The adjacent **PLUMAS COUNTY MUSEUM** (500 Jackson St; 530/283-6320) is a gem, with handsomely displayed early California artifacts. There's one 1930s art deco movie theater, playing one movie—the essence of small-town living (**TOWN HALL THEATER**; 530/283-1140). That essential element of civilized living, a decent bookstore, is satisfactorily provided by the **BOOKSHELF** (373 Main St; 530/283-BOOK), and there's a variety of interesting downtown restaurants (see reviews, below). The surrounding wilderness, punctuated by numerous lakes and streams, is perfect for every kind of outdoor recreation you can think of, particularly if you're looking for solitude. This is still a relatively remote area of California, and that is part of its appeal.

RESTAURANTS

Moon's / ★

497 LAWRENCE ST, QUINCY; 530/283-0765 A popular local hangout since the mid-'70s, Moon's is a roomy, ramshackle, rustic wooden building with four separate dining areas, including a formal dining room and an open-air patio covered with lush plants. The strong scent of garlic and yeast is a dead giveaway to the house specialties: pizza, pasta, and other classic Italian dishes. The thick lasagne, heavily laden with sausage, and some of the beef entrees are among the kitchen's best efforts. Another favorite is the Mushrooms St. Thomas—a spinach, mushroom, and Italian-sausage casserole. Moon's is ideal for families, offering something to suit just about every taste. *$; AE, MC, V; checks OK; dinner Tues–Sun; beer and wine; reservations recommended; at Plymouth St.* &

Morning Thunder Cafe / ★

557 LAWRENCE ST, QUINCY; 530/283-1310 With its stained-glass window, vine-laced trellis, and macramé plant holder, the Morning Thunder Cafe may look a bit like a hippie haven, but those details are just leftovers from its impetuous youth. Breakfast has always been the draw here, with dishes like biscuits and gravy, huevos rancheros, and three-egg spinach, cheese, and mushroom omelets. The portions are huge, and the biscuits are as large as a prizefighter's fist. The restaurant also serves lunches of enormous hamburgers and freshly made soups. In fact, the delicious Boston clam chowder has become such a hit that the cafe's regulars insist on having it every Friday. *$; MC, V; no checks; breakfast, lunch every day; beer and wine; reservations not accepted on weekends; downtown.*

Sweet Lorraine's / ★

384 MAIN ST, QUINCY; 530/283-5300 On a sunny day in Quincy, the patio at Sweet Lorraine's is this little town's best spot to kick back after touring the nearby Plumas County Museum—a small jewel (530/283-6320)—or the shops along Main Street. The cook here sticks to simple dishes, nicely prepared, such as grilled steaks, chicken marsala, sautéed shrimp, and several pastas. The pan-seared salmon with portobello mushroom ragù and roasted garlic mashed potatoes is a good choice. Soups, breads, and desserts are freshly prepared in-house, and there's beer on tap and a selection of wines. Relax and enjoy small pleasures in a peaceful, picturesque little town. *$–$$; MC, V; checks only; lunch Mon–Fri, dinner Mon–Sat; beer and wine; reservations recommended; downtown.*

LODGINGS

The Feather Bed / ★

542 JACKSON ST, QUINCY; 530/283-0102 OR 800/696-8624 This 1893 Victorian inn, proudly punctuated with colonnades on its teal-and-peach front porch, features five cozy, turn-of-the-century country-style guest rooms with private baths. There are also two quaint little cottages set behind the house. Floral-print wallpaper and beautiful patchwork quilts give the rooms a homey, old-fashioned feel. Some rooms have terrific deep claw-footed soaking tubs; others have gas fireplaces. After refueling on the full breakfast served in the dining room, borrow a bike from proprietor Bob Janowski and take a spin around Quincy. You can also easily walk from the Feather Bed to the heart of the quaint town. *$$–$$$; AE, DC, DIS, MC, V; checks OK; www.featherbedinn.com; at Court St, 1 block S of Hwy 70.* &

Crescent Mills

RESTAURANTS

Crescent Hotel / ★

MAIN ST, HWY 89, CRESCENT MILLS; 530/284-0879 The tiny community of Crescent Mills was a mining boomtown between 1862 and 1882, springing up around a 30-stamp crushing mill. Among the town's few commercial establishments remaining is the family owned and operated Crescent Hotel, which has a solid reputation as one of the better places to dine in the Indian Valley. The hotel dining room's menu ranges from "light" fare—prime rib sandwiches, cheeseburgers, and buffalo burgers—to 16-ounce T-bones, meat loaf, duck, shrimp, or your own catch prepared to your liking. The locals say their Saturday-night rack of lamb is the best around. There's a children's menu, too. If you've eaten yourself into a daze, you can always check yourself into one of the guest rooms at this authentic Gold Rush–era hotel. *$$–$$$; MC, V; checks OK; dinner Thurs–Sun in summer (winter hours vary); full bar; reservations requested on weekends; www.crescenthotel.net; Hwy 89 in Crescent Mills.* &*(restaurant only)*

Greenville

LODGINGS

Yorkshire House Bed and Breakfast / ★

421 MAIN ST, GREENVILLE; 530/284-1794 If you really want to get off the beaten path, explore Indian Valley, a mountainous meadowland tucked between the Feather River and Lake Almanor. It's the site of a handful of very small yet interesting and largely unspoiled towns, the largest being Greenville (population 2,000), a 10-minute drive from the 26,000-acre Lake Almanor. While there are all sorts of campgrounds and motels around the lake, you and your honey might delight in the comforts of this cute little bed-and-breakfast, named by co-owner Angie Dalton for her birthplace in England. With four suites to choose from, friendly hosts, and a full breakfast of yogurt, fruit, locally made sausages, and fresh muffins—all for a modest price—you may think about moving in permanently. This is fisher-folk heaven, with lots of lakes and reservoirs offering both native and planted trout as well as bass. Just 4 miles away, Round Valley Reservoir, a warmwater fishery and Greenville's source of water, shelters more than 100 resident species of birds. *$–$$; AE, MC, V; checks OK; www.yorkshirehousebb.com; 2 blocks east of Hwy 89.*

Bear Valley Area

Tucked away in the central Sierra Nevada some 7,000 feet above sea level is the small town of Bear Valley, home of the popular **BEAR VALLEY MOUNTAIN RESORT COMPANY** and the **BEAR VALLEY CROSS-COUNTRY AREA**. (See Skiing the Sierra Nevada at the end of this chapter for contact information.) In the summer, more than 100 miles of the cross-country ski trails become prime mountain-biking territory.

Bear Valley

LODGINGS

Bear Valley Lodge and Restaurant / ★★

BEAR VALLEY RD, BEAR VALLEY; 209/753-2327 Bear Valley Lodge, the center of this small mountain community, is a full-service year-round resort catering to families and sports enthusiasts. There are cross-country and downhill ski facilities nearby (ask about the great skiing/lodging package deals here) and plenty of mountains, trails, lakes, and streams to explore. Another bonus is the resort's high 7,000-foot elevation, which helps keep the scorching summer heat at bay. There are 51 guest rooms (including three suites), a restaurant and bar, and a heated swimming pool (open in summer only). Bear Valley Lodge Restaurant, catering to a mostly captive audience, offers California cuisine—steak, fish, chicken, pasta, vegetarian entrees, salads—and a children's menu. White tablecloths and candles set the mood in the dining room, although the dress code is casual. *$$; AE, MC, V; checks OK; stay@bearvalleylodge.com; www.bearvalleylodge.com; from Hwy 4E go left on Bear Valley Rd.* &

Lake Alpine Lodge / ★

4000 HWY 4, BEAR VALLEY; 209/753-6358 This quaint Sierra summer resort situated on Lake Alpine is an excellent choice for families looking to get up into the mountains for a long weekend. It features lodgepole pine pillars, a fireplace so large you can walk into it, a spacious deck overlooking the lake, and a game room equipped with a pool table and video games. Eight of the nine rustic, fully equipped cabins have kitchens and outdoor barbecues, and all come with a shower, a deck, and a view of the lake. The lodge also offers "upscale camping" via several cabins, each furnished with four twin beds, a barbecue ring, and access to public bathrooms (available mid-June–Labor Day only). The Lake Alpine Lodge Cafe serves breakfast, lunch, and dinner in the summer (pancakes, burgers, sandwiches, and the like), and there's a small saloon as well as a convenience market that sells bait, tackle, and camping equipment. A laundromat and public showers are also available, as are boats and mountain bike rentals. *$$; MC, V; local checks only; open May 1–Oct 1; info@lakealpinelodge.com; www.lakealpinelodge.com; at Ebbets Pass/Lake Alpine.* &

Dorrington

LODGINGS

The Dorrington Hotel and Restaurant / ★★

3431 HWY 4, DORRINGTON; 209/795-5800 OR 866/995-5800 A few miles from magnificent Calaveras Big Trees State Park sits the Dorrington Hotel, built in 1852 and used as a stagecoach stop, a depot for stockmen, and—because of its 5,000-foot elevation—a summer resort where people could beat the heat. The country hotel, surrounded by some of the largest pines and sequoias in California, has been dressed up with lace curtains, period wallpaper, and decorative pillows (be sure to inquire about the resident ghost). The five antique-filled rooms, which share bathrooms, have brass beds with homemade quilts. There's also a one-room cabin next door with a kitchenette, a large stone fireplace, and a spa tub. Complimentary sherry and fruit are left in the room, and a continental breakfast is served there in the morning. The hotel's casual dining room offers northern Italian–style dinners in the $15 to $21 range. *$$; DIS, MC, V; checks OK; info@dorringtonhotel.com; www.dorringtonhotel.com; near Board's Crossing.*

Arnold

RESTAURANTS

Tallahan's Cafe / ★★★

1225 OAK CIRCLE, ARNOLD; 209/795-4005 For years partners Kathleen Minahan and Bruce Tallakson have been serving up hearty yet sophisticated fare in their comfortable country cafe, a happy surprise in this rustic setting. Appetizers include grilled polenta and roasted veggie "pot stickers" with balsamic chile sauce. For dinner, try the red chard and onion ravioli with mushrooms, dried cherries, white wine, and feta cheese or the risotto with tiger prawns and New Mexico sausage. Even sandwiches are imaginative creations here, such as the thinly sliced tri-tip with red onion, spinach, avocado, cheddar cheese, and red-chile aioli in a chipotle chile tortilla. The best spot to dine is on the deck, if weather permits. Desserts include bread pudding and pumpkin cheesecake that you can walk off on a stroll through the Harbinger Gallery across the street. *$$; AE, DIS, MC, V; local checks OK; lunch, dinner Fri–Tues (closed 2 weeks in mid-Nov and 3rd week in May); beer and wine; reservations recommended; off Hwy 4 at Cedar Center.* ঐ

Pinecrest

RESTAURANTS

Steam Donkey Restaurant / ★

421 PINECREST LAKE RD, PINECREST; 209/965-3117 Named after a steam-powered logging machine used to drag timber from the woods to the railroad, this popular barbecue house is usually packed with Sonorans, who make the 32-mile trek up to Dodge Ridge every weekend for the Steam Donkey's highly rated ribs, steaks, and chicken. Many of the regular patrons are ex-loggers, who likely feel right at home amid all the logging memorabilia scattered throughout the restaurant. *$–$$; MC, V; checks OK; lunch Sat–Sun (every day in summer), dinner every day; full bar; reservations recommended; off Pinecrest Ave and Hwy 108.* ⅃

Yosemite National Park and Beyond

What was once the beloved home of the Ahwahneechee, Miwok, and Paiute Indians is now a spectacular international playground for 4 million annual visitors. Designated a national park in 1890, thanks in part to Sierra Club founder John Muir, 1,170-square-mile Yosemite is only slightly smaller than the state of Rhode Island. During the peak season, however, Yosemite seems more like a 1,200-square-foot park. Crowds more typical of Disney World clog the 7-square-mile valley for a glimpse of some of nature's most incredible creations, including 4,500-foot-high **EL CAPITAN,** the largest piece of exposed granite on earth, and 2,425-foot-high **YOSEMITE FALLS,** the highest waterfall in North America and fifth highest in the world.

The Yosemite area also offers access to the bird-watching shores of **MONO LAKE** and the outdoor haven of the **MAMMOTH LAKES** region.

Yosemite National Park

To avoid most of the crowds, visit Yosemite in the spring or early fall, when the wildflowers are plentiful and the weather is usually mild. You can virtually escape civilization by setting up a tent in Tuolumne Meadows (closed in winter), where numerous trails wind through the densely forested and sparsely populated high country. This grande dame of national parks is actually most dazzling—and least crowded—in the winter, the time of year Ansel Adams shot those world-renowned photographs of the snow-laced valley. Unfortunately, most of the hiking trails (and Tuolumne Meadows) will be inaccessible then, and the drive may be treacherous. Snow and ice limit access to the park, and many of the eastern passes are closed; call for **HIGHWAY CONDITIONS** (800/427-ROAD). Those who do brave the elements, however, will be rewarded with a truly unforgettable winter vista.

No matter what the time of year, visitors to Yosemite National Park must pay its friendly rangers a $20-per-car entrance fee or $10 per person (17 years and older) per week for visitors on foot, horseback, motorcycle, or bus (annual Yosemite Passes are a bargain at only $40). In return, you receive a seven-day pass, a detailed park map, and the Yosemite Guide, a handy tabloid featuring the park's rules, rates, attractions, and current exhibits. One of the best ways to sightsee on the valley floor is by bike. **CURRY VILLAGE** (209/372-8319) and **YOSEMITE LODGE** (209/372-1208) have bike stands that rent one-speed cruisers (and helmets) daily. More than 8 miles of paved bicycle paths wind through the eastern end of the valley, but bicycles (including mountain bikes) are not allowed on the hiking trails.

Day hikers in the valley have a wide variety of trails to choose from and all are well-charted on the visitors' map. The best easy hike is the **MIRROR LAKE/MEADOW TRAIL,** a 2-mile round-trip walk (5 miles if you circle the lake) that provides a magnificent view of Half Dome. More strenuous is the popular hike to **UPPER YOSEMITE FALLS,** a 7.2-mile round-trip trek with a spectacular overview of the 2,425-foot drop. (Don't wander off the trail, or you may join the unlucky souls who have tumbled off the cliffs to their deaths.) The granddaddy of Yosemite hikes is the very steep ascent to the top of 8,840-foot **HALF DOME,** a 17-mile, round-trip, 10- to 12-hour-long thigh-burner that requires Schwarzenegger-like gusto and the nerve to hang on to climbing cables anchored in granite—clearly not a jaunt for everyone. When the snowstorm season hits, many people haul out their snowshoes or cross-country skis for valley excursions, or snap on their alpine skis and schuss down the groomed beginner/intermediate hills of **BADGER PASS SKI** (Glacier Point Rd; 209/372-8430).

If you'd rather keep your feet firmly planted on lower ground, tour the **YOSEMITE VALLEY VISITORS CENTER** (Village Mall, Yosemite Valley; 209/372-0200; www.nps.gov/yose), which houses some mildly interesting galleries and museums. The center's Indian Cultural Museum hosts live demonstrations of the native Miwok and Paiute methods of basket weaving, jewelry making, and other crafts. Nearby are a reconstructed Miwok-Paiute village, a self-guided nature trail, and an art gallery showcasing the master photographer whose name is almost synonymous with this place: Ansel Adams.

Unless bumper-to-bumper traffic is your idea of a vacation in the woods, skip Yosemite Valley during summer weekends and join the rebel minority who know there's more than one way to view the area. **GLACIER POINT** (at the end of Glacier Point Rd), a rocky ledge 3,215 feet above the valley floor, has what many consider one of the best vistas on the continent: a bird's-eye view of the entire valley and a panoramic expanse of the High Sierra. The view is particularly striking at sunset and under a full moon. The point is open only in the summer.

At the southern entrance to the park, 35 miles south of the valley, lies **MARIPOSA GROVE,** home to some of the planet's largest and most ancient living things. The most popular attraction is the 2,700-year-old **GRIZZLY GIANT,** the world's oldest sequoia. Pick up a self-guided trail map in the box at the grove trailhead or attend one of the free ranger-led walks, offered regularly; check the Yosemite Guide for current schedules.

Due north of Yosemite Valley is the famous **TIOGA PASS** (Hwy 120), the highest automobile pass in California, which crests at 9,945 feet (and is closed in the winter). The ideal time to tour the 60-mile east-west stretch is in early summer, when the meadows are dotted with wildflowers and you can occasionally spot some wildlife lingering near the lakes and exposed granite slopes. Numerous turnouts offer prime photo opportunities, and roadside picnic areas are located at **LEMBERT DOME** and **TENAYA LAKE**. This is also the route to **TUOLUMNE MEADOWS,** the gorgeous sub-alpine meadows along the Tuolumne River. The meadows are a popular camping area (half the campsites are available on a first-come, first-served basis and half require reservations) and the base for backpackers heading into Yosemite's beautiful high country.

Backpackers are required to obtain a **WILDERNESS PERMIT** in person (call 209/372-0740 for more information). The permits are free, but only a limited number are distributed. The 3½-mile hike to **MAY LAKE** is a favorite route for back-packers, and the 6-mile hike to the **GLEN AULIN HIGH SIERRA BACKPACKER'S CAMP** offers a spectacular spot for pitching a tent. Five clusters of canvas cabins (call 559/253-5674 for details), for four to six occupants, are available to backpackers in the High Sierra region; prices average $110 per person per night and include break-fast, dinner, and a shower. These cabins are booked through an annual lottery each fall.

If you're partial to viewing Yosemite by car, pick up a copy of the **YOSEMITE ROAD GUIDE** or the *Yosemite Valley Tour* cassette tape at the Yosemite Valley Vis-itors Center. It's almost as good as having Ranger Rick in the back seat of your car. City slickers might also want to consider seeing the park on **HORSEBACK;** the thrill (and ease) of riding a horse into Yosemite's beautiful backcountry just might be worth the splurge. Select a stable in either Yosemite Valley, Wawona, or Tuolumne Meadows, then call 209/372-8348, 209/375-6502, or 209/372-8427 to make a reservation.

While the sightseeing in Yosemite is unparalleled, the dining is not. Bring as much of your own food as possible, because most of the park's restaurants offer mediocre (or worse) cafeteria-style food; the only exception is the lofty Ahwahnee Restaurant, but you'll have to fork over a bundle to eat there.

Park accommodations range from less than $18 per night for a campsite to more than $200 nightly for a room at the Ahwahnee Hotel. Reservations are required for most Yosemite **CAMPSITES**—only a few are available on a first-come, first-served basis. The valley campsites near the Merced River offer easy access to the park's most sought-after attractions, but not much in the way of privacy. Moderately priced **MOTEL ROOMS** are available at the valley's bare-bones but adequate Yosemite Lodge (a quick walk from Lower Yosemite Falls). Spartan **CABINS** (some are nothing more than wood frames with canvas covers; others are heated in the winter) offer inexpensive alternatives to camping, and they're popular with families. Curry Village has 427 canvas tent cabins (about $60 a night) that sleep up to five people. Bathroom facilities are shared and, to avoid tempting the always-hungry bears, no food or cooking is allowed. These lodgings are actually just a step up from camping, but if you adopt the right "roughing it" attitude, they can be a lot of fun—sort of like summer camp. There are also tent cabins at Tuolumne Meadows Lodge and Yosemite Lodge. Campgrounds in Yosemite can be reserved up to five months in advance through the National Park Reservation Service (800/436-7275; http://reser-

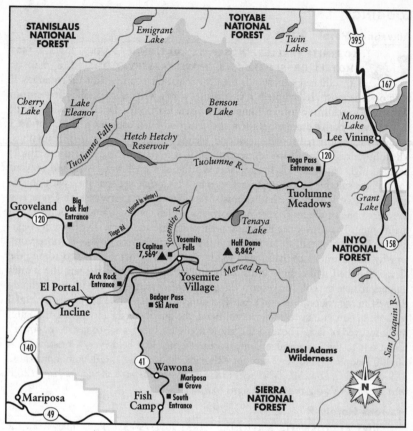

STANISLAUS
NATIONAL
FOREST

TOIYABE
NATIONAL
FOREST

Emigrant
Lake

Twin
Lakes

395

167

Cherry
Lake

Lake
Eleanor

Benson
Lake

Mono
Lake

Lee Vining

Tuolumne Falls

Hetch Hetchy
Reservoir

Tuolumne R.

Tioga Pass
Entrance

120

Tuolumne
Meadows

Grant
Lake

Groveland

120

Big
Oak Flat
Entrance

Tioga Rd (closed in winter)

Yosemite R.

Tenaya
Lake

INYO
NATIONAL
FOREST

158

El Capitan
7,569'

Yosemite
Falls

Half Dome
8,842'

Merced R.

San Joaquin R.

El Portal

Arch Rock
Entrance

Yosemite
Village

Incline

Badger Pass
Ski Area

Ansel Adams
Wilderness

N

140

41

Wawona

Mariposa
Grove

SIERRA
NATIONAL
FOREST

Mariposa

Fish
Camp

South
Entrance

49

YOSEMITE NATIONAL PARK

vations.nps.gov). During the busy season, all valley campsites sell out within hours of becoming available on the service. For reservations at all other Yosemite National Park accommodations, call Yosemite Concessions Services at 559/252-4848. Online reservations may be booked through www.yosemitepark.com. Keep in mind that reservations held without deposit must be confirmed on the scheduled day of arrival by 4pm. Otherwise, you'll lose your reservation. Vacation-home rentals (with full kitchens) can also be reserved, but they cost a pretty penny; for more information call **YOSEMITE WEST COTTAGES AND VACATION HOME RENTALS** (559/642-2211; www.yosemitewestreservations.com). Additional information on Yosemite National Park is available on the park's Web page at www.yosemitepark.com and www.nps.gov/yose. There's also a central, 24-hour recorded information line for the park at 209/372-0200.

LODGINGS

Ahwahnee Hotel / ★★★

YOSEMITE VALLEY, YOSEMITE NATIONAL PARK; 209/372-1407 (HOTEL) OR 559/252-4848 (HOTEL RESERVATIONS) The majestic Ahwahnee Hotel stands regally against the soaring cliffs of Yosemite. It is among the most idyllic hotels in California, with a VIP guest list that ranges from Winston Churchill and John F. Kennedy to Greta Garbo and Queen Elizabeth. Built in 1927 with native granite boulders and redwood-hued concrete at a cost of $1.5 million, the multitiered six-story building blends comfortably into its surroundings. The lobby, dressed in a Native American motif, is oversized in all dimensions: thick-beamed high ceilings, walk-in fireplaces worthy of a medieval castle, and opulent chandeliers suitable for an opera house. The 123 rooms are spacious, with double or king-size beds and large bathrooms; a few even boast a view of Half Dome (try to reserve one of the more spacious cottages, which cost the same as rooms in the main hotel). The Ahwahnee Restaurant—an immense and impressive chamber highlighted by 50-foot-tall, floor-to-cathedral-ceiling leaded windows—is more noteworthy for its ambiance than for its food (arrive well before nightfall to admire the view). Starched white tablecloths, tall candles, and a pianist tickling the ivories manage to give the colossal room a warm, almost intimate feel. The food is certainly the best in the region, but don't expect a gourmet affair; while the prices are equal to those of San Francisco's finer restaurants, the quality of the fare is not, though it has improved of late. Those in the know apply far in advance to get in the lottery for tickets to the Bracebridge Dinner, a three-hour feast held every Christmas that 60,000 people try to sign up for—though, alas, only 1,750 gain admission. *$$$–$$$$; DC, DIS, MC, V; checks OK; www.yosemitepark.com; take Hwy 120 E into Yosemite Valley and follow signs to hotel.* ♿

Wawona Hotel / ★

HWY 41, YOSEMITE NATIONAL PARK; 209/375-6556 Four miles from the park's entrance, the Wawona—the Ahwahnee Hotel's more rustic cousin—is the oldest resort hotel in the state. A pair of century-old white buildings, adorned by pillars and a veranda, face an expansive manicured lawn, giving the Wawona the look of an antebellum mansion (you almost expect to see Scarlett O'Hara gracing the entryway). The majority of its 104 rooms are small, and only about half of them have private bathrooms. This National Historic Landmark's biggest drawback is its lengthy distance from the park's most popular attractions. The giant sequoias in the nearby Mariposa Grove are inviting, but they don't compare to the cliffs and vistas elsewhere in Yosemite. Amenities include a nine-hole golf course, a tennis court, a riding stable, and a 1917 "swimming tank." For all its pretensions, the Wawona Hotel dining room has usually offered little more than upscale institutional food, though lately the quality has improved considerably. However, the Wawona's year-round Sunday brunch and the Saturday-evening summer lawn barbecues are a treat. *$$; AE, DC, DIS, MC, V; checks OK; www.yosemitepark.com; SW corner of the park, 27 miles from Yosemite Valley.* ♿

Groveland

LODGINGS

Berkshire Inn / ★★

19950 HWY 120, GROVELAND; 209/962-6744 OR 888/225-2064 Most guests come to the Berkshire Inn for a weekend of white-water rafting on the Tuolumne River; for boating, golfing, or hiking at nearby Pine Mountain Lake Recreation Area; or for an overnight stop on their way to Yosemite. Situated on 20 wooded acres, this sprawling open-beam lodge has six large guest rooms and four suites, all with private bathrooms and private entrances from outside via French doors; some also have decks. Guests are encouraged to relax at the inn's wood decks overlooking the surrounding mountains, as well as in two large common areas with comfy couches, TVs, and VCRs. Guests share access to the large gazebo overlooking the countryside. Other perks include complimentary wine and a large continental breakfast. It's a warm, friendly place that's perfect for families, hikers, or groups of rafters. *$$; AE, DIS, MC, V; checks OK; berkshireinn@bigvalley.net; www.berkshireinn.net; 2 miles E of town, look for the international flags.*

Evergreen Lodge / ★★

33160 EVERGREEN RD, GROVELAND; 209/379-2606 OR 800/935-6343 The key to truly enjoying Yosemite National Park is to stay clear of the brutal crowds in the valley, particularly on summer weekends. You accomplish this by booking a rustic little cabin at the Evergreen Lodge, which is located just a few miles from both the Groveland and Hetch Hetchy gateways to the park. For more than 80 years this idyllic mountain hideaway has offered affordable lodging and easy access to everything Yosemite has to offer. You'll instantly feel at home here as you down a cold beer at the classic old bar or play table tennis under the barbecue tent. The 18 recently renovated cabins are scattered throughout a wooded grove of towering pines; each comes with a private bathroom, rocking chairs on the front porch, and TVs. Rates include a continental breakfast; dinner is served daily at the lodge's restaurant. There's also a small general store and deli. The lodge is surrounded by numerous hiking trails; access to tennis courts, a pool, and horseback riding are right down the road at neighboring Camp Mather. "Evergreen Dan" Braun, an Evergreen owner and former Yosemite backpack outfitter, is in charge of the lodge's many outdoor programs and is chock-full of advice on where to spend the day. By late 2004 the lodge will add 52 more cabin units, a beer garden, outdoor dining, a hot tub area, a campfire/amphitheater area, a recreation center, and guided trips in and around Yosemite. *$–$$; AE, DIS, MC, V; checks OK; info@evergreenlodge.com; www.evergreenlodge.com; off Hwy 120, turn left at Hetch Hetchy/Evergreen Rd.*

Groveland Hotel / ★★

18767 MAIN ST, GROVELAND; 209/962-4000 OR 800/273-3314 Constructed in 1849, the adobe Groveland Hotel is one of the region's oldest buildings. Several years ago, the hotel underwent a million-dollar renovation, adding a modern conference center and a saloon. Despite the costly upgrades, the place still manages to retain some of the charm of yesteryear. Its 17 guest rooms aren't large, but down comforters and private baths make them quite comfortable, and they're furnished with attractive European antiques. The best rooms are the two-room suites equipped with spa tubs and fireplaces. Along with an authentic Gold Rush–era saloon, the hotel has an old-fashioned restaurant serving American classics such as rack of lamb, baby back ribs, fresh fish, and pasta, and the wine list has won *Wine Spectator* Award of Excellence. Another plus: The hotel is pet-friendly. *$$$; AE, DC, DIS, MC, V; checks OK; info@groveland.com; www.groveland.com; downtown, E side's of Main St.* &

Fish Camp

RESTAURANTS

Narrow Gauge Inn / ★★

48571 HWY 41, FISH CAMP; 559/683-7720 An attractive old inn and restaurant nestled in the thick of the Sierra National Forest at a 4,800-foot elevation, the Narrow Gauge is one of the Mariposa Grove area's best restaurants. You'll find down-home service here, as well as views of Mount Raymond and a cozy country ambiance enhanced by candlelight and a crackling fire. The inn's specialty is thick cuts of well-prepared meats: charbroiled rib eye, slow-roasted prime rib, bacon-wrapped filet mignon, venison steak, and even fillet of ostrich. Pasta, chicken, and seafood are available as well, but it's the red meat that everyone comes here for. All dinners include a house-made soup or salad, fresh vegetables, and rice or potatoes (baked or garlic mashed). There's a well-edited wine list, too. The inn offers 26 rooms with balconies; ask for one of the four creekside rooms, which have particularly splendid views. Narrow Gauge also offers a heated swimming pool and a spa. *$$; DIS, MC, V; no checks; dinner every day (open Apr 9–Oct 20); full bar; reservations recommended; ngi@sierratel.com; www.narrowgaugeinn.com; 4 miles S of Yosemite National Park's S gate.*

LODGINGS

Tenaya Lodge at Yosemite / ★★★

1122 HWY 41, FISH CAMP; 559/683-6555 OR 800/514-2167 Tenaya Lodge is a full-service resort that offers just about everything, and its location is just 2 miles from the entrance to Yosemite National Park. Built in 1990 and rebuilt in 1999, the lodge has 244 rooms, all with mountain and forest views, private baths, and tasteful Southwestern decor. The lodge's showpiece is the immense front lobby, with its stone floors, high ceiling, huge fireplace, and Native American motif. Amenities include outdoor and indoor pools and a small fitness center with a steam room, sauna, and whirlpool. Sierra Restaurant offers breakfast and such Cal-Ital entrees as grilled sterling salmon, New York pepper steak, and lobster with orecchiette pasta for dinner. The Parkside Deli specializes in picnic lunches to go, and Jackalope's Bar and Grill offers more casual fare like pizza, pasta, and burgers. At the lodge's events desk you can sign up for mountain bike rentals, tours of Yosemite, white-water rafting, rock climbing, horseback riding, and other outdoor activities. The lodge is idyllic for families: Camp Tenaya offers nature walks, arts and crafts, and music for kids, and lodge personnel can arrange daily baby-sitting services for infants. *$$$; AE, DC, DIS, MC, V; checks OK; www.tenayalodge.com; 2 miles S of Yosemite National Park's SW gate.* &

Bridgeport

LODGINGS

The Cain House: A Country Inn / ★★

340 MAIN ST, BRIDGEPORT; 760/932-7040 OR 800/433-2246 James Stuart Cain made his fortune as the principal landowner in the rough-and-tumble boomtown of Bodie (known in its day as the wickedest town in the West). However, later generations of Cains (perhaps weary of Bodie's sanitation problems and the proliferation of brothels) moved over the hill to the comparatively genteel cowtown of Bridgeport. Set in one of the most picturesque valleys in the eastern Sierra, Bridgeport is backed by granite peaks in the west and by round sage- and piñon-covered desert hills in the east. This modest turn-of-the-century inn, owned by the obliging Marachal Gohlich, is a tribute to Cain. It combines European elegance with a Western atmosphere, and each of the seven individually decorated guest rooms has a private bath, a king- or queen-size bed with a quilt and down comforter, and a TV tucked inside an armoire. In the morning expect good, dark coffee (a rare treat on this side of the Sierra) and a hearty full breakfast, including house-made muffins. *$$; AE, DIS, MC, V; checks OK; info@cainhouse.com; www.cainhouse.com; at the N end of town.*

Mono Lake

Set at the eastern foot of the craggy Sierra Nevada and ringed with fragile limestone tufa spires, this hauntingly beautiful 60-square-mile desert salt lake is a stopover for millions of migratory birds that arrive each year to feed on the lake's trillions of brine shrimp and alkali flies (mono means "flies" in the language of the Yokuts, the Native Americans who live just south of this region). While numerous streams empty into Mono (pronounced "MOE-no") Lake, there is no outlet. Instead, the lake water evaporates, leaving behind minerals washed down from the surrounding mountains. The result is an alkaline and saline content that is too high for fish but ideal for shrimp, flies, and swimmers (the brackish water is three times saltier than the sea). Right off Highway 395 is the **MONO BASIN SCENIC AREA VISITORS CENTER** (760/647-3044; www.monolake.org; open every day in summer, Thurs–Mon in winter), a modern, high-tech edifice that would make any taxpayer proud. The center offers scheduled walks and talks, and it has an outstanding environmental and historical display with hands-on exhibits that will even entertain the kids. After touring the visitors center, head for the **SOUTH TUFA AREA** at the southern end of the lake and get a closer look at the tufa formations and briny water.

RESTAURANTS

The Mono Inn / ★★★

HWY 395, MONO LAKE; 760/647-6581 After years of neglect, the historic Mono Inn, a popular respite for travelers to the Mono Lake region since 1922, was purchased several years ago by the Adams family (relatives of legendary photographer Ansel Adams). They hired architect Peter Bolin to revamp the aging structure to include a restaurant, an arts and crafts gallery, and a lounge, yet still retain the rustic charm and stellar views of Mono Lake. Proprietor Sarah Adams (Ansel's granddaughter) oversees the upper-level gallery/lounge and lower-level dining room, while chef Fernando Madrigal runs the kitchen, preparing hearty California and Latin American cuisine ranging from broiled filet mignon—served with a burgundy sauce, smoked glazed apples, and garlic mashed potatoes—to fresh poblano chilies stuffed with corn, zucchini, onions, mushrooms, and Monterey Jack cheese. Other menu choices include broiled salmon fillet, polenta tamales, a daily vegetarian special, and a few kids-only dishes. Madrigal continues a 50-year Friday- and Saturday-night tradition of serving well-seasoned prime rib. There's also a good wine list. Be sure to arrive early to admire the gallery (featuring original Ansel Adams photographs) and the panoramic view from the cocktail lounge—and beg for a dinner table near the window, particularly on moonlit nights when Mono Lake is most dazzling. Note: Operating hours vary seasonally, so be sure to call ahead. *$$; AE, CB, DIS, MC, V; checks OK; dinner Wed–Mon (mid-May–Nov 2), Thurs–Sun (Dec–mid-May); full bar; reservations recommended; sarah@anseladams.com; www.monoinn.com; 4 miles N of Lee Vining.*

June Lake

RESTAURANTS

Carson Peak Inn / ★★

JUNE LAKE LOOP, JUNE LAKE; 760/648-7575 This barn-red building, located a few miles past the town of June Lake, has led several former lives, most recently as an American Legion headquarters, a dance hall, and a pizza parlor. Now it's one of the better restaurants in the area, serving hearty dinners such as steak-and-lobster brochette, barbecued ribs, and a melt-in-your-mouth filet mignon smothered with sautéed mushrooms. Many regulars come for the Australian lobster tail (a rarity in these parts). Fish, chicken, and pork are served broiled, deep-fried, pan-fried, or barbecued. Portions are large, so arrive hungry. They also offer a vegetarian plate and a special menu for kids. *$–$$$; AE, DIS, MC, V; checks OK; dinner every day; beer and wine; reservations recommended; off Hwy 395.* &

Mammoth Lakes

At the base of 11,053-foot Mammoth Mountain are nearly a dozen alpine lakes and the sprawling town of Mammoth Lakes—a mishmash of inns, motels, and restaurants primarily built to serve patrons of the popular Mammoth Mountain Ski Area. Ever since founder Dave McCoy mortgaged his motorcycle for $85 in 1938 to buy his first ski lift, folks have been coming here in droves (particularly from Southern California) to carve turns and navigate the moguls at one of the best downhill ski areas in the United States. In addition to skiing, this section of the eastern Sierra Nevada has been famous for decades for its fantastic fishing holes. In fact, the trout is king here, and several fishing derbies celebrate its royal status. This natural kingdom is no longer the exclusive domain of anglers and skiers, however. Word has gotten out about Mammoth's charms, attracting every kind of outdoor enthusiast and adventurer to this spectacular region in the heart of the High Sierra.

Whether you've migrated to the Mammoth area to ski, fish, golf, play, or simply rest your weary bones, stop by the **MAMMOTH LAKES VISITORS CENTER/RANGER STATION** (Hwy 203, just before the town of Mammoth Lakes; 760/924-5500), or contact the **MAMMOTH LAKES VISITORS BUREAU** (760/934-2712 or 888-GO-MAMMOTH; www.visitmammoth.com). You'll find wall-to-wall maps, brochures, and day planners, as well as copies of the Forest Service's excellent (and free) "Winter Recreation Map" and "Summer Recreation Map," which show the area's best routes for hiking, biking, sledding, snowmobiling, and cross-country skiing. If you need to rent ski gear or practically any other athletic or outdoor equipment, visit the bustling **KITTREDGE SPORTS** shop (3218 Main S, next to the Chevron gas station, Mammoth Lakes; 760/934-7566; www.kittredgesports.com).

Once you've unpacked your bags, it's time to lace up your hiking boots and explore. A top attraction is **DEVILS POSTPILE NATIONAL MONUMENT** (760/934-2289 in summer, 760/872-4881 in winter), one of the world's premier examples of basalt columns. The 60-foot-tall, slender rock columns rise 7,560 feet above sea level and were formed nearly 100,000 years ago when molten lava from the erupting Mammoth Mountain cooled and fractured into multisided forms; they've become such a popular attraction that between June 15 and September 15, rangers close the access road to daytime traffic and require visitors without a special permit to travel by shuttle. Shuttles pick up riders every 15 minutes at the Mammoth Mountain Ski Area parking lot on Minaret Road, off Highway 203 West, and drop them off at a riverside trail for the less-than-half-mile walk to the monument. (To reach the access road, take Hwy 203 W from US 395, go through the town of Mammoth, and continue 17 miles W.)

After you've seen the Postpile, follow the trail for another 2 miles to the beautiful **RAINBOW FALLS**, where the **SAN JOAQUIN RIVER** plunges 101 feet over an ancient lava flow into a deep pool, often creating rainbows in the mist. If you follow the trail another 3 miles to **REDS MEADOW**, you'll be at one of the entrance points to the 228,500-acre **ANSEL ADAMS WILDERNESS**, a popular backpacking destination highlighted by the jagged **MINARETS**, a series of steep, narrow volcanic ridges just south of massive Mount Ritter.

MADAME MOUSTACHE AND
THE ITALIAN GHOST

"Good-bye God, I'm going to Bodie," wrote a little girl whose family was moving to the most infamous Gold Rush boomtown in California.

Located in high desert country along the western slopes of the Sierra Nevada mountain range, Bodie had a population of about 8,000 brave souls in 1879 and a lurid history of stagecoach holdups, robberies, killings, saloons and dance halls, and loose women (Madame Moustache was a favorite). During one brief lull in the action, the local newspaper, tongue in cheek, commented, "Bodie is becoming a summer resort—no one killed here last week."

The town bustled with white-topped prairie schooners, horses and wagons filled with ore, wood, hay, and lumber, and daily stages carrying bars of gold bullion guarded by men with sawed-off shotguns. Some $32 million in gold was mined in the Bodie hills in the area's intense but short heyday. After the mines played out, the town went into decline, and by 1882 most of the townsfolk had moved on. Fires finished off a large number of the remaining buildings. Today Bodie is a ghost town, designated a National Historic Site and State Historic Park. It is maintained in a state of "arrested decay," which means the remaining buildings are preserved but not rebuilt or changed in any way.

What you see is so eerily authentic and strange—pants still hanging next to a steamer trunk, dusty schoolbooks tossed on desks, desert winds howling through a town jail known for vigilante justice—that ghost stories naturally abound. A little girl, buried in the cemetery and known as "the Angel of Bodie," has been heard calling for her daddy and plays with the occasional unsuspecting visitor's child. Park aides tossing rocks down a mine shaft claim to have heard a calm voice saying "Hey, you," coming from within the blocked-up, caved-in mine. Another park employee opened a house that had been locked up for the winter and smelled fresh-cooked Italian food.

In addition to its ghostly inhabitants, Bodie is open to visitors all year, but winters can be fierce. At 9,000 feet, even summer months can get chilly. Mark Twain once said that the breaking up of one winter and the beginning of the next were the only two seasons he could distinguish in Bodie. The *Carson Tribune* observed, "The weather is so cold in Bodie that four pairs of blankets and three in a bed is not sufficient to promote warmth." There's no food, drink, or tourist accommodations in the park either—just the pure remains of the wild, wild West.

To get to Bodie, take US 395; 7 miles south of Bridgeport, take State Route 270. Go 10 miles to the end of the paved road and continue 3 more miles on the unfinished road to Bodie. Call ahead (760/647-6445) for road and weather conditions. Admission is $2 per person 17 and older; free for 16 and under. For more information, visit www.bodie.com.

True to its name, the Mammoth Lakes area boasts 10 lakes (none of which, oddly enough, are named Mammoth). The largest and one of the most striking is **LAKE MARY** (head W on Main St, which turns into Lake Mary Rd, drive past Twin Lakes, and continue on until you see it), and even though it's set high in the mountains, it's easy to get to. Numerous hiking trails at Lake Mary lead to nearby smaller, less-crowded lakes, including **HORSESHOE LAKE,** a great place for swimming (the water is slightly warmer than in neighboring lakes). Trout fishers frequently try their luck at Lake Mary, although most anglers prefer to cast their lines in **CONVICT LAKE,** where you can rent a boat and stock up at the Convict Lake Resort's tackle shop (from Hwy 395 a few miles S of town, take the Convict Lake Rd exit, just S of Mammoth Lakes Airport; 760/934-3800). Another hot spot for snagging some meaty trout is **HOT CREEK** (on Hot Creek Hatchery Rd, just off Hwy 395 at the N end of Mammoth Lakes Airport), the most popular catch-and-release fishery in California (on average, each trout is caught and released five to six times a month). Only a few miles of the creek are accessible to the public—the rest is private property.

MOUNTAIN BIKING is another hugely popular sport here in the summer, when the entire Mammoth Mountain Ski Area is transformed into one of the top bike parks in the country. The national Norba mountain bike championship race (on Minaret Rd, off Hwy 203 W) takes place here, too; call the Mammoth Lakes Visitors Bureau for details. You can buy an all-day pass to 60 miles of single-track trails and a gondola that will zip you and your bike up to the top of the mountain. From there it's downhill all the way (be sure to wear a helmet), with trails ranging in difficulty from the mellow "Paper Route" ride to the infamous "Kamikaze" wheelspinner. If you don't want to pay to ride a bike, there are dozens of great trails in the area where mountain bikes are permitted. There's a variety of rent-and-ride packages available; for more information, call 800/MAMMOTH or log onto www.mammothmountain.com.

With winter comes an onslaught of downhill skiers, who journey here to schuss the slopes of **MAMMOTH MOUNTAIN SKI AREA** (see Skiing the Sierra Nevada). Unfortunately, it can be one of the country's most crowded ski areas, particularly on weekends, when more than 10,000 Los Angelenos make the lengthy commute. (Tip: About 90 percent of the skiers arrive on Friday night and leave Sunday afternoon, so come on a weekday.) If you've ever seen the several-mile-long traffic jams converging on the ski area's parking lot, then you know why veteran Mammoth skiers always park their wheels in town and take the shuttle to the resort. These shuttles are not only convenient, they're also free. And no matter where you're staying in Mammoth Lakes, a **MAMMOTH AREA SHUTTLE** (MAS; www.mammothweb.com/shuttlemap) stop is most likely nearby. The ubiquitous buses run from 7am to 5:30pm every day during the ski season, and they swing by their stops every 15 minutes to shuttle skiers to one of the resort's three entrances.

Mammoth Lakes also has mile upon mile of perfectly groomed cross-country ski trails, winding through gorgeous stretches of national forest and immense meadows. Nordic skiers of all levels favor the **TAMARACK CROSS-COUNTRY SKI CENTER** (Lake Mary Rd, 2½ miles SW of town; 760/934-2442; www.tamaracklodge.com) at

Tamarack Lodge in Twin Lakes, which offers 25 miles of groomed trails, extensive backcountry trails, lessons, rentals, and tours.

Dozens of natural hot springs dot the Mammoth area, although most of the remote ones are kept secret by tourist-weary locals who probably wouldn't make you feel very welcome even if you discovered one. Visitors are definitely welcome, however, at the more accessible springs, including the free **HOT CREEK GEOLOGIC SITE** (take the Hot Creek Hatchery Rd exit off Hwy 395, at the N end of Mammoth Lakes Airport, and follow the signs), where the narrow creek feeds into a series of artificial pools—some only big enough for two, others family size. These pools are equipped with cold-water pipes that usually keep the water temperature toasty yet not unbearably hot. The Forest Service discourages soaking in the pools because of sporadic spurts of scalding water—yes, there is a small risk of getting your buns poached—but most people are more concerned about whether or not to show off their birthday suit (swimsuits are optional). Call the Mammoth Lakes Visitors Bureau for more details.

Granted, life is often one big outdoor party in Mammoth Lakes, but when the annual **MAMMOTH LAKES JAZZ JUBILEE** (www.mammothjazz.org) swings into gear in July, hold on to your Tevas—nearly everyone in this toe-tapping town starts kicking up their heels when a dozen world-class bands start tootin' their horns. This three-day jazz extravaganza usually happens the first weekend after the Fourth of July. A much more sedate but definitely worthwhile musical event is the annual **SIERRA SUMMER FESTIVAL** (www.sierrasummerfestival.org), a tribute to everything from chamber to classical music that begins in late July and winds down in early August. For a full list of the town's many annual events, log onto www.visit mammoth.com.

RESTAURANTS

The Mogul / ★

1528 TAVERN RD, MAMMOTH LAKES; 760/934-3039 Your server skillfully charbroils fresh fish, shrimp, and steak under your watchful eye here at the Mogul, the steak house voted Mammoth's best several years in a row by *Mammoth Times* readers. Although it's not cooked at the table, the "Mammoth" cut of prime rib is a local favorite; top sirloin, New York strip steak, filet mignon, and porterhouse are your other beefy choices. The restaurant's success is based in part on large portions and the use of old family recipes for such favorites as baked beans and sweet Cinnamon Charlotte, a cupcake topped with ice cream and cinnamon sauce. Kids get their own menu and a Mogul balloon. *$$; AE, DIS, MC, V; no checks; dinner every day; full bar; reservations recommended; Reservations@the-mogul.com; 1 block S of Main St, off Old Mammoth Rd.*

Nevados / ★★

ON MAIN ST, MAMMOTH LAKES; 760/934-4466 One of Mammoth's finest restaurants is packed almost every night with an equal split of locals and Los Angelenos on their annual ski or summer holiday. The entrees are so utterly satisfying—and reasonably priced—that nary a complaint is heard about the food or service (that is, if you keep in mind that your server is a skier first, a waitperson second). A cheerful trompe l'oeil of a European village is painted on the dining room walls and melds well with the often crowded and boisterous dinner scene. Though all menu items are available à la carte, for only a few dollars more you can enjoy a prix-fixe three-course meal with any dish on the three-part menu. A recommended trio is the strudel appetizer of wild mushrooms and rabbit with roasted shallots and grilled scallions, followed by an entree of braised Provimi veal shank with roasted tomatoes and garlic mashed potatoes and, for dessert, a fantastic warm pear and almond tart sweetened with caramel sauce and vanilla bean ice cream. Other commendable choices include the tuna tartare and tuna sashimi layered with wonton skins and wasabi aioli, the duck confit and grilled duck breast with plum wine sauce and duck fried rice, or the chocolate tiramisu in a chocolate cup with espresso ladyfingers. $$–$$$; AE, MC, V; checks OK; dinner every day; full bar; reservations recommended; at Minaret Rd.

Skadi / ★★

587 OLD MAMMOTH RD, MAMMOTH LAKES; 760/934-3902 Ian Algerøen, chef-owner of Skadi, was formerly chef at the popular Nevados (see review, above), then moved on to realize his own unique culinary vision. The food here is a mix of Scandinavian and Italian Alpine, with a bit of San Francisco thrown in. *Bon Appétit* magazine has called Skadi (named for the Viking goddess of hunting and skiing) "the most inventive restaurant in Mammoth," and so it is. The appetizers range from a Caprese salad of fresh mozzarella, tomatoes, and basil to a smorgasbord plate of Norwegian-style gravlax, smoked red trout with horseradish, dilled shrimp steamed in Carlsberg beer, and ahi tuna tartare. Entrees include lamb shanks braised in zinfandel, garlic, and rosemary with rosemary-garlic mashed potatoes and a side of garlic confit; roast maple leaf duck with juniper, aquavit, and lingonberries; and pan-roasted, crispy-skin salmon with horseradish and chives, served with mashed potatoes and roasted beets. The desserts are noteworthy, particularly the special tasting of four of the house-made chocolate delights and the wild honey roasted strawberries with passion fruit sorbet. $$$; AE, MC, V; checks OK; dinner every day; beer and wine; reservations recommended; corner of Chateau and Old Mammoth Rds.

Whiskey Creek Mountain Bistro / ★

24 LAKE MARY RD, MAMMOTH LAKES; 760/934-2555 Both skiers and locals head to Whiskey Creek for only two things: great steaks and a swinging bar scene. In the '70s this place was a raging singles hangout for the juiced-up L.A. crowd, and though it's calmed down a bit since then, it's still the most rockin' restaurant in Mammoth. Wraparound windows encompass a pretty view of the snow-clad mountains at the downstairs dining room, which serves big portions of steak, prime rib, pasta, seafood, and Signature Sides such as Dry Jack macaroni and cheese and Cajun creamed corn. The most popular entrees are the bacon-wrapped meat loaf, South Carolina pork chops, and barbecued pork spareribs, all served with a side of roasted garlic mashed potatoes. After dinner, head upstairs and enjoy live music every night from 9pm until at least 1am—and don't forget to dust off your old cheesy come-on lines. $$; AE, DC, DIS, MC, V; local checks only; dinner every day; full bar; reservations recommended; at Minaret Rd.

LODGINGS

Mammoth Mountain Inn / ★

MINARET RD, MAMMOTH LAKES; 760/934-2581 OR 800/228-4947 This mammoth-sized inn is a popular haven for downhill skiers—it's just steps away from the chairlifts at Mammoth Mountain Ski Area—and in the summer the guests are primarily mountain bikers, fly fishers, hikers, and horseback riders. The 173 guest rooms were recently upgraded with new carpets and furnishings and come with all the usual amenities—telephones, TVs, and queen-size or double beds—but suffer from thin walls and a rather uninspired decor. Your best bet is to rent a junior suite in the refurbished section that has a view of the ski area or, if you're bringing the family, one of the 40 condo units, which can house up to 13 guests. Other perks include a whirlpool spa, child-care facilities, a game room, a playground, and shuttle-bus service. The only downside is the 10-minute drive into town, but if your goal is to ski till you drop, you can't get any closer to the slopes. The hotel's Yodler Pub, Mountainside Grill—a semiformal restaurant serving pasta, seafood, lamb, chicken, and prime rib—and Dry Creek Bar are open year-round. *$$–$$$; AE, MC, V; checks OK; mcv@mammoth-mtn.com; www.mammothmountain.com; at Mammoth Mountain Ski Area, 4 miles from downtown.*

Sierra Lodge / ★★

3540 MAIN ST, MAMMOTH LAKES; 760/934-8881 OR 800/356-5711 Unlike most lodges in the area, Sierra Lodge, built in 1991, has no rustic elements in any of its 35 spacious rooms. The decor here is quite contemporary: soothing earth tones, framed modern prints, track lighting, blond wood furnishings, and big comfy beds. Amenities include cable TV, telephones, kitchenettes, and partial mountain views from your private balcony. The two-bedroom suite—equipped with two queen beds and a full-size pull-out sofa—is ideal for groups or families. After a hard day of skiing, relax your bones in the lodge's outdoor Jacuzzi, then kick back by the fireplace for a game of backgammon in the cozy Fireside Room. Skiers are pampered with their own ski locker; all guests enjoy free covered parking and a continental breakfast. Other perks include free shuttle service right outside the front door, and Mammoth's best restaurant, Nevados (see review, above), is within easy walking distance. *$–$$; AE, DIS, MC, V; checks OK; info@sierralodge.com; www.sierralodge. com; at Sierra St.*

Tamarack Lodge Resort / ★★

TWIN LAKE RD, MAMMOTH LAKES; 760/934-2442 OR 800/MAMMOTH Built in 1924 by the movie-star Foy family of Los Angeles, the 6-acre Tamarack Lodge sits at an elevation of 8,600 feet on the edge of Twin Lake. Come summer or winter, it's an extremely romantic retreat, nestled deep within the pines and overlooking a serene alpine lake. The resort offers 11 lodge rooms (some with shared bath) and 27 cabins that come in a variety of configurations—from studios to two-bedroom/two-bathroom suites that sleep up to nine people. All have kitchens, private bathrooms, heat, and telephones; wood is provided for the cabins that have wood-burning stoves. The best units are the lakefront cabins, so be sure to request one with a lake view. The rustic Lakefront Restaurant, with its antique furnishings and fringed lamps, offers the most romantic dinner setting in Mammoth Lakes. Its seasonally changing menu may feature such well-prepared fare as grilled medallions of elk fillet with a blueberry–juniper berry sauce, veal tenderloin, and fresh sea scallops in a caper-chardonnay-tarragon beurre blanc, and the restaurant gets an air-shipment of fresh Hawaiian fish daily. In the winter, the lodge opens the Tamarack Cross-Country Ski Center, with 25 miles of groomed trails, lessons, rentals, and tours. *$$–$$$; AE, MC, V; checks OK; info@tamaracklodge.com; www.tamaracklodge.com; off Lake Mary Rd, 2½ miles above town.*

Convict Lake

RESTAURANTS

The Restaurant at Convict Lake / ★★★

AT CONVICT LAKE, CONVICT LAKE; 760/934-3803 The anglers who toss their lines into Convict Lake to catch rainbow and German brown trout have kept this restaurant to themselves for many years. Their secret, however, is yet another big one that got away as others have begun to journey here for a meal at this glorious lakeside spot. The lounge's open-beam ceiling and bare wood floors are warmed by a wood-burning stove and overstuffed chairs and sofas. Some patrons make a meal out of the appetizers at the bar, while others settle into the cozy booths in the elegant dining area, where a freestanding fireplace with a glistening copper chimney glows in the center of the room. The chef's specials might include Chilean sea bass with mango-pineapple-cilantro relish or lamb loin in a hazelnut-and-rosemary sauce. Popular entrees from the seasonal menu include Beef Wellington, local Alpers Ranch rainbow trout, and duck confit flavored with sundried cherry sauce and garnished with candied orange zest. For dessert try the tasty meringue topped with kiwifruit and whipped cream or the bananas Foster flambé. *$$$; AE, DIS, MC, V; checks OK; dinner every day; full bar; reservations recommended; www.convictlake.com; from Hwy 395 take the Convict Lake exit; 3½ miles S of Mammoth Lakes.* &

Skiing the Sierra Nevada

When the Golden State's denizens gear up for the ski season, they all usually have one destination in mind: **LAKE TAHOE,** the premier winter playground for deranged daredevils and cautious snowplowers alike. Whether you're a 6-year-old hotshot schussing down chutes and cornices, a 60-year-old granddaddy trekking through cross-country tracks in a serene Sierra valley, or someone in between, the Tahoe region will surely please you. A smorgasbord of downhill slopes encircles the famous twinkling alpine lake, while the cross-country ski trails are some of the most scenic and challenging in the country.

Tops on the list of **CROSS-COUNTRY FAVORITES** is the North Shore's **ROYAL GORGE** (Soda Springs exit off I-80; 800/500-3871 or 800/666-3871 in Northern

California; www.royalgorge.com), the largest cross-country ski resort in North America, with 200 miles of trails for skiers of all levels, 9,172 acres of skiable terrain, an average annual snowfall of more than 650 inches, 10 warming huts (for defrosting those frozen fingers and toes), and two lodges. More experienced Nordic skiers should head over to **EAGLE MOUNTAIN** (from I-80, exit at Yuba Gap, turn right, and follow the signs; 530/389-2254 or 800/391-2254), one of the area's best-kept secrets, which offers 47 miles of challenging trails with fantastic Sierra vistas. The South Shore's choicest cross-country tracks are at Sorensen's Resort in **HOPE VALLEY**, and they're open to the public at no charge. You'll find more than 60 miles of trails winding through the **TOIYABE NATIONAL FOREST**—plenty of room for mastering that telemark turn and escaping the Tahoe crowds. Rentals, lessons, tours, and trail maps are available at the **HOPE VALLEY OUTDOOR CENTER** (from Hwy 50 in Myers, take Hwy 89 S over the Luther Pass to the Hwy 88/89 intersection, turn left, and continue to 14655 Hwy 88; 530/694-2266; www.hopevalley outdoors.com), located 300 yards east of Sorensen's Resort. Farther south is the **BEAR VALLEY CROSS-COUNTRY** area (209/753-2834; www.bearvalleyxc.com; off Hwy 4), with 43 miles of groomed Nordic track—one of the largest track systems in the United States. **YOSEMITE CROSS-COUNTRY CENTER** (209/372-8444), at **BADGER PASS SKI AREA** (off SR 41), offers rentals, lessons, and excursions on 90 miles of groomed trails (there's a total of 350 miles of cross-country trails in the park). There are also two major cross-country ski centers at **MAMMOTH MOUNTAIN SKI AREA** (off Hwy 395), where L.A. folk flock on winter weekends; for more information, call the Mammoth Lakes Visitors Bureau (760/934-2712 or 800/367-6572).

For **DOWNHILL** thrill-seekers, Lake Tahoe offers a plethora of first-rate resorts that cater to every age, ability, and whim. Families fare best at **NORTHSTAR**, while serious skiers find the most challenging terrain at **SQUAW VALLEY USA, KIRKWOOD, HEAVENLY SKI RESORT**, and **ALPINE MEADOWS**. Wherever you're staying, be sure to inquire about ski-package deals. Although most Northern Californians rarely tote their skis beyond Tahoe's sunny slopes, a host of top-notch ski resorts dot the landscape south of the lake, including one of the state's best: **MAMMOTH MOUNTAIN SKI AREA**. Aside from Mammoth, these south-of-Tahoe ski spots are often less crowded and less expensive than their lakeside counterparts. Here's a roundup of the Sierra's major downhill ski areas, from the outer reaches of North Lake Tahoe to as far south as Badger Pass, just outside Yosemite National Park.

Lake Tahoe Ski Resorts

ALPINE MEADOWS (off Hwy 89; 530/583-4232 or 800/441-4423; www.skialpine. com). A favorite among locals, Alpine has runs on a par with Squaw Valley's best, but all you really need to know is that, as most other of the major ski resorts are raising their lift ticket prices to the $65 range, Alpine Meadows is lowering theirs to $39. It's a gamble that may or may not pay off for the ski company, but for now it's a deal you just can't pass up. Highlights include an excellent snowboarding-terrain park and superpipe, snow play areas, a family ski zone, unique kids' programs, and plenty of black diamond runs. Alpine Meadows also offers Beds & Boards combo ski/lodging packages, which are outstanding values.

BOREAL (off I-80; 530/426-3666; www.skiboreal.com). Small, easy to ski, and easy to get to (right off I-80 well before the Lake Tahoe exit), Boreal is a good beginner's resort and, with eight terrain parks offering slide rails, ride pipes, and plenty of big-air opportunities, it's also a mecca for snowboarders. It's one of the few places in the Lake Tahoe area that offers night skiing (open until 9pm) and, thanks to its extensive snowmaking equipment, is usually one of the first ski areas to open.

DIAMOND PEAK (from Hwy 28, exit on Country Club Dr, turn right on Sky Wy, and drive to Incline Village; 775/832-1177; www.diamondpeak.com). Located in Incline Village on the Nevada side of Tahoe's North Shore, this small family-oriented ski resort guarantees good skiing—if you don't like the conditions, you can turn in your ticket within the first hour for a full refund. The resort has spectacular lake views and excellent kids' programs, including a snowboard park and sledding area.

DONNER SKI RANCH (Soda Springs exit off I-80; 530/426-3635; www.donner skiranch.com). Just up the road from Sugar Bowl is Donner, where a ski pass costs about half of what you'd pay at neighboring resorts. And despite its small size, this unpretentious ski area has a lot to offer skiers of all levels: tree skiing, groomed trails, and a few steeps and jumps, not to mention convenient parking and a cozy, down-home lodge.

GRANLIBAKKEN (off Hwy 89 at the junction of Hwy 28; 530/583-4242 or 800/543-3221; www.granlibakken.com). Tiny and mainly for tots, this is a great place to teach kids the fundamentals. A rental shop, ski school, snow play area, warming hut, and snack bar are all on the premises. Later, when you'll surely need a drink, you won't have far to go to find the Tahoe City nightspots.

HEAVENLY SKI RESORT (off Hwy 50; 702/586-7000 or 800/2-HEAVEN; www.skiheavenly.com). South Lake Tahoe's pride and joy has something for skiers of all levels. Heavenly is so immense that it straddles two states (California and Nevada); those in the know park on the Nevada side to avoid the weekend crowds. With a snowboard park and specially constructed terrain features, combined with nearby arcades, recreation centers, bowling alleys, and movie theaters, this is a good choice if you have teenagers or like to play the casinos. Heavenly offers day care for infants, child care, and full-day programs for older kids.

HOMEWOOD MOUNTAIN RESORT (off Hwy 89; 530/525-2992; www.ski homewood.com). This underrated midsize resort is a locals' favorite because it has a little of everything for skiers of all levels (and without the crowds), as well as one of the best views of Lake Tahoe. Midweek specials often knock down the price of a ticket by as much as 50 percent (call ahead for quotes), and children under 10 ski free when accompanied by an adult—easily the best deal around.

KIRKWOOD (off Hwy 88; 209/258-6000; www.kirkwood.com). When skiing conditions just don't get any better, Tahoe locals make the pilgrimage over the passes to where the snow is the deepest and the skiing is the sweetest. The only drawback is that it's 30 miles south of South Lake Tahoe (though the resort offers free shuttle service to and from South Lake Tahoe); otherwise, it's one of the top ski areas in Tahoe, with lots of snow and excellent spring skiing. The **KIRKWOOD CROSS**

COUNTRY SKI CENTER (209/258-7248) is one of the best in the state and offers lessons for all ages. Kirkwood also offers some very tempting ski/lodging packages.

NORTHSTAR-AT-TAHOE (off Hwy 267; 530/562-1010 or 800/466-6784; www.northstarattahoe.com). Northstar is consistently rated one of the best family ski resorts in the nation thanks to its numerous kids' programs and 2,400 acres of skiable terrain. It also has the dubious honor of being called "Flatstar" by the locals because of its penchant for grooming, but several new black diamond runs are starting to erase its low-thrills reputation. It's a completely self-contained ski resort (you'll find everything from lodgings to stores to a gas station here), so you can park your car and leave it in the same spot for the duration of your stay.

SIERRA-AT-TAHOE (off Hwy 50; 530/659-7453; www.sierratahoe.com). Formerly named Sierra Ski Ranch, Tahoe's third-largest ski area is a good all-around resort, offering a slightly better price than most comparable places in the area. It's not worth the drive from the North Shore, but it's a good alternative to Heavenly Ski Resort if you want a change of venue near the South Shore.

SQUAW VALLEY USA (off Hwy 89; 530/583-6985 or 800/545-4350; www.squaw.com). Site of the 1960 Winter Olympic Games, Squaw is one of the world's top ski resorts, the kind of place people either love (because it has everything a skier could hope for) or hate (because it's gone the mega-corporate route with Aspen-like ski villages and expensive everything). Squaw offers some of the country's most challenging terrain, excellent ski-school programs for kids and teens, top-of-the-line chairlifts, night skiing from 4pm to 9pm, and a snowboard park, plus a variety of nonskiing activities including ice skating, swimming, and even bungee jumping.

SUGAR BOWL (Soda Springs exit off I-80; 530/426-9000; www.sugarbowl.com). Here's another good all-around midsize ski resort, with about 50 runs on 1,500 skiable acres. Sugar Bowl's most popular feature, however, is its accessibility—it's the closest resort from the valley off Interstate 80, about 40 minutes closer than Squaw Valley USA (and several bucks less a pass, thank you). Whether it's worth the drive from the North Shore, however, is questionable.

TAHOE DONNER SKI AREA (from I-80, take the Donner State Park exit, turn left on Donner Pass Rd, and go left on Northwoods Blvd; 530/587-9400; www.tahoe donner.com). If you're a beginner or a beginner/intermediate skier and are staying on the North Shore, Tahoe Donner is a viable option, offering short lift lines, no car traffic, and relatively low prices.

South-of-Tahoe Ski Resorts

BADGER PASS SKI AREA (off SR 41; 209/372-8430; www.yosemitepark.com). Unpretentious, friendly, and affordable, Badger Pass—located 23 miles from Yosemite Valley inside Yosemite National Park—keeps its predominantly intermediate ski and snowboard runs well-manicured and offers some unique family activities, such as daily snowshoe walks led by a ranger/naturalist, excellent cross-country skiing, tubing, and ice skating in the shadow of Half Dome. Established in 1935, it's California's oldest operating ski area.

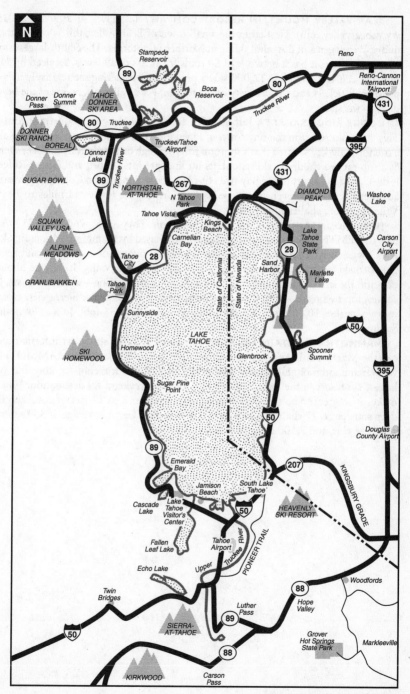

LAKE TAHOE SKI RESORTS

BEAR VALLEY MOUNTAIN RESORT COMPANY (off Hwy 4; 209/753-2301; www.bearvalley.com). Nestled in the small town of Bear Valley, this is one of the undiscovered gems of downhill skiing in Northern California. The eighth-largest ski area in the state, it has a network of 60 trails for skiers of all levels, serviced by 11 lifts that can accommodate 12,000 skiers per hour. Considering the relatively inexpensive lift tickets and the diversity of the terrain, Bear Valley offers one of the best deals in the state.

DODGE RIDGE SKI AREA (off SR 108; 209/965-3474; www.dodgeridge.com). This small ski resort in the tiny town of Pinecrest has a decades-long reputation as a friendly, low-key ski area that's short on frills but high on family conveniences such as a top-ranked children's ski school. Its lift lines are often short, and Dodge Ridge is the closest ski resort to the Bay Area (it's just above Sonora and Columbia). More advanced skiers, however, would be happier driving the few extra miles to Bear Valley for more challenging terrain.

JUNE MOUNTAIN (on June Lake Loop off Hwy 395; 760/648-7733 or 888/JUNEMTN; www.junemountain.com). Purchased by Mammoth Mountain Ski Area owner Dave McCoy in 1986, June Mountain offers skiers a calmer and less-crowded ski experience than its colossal cousin across the valley. It may be about one-fifth the size of Mammoth, but June also offers great skiing—wide bowls, steep chutes, forested trails—with the added attraction of a spectacular Sierra view from its two peaks: 10,050-foot Rainbow Summit and 10,135-foot June Mountain Summit.

MAMMOTH MOUNTAIN SKI AREA (off Hwy 395; for ski-resort information, call the Mammoth Lakes Visitors Bureau at 760/934-8006 or 800/MAMMOTH; www.mammothmountain.com). Mammoth vies with Heavenly for the title of largest ski resort in the state, and it's L.A.'s prime weekend ski destination. What makes it so great? The numbers speak for themselves: 8 to 12 feet of consistently deep snowpack, 27 chairlifts, 150 runs, 3,100 vertical feet, an average of 300 sunny skies per year, and 3,500 acres of skiable terrain.

GOLD COUNTRY

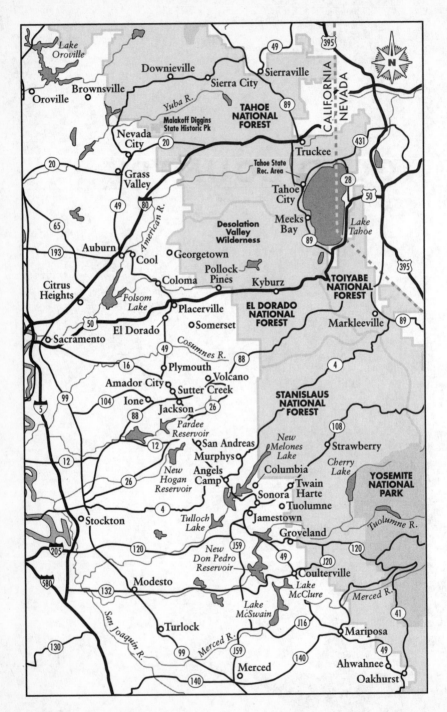

GOLD COUNTRY

On the morning of January 24, 1848, a carpenter named James Marshall was working on John Sutter's mill in Coloma when he stumbled upon a gold nugget on the south fork of the American River. Despite Sutter's efforts to keep the find a secret, word leaked out that the hills of California were littered with gold.

By 1849, word had spread quickly throughout the United States, Europe, and other corners of the globe that gold miners in California were becoming millionaires overnight. In just one year, more than 80,000 eager souls stampeded across water and land to reach the hilly terrain now known as the Gold Country and the Mother Lode. By 1852, more than 200,000 men were working the mines. Many of the "forty-niners" had to fight for their claims to the land, claims that left the average miner with little more than dirt and grime in his pocket. Crime and starvation were rampant, and when the exhausted miners put away their picks and pans for the night, most sought comfort in drinking, gambling, and prostitutes. It was a wild and heady time that brought riches to relatively few but changed the Golden State forever.

During the next 50 years, 125 million ounces of gold were mined from the Sierra foothills, an amount worth a staggering $50 billion today. You can follow in the miners' footsteps (geographically, at least) by cruising along the aptly numbered Highway 49, the zigzagging, 321-mile Gold Rush road that links many of the mining towns. Yep, there's still many a precious nugget in them thar hills and cricks, and you can hire a prospector to show you how and where to try your luck. But spend any time in the Sierra foothills and you'll soon discover that the real gold lies in the history of the tiny towns that characterize this region and in the grassy foothills that turn golden beneath the summer sun.

ACCESS AND INFORMATION

Today, the Gold Country is truly a region for all seasons, with wineries, antique shops, historic parks, caverns, and museums open throughout the year. Late spring and early summer bring explosions of wildflowers and rafting down the American, Merced, Tuolumne, and Yuba Rivers. The crisp air of autumn ushers in apple and grape harvests and the vibrant turning of leaves on the Chinese pistache, dogwood, and maple trees. During the winter, when the Sacramento and San Joaquin valleys are shrouded in fog, the sun is often shining in the Gold Country, and the region is only a short drive away from most ski resorts. On the other hand, you'll want an air-conditioned room on the hottest summer days and tire chains in the winter if you're heading up to Kyburz or Sierra City.

If, like most visitors to the area, you decide to drive, there are several ways to enter the region. With **INTERSTATE 5** or **HIGHWAY 99** as your motoring-off point, you will find a slew of highways and county roads (marked with a "J") running east toward **HIGHWAY 49**. A California map or Gold Country region map are your best bets for finding the quickest route as well as for deciphering all those tempting side roads that pop up along the way.

Though the easiest way to explore the towns on and off Highway 49 is by car or motorcycle, there are a few other ways to reach the area. **AMTRAK'S CAPITAL CORRIDOR** train (800/872-7245; www.amtrak.com) runs daily from the Bay Area to Sacramento, but the only stop it makes in the Gold Country is the town of Auburn.

Nine noncommercial small-passenger and private plane airports dot the Gold Country from Nevada City to Mariposa. Check your **AOPA DIRECTORY** or **WESTERN FLIGHT GUIDE** (or even a California road map) for locations. **COLUMBIA AIRPORT** (10767 Airport Rd, Columbia; 209/533-5685) is an easy half-mile walk away from Columbia State Historic Park, and you can borrow a car at **CALAVERAS AIRPORT** (3600 Carol Kennedy, San Andreas; 209/736-2501) for a few hours on weekdays if you let them know ahead of time. Staff at most of the other airports can help you arrange for a taxi or rental car (best to call ahead) if you don't want to walk the 2 to 5 miles into town.

Northern Gold Country

You'll find some of the most authentically preserved towns in the Northern Gold Country, including Grass Valley, where more than a billion dollars in gold was extracted, and Nevada City, former home of one of the region's more famous miners, President Herbert Hoover. The farther east you travel in the Gold Country, the closer you move toward the Sierra Nevada mountains. In towns like Downieville, Sierra City, Kyburz, and Twain Harte, the Gold Country foothills begin to lose their gentle climb; slopes get steeper, oak trees fade into forests of fir and pine.

Sierra City

Upon entering Sierra City, the first thing all visitors do is tilt their heads back to take in the magnificent view of the **SIERRA BUTTES** towering above them. Don't worry if you forgot your binoculars: just about every restaurant and lodging in town has a telescope pointing straight up at these majestic mountains. Black bear lumber through this little town on a daily basis, so unless you are willing to sacrifice a back window, be careful not to leave any food in your automobile. Dozens of nearby hiking and cross-country-ski trails wind through Tahoe National Forest to more than 30 mountain lakes, which offer great trout fishing. Local activities include mountain biking, horseback riding, kayaking, snowmobiling, and enjoying the pristine scenery. For more information about Sierra City, log onto www.sierracity.com.

RESTAURANTS

Buckhorn Lodge Restaurant and Tavern / ★★

225 MAIN ST, SIERRA CITY; 530/862-1171 This classic 1889 tavern is the most popular bar and restaurant in Sierra City, particularly when the 49ers are playing. It's also the only restaurant in California we know of that has creek-side dining on a terraced garden patio. On a warm summer evening it's the pefect setting for digging into a New York steak, charbroiled salmon, or barbecued ribs. Daily specials are always of the meat-and-potatoes variety and range from braised Bavarian pork to roasted leg of lamb and bacon-wrapped filet mignon. On summer Saturdays they host a barbecue in the garden. The days of operation vary seasonally, so be sure to call ahead. *$$; MC, V; checks OK; dinner Wed–Sun (Fri–Sat, Dec–May); full bar; reservations recommended; jpatheal@aol.com; downtown.*

Herrington's Sierra Pines Resort / ★★

104 MAIN ST, SIERRA CITY; 530/862-1151 OR 800/682-9848 Rainbow trout amandine straight from the resort's trout pond is the specialty at this cozy log- and wood-paneled dining room situated on the north fork of the Yuba River. The dinner menu also offers New York steaks, charbroiled center-cut pork chops, clam linguine, honey-dipped deep-fried chicken, and an assortment of other high-calorie dishes that'll satisfy a mountain man's appetite. The Saturday-night special is slow-roasted prime rib au jus, and all entrees come with a hot loaf of house-baked bread. The lodge serves breakfast as well: pork chops and eggs with biscuits and gravy should keep you going until dinner. From mid-April to mid-November the pet-friendly resort also offers 21 motel-style units with covered decks, and most have views of the Yuba River. *$$; DIS, MC, V; checks OK; breakfast, dinner every day (closed mid-Oct–mid-May); full bar; reservations recommended; www.herringtonssierra pines.com; S side of Hwy 49 at the W end of town.*

LODGINGS

High Country Inn / ★★★

100 GREENE RD, SIERRA CITY; 530/862-1530 OR 800/862-1530 The highlight of the High Country Inn is the spectacular view of the Sierra Buttes and the grove of aspens fluttering in the breeze along the north fork of the Yuba River. The B&B's five individually decorated guest rooms come with king or queen beds, antique furnishings, and beautiful views of the buttes, river, and private trout pond. The best and largest room is the Sierra Butte Suite, which encompasses the entire second floor and has a king-size bed and fireplace (the bathroom is almost a suite of its own, with a 6½-foot-long 1846 bathtub and a dressing room complete with terry-cloth robes). Families often opt for the spacious Howard Creek Room because it has both a king-size and a double bed, as well as room for a roll-away. Room rates include a full country breakfast in addition to the tray of coffee and tea that's set outside each room by 7am for those who want to get an early start. *$$$; AE, DIS, MC, V; checks OK; info@hicountryinn.com; www.hicountryinn.com; 5 miles E of town, on the S side of Hwy 49 and Gold Lake Rd.*

Holly House / ★★★

119 MAIN ST, SIERRA CITY; 530/862-1123 Tucked beneath the breathtaking Sierra Buttes, this carefully restored Italianate Victorian, owned and run by Mary and Rich Nourse, is sure to bring welcome relief to the road-weary traveler. High medallioned ceilings, classic antiques, and a wraparound porch add to the charm and elegance of the six-bedroom air-conditioned B&B. The grandest guest room in the house is The Engel, decorated in pale blues and white, with a large mirrored armoire, a love seat/hide-a-bed in the bay window, and a luxurious private bath with a claw-footed tub and shower. The red plaid wallpaper bordered by wide white molding in the downstairs H. Watt Hughes Room (also known as the Fire

Room) is more charming than alarming, and the double-size spa in the private bath is a perfect place to relax those muscles after a day of exploring the great outdoors. Guests are welcome to enjoy their evening wine and hors d'oeuvres in the parlor and have their breakfast in the formal dining room, but most eventually end up at the large table in the spacious country kitchen or out on the shaded patio. *$$; MC, V; checks OK; open June–Sept; holly@hollyhouse.com; www.hollyhouse.com; W of downtown, on the N side of Hwy 49.*

Downieville

This scenic little mountain town at the junction of the Yuba and Downie rivers hasn't changed much since the 1850s: venerable buildings still line the boardwalks along crooked Main Street, and trim homes are cut into the canyon walls above. Downieville's population hovers around 350 now (closer to 500 in the summer), though during its heyday 5,000 prospectors panned the streams and worked the mines here. The lusty gold camp even had the dubious distinction of being the only place in California where a woman was lynched.

A former Gold Rush–era Chinese store houses the **DOWNIEVILLE MUSEUM** (330 Main St; open 10am–5pm Wed–Sun, May–Oct). For guided tours of the museum call 530/289-3423. The **SIERRA COUNTY COURTHOUSE** (100 Courthouse Sq; 530/289-3698) displays gold dug out of the rich Ruby Mine, and next door stands the only original gallows in the Gold Country. For more Gold Rush history and lore, check out the **SIERRA COUNTY HISTORICAL PARK** (530/862-1310) on Highway 99, 1 mile north of Sierra City, where the restored Kentucky Mine and a stamp mill still stand. It's open Wednesday through Sunday, Memorial Day through September, and on weekends in October, weather permitting.

For local news and current Downieville events, pick up a copy of the **MOUNTAIN MESSENGER** (100 Main St; 530/289-3262), California's oldest weekly newspaper, published since 1853. To tour this scenic area by mountain bike, visit the friendly guys at **YUBA EXPEDITIONS** (105 Commercial St at Main St; 530/289-3110; www.yubaexpeditions.com). They rent demos, shuttle mountain bikers to the top of the mountain, and offer guided mountain-biking trips.

Brownsville

If you're driving anywhere near this remote region of the Gold Country, consider making a reservation for a tour of the **RENAISSANCE VINEYARD & WINERY** (12585 Rice's Crossing Rd, Oregon House; 800/655-3277; sales@rvw.com; www.renaissancewinery.com; 7 miles S of Brownsville, call for directions), a spectacular 365-acre winery with rose gardens fit for a queen's palace. Located in the nearby village of Oregon House, Renaissance is at an elevation of 2,300 feet and is one of the largest mountain vineyards in North America. The visitors' schedule is subject to change, but tours and tastings are usually available on Friday and Saturday, and appointments are essential, even if you just want to smell the roses. Three-course wine-tasting lunches are offered by reservation only (530/692-8231) at the winery's French bistro.

For a glimpse of life in the 1800s, visit the **YUBA FEATHER MUSEUM** (19096 New York Flat Rd, Forbestown; 530/675-1025; www.YFHmuseum.org), just 15 minutes outside of Brownsville. The museum features more than 3,000 photographs and life-size exhibits, including a schoolhouse, barbershop, jail, Native American Maidu village, and Chinese laundry. This miniature town of yesteryear is open only on the weekends from noon to 4pm, June 7 through August 30.

Nevada City

Established in 1849 when miners found gold in Deer Creek, Nevada City occupies one of the most picturesque sites in the Sierra foothills. When the sugar maples blaze in autumn, the town resembles a small New England village, making it hard to believe this was once the third-largest city in California. This is also B&B heaven, and with so many beautifully restored houses to choose from, you'll have a tough time selecting a favorite. To understand the lay of the land, put on your walking shoes and pick up a **FREE WALKING-TOUR MAP** at the Chamber of Commerce (132 Main St at Coyote St; 530/265-2692 or 800/655-NJOY; www.nevadacity chamber.com). Town highlights include the **NATIONAL HOTEL,** where the cozy Gold Rush–era bar is ideal for a cocktail or two, and the white, cupola-topped **FIRE-HOUSE NUMBER 1 MUSEUM** (214 Main St at Commercial St; 530/265-5468), featuring Gold Rush memorabilia, rare Indian baskets, a fine Chinese altar from a local 1860s joss house, and relics from the infamous and ill-fated Donner Party. The museum is open from 11am to 4pm daily in summer and from 11:30am to 4pm Thursday through Sunday, November 1 to May 1.

North of Nevada City is the 3,000-acre **MALAKOFF DIGGINS STATE HISTORIC PARK** (530/265-2740), home of the world's largest hydraulic gold mine and a monument to mining's devastating results. During the Gold Rush days, nearly half a mountain was washed away with powerful jets of pressurized water, leaving behind a 600-foot-deep canyon of minaret-shaped, rust-colored rocks—eerily beautiful to some but an eyesore to most. Inside the park is the semirestored mining town of North Bloomfield, where you can hike along a 3-mile loop trail that features hydraulic-mining memorabilia. The easiest way to reach the park is to drive on Highway 49 north, 5 miles past the Yuba River, turn right on Tyler-Foote Crossing, then continue up 14 miles to the park.

RESTAURANTS

Citronée Bistro & Wine Bar / ★★★

320 BROAD ST, NEVADA CITY; 530/265-5697 Whether you are seated in the bistro-like room upstairs or in the more intimate back room downstairs, you will soon understand why this Nevada City restaurant was recommended by the *New York Times*. The menu offers American regional cuisine with Mediterranean, Mexican, and Asian influences. For lunch you'll want to order the barbecued brisket sandwich topped with white cheddar cheese on chipotle focaccia served

GOLD COUNTRY THREE-DAY TOUR

DAY ONE: The northern highlights. Get on the road early, drive north on Highway 49 to Nevada City, and check in at the **EMMA NEVADA HOUSE**. While you're at it, have the innkeeper make dinner reservations for you at the **CITRONÉE BISTRO** or **NEW MOON CAFE**. Have an alfresco lunch at the **COUNTRY ROSE CAFE**, then walk over to the Chamber of Commerce and pick up a free walking-tour map. After touring the town highlights, continue north on Highway 49 to **DOWNIEVILLE**, one of the most scenic little mountain towns in California. Take a guided tour of the **DOWN-IEVILLE MUSEUM**, then head back toward Nevada City to tour the 3,000-acre **MALAKOFF DIGGINS STATE HISTORIC PARK**. By now you've worked up an appetite. After an early dinner, return to the Emma Nevada House and relax with a good book on the B&B's wraparound porch (the Gold Country's warm summer nights are wonderful).

DAY TWO: Laughter to the rafters. After a gourmet breakfast at Emma Nevada House, drive south on Highway 49 to the **MARSHALL GOLD DISCOVERY STATE HISTORIC PARK** in Coloma. Spend about an hour wandering through the historic buildings and the site where gold was first discovered or, better yet, spend the day white-water rafting down the south fork of the American River by booking a trip with **WHITE WATER CONNECTION**. You'll be plenty hungry after shooting the rapids, so hop in the

with cayenne-dusted waffle potato chips. Recommended starters on the evening menu are the seared ahi appetizer with chile soy dip and wasabi crème fraîche, and the hazelnut-breaded goat cheese served warm with homemade mango chutney and Tuscan white beans. Entrees include sautéed sea bass served with wasabi mashed potatoes and lamb shanks braised with lambrusco and served with porcini risotto. If you're feeling a bit adventurous, request the menu *gastronomique*, a five-course menu specially chosen each night. *Wine Spectator* magazine recently gave Citronée an award of excellence for their selection of more than 150 wines. *$$$; AE, MC, V; local checks; lunch Mon–Fri, dinner Mon–Sat; beer and wine; reservations recommended; across from City Hall.*

Country Rose Cafe / ★★

300 COMMERCIAL ST, NEVADA CITY; 530/265-6248 Within this tall, stately brick building you'll find chef-owner Michael Johns cooking some mighty fine French country fare. After seating you, one of the cheerful wait staff lugs over a large chalkboard that lists the day's specials, which are mostly French with a smattering of Italian, Mexican, and American dishes. The afternoon offerings usually include great sandwiches—such as the savory salmon-cucumber sandwich served on a baguette with an herb spread—along with ratatouille, beef stroganoff, and a delicate salmon quiche. For dinner, Johns's specialty is fresh fish—swordfish oscar, filet of sole doré, car and have an early dinner at either **ZACHARY JACQUES** in Placerville or **POOR RED'S** in El Dorado. After dinner, check into the **SHAFSKY HOUSE** and relax.

DAY THREE: South to Sutter Creek. After breakfast at the Shafsky House, take a leisurely drive south on Highway 49 for a day of antiquing in **AMADOR CITY** and **SUTTER CREEK**. Be sure to stop at the **SUTTER GOLD MINE** and take a guided tour. Drop off your luggage at **THE FOXES IN SUTTER CREEK BED & BREAKFAST INN**, make a reservation for dinner at **ZINFANDELS**, then walk down the street to **SUSAN'S PLACE** for lunch. Next, take the 12-mile scenic Sutter Creek-Volcano Road into **VOLCANO** and have a cocktail at the **ST. GEORGE HOTEL'S WHISKEY FLAT SALOON**. If it's between mid-March and mid-April, drive 3 miles north on Ram's Horn Grade over to **DAFFODIL HILL** to admire the half-million daffodils in bloom on this 4-acre ranch north of Volcano (follow the signs). If there's still time, make a short stop along the way back at Indian Grinding Rock State Historic Park, and take a moment to stretch your legs on the half-mile nature trail where the Miwok once walked, hundreds of years before anyone in the region even cared about that shiny stuff shimmering in the creeks. Head back to Sutter Creek via Pine Grove–Volcano Road to **ZINFANDELS** for dinner (and breakfast in bed at the Foxes the following morning). Spend the rest of the next day touring the charming towns of **ANGELS CAMP, MURPHYS, SONORA**, and **JAMESTOWN**. Now that's a Gold Country vacation.

sea bass with garlic-basil sauce—but he also makes a mean rack of lamb, beef tournedos, and roasted game hen. Fortunately, sunny days are in abundance here, enabling diners to sit on the cafe's pretty walled-in garden patio. The wine and beer lists are terrific, and more than a dozen wines are poured by the glass. *$$$; AE, DC, MC, V; local checks only; lunch, dinner every day, brunch Sun; beer and wine; reservations recommended; near the center of town at Commercial and Pine Sts.* &

Kirby's Creekside Restaurant & Bar / ★★

101 BROAD ST, NEVADA CITY; 530/265-3445 Deer Creek calmly flows underneath the large sun-filled deck at Kirby's Creekside, one of Nevada City's most popular restaurants. If possible, forgo the low-ceilinged dining room for a far more romantic table on the deck. The lunch menu offers large selection of salads and sandwiches, as well as heartier entrees such as meat loaf with garlic mashed potatoes and daily seafood specials. Dinner is a more elaborate affair, kicked off with appetizers such as the marinated portobello mushrooms served with roasted tomato aioli, or the steamed mussels in a chardonnay-tomato coulis. For your next course, select from one of a half-dozen pasta dishes and entrees such as braised beef in a red wine sauce, stuffed pork loin in crème de cassis sauce, or roasted leg of lamb. Prix-fixe multicourse dinners are also available, and children can choose from the kids' menu. Kirby's takes its wine list as seriously as its food and maintains a very good selection. The wine and beer bar, located on the main floor, offers live music Tuesday through Saturday. The main restaurant is downstairs, but dinner can also be served at the bar. *$$–$$$; AE, DIS, MC, V; checks OK; lunch Mon–Sat, dinner every day; beer and wine; reservations recommended; W side of Hwy 49 at Broad and Sacramento Sts.* &

New Moon Cafe / ★★★

203 YORK ST, NEVADA CITY; 530/265-6399 Set inside a cedar cabin lined with glass windows and decorated with Mediterranean touches and large paintings from local artists, this restaurant is popular with locals and tourists alike. But it isn't just the pleasant ambiance that keeps folks coming back. Everything, from the organic-grain bread to the handmade ravioli, is made from scratch. Whenever possible, the food is purchased locally, and the meat dishes are always free-range and antibiotic-free, such as the Niman Ranch top sirloin grilled with a roasted garlic, zinfandel, and rosemary sauce, and the fresh line-caught wild salmon pan-seared with julienne vegetables and a beurre blanc verjus. Five to seven fresh vegetables are served with every entree, including the sumptuous Navarro Scampi and the vegetarian wild mushroom lasagne, made with New Moon's own fresh pasta, three different Italian cheeses, and a smoked tomato sauce. Our favorite among the house-made desserts is the fantastic fresh strawberry napoleon. *$$$; DC, MC, V; checks OK; lunch Tues–Fri, dinner Tues–Sun; beer and wine; reservations recommended; 1 block from Broad St.* &

LODGINGS

Deer Creek Inn Bed & Breakfast / ★★★

116 NEVADA ST, NEVADA CITY; 530/265-0363 OR 800/655-0363 Perched on the banks of Deer Creek, which was famous in the Gold Rush days as a "pound-a-day" source for gold panners, this three-story Queen Anne Victorian house has been completely restored and attractively decorated as a bed-and-breakfast. The five guest rooms have either king- or queen-size four-poster or canopy beds with down comforters, private baths with marble or claw-footed tubs, and private verandas or patios facing the creek or town. If you're contemplating getting engaged, you might be interested to know that Winifred's Room has been the site of at least a half-dozen marriage proposals (Perhaps it's the romantic veranda overlooking the creek that inspires couples to commit?). In the morning, guests are treated to a gourmet breakfast served on the deck overlooking the creek and rose garden or in the formal dining room. Wine and hors d'oeuvres are served each evening. There's a two-night minimum stay on weekends. *$$$; AE, MC, V; checks OK; deercreek@gv.net; www.deercreekinn.com; at Nevada and Broad Sts.*

Emma Nevada House / ★★★★

528 E BROAD ST, NEVADA CITY; 530/265-4415 OR 800/916-3662 Built in 1856, the immaculately restored Emma Nevada House (the childhood home and namesake of 19th-century opera star Emma Nevada) is one of the finest bed-and-breakfast inns in the Gold Country. On summer days you can't help but relax and enjoy the warm sunshine on the inn's deck and wraparound porch. Many of the home's antique fixtures, such as the gas-lit chandeliers, claw-footed bathtubs,

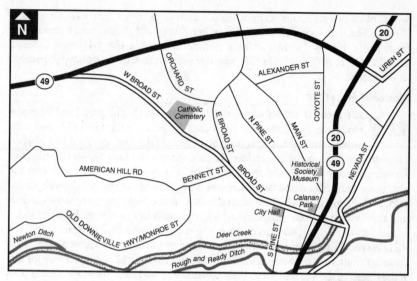

transoms, and doors, have been refurbished and modernized, and the six guest rooms all have private baths and queen-size beds. One of the preferred units is Nightingale's Bower, a room on the main floor with bay windows, a fireplace, elegant Italian bedding, and a Jacuzzi. Another popular choice for honeymooners is the romantic Empress's Chamber with its large wall of windows, soothing ivory and burgundy tones, and Jacuzzi tub for two. A full breakfast of fresh fruit, juices, muffins or scones, and an entree such as onion-caraway quiche, pumpkin waffles, or Emma's special cobbler, is served in the dining room or sunroom overlooking the garden. The shops and restaurants of Nevada City's Historic District are only a short walk away. *$$$; AE, DC, MC, V; checks OK; mail@emmanevadahouse.com; www.nevadacityinns.com; right fork of the "Y" at the top of Broad St.*

The Grandmère's Inn / ★★★½

449 BROAD ST, NEVADA CITY; 530/265-4660 Generally considered the grande dame of Nevada City's hostelries, the Grandmère's Inn is indeed a showplace, with quite a history to boot. This three-story Colonial Revival mansion, set on a half-acre of beautifully manicured gardens, was once owned by Aaron and Ellen Clark Sargent, and Susan B. Anthony was a regular guest. A suffragette, Ellen helped champion women's rights, while Aaron, a U.S. senator, authored the legislation that ultimately allowed women to vote; he was also a major catalyst in the founding of the Transcontinental Railroad. The mansion is set amid old terraced gardens and offers six guest rooms, all with high ceilings, private baths, and queen-size beds with handmade quilts. The downstairs Senator's Chambers suite is the finest, with blond hardwood floors, a sitting area, an antique pine bed, and a private porch. If you want a bit more privacy, ask for Ellen's Garden Room, which has a private garden entrance and a bathroom with a deep soaking tub and shower. The wonderful breakfast spread consists of hot dishes, baked goods, and fresh fruits. It's also within walking distanc of Nevada City's Historic District. *$$$–$$$$; AE, MC, V; checks OK; www.grandmeresinn.com; left side of Broad St at Bennett St.*

National Hotel / ★

211 BROAD ST, NEVADA CITY; 530/265-4551 The grand old National Hotel is truly a California institution. It opened in the mid-1850s and is the oldest continuously operating hotel west of the Rockies. President Herbert Hoover slept here, as did entertainers Lotta Crabtree and Lola Montez. Heck, even former governor Jerry Brown spent the night, presumably in a four-poster bed and not on the floor. It's located near what was once the center of the town's red-light district, and the lobby is full of mementos from that era. Sure, the place shows its age, and the decor (particularly the carpets) is a mishmash from every era from the 1850s to the 1950s. But, hey, such color keeps the fastidious and faint of heart away. The 42 guest rooms are furnished with antiques, and all but eight units have private bathrooms. Families are welcome at the National, and children 12 and under stay for free if they sleep in the same room as their parents. The hotel also has a swimming pool filled with cool mountain water (a welcome relief on those scorching summer days) and a Victorian-era dining room serving traditional American fare—such as prime rib, steak, and lobster tail—as well as homemade desserts. The hotel features live music on Friday and Saturday, and a popular Sunday brunch. *$$; AE, MC, V; local checks only; www.thenationalhotel.com; located at the center of town.* &

Parsonage Bed and Breakfast Inn / ★★

427 BROAD ST, NEVADA CITY; 530/265-9478 OR 877/265-9499 Once home to the ministers of the Nevada City Methodist Church, the Parsonage is quiet, unassuming, and an essential stop for California history buffs. Owned and operated by a great-granddaughter of California pioneer Ezra Dane, the place is something of a living museum. Deborah Dane lovingly maintains the home, which is decorated with collections from three generations of Californians—everything from a Sheraton dining room set to Chinese rice-paper-and-silk peacock screens. All six guest rooms have private baths and are furnished with the family's museum-quality heritage antiques. The Mouse House, a cute cottage that was originally an old woodshed, is set apart from the inn, making it ideal for honeymooners seeking privacy or for couples with a rambunctious child. *$$; MC, V; checks OK; www.theparsonage.net; in historic downtown.*

Piety Hill Cottages / ★★★

523 SACRAMENTO ST, NEVADA CITY; 530/265-2245 OR 800/443-2245 Originally built in 1933 as an auto court, Piety Hill Cottages has been imaginatively and charmingly restored and redecorated by owners/innkeepers Joan and Steve Oas. The inn consists of nine cottages clustered around a grassy, tree-shaded courtyard and garden. Each of the one-, two-, and three-room cottages has a kitchenette stocked with complimentary hot and cold beverages, at least one king- or queen-size bed, a private bath, cable TV, and air conditioning. One unit also has a wood-burning stove. Between

8:30am and 10am (you pick the exact time), the innkeeper delivers a breakfast basket filled with juice, fresh fruit, and lemon poppy seed bread or orange sourdough French toast. Guests are free to linger in the lodge-style living room, soak in the gazebo-sheltered spa nestled among cedars, and barbecue on the outdoor grills. The larger cottages may be rented by the week in the summer. *$$–$$$; AE, MC, V; checks OK; www.pietyhillcottages.com; 2 blocks SE of Hwy 49.*

The Red Castle Historic Lodging / ★★★☆

109 PROSPECT ST, NEVADA CITY; 530/265-5135 OR 800/761-4766 A towering, four-story red brick manse detailed with lacy white icicle trim, the Red Castle is a Gothic Revival gem. Located on a quiet tree-lined street and surrounded by terraced gardens, the B&B still boasts much of its original woodwork, plaster moldings, ceiling medallions, and handmade glass from the 1860s. The seven high-ceilinged guest rooms (three are suites) have either a private or shared veranda that overlooks the rose garden, and all have private bathrooms that have been restyled in Gold Rush–era fashion. The oft-photographed Garden Room on the mansion's entry level is furnished with a canopy bed, French doors, and two mannequin arms that reach out for your towels in the bathroom. Smaller quarters are upstairs on the former nursery floor, but climb a bit higher and you'll find the three-room Garret Suite, where the private veranda provides a superb view of Nevada City. The Red Castle's ever-changing five-course buffet breakfast (prepared by an in-house chef) is a feast, and the afternoon tea is a great way to meet the other guests. *$$$; MC, V; checks OK; www.redcastleinn.com; call for directions.*

Grass Valley

Once known for rich quartz mines, Cornish pasties, and Gold Rush entertainers like Lola Montez and Lotta Crabtree, Grass Valley has a historic and slightly scruffy downtown that's a pleasure to explore, as well as elegant bed-and-breakfasts and good restaurants. Stop at the **CHAMBER OF COMMERCE** (248 Mill St; 530/273-4667 or 800/655-4667; info@gvncchamber.org; www.gvncchamber.org), site of the Lola Montez home, for a free walking-tour map of the town and two terrific brochures listing more than two dozen scenic walking, hiking, and mountain-biking trails. As you tour the town, be sure to stop at the 10-ton Pelton Waterwheel (at 30 feet in diameter, it's the world's largest) on display at the exemplary **NORTH STAR MUSEUM AND PELTON WHEEL EXHIBIT** (S end of Mill St at McCourtney Rd; 530/273-4255). The museum building, open daily May through October, was once the powerhouse for the North Star Mine. Part of the park is wheelchair accessible.

Just outside of town is the 785-acre **EMPIRE MINE STATE HISTORIC PARK** (10791 E Empire St; 530/273-8522; www.cal-parks.ca.gov), the oldest, largest, deepest, and richest gold mine in California. Its underground passages once extended 367 miles, descended 11,007 feet into the ground, and produced an estimated 5.8 million ounces of gold between 1850 and 1956, when it closed. A museum occupies a former stable, and the impressive granite and red brick **EMPIRE COTTAGE**, designed by San Francisco architect Willis Polk in 1897 for the mine's owner, is a prime example of what all that gold dust could buy. For the most part, the park is wheelchair accessible, and dogs on a leash are OK. From March to November, tours are given daily, and a mining movie is shown.

After touring Grass Valley, head about 5 miles west on Highway 20 for a pleasant side trip to the tiny town of **ROUGH AND READY,** which once chose to secede from the Union rather than pay a mining tax. Then continue on Highway 20 for another couple of miles and turn north on Pleasant Valley Road; 15 miles up the road is **BRIDGEPORT,** home of California's longest covered bridge. Built in 1862, the bridge provides a good spot for dangling your fishing line.

RESTAURANTS

212 Bistro at the Holbrooke / ★★

212 W MAIN ST (THE HOLBROOKE HOTEL), GRASS VALLEY; 530/273-1353 OR 800/933-7077 The most formal restaurant in Grass Valley is at the elegant dining room at the Holbrooke Hotel, which is kind of ironic considering it used to be a Gold Rush–era saloon and a flophouse for drunken miners. Lunch offerings range from a tri-tip sandwich and Holbrooke Hamburger to Chinese chicken salad; dinner entrees include mesquite-smoked prime rib, Cajun-rubbed New York steak, and seared salmon fillet encrusted with a cashew-coconut herb and lime-hibiscus sauce. Polish the evening off with an after-dinner cocktail at the hotel's Golden Gate Saloon, one of the longest continually operating saloons west of the Mississippi. *$$$; AE, DC, DIS, MC, V; checks OK; lunch, dinner every day; full bar; reservations recommended; holbrooke@holbrooke.com; www.holbrooke.com; between S Church and Mill Sts, inside the Holbrooke Hotel.* &

Tofanelli's / ★★

302 W MAIN ST, GRASS VALLEY; 530/272-1468 Tofanelli's is one of Grass Valley's cultural and culinary meeting places. The restaurant consists of a bright, cheery trio of dining areas—atrium, outdoor patio, and dining room—separated by exposed brick walls and decorated with prints and paintings. When the locals convene here for lunch, they often order the restaurant's famous veggie burger. The tostadas also make a very good lunch, including the version topped with marinated chicken breast (or marinated tofu), brown rice, the house pinto beans, greens, carrots, and tomatoes. Tofanelli's whips up several vegetarian dishes, but the kitchen can also turn out a mean hamburger and Reuben sandwich. Each week the chefs prepare a new dinner menu, which might feature Brie chicken breast with pesto, red peppers, and garlic (also served as a sandwich for lunch); Gorgonzola ravioli topped with garlic cream sauce; or the popular Linda's Vegetarian Lasagne with three cheeses, fresh spinach, and house-made marinara. Be sure to save room for Katherine's Chocolate Cake, complemented perfectly by one of Tofanelli's dozen coffee or espresso drinks. *$; AE, MC, V; checks OK; breakfast, lunch, dinner Tues–Sun; beer and wine; reservations required for parties of 6 or more; next to the Holbrooke Hotel.* &

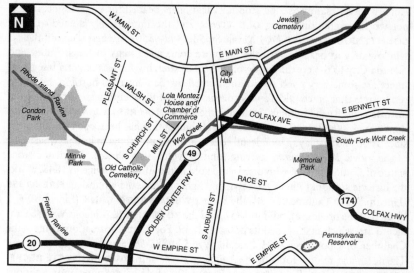

GRASS VALLEY

LODGINGS

The Holbrooke Hotel / ★★★

212 W MAIN ST, GRASS VALLEY; 530/273-1353 OR 800/933-7077 Mark Twain slept at this Victorian-era white-clapboard building, the oldest and most historic hotel in town. So did entertainers Lola Montez and Lotta Crabtree, as well as the notorious gentleman-bandit Black Bart. Other heavyweight visitors to this historic Gold Rush hostelry include champion boxers Gentleman Jim Corbett and Bob Fitzsimmons, and political prizefighters Ulysses S. Grant, Benjamin Harrison, Herbert Hoover, and Grover Cleveland. But don't be intimidated; despite its rugged Gold Rush grandeur, the 140-year-old brick Holbrooke Hotel is a relaxed and accommodating establishment. Many of the 28 guest rooms have private balconies, and all contain Gold Rush–era furniture and antiques, cable TVs tucked away in armoires, and contemporary bathrooms (most with claw-footed bathtubs). The best rooms are the larger Veranda rooms that face Main Street and have access to the balconies. A continental breakfast is served in the library. The hotel's restaurant, 212 Bistro, offers upscale American fare, and the Holbrooke's Golden Gate Saloon is the best bar on Main Street, so light sleepers should request a suite far from the libations. *$$; AE, DC, DIS, MC, V; checks OK; holbrooke@holbrooke. com; www.holbrooke.com; between S Church and Mill Sts.* &

Auburn

The Gold Country's largest town, Auburn is sprawled on a bluff overlooking the American River and has been the seat of Placer County since 1850. Nowadays,

Auburn serves mainly as a pit stop for vacationers headed for Lake Tahoe. Its few noteworthy sights, including **OLD TOWN** and the impressively domed **PLACER COUNTY COURTHOUSE** (101 Maple St; 530/889-6550), are best seen out the car window as you head toward the far more congenial towns of Grass Valley and Nevada City to the north. But if you're here to stretch your legs or get a bite to eat (there are some very good restaurants), stroll by the numerous bustling shops and restaurants that grace Old Town's streets. Many of these enterprises are housed in historic Gold Rush buildings, including the **SHANGHAI RESTAURANT** (289 Washington St; 530/823-2613), a Chinese establishment that has been open continuously since 1906 and displays a wonderful collection of memorabilia in its bar (where part of the movie *Phenomenon,* starring John Travolta, was filmed). A gigantic stone statue of Claude Chana, who discovered gold in the Auburn Ravine in 1848, marks the historic section. Other Old Town highlights include the whimsical **FIREHOUSE** (Lincoln Wy at Commercial St), the former **WELLS FARGO BANK** (Lincoln Wy, 1 block S of the firehouse), built in 1852, and the **POST OFFICE** (Lincoln Wy at Sacramento St), which first opened its doors in 1849. For more information, contact the Chamber of Commerce (601 Lincoln Wy; 530/885-5616; www.visitplacer.com). The north and middle forks of the American River in the **AUBURN STATE RECREATION AREA** (Hwy 49, 1 mile S of Auburn; 530/885-4527) are popular destinations for gold panners, swimmers, picnickers, and rafters. The recreation area also has great camping sites, hiking trails, equestrian trails, and mountain-biking routes.

RESTAURANTS

Bootlegger's Old Town Tavern & Grill / ★★☆

210 WASHINGTON ST, AUBURN; 530/889-2229 Located in a handsome old brick building in the heart of Auburn's historic center, Bootlegger's offers a large, eclectic seasonal menu that's chock-full of tempting choices. Two lunchtime winners are the spicy Creole chicken gumbo and the fish tacos—marinated white fish on white corn tortillas with Jack cheese, Napa cabbage, and a jalapeño cilantro aioli, topped with pico de gallo. For dinner, choose from an expansive menu of pastas, grilled steak, ribs, lamb, or chicken, including Southern fried chicken, Mom's Meat Loaf, Maryland-style crab cakes, and sautéed pork loin with fresh pineapple and crimini mushrooms in a rosemary demi-glace. *$$; AE, DIS, MC, V; checks OK; lunch Tues–Sat, dinner Tues–Sun; beer and wine; reservations recommended; bootlegg@foothill.net; www.bootleggers.com; in Old Town.* ⅄

Latitudes / ★★

130 MAPLE ST #200, AUBURN; 530/885-9535 Latitudes, which chef-owners Pat and Pete Enochs call their "World Kitchen," is located in a pretty Victorian building just above Auburn's Old Town. Every month the menu takes on the cuisine from a foreign country (for example, our October visit was "German Cuisine" month with plenty of schnitzel, sauerbraten, and German Oktoberfest sausage for all), reflecting the Enochs' desire to encourage people to try foods from other cultures. The lunch menu includes a terrific tofu Florentine (grilled with cashews, green onions, and spinach), a tenderloin fajita (pepper-coated tenderloin strips grilled with vegetables and red wine, served in a sun-dried tomato tortilla with lettuce and Caesar dressing), and a first-rate burger served with the best fries in town. Dinner is equally rewarding, with a juicy fillet of fresh Atlantic salmon, gingered prawns, East Indian curried tofu, and a fork-tender filet mignon. (If you bring the kids, ask for the children's menu.) The extensive wine and beer lists feature brands from around the world. And as if the great food weren't enough, Latitudes often has live music in its downstairs bar on Fridays and Saturdays. *$$; AE, DIS, MC, V; local checks only; lunch Wed–Sat, dinner Wed–Sun, brunch Sun; full bar; reservations recommended; patandpete@latitudesrestaurant.com; www.latitudesrestaurant.com; across from the courthouse.* &

Le Bilig / ★★★

11750 ATWOOD RD, AUBURN; 530/888-1491 This intimate little French bistro is the creation of husband-and-wife team Marc and Monica Deconinck. Marc is an accomplished and dedicated chef from Lille in northern France, and his specialty is hearty, rustic French comfort food—not unctuous, sauced French fare or prissy nouvelle cuisine. In winter, Deconinck might be dishing out a definitive French onion soup or ham hocks with lentils; in early spring, look for his lamb shanks roasted with fennel and thyme-scented tomatoes. There are also a few house specialties served nearly year-round—steak with Belgian fries, and Brittany-style whole-wheat or buckwheat crepes (*le bilig* is a French cast-iron crepe pan) with savory fillings like poached fresh salmon. The wine list has some rarities and bargains, including reasonably priced French bottles from the '70s and '80s as well as some local wines from El Dorado and Amador counties. A few divine desserts are offered, such as the classic crème caramel and crepes suzette. For a great culinary treat, visit Le Bilig on the second Sunday of each month, when the Deconincks serve a prix-fixe French country feast. *$$$; MC, V; checks OK; dinner Wed–Sun; beer and wine; reservations recommended; off Hwy 49, 1 block W of the Bel Air Shopping Center, at the N end of town.* &

Georgetown

When the tent city located here burned in 1852, this mountain town was rebuilt with much wider streets, which are now graced by a few noteworthy old buildings: **I.O.O.F. HALL** (at Main St and Hwy 193), **GEORGETOWN HOTEL** (6260 Main St), and the **AMERICAN RIVER INN** (see review, below), which had an earlier life as a boardinghouse. In the spring, spectacular displays of wild Scotch broom cover the Georgetown hillsides. At first glance there isn't much to do in this town, and after you've examined the **SIGNPOST FOREST** pointing the way to at least a dozen destinations out of town (feel free to put up your own) and sipped on a beverage at the karaoke bar in the Georgetown Hotel, you'll realize there isn't much to do at second glance either. But that's what your car is for, and if you want to experience small-town life in the foothills or, like Garbo, you just want to be alone, Georgetown is the place to be.

LODGINGS

American River Inn / ★★

CORNER OF MAIN AND ORLEANS STS, GEORGETOWN; 530/333-4499 OR 800/245-6566 This is the hotel that gold built. In the nearby community of Growlersburg, the gold nuggets were so big they growled as they rolled around the miners' pans. One nugget taken from the Woodside Gold Mine (which has tunnels running underneath the inn) weighed 126 ounces—the equivalent of winning the Super Lotto today. The inn originally served as a stagecoach stop and a boarding-house for miners, and today innkeepers Will and Maria Collin have done an exemplary job of maintaining this inn's 13 guest rooms, each replete with Victorian flourishes and antiques, feather beds, and down comforters; a few share bathrooms. Once you make your way past the ceramic masks, teddy bears, and Elvis jigsaw puzzles spilling out into the hallway from the gift shop, you will soon notice that most of the inn is filled with interesting and beautiful antiques. The individually decorated guest rooms vary dramatically in price, decor, and amenities, so be sure to ask the innkeepers which room is best for you. The inn has a pool and a 50-jet eight-person hot tub surrounded by a Victorian garden, as well as mountain bikes, a putting green, horseshoes, table tennis, badminton, a driving range, and a croquet ground. Rates include a full breakfast for two and wine and hors d'oeuvres each afternoon. If you arrive in Georgetown by plane, take advantage of the inn's free airport limo. *$$; AE, MC, V; checks OK; stay@americanriverinn.com; www.americanriverinn.com; corner of Main and Orleans Sts.* &

Coloma

As every Sacramento schoolchild knows (or should know), the Gold Rush began here when carpenter James Marshall found traces of the precious metal on January 24, 1848, at the sawmill he and John Sutter owned. A full-scale working replica of the famous sawmill and other gold-related exhibits are displayed at **MARSHALL GOLD DISCOVERY STATE HISTORIC PARK** (Hwy 49; 530/622-3470; www.coloma.com/gold), a 280-acre expanse of shaded lawns and picnic tables that extends through three-quarters of the town. Stop at the park's small **GOLD DISCOVERY MUSEUM** for a look at Native American artifacts and James Marshall memorabilia, and pick up the self-guided tour pamphlet outlining the park's highlights.

Coloma is thick with tourists and river rafters on summer weekends, so try to plan your visit during the week, when you can picnic in peace and float down the **AMERICAN RIVER** without fear of colliding into others. To plan your river rafting trip, contact **WHITE WATER CONNECTION** in Coloma (530/622-6446 or 800/336-7238; www.whitewaterconnection.com), which offers ½- to 2-day trips down the rapids of the American River. For a more mellow but certainly no less dramatic experience, attend an audience-participation melodrama at the **OLDE COLOMA THEATER** (380 Monument Blvd; 530/626-5282; www.oldecolomatheatre.com). Performances are Friday and Saturday nights, Memorial Day through late December. Popcorn throwing and booing are required.

LODGINGS

Coloma Country Inn / ★★★

345 HIGH ST, COLOMA; 530/622-6919 Candi and Kerry Bliss are the owners and innkeepers of this winsome five-room B&B set on 5 private acres in the heart of the Marshall Gold Discovery State Historic Park. The gray and white 1852 clapboard farmhouse provides a tranquil retreat from the summer crowds. Each of the five rooms is individually decorated with turn-of-the-century antiques, handmade quilts, and fresh flowers. The Rose room has both a private bath and its own patio, while the lavender Eastlake room comes with a private balcony and a view of the garden, as well as a private bath. Families might prefer the detatched Cottage Suite within the 1888 Carriage House, which comes with a queen-size bed and a daybed fitted with a trundle that can be used in combination to make a king-size bed. The suite also has a kitchenette, a sitting area, and a private courtyard. Every day ends in a most civilized manner with iced tea and homemade cookies in the garden gazebo. *$$–$$$; no credit cards; checks OK; info@colomacountryinn.com; www.colomacountryinn.com; in Marshall Gold Discovery State Historic Park.*

El Dorado

Three miles south of Placerville on Highway 49 sits the small town of El Dorado, whose denizens tolerate but in no way cultivate tourism. In fact, most travelers pass right on through—except for those who know about Poor Red's (see review, below), a bar and restaurant that may not look like much from the outside (or the inside, for that matter) but is known throughout the land for its famous cocktail.

RESTAURANTS

Poor Red's / ★

6221 PLEASANT VALLEY RD, EL DORADO; 530/622-2901 It's not often that small-town bars garner an international reputation, but this Cheers of the Gold Country has had its name translated into more tongues than a Robert Ludlum novel. It all started one night when the proud new owners of a gold-colored Cadillac asked the bartender to whip up a commemorative drink to celebrate their purchase. Grabbing the only thing behind the bar that was gold-colored (Galliano liqueur), the bartender dusted off the bottle, added a shot of this and a jigger of that, and—eureka!—the frothy Golden Cadillac was born. By alchemic accident, this tiny Golden State saloon soon became the largest user of Galliano in North America (as the gilded plaque, sent from Italy and proudly displayed behind a glass showcase, attests). Legend has it that during Poor Red's, er, golden era, dozens of bottles were emptied per day as celebrities, dignitaries, and plain folks all queued up at the door for a chance to squeeze inside. Nowadays a line of motorcycles might be parked outside the bar on a weekend night, but inside, the bar will be packed with friendly tourists and locals. The days are a bit more placid, with lawyers, doctors, and ranchers in baseball caps and boots politely ordering from a memorized menu of barbecued steak, ham, chicken, and pork (all in country-sized portions). *$; AE, DC, DIS, MC, V; checks OK; lunch Mon–Fri, dinner every day; full bar; no reservations; downtown.*

Placerville

One of the first camps settled by miners who branched out from Coloma, Placerville was dubbed Dry Diggins because of a lack of water. Its name was changed to Hangtown in 1849 after a series of grisly lynchings; it became Placerville in 1854 to satisfy local pride. Among the town's historical highlights are the brick-and-stone **CITY HALL** (487 Main St; 530/642-5200), which was built in 1860 and originally served as the town's firehouse, and the **HISTORIC SODA WORKS** building, home of the 150-foot gold mine. Another noteworthy edifice is the **HISTORIC CARY HOUSE HOTEL** (see review, below), where Mark Twain once lodged. Across the street, note the dangling dummy that marks the location of the town's infamous hanging tree. If you get a sudden longing for the *Wall Street Journal* or the *New York Times,* step into **PLACERVILLE NEWS** (409 Main St; 530/622-4510). The store has been run by the same family since 1912. Just a few doors down is **PLACERVILLE HARDWARE** (441 Main St; 530/622-1151), established in 1852. A single brass tack marks each foot along a section of the 100-foot-long store (two tacks mark every 5 feet), which is handy for measuring lumber or lengths of rope, and may just explain the origins of the expression "getting down to brass tacks."

A mile north of downtown Placerville is **GOLD BUG PARK,** home of the city-owned **GOLD BUG MINE** (Bedford Ave; 530/642-5238; www.goldbugpark.org). Tours of the mine lead you deep into the cool, lighted shafts. **EL DORADO COUNTY HISTORICAL MUSEUM** (104 Placerville Dr; 530/621-5865; www.co.el-dorado.ca.us/museum), adjacent to the county fairgrounds, is open Wednesday through Sunday and showcases Pony Express paraphernalia, an original Studebaker wheelbarrow, a replica of a 19th-century general store, and a restored Concord stagecoach, plus other mining-era relics.

Every autumn, droves of people—about half a million each year—come to a small ridge just east of Placerville called **APPLE HILL ORCHARDS** (from Hwy 50, take the Carson Rd exit and follow the signs; www.applehill.biz).What's the attraction? Why, apples, of course. Baked, fried, buttered, canned, candied, and caramelized apples, to name just a few variations. Dozens of vendors sell their special apple concoctions, and in September and October (peak apple-harvest season), if you don't mind the crowds, it's definitely worth a stop.

RESTAURANTS

Sweetie Pies / ★★

577 MAIN ST, PLACERVILLE; 530/642-0128 If you're passing through Placerville on your way to Tahoe and want to stop for breakfast or lunch, this little cafe and bakery on Main Street is the place to go. A bowl of freshly made soup served with house-baked sourdough bread makes a great light meal. Or you might fancy a slice of vegetable quiche with a freshly tossed garden salad. Whatever you choose, save room for the pie. Better yet, eat dessert first—it's that good. Don't miss the knockout thick, rich olallieberry pie or the rhubarb pie filled with tart chunks of the real thing. Other sweet-tooth temptations include cream pies and cinnamon and pecan rolls. Should you need more than a sugar rush to get you pumped, various coffee drinks are offered as well. Breakfasts at Sweetie Pies can be rich and filling: waffles, pancakes, egg dishes, and biscuits topped with a spicy sausage gravy (and, of course, a pie to go). *$; MC, V; checks OK; breakfast, lunch every day; beer and wine; no reservations on weekends; across from the Historic Soda Works building.* &

Zachary Jacques / ★★★

1821 PLEASANT VALLEY RD, PLACERVILLE; 530/626-8045 For more than 15 years Zachary Jacques has been one of Placerville's best restaurants. The cozy faux-French country decor is a suitable setting for French country cuisine. The seasonal menus—both à la carte and prix fixe—feature such provincial classics as Burgundy-style escargots with garlic butter and parsley to *saumon en croûte,* a fresh filet of king salmon baked in puff pastry with basil and mushrooms. Other popular dishes include roast pork tenderloin served in garlic, honey, and rosemary, and a lamb tenderloin in a Côtes du Rhone sauce, served with ratatouille and potato pancake. Every Sunday the restaurant hosts a "Sunday in the Country" menu that's always different but always a bargain at $24. Finding the perfect bottle of wine to accompany your order is never a problem: the wine list, which received an award of excellence from the highly respected *Wine Spectator* magazine, features more than 300 French and American labels. *$$$; AE, MC, V; no checks; dinner Wed–Sun; beer and wine; reservations recommended; 3 miles E of Diamond Springs.* &

LODGINGS

Chichester-McKee House / ★★

800 SPRING ST, PLACERVILLE; 530/626-1882 OR 800/831-4008 This stately Victorian home, built in 1892 by lumber baron D. W. Chichester, was the finest house in Placerville at the time and the first to have the luxury of indoor plumbing. Today the refurbished home still has the look and feel of the late 1800s—except, of course, for its updated plumbing. All four individually decorated guest rooms have queen-size, Victorian-era bedsteads, stained-glass windows; fireplaces trimmed with carved wood and marble, and private baths. In the winter you'll want to reserve the Chichester Suite, the only guest room with a fireplace. You won't find televisions in the guest rooms of this B&B, but the grand old house offers something even better—a library. And despite the location on occasionally busy Spring Street, all is peaceful inside Chichester-McKee. Guests can munch on homemade caramel brownies in the evening and feast in the morning on a full breakfast served in the dining room. *$$; AE, DIS, MC, V; checks OK; info@innlover.com; www.innlover.com; on Hwy 49, 1½ blocks N of Hwy 50.*

Historic Cary House Hotel / ★★

300 MAIN ST, PLACERVILLE; 530/622-4271 Originally built in 1857, the Cary House is a historically significant Victorian inn centrally located on Main Street. The four-story brick building was the headquarters of the Wells Fargo stage lines during the Gold Rush, and according to local lore, $90 million worth of bullion was dumped over time on the hotel's porch before it was transported to the U.S. Mint in San Francisco. Years later, newspaper editor Horace Greeley used the balcony above the porch to make his "Go West, young man" presidential campaign speech to miners. All 37 of the individually decorated guest rooms have vintage furnishings along with modern comforts such as air conditioning, private baths, TVs, and phones; many units have kitchenettes as well. A continental breakfast is served in the pantry. *$$$; AE, DIS, MC, V; no checks; hchh@caryhouse.com; www.cary house.com; between Bedford and Spring Sts.*

The Shafsky House / ★★

2942 COLOMA ST, PLACERVILLE; 530/642-2776 A cool refreshment and a pair of slippers await new arrivals as they step out of their shoes and into the early 1900s when they enter this absolutely charming 1902 Queen Anne Victorian. Lining the walls of the stairway to the second floor are photographs of the Shafsky family, including Albert Shafsky, who came to the United States from Moldavia in the late 1800s, and his daughter Alberta Shafsky. Uniquely decorated with period antiques, the three guest rooms come with private baths and king- or queen-size beds (with featherbeds and goose-down comforters in the winter months). Room rates include a fantastic gourmet breakfast of cranberry banana nut bread, oven-baked apple pancakes, and other Shafsky House specialties served on china and silver in the elegant dining room. *$$; DIS, MC, V; local checks only; shafsky@directcon.net; www.shafsky.com; 1 block N of Hwy 50, at the corner of Spring and Coloma Sts.*

Kyburz

LODGINGS

Strawberry Lodge / ★★

17510 HWY 50, KYBURZ; 530/659-7200 Wedged between the giant conifers and granite headwalls of Lake Tahoe's southwestern rim, the barnlike Strawberry Lodge has been the headquarters for a cornucopia of year-round outdoor activities for more than a century. Named for the wild strawberry patches that once covered the area, the lodge has 44 rooms (most with private baths) that often get booked up during the peak months of summer and winter (the place does a fierce wedding business). The rooms overlooking the river are the quietest. In the newer section (built in 1997), the rooms feature cabin-style log furniture and private baths. The rooms in Annex Lodge (across the highway) vary in size, also come with private baths, and are among the least expensive. Families or small groups might prefer the Hawks Nest, with two queen-size beds and a single, in the newer wing of the lodge, or the River Cabin, perched at the edge of the American River's south fork. The Strawberry Lodge's dining room serves breakfast, lunch, and dinner and offers fresh-baked bread, steaks, chicken, seafood, and a daily pasta special. The lodge also has a full-service bar and a large patio with beautiful views of the Sierra Nevada mountains. *$$; AE, MC, V; no checks; www.strawberry-lodge.com; 43 miles E of Placerville, 9 miles E of Kyburz.*

Somerset

LODGINGS

Fitzpatrick Winery and Lodge / ★★

7740 FAIRPLAY RD, SOMERSET; 530/620-3248 OR 800/245-9166 If you've never experienced true Irish hospitality, reserve a night at Brian and Diana Fitzpatrick's country-style winery and lodge. Sitting atop a hill with a commanding 360-degree view of the countryside, their 40-acre retreat has five sun-filled guest rooms, all with a combination of antique and modern furnishings, oodles of exposed wood (the rustic Log Suite is our favorite), and private baths. Guests may also dive into the 25-meter lap pool, take a soak in the spa, relax by the fire in the Great Room, or bask in the sun at tables on the expanded deck, where chefs cook meats and breads in the outdoor wood-fired oven. A full breakfast and complimentary glasses of the Fitzpatricks' wine are included in the room rate. On Friday nights during the extended evenings of daylight savings time, the Fitzpatricks serve pizza, salad, cheesecake, and, of course, handcrafted, organically grown wine. *$$–$$$; AE, DC, DIS, MC, V; checks OK; brian@fitzpatrickwinery.com; www.fitzpatrickwinery.com; off Mt Aukum Rd, 6 miles SE of town.* &

Southern Gold Country

Placerville may be the center of the Gold Country, but it's not the prettiest town by a long shot. Rather, the Gold Rush towns a few miles to the south (Amador City, Sutter Creek, and Jackson) are far more appealing destinations. The rolling hills and majestic oaks of the southern Gold Country are honeycombed with mysterious caverns and abandoned mines, including the deepest gold mines on the continent. The mining boom went bust by 1860, and most of the Gold Rush towns were abandoned by the 1870s. Some towns have survived by mining for tourist dollars. Along with sightseeing and B&B hopping, most visitors journey to this area for the fishing, camping, hiking, rafting, and mountain biking. And yes, some diehards still come just to pan for gold.

The first town you'll pass heading south is Plymouth, the starting point of the **AMADOR COUNTRY WINERIES** (209/267-2297; www.amadorwine.com), located along the Shenandoah Valley Road. The town's **POKERVILLE MARKET** (18170 Hwy 49; 209/245-6986) carries almost all of the wines produced in the area and sells them at low prices. If you are planning to visit the wineries, the market's deli is a great place to pick up a picnic lunch to take with you.

For more information about the southern Gold Country, contact the **AMADOR COUNTY CHAMBER OF COMMERCE** at 209/223-0350 or www.amadorcounty chamber.com.

THE HEROES AND VILLAINS OF THE GOLD RUSH ERA

Gold! From Sutter's Mill the word spread like wildfire, bringing hordes of fortune seekers and adventurers from around the world to the Sierra foothills. But who would write their stories? Who would entertain them? And who would rob them of their gold?

It was "The Celebrated Jumping Frog of Calaveras County" that first brought international fame to **MARK TWAIN**—and he heard the story while drinking in a saloon in Angels Camp. Between writing for newspapers in San Francisco and Carson City, Nevada, Twain hung out with his mining buddies on Mokelumne Hill near Jackson. This author and humorist has since become the George Washington of the Sierra foothills, with seemingly every third lodging claiming that "Mark Twain slept here."

Once mistress to Czar Nicholas I and the lunatic King Ludwig I of Bavaria, the beautiful and voluptuous **LOLA MONTEZ** arrived in Grass Valley on the arm of her second husband. But after she threw him out, she returned to doing what she thought she knew best—the Spider Dance. Wearing a scandalous knee-length skirt covered with cork tarantulas, Lola could always pack a theater—for one night. Despite her lack of talent, Lola took her act on the road, where the miners she entertained in the camps loved her—and Lola, in turn, loved them back.

Whatever Lola Montez lacked in talent, her Grass Valley neighbor **LOTTA CRAB-TREE** had in spades. Pushed by her mother, the gifted little girl performed in mining camps throughout the Sierras before moving to Boston, where she became a famous actress and the first female millionaire in the country.

Amador City

Once a bustling mining town, Amador City is now the smallest incorporated city in California. Lined with false-fronted antique and specialty boutiques—handcrafted furniture, Gold Rush memorabilia, rare books, Native American crafts—this block-long non-metropolis is a good place to stop, stretch your legs, and window-shop along the boardwalk. Parking can be difficult, particularly on summer weekends.

RESTAURANTS

Imperial Hotel Restaurant / ★★★

14202 HWY 49, AMADOR CITY; 209/267-9172 OR 800/242-5594 This elegant restaurant within the Imperial Hotel has earned a solid reputation for serving superb California-Mediterranean cuisine in a relaxed setting. The menu changes seasonally (and, apparently, so do the chefs). A fall menu might include a smoked pork chop with fig and onion confit or the pan-broiled rib eye with a Provençal herb crust. Fresh seafood is offered nightly, such as lemon-baked sea bass wrapped in parchment and served with a wilted spinach salad. The dessert selection is impressive as well: crème brûlée, custom-made ice cream, and a selection

Famous for saying "please" when he pointed his (empty) double-barreled shotgun at Wells Fargo stage coach drivers and demanded their strongbox full of gold, **BLACK BART**—the "gentleman bandit"—never stole from the passengers riding the stage. Much of his success as a thief can be attributed to his skill as a backwoodsman and to his double life as a distinguished gentleman living in San Francisco, where he was known only as Charles E. Bolton.

The murderous activities attributed to outlaw **JOAQUIN MURIETA** may have been the work of as many as five different Joaquins. More myth than man, and much romanticized in an 1854 biography, "Murieta" was a name soon whispered in fear by miners and printed in newspapers throughout California whenever gold was missing and bodies were found. Eventually killed by the California Rangers, Murieta had his head lopped off and placed in a jar. For years it toured the West via local fairs and celebrations, where for a dollar you could see what was left of the notorious bandit king. But was it Murieta's head, or that of another Joaquin?

The foothills are filled with stories of Gold Rush heroes whose fame may not have crossed the Sierra Nevada—like one-eyed **CHARLEY PARKER**, the woman who handled the reins of Wells Fargo stagecoaches in the guise of a man, and **SNOWSHOE THOMPSON**, who carried the miners' mail to Nevada and back over the snow-covered Sierra. Theirs are the stories that make up the lore of this region, and they can be heard in every town along the forty-niner trail.

of cakes and tortes. On warm summer evenings, be sure to request a table on the back patio. *$$$; AE, DIS, MC, V; checks OK; dinner Wed–Sun, brunch Mother's Day and Easter; full bar; reservations recommended; www.imperialamador.com; downtown.* &

LODGINGS

Imperial Hotel / ★★★

14202 HWY 49, AMADOR CITY; 209/267-9172 OR 800/242-5594 This beautifully restored 1879 brick hotel, located at the foot of Main Street overlooking Amador City, strikes a marvelous balance between elegance and whimsy. One example is displayed inside the Oasis Bar: a fresco fantasy of a Saharan oasis complete with palm trees, belly dancers, and camels. The six upstairs guest rooms house numerous antiques as well as hand-painted furnishings by local artists. Room 6 is one of the quietest, but room 1 is everyone's favorite, with its high ceiling, hand-painted queen-size canopy bed, art deco appointments, giant windows, and French doors that open onto a private balcony overlooking Main Street (granted, you have to put up with some traffic noise, but the old brick hotel is located on a slow curve, so no one's going terribly fast). All of the rooms are furnished with brass, iron, or pine beds and have private bathrooms. Breakfast is served downstairs, in your room, or on the patio or balcony. *$$; AE, DIS, MC, V; checks OK; rooms@imperialamador; www.imperialamador.com; downtown.*

Sutter Creek

"Big Four" railroad baron Leland Stanford made his millions at Sutter Creek's Lincoln Mine, then used his windfall to invest in the Transcontinental Railroad and fund his successful campaign to become governor of California. Sutter Creek is the self-proclaimed "nicest little town in the Mother Lode" and was named after sawmill owner John Sutter. It boasts some beautiful 19th-century buildings, including the recently reopened landmark **KNIGHT'S FOUNDRY HISTORIC WATER-POWERED IRON WORKS** (81 Eureka St; 209/267-0201), the last water-powered foundry and machine shop in the nation, and the **DOWNS MANSION** (Spanish St, across from the Immaculate Conception Church), the former home of the foreman at Leland Stanford's mine. Also worth exploring is the **SUTTER GOLD MINE** (13660 Hwy 49; 209/736-2708 or 866/762-2837; www.suttergold.com), where you can take a guided tour into the bowels of a modern hard-rock gold mine, then pan for real gold using gold pans or sluice boxes ($5 bags of ore sold at the gift shop are guaranteed to hold either gold or gemstones). It's a great way to learn about geology and the history of mining technology, and kids get a kick out of panning for real gold. It's open daily year-round from 9am to 5pm in the summer and 10am to 4pm October through May. It's located at 13660 Hwy 49, about ½ mile south of Amador City.

RESTAURANTS

Zinfandels / ★★★

51 HANFORD ST, SUTTER CREEK; 209/267-5008 Chef Gregory West, a six-year veteran of Greens (San Francisco's most famous vegetarian restaurant), has been earning kudos from Gold Country locals since 1996 with his version of light California cuisine. West's menu changes monthly, incorporating the best local farm produce and seasonal ingredients. A made-from-scratch meal might begin with two popular appetizers: the crisp polenta topped with mushrooms, garlic, shallots, and fresh herbs and cream; and the Medicated Goo—a small round of homemade bread hollowed out and filled with blue Castello cheese, toasted walnuts, pan-fried garlic, and fresh herbs. For the main course, standouts include a butternut squash risotto with pancetta, leeks, crimini mushrooms, and spinach; and the Copper River salmon topped with Morello cherry *beurre rouge* (red butter) and served with orange pumpkin seeds, wild rice, and basmati rice pilaf. Zinfandels also offers a well-edited list of locally produced wines, and the chef thoughtfully highlights the perfect wine to accompany each dish on the menu. If you're not up for a full sit-down dinner, opt for a bit of wine-tasting, appetizers, and dessert in the wine bar downstairs. *$$$; AE, DIS, MC, V; checks OK; dinner Thurs–Sun; beer and wine; reservations recommended; www.zinfood.com; N end of downtown.*

LODGINGS

Eureka Street Inn Bed and Breakfast / ★★

55 EUREKA ST, SUTTER CREEK; 209/267-5500 OR 800/399-2389 Chuck and Sandy Anderson, quite the warm and friendly couple, have been making new friends as innkeepers of this quaint Craftsman-style inn since 1999. Step into the living room with its overstuffed leather sofa and stained-glass windows, and you'll instantly feel at home. The downstairs common areas are comfortable and cozy, and the four guest rooms on the second floor are bright, cheerful, and tastefully decorated with Gold Rush–era antiques; all have private bathrooms, gas fireplaces or stoves, and air conditioning (a must in the midsummer). Chuck is in charge of the gourmet breakfasts—eggs Benedict on artichoke hearts, cheese blintzes, French toast, and poached pears—served in the formal dining room. *$$; DIS, MC, V; checks OK; may be closed last 2 weeks of Dec and all of Jan; innkeepers@eurekastreetinn.com; www.eureka streetinn.com; 1½ blocks off Main St, near the Foundry.*

The Foxes in Sutter Creek Bed and Breakfast Inn / ★★★

77 MAIN ST, SUTTER CREEK; 209/267-5882 OR 800/987-3344 This is, without question, one of the finest B&Bs in the Gold Country. An immaculate garden fronts the Gold Rush–era foundation, and from there it only gets better. Each of the seven guest rooms is beautifully furnished with antiques, including massive, elaborate Victorian headboards and armoires that seem too priceless to actually use. All of the rooms have private baths, and five have fireplaces. What helps account for this B&B's popularity is the breakfast experience: a hearty spread, chosen by you from the B&B's breakfast menu, is delivered with the morning paper on a silver platter to your room or at the garden gazebo (why can't life always be like this?). Located on Main Street, the inn is only steps away from Sutter Creek's shops and restaurants. Reserve early to avoid a two-month wait for weekend stays during peak seasons. *$$$; DIS, MC, V; checks OK; innkeeper@foxesinn.com; www.foxesinn.com; downtown.*

Grey Gables Inn / ★★★

161 HANFORD ST, SUTTER CREEK; 209/267-1039 OR 800/473-9422 Surrounded by terraces of colorful and meticulously manicured gardens, this adorable three-story Victorian retreat offers eight plushly carpeted guest rooms named after British poets and writers. Our favorite, the Byron Room, is bedecked in hues of deep green and Normandy rose, which pairs well with the dark wood furnishings and Renaissance Revival bed. Aside from the king-size bed in the Brontë Room, all of the boudoirs have queen-size beds, gas-log fireplaces, large armoires, air conditioning, and private baths (a few with claw-footed tubs). A bounteous breakfast, delivered on fine English bone china, is served either in the formal dining room or in your room. And in true English fashion, there is an informal tea every afternoon from 3pm to 4pm; wine and cheese is served daily from 6pm to 7pm. The only drawback to this English Eden is that the house abuts heavily traveled Highway 49, though the rooms are soundproofed. On the plus side, Sutter Creek's shops and restaurants are only a short walk away. *$$$; AE, DIS, MC, V; checks OK; reservations@grey gables.com; www.greygables.com; on Hwy 49, at the N end of town.* ♿

Jackson

Just beyond an enormous Georgia-Pacific lumber mill lies Jackson, the seat of Amador County. Jackson hides most of its rowdy past behind modern facades, but old-timers know the town (once called "little Reno") as the last place in California to outlaw prostitution. For a trip back in time, take a gander at the **NATIONAL HOTEL** (2 Water St; 209/223-0500; www.national-hotel.com), which has been in continuous operation since 1862 and has built up quite a guest list: Will Rogers, John Wayne, Leland Stanford and almost every other California governor in the 19th century. Ragtime tunes and classic oldie sing-alongs are played on the grand piano, and guests register for the spartan rooms with the bartender through a wooden cage at the back of the saloon.

Gold Rush buffs shouldn't miss the **AMADOR COUNTY MUSEUM** (225 Church St; 209/223-6386), which has scale models of the local Kennedy and Argonaut hard-rock mines, among the deepest and richest in the nation (this is also where Will Rogers filmed *Boys Will Be Boys* in 1920). It's open Wednesday through Sunday; tours of the museum are offered Saturday and Sunday on the hour from 11am to 3pm.

There's also **KENNEDY TAILING WHEELS PARK** (take Main St to Jackson Gate Rd, just N of Jackson; no phone), site of the Kennedy and Argonaut mines, the Mother Lode's deepest. Though these mines have been closed for decades, their head frames and huge tailing wheels (some are 58 feet in diameter) remain to help show how waste from the mines was conveyed over the hills to a settling pond.

A few miles south of Jackson is the "Historic 49" turnoff to **MOKELUMNE HILL**, a town once so rich with gold that claims were limited in size to 16 square feet and the hill was covered with tents and wood-and-tar-paper shacks. Although there's little going on these days in this sleepy block-long town—try to imagine a past population of 15,000, including an old French quarter and a Chinatown—it's still a pleasant 15-minute drive through Mokelumne's green pastures, along its historic but minuscule Main Street, past the Protestant, Jewish, and Catholic cemeteries of its former residents, and back onto the highway.

If all this touring has given you a forty-niner-size appetite, indulge in a messy Moo-Burger and shake at **MEL AND FAYE'S DINER** (205 Hwy 49, Jackson; 209/223-0853), a local landmark since 1956.

RESTAURANTS

Upstairs Restaurant & Streetside Bistro / ★★

164 MAIN ST, JACKSON; 209/223-3342 Chef Layne McCollum, who learned his trade at the California Culinary Academy, presides over this two-story restaurant housed in a handsome Gold Rush–era building made of exposed brick and petrified wood. The bright, cheery Streetside Bistro—tastefully decorated with wrought-iron furniture, tile flooring, and colorful oil paintings—offers quiche, soups, salads, and gourmet sandwiches such as smoked pork loin with red chile pesto for lunch. For dinner, take the stairway to the Upstairs Restaurant, a long, narrow room of exposed brick and glass furnished with white-linen-topped tables graced with fresh flowers and oil lamps. McCollum's small, contemporary

American menu changes weekly, though you might encounter pasta puttanesca prepared with tomato-basil fettuccine, smoked vegetables grilled with pesto, or grilled boneless breast of duck topped with blackberry-ginger sauce. A prix-fixe five-course special is offered on every menu. *$$$; AE, DIS, MC, V; checks OK; lunch, dinner Wed–Sun; beer and wine; reservations recommended; downtown.*

LODGINGS

Court Street Inn / ★★☆

215 COURT ST, JACKSON; 209/223-0416 OR 800/200-0416 Dave and Nancy Butow's pretty 1872 Victorian, with its embossed tin ceilings, eyelash shutters, redwood staircase, and marble fireplace, has earned a well-deserved spot on the National Register of Historic Places. A two-minute stroll from Main Street, the inn is loaded with vintage furnishings in each of the seven guest rooms, all of which come with private bathrooms, down comforters, and gas or electric fireplaces; some have whirlpool or claw-footed tubs. The Bordeaux Court room has an adjoining sitting room that's perfect for a lazy read of the morning paper, though our favorite room is Burgundy Court, with its oak-manteled fireplace and handsome four-poster king-size bed. The rustic Indian House is a two-story private cottage with a fireplace, cozy furniture, a porch swing, and an enormous 61-inch TV with VCR and cable that's discreetly screened off for anti-TV types; two separate bedrooms allow up to four people. On warm summer mornings, a bounteous Butow breakfast is served on the back garden patio—a big hit with their guests (as is the hot tub). Complimentary evening refreshments are included as well. *$$; AE, DIS, MC, V; checks OK; dave@courtstreetinn.com; www.courtstreetinn.com; just off Church St.*

Volcano

This tiny town with fewer than 100 residents is so wonderfully authentic that it borders on decrepit (it doesn't get more Gold Rush–genuine than this, folks). During the heady mining days, this unusually sophisticated town built the state's first library and its first astronomical observatory. Nowadays you can see some preserved buildings and artifacts, including a Civil War cannon. The town got its name in 1848 after miners mistook the enormous craggy boulders that lie in the center of town for volcanic rock. An outdoor amphitheater, hidden behind stone facades along Main Street, is the site of popular summer theatricals performed by the **VOLCANO THEATRE COMPANY** (on Main St, 1 block N of the St. George Hotel; www.volcanotheatre.org). Watching a play under the stars is a wonderful Gold Country experience; purchase tickets online at www.high sierratickets.com or call 866/463-8659. And at nearby **INDIAN GRINDING ROCK STATE HISTORIC PARK** (located 1 mile S of Volcano off Pine Grove/Volcano Rd; 209/296-7488), you'll find 3,000-year-old petroglyphs and an enormous limestone outcropping—the largest of its kind in America—dotted with thousands of holes created by generations of native Miwoks who ground their acorn meal on the rock here. The park also has a fine Indian artifacts museum and a replica of a Miwok ceremonial roundhouse. After touring the town, take the side trip up winding Ram's Horn Grade to cool off in the funky, friendly bar at the **ST. GEORGE HOTEL**. Or, in early spring from mid-March through mid-April, picnic amid the nearly half-million daffodils (more than 100 varieties) in bloom on **DAFFODIL HILL**, a 4-acre ranch 3 miles north of Volcano (follow the signs on Ram's Horn Grade; 209/296-7048; www.comspark.com/daffodil hill). Entrance to the ranch is free, but donations are accepted.

RESTAURANTS

The St. George Hotel Restaurant / ★★★

16104 MAIN ST, VOLCANO; 209/296-4458 Voted the number one restaurant in Amador County by readers of the *Amador Ledger Dispatch,* the St. George's seasonally changing menu offers some of the finest cuisine in the region. Whenever possible, the kitchen staff uses locally grown produce and herbs from the hotel's garden. Be sure to start the feast with the St. George ravioli appetizer: crisp wontons layered with sautéed mushrooms and spinach over a chicken sun-dried-tomato galantine, resting on a bed of roasted red-pepper pesto and braised leek sauce. Locals drive in from Jackson for lamb and fish entrees like the South of the Border grilled salmon topped with mango salsa or the Trujillo pork loin topped with a citrus-avocado relish and a spicy guava barbecue sauce. For those who long for that traditional slab of meat, there's always the saffron-infused roasted rack of lamb or the New York steak topped with rich mushroom sauce, both served with a side of mashed Yukon gold potatoes. Choosing from the dessert menu isn't easy, but the frozen chocolate nut mousse with macadamia nut filling and Oreo cookie crust is definitely something to sigh over. *$$$; AE, MC, V; checks OK; dinner Thurs–Sun, brunch Sun (closed 3 weeks in Jan or Feb); full bar; reservations recommended; stgeorge@stgeorgehotel.com; www.stgeorgehotel.com; downtown.*

LODGINGS

The St. George Hotel / ★★

16104 MAIN ST, VOLCANO; 209/296-4458 In its heyday in the 1860s, the burgeoning village of Volcano offered a tired miner his choice of 17 hotels. Those whose pockets held the largest nuggets chose the St. George. Voted "Best Hotel" for the third year in a row by residents of Amador County, the St. George Hotel—wrapped with balconies and entwined with Virginia creeper—is still a gold mine for anyone spending an evening in this little town. Owners Tracey and Mark Berkner have spent the past few years recapturing some the hotel's original charm: the restaurant (see review, above) is delightful, the parlor and grounds exquisite (think weddings), and the Bungalow Rooms in the modernized annex are bright and comfortable. The guest rooms in the main building are by far the most interesting. Each room is decorated with antiques and personal effects donated by admired friends and relatives. The rooms in back have great views of the garden and are perfect for morning people who like to rise with the sun. Otherwise, your best bet is to ask for a balcony room in front. On the downside, all rooms in the main lodge share a total of five bathrooms. A continental breakfast, served in the large downstairs parlor, can also be enjoyed in the garden. *$$; AE, MC, V; checks OK; open Wed–Sun (closed 3 weeks in Jan or Feb); stgeorge@volcano.net; www.stgeorgehotel.com; downtown.* &

Angels Camp

Cruise right through the overcommercialized and truly uninspiring town of San Andreas and you'll eventually pull into Angels Camp, made famous by Mark Twain's short story "The Celebrated Jumping Frog of Calaveras County." Every year on the third weekend in May, thousands of frog fans flock to the **CALAVERAS COUNTY FAIR** (at the county fairgrounds, 2 miles S of town; 209/736-2561; www.frogtown.org) to witness the **JUMPING FROG JUBILEE,** one of the premier frog-jumping contests in the world and a truly ribbiting competition. The festival, started in 1928 to mark the paving of the town's streets, also features livestock exhibitions, pageants, cook-offs, arm-wrestling tournaments, carnival rides, live music, a rodeo, and—for those of you who forgot to bring one—frogs for rent. The record, by the way, is 21 feet, 5¾ inches, jumped in 1986 by "Rosie the Ribbiter," beating the old world record by 4½ inches.

RESTAURANTS

CAMPS / ★★★

676 MCCAULEY RANCH RD, ANGELS CAMP; 209/736-8181 A bit hard to find, CAMPS is ensconced within sprawling Greenhorn Creek golf resort on the western fringes of Angels Camp. Designed to meld into the natural surroundings thanks to its outer walls, which are made from locally mined rhyolite, the restaurant's natural earth tones and wicker and wood furniture offer a relaxing atmosphere where you can contemplate the many problems with your golf swing. The best seats in the house are on the spacious veranda overlooking the course, a fine venue for the traditional California cuisine. The menu changes frequently, but you can count on a variety of cuts of certified Angus beef, fresh fish, and organically grown vegetables. A typical dinner may start with house salad with American field greens, toasted pistachios, julienned red onions, and a raspberry vinaigrette, followed by macadamia-crusted halibut with a mandarin orange beurre blanc or crisp roasted duck with kumquat and sun-dried tomatoes. It shouldn't be a problem finding the right wine to pair with your meal, as the wine list has been given *Wine Spectator's* Award of Excellence for the last three years. And CAMPS offers kids' meals for around $5. *$$$; AE, MC, V; checks OK; breakfast, lunch, dinner every day, brunch Sun; full bar; reservations recommended; www.greenhorncreek.com; ½ mile W on Hwy 4, from N junction of Hwys 4 and 49.* &

LODGINGS

The Cottages at Greenhorn Creek / ★★★

626 MCCAULEY RANCH RD, ANGELS CAMP; 209/736-8120 OR 888/736-5900 A variety of guest rooms within 27 individual cottages are available for rent on a daily basis at the quiet Greenhorn Creek resort. Each cottage is roughly 1,300 square feet, with two master suites, two bathrooms, and a fully equipped kitchen in a "great room" that includes a dining area and a comfortable living room complete with TV and VCR, cathedral ceilings, fireplace, and private deck or patio. If an entire house is more than you need, each cottage can be separated into a one-bedroom suite or a one-bedroom hotel room with the turn of a key. It's not exactly the traditional Gold Country B&B experience, but if you've ever wanted to spend your vacation at a golf resort, these cottages are ideal. Not only is the restaurant CAMPS (see review, above) within walking distance, but also guests have access to the swimming pool and fitness center. *$$$$; AE, MC, V; checks OK; request@greenhorncreek.com; www.greenhorncreek.com; ½ mile W on Hwy 4, from N junction of Hwys 4 and 49.*

Murphys

Gingerbread Victorian homes behind white picket fences and tall locust trees border the streets in Murphys, a former trading post set up by brothers Dan and John Murphy in cooperation with local Native Americans (John married the chief's daughter). It's worth taking the detour off Highway 49 just to stroll down Murphys' tree-lined Main Street—or, better yet, to sample the regions' brews at **MURPHY'S BREWING COMPANY** within Murphys Historic Hotel & Lodge (see review, below). Most of the **CALAVERAS WINERIES** (209/736-6722 or 800/225-3764, ext. 25; www.calaveras wines.org) have tasting rooms right in the heart of town. Peer below the foundations of **MURPHYS CREEK ANTIQUES** next to the hotel to find the cavelike interior of the tasting room at **ZUCCA** (209/728-1623; www.zuccawines.com). Just a few steps farther and you'll find **MALVADINO'S** (209/728-9030; www.malvadino.com). Pick up a map in town to visit the wineries located just outside of town.

Eighteen miles northeast of Murphys on Highway 4 is **CALAVERAS BIG TREES STATE PARK** (209/795-2334; www.bigtrees.org), where you can see giant sequoias that are among the biggest and oldest living things on earth. It's also a popular summer retreat that offers camping, swimming, hiking, and fishing along the Stanislaus River. Many of the numerous caverns in the area were discovered in the mid-1800s by gold prospectors and can now be toured, including **MERCER CAVERNS** (209/728-2101; www.mercercaverns.com), which has crystalline stalactites and stalagmites in a series of descending chambers; **MOANING CAVERN** (209/736-2708; www.caverntours.com), where a 100-foot stairway spirals down into a limestone chamber so huge it could house the Statue of Liberty (it's also a great place to try out your rappelling skills); and **CALIFORNIA CAVERNS** (209/736-2708; www.cavern tours.com), the West's first commercially developed cave and the largest single cave system in Northern California. It has yet to be fully explored.

RESTAURANTS

Grounds / ★★

402 MAIN ST, MURPHYS; 209/728-8663 River Klass, a gregarious transplant from the East Coast, opened this hugely popular coffeehouse and cafe in 1993. It was quickly nicknamed the "Rude Boy Cafe" after Klass's acerbic wit, but all you're likely to encounter is a cheerful staff and a room full of locals who are addicted to the Grounds' potato pancakes (served with every made-to-order omelet), freshly baked breads, free-range egg dishes, and rich coffee. Lunch favorites include the grilled eggplant sandwich stuffed with smoked mozzarella and fresh basil and the sausage sandwich on house-baked bread. The dinner menu, which changes about twice a week, offers a wide range of entrees—everything from grilled halibut served with rock shrimp and spinach dumplings to fettuccine topped with sautéed shrimp, halibut, and mussels in a garlic cream sauce. Other popular entrees are the juicy pot roast with steamed red potatoes, oven-roasted sweetheart ham with glazed yams, and a good ol' New York steak with caramelized onions and horseradish mashed potatoes. The wine list is equally impressive and very reasonably priced. The long, narrow dining rooms are bright and airy, with pine furnishings, wood floors, and an open kitchen. If the weather is warm, ask for a table on the back patio. *$$; AE, DIS, MC, V; checks OK; breakfast, lunch every day, dinner Wed–Sun; beer and wine; reservations recommended; E side of street, center of town.* &

LODGINGS

Dunbar House, 1880 / ★★★

271 JONES ST, MURPHYS; 209/728-2897 OR 800/692-6006 Without question, Dunbar House is among the finest B&Bs in the Gold Country. Century-old gardens adorn this lovely Italianate home built in 1880 by Willis Dunbar, a superintendent for the Utica Water Company, for his bride. The lush grounds are complemented by a two-person hammock, a gazebo, a rose garden with benches, and a swing. All five guest rooms are furnished with gas-burning fireplaces, heirloom antiques, down pillows and comforters, 350-thread-count Egyptian cotton bed linens, thick Egyptian cotton towels imported from England, and vases of fresh flowers for dashes of vibrant color. The Cedar Room offers a private sunporch and a two-person whirlpool bath, while the two-room Sugar Pine suite comes with English towel warmers, a CD/stereo system, and a balcony perched among the elm trees. For breakfast, fresh juices, coffee, house-made pastries, and a main dish such as the fabulous concoction of crab and cheese atop an English muffin are served in your room, at the dining room table, or in the gorgeous garden. Really, it's impossible not to indulge yourself at this wonderful B&B. *$$$–$$$$; AE, MC, V; checks OK; innkeep@ dunbarhouse.com; www.dunbarhouse.com; just off Main St at S end of town.*

Murphys Historic Hotel & Lodge / ★

457 MAIN ST, MURPHYS; 209/728-3444 OR 800/532-7684 When this hotel opened in 1856, who could have known what kind of characters would pass through its doors? The illustrious guest register includes Ulysses S. Grant, Mark Twain, Horatio Alger, Susan B. Anthony, and Black Bart, to name just a few. Although its days of housing dignitaries are long past, this national- and state-registered landmark still maintains its hold as Murphys's social center. Any time of day or night you'll find a few locals here hunched over stools at the old-fashioned saloon, voicing their opinions and politely ignoring the tourists who stop in for a beer. The main building has 9 historic guest rooms that reflect turn-of-the-century lifestyles (that is, thin walls and no phones, televisions, or private baths), while the newer building offers 20 modern rooms with private bathrooms and hair dryers. In the dining area—open for breakfast, lunch, and dinner—you'll find huge platters of chicken, beef, seafood, and pasta, but the lackluster service and mediocre cuisine usually discourages most visitors from coming back (especially with the estimable Grounds restaurant just down the street). *$$; AE, DC, DIS, MC, V; checks OK; mhotel@caltel.com; www.murphyshotel.com; downtown.* &

Victorian Inn / ★★

402 MAIN ST, MURPHYS; 209/728-8933 A town in need of more luxury accommodations, Murphys hadn't celebrated the opening of a new inn in more than a century until 1993, when this two-story shingle and rock charmer opened its doors onto Main Street. Each of the 14 individually decorated guest rooms has an eclectic mix of Victorian and modern amenities: fireplaces or woodstoves, claw-footed tubs or spas, and brass or antique beds. The two best rooms for romance are the Wisteria, with its king bed, fireplace, wet bar, spa tub for two, and private porch overlooking the garden, and the Anniversary Suite, which features a private balcony, wet bar, double-sided fireplace, king-size sleigh bed, and enormous spa tub. You'll like the location as well, right on Murphys' lively section of Main Street. *$$–$$$$; DIS, MC, V; checks OK; info@victoriainn-murphys.com; www.victoriainn-murphys.com; in the Miner's Exchange Complex.* &

Columbia

Some mighty fortunate forty-niners unearthed a staggering $87 million in gold in this former boisterous mining town, once the state's second-largest city (it was only two votes shy of becoming the state capital over Sacramento). But when the gold no longer panned out in the late 1850s, Columbia's population of 15,000 nearly vanished. In 1945 the entire town was turned into **COLUMBIA STATE HISTORIC PARK** (209/532-4301 or 209/532-0150). This is the Mother Lode's best-preserved park, filled with Western-style Victorian hotels and saloons, a newspaper office, a working blacksmith's forge, stagecoaches, and numerous other relics of California's early mining days. Follow the free, short, self-guided park tour, and don't miss the **WELLS FARGO EXPRESS OFFICE**, a former stagecoach center, and the restored **COLUMBIA SCHOOLHOUSE**, which was in use until 1937. Big-time Gold Rush buffs who want more area history should pick up the inexpensive walking-tour booklet at the visitors center or sign up for a 45-minute guided mine tour. For a more leisurely view of the park, hop aboard one of the horse-drawn stagecoaches. And to learn how to pan for gold, stop by **HIDDEN TREASURE GOLD MINE TOURS** (209/532-9693) at the corner of Main and Stage streets.

RESTAURANTS

The City Hotel Restaurant / ★★

MAIN ST, COLUMBIA; 209/532-1479 OR 800/532-1479 The City Hotel Restaurant is a rarity—a culinary palace in the heart of a state park. Inside, it's decked out with red velvet drapes, oil paintings, and antique furniture topped with crisp linens and flowers. The restaurant and hotel are a hotel-hospitality training center for nearby Columbia College, and the students assist the staff here. If this is Hotel Hospitality 101, these are 4.0 students—the serving staff even dresses in period costumes. You may order from the small prix-fixe or à la carte menus featuring dishes like grilled tournedos of beef tenderloin with potato and blue cheese twice-baked soufflé, or pan-seared fillet of salmon over stir-fried vegetables with shiitake mushroom compote. For dessert, diners who can wait 30 minutes will be justly rewarded with a lemon soufflé crowned with Grand Marnier sauce. California vintages feature prominently on the wine list. While you wait for your dinner table, spend some time in What Cheer, the hotel's saloon. *$$$; AE, DIS, MC, V; checks OK; dinner Tues–Sun, brunch Sun; full bar; reservations required on weekends, recommended on weekdays; info@cityhotel.com; www.cityhotel.com; between Jackson and State Sts.*

LODGINGS

City Hotel / ★★

MAIN ST, COLUMBIA; 209/532-1479 OR 800/532-1479 City folk who frequented this opulent hotel in 1856 called it the Gem of the Southern Mines. Predictably, the building has gone through several incarnations since then, including stints as a gold-assay shop and a dance hall. When the town was turned into a state historic park in 1945, visitors once again returned to this venerable landmark. In the '70s, nearby Columbia College obtained grant money to renovate the structure and turn it into a hotel-hospitality training center, and now students assist the staff here. The lobby is fitted with period settees and marble-topped tables, and 6 of the 10 high-ceilinged rooms face a central parlor where you can relax and read the newspaper or chat with fellow guests. Rooms 1 and 2 are the largest and have balconies overlooking Main Street. All of the rooms are nicely furnished with Renaissance Revival beds and antiques, but they also only have half-baths—the showers are down the hall (the hotel provides comfy robes, slippers, and wicker baskets full of toiletries to ease the trip). *$$; AE, DIS, MC, V; checks OK; info@cityhotel.com; www.cityhotel.com; between Jackson and State Sts.*

Twain Harte

LODGINGS

McCaffrey House Bed & Breakfast Inn / ★★★☆

23251 HWY 108, TWAIN HARTE; 209/586-0757 OR 888/586-0757 Located in the Stanislaus National Forest, this gorgeous, sprawling three-story country home was built specifically as a B&B, and it's one of the top 10 in the Gold Country. Each of the seven immaculate guest rooms has its own bath with a shower and tub, a blow dryer, an individually controlled thermostat, access to a video library of 400 movies, and a private phone and modem jacks. All but two units have private decks. But it's the details that make the difference: a nearby creek to lull you to sleep; a view of the forest from your deck; queen-size quilts handmade by the Amish of Pennsylvania; a black iron stove in every room; exceptional gallery-quality art adorning the walls; TVs with VCRs stored in pine wood armoires; a library of paperbacks that are yours to keep; an outdoor hot tub perfectly situated to watch the full moon passing overhead—and more. In the summer, breakfast and hors d'oeuvres, wine, and sparkling cider are served on the huge redwood deck, which surrounds the house and overlooks the verdant hollow. Winter attracts families of

PURPLE GOLD: THERE'S WINE IN THEM
THAR HILLS

During the Gold Rush, dozens of wineries existed in the Sierra foothills, started mainly by Italian immigrants. Sadly, the end of the mining boom and Prohibition brought a severe wine-making drought to the region. Today, however, there are more than 60 wineries in the area from Mariposa to Nevada county, producing, naturally enough, gold-medal-winning wines. Most are small, family-owned establishments offering free public tours, tastings, and picnic sites.

Thirty-two varietals flourish within the microclimates of the foothills, resulting in everything from rich, spicy zinfandels to full-bodied chardonnays and fruity Rieslings. Fortunately, wine enthusiasts don't have to travel all over the counties and down isolated roads to taste them. Most of the **AMADOR COUNTY WINERIES** (209/267-2297; www.amadorwine.com) are situated along the Shenandoah Valley Road out of Plymouth. The nine wineries in **CALAVERAS COUNTY** (800/225-3764, ext. 25; www.calaveraswines.org) are within a 3-mile radius of the town of Murphys, and five tasting rooms are right in town. The majority of wineries in **EL DORADO COUNTY** (800/306-3956; www.eldoradowines.org) are centered around the Apple Hill area and between the towns of Fairplay and Mount Akum. A map to all the wineries can be found throughout the region in the **VINE TIMES** (www.thevinetimes.com), a complimentary wine newspaper, and county winery maps can be picked up in visitors centers and in most lodgings. Many of the wineries are open daily and most offer free wine tasting, with a friendly staff ready to answer all your questions.

While the "quaint" factor of the tasting rooms has little to do with how a wine tastes, the atmosphere surrounding the wine adds to the wine taster's experience. Listed below are just a few among the more interesting to see.

skiers, who opt for McCaffrey House's ski packages to make use of nearby resorts (also ask about its theater and fishing packages). Every room in this B&B is a winner, but top honors go to the Evergreen and Burgundy boudoirs, which have unobstructed views of the forest. Owners Michael and Stephanie McCaffrey and their gaggle of pets are all incredibly friendly—reason enough to return again and again. *$$$; AE, MC, V; checks OK; innkeeper@mccaffreyhouse.com; www.mccaffrey house.com; 11 miles E of Sonora.*

Sonora

When the traffic starts to crawl along Highway 49, you're probably closing in on Sonora. In forty-niner days, Sonora competed with Columbia for the title of wealthiest city in the southern Mother Lode. Today, it is the Gold Country's largest and most

BOEGER (1709 Carson Rd, Placerville; 530/622-8094; www.boegerwinery.com). Started by the Lamardo Fossati Family in 1850, this winery is surrounded by both vineyards and pear orchards—a perfect picnic spot. Try the Gold Medal barbera served in the 1857 Swiss Italian stone wine cellar and tasting room.

SIERRA VISTA (4560 Cabernet Wy, end of Leisure Ln; 530/622-7221; www.sierra vistawinery.com). Taste the flagship Rhône-style wines of this family-operated winery while gazing at the magnificent view of the snowcapped Sierra Nevada Mountains. Picnic tables rest on the shaded lawn, circled by a flower garden. Winery tours are available by appointment.

STEVENOT (2690 San Domingo Rd, Murphys; 209/728-0638; www.stevenot winery.com). Guests can sip the winery's signature chardonnay in the 1887 Shaw ranch house. Grapevines grow so close to the building, you'll be tempted to pick the grapes yourself. During the summer, Shakespearean plays are performed on the pretty lawn.

STORY WINERY (10525 Bell Rd, Plymouth; 209/245-6208; www.zin.com). Hundred-year-old Mission grapevines grow in the vineyards of this family-operated winery that produces Mission, zinfandel, and chenin blanc wines. The cabinlike tasting room and picnic area are dramatically perched above the Cosumnes River, offering visitors an exciting view of the canyon.

VILLA TOSCANO (106000 Shenandoah School House Rd; 209/245-3800; www.villatoscano.com). The faux-red-clay tasting room rises above the formal grounds of this Tuscan-style villa with two koi ponds, roses, and round mosaic cafe tables. This is one of the newest wineries in the region, and it produces barbera and sangiovese, among other wines.

crowded town and the Tuolumne County seat, with dozens of stores and small cafes lining the main thoroughfare. If you have time to spare, search for a parking space along Washington Street (no easy feat on weekends) or park in one of the lots a block east of Washington on Stewart Street, and take a look at the well-preserved 19th-century **ST. JAMES EPISCOPAL CHURCH,** at the top of Washington Street, and the **TUOLUMNE COUNTY MUSEUM AND HISTORY CENTER** (158 W Bradford St; 209/532-1317), located in the century-old jail. In the charming old lumber town of Standard, now part of East Sonora, is the **SNOWSHOE BREWING COMPANY** (19040 Standard Rd; 209/536-1445), housed in the spacious former office of the now-defunct Standard Lumber Company and serving up its own Grizzly Brown and ESB (Extra Special Blizzard) brews along with several specialty beers. If you have time to kill, take a leisurely drive along the picturesque **DETOUR ROUTE 108,** which heads west into the Sierra Nevada over **SONORA PASS** and through several scenic alpine communities.

RESTAURANTS

Banny's / ★★

83 S STEWART ST, SONORA; 209/533-4709 French innkeeper Bruno Trial at Barretta Gardens Inn (see review, below) not only sends his guests here, he and his wife, Sherri, often eat here themselves. The decor may be simple, but chef-owner Rob Bannworth's menu is quite sophisticated. He's a passionate cook who takes his sauces seriously, and you certainly can't complain about the reasonable prices for entrees such as pan-roasted duckling with apricot port wine sauce; spicy Moroccan lamb chops; grilled salmon topped with a wasabi ginger soy aioli sauce; and filet mignon grilled with roasted shiitake mushrooms, herb butter, and a red wine demi-glace. With entrees ranging from $11 to $15, you'll spend only about half of what you'd have to shell out in the Bay Area for fare of equal quality. Please note that service can be slow at times, so we don't recommend dining here if you're in a hurry. *$$; DIS, MC, V; checks OK; lunch Mon–Sat, dinner every day; beer and wine; reservations recommended; www.bannyscafe.com; in Old Town.*

LODGINGS

Barretta Gardens Inn / ★★

700 S BARRETTA ST, SONORA; 209/532-6039 OR 800/206-3333 There is always something blooming in the expansive gardens of native flowering shrubs surrounding this small country inn, which is perched on a hillside southeast of downtown Sonora. The wraparound porch is perfect for curling up with a good book (or your honey) in spring or autumn. Winter conversation takes place on soft sofas around the fireplace in the comfortable living room. The inn has five individually decorated guest rooms, and the most impressive is the pretty Odette room, fashioned after a late-18th-century Italian suite. All guest rooms come with fresh flowers, TVs and VCRs (and a library of 250 videos available for guests' use), soft terry-lined bathrobes, and small refrigerators stocked with beverages. Coffee, tea, and juice are delivered to your room at your convenience in the morning. Innkeepers Sally and Bruno Trial greet guests in the afternoon with beverages and treat them the following morning to a generous breakfast of apple puff pancakes, freshly baked French pastries prepared by Bruno, and fresh-squeezed juices—all served in the dining room or, when it's warm, on the screened-in breakfast porch. *$$–$$$; AE, MC, V; checks OK; barrettagardens@ hotmail.com; www.barrettagardens.com; a few blocks E of Washington St.*

Jamestown

Jamestown has been preoccupied with gold since the first fleck was taken out of Woods Creek in 1848; a marker even commemorates the discovery of a 75-pound nugget. For a fee, you can pan for gold at troughs on Main Street or go prospecting with a guide. But gold isn't Jamestown's only claim to fame. For decades, this four-block-long town lined with picturesque buildings has been Hollywood's favorite Western movie set: scenes from famous flicks like *Butch Cassidy and the Sundance Kid* were shot here, and vintage railway cars and steam locomotives used in such TV classics as *Little House on the Prairie, Bonanza,* and *High Noon* are on display at the **RAILTOWN 1897 STATE HISTORIC PARK** (5th Ave at Reservoir Rd, near the center of town; 209/984-3953; www.csrmf.org/railtown). You can view the vehicles at the roundhouse daily or ride the rails on weekends from April through October and during holiday events, such as the Santa Train ride in December.

RESTAURANTS

Michelangelo Ristorante Italiano / ★★

18228 MAIN ST, JAMESTOWN; 209/984-4830 For three years the town watched the large round Michelangelo's sign hang in front of its abandoned restaurant, a cruel reminder of the Italian dinners they had to go without. Then in 1999, Neal Parrish rode into town and reopened their beloved Michelangelo, saving the town from their painful marinara withdrawal. Locals from all over come to the region to sit beneath the white tin ceiling of this old Gold Rush–era building and just breathe in the divine aromas of the roasted garlic and marsala wine sauces. The most popular dishes on the menu are the chicken parmigiana, spaghetti bolognese, Cajun andouille pasta, and the pancetta-wrapped prawns appetizer. The pastas, salads, and thin-crust pizzas are also quite good and reasonably priced. Focaccia herb bread is served with all the entrees, and wines from the Gold Country are available from the bar at the side of the restaurant. *$$; AE, DIS, MC, V; checks OK; dinner Wed–Sun; full bar; reservations recommended; downtown.*

LODGINGS

The Historic National Hotel & Restaurant / ★★

18183 MAIN ST, JAMESTOWN; 209/984-3446 OR 800/894-3446 The restoration of the 1859 National Hotel was so impressive that both the Tuolumne Visitors Bureau and the Tuolumne County Lodging Association bestowed awards for its new look. The restorers of the nine guest rooms did an admirable job of blending 19th-century details (handmade quilts, lace curtains, brass beds) with 20th-century comforts (private bathrooms). The original Gold Rush saloon, with its handsome redwood bar, is the best place in town to eavesdrop on local gossip. A generous continental breakfast includes cereals, house-made muffins, hard-boiled eggs, fresh fruit, fresh-squeezed juices, coffee and tea, and the morning paper. Brunch, lunch, and dinner are served to the public in the handsome old-fashioned dining room, replete with antiques, old photos, and Gold Rush memorabilia. You'll find an extensive array of hearty steak, prime rib, chicken, seafood, and pasta dishes, as well as numerous fine wines from their award-winning wine list and house-made desserts. On sunny days or warm summer nights, ask for a table in the Garden Courtyard, draped by vines from a century-old grape arbor. *$$; AE, DC, DIS, MC, V; checks OK; info@national-hotel.com; www.national-hotel.com; downtown.*

Jamestown Hotel & Restaurant / ★★

18153 MAIN ST, JAMESTOWN; 209/984-3902 OR 800/205-4901 Built at the turn of the last century and converted into a hospital in the 1920s, this two-story brick charmer with its Western facade and wood veranda was transformed into one of the most authenic Gold Rush–era hotels in the Gold Country. The 11 engaging guest rooms—named after female Gold Rush personalities—are filled with antiques and luxuriously appointed with either claw-footed or whirlpool tubs, air conditioning, in-room hair dryers, and Turkish cotton bathrobes. The romantic Lotta Crabtree suite is furnished with lots of wicker, floral fabrics, a beautiful wrought-iron queen-size bed, and a claw-footed tub. A separate sitting room and claw-footed tub are part of the fiery Lola Montez suite, which is rumored to be haunted by the countess herself (more likely a ghostly impersonator, as no one can confirm that the lady ever stayed at the hotel). A full breakfast is included in the room rate. Downstairs is a classic Western-style bar that's worth a gander even if you're just passing through. The dining room is open Thursday through Monday for lunch and dinner, offering hearty dishes such as bacon-wrapped filet mignon, salmon steak poached in white wine, prime rib, and charbroiled rib eye with Yukon gold mashed potatoes. If you're staying for the weekend, be sure to attend the hotel's popular Sunday champagne brunch. *$$; AE, DC, DIS, MC, V; no checks; Info@JamestownHotel.com; www.jamestownhotel.com; downtown.* &

Mariposa

The town clock in the two-story **MARIPOSA COUNTY COURTHOUSE** (Bullion St between 9th and 10th Sts) has been marking time since 1866. Another town landmark is **ST. JOSEPH'S CATHOLIC CHURCH** (4985 Bullion St), built in 1863; and behind it lies the entrance to the **MARIPOSA MINE**, discovered by Kit Carson in 1849 and later purchased by John C. Frémont, who owned most of the land around these parts.

Two miles south of Mariposa at the Mariposa County Fairgrounds is the **CALIFORNIA STATE MINING AND MINERAL MUSEUM** (5007 Fairgrounds Rd; 209/742-7625), a state geology center with one of the country's finest collections of gems and minerals. One wing showcases 20,000 glittering gems and minerals; another holds artifacts and photos that tell California's mining story.

A side trip off Highway 49 leads to **HORNITOS** (Spanish for "little ovens"), a name that refers to the shape of the tombs on Boot Hill. This formerly lawless burg is nearly a ghost town, though it was once a favorite haunt of Gold Country bandito Joaquin Murieta, whose pickled head was turned over to state authorities in a glass jar for a $1,000 reward in 1853. Weathered old buildings (saloons, fandango halls, and gambling dens) stand around the plaza, some flaunting bullet holes from bygone battles.

RESTAURANTS

Charles Street Dinner House / ★★

5043 CHARLES ST, MARIPOSA; 209/966-2366 This 18-year-old landmark isn't as formal as its name might suggest. Rather, it's a place where the Old West reigns over decor, food, and service. The wait staff are dressed in period costume and look as though they just stepped out of the historic photos on the wall. Although the culinary offerings—steaks, chops, chicken, fresh seafood—are fairly common fare, they are skillfully prepared and well presented. Dinner specials might include broiled chicken breast, rack of lamb, duck, lobster, scampi, or prime rib, and all dinners are served with soup and salad. The 2,000-bottle wine cellar offers an impressive array of vintages. *$$; AE, DIS, MC, V; local checks only; dinner Wed–Sun; beer and wine; reservations recommended; www.charlesstreetdinnerhouse.com; Hwy 140 and 7th St.*

Ocean Sierra / ★★

3292 E WESTFALL RD, MARIPOSA; 209/742-7050 This little cabin in the woods is home to some of the best cuisine in the county. Dinner begins with a soup (the spicy gazpacho is fantastic) and a green salad served with a chilled fork. Entrees include lemon grilled prawns, New York pepper steak, a savory vegetarian stir-fry, and Australian lobster. Complete your meal with homemade ice cream, the oh-so-tasty So Slim Key Lime Cheesecake, or other desserts of the day. The restaurant, with its high pine ceiling, chipped-wood walls, brick fireplace, and white linen tablecloths, has the feel of a French inn in the mountains. Even the deer come by at dusk to graze on the lawn. *$$$; DIS, MC, V; checks OK; dinner Fri–Sun; beer and wine; reservations recommended; osierra@yosemite.net; www.yosemite.net/ocean sierra; at Triangle and E Westfall Rds.*

LODGINGS

Meadow Creek Ranch / ★★

2669 TRIANGLE RD, MARIPOSA; 209/966-3843 OR 800/853-2057 A stage stop in the 1850s, this refurbished ranch house is one of the most secluded bed-and-breakfasts in the Gold Country—a good choice for those looking for romantic solitude. There are only two guest rooms, each decorated in an Early American style. The Garden Gate Room, located in an annex to the main house with a private entrance, offers a queen-size bed, a twin bed in the alcove, sitting area, private bath, and a patio that overlooks the meadow. The cozy Country Cottage Room, a converted chicken coop—stay with us here—that has been beautifully decorated in mahogany, has a queen-size bed imported from Austria, a private bath with a claw-footed tub, and a sitting area. As you enjoy that early-morning cup of coffee, wander around the waterwheel and arbor or take a seat on the patio and soak in the scenic surroundings. A hearty breakfast is served family style in the ranch house's spacious dining room. *$$; AE, DIS, MC, V; checks OK; meadow creekranch@sierratel.com; www.sierranet.net/web/meadow; about 11½ miles S of Mariposa on Hwy 49.* &

Oakhurst

RESTAURANTS

Erna's Elderberry House / ★★★★

48688 VICTORIA LN, OAKHURST; 559/683-6800 Vienna-born Erna Kubin-Clanin selected this Oakhurst hillside in 1984 as the site for her now-famous restaurant and inn. The location is reminiscent of a corner of Provence, and, indeed, after indulging in one of her meals you'll think you've been transported to some European gastronomical paradise. Ever since the *New York Times* praised Erna's Elderberry House as "one of the most elegant and stylish restaurants in the nation," epicureans from around the world have made the pilgrimage to the elaborate Mediterranean-style dining room ensconced among pine trees and elderberry bushes. The prix-fixe dinner is a six-course affair that changes daily. A meal might begin with a grilled vegetable and goat cheese terrine, followed by chilled Yukon gold potato soup, then onto the main courses: Dungeness crab sandwich served with yucca root cake, avocado, and saffron aioli; foie gras–apricot spaetzle; or curry-roasted pork tenderloin. The sweet finale might be a caramelized banana-chocolate tart. Order a bottle of wine from sommelier Renée-Nicole Kubin's—yes, Erna's daughter—award-winning list to match the vintage to the course. If you prefer a more casual meal, the château's Restaurant-Cellar Bar offers a small bistro-style menu. Erna also runs the spectacular Château du Sureau (see review, below). *$$$$; AE, DIS, MC, V; no checks; dinner every day, brunch Sun; full bar; reservations recommended; chateaux@chateauxsureau.com; www.elderberryhouse.com; off Hwy 41, just W of town.* &

LODGINGS

Château du Sureau / ★★★★

48688 VICTORIA LN, OAKHURST; 559/683-6860 In 1991, when the opulent Château du Sureau was completed (*sureau* is French for "elderberry"), Erna Kubin-Clanin was able to offer her guests a magnificent place to stay after indulging in the exquisite cuisine at her Elderberry House (see review, above). Erna's desire for perfection doesn't stop in the kitchen, as you'll instantly notice once you see the château's massive chandeliers and 19th-century paintings, the cathedral windows framing grand Sierra views, and the imported tiles that complement the limestone in the baths. The 10 guest rooms come replete with goose-down comforters, canopy beds, antiques, Provençal fabrics, tapestries, fresh flowers, and a CD sound system. The elegant Thyme Room is designed to easily accommodate wheelchairs; the Mint Room has a private entrance for those seeking seclusion; and the Saffron Room has a breathtaking Napoleon III–era bedroom set made of ebony and inlaid ivory. A European-style breakfast is served to all château guests in the cozy breakfast room or alfresco on the patio. Elsewhere on the grounds lie a fountain, a swimming pool, and a giant outdoor chess court with 3-foot-tall pieces. There's even a tiny chapel where wedding bells occasionally ring. If you find the exquisite decor still too mundane for your tastes, you might be interested in the château's pièce de résistance—the Villa Sureau, a private two-bedroom, two-bath guest residence, featuring a salon, a library, and authentic antique furnishings and original artwork from the early 19th century. Outside the villa is a private Roman spa, where you can soak under the stars or receive a massage to relax all those muscles you used picking up the phone to call your butler. (Oh yes, the villa comes with a 24-hour butler.) If you feel you can do without the use of Jeeves, you are welcome to rent only half the villa. All this luxury comes at a price, of course. But the Elderberry House and Château du Sureau are one-of-a-kind Gold Country finds—and just about as precious and rare as those golden nuggets in the surrounding countryside. *$$$$; AE, MC, V; no checks; chateaux@chateauxsureau.com; www.chateaudusureau.com; off Hwy 41, just W of town.* &

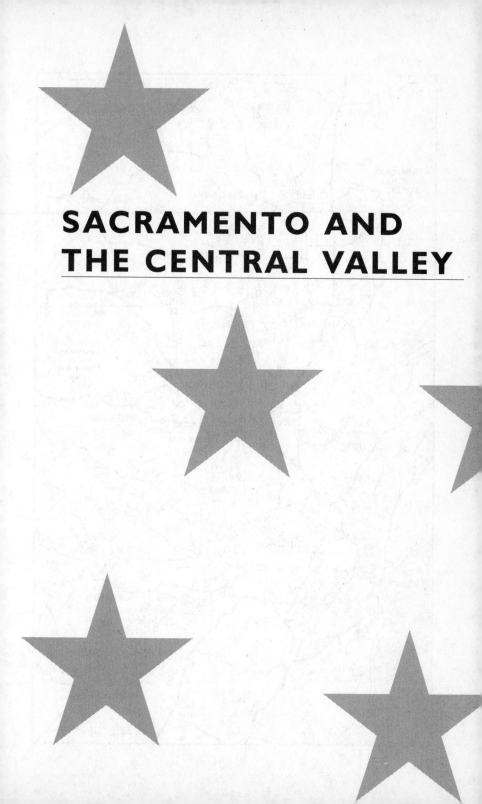

SACRAMENTO AND THE CENTRAL VALLEY

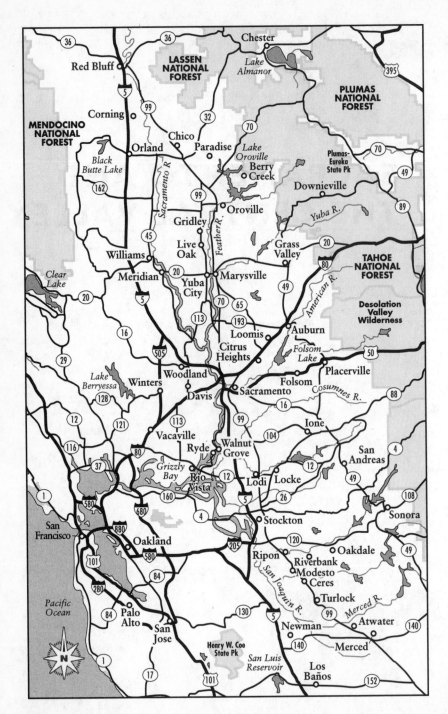

SACRAMENTO AND THE CENTRAL VALLEY

Here's a bit of trivia you probably didn't know: California's Central Valley is the largest expanse of flatland west of the Continental Divide—nearly 300 miles long and 50 miles wide. Stretching from Los Banos in the south to Red Bluff in the north, this mighty plain is bordered by the Sierra Nevada Mountains on the eastern flank and the Coast Ranges to the west. At the heart lies the capital city, Sacramento, the legislative pulse of the state. For the most part, the Central Valley is slightly above sea level, with the exception of the Sutter Buttes (the world's smallest mountain range), located just north of Sacramento, and the Sacramento River Delta, which is largely below sea level. Like a huge patchwork quilt, the Central Valley encompasses miles of farmland, orchards, and vineyards, stitched with irrigation canals, lakes, and rivers.

ACCESS AND INFORMATION

INTERSTATE 5 AND HIGHWAY 99 are the primary north-south routes through the Central Valley. Among the many east-west arteries are Highway 152 between Los Banos and Merced, and Highway 132 between the Altamont Pass and Modesto in the south, while to the north, Highway 20 serves as an artery from the foothills near Grass Valley to Clear Lake. Interstate 5 provides easy access to **SACRAMENTO INTERNATIONAL AIRPORT,** while Interstate 80 will take you east to the Reno/Lake Tahoe region or west to San Francisco. Through the Delta, Highway 12 is the major thoroughfare from 99 or Interstate 5, and from Sacramento, Highway 160 winds along the Sacramento River, across drawbridges and swing bridges, and is by far the most scenic. There is no public transportation system for the region (only within the cities), so it is best to explore this area by car. However, take notice that the Central Valley is often blanketed with thick fog during the winter months (December through February is the worst). Driving can be hazardous, and often flights are delayed at Sacramento's International Airport due to poor visibility. Always call the airline to confirm schedules, and for news on current road conditions throughout the Central Valley and the state, visit www.dot.ca.gov or call 800/427-ROAD.

Stockton and the South Central Valley

The communities between Los Banos and Stockton—some tiny, some rapidly developing (like Modesto)—are worth exploring. This region of the Central Valley can be defined as the east-west midway point between Yosemite National Park and the San Francisco Bay Area. Closer inspection, however, finds this agriculturally abundant area rich in history, cultural diversity, and small-town flavor.

Merced

Merced has claimed the title "Gateway to Yosemite" for more than a century, and the majority of its visitors are San Francisco Bay Area residents just passing through. Those who stop long enough to look around usually end up at **APPLEGATE PARK** (between M and R Sts), a 23-acre greenbelt with more than 60 varieties of trees, an immaculate rose garden, a small, free zoo, and, in the summer, amusement rides to whirl and twirl you and the kids. On Thursday evenings, local farmers sell their fresh produce from 6pm to 9pm on Main Street (between N and K Sts), a good place to buy picnic basket ingredients. One of the more interesting sights in the area is the **MERCED COUNTY COURTHOUSE MUSEUM** (21st and N Sts; 209/723-2401), the pride and joy of Merced and a monument to the early settlers of the great Central Valley.

RESTAURANTS

Branding Iron Restaurant / ★★

640 W 16TH ST, MERCED; 209/722-1822 This paean to the American Beef Council has satiated Mercedites for nearly half a century, thanks in part to chef Bob Freitas, who has presided over the kitchen for almost three decades. Owners Kara and Greg Parle have added to the Branding Iron's Old West ambiance by decorating its rough-hewn redwood walls with registered livestock brands from all over California. Dinner begins with soup and salad, followed by such carnivorous delights as a thick cut of choice prime rib seasoned with coarse-ground pepper, garlic, rosemary, and thyme, and a large baked potato with all the fixins. If your stomach (or waistline) will allow it, finish the evening with a sweet treat from the well-stocked dessert tray. *$$; AE, MC, V; local checks only; lunch Mon–Fri, dinner every day; full bar; reservations recommended; at W 16th and M Sts.* &

Atwater

RESTAURANTS

Out to Lunch / ★★

1301 WINTON WY, ATWATER; 209/357-1170 Word got out a long time ago about the superb, thick sandwiches that emerge from this little veranda-wrapped cottage. Almost anything piled between the warm, sweetly spiced slices of house-made zucchini bread is a good bet, including the crunchy veggie sandwich with cream cheese, cucumbers, bell peppers, shredded carrots, avocado, and sprouts. Other great choices are the English muffin topped with sautéed mushrooms, Jack cheese, and crumbled bacon or any of the house-made quiches. No alcohol is served here, but you're welcome to bring your own bottle of wine. If you're en route by car from Los Angeles to the Sacramento area (or vice versa), this is one of the best places for a lunch break—and it's just a minute away from the highway. *$; MC, V; checks OK; lunch Mon–Fri; no alcohol; no reservations; at Drakely St: from Hwy 99, take the Applegate exit.* &

Turlock

RESTAURANTS

El Jardín / ★★

409 E OLIVE ST, TURLOCK; 209/632-0932 True to its name, El Jardín has a fragrant, colorful flower garden surrounded by several outdoor tables—the place to sit when the weather is mild. The authentic south-of-the-border fare—all offered at south-of-the-border prices—includes such house specials as the Milanesa breaded beef fillet with fresh green salsa and the tender and tasty *pollo a la parilla* (grilled chicken breast). For *los niños* there are kid-size enchiladas, quesadillas, taquitos, burritos, and tostadas served with rice and beans. *$; V; no checks; lunch, dinner every day; beer and wine; reservations recommended; 1 block W of Golden State Blvd, 1 block N of Main St.* &

Modesto

RESTAURANTS

Hazel's / ★★

431 12TH ST, MODESTO; 209/578-3463 This popular continental restaurant has been around almost 40 years and is a favorite romantic weekend retreat for both residents and visitors in the Modesto area. Owner Jeff Morey, a graduate of the California Culinary Academy, maintains original owner Hazel Saylor's time-honored menu, featuring dishes as simple as liver and onions topped with sautéed mushrooms and as deluxe as the Australian lobster tail. Hazel's version of cannelloni, stuffed with seasoned veal, chicken, and mushrooms, is still a lunchtime favorite. The wine list is well edited and reasonably priced, with several selections available by the glass. *$$–$$$; AE, DC, DIS, MC, V; local checks only; lunch Tues–Fri, dinner Tues–Sat; full bar; reservations recommended; jeffhazel@softcom.net; www.hazelsmodesto.com; corner of 12th and E Sts.* &

Tresetti's World Caffe / ★★

927 11TH ST, MODESTO; 209/572-2990 Located a few blocks from City Hall, this popular hangout attracts a steady gaggle of lawyers, lobbyists, politicians, and other professionals who congregate at the stylish galvanized steel and polished-wood wine bar. The adjacent high-ceilinged dining room is equally chic, with its burgundy drapes, matching cement floor, pale yellow walls, glass facade overlooking downtown Modesto, and only a dozen tables. The chef strives for a global culinary theme, focusing on classic dishes from around the world. Offerings range from baked Moroccan chicken with currant couscous and a curry-lime yogurt, to potato-encrusted Australian lamb loin with Shiraz balsamic demi-glace and a cilantro-lime-Dijon aioli on roasted garlic mashed potatoes. Tresetti's also has a large assortment of single-malt whiskeys and ports. *$$; AE, DC, DIS, MC, V; checks OK; lunch, dinner Mon–Sat; full bar; reservations recommended; www.tresetti.com; corner of 11th and J Sts.* &

LODGINGS

Doubletree Hotel Modesto / ★

1150 9TH ST, MODESTO; 209/526-6000 OR 800/222-TREE Towering 14 stories above the Modesto landscape, the Doubletree is the Central Valley's premier business/luxury accommodation. Guests are pampered with such amenities as a spa, sauna, sundeck, heated outdoor pool, weight room, restaurant, two bars, and extensive conference facilities. Each of the 258 comfortable guest rooms (including 6 suites) are equipped with a TV, three telephones with a fax/PC data port and direct inward dialing, a king- or queen-size bed, a separate desk and table, a coffeemaker, an iron and ironing board, and a hair dryer. A free shuttle will whisk you to the Modesto airport; if you have your own wheels, take advantage of the free parking in the sheltered lot. *$$$; AE, DC, DIS, MC, V; checks OK; www.doubletree hotels.com; at K St.* &

Oakdale

Sitting on Highway 120, en route to Yosemite, this "Cowboy Capital of the World" is the home of the **OAKDALE COWBOY MUSEUM** (355 East F St; 209/847-7049), which houses items from world-renowned rodeo champions. Succulent lovers—and who isn't?—shouldn't miss **POOT'S HOUSE OF CACTUS** (on the way to Oakdale, 5 miles E of Hwy 99; 17229 E Hwy 120; 209/599-7241)—a bristling collection of cactus and unusual plants from around the world. Another town highlight is the **SATURDAY OAKDALE LIVESTOCK AUCTION** (6001 Albers Rd; 209/847-1033). Just be careful not to scratch your nose—you could become the dumbstruck new owner of a 600-pound Black Angus.

RESTAURANTS

H-B Saloon and Bachi's Family Restaurant / ★

401 EAST F ST, OAKDALE; 209/847-2985 For a real Central Valley experience, don your shit-kickers and cowboy hat and head for the H-B Saloon, a decidedly funky old bar and restaurant festooned with faded photos of ranches and rodeos, mounted game, old-fashioned tack, branded wainscoting, and other mementos of ranching life. During any time of the day or night you'll find aging cattlemen in baseball caps and cowboy hats playing shuffleboard or poker in the saloon, drinking $1.75 beers, listening to Johnny Cash on the jukebox, and doing their best to ignore the occasional wayward tourist. Dinner, served family-style in the adjacent Bachi's Restaurant, will satisfy even the hungriest cowboy: choose from rib-eye steak, pork chops, lamb chops, chicken, baby back ribs, halibut, and prime rib. Each inexpensive meal includes red wine, soup, salad, French fries, bread, beans, and potato salad. *$; AE, DIS, MC, V; local checks only; lunch Mon–Fri, dinner Wed–Sat; full bar; no reservations; next to the Hershey Visitors Center.* &

Stockton

The birthplace of Caterpillar tractor inventor Benjamin Holt, and heartthrob rock star Chris Isaak, and summer home of the San Francisco 49ers, Stockton used to be a simple, blue-collar town. In 1999, it was chosen as an All-American City by the National Civic League. A multicultural blend of European, Mexican, and Asian immigrants who own businesses and provide services and labor in this agriculturally abundant region make diversity a watchword here. Some 75 languages are spoken within the city limits.

For a taste of regional history and fine art, a visit to the **HAGGIN MUSEUM** (1201 N Pershing Ave; 209/940-6300; www.hagginmuseum.org) is a must. Maestro Peter Jaffe conducts the innovative **STOCKTON SYMPHONY** (209/951-0196; www.stockton symphony.org) along with high-caliber guest artists. The **STOCKTON CIVIC THEATRE** (2312 Rose Marie Ln; 209/473-2424; www.california mall.com/SCT/) puts on affordable, quality productions, and the historic **FOX THEATRE** (242 E Main; 209/462-2694; www.stocktongov.com/foxtheatre/) is the place to see big-name performers.

On those scorching summer days, what better way to cool off than a trip to the **OAK PARK ICE ARENA** (3545 Alvarado St; 209/937-7433). The **CHILDREN'S MUSEUM OF STOCKTON** (402 W Weber Ave; 209/465-4386; www.stockton gov.com/childrensmuseum/) is a hands-on discovery and learning center for kids as well as parents. **MICKE GROVE PARK & ZOO** (11793 N Micke Grove Rd, take the Eight-Mile Rd exit from Hwy 99; 209/331-7270; www.mgzoo.com) is shaded by huge oak trees—a great place to picnic. It also features a zoo known for its endangered species breeding program, a golf course, a driving range, Japanese gardens, and a small amusement park for the younger ones. For a rundown on the agricultural history of the San Joaquin Valley, check out the **SAN JOAQUIN COUNTY HISTORICAL MUSEUM** (located inside Micke Grove Park; 209/331-2055; www.sanjoaquinhistory.org).

From May through October the **STOCKTON CERTIFIED FARMERS MARKETS** (209/943-1830) offer superb local produce and are held Thursday through Sunday mornings at various locations around town. And speaking of produce, the annual **STOCKTON ASPARAGUS FESTIVAL** (Oak Grove Regional Park, Eight-Mile Rd exit off I-5), held every fourth weekend in April, has grown into one of the most popular food and entertainment events in Northern California. This three-day event features more than 50 entertainers, gourmet asparagus dishes, a wine and beer pavilion, a classic car show, a 5K run, and more, all celebrating—you guessed it—asparagus. For more information on this event or other activities in the Stockton area, call the **SAN JOAQUIN CONVENTION AND VISITORS BUREAU** (46 W Fremont St; 800/350-1987; www.visitstockton.com).

RESTAURANTS

Ernie's on the Brick Walk / ★★

296 LINCOLN CENTER N, STOCKTON; 209/951-3311 In 1994, chef-owner Warren K. Ito moved his Ernie's Pasta Barn from the country northeast of Stockton to this brick walk location, tucked among the coffeehouses and gift shops of Lincoln Center North. Ernie's concise menu still reflects quality as opposed to quantity (that applies to portions as well). For starters try the polenta Castello, topped with melted blue cheese, sautéed mushrooms, and marsala sauce. The mixed mushroom fusilli is tossed with a light roasted garlic–cream sauce with shiitake, oyster, portobello, and porcini mushrooms. If you're craving something more filling, try the New Zealand lamb chops with kalamata olive and rosemary soubise. The restaurant also offers nightly specials and an impressive wine list with the largest selection of ports in the area. *$$; AE, DIS, MC, V; no checks; lunch Mon–Fri, dinner every day; full bar; reservations recommended; center of Lincoln Center N at Benjamin Holt Dr.* &

Sho Mi Japanese Cuisine / ★★

419 LINCOLN CENTER, STOCKTON; 209/951/3525 When you go to Sho Mi, whether for lunch or dinner, be prepared to stand in line. After expanding the place once in 1999, Shoji Akai and his team of talented sushi chefs and prep cooks continue to pack 'em in at this unassuming Japanese restaurant. Akai, the proprietor, a 1994 transplant from Shiba City, Japan, has been creating artistic delicacies for more than two decades. Order first and wait for a table, or seat yourself at the L-shaped sushi bar and observe the efficiency of this extremely popular eatery. Try the spicy shrimp eel roll or one of the daily specials. If sushi is not your thing, the ginger pork or chicken combines tender pieces of browned meat with zucchini and mushrooms in a potent ginger-teriyaki sauce. The combination plates are guaranteed to satisfy even the biggest appetites. Everything at Sho Mi is consistently fresh and flavorful, the portions are generous, and drinks (nonalcoholic) are included with all meals over $5.75. *$; cash only; lunch, dinner Mon–Sat; beer and wine; no reservations; SW corner of Lincoln Center at Benjamin Holt Dr.* &

Lodi

For more than a century, vineyards have thrived in Lodi. Situated just east of the fertile Sacramento River Delta and west of the Sierra Nevada foothills, with alluvial soil, abundant water, warm days, and cool nights (thanks to the Delta breezes), Lodi is geographically ideal for growing wine grapes. Check out the **LODI GRAPE FESTIVAL AND HARVEST FAIR** (209/369-2771; www.lodifestival.com), held each third weekend in September. The **DISCOVER LODI! WINE AND VISITOR'S CENTER** (2545 Turner Rd; 209/367-4727; www.lodiwine.com) is a great place to pick up a map and learn more about Lodi-area wines and wineries.

RESTAURANTS

Wine and Roses Country Inn / ★★★

2505 TURNER RD, LODI; 209/334-6988 Talented chef John Hitchcock, a graduate of the world-renowned Culinary Institute of America in Hyde Park, New York, consistently presents delectable creations with attention to detail at this 1902 homestead estate (listed with the San Joaquin County Historical Society). For lunch, try the classic Caesar salad or the grilled boneless quail with warm poblano peppers and sweet corn salad. The dinner menu will tempt you with grilled New York steak with truffle mashed potatoes, *haricots verts,* and Madeira sauce, or grilled hen duck breast, marinated and served with Asian greens, five-spice sauce, jasmine rice, and crispy duck spring rolls. Order a bottle of one of the increasingly popular Lodi wines to round out the meal. Be sure to leave room for dessert, such as the Madagascar vanilla poached pear wrapped in puff pastry with vanilla-bean crème anglaise and a port wine reduction. The inn hosts special events including musical and theatrical productions in the garden between June and September. During these affairs a grand buffet is served in place of the regular menu, and reservations are required. *$$; AE, DC, DIS, MC, V; checks OK; lunch and dinner daily, breakfast Sat, brunch Sun; full bar; reservations required; www.winerose.com; 5 miles E of I-5, 2 miles W of Hwy 99, at Turner and Lower Sacramento Rds.* &

LODGINGS

Wine and Roses Country Inn / ★★★

2505 W TURNER RD, LODI; 209/334-6988 Martha Stewart and former British prime minister Lady Margaret Thatcher are among the guests who've signed the register at this tasteful country inn situated on 5 acres of towering 100-year-old deodar cedars, cherry trees, and beautifully landscaped gardens. The 1902 estate, owned and operated by Del and Sherri Smith and their partners Russ and Kathryn Munson, has recently expanded. Included in this $5 million project are the Discover Lodi! Wine & Visitor's Center (see above); 36 new rooms, each with private courtyard entries, spa tubs, fireplaces, large televisions, garden verandas, and room service; two 5,000-square-foot banquet facilities; a spa and therapy center; a flower shop; a pool; a Jacuzzi; a large catering kitchen; and a small cafe. The 10 original rooms (named after songs) have queen-size beds, turn-of-the-century decor, and handmade comforters. In the rose-toned sitting room, camelback couches and wing chairs are clustered around a wide fireplace that's always ablaze in the winter. Guests are treated to evening wine and a gourmet breakfast served in the popular restaurant, located on the ground floor. *$$–$$$; AE, DC, DIS, MC, V; checks OK; www.winerose.com; 5 miles E of I-5, 2 miles W of Hwy 99; at Turner and Lower Sacramento Rds.* &

SACRAMENTO AREA THREE-DAY TOUR

DAY ONE: Just like old times. After breakfast at the **FOX AND GOOSE**, start your first day in Old Sacramento with a stop at the visitor center on Second Street; pick up a map of attractions. Spend some time exploring the **CALIFORNIA STATE RAILROAD MUSEUM**, for an understanding of how the railroads shaped California history. Browse the rest of **OLD SACRAMENTO** by foot, or consider a **PADDLE WHEEL SIGHTSEEING CRUISE** (916/552-2933 or 800/433-0263) aboard either the historic *Spirit of Sacramento* or the *Matthew McKinley*. Wander over to the **RIO CITY CAFE** for lunch with a view of the river, on the deck, weather permitting. If you're ready for more history, don't miss the **CROCKER ART MUSEUM**, or if you've got small kids along, visit the **SACRAMENTO ZOO** and the adjacent **FAIRY TALE TOWN AND FUNDERLAND** amusement park. When you're ready to kick back, board the *Delta King* and head for the fourth-floor lounge for an early-evening aperitif and view of the sunset. Lodging at the centrally located **STERLING HOTEL** is highly recommended. Enjoy tonight's dinner at **PARAGARY'S BAR AND OVEN**.

DAY TWO: State of the arts. Begin today with breakfast and people-watching at the **TOWER CAFE** (1518 Broadway; 916/441-0222). You may be interested to know you're sitting in the birthplace of Tower Records. Choose a table on the green outdoor patio, space and weather permitting. Then head over to **SUTTER'S FORT** and the **CALIFORNIA STATE INDIAN MUSEUM**. Arrive at the Pavilions Shopping Mall before the lunch crowd for a remarkable deli experience at **DAVID BERKLEY**. Dine there and browse the small, but interesting shopping center, or pack a picnic and head for **CAPITOL PARK** for lunch under the huge trees. From here, take the **STATE CAPITOL TOUR** (free), then walk to the poignant **CALIFORNIA VIETNAM**

Sacramento and the Delta Region

Five rivers, 57 islands, and 1,000 miles of navigable waterways make up the Sacramento River Delta, which is easily mistaken at high tide for a vast inland lake. It's the largest estuary on the West Coast, touching six counties and containing half the freshwater runoff in California. After the completion of the Transcontinental Railroad in 1869, a workforce of some 10,000 Chinese laborers began work on the levee system, reclaiming the fertile farmland. Today's Delta is dotted with old-fashioned island towns—from Rio Vista to the tiny hamlets just south of Sacramento—connected by drawbridges, ferries, and winding levee roads. For a true Delta experience, rent a houseboat and cruise this labyrinth of waterways for a few days. **HOUSEBOAT, SKI-BOAT, AND WAVE-RUNNER RENTALS** are available several miles north of Stockton at **HERMAN AND HELEN'S MARINA** (off I-5, at the W end of Eight-Mile Rd; 209/951-4634; www.houseboats.com) and **PARADISE POINT MARINA** (8095

VETERANS MEMORIAL. For dinner with music (Spanish classical and flamenco guitar), try **TAPA THE WORLD**, or for a wonderfully elegant and exotic meal, try Sacramento's famous **LEMON GRASS**.

DAY THREE: Cruisin' country roads. After breakfast at **33RD STREET BISTRO**, leave the city for a tour of the rural levee roads of the **SACRAMENTO RIVER DELTA** and the century-old vineyards of Lodi. From Sacramento, take scenic Highway 160 S through Freeport and Hood. Explore the tiny town of **LOCKE**, built by Chinese immigrants in 1915. Have lunch at the popular **ORILLA DEL RIO** in Walnut Grove. Cross the Sacramento River just past town and head south. If it's the weekend, visit the **LEVEE GALLERY** (14151 River Rd, Walnut Grove; 916/776-1282), displaying peaceful Delta landscapes captured on canvas by local artist Marty Stanley, and don't miss the **RYDE HOTEL**, a former boardinghouse/speakeasy. Turn west between the gallery and the Ryde Hotel and head toward the **GRAND ISLAND MANSION** (13415 Grand Island Rd, Walnut Grove; 916/775-1706), a 1917 Italian Renaissance–style inn with lush gardens. Just south of the mansion, hop on the **J-MACK FERRY** (free) and cross Steamboat Slough. Turn left and follow the water to the next ferry crossing—the *Real McCoy*. This ferry (also free) takes you across Cache Slough, where you disembark just a few miles from the town of **RIO VISTA**. On Highway 12, head east toward Lodi, driving over drawbridges and through patchworks of sunflowers, vineyards, and corn. Between Interstate 5 and Lodi, stop in at **MICHAEL DAVIS FARM** and again at the **VAN RUITEN FAMILY WINERY** (340 W Hwy 12; 209/334-5722) to sample or purchase some of Lodi's respected and popular varietals. Finish the long day with a relaxing dinner and pampered lodging at Lodi's **WINE AND ROSES COUNTRY INN**.

Rio Blanco; 209/952-1000 or 800/752-9669; www.paradisepointmarina.com). If you'd rather explore by car, keep in mind that many folks miss the beauty of the Delta as they speed along the rivers of highway that bisect this unique and delicate ecosystem. Slow down, relax a bit, and get on "Delta time."

Rio Vista

This slow-paced Delta town, located at the junction of Highways 12 and 160, is considered by many to be the heart of the Delta. With a population of 5,000, its residents include speed demon Craig Breedlove—former land-speed record holder—and Dennis Hope of Lunar Embassy–Celestial Property Sales, who can sell you a piece of property anywhere in the universe. There's not much to do in town—the river is the main attraction here—although you might check out the **RIO VISTA MUSEUM** (16 N Front St; 707/374-5169; weekends only) for a rundown on the history of farming and dredging in the area. Even if you don't have the nerve to eat at **FOSTER'S BIGHORN** (143 Main St; 707/374-2511), it's worth a peek. This stuffy bar and restaurant displays some 300 wild game trophies from Bill Foster's private collection, including a full-grown bull elephant—complete with ivory tusks—and a giraffe (who could shoot a giraffe?). Humphrey the wayward humpback whale cruised this part of the river back in 1985 (good thing Foster was already dead), and there's a stone monument to Humphrey on the waterfront, adjacent to city hall.

Isleton

Once the asparagus capital of the world and an original stop for the *Delta King* river boat, Isleton today is known as **CRAWDAD TOWN USA**—home of the Crawdad Festival each Father's Day weekend (www.isletoncoc.org/crawdad.htm). This sleepy little town on Highway 160 has a sense of humor (the local bait shop is the "Master-Baiter") and a Chinatown, where decrepit buildings stand beside refurbished ones.

RESTAURANTS

Riverboat II / ★★

106 W BRANNAN ISLAND RD, ISLETON; 916/777-6972 High ceilings and a nautical theme set the mood for this casual-yet-stylish floating restaurant. Formerly Moore's Riverboat (which burned in 1993), Riverboat II, located on the scenic "Delta loop," offers fine dining, excellent service, and a pretty good wine list. New owner Gary Cammack specializes in Italian cooking, offering a variety of freshly prepared pasta dishes and veal specialties; he also serves well-prepared versions of the tried-and-true that patrons keep coming back for: fresh fish, prawns, and scallops, along with a half-dozen cuts of tender beef. If you just want to hang out for a while in a pleasant river setting, there are plenty of appetizers to nosh on, including prawn, shrimp, and crab cocktails; fried calamari or fried mushrooms; zucchini sticks; and hot wings Cajun-style. $$; AE, MC, V; *local checks only; lunch Mon–Sat, dinner every day, brunch Sun; full bar; reservations recommended; www.riverboat2.com; 3.5 miles off Hwy 12.* &

Ryde

RESTAURANTS

The Ryde Hotel / ★★

14340 HWY 160, RYDE; 916/776-1318 OR 888/717-RYDE Walk past the lively fountain, under the black awning, and into another era. This art deco–themed restaurant with its grand piano and black-lacquered bar will transport you to a day when liquor was illegal and grand steamships regularly cruised this part of the Sacramento River. Look out over the golf course through expansive windows, or watch the sunset paint magenta hues along the river as you dine alfresco. The menu showcases fresh local ingredients, and dinner entrees are elegant in both taste and presentation. Try the andouille sausage and prawns, sautéed with white wine, bell peppers, and onions and finished with roasted tomato sauce and seared polenta. Complement your dinner with a glass of the highly regarded Bogle chardonnay—the vineyards are just upriver in Clarksburg. There's live jazz on Saturday nights, and if you plan to partake of the extremely popular Sunday brunch, bring your appetite and make sure you have reservations. *$$–$$$; AE, DIS, MC, V; no checks; dinner Fri–Sat (Apr–Nov), brunch Sun; full bar; reservations required; rydehotel@hotmail.com; www.rydehotel.com; 3 miles S of Walnut Grove on the W bank of the Sacramento River.* ♿

LODGINGS

The Ryde Hotel / ★★

14340 HWY 160, RYDE; 916/776-1318 OR 888/717-RYDE Originally built as a boardinghouse, this four-story peach stucco inn on the banks of the Sacramento River became famous as a speakeasy during Prohibition, when steamers and paddleboats brought crowds of city folk in search of jazz and illicit liquor. The Ryde attracted movie stars, politicians, and presidents: Herbert Hoover announced his candidacy here in 1940. In 1997, the hotel changed hands and underwent major renovations. The new owners, Jan LeRoy and Cathy Hartrich, have managed to maintain the original historic design while integrating modern amenities. The hotel now has 32 guest rooms decorated in a 1920s art deco style with a mauve, gray, and black color scheme. The two master suites offer sweeping views and are furnished with antique armoires and large Jacuzzi tubs that overlook the river. Two golf suites face the executive nine-hole golf course, which winds through a stately pear orchard. Four of the rooms exemplify the original European-style accommodations, with shared bathroom facilities. Continental breakfast is included and is served in the salon or outside on one of the patios. (The Ryde's trendy restaurant, located inside the main entrance facing the river, is open on weekends.) Hotel and restaurant guests may arrive by car or tie their vessels at the private boat dock. *$$–$$$; MC, V; checks OK; rydehotel@hotmail.com; www.rydehotel.com; 3 miles S of Walnut Grove.*

Walnut Grove

RESTAURANTS

Orilla del Rio / ★★

14133 MARKET ST, WALNUT GROVE; 916/776-2007 This family-owned restaurant pumps out the best Mexican food in the Delta. Meals seem to be health-conscious, so if you order wisely, your cholesterol count won't skyrocket too seriously. Try the chile-lime chicken wings for starters and the alligator tacos for something totally different. The chile verde, made with lean pork, is very good. A variety of house-made salsas are always available at the salsa bar, and if you're really not watching that cholesterol, finish off your meal with an order of the delightfully rich flan. *$; no credit cards; checks OK; breakfast Sun, lunch Tues–Fri and Sun, dinner Tues–Sun; beer and wine; no reservations; 1 block E of Hwy 160.* ♿

Locke

The town of Locke was established in 1915, soon after a devastating fire destroyed the neighboring Chinese community of Walnut Grove. Since Asian Americans at that time couldn't legally own property, a committee of Chinese merchants led by (Charlie) Lee Bing approached landowner George Locke and persuaded him to allow a new community to be built on his land. Chinese architects designed Lockeport, which became Locke as it exists today. At one time this hamlet claimed more than 600 permanent residents. Businesses flourished, including illicit activities that thrived in the form of gambling houses, brothels, speakeasies, and opium dens.

Locke was also the educational center for the region. The Joe Shoong Chinese School was built in 1926, with funding from Joe Shoong, the millionaire who founded National Dollar Stores. Shoong endorsed Chinese language, art, and culture in schools built specifically for Chinese youth. Located at the north end of town, the school is still in use today and is open for public viewing. Next door, **YUEN CHONG MARKET,** established in 1916 by a Chinese cooperative, stocks a wide selection of cold drinks. Today, you can wander Locke's Main Street and easily imagine what it must have been like in the days of Prohibition. Notice the worn wooden sidewalks; like the town, they seem warped in time. Visit the **DAI LOY GAMBLING HOUSE MUSEUM,** and step into **AL THE WOP'S,** Lee Bing's original restaurant. For information regarding a guided tour of Locke, given by a resident historian, stop in at **LOCKE ART CENTER** (916/776-1661).

RESTAURANTS

Al the Wop's / ★

13943 MAIN ST, LOCKE; 916/776-1800 Al Adami bought this former Chinese restaurant in 1934. When Al died in 1961, his bartender, Ralph Santos Sr., took over this venerable and legendary Delta institution. Ralph, in turn, was succeeded by his son in 1981, who changed the name of this restaurant to Al's Place—a more politically correct moniker. Alas, the name change didn't go over too well, in part because people drove the phone company crazy asking for "Al the Wop's" and got very surly when the name didn't come up in the database. In 1995, Ralph's nephews, Lorenzo and Steve Giannetti, took over the place and, by popular demand, reinstated the old name. Everything else here remains pretty much the same. The low-ceilinged dining room in the back of the building is furnished with long tables and benches—just as it was in the '30s. The food is simple but adequate, and the assorted tourists, boaters, and local characters who hang out here like it that way. For lunch, try Al's traditional steak or chicken dishes or one of the newer menu items: hamburgers and cheeseburgers. Tuesdays and Fridays are steak and lobster nights; otherwise, Al's dinners are limited to chicken and New York steaks (12 or 18 ounces) served with a side of spaghetti or French fries and maybe a bowl of homemade minestrone. $; *no credit cards; checks OK; lunch, dinner every day; full bar; no reservations; middle of Main St.*

Sacramento

Heart and center of the Central Valley and capital city of the state, Sacramento has long been regarded as the second-class stepsister of San Francisco. But with its increasing number of skyscrapers, upscale restaurants, and swanky hotels (as well as the NBA's Sacramento Kings, the women's NBA Sacramento Monarchs, and Class AAA baseball's Rivercats), California's capital city is no longer the sleepy little valley town folks whiz through on their way to Lake Tahoe. Located 90 miles northeast of the Bay Area, the city is best known for its dual status as the seat of state government and the epicenter of California's biggest industry—agriculture. But disregard any disparaging words you may have heard about this fertile hot spot: there are no cows (or even cowboy hats) within city limits, and most of the city slickers don't pick tomatoes for a living.

A former Gold Rush boomtown, Sacramento sprang up where the American and Sacramento Rivers meet—a tourist area now known as Old Sacramento. In 1839 Swiss immigrant John Sutter traversed both waterways, built his famous fort, and established his colony called New Helvetia (New Switzerland). But his hopes that the thriving colony would evolve into his own vast empire were dashed when gold was discovered up near his sawmill in 1848. Sutter's colonists deserted New Helvetia to search for the precious nuggets, and as word of the discovery spread, thousands more wound their way to the hills above Sacramento to seek their fortune. Ironically, Sutter himself never prospered from the Gold Rush, and he died a bitter, penniless man.

Today, Sacramento is home to more than a million people, many of who play politics with the capital crowd or practice law. They dote on their spectacular Victorian homes and fine Craftsman-style bungalows, and are justly proud of the tree-lined streets and thick carpets of grass that surround their houses and parks.

In the scorching summer months, when thermometers often soar above three digits for days, many folks beat the heat by diving into swimming pools, chugging around the Delta on a houseboat, or floating down the American River in a raft or inner tube. Once the sun sets, however, things usually cool off dramatically. Winters are punctuated by the famous tule fog—so thick it can block the sun for weeks at a time. But as all ski buffs know, Sacramentans get the jump on their Bay Area neighbors racing to the snowy slopes of Tahoe, thanks to the city's proximity to the Sierra Nevada.

ACCESS AND INFORMATION

Conveniently located just 15 minutes north of downtown, the **SACRAMENTO INTERNATIONAL AIRPORT** is easily accessible from Interstate 5. **SUPERSHUTTLE** Sacramento (www.supershuttle.com; 800/BLUE-VAN) provides door-to-door service, while taxi and van service is available 24 hours a day from **SACRAMENTO INDEPENDENT TAXI** (916/457-4862) and **YELLOW CAB** (916/444-2222). **AMTRAK'S CAPITOL ROUTES** (5th and I Sts; 800/872-7245; www.amtrak.com) connect Sacramento and the Bay Area several times a day. **CITY BUS** and **LIGHT RAIL** service is operated by **SACRAMENTO REGIONAL TRANSIT DISTRICT** (916/321-BUSS), and the **GREYHOUND** terminal (7th and L Sts; 800/231-2222) is open 24 hours and can connect you to just about anywhere. By car, Interstate 5 and US Highway 99 reach Sacramento on the north-south route; Interstate 80 is a direct route from the Bay Area, and US Highway 50 will get you there from Lake Tahoe/Reno. Once downtown, it's nice to know that the "lettered" city streets (C–Z) run from north to south, with M Street also being known as Capitol, and the "numbered" streets (2nd–29th) run west to east, with First Street referred to as Front Street due to its location on the waterfront. **PARKING** can be a challenge along the streets, so look for the large public lots, which usually have spaces available. For more information, contact the **SACRAMENTO CONVENTION AND VISITORS BUREAU** (1303 J St, Ste 600; 916/264-7777; wwwdiscovergold.org) or drop in at the **VISITOR INFORMATION CENTER** (1002 2nd St; 916/442-7644), located in Old Sacramento.

MAJOR ATTRACTIONS

To best appreciate this thriving city, visit **OLD SACRAMENTO** (a.k.a. Old Sac), the historic district. Perched along the Sacramento River, this four-block-long stretch is filled with dozens of restaurants, gift shops, and saloons. An Old Sac highlight is the **CALIFORNIA STATE RAILROAD MUSEUM** (125 I St at 2nd St; 916/323-9280; www.californiastaterailroadmuseum.org), a grand monument to the glory days of locomotion and the Big Four; it's the largest museum of its kind in the nation. The granddaddy of Old Sac attractions is the **SACRAMENTO JAZZ JUBILEE,** the world's largest jazz festival, which attracts thousands of toe-tappers and bands from around the world each Memorial Day weekend (916/372-5277; www.sacjazz.com). One mile south of this historic district is the **TOWE AUTO MUSEUM** (2200 Front St; 916/442-6802; www.toweautomuseum.org), which displays over 150 classic, vintage, and collector cars. Nearby is the **CROCKER ART MUSEUM** (216 O St at 3rd St; 916/264-5423; www.crockerartmuseum.org), home of the region's largest art collection, including stunning European master drawings and contemporary California art by local talents who made the big time, such as Wayne Thiebaud and Robert Arneson. **LA RAZA GALLERIA POSADA** (1720 15th St; 916/446-5133; www.galleria posada.org) is a Chicano, Latino, and indigenous American arts center located in a beautifully restored warehouse. Within this complex are a cultural center, a contemporary art gallery, a bookstore, and a gift shop stocked with wonderful Mexican/Latin American folk art.

A few blocks northeast of the gallery is the awe-inspiring **STATE CAPITOL** (10th St, between L and N Sts; 916/324-0333; www.capitolmuseum.ca.org), restored in the 1970s to its original turn-of-the-century magnificence with $67.8 million in taxpayers' dollars (so come see what you paid for). You may wander around the building on your own, but you really shouldn't miss the free tours given daily every hour between 9am and 4pm. Tours include an overview of the legislative process and, if you're lucky, a chance to see the political hotshots in action—including, of course, Arnold and Maria, Sacramento's newest tourist attractions. Tickets are handed out a half hour before the tour on a first-come, first-served basis in the basement of room B-27 in the capitol. While you're getting your tickets, pick up a copy of the **STATE CAPITOL TREE TOUR** brochure so you can saunter through marvelous **CAPITOL PARK** and admire more than 340 varieties of trees from around the world.

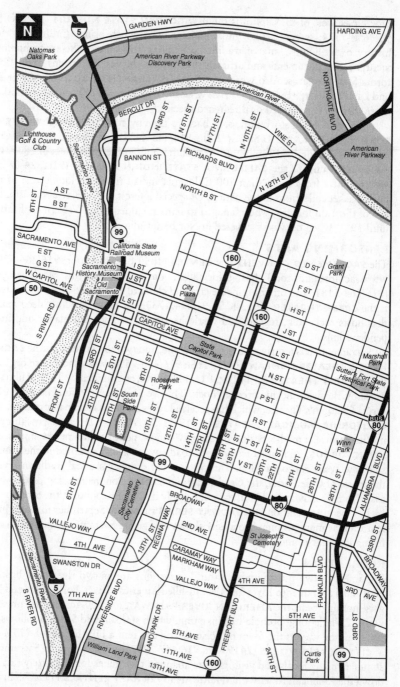

DOWNTOWN SACRAMENTO

One block west of the capitol is the new **GOLDEN STATE MUSEUM** (1020 O St; 916/653-7524; www.ss.ca.gov/museum/intro.htm) which brings California's rich history to life with a mix of traditional exhibits and state-of-the-art technology incorporating documents and artifacts drawn from the vast collections of the California State Archives. Also worth a visit, the **SACRAMENTO ZOO** (Sutterville Rd and Land Park Dr; 916/264-5888; www.saczoo.com) houses 400 animals, including more than 40 endangered or threatened species.

If you're a big history buff, step back in time by strolling through **SUTTER'S FORT** (between K and L Sts, at 27th; 916/445-4422), where you can view the restored, self-contained community that Sutter built in the wilderness in 1839. On the same grounds is the **CALIFORNIA STATE INDIAN MUSEUM** (916/324-0539), with artifacts from more than 100 California Indian tribes, including one of the finest basket collections in the nation. Of special interest is a display about Ishi, the last of the Yahi Indians, who managed to remain hidden from Western civilization until 1911, when he was discovered in Northern California.

PERFORMING ARTS

The **SACRAMENTO CONVENTION CENTER** (1030 J St, 2nd floor; 916/264-5291; www.sacramenities.com) has information on the Sacramento Philharmonic (916/264-5181) and other big-name jazz and classical performers. Just up the road is the **CREST THEATER** (1013 K St; 916/442-7378), a refurbished art deco palace that hosts rock, folk, reggae, and world-beat concerts and runs classic and independent films.

Sacramento has a thriving live theater scene, and two top venues are the **SACRAMENTO THEATER COMPANY** (1419 H St; 916/446-7501; www.sactheatre.org) and the **B STREET THEATER** (2711 B St; 916/443-5300), co-founded by TV and film star Timothy Busfield and his brother Buck. They've also recently launched the California Children's Theatre, which has received raves from kids and parents alike. The **CALIFORNIA MUSICAL THEATRE** (1419 H St; 916/557-1999; www.california musicaltheatre.com) hosts one of the city's most popular summer pastimes, the **MUSIC CIRCUS,** an annual festival of Broadway musicals presented in the impressive new Wells Fargo Pavilion. This 50-year-old summer musical tradition revives the music of Cole Porter, the Gershwins, and Stephen Sondheim using professional casts from Broadway and Hollywood. Equally if not more popular, the Sacramento Light Opera Association's **BROADWAY SERIES** runs from September through June, featuring as many as nine Broadway shows and giving Sacramento top-notch performances year-round.

RECREATION

Sacramento's two most notable natural attractions are its two rivers: the bustling boat-filled Sacramento River and the raft-filled American River. For cyclists and joggers, nothing beats the **AMERICAN RIVER PARKWAY,** a 5,000-acre nature preserve with a 22-mile-long, pothole-free bike trail, which starts in Old Sac and follows the water all the way to the town of Folsom. You can rent a bike for about $15 a day at **CITY BICYCLE WORKS** (2419 K St; 916/447-2453). In the sweltering Sacramento summers many locals and visitors alike abandon their bikes for a leisurely raft trip down the American River with **AMERICAN RIVER RAFT RENTALS** (11257 S Bridge

St, Rancho Cordova; 916/635-6400) or head for **SIX FLAGS–WATERWORLD USA** (1600 Exposition Blvd; 916/924-0556; www.sixflags.com). **SHADOW GLEN RIDING STABLES** (4854 Main Ave, Orangevale; 916/989-1826) offers hourly horseback riding and guided trail rides around Folsom Lake from April to October, and the **ICELAND** ice skating rink (1430 Del Paso Blvd; 916/925-3121) provides a cool indoor alternative. If you're cruising through town during the last two weeks of August, set aside a day or night to visit the **CALIFORNIA STATE FAIR** (916/263-3000; www.bigfun.org), Sacramento's grandest party. The carnival area is predictably cheesy, but the livestock exhibits and wine tasting are worth the admission price. Located at Cal Expo (at Expo Blvd, off the I-80/Capital City Fwy).

RESTAURANTS

Biba / ★★★★

2801 CAPITOL AVE, SACRAMENTO; 916/455-2422 Biba is a study in understated neo-deco design, the sort of place where you'd expect precious, trendy foods to dominate the menu. Fortunately, they don't. Bologna-born chef-owner Biba Caggiano is a traditionalist to the core, and what comes out of her kitchen is exactly what she learned at her mother's elbow: classical Italian cooking based on the finest ingredients available and a painstaking attention to detail. The menu changes seasonally, but expect to find such entrees as grilled shrimp wrapped in basil and Parma ham, melt-in-your-mouth shiitake ravioli with pancetta and sage, hand-made garganelli pasta in a slowly simmered Bolognese meat ragù, a phenomenal shrimp-studded linguine, duck cooked with port and Italian cherries, and rosemary-infused lamb chops. As if all that weren't enough, the service is superb and the long list of domestic and Italian wines should please even the snootiest connoisseur. Top off your marvelous meal with Biba's divine double-chocolate trifle. In addition to running one of the region's finest restaurants, Biba has written more than a half-dozen books on Italian cooking—her latest is *A Taste of Italy*—that are filled with recipes from the homes, trattorie, and restaurants of Emilia Romagna. *$$$; AE, DC, MC, V; no checks; lunch Mon–Fri, dinner Mon–Sat; full bar; reservations recommended; www.biba-restaurant.com; at 28th St.* &

David Berkley / ★★★

515 PAVILIONS LN, SACRAMENTO; 916/929-4422 Located in the Pavilions, Sacramento's most upscale shopping center, David Berkley is essentially a delicatessen—but, wow, what a deli! Just about everything served here is perfect. There's one of the region's best selections of wine and beer (the owner is often called on to select wines for White House dinners), and the deli section offers nearly two dozen different salads every day, including several low-fat options. Try sinking your teeth into the savory smoked-chicken salad; the wild rice and pear salad; or the luscious shrimp, avocado, cucumber, and fresh dill combination. David Berkley (named after the owner) also offers a takeout dinner menu, which changes weekly and features four main courses and a selection of starters and side dishes. A takeout meal might include a salad of jicama and orange slices tossed with a citrus vinaigrette; a thick, grilled New York steak crusted with Dijon mustard and horseradish; herbed mashed potatoes; and sautéed baby vegetables. Finish your feast with a decadent cheesecake or tart. Arrive early if you're planning to eat here, since seating is limited (most tables are outdoors) and this place packs 'em in. *$$; AE, MC, V; checks OK; lunch every day; beer and wine; no reservations; dberkley@dberkley.com; www.dberkley.com; in the Pavilions shopping center, on the N side of Fair Oaks Blvd, between Howe and Fulton Aves.* &

Dos Coyotes Border Cafe / ★★

1735 ARDEN WY, SACRAMENTO; 916/927-0377 With its leaping lizards and chile pepper decor, this Arden Fair branch of the popular eatery in Davis is always hopping, serving up consistently fresh and creative fare like mango-charbroiled chicken quesadillas or paella burritos. For a full review, see the Restaurants section of Davis. *$; AE, MC, V; no checks; lunch, dinner every day; beer and wine; no reservations; at Market Square in the Arden Fair shopping mall.* &

The Fox and Goose / ★★

1001 R ST, SACRAMENTO; 916/443-8825 You'll see chaps chugging down pints of bitter and having a jolly good time over a game of darts at this bustling British pub, almost as genuine as any neighborhood spot you're likely to find in the United Kingdom. Owned by Allyson Dalton, the Fox and Goose is a River City institution, offering a wee bit of everything—beer, breakfast, lunch, and live music—and doing it all wonderfully. There are 13 beers on tap, including brews from England, Ireland, and Scotland. For breakfast, choose from a variety of omelets as well as kippers (Atlantic herring), grilled tomatoes, crumpets, and such authentic English treats as bangers and mash; or you can take the California-cuisine route and order the vegetarian pub grill (scrambled tofu mixed with pesto and red onions or curry and green onions). The Fox and Goose is famous for its burnt cream—a rich, velvety custard topped with caramelized brown sugar—but the other desserts are equally delectable. Be forewarned: This is a popular pub and reservations are not accepted, so arrive a little early, particularly for lunch. At night the place swings to folk, jazz, and bluegrass tunes. *$; AE, MC, V; local checks only; breakfast, lunch every day, dinner Mon–Sat; beer and wine; no reservations; www.foxandgoose.com; at 12th St, just S of the capitol.* &

Lemon Grass / ★★★★

601 MONROE ST, SACRAMENTO; 916/486-4891 This elegant restaurant, offering a unique blend of Vietnamese and Thai cooking, keeps getting better and better and is approaching nirvana. Owner Mai Pham uses local organically grown produce whenever possible, fresh seafood, Petaluma free-range chicken, and little or no oil in many of her culinary masterpieces. The Siamese Seafood Feast, a Thai bouillabaisse, comes bubbling with fresh clams, sea scallops, mussels, and prawns in a spicy, hot-and-sour broth infused with lemongrass, galangal (Thai ginger), kaffir lime leaves, and chilies. Other standout dishes include the fillet of farm-raised catfish cooked in a caramelized garlic sauce and the Thai green curry, made with slices of chicken breast, bamboo shoots, and peas simmered in a curry-based coconut milk. The wide-ranging dessert menu features such delicacies as Saigon by Night, a blend of Vietnamese espresso, hazelnut syrup, whipped cream, and vanilla ice cream; a silky house-made caramelized Australian ginger ice cream with Grand Marnier sauce; and a banana cheesecake topped with a scoop of coconut sorbet. Mai, a best-selling author, has been featured in *Martha Stewart Living* magazine and on National Public Radio's program *Fresh Air*. Her latest cookbook is entitled *Pleasures of the Vietnamese Table*. *$$; AE, DC, MC, V; no checks; lunch Mon–Fri, dinner Mon–Sat; full bar; reservations recommended; www.lemongrassrestaurant.com; just N of Fair Oaks Blvd, near Loehmann's Plaza shopping center.* &

Paragary's Bar and Oven / ★★★★

1401 28TH ST, SACRAMENTO; 916/485-7100 / 2220 GOLD SPRINGS CT, SACRAMENTO; 916/852-0214 Paragary's Bar and Oven restaurants (there are two in Sacramento alone) were voted Best Overall Restaurants by the readers of the *Sacramento Bee* and *Sacramento Magazine*. The 28th Street branch is the small chain's flagship. Both locations are well known for zesty pizzas cooked in wood-burning ovens, mesquite-grilled entrées that typically have a strong Italian accent, and freshly made pastas and desserts. Part of the Randy Paragary empire, each Sacramento branch has different and wonderfully imaginative menus that change frequently and feature produce from the restaurant's own garden. Recent offerings included a salad of sliced mushrooms with Jarlsberg cheese, parsley, lemon, and olive oil; a pizza with Italian sausage, cilantro pesto, sautéed red onions, and sweet peppers with mozzarella; and a Niman Ranch pork chop with fresh corn polenta, cornmeal-crusted zucchini, and sweet onion jam. The 28th Street location has a lovely courtyard and a well-stocked bar. *$$$; AE, DC, MC, V; no checks; lunch Mon–Fri, dinner every day; full bar; reservations recommended; www.paragarys.com; at N St.* &

Rio City Cafe / ★

1110 FRONT ST, SACRAMENTO; 916/442-8226 Located on the Sacramento River smack-dab in the middle of "Old Sac," the city's premier tourist attraction, the Rio City Cafe has a commanding view up and down this Old Man River. The pleasantly light, airy, and attractive dining room also offers a view of the glassed-in kitchen so you can watch the cooks as they sauté and grill the evening's entrees. The fare here is primarily Southwestern with a dash of California. For lunch, expect a large variety of soups, salads, and sandwiches; the dinner entrees change as regularly as the delta tides. Rio's extensive wine list features a thoughtful collection of California vintages. *$$; AE, DC, DIS, MC, V; no checks; lunch, dinner every day; full bar; reservations recommended; between J and K Sts.* &

Tapa the World / ★★

2115 J ST, SACRAMENTO; 916/442-4353 Choose from a wide selection of flavorful tapas (Spanish appetizers) and other specialties at this extremely popular dinner house, one of the few in Sacramento that serves from noon until midnight. Tapa your feet to the live Spanish and flamenco guitar performances every night of the week. The wine list offers numerous varietals from both Spain and California to complement your meal. Try one of the paellas; the deep-dish, saffron-simmered rice feasts, available in *mariscos* (seafood), *mixta* (combination of chicken, seafood, and chorizo), or vegetarian versions; or the *lomo de cordero*, marinated grilled lamb loin served with wild mushroom rice and three specialty sauces—Rioja wine, avocado, and balsamic. The menu also features a braised tri-tip dinner and a nightly grilled venison special. They also serve the oh-so-dear and oh-so-delicious Kobe beef. And don't miss the most popular dessert specialty, Chocolate Addiction—a double-layered chocolate mousse cake topped with a warm simmered and reduced sangría and fresh strawberries. *$$; AE, DIS, MC, V; no checks; lunch, dinner every day; full bar; no reservations; on J St between 21st and 22nd Sts.* &

33rd Street Bistro / ★★

3301 FOLSOM BLVD, SACRAMENTO; 916/455-2282 The 33rd Street Bistro was a huge success right from the start, and it just keeps getting better. Chef-owner Fred Haines has combined a casual, trendy ambiance—a handsome red brick wall, high ceilings, and vibrant oversize paintings of vegetables—with terrific food at reasonable prices. You can order the excellent salads in a large or "lite" size, including a knockout Mediterranean salad tossed with wood-roasted chicken, sweet red peppers, red onions, white beans, and feta. The entrees, called "large plates," usually include your choice of salmon, chicken, or pork and are served with grilled or sautéed seasonal vegetables. The daily soups are always outstanding, and so are the seasonal desserts. Expect a crowd during peak dining hours. *$$; AE, MC, V; checks OK; breakfast, lunch, dinner every day; full bar; no reservations; at 33rd St.* &

The Waterboy / ★★★★

2000 CAPITOL AVE, SACRAMENTO; 916/498-9891 Chef-owner Rick Mahan insists on fresh, high-quality ingredients like naturally raised beef from Niman Ranch and lamb from James Ranch, organic produce from Full Belly Farms and Live Oak Farm, and outstanding breads from Grateful Bread. Named after the Celtic rock band the Waterboys, this midtown restaurant is a bright and cheery gem, serving bold and imaginative dishes inspired by recipes from southern France and northern Italy. The menu changes monthly to stay in sync with the seasons. A recent dinner menu included handmade potato gnocchi with pesto and vine-ripe cherry tomatoes; carnaroli risotto with oxtails, porcini mushrooms, tomatoes, Reggiano, and sage; and a sweet corn soup. If there's room for dessert, don't miss Edie Stewart's heavenly creations, like the warm fruit crostada with vanilla-bean ice cream and caramel. The wine list promotes fine California varietals and ports with choices available by the bottle, glass, or half-glass. *$$–$$$; AE, DC, DIS, MC, V; no checks; lunch Tues–Fri, dinner Tues–Sun; beer and wine; reservations recommended; info@waterboyrestaurant.com; www.waterboyrestaurant.com; at 20th St and Capitol Ave.* &

Zinfandel Grille / ★★★

2384 FAIR OAKS BLVD, SACRAMENTO; 916/485-7100 There are three Zinfandel Grilles—the original on Fair Oaks Boulevard, a second in Folsom (see review in the Restaurants section of Folsom), and one newly opened in the foothill town of Rocklin, just east of Roseville—a proliferation due to their history of consistently good and imaginative food. The menu (which changes every two months) still shines with the creative talents of executive chef Doug Eby. Readers of the *Sacramento Bee* have voted this establishment "Best American," and Eby and his staff continue to please the population with entrees like four-mushroom lasagne (porcini, oyster, crimini, and shiitake), with beautifully blended flavors and béchamel sauce; or grilled, spice-crusted pork tenderloin with Anaheim chiles and zucchini, cilantro pesto, and fried polenta. And don't miss the opportunity to try one (or more) of the award-winning desserts from pastry chef Pat Conroy—seasonal crème brûlée, tiramisu, Boston cream pie—any of which will leave you speechless. *$$$; AE, MC, V; no checks; lunch, dinner every day; full bar; reservations recommended; between Howe and Fulton Aves.* &

LODGINGS

Amber House / ★★★

1315 22ND ST, SACRAMENTO; 916/444-8085 OR 800/755-6526 Amber House is actually three restored historic homes—two set side by side (a 1905 Craftsman and a 1913 Mediterranean) and one across the street (an 1895 Colonial Revival). The 14 guest rooms, named after artists, poets, and musicians, have private, Italian-marble-tiled baths stocked with plush robes (11 also have Jacuzzi tubs for two), private phones with voice mail, cable TVs with VCRs, and CD players. The Van Gogh Room offers a spectacular bathroom with a heart-shaped Jacuzzi for two that perhaps even Vincent would have liked. Guests may enjoy their gourmet breakfast at whatever time they wish, served in their room, the dining room, or in one of the inn's several delightful gardens. Amber House is located on a quiet, shady street eight blocks from the capitol and is within easy walking distance of half a dozen of Sacramento's finest restaurants. *$$; AE, DC, DIS, MC, V; checks OK; innkeeper@amberhouse.com; www.amberhouse.com; between Capitol Ave and N St.*

Hyatt Regency Sacramento / ★★★

1209 L ST, SACRAMENTO; 916/443-1234 OR 800/233-1234 The Hyatt and the nearby Sheraton Grand Sacramento (see review, below) are the only lodgings in Sacramento that truly feel like big-city hotels. The Hyatt boasts a vaulted marble entryway; a sumptuous, light-filled atrium lounge; 500 beautifully appointed rooms with pretty views of palm-tree-lined Capitol Park; and excellent service. There are two fine restaurants on the hotel's main floor: Dawson's American Bistro and Martini Bar, featuring comfort foods as well as martinis both classic and modern, and Vines, an all-seasons cafe featuring local Sacramento produce. The outstanding artwork displayed throughout the hotel—murals, paintings, and wrought-iron railings and banisters—is by local artists. *$$$; AE, DC, DIS, MC, V; checks OK; www.sacramento.hyatt.com; at 12th St, across from the capitol.* &

Sheraton Grand Sacramento Hotel / ★★★

1230 J ST, SACRAMENTO; 916/447-1700 OR 800/325-3535 The latest addition to downtown Sacramento's glitzy and glamorous overhaul, this 26-floor conversion of a historic Public Market Building (designed in 1923 by renowned architect Julia Morgan) is a charmer. It's close to everything: the Sacramento Convention Center, the State Capitol complex, and some good restaurants and hot night spots (yes, you Bay Area snobs, hot night spots in Sacramento!). The Public Market Bar has become one of the places trendy folks gather after work to eye one another. The 500 attractive guest rooms offer all the standard luxury amenities, plus one you won't find at almost any other major hotel—Sheraton's own Sweet Sleeper Dog Beds. The hotel has two restaurants: the Morgan Central Valley Bistro, with a splendid view of the

THE LODI ON WINES

DELICATO WINERY (12001 Hwy 99, Manteca; 800/924-2024; www.delicato.com). Established in 1924 by Gaspare Indelicato, this large vineyard and winery is presently run by Gaspare's three sons. Delicato has a busy gift shop/tasting room filled with cutesy merchandise and medal-draped bottles displaying awards from various wine competitions. Tasting 9am–5:30pm, tours at 11am every day.

THE LUCAS WINERY (18196 N Davis Rd, Lodi; 209/368-2006; www.lucas winery.com). This charming winery was built specifically for the gentle handling of classic, old-vine zinfandel wine grapes from the famous 72-year-old Zinstar vineyards. The trendy tasting room (a former tractor barn) sits next to a climate-controlled, gravel-floored aging room known as the Grand Chai (French for "barrel room"). Tasting and short tour noon–5pm Thurs–Sun.

MICHAEL DAVID VINEYARDS (4580 W Hwy 12, Lodi; 209/368-7384; www.lodivineyards.com). These award-winning wines are available to sample at the Phillips Farm Produce Market, packed full of fresh asparagus, sweet corn, cherries, and whatever else is in season. A branch of Phillips Farms, Michael David specializes in Rhône varietals and blends. The small cafe serves burgers made with Phillips's own range-fed beef, along with killer fresh-fruit milk shakes and pies. Tasting 10am–5pm daily; tours by appointment only.

OAK RIDGE WINERY (6100 E Hwy 12, Lodi; 209/369-4758; www.oakridge winery.com). This winery was founded in 1934, just after the repeal of Prohibition. Step

soaring atrium, open for breakfast, lunch, and dinner; and the more casual Glide's Market Café, open until 3pm, with indoor and outdoor seating and wireless access in case your date is a laptop. *$$$; AE, DC, DIS, MC, V; checks OK; www. starwood.com/sheraton; on J St between 12th and 13th Sts.* &

Sterling Hotel / ★★★

1300 H ST, SACRAMENTO; 916/448-1300 OR 800/365-7660 From the outside, this striking, turn-of-the-century Victorian inn with its beautiful garden and manicured lawn immediately draws the attention of all who pass by. Inside, it's a sleek luxury hotel aimed at the upper echelon of corporate travelers. The Sterling's interior is awash in Asian-influenced, neo-deco flourishes, and the artwork has a decidedly Zen twist. The 17 guest rooms are large, airy, and spotless; each has a marble bathroom equipped with a Jacuzzi, replicas of antique furniture, big, CEO-style desks, voice mail and data ports, and numerous brass fixtures. Chanterelle, the hotel's small but highly regarded restaurant, is located on the ground floor with a charming patio for fair-weather dining. *$$$; AE, DC, MC, V; checks OK when mailed in advance; www.sterlinghotel.com; at 13th St.* &

inside the 50,000-gallon redwood-barrel tasting room and sample their reds and whites. Picnic tables are available, surrounded by colorful gardens. Tasting 11am–4pm Thurs–Sun; tours by appointment only.

PEIRANO ESTATE (21831 N Highway 99, Acampo; 209/369-9463; www.peirano.com). Conveniently located on the Highway 99 frontage road, Peirano owns the largest single block of head-trained, natural-rooted zinfandel remaining in the country. The cheerful tasting room is actually the remodeled Peirano Estate farmhouse, built in 1904. Enjoy a picnic among the 90-year-old vines or browse the gift shop while you sample the popular wines. Tasting noon–4:30pm Wed–Sun.

THE VAN RUITEN FAMILY WINERY (340 W Hwy 12, Lodi; 209/334-5722; www.vrt.com). In 1998, John Van Ruiten and his family, generations-old Lodi-area grape growers, created this state-of-the-art winery. Surrounded by vineyards and featuring a glass-fronted, two-story tasting room, Van Ruiten offers one of the first cab-shiraz wines produced in this country along with old-vine zins and a chardonnay. Tasting 11am–5pm Tues–Sun; tours by appointment.

WOODBRIDGE BY ROBERT MONDAVI (5950 E. Woodbridge Rd, Acampo; 209/365-2839; www.robertmondavi.com). Robert Mondavi was raised among the vineyards of Lodi. In 1979 he established Woodbridge, just northeast of town. Here Mondavi produces cabernet sauvignon, chardonnay, merlot, muscat, sauvignon blanc, white zinfandel, and a specialty dessert wine called Portacinco. Tasting and retail sales 10:30am–4:30pm Tues–Sun, tours 9:30am and 1:30pm Tues–Sun.

Northern Central Valley

Leaving the urban, political sprawl of Sacramento, the Northern Central Valley opens into a patchwork of farmland and orchards, stitched together by country roads and small towns. From historic Sutter Street in Folsom to the charming college town of Chico, with its abundance of outdoor-activity options, this region of the Golden State has something for everyone.

Folsom

RESTAURANTS
Zinfandel Grille / ★★★

705 GOLD LAKE DR, FOLSOM; 916/985-3321 Located near Lake Natoma, this branch of the well-liked restaurant in Sacramento is very popular, even at lunchtime, so reservations are strongly advised. On a par with the other fine dining establishments in Folsom, the Zinfandel serves such culinary delights as grilled portobello mushrooms and sweet onion risotto-fontina cake with a balsamic vinegar sauce for starters, followed by main courses such as spinach linguine with smoked salmon and mussels with leeks, fresh dill, shallots, and a touch of vermouth. For a full review, see the Restaurants section of Sacramento, home of the main branch. *$$$; AE, MC, V; no checks; lunch, dinner every day; full bar; reservations recommended; in the Lakes shopping center.* &

Loomis

LODGINGS

Emma's Bed and Breakfast / ★★★

3137 TAYLOR RD, LOOMIS; 916/652-1392 Perched on a hill overlooking apple, walnut, and mandarin orange orchards, this stately manor situated on 45 acres is impressively furnished and decorated. It has five guest suites with opulent private baths, down-filled duvets, TVs with VCRs, and fax/PC ports. Three of the suites are in the immaculately renovated 1912 farmhouse, and two are in a new matching building next door. The Orchard Suite features mahogany antiques, including a beautiful Louis XV queen-size bed. Lovebirds may opt for the luxurious Honeymoon Suite. The full breakfasts are different every day and include juice, an entree such as German pancakes, and coffee or tea. *$$; DIS, MC, V; checks OK; info@emmasbnb.com; www.emmasbnb.com; between King and Penryn Rds.* &

The Old Flower Farm Bed and Breakfast Inn / ★★★

4150 AUBURN–FOLSOM RD, LOOMIS; 916/652-4200 Set in a bucolic countryside and oozing charm from every 100-year-old board, the Old Flower Farm looks out over (what else?) a flower farm. With its century-old architecture lovingly painted and restored, it looks like a cover shot for *Sunset* magazine. And inside it's even more impressive. Owner Jenny Leonard, a longtime professional decorator, has turned this into a special place indeed. The living room's focal point is a red Vermont stove set on a rock hearth, which, with the two antique wing-back chairs, a large upright wicker chair, and an overstuffed celadon green sofa, cry out for a good book and a willing reader. Upstairs are three guest bedrooms, each with a queen-size bed topped with overstuffed down comforter and a private bath with a claw-footed tub and shower. The largest unit, the Country Checker Room, is filled with antiques, a white wicker chaise lounge, a high poster bed with a Victorian dresser, and red-and white-checked curtains. Adjacent to the main house is the Honeymoon Cottage, decorated in a celadon green with a white, net-draped queen-size bed. The swimming pool beckons on hot summer days, and Folsom Lake, a mecca for boaters and anglers, is only a five-minute drive away. Breakfasts are healthy and hearty, served with fresh fruit, homemade jams, and juices made from the farm's own produce. *$$–$$$; AE, MC, V; checks OK; www.oldflowerfarm.com; halfway between the towns of Auburn and Folsom, at Horseshoe Bar.*

Davis

The **UNIVERSITY OF CALIFORNIA AT DAVIS (UCD)** is this little city's claim to fame, particularly the college's respected veterinary science and enology schools. A former farming town, Davis is also famous for its city officials who pride themselves on finding more ecological ways of living on the planet. For example, to encourage people to cut down on fuel consumption, the city has built 67 miles of bike lanes and trails. The urban-village atmosphere of downtown Davis draws shoppers, diners, and browsers to its charming streets. Great minds of Davis get their world-shaking ideas while sipping espresso at **MISHKA'S CAFE** (514 2nd St; 530/759-0811); they spend hours studying the works of other great minds at the **AVID READER** (617 2nd St; 530/758-4040); and they take out their aggressions by climbing the walls (literally) at **ROCKNASIUM** (720 Olive Dr; 530/757-2902). The new, $57-million **MONDAVI CENTER FOR THE PERFORMING ARTS** (at the SW corner of UC Davis, I-80 exit UCD/Mondavi Center; 530/754-ARTS; 866-754-ARTS; www.mondaviarts.org) is the premier performance venue in the Sacramento Valley, with two theaters featuring world-famous personalities, musicians, dancers, and performance artists. Davis boasts one of the most appealing **FARMERS' MARKETS** in the nation, with lots of produce for purchase—mostly organic, naturally—but with other gourmet foods prepared on the spot, as well as musicians and stuff for kids (Central Park, 3rd and B Sts, Sat mornings and Wed evenings). Or, if you've always wanted to jump out of an airplane, try **SKYDANCE SKYDIVING** (Yolo County Airport; 800/759-3483; www.1800skydance.net). For more information on what to see and do in Davis, call the **DAVIS CONFERENCE AND VISITORS BUREAU** (530/297-1900; 877/71DAVIS; www.davisvisitor.org).

RESTAURANTS

Dos Coyotes Border Cafe / ★★

1411 W COVELL BLVD #108, DAVIS; 530/753-0922 / 2191 COWELL BLVD #A, DAVIS; 530/753-0922 This distant outpost of Southwestern cuisine is one of the hottest restaurants in Davis. The crowds come for the fresh, consistently good food, such as the house-made salsas (help yourself to the salsa bar), shrimp tacos, and ranchero burritos with marinated steak, chicken, or vegetarian fillings. Equally good are the more unconventional offerings, such as the mahimahi taco or the Yucatan salad with marinated, charbroiled chicken breast, black beans, red onion, carrots, cabbage, sweet peppers, and corn served on a flour tortilla. Owner Bobby Coyote has turned his cafe into a howling success—even the branch in Sacramento (1735 Arden Wy; 916/927-0377) attracts crowds. $; AE, MC, V; no checks; lunch, dinner every day; beer and wine; reservations not necessary; www.doscoyotes.net; in the Marketplace shopping center, just E of Hwy 113. &

Soga's Restaurant / ★★★

217 E ST, DAVIS; 530/757-1733 If you didn't know about this exquisite slip of a restaurant, you might pass right by it. Word of mouth has transformed the classy spot into a bustling establishment where reservations are highly recommended. Chef-owner Matt Soga prepares innovative appetizers such as smoked salmon

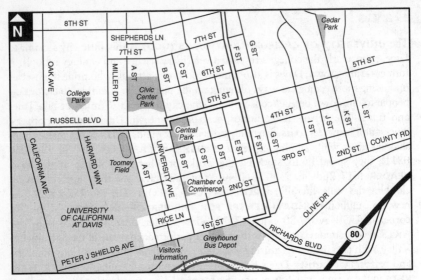

DAVIS

served alongside cornmeal pancakes smeared with cream cheese, onions, and chives, and medallions of lamb with fresh artichoke hearts, tomatoes, and mushrooms. He also makes a superb double-thick pork chop that's marinated for 48 hours, roasted to perfection, and served with garlic mashed potatoes and gravy. Desserts are simple but heartwarming: strawberry shortcake, warm apple crisp, and lemon-mint sorbet scooped onto a cookie shell and topped with a raspberry purée. *$$; AE, DIS, MC, V; local checks only; lunch Mon–Fri, dinner Mon–Sat; full bar; reservations recommended; between 2nd and 3rd Sts.* &

LODGINGS

Hotel Palm Court / ★★★

234 D ST, DAVIS; 530/753-7100 OR 800/528-1234 This chic, unobtrusive jewel is reminiscent of a fine little boutique hotel. The lobby is small and intimate with a kind of Raffles Hotel look—English with a dash of East Indian. The 27 suites (all for nonsmokers) have lots of goodies for the serious traveler, including irons and ironing boards, hair dryers, two TVs and telephones in every room, office desks, and sofa beds (in addition to the beds in the adjoining rooms). The two Palm Suites are the ritziest, with fireplaces, marble bathrooms with whirlpool baths, and full-length balconies. The decor in the rooms has an East Indian/English flair, too, with dark wooden blinds; Regency furnishings in hues of rust, maroon, and gold; and handsome armoires that conceal TVs, honor bars, and refrigerators. *$$; AE, DC, DIS, MC, V; no checks; www.stayanight.com/palmcourt; at 3rd St.* &

Woodland

RESTAURANTS

Morrison's Upstairs / ★★

428½ 1ST ST, WOODLAND; 530/666-6176 Tucked into the attic of one of Woodland's most striking buildings, an 1891 Queen Anne Victorian that was originally a luxury apartment house, Morrison's Upstairs combines old-fashioned elegance with a predinner aerobic workout; guests must climb three flights of stairs to reach the dining room. (The elevator is an option for those who are easily winded.) Favorite entrees include an abundance of creatively prepared fresh fish dishes, plump beer-batter prawns, fettuccine with prawns in a Parmesan cream sauce, perfectly cooked prime rib, and steak Morrison—a 12-ounce prime-cut New York strip smothered with mushrooms and shallots. Early birds dining between 5pm and 6pm Monday through Thursday get the same fare at bargain prices. Morrison's wine list is the best in town. *$$; AE, DC, DIS, MC, V; local checks only; lunch Mon–Fri, dinner every day; full bar; reservations recommended; at Bush St.* &

Yuba City

RESTAURANTS

City Cafe / ★★

667 PLUMAS ST, YUBA CITY; 530/671-1501 By golly, sleepy Yuba City's gone trendy with this chic little cafe smack-dab in the middle of the town's historic section. Take a seat inside the bistro-like dining room (a bit cramped) or sit outside in the courtyard in front of the restaurant, where you have more legroom. The lunch menu focuses on an assortment of panini prepared with focaccia and herb mayo, including the popular grilled eggplant, sautéed spinach, mild banana pepper, and feta sandwich. Dinner is a more ambitious affair, with such items as Cajun jambalaya with prawns, chicken, smoked ham, and sausage in a tomato broth over rice, and charbroiled filet steak in a cherry pepper and miso demi-glace served with grilled bok choy and mashed potatoes. City Cafe has a good selection of beer and wine, with many wines available by the glass. *$$; DIS, MC, V; no checks; lunch Mon–Fri, dinner Mon–Sat; full bar; reservations recommended; at Colusa Hwy.* &

Ruthy's Bar and Oven / ★★

229 CLARK AVE, YUBA CITY; 530/674-2611 If you're a big breakfast eater, make a beeline to Ruthy's. You'll find such belly-packing fare as French toast made with Ruthy's own cinnamon-raisin bread, terrific whole-wheat and buttermilk pancakes, and creative egg dishes such as the omelet stuffed with Monterey Jack cheese and prawns sautéed in garlic-herb butter. For lunch, head straight for the salad bar or order a sandwich served on house-made bread. Dinner is more elaborate, with interesting appetizers like little chicken quesadillas, tiny New Zealand clams steamed in a garlic and white wine sauce, and spicy Cajun prawns in a garlic red pepper sauce.

Entrees vary from house-made fettuccine tossed with house-smoked salmon to a spicy chicken stir-fry. *$$; AE, DIS, MC, V; checks OK; breakfast Sat–Sun, lunch, dinner Tues–Sat, brunch Sun; full bar; reservations not necessary; in the Hillcrest Plaza mini-mall, S of Franklin Rd.* &

LODGINGS

Harkey House / ★★

212 C ST, YUBA CITY; 530/674-1942 Sitting just a few hundred feet from the Yuba River, this cream-colored 1874 Victorian Gothic B&B trimmed in gold offers three guest rooms with private baths, a cottage, and diversions such as a spa, a chess table, and an antique Chickering piano. Outside there is a garden with a swimming pool, deck furniture, and a hammock. The spacious Camilla's Cottage guest room has a fireplace, Oriental rugs, TV/VCR/CD player, a small kitchen, and a two-person shower (so who needs a VCR?). The soft green Empress Room features a gas fireplace and a water fountain. In the solarium-style dining area guests are treated to a full breakfast, including treats like Belgian waffles, zucchini croquettes, Canadian bacon, fresh fruit, and scones. *$$; AE, DIS, MC, V; checks OK; www.harkey house.com; in Old Town, across from the courthouse.*

Marysville

RESTAURANTS

Silver Dollar Saloon / ★

330 1ST ST, MARYSVILLE; 530/743-0507 As you amble up to the Silver Dollar Saloon, be sure to pay your respects to the massive wooden cowboy standing guard at the entrance. This restaurant and saloon is a lively relic of Marysville's frontier past, with Western memorabilia scattered throughout the building. The Silver Dollar's menu features terrific grilled steaks and steak sandwiches, grilled chicken, hot pastrami sandwiches, and delectable barbecued ribs. For those craving a lighter meal, they also serve up some tasty grilled vegetables, and to give the place a hint of multiculturalism, the Honolulu-born owner has added some Hawaiian specialties— just in case any Kona cowpokes show up. On Friday and Saturday nights the place is packed with cowpokes tappin' their boots to the beat of country music mixed by a DJ. *$; MC, V; no checks; lunch, dinner Mon–Sat; full bar; no reservations; in Old Town, between C and D Sts.* &

Williams

LODGINGS

Wilbur Hot Springs / ★★

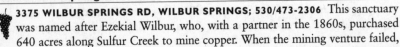

3375 WILBUR SPRINGS RD, WILBUR SPRINGS; 530/473-2306 This sanctuary was named after Ezekial Wilbur, who, with a partner in the 1860s, purchased 640 acres along Sulfur Creek to mine copper. When the mining venture failed,

Wilbur bought out his partner, built a small wooden hotel, and opened Wilbur Hot Springs. The current owner purchased the retreat in the 1970s, restored the hotel, added a third floor, and managed to keep its original charm and simplicity. Today Wilbur sits 22 miles west of Williams, on private property within a 15,000-acre nature preserve. You'll find no electricity here—the hotel is softly lit with solar power and warmed by centrally located gas fireplaces. There are 17 private guest rooms (toilets are located, European style, throughout the hotel), a spacious suite with private bath and kitchen, and a comfortable 11-bed bunk room. Since there is no restaurant at Wilbur, guests bring their own groceries and use the well-equipped commercial kitchen, where dry spices, cookware, utensils, dishes, and refrigeration/freezer storage are supplied. The hot springs area (the highlight of your stay) is dimly lit with Japanese lanterns and sheltered by a cedar A-framed bathhouse where clothing is optional and noise is a no-no. Registered guests have 24-hour access to the hot springs. A spacious redwood deck surrounds the bathhouse and leads to an 80°F outdoor pool, a dry sauna, and private outdoor showers. *$$–$$$; MC, V; checks OK; www.wilburhotsprings.com; from I-5, take Hwy 20 W, N on Bear Valley Rd (go 4 miles), turn left onto Wilbur Springs Rd at the Wilbur Silver Bridge, drive 1 mile, and enter gate.*

Oroville

Oroville has been largely, and undeservedly, overlooked by tourists. This historic **GOLD RUSH** town is the site of the second major gold discovery after Coloma and the center of a rich agricultural industry (specializing in cattle, citrus, nuts, and olives). The **OROVILLE CHINESE TEMPLE AND GARDEN** (1500 Broderick St; 530/538-2496) was built in 1863 to serve the 10,000 Chinese who worked the mines here. It has an extensive collection of tapestries, costumes, and puppets used in Chinese opera, and its lovely gardens, planted exclusively with plants from China, offer a great place for meditation. The 770-foot-tall **OROVILLE DAM** (from Hwy 70, head E on Oroville Dam Blvd) is the tallest earthen dam in the country, and **LAKE OROVILLE** (530/538-2219) is regularly rated as one of the best bass fishing spots in the United States. It is also a houseboaters' paradise, with 24 square miles of surface area and 167 miles of shoreline. Just south of the dam you can rent a houseboat, ski boat, or wave-runner and find out where to reel in the big ones by visiting the folks at **BIDWELL CANYON MARINA** (801 Bidwell Canyon Rd; 530/589-3165). The 640-foot-high **FEATHER FALLS,** the sixth-tallest waterfall in the country, is a worthy side trip if you're up for a moderately strenuous hike. Your reward: spectacular views of the falls, the Sacramento Valley, and the Coast Range; for directions and details, call the **OROVILLE AREA CHAMBER OF COMMERCE** (530/538-2542; www.orovillechamber.net).

Berry Creek

LODGINGS

Lake Oroville Bed and Breakfast / ★★★

240 SUNDAY DR, BERRY CREEK; 530/589-0700 OR 800/455-LAKE
"Silent, upon a peak in Darien. . . ." With apologies to Mr. Keats, make that "upon the outskirts of Oroville" and you have a pretty fair description of the Lake Oroville Bed and Breakfast, sitting in lonely yellow splendor on 40 acres high above the lake, with views in every direction. Built in 1992 specifically to be an inn (as opposed to a reconfigured residence), the B&B has six guest bedrooms with private entrances and baths, and five of them have whirlpool tubs. The Rose Petal Room is appropriately covered with rose print wallpaper, and a white Battenberg bedspread is draped over the king-size bed, from which you have a view of the lake, as you do from the Victorian Room. The Monet Room, Max's Room, the Arbor Room, and the Vine Room all have queen-size beds and views of the surrounding woods. Breakfast is a hearty affair, with a choice of quiche, eggs Benedict, crepes, waffles, or French toast. Proprietors Ron and Cheryl Damberger welcome children and maintain a small playroom for them, and they like to host family reunions and other group events, too. A gas grill is available for guests who get so downright relaxed they'd rather barbecue than drive into town for dinner. Pets are welcome. *$$; AE, DIS, MC, V; checks OK; www.lakeorovillebedandbreakfast.com; from Hwy 70 take Oroville Dam Blvd/Hwy 162 E for 1.7 miles, turn right at Olive Hwy, continue for 13½ miles, then turn left at Bell Ranch Rd, bear right, and go ½ mile to Sunday Dr.* &

Chico

This charming little city was founded in 1860 by John Bidwell, a member of the first wagon-train expedition to reach California. After he struck gold near Oroville and purchased land along Chico Creek, he built a three-story Italian villa–style mansion. After Bidwell's death, the mansion and its surrounding grounds were donated for the establishment of a Christian school and later became California State University–Chico (Chico State). Today, **BIDWELL MANSION STATE HISTORIC PARK** stands adjacent to the beautifully landscaped campus grounds surrounded by hundreds of varieties of trees Bidwell introduced to the area. Across town, Bidwell Park is a 3,600-acre playground for outdoor enthusiasts, with swimming holes, hiking, biking and equestrian trails, picnic areas, and facilities for organized sports. These days, Chico, once known as the nation's number-one party school, has a new designation as the nation's number-one bike town, with user-friendly bike paths leading both in and out of town. **UPPER BIDWELL PARK** has become somewhat of a mecca for mountain bikers.

To find out what's currently going on around town, settle in at one of the espresso bars and thumb through the *Chico News and Review* (642 W 5th St; 530/894-2300; www.newsreview.com), the city's fine alternative-press newspaper. Or simply relax

THE BOK-BOK MAN

Bok . . . bok . . . bok . . . the hollow sound of bamboo mallet on wooden box echoed through the darkness. Residents of the small Delta town of Locke, knowing he was there, rested peacefully. Every hour on the hour, year after year, through heavy rain, winter fog, and summer winds, he walked up and down Main Street. Today, no one remembers his name—he is simply the bok-bok man. Because of the fire hazard associated with numerous households living in tightly packed wooden-framed buildings, the town of Locke hired this man to walk Main Street every night and serve as a night fire-watchman. He could very well be the reason that Locke, the only town built by the Chinese for the Chinese, still stands today. Other Chinese communities in the Delta were destroyed by major fires, some of them twice.

The small, rectangular bok-bok box was hand-carried and struck on the hour (the number of hits reflected the hour) beginning at 1am and continuing through the early morning until 5am. The sound could be heard for surprisingly long distances and served as the signal that all was well. For many residents, especially the farmworkers, the bok-bok man was an alarm clock. His salary was collected from the community: 25 cents per month, per household. The bok-bok man patrolled Locke until his death in 1955. His original bok-bok box and mallet are on display at the Dai Loy Gambling House Museum on Main Street (13951 Main St, Locke; 916/776-1661).

à la Chico by observing the brewing-to-bottling process and sampling the award-winning ales and lagers at **SIERRA NEVADA BREWING COMPANY** (1075 E 20th St; 530/893-3520; www.sierra-nevada.com); free tours are offered at 2:30pm Tuesday through Friday and noon to 3pm on Saturday.

RESTAURANTS

The Albatross / ★★

3312 THE ESPLANADE, CHICO; 530/345-6037 Set in a neighborhood of old mansions, the Albatross was a private home before it was converted into a dinner house with several small, casual dining rooms and a wonderfully landscaped garden patio. The service is excellent, and despite the wait staff's aloha attire and the restaurant's tropical decor, you won't find any pounded taro root or papaya salsa on the menu. What you will find is well-prepared mahimahi, fresh salmon topped with champagne butter, and blackened swordfish, as well as steak and slow-roasted prime rib. All the entrees come with steaming hot sourdough and squaw bread and choice of potato and include unlimited trips to the first-rate salad bar. Top off your meal with the ultra-rich Island Pie: macadamia-nut ice cream piled onto a cookie-crumb crust and smothered with fudge, whipped cream, and a sprinkling of almonds. *$$; AE, MC, V; checks OK; dinner Tues–Sun; full bar; reservations recommended; N of downtown.* ⅃

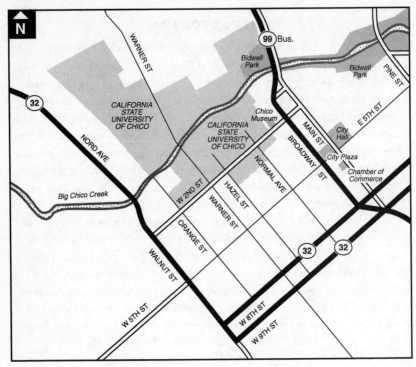

CHICO

The Black Crow Grill and Taproom / ★★★

209 SALEM ST, CHICO; 530/892-1392 Voted "Best Dinner Place" four years in a row by the *Chico News and Review,* this popular downtown restaurant has reasonably priced meals, good service, and a lively atmosphere. Check the daily specials menu, which features a choice of wines, starters, entrees, and desserts. Try the Fuji apple salad with organic baby greens, blue cheese, currants, and caramelized walnuts with aged balsamic vinaigrette for a start. Entrees include house-made linguine with bay scallops, corn, roasted tomato, and a white wine–artichoke basil pesto sauce; lemon roasted half chicken served with garlic mashed potatoes and herbed pan gravy; and pan-roasted Atlantic salmon, seared and smothered with an orange stone-ground mustard butter sauce. And if it's on the menu, don't miss their creamy lemon brûlée, a perfect end to a satisfying meal. *$$; AE, MC, V; checks OK; lunch Mon–Sat, dinner every day; full bar; reservations recommended; www.theblackcrow.com; corner of 2nd and Salem Sts.* &

Kramore Inn / ★★

1903 PARK AVE, CHICO; 530/343-3701 Owner Bill Theller started at the Kramore as a dishwasher, worked his way up to become cook and manager, then bought the place and clearly figured out how to keep his customers happy: the inn's food has kept people coming back for more than 20 years. The

Kramore specialty is crepes. You'll find 30 different kinds—everything from a Cajun seafood crepe to the old favorite ham-and-cheese. There are plenty of vegetarian varieties as well (to keep the conscience as pure as the body), and the Kramore serves organic and pesticide-free vegetables whenever possible. Other good dishes on the lengthy menu are the Italian roast chicken, the Hungarian mushroom soup, and the daily stir-fries. The excellent breads, pasta, and ice creams are made locally. For a sweet finale, top off your meal with the decadent chocolate mousse crepe. *$; AE, DIS, MC, V; local checks only; dinner every day, brunch Sun; beer and wine; reservations recommended; jpw@cmc.net; at W 19th St.* &

LODGINGS

The Esplanade Bed and Breakfast / ★★

620 THE ESPLANADE, CHICO; 530/345-8084 This B&B is located on one of Chico's most beautiful boulevards, The Esplanade, which is lined on both sides with lush lawns, tall trees, and stately Victorian mansions. The charming turn-of-the-century house sits across the street from the famous Bidwell Mansion and is close to downtown and the university. Five guest rooms are offered here, each with a cable TV and a private bath. Susan's Room is a favorite, with its luxurious queen-size poster bed and a great view of the Bidwell Mansion. Natalie's Room is downstairs and has lavender decor and a bay window. The attached bathroom features a Jacuzzi tub situated under a stained-glass window. Proprietor Lois Kloss pampers her guests with a hearty breakfast in the formal dining room, and she pours everyone a glass of wine each evening in the parlor or on the garden patio. *$; DIS, MC, V; checks OK; www.northvalley.net/esplanade; near Memorial Wy.*

Johnson's Country Inn / ★★★★

3935 MOOREHEAD AVE, CHICO; 530/345-7829 OR 866/872-7780 Set in the heart of a picture-perfect almond orchard, this Victorian-style farmhouse is an ideal place for a wedding, an anniversary, or simply a peaceful retreat—and you'd never notice that it's only five minutes from downtown Chico. Built specifically as a B&B in 1992, the inn has four guest rooms, all with private baths. The Icart Room, named after Louis Icart, a Parisian art-deco artist, is furnished in a French country style in shades of green, blue, and rose (and it's wheelchair accessible). The Jarrett Room, adorned with paintings by the 1930s San Francisco artist Charles "Dixie" Jarrett, is decorated in soft greens and blues and has a view of the orchard from an upstairs window. Named after a family member, the Sexton Room is decked out in floral hues of rose, beige, and blue with furnishings designed by William Morris, the famous pre-Raphaelite English artist and poet. The romantic Harrison Room, named after the owners' great-great-great-great-grandfather, the 23rd president, has an 1860s Victorian double bed, a fireplace, and a private Jacuzzi. Owners David and Joan Johnson provide a coffee and juice tray for each room early in the morning, then later bring out an ample country breakfast, including locally made apple sausages, peach French toast, frittata, and almond coffee cakes (you can guess where the almonds come from—as do many of the fresh fruits and herbs in season). Wine is provided each afternoon to allow guests to decompress from a hard day on the croquet court. *$$; AE, MC, V; checks OK; j.c.inn@pobox.com; www.chico.com/johnsonsinn; travel W on W 5th St for 1 mile, past Walnut to Moorhead Ave.* &

Orland

LODGINGS

The Inn at Shallow Creek Farm / ★★

🐷 **4712 COUNTY RD, ORLAND; 530/865-4093 OR 800/865-4093** Who would have thought there'd be an elegant and absolutely peaceful refuge so close to Interstate 5? Mary and Kurt Glaeseman are the proprietors of this gray-and-white, ivy-covered farmhouse surrounded by citrus trees and set at the end of a long drive lined with fruit and nut trees. The inn offers four guest rooms, including the Heritage Room upstairs, a favorite with its striking morning-glory wallpaper and wonderful antiques. The Brookdale Room has twin beds and a wide window overlooking the wild, verdant tangle along the creek. If total privacy is what you're after, stay in the four-room Cottage, with a fully equipped kitchen, a sunporch, and a wood-burning stove. Mary serves a breakfast of home-baked breads and muffins, fresh fruit from the farm's orchards, juice, and coffee. When the day turns cold and wintry, sink into one of the overstuffed sofas in front of the roaring fire with a good book and nibble on some mandarin oranges—a local delicacy. *$; MC, V; checks OK; inn-farm@orland.net; take the Chico/Orland exit off I-5, drive 2½ miles W, then turn right on County Rd DD and drive ½ mile.*

Red Bluff

LODGINGS

Jeter Victorian Inn / ★★

🐷 **1107 JEFFERSON ST, RED BLUFF; 530/527-7574** If you're a fan of true Victoriana, this is your place. Completely furnished in authentic antiques, this warm and appealing bed-and-breakfast features five guest rooms filled with the period art and furniture that owner Mary Dunlap has collected for 46 years. The inn is on a quiet, tree-lined street, in a lovely garden setting, where, weather permitting, bountiful breakfasts are served alfresco. Red Bluff is noted for its antique shops and Victorian-era museums. Spending the night in one is even better. *$$; MC, V; checks OK; www.jetervictorianinn.com; corner of Union and Jefferson Sts, 2 blocks E of Union.*

Index